FUN學

美國英語閱讀課本

各學科實用課文 二版

9

附 **Workbook** +MP3

AMERICAN SCHOOL TEXTBOOK

READING KEY

作者 Michael A. Putlack & e-Creative Contents　　譯者 邱佳皇

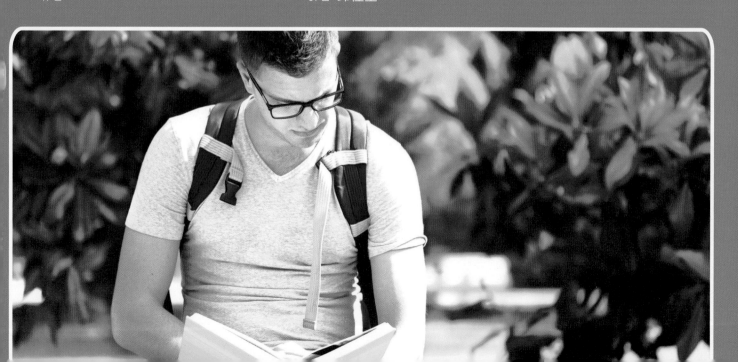

The Best Preparation for Building Academic Reading Skills and Vocabulary

The Reading Key series is designed to help students to understand American school textbooks and to develop background knowledge in a wide variety of academic topics. This series also provides learners with the opportunity to enhance their reading comprehension skills and vocabulary, which will assist them when they take various English exams.

Reading Key <Volume 1–3> is
a three-book series designed for beginner to intermediate learners.

Reading Key <Volume 4–6> is
a three-book series designed for intermediate to high-intermediate learners.

Reading Key <Volume 7–9> is
a three-book series designed for high-intermediate learners.

Features

- A wide variety of topics that cover American school subjects
  helps learners expand their knowledge of academic topics through interdisciplinary studies

- Intensive practice for reading skill development
  helps learners prepare for various English exams

- Building vocabulary by school subjects and themed texts
  helps learners expand their vocabulary and reading skills in each subject

- Graphic organizers for each passage
  show the structure of the passage and help to build summary skills

- Captivating pictures and illustrations related
  to the topics help learners gain a broader understanding
  of the topics and key concepts

Table of Contents

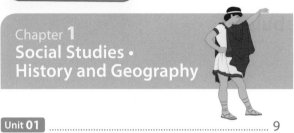

Chapter 1
Social Studies •
History and Geography

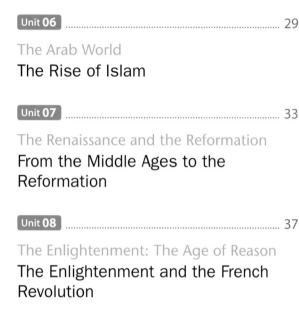

Chapter 2
Science

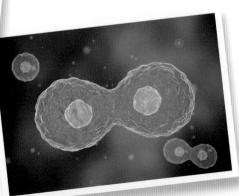

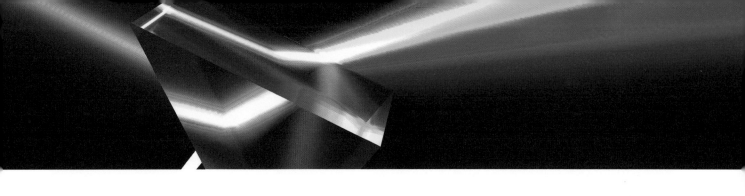

Chapter 3
Mathematics • Language • Visual Arts • Music

Workbook for Daily Review

Syllabus Vol. 9

Subject	Topic & Area	Title
Social Studies ★ History and Geography	World History and Culture	Early People
	World History and Culture	The Fertile Crescent and the Kingdoms of Egypt
	World History and Culture	The Indus Civilization
	World History and Culture	Ancient Greece
	World History and Culture	The Roman Empire
	World History and Culture	The Rise of Islam
	World History and Culture	From the Middle Ages to the Reformation
	World History and Culture	The Enlightenment and the French Revolution
Science	A World of Living Things	Cells, Reproduction, and Heredity
	The Earth's Oceans	Oceans and Ocean Life
	Our Earth	What We Can Learn From Fossils
	Force and Motion	Newton's Laws
	Matter and Energy	Light Energy
	The Universe	Eclipses
	The Human Body	Diseases and the Immune System
Mathematics	Numbers and Computation	Factors, Prime Numbers, and Exponents
	Geometry	Dimensions
Language and Literature	Literature	Pygmalion
	Language Arts	Sentences
Visual Arts	Visual Arts	From Baroque Art to Pop Art
Music	A World of Music	Gregorian Chants and Polyphonic Music

1

- **Social Studies**
- **History and Geography**

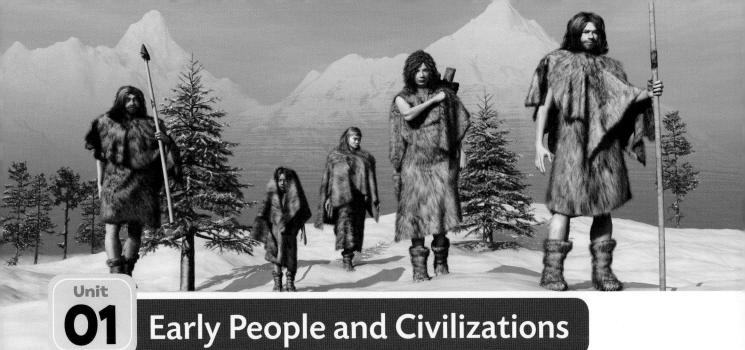

Unit 01   Early People and Civilizations

Visual Preview What are some of the prehistoric ages in human history?

During the Stone Age, humans were hunter-gatherers who made simple tools from stone.

During the Bronze Age, humans learned to make tools from bronze.

During the Iron Age, humans learned to make tools from iron and began to develop real civilizations.

Vocabulary Preview   Write the correct word and the meaning in Chinese next to its meaning.

| Ice Age | Bronze Age | domesticate | primitive | hunter-gatherer |

1 _____ : the period when much of the earth was cold and covered with glaciers

2 _____ : to train an animal to live with or work for humans

3 _____ : the period when humans learned to work with copper and tin

4 _____ : relating to a very early stage in the development of humans, animals, or plants

5 _____ : a person who hunts animals and gathers wild plants for food

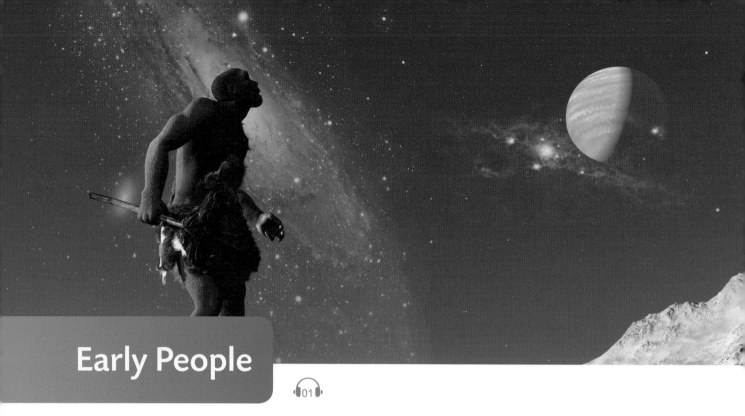

Early People

▲ primitive human

▲ vessel from the Stone Age

A couple of million years ago, **primitive** humans were nothing like the modern humans of today. They were simplistic creatures that shared characteristics with both humans and apes. For much of this time, the earth was extremely cold. It endured a very long **Ice Age**. During the Ice Age, much of the earth's surface was covered by huge sheets of ice called glaciers. However, around 12,500 years ago, the Ice Age ended. The ice and glaciers receded. And humans began to evolve, to spread out, and to become more civilized.

Archaeologists have created a three-age system to describe **prehistoric** cultures. They are the Stone Age, the Bronze Age, and the Iron Age.

The **Stone Age** is often divided into the Old Stone Age and the New Stone Age. The Old Stone Age was the first part of the Stone Age and began around 2,000,000 B.C. The New Stone Age was the last part of the Stone Age and began around 10,000 B.C.

During the Old Stone Age, humans lived as **hunter-gatherers**. They hunted animals and gathered wild plants for food. People could only make simple tools out of stone. Yet people learned how to make fire during this age. Having fire changed human life a lot. Fire provided light and helped people stay warm. Most of all, people could cook their food.

▲ **People learned how to make fire during the Old Stone Age.**

In the New Stone Age, there began to be some more improvements. People learned to farm the land. People also learned to **domesticate** wild animals such as dogs, sheep, and goats. Some people began to settle in villages where there was **fertile soil** for farming. Since they could grow their own crops and raise their own animals, they no longer had to live as **nomads**. However, they still used stone tools, so this time is called the New Stone Age.

▲ **primitive art**

Around 3000 B.C., the **Bronze Age** began in some parts of the world. During it, humans started working with soft metals such as copper and tin. They learned how to create tools and weapons out of bronze. And pottery became more common during this time.

Around 1500 B.C., the **Iron Age** began in Europe. Of course, it started earlier in some places and later in other places. During the Iron Age, humans began working with iron. Also, the first real cities began to appear, and trade between cities became more commonplace. It was during this age that human civilization started to develop much more quickly than ever before.

from the Stone Age

from the Bronze Age

from the Iron Age

▲ **primitive tools**

◄ **the evolution of human beings**

Quick Check Check T (True) or F (False).

1 The Stone Age happened before the Iron Age. ⬜T ⬜F
2 During the New Stone Age, people learned to tame some animals. ⬜T ⬜F
3 The Iron Age began in Europe around 3000 B.C. ⬜T ⬜F

1 **What is the passage mainly about?**
a. The different ages that prehistoric humans lived in.
b. The achievements of Bronze and Iron Age humans.
c. How the Ice Age affected the progress of humans.

2 **People learned to farm and started to live in villages in the _____.**
a. Old Stone Age   b. New Stone Age   c. Bronze Age

3 **How did fire help change humans' lives?**
a. They used it to farm the land.
b. They were able to cook their food with it.
c. They stopped living lives as nomads.

4 **What does endured mean?**
a. Approached.   b. Practiced.   c. Experienced.

5 **Complete the sentences.**
a. When the Ice Age ended, the ice and _____ began to recede.
b. During the _____ _____, humans learned to make tools out of copper and tin.
c. The first real cities started to appear during the _____ _____.

6 **Complete the outline.**

Stone Age
• Lasted from 2,000,000 B.C. to 3000 B.C.
Old Stone Age
• Humans were hunter-gatherers.
• Made simple tools of ^a_____ and learned to make fire
New Stone Age
• Learned to farm and how to ^b_____ animals

Bronze Age
• Began around 3000 B.C.
• Worked with soft metals like ^c_____ and tin
• Learned to make bronze tools and weapons
• ^d_____ became more common.

Iron Age
• Began around 1500 B.C. in Europe
• Began to work with ^e_____
• The first real cities appeared.
• Trade became more common.
• Civilization developed more quickly.

Complete each sentence. Change the form if necessary.

primitive   prehistoric   domesticate   fertile soil   nomad

1 Because some areas had _____ _____, humans could easily farm the land.

2 The _____ wandered on the grasslands while following herds of animals.

3 During _____ times, there were no written records of human accomplishments.

4 The word _____ means to tame or raise animals.

5 _____ humans were simple hunter-gatherers who had few skills.

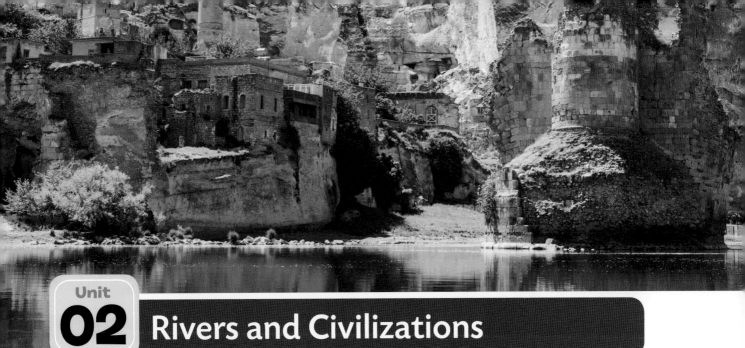

Rivers and Civilizations

What are some ancient civilizations that were located beside rivers?

Ancient Mesopotamia was located between the Tigris and Euphrates rivers.

Sumer was also located by the Tigris and Euphrates rivers.

The civilization of ancient Egypt arose around the Nile River in Africa.

Vocabulary Preview **Write the correct word and the meaning in Chinese next to its meaning.**

Mesopotamia ziggurat irrigate cuneiform polytheism

1 _____ : to bring water to land through a system of pipes, ditches, etc. in order to make crops grow

2 _____ : an early civilization in the Fertile Crescent whose name means "the land between two rivers"

3 _____ : a rectangular stepped tower, sometimes surmounted by a temple

4 _____ : the belief in many gods and goddesses

5 _____ : a writing system created by the Sumerians

The Fertile Crescent and the Kingdoms of Egypt

▲ Fertile Crescent

One of the world's first civilizations began in the **Fertile Crescent** in Southwest Asia. The Fertile Crescent region lies between the Tigris and Euphrates rivers. Later, people called this area **Mesopotamia**, which means "the land between two rivers." Today, we call this area the Middle East.

The two rivers were extremely important to the people of Mesopotamia. When these rivers flooded, they left rich soil that was good for farming. It led an early farming civilization to arise in this region. The Mesopotamians also used their geography and resources to their advantage. Mesopotamian farmers learned to use the waters of the Tigris and Euphrates to **irrigate** dry fields by using canals and pipes. They also constructed dams to store water in artificial lakes. They caught fish in the rivers and raised animals for food and clothing as well. By 3000 B.C., Mesopotamia's villages had grown into larger cities and eventually developed into city-states. Many of these city-states in southern Mesopotamia became known as Sumer.

The Sumerians had a very advanced civilization. They developed a **writing system** called **cuneiform** even before the ancient Egyptians created hieroglyphics. They practiced

▲ ziggurat

polytheism and built a massive **ziggurat** for their gods and goddesses in each city. They also developed basic mathematics and created the 12-month calendar that we use today. After the fall of Sumer, many empires rose and fell in Mesopotamia. Babylonia, Assyria, Hittite, and ancient Israel were all civilizations that were established there.

▲ cuneiform

Around the same time, another great civilization was being developed in Africa. Sometime around 4000 B.C., people started to settle down and found villages and towns in areas alongside the Nile River in Egypt. This was **ancient Egypt**.

▲ hieroglyphics

Life in ancient Egypt was centered on the Nile River. Like the rivers in Mesopotamia, the land around the Nile was very fertile because the river flooded every summer. After the Nile flooded, the soil along the river was full of minerals and other nutrients that helped many crops grow. Soon, Egypt had a large population and a strong farming economy.

Ancient Egypt lasted from around 3100 B.C. until it was conquered by Alexander the Great in 332 B.C. Egyptian history is often divided into three time periods: the Old Kingdom, the Middle Kingdom, and the New Kingdom.

▲ ancient Egypt

The **Old Kingdom** lasted from around 3100 B.C. to 2200 B.C. About 3100 B.C., the ruler of Upper Egypt, Menes, conquered Lower Egypt and united it. He became the first pharaoh of Egypt. The Old Kingdom was the age when the pharaohs became very powerful and were worshipped as living **god-kings**. The pyramids, stone tombs for the pharaohs, were built then. The **Middle Kingdom** lasted from around 2100 B.C. to about 1700 B.C. Many people consider this the golden age of ancient Egypt. Trade **flourished** during this period. And there were great advances made in art, mathematics, and science. As for the **New Kingdom**, it lasted from around 1500 B.C. to 1000 B.C. The pharaohs Amenhotep II and Ramses II both ruled during the New Kingdom. Egypt expanded its territory and reached the peak of its power during this period.

Quick Check Check T (True) or F (False).

1 An early civilization arose in Mesopotamia. T F
2 Egyptian history is divided into three kingdoms. T F
3 The Middle Kingdom in Egypt lasted from 2100 B.C. to 1500 B.C. T F

1   What is the passage mainly about?
   a. The rise and fall of ancient Egypt.
   b. The differences between Mesopotamia and Sumer.
   c. Some early civilizations in Asia and Africa.

2   The _____ were built by the pharaohs during the Old Kingdom.
   a. pyramids   **b.** city-states   **c.** artificial lakes

3   What was cuneiform?
   a. The language spoken by the ancient Egyptians.
   b. The writing system invented by the Sumerians.
   c. The name of the calendar that the Sumerians used.

4   What does arise mean?
   a. Flood.   **b.** Locate.   **c.** Begin.

5   According to the passage, which statement is true?
   a. A part of the Fertile Crescent is located in Egypt.
   b. The Tigris, Euphrates, and Nile rivers all flooded yearly.
   c. Alexander the Great was a famous pharaoh from Egypt.

6   Complete the outline.

Mesopotamia	**Sumer**	**Ancient Egypt**
• Was in the Fertile Crescent between the ^{a}_____ and Euphrates rivers • Farmers ^{b}_____ their fields with the rivers' waters. • Caught fish and raised animals • Had large cities by 3000 B.C.	• Was a group of city-states in southern Mesopotamia • Had a writing system called cuneiform • Practiced ^{c}_____ and built ziggurats • Used a 12-month ^{d}_____	• Developed by the Nile River Old Kingdom = 3100 B.C. to 2200 B.C. • Pharaohs became very powerful and built the ^{e}_____ Middle Kingdom = 2100 B.C. to 1700 B.C. • Was the golden age of Egypt ^{f}_____ _____ = 1500 B.C. to 1000 B.C. • Was the most powerful

Complete each sentence. Change the form if necessary.

irrigate   writing system   ziggurat   flourish   god-king

1   A _____ was a massive temple built by the Sumerians.

2   Mesopotamian farmers used river water to _____ their fields.

3   Pharaohs, the _____ rulers of ancient Egypt, controlled Egypt for 2,000 years.

4   Hieroglyphics and cuneiform were two _____ _____ from the ancient world.

5   Many civilizations _____ after people began to build cities.

Unit 03 Asian Civilizations

What were some features of the Indus Valley Civilization?

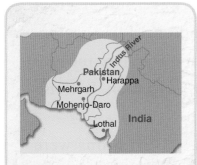

The Indus Valley cities were well organized and built in a grid pattern.

Harappan artifacts include pots, toys, statues, and tools from clay and copper.

Hinduism, one of the world's oldest religions, was born and developed in ancient India.

Vocabulary Preview   Write the correct word and the meaning in Chinese next to its meaning.

| Indus Valley Civilization   monsoon   sewage system   Indus script   decline |

1 _____ : a system that can remove human and animal waste

2 _____ : to become worse in condition or quality

3 _____ : the ancient civilization that arose in the Indus Valley

4 _____ : the writing system used by the Indus people

5 _____ : a wind in the Indian Ocean and southern Asia that brings heavy rains in the summer

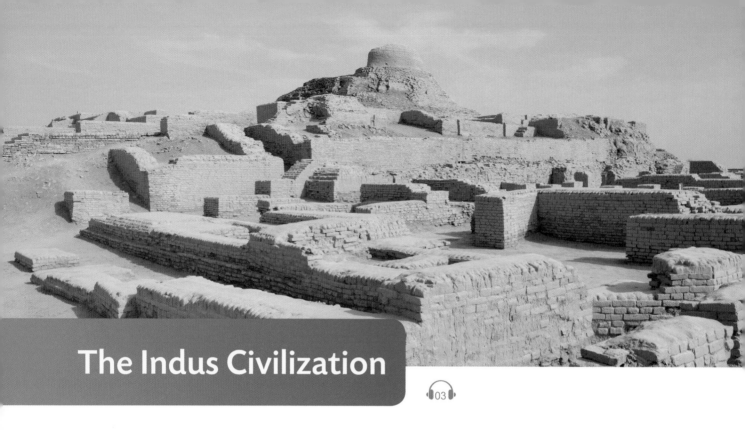

The Indus Civilization

🎧 03

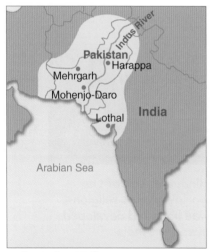

▲ the Indus Valley Civilization

▲ Indus script

Around 2500 B.C., there was another great civilization rising in the Indus River region, which is in modern-day India and Pakistan. Today, it is known as the **Indus Valley Civilization**. It is also called the Harappan Civilization.

Much like the other great civilizations were established beside rivers, the Indus Valley people built their villages, towns, and cities along the Indus River. In doing so, they gained easy access to water for drinking, farming, and raising animals. Today, two of these cities are called Harappa and Mohenjo-Daro.

Archaeologists have unearthed more than 1,000 different settlements from the Indus Valley Civilization. By studying **artifacts**, archaeologists have learned that the Indus Valley Civilization was well organized. For instance, its cities were **laid out** in a grid pattern in the shape of a rectangle. Within the cities were palaces, temples, granaries, bathhouses, and wide paved streets. They even had **sewage systems**.

The Indus Valley people knew about agriculture. The Indus River and **monsoons**—seasonal winds that cause heavy rains during summer—influenced Indian life. Harappan farmers learned to take advantage of this weather, so they grew a variety of crops. Surplus grain was stored **in case of** droughts. They also domesticated sheep, cattle, and pigs. They made pots and tools from clay and copper. They even **engaged in** trade with other places such as Mesopotamia. While they had a writing system called **Indus script**, historians have not been able to read it yet.

▲ the ruins of Harappa

▲ the ruins of Mohenjo-Daro

The Indus Civilization lasted more than 1,000 years. Historians are not sure why the Indus Civilization **declined**. But, for some reason, the people began to leave the cities along the Indus River. A new civilization developed along the Ganges River in another part of India. But then new people, called Aryans, came from the northwest and settled in the region. They conquered and ruled the Indian people. Over many years, the Aryans changed the way that the Indian people lived. One of the biggest changes was the birth of **Hinduism**. The Aryans combined their gods with the gods worshipped by the Indian people. Hinduism is now one of the world's oldest religions. Today, more than 850 million people in India are Hindus.

Brahma
Vishnu
▲ Hinduism

Quick Check   Check T (True) or F (False).

1   Mohenjo-Daro was a city that was in the Indus Valley Civilization.   ☐ T   ☐ F

2   The people in the Indus Valley did not know how to farm the land.   ☐ T   ☐ F

3   The Aryans were the original people who lived in the Indus Valley.   ☐ T   ☐ F

1 **What is the main idea of the passage?**
  a. The Indus Valley was where the first human civilization was founded.
  b. The Aryans were the most important people in the Indus Valley.
  c. The people in the Indus Valley formed an advanced civilization.

2 **The cities in the Indus Valley Civilization were shaped like a _____.**
  a. circle   **b.** triangle   **c.** rectangle

3 **What let Harappan farmers grow many kinds of crops?**
  a. Advanced farming methods.   **b.** Monsoon rains.   **c.** Very fertile soil.

4 **What does unearthed mean?**
  a. Found.   **b.** Dug up.   **c.** Built up.

5 **Answer the questions.**
  a. What is the writing system that the Indus Valley people used called? _____
  b. What animals did the Harappans domesticate? _____
  c. How long did the Indus Civilization last? _____

6 **Complete the outline.**

Indus Valley Civilization
• Was by the ᵃ_____ _____
• Had well-organized cities laid out in grid patterns
• Cities had palaces, temples, granaries, bathhouses, wide paved streets, and ᵇ_____ systems
• The Indus River and ᶜ_____ influenced Indian life.
• Had Indus script as a writing system

Aryans
• Came from the ᵈ_____
• Conquered the Indus Valley area and ruled the people
• Changed how the Indian people lived
• Combined their gods with the gods worshipped in India and formed ᵉ_____

Complete each sentence. Change the form if necessary.

monsoon   lay out   in case of   engage in   decline

1 The merchants _____ _____ trade with people from Mesopotamia.

2 The civilization began to _____ after the people were defeated by invading armies.

3 Harappan cities were _____ _____ in the form of a rectangle, which made them well organized.

4 A _____ caused heavy rains in India during summer.

5 Surplus grain was stored in granaries _____ _____ _____ crop failures.

Unit 04 The Ancient World

Visual Preview What were some important features of ancient Greece?

The Greeks frequently traded with other cultures around the Mediterranean Sea.

Athens and other Greek city-states practiced democracy as their form of government.

The Greek city-states often fought each other, such as during the Peloponnesian War.

Vocabulary Preview Write the correct word and the meaning in Chinese next to its meaning.

| ambitious | city-state | monarchy | oligarchy | Peloponnesian War |

1 _____ : a war between Athens and Sparta that lasted almost thirty years

2 _____ : determined to be successful, rich, famous, etc.

3 _____ : a form of government in which a small group of rich men rule

4 _____ : a form of government in which the ruler is a king

5 _____ : a great independent city in the ancient world, such as Athens and Sparta

Ancient Greece

🎧 04

Ancient Greece was made up of two peninsulas in the **Mediterranean Sea**: Attica and Peloponnesus. There were also more than 400 islands along the coast of the Mediterranean Sea. Greece had no flooding river like the Nile, and much of its mainland was covered with hills and mountains. Its rocky, dry soil was not **suitable for** farming, so the ancient Greeks depended on the sea for food and trade.

Three earlier Mediterranean civilizations **influenced** the ancient Greek culture. They were the Minoans of the island of Crete, the Mycenaeans, who came from central Asia and conquered the Minoans, and the Phoenicians of the eastern Mediterranean. They sailed across the Mediterranean as traders and spread their cultures and ideas along with their trade goods. The Phoenicians invented the alphabet which became the basis for the alphabet we use today.

The Greeks **practiced** many new ideas and various government systems. The Greeks lived in separate **city-states**. These city-states remained independent of each other, but the people living in them all spoke the same Greek language.

▼ ancient Greece

22

Some city-states were ruled by a king. This kind of government is called a **monarchy**. Other city-states were ruled by groups of rich men. This kind of government is called an **oligarchy**. A few city-states practiced democracy, in which all of the citizens took part in the government and chose their leaders. The Athenians led the way. But only men could be citizens. Women and slaves were not citizens, so they could not vote. Even though democracy in Athens was not perfect, it still influenced many nations in later times. Today, we call Athens the **birthplace** of democracy.

▲ The Athenians practiced democracy.

By about 500 B.C., the two most powerful city-states in Greece were Athens and Sparta. They had different values and cultures. Athens practiced democracy and was a great sea power. The Spartans were excellent warriors and had a powerful army. From 431 B.C. to 404 B.C., Athens and Sparta fought one another in the **Peloponnesian War**. Eventually, Sparta won, and Athens ceased to be a great power.

▲ The Spartans constantly trained for war.

Many other Greek city-states were also involved in the Peloponnesian War. After it ended, these city-states were all weak. North of Greece was Macedon. It was led by King Philip. He began to conquer many Greek city-states, including Athens. Philip was murdered in 336 B.C., and his son Alexander became the king. Alexander quickly defeated the rest of the Greek peninsula. However, he was an **ambitious** young man. Alexander took his army eastward. By the time Alexander the Great died in 323 B.C., he had destroyed the Persian Empire and conquered much of Western Asia and Northern Africa. He was the ruler of the largest empire in the world when he died.

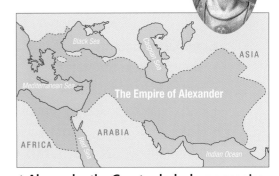
▲ Alexander the Great ruled a large empire.

Quick Check　Check T (True) or F (False).

1　The Mycenaeans invented the alphabet that the ancient Greeks used.　T　F

2　Sparta was a city-state where the people practiced democracy.　T　F

3　Alexander the Great managed to conquer all of Greece.　T　F

1 **What is the passage mainly about?**
   a. The rivalry between Athens and Sparta.
   b. The history and culture of ancient Greece.
   c. The forms of government the ancient Greeks practiced.

2 **The city-state known as the birthplace of democracy was _____ .**
   a. Sparta   **b.** Thebes   **c.** Athens

3 **Who was King Philip?**
   a. The father of Alexander the Great.   **b.** The first king of ancient Greece.
   c. One of the kings of Persia.

4 **What does took part mean?**
   a. Practiced.   **b.** Participated.   **c.** Supported.

5 **Complete the sentences.**
   a. Ancient Greece was made up of the Attica and Peloponnesus _____ .
   b. In Athens, only men were considered _____ and therefore allowed to vote.
   c. Sparta defeated Athens during the _____ War.

6 **Complete the outline.**

Greek Civilizations

Earlier Civilizations
• Minoan civilization • Mycenaean civilization
• ᵃ_____ civilization
Greek Governments
• Greeks lived in city-states.
• Had monarchies ruled by ᵇ_____
• Had oligarchies ruled by groups of rich men
• Had ᶜ_____ , in which citizens
  participated in the government

Two Powerful City-States and Macedon

Athens
• Practiced democracy • Was a great sea power
Sparta
• Had great warriors • Had a powerful army
• Defeated ᵈ_____ in the Peloponnesian War
Macedon
• King Philip and ᵉ_____ the Great
  conquered Greece.

Complete each sentence. Change the form if necessary.

| suitable for | influence | practice | birthplace | ambitious |

1 Athens and some other city-states in ancient Greece _____ democracy.

2 Alexander the Great was very _____ , so he invaded many countries.

3 The _____ of democracy is considered to be Athens.

4 Athens and Sparta both _____ many of the city-states throughout Greece.

5 The rocky soil was mostly not _____ _____ farming, so Greek farmers grew olives.

Visual Preview What were some important events in the history of ancient Rome?

Rome defeated Carthage in the Punic Wars.

Julius Caesar was assassinated in the Roman Senate.

Octavian defeated Antony and Cleopatra and became the first emperor of Rome.

Vocabulary Preview Write the correct word and the meaning in Chinese next to its meaning.

> triumvirate   Punic Wars   tribune   triumphant   Pax Romana

1 _____ : a group of three powerful people, especially people in charge of something

2 _____ : a plebeian who took part in the government during the Roman Republic

3 _____ : showing that you are very pleased or excited about a victory or success

4 _____ : three wars that were fought between Rome and Carthage

5 _____ : the Roman peace; the long period of stability under the Roman Empire

The Roman Empire

05

According to legend, Rome was founded by the brothers Romulus and Remus on the Italian peninsula in 753 B.C. It was a small city located on seven hills along the Tiber River, but, as it grew, Rome became the center of a vast empire. At its height, the Roman Empire included most of modern-day Europe and some of Africa and the Middle East.

▲ the ancient Romans

Early in its history, Rome was ruled by Etruscan kings for 250 years. In 510 B.C., the Romans **drove away** these kings and founded a new form of government called a republic. Thus, the Roman Republic was born. In a republic, people choose representatives, who make political decisions for them. Every year, the wealthy men in the Roman Republic, known as **patricians**, selected two leaders, called consuls. They also elected **senators**, who advised the consuls and served in the Roman Senate. Together, they ruled Rome and made important decisions concerning the city. Later, the **plebeians**—the poor farmers and shopkeepers—were given a plebeian assembly to elect 10 plebeian **tribunes**. These tribunes had **veto power** and defended the plebeians' rights.

Over the years, Rome's power grew. By 300 B.C., Rome controlled most of the Italian peninsula and was a major power on the Mediterranean Sea. But Rome had a rival across the Mediterranean: the city of Carthage. Beginning in 275 B.C., the Romans battled Carthage in three separate wars, called the **Punic Wars**. The Third Punic War ended in 146 B.C. After winning the Punic Wars, the Romans became the masters of the Mediterranean region.

▲ the second Punic War

Rome continued expanding its territory. It took over very much land in Europe, Asia, and Africa. But after the Punic Wars ended, several **civil wars** erupted between wealthy Romans and powerful generals. Eventually, Pompey, Crassus, and Julius Caesar formed a **triumvirate** to rule Rome. This lasted for around a decade until the three men started fighting. Julius Caesar **emerged triumphant**, but he was assassinated in the Roman Senate in 44 B.C.

After Caesar's death, there was more fighting until 31 B.C., when Octavian defeated Anthony and Cleopatra. After his victory, Octavian became emperor. The Roman Republic ended, and the Roman Empire began with Octavian, now called Augustus, as the first emperor. Augustus's rule began the **Pax Romana**, the "Roman Peace." This peace lasted nearly 200 years.

▲ Augustus (= Octavian), the first Roman emperor

Over time, the empire became too big for one man to rule. In 293 A.D., Diocletian split the empire into eastern and western parts. His goal was to make ruling the empire easier. However, this led to the complete split of the Roman Empire under Constantine I. In 324, Constantine I moved the center of power to Byzantium and renamed the city Constantinople. This would become the Byzantine Empire.

▼ the Roman Empire

The Western Roman Empire grew weaker after the split. Finally, in 476, Germanic invaders conquered the city of Rome. But the Byzantine Empire lasted for almost one thousand more years.

Quick Check   Check T (True) or F (False).

1   Rome was supposedly founded in 753 A.D.   ☐ T   ☐ F
2   Rome defeated Carthage in the Punic Wars.   ☐ T   ☐ F
3   The Pax Romana began during the rule of Constantine I.   ☐ T   ☐ F

1 **What is the passage mainly about?**
   a. The founding of Rome and the Pax Romana.
   b. Roman history from republic to empire.
   c. The fighting between Rome and Carthage.

2 **The emperor who divided Rome into eastern and western parts was _____.**
   a. Constantine I   **b.** Augustus   **c.** Diocletian

3 **What happened in Rome after the Punic Wars ended?**
   a. There were several civil wars.
   b. Rome finally became a republic.
   c. Rome was broken into two countries.

4 **What does took over mean?**
   a. Captured.   **b.** Defeated.   **c.** Ruled.

5 **According to the passage, which statement is true?**
   a. The Byzantine Empire was conquered by Germanic invaders.
   b. Roman patricians elected both the consuls and the senators.
   c. Julius Caesar ruled Rome and became the first emperor.

6 **Complete the outline.**

The Roman Republic
- Was founded in 510 B.C. when the Romans drove away the Etruscans
- The people chose representatives.
- Was led by 2 ᵃ_____
- Had senators and ᵇ_____
- Won the Punic Wars
- Civil wars erupted until 31 B.C.

The Roman Empire
- Began when Octavian became emperor
- Started the Pax Romana
- The empire became too big.
- Was divided into ᶜ_____ and western parts
- Split into the Western Roman Empire and the ᵈ_____ _____ under Constantine I
- The Western Roman Empire was conquered in 476 by ᵉ_____ invaders.

Complete each sentence. Change the form if necessary.

> drive away   triumvirate   senator   civil war   emerge triumphant

1 The people of Rome managed to _____ _____ the Etruscans and win their freedom.

2 _____ advised the consuls and served in the Roman Senate in ancient Rome.

3 During the _____ _____, many Romans were killed in the fighting.

4 The _____ refers to the joint rule by three men in ancient Rome.

5 Octavian _____ _____ in the civil war and became the first emperor.

Unit 06 The Arab World

What are some of the basic duties of all Muslims?

Muslims must face Mecca and pray five times a day.

fasting time

Muslims cannot eat in the daylight hours during the month of Ramadan.

Muslims must make a pilgrimage to the city of Mecca at least once in their lives.

Vocabulary Preview

Write the correct word and the meaning in Chinese next to its meaning.

| prophet | fast | holy book | caliph | crusade |

1 _____ : a Muslim leader who was selected as a successor of Muhammad

2 _____ : a holy war

3 _____ : a member of some religions (such as Islam) who delivers messages that are believed to have come from God

4 _____ : scripture; a book important to a religion

5 _____ : to eat no food or very little food for a period of time, often for religious reasons

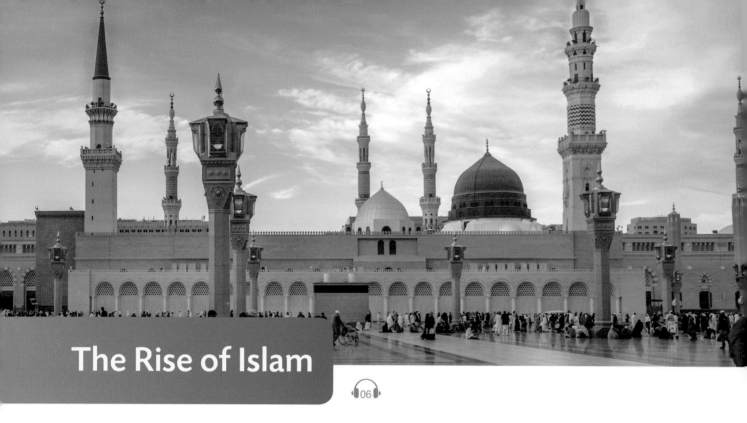

The Rise of Islam

🎧 06

The Arabian Peninsula has some of the world's largest desert areas. Much of the region is very dry and hot. Yet people have lived on the Arabian Peninsula for thousands of years, and wonderful civilizations have flourished there. We call the people who have lived there for more than 3,000 years Arabs.

Islam developed on the Arabian Peninsula starting in 610 and grew rapidly. Muhammad (= Mohammad), the founder of Islam, was born in the city of **Mecca** (= Makkah) in the Arabian Peninsula around 570. Muslims, Islam's followers, believe that Muhammad was visited by the angel Gabriel with a message from Allah in 610. Allah is the Arabic word for God.

According to Islamic tradition, after Muhammad had a vision of the angel Gabriel, he began preaching to other Arabs. He preached that they should worship only one god: Allah. He taught that all people are equal and that the rich should take care of the poor. After Muhammad's death, his teachings were written down by his

▼ the Koran,
   the holy book of Islam

followers, and they became the **holy book** of Islam, called the Koran (= Quran). There are five basic duties in Islam. These are called the Five Pillars of Islam. They are:

1. **Testify** that there is no god but Allah and that Muhammad is Allah's **prophet**.

2. Make prayers five times a day while facing Mecca.

3. **Give charity** to the poor and the needy.

4. **Fast**, which means not to eat or drink anything, during the daytime in the holy month of Ramadan.

5. Make a Hajj, which means to make a pilgrimage to Mecca, during one's lifetime.

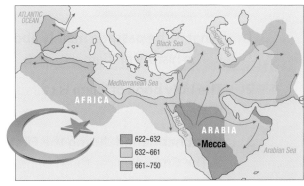
▲ the spread of Islam

After Muhammad died in 632, Muslim leaders selected **caliphs** to govern the Muslim community. A caliph was a Muslim political and religious leader who was selected as a successor of Muhammad. From 632 to 661, there were four caliphs. Under them, Islam spread rapidly. Muslim armies conquered Christian cities such as Alexandria, Jerusalem, and Damascus. They took over land in western Asia, North Africa, and Spain. They went north up to France, but they were defeated by Charles Martel in 732. In the east, they reached the gates of Constantinople, the capital of the Byzantine Empire, before they were pushed back.

The spread of Islam alarmed many people in the West. So, in the late eleventh century, the pope urged Christians in Western Europe to send armies to Jerusalem to free the Holy Land. This began the **Crusades**. In 1099, during the First Crusade, the Crusaders **captured** Jerusalem. For the next 200 years, there were several Crusades. In the end, though, the Crusaders were defeated, and the Muslims recaptured all of the lands that they had lost during the Crusades.

▲ Crusaders in battle

Later, the **Ottoman Empire** arose during the 1200s. It became extremely powerful. In 1453, the Ottoman Empire captured Constantinople and destroyed the Byzantine Empire. The Ottoman Empire survived up until the end of World War I.

▲ the Ottoman Empire at its peak

Quick Check Check T (True) or F (False).

1 Muslims believe that Allah appeared and spoke to Muhammad in 610. ☐ T ☐ F
2 Four caliphs ruled the Islamic world from 632 to 661. ☐ T ☐ F
3 The Ottoman Empire defeated the Byzantine Empire. ☐ T ☐ F

1 **What is the passage mainly about?**
a. The history of Islam.   b. The Five Pillars of Islam.   c. The life of Muhammad.

2 **The holy book of Islam is called the _____.**
a. Hajj   b. Koran   c. Allah

3 **What happened during the First Crusade?**
a. The Crusaders captured Damascus.
b. The Crusaders captured Jerusalem.
c. The Crusaders captured Constantinople.

4 **What does urged mean?**
a. Begged.   b. Preached.   c. Announced.

5 **Answer the questions.**
a. What is a Hajj? _____
b. What did Charles Martel do? _____
c. What did the Ottoman Empire do in 1453?

_____

6 **Complete the outline.**

The Rise of Islam
• Was founded by a_____ • Koran = the holy book of Islam **The Five Pillars of Islam** • There is no god but Allah, and Muhammad is Allah's b_____. • Pray toward Mecca five times a day • Give charity to the poor and the needy • Fast during c_____ • Make a Hajj to Mecca

The History of Islam
• 610 = Muhammad founded d_____ • 632 = Muhammad died • 632–661 = Islam spread rapidly in western Asia, North Africa, and Spain • 732 = Charles Martel stopped an Islamic army in France • 1099–1300 = Crusades • 1453 = The e_____ _____ captured Constantinople

Complete each sentence. Change the form if necessary.

give charity   testify   fast   capture   prophet

1 Islamic armies _____ a large number of Christian cities.

2 The followers of Islam must _____ about their beliefs.

3 The Five Pillars of Islam speaks of _____ _____ to the needy.

4 A _____ is a person who is believed to have been chosen by God to speak for God.

5 Muslims have to _____ for most of the day during Ramadan.

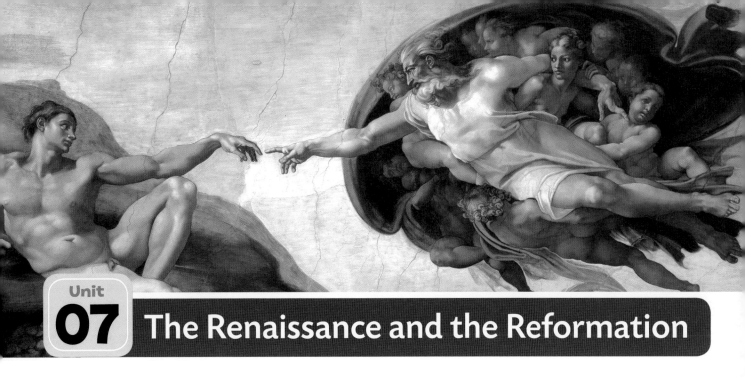

Visual Preview What were some of the main features of the Renaissance and the Reformation?

People studied works from ancient Greece and Rome during the Renaissance.

People focused on humans more than religion in the Renaissance.

Men like Martin Luther felt that the Church was corrupt during the Reformation.

Vocabulary Preview Write the correct word and the meaning in Chinese next to its meaning.

| sect Black Death Protestant Reformation indulgence thesis |

1 _____ : a group of people with somewhat different religious beliefs from those of a larger group to which they belong

2 _____ : the movement to reform the Catholic Church in the sixteenth century

3 _____ : a proposal; an argument

4 _____ : a plague in the 1300s that killed millions of people in Europe

5 _____ : forgiveness for one's sins

From the Middle Ages to the Reformation

🎧 07

The Roman Empire had controlled all of the land along the coast of the Mediterranean Sea and most places in Europe. Under the Pax Romana, Rome's soldiers had kept the peace for centuries. After the vast Roman Empire collapsed in 476, Europe suffered almost constant war. The period between the fall of Rome and the 1400s is called the Middle Ages.

For most Europeans, life was hard during the Middle Ages. Medieval society was like a pyramid based on **feudalism**: the kings and lords were on top, the knights were below them, and the peasants, or serfs, were on the bottom. People suffered from terrible wars and hunger, and diseases killed thousands of people. There were few advances in science, literature, art, and other fields.

However, for the Christian Church, the Middle Ages were a time of growth. Since Christianity became the official religion of the Roman Empire in 313, the Church continued to expand even after the Western Roman Empire collapsed. By the year 1000, most Europeans were Christians, and the Church dominated people's daily lives. This is why the Middle Ages is sometimes called the Age of Faith.

▲ the Black Death

In the 1300s, a plague, called the **Black Death**, struck Europe. It killed millions of people. The deaths of so many people changed Europe's economy and **sped up** the end of feudalism in Europe. So many serfs died that lords had to pay workers on their manors.

Around 1400, the Middle Ages came to an end, and the Renaissance began in Italy. The word Renaissance

34

means "rebirth." During this period, people began to rediscover and value art, science, literature, and the ideas of ancient Greece and Rome. This led them to make new discoveries of their own. **Humanists** led the way. They studied ancient Greek and Roman writings and focused on humans more than religion. There were numerous advances made in science, art, literature, music, and other fields. People

like Leonardo da Vinci and Michelangelo became Renaissance Men—men with curiosity and talents in many fields.

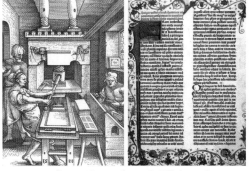
▲ a page from Gutenberg's Bible using movable type

The Renaissance spread throughout Europe. During it, there was one important invention that greatly altered society. It was the printing press. Johannes Gutenberg invented **movable type** in the 1450s. His invention made books more accessible. Books became cheaper and easier to make, so more people learned to read. This let more people read the Bible for themselves. Previously, only priests and the rich could read it. But, now, common people could read the Bible and come up with their own interpretations of it. This helped lead to the **Protestant Reformation**.

▲ Martin Luther and German Protestant reformers

During the Renaissance, the Catholic Church still had great power. Some popes and bishops became powerful political rulers. But Martin Luther, a German priest, thought that the Church was too corrupt. He was especially upset that the Church sold **indulgences** to rebuild St. Peter's Church in Rome. In 1517, he went to a church and **nailed** a paper with ninety-five **theses** on it. His actions resulted in the Protestant Reformation.

Many others felt the same as Luther. They thought the Church needed to be reformed. The ideas of the Reformation rapidly spread from Germany to Switzerland, the Netherlands, France, and England. More people left the Catholic Church and founded their own Christian **sects**. Even King Henry VIII of England split with the Catholic Church and established the Anglican Church in the 1530s. The Lutheran, Presbyterian, and Anabaptist sects were all founded during this time.

Quick Check | Check T (True) or F (False).

1 The fall of the Roman Empire happened during the Middle Ages. T F
2 Michelangelo and Leonardo da Vinci were both Renaissance Men. T F
3 The Anglican Church was created by King Henry VIII. T F

1 **What is the passage mainly about?**
  a. The reasons why the Protestant Reformation occurred.
  b. Medieval European and how it moved to the Renaissance.
  c. Human progress from the Middle Ages to the Reformation.

2 **The Black Death happened during the** _____ .
  a. Reformation   b. Middle Ages   c. Renaissance

3 **Why did Martin Luther nail the paper with ninety-five theses to a church?**
  a. He was protesting the role of priests in the Church.
  b. He believed that the Church had become corrupt.
  c. He wanted to found a new church of his own.

4 **What does interpretations mean?**
  a. Explanations.   b. Purchases.   c. Translations.

5 **Complete the sentences.**
  a. In _____, the king was at the top while the peasants were at the bottom of society.
  b. People who focused more on humans than religion were called _____.
  c. The Protestant Reformation began in _____ but spread to other European countries.

6 **Complete the outline.**

Renaissance
• Began in ᵃ_____ around 1400
• People rediscovered art, science, literature, and the ideas of ancient Greece and Rome.
• Was led by ᵇ_____
• Focused less on religion
• There were many advances.
• ᶜ_____ studied many different fields.
• Invention of movable type = more people could read

Reformation
• Martin Luther thought the Catholic Church was corrupt.
• Nailed 95 ᵈ_____ to a church
• Others thought the Church needed to be reformed.
• The Reformation spread to many countries.
• Henry VIII founded the ᵉ_____ _____.
• The Lutheran, Presbyterian, and Anabaptist ᶠ_____ were founded.

Complete each sentence. Change the form if necessary.

speed up   humanist   movable type   nail   sect

1 The invention of _____ _____ greatly changed European society.

2 Martin Luther _____ his ninety-five theses to a church and started the Reformation.

3 Gutenberg press helped _____ _____ the Reformation.

4 Many Christian _____ were established during the Reformation.

5 The ideas of the _____ were inspired by the cultures of ancient Greece and Rome.

Unit 08
The Enlightenment: The Age of Reason

What were some of the results of the Enlightenment?

New inventions and new ideas swept over Europe during the 1600s and 1700s.

The American colonists used the ideas of the Enlightenment to rebel against England.

The people of France rebelled against the French monarchy in 1789.

Write the correct word and the meaning in Chinese next to its meaning.

| Enlightenment | remarkable | heliocentric | divine right | Three Estates |

1 _____ : sun-centered

2 _____ : a period of scientific discoveries and new ideas in Europe during the 1600s and 1700s

3 _____ : the three classes of people in eighteenth-century France

4 _____ : unusual in a way that surprises or impresses you

5 _____ : the concept that the king's right to rule comes from God

The Enlightenment and the French Revolution

🎧 08

During the 1600s and 1700s, new ideas about the world and scientific discoveries **swept over** Europe. This was the **Enlightenment**. It is also called the Age of **Reason**.

During the Enlightenment, scientists developed a process called the scientific method and began to ask questions about everything. As a result, there were many **remarkable** scientific discoveries. Galileo Galilei improved the early telescope and studied the solar system. He supported Nicolaus Copernicus's **heliocentric**, sun-centered theory. Isaac Newton invented calculus, a new kind of mathematics, and discovered gravity and the laws of motion. Doctors improved medicine with new ideas and methods. The French philosopher René Descartes developed a philosophy based on logic and reason. Philosophers such as Thomas Hobbes, John Locke, and Baron Montesquieu expounded on governments and people's basic rights.

The ideas of the Enlightenment changed how people understood society and government. Eventually, these ideas would lead to war and revolution in England, the United States, and France.

In the 1600s, Europe's kings were very powerful. They claimed that they ruled by **divine right**. They insisted that God had chosen them to be kings, so they had the right to rule the country in any way they wanted. But the new ideas about the government and equality no longer accepted the concept of divine

▲ Galilei demonstrating his telescope

right. As a result, the conflict between the English King Charles I and Parliament led to a civil war in England in 1642. In 1649, Charles I was defeated, and the English kings were forced to respect the laws passed by Parliament.

The ideas of the Enlightenment were also very **influential** to the American Revolution, which began in 1775. In 1763, the English government wanted the American colonies to pay off the debt caused by an expensive war with France. But the colonists protested. In 1776, the colonists separated from Great Britain and later established the United States of America. The American Founding Fathers based their ideas on freedom on the works of Enlightenment scholars.

A few years later, in 1789, the French Revolution began. It too was influenced by the Enlightenment. The kingdom of France was divided into three "estates," or classes. The First Estate was the **clergy** in the Catholic Church. The Second Estate was the nobility. The Third Estate was everybody else. The Third Estate included about 98 percent of population. Most of these people were poor peasants. They paid the majority of the taxes but had no role in the government.

According to French law, each of the **Three Estates** had the right to elect representatives to send to the **Estates General**, an assembly. However, no French king had called a meeting of the Estates General since 1614. By 1789, France was nearing bankruptcy. King Louis XVI called the Estates General in order to levy more taxes. The Third Estate was upset. They rebelled and formed a National Assembly. They stormed the Bastille, a prison in Paris, and took weapons that were there to defend their rights. "Liberty! Equality! Fraternity!" was the slogan of the French Revolution. In 1792, the National Convention ended the monarchy and established a republic.

Isaac Newton,
the discoverer of the laws of motion

René Descartes,
the founder of modern philosophy

King Louis XVI

▲ **Parisians storming the Bastille**

| Quick Check | Check T (True) or F (False). |

1 René Descartes was a philosopher who wrote about logic and reason. ☐T ☐F
2 In the Enlightenment, people no longer accepted the concept of divine right. ☐T ☐F
3 The First Estate in France was the nobility. ☐T ☐F

1 **What is the passage mainly about?**
   a. The most important scientists and philosophers in the Enlightenment.
   b. The results of the American and French Revolutions.
   c. The Enlightenment and how it changed Europe afterward.

2 **One famous philosopher from the Enlightenment was _____.**
   a. John Locke   **b.** Nicolaus Copernicus   **c.** Galileo Galilei

3 **Which event started in 1789?**
   a. The American Revolution.   **b.** The French Revolution.   **c.** The English Civil War.

4 **What does stormed mean?**
   a. Attacked.   **b.** Purchased.   **c.** Burned.

5 **According to the passage, which statement is true?**
   a. The Enlightenment started in the sixteenth century.
   b. The English kings had to listen to Parliament starting in 1649.
   c. Soldiers for King Louis XVI attacked the Bastille in 1789.

6 **Complete the outline.**

Enlightenment
• Lasted from 1600s to 1700s
• Many great scientists = Galileo Galilei, Nicolaus Copernicus, and Isaac Newton
• Many great ª_____ = René Descartes, Thomas Hobbes, John Locke, and Baron Montesquieu
• New ideas led to revolutions.

War and Revolution
The English Civil War
• People no longer accepted "ᵇ_____ _____."
• English kings were forced to respect the laws of Parliament.
American Revolution
• The Founding Fathers based their ideas on the ᶜ_____.
French Revolution
• 1789 = the Estates General was called
• The Third Estate stormed the ᵈ_____
• 1792 = The ᵉ_____ ended, and a republic was founded.

Complete each sentence. Change the form if necessary.

sweep over   remarkable   influential   clergy   Estates General

1 The work that Isaac Newton did in the field of physics was _____.

2 The _____ are members of the church such as priests and bishops.

3 George Washington was a very _____ person in the American Revolution.

4 Many changes _____ _____ Europe and altered how people thought about the world.

5 The French kings rarely called the _____ _____ to order.

A

Complete each sentence with the correct word. Change the form if necessary.

| New Stone Age | three-age | lie | ziggurat | artifact |
| hunter-gatherer | Old Kingdom | influence | practice | worship |

1   Archaeologists have created a _____ system to describe prehistoric cultures.

2   During the Old Stone Age, humans lived as _____.

3   In the _____ _____ _____, people also learned to domesticate wild animals.

4   The Fertile Crescent region _____ between the Tigris and Euphrates rivers.

5   The Sumerians practiced polytheism and built a massive _____ for their gods and goddesses in each city.

6   Egyptian history is often divided into three time periods: the _____ _____, the Middle Kingdom, and the New Kingdom.

7   By studying _____, archaeologists have learned that the Indus Valley Civilization was well organized.

8   The Aryans combined their gods with the gods _____ by the Indian people.

9   Three earlier Mediterranean civilizations _____ the ancient Greek culture.

10   The Greeks _____ many new ideas and various government systems.

B

Complete each sentence with the correct word. Change the form if necessary.

| Arabian | height | Pax Romana | Mediterranean | knight |
| capture | nail | sweep over | Muhammad | slogan |

1   At its _____, the Roman Empire included most of modern-day Europe and some of Africa and the Middle East.

2   After winning the Punic Wars, the Romans became the masters of the _____ region.

3   Augustus's rule began the _____ _____, the "Roman Peace."

4   Islam developed on the _____ Peninsula starting in 610 and grew rapidly.

5   After _____ died in 632, Muslim leaders selected caliphs to govern the Muslim community.

6   In 1099, during the First Crusade, the Crusaders _____ Jerusalem.

7   Medieval society was like a pyramid based on feudalism: the kings and lords were on top, the _____ were below them, and the peasants were on the bottom.

8   In 1517, Martin Luther went to a church and _____ a paper with ninety-five theses on it.

9   During the Enlightenment, new ideas about the world and scientific discoveries _____ _____ Europe.

10   "Liberty! Equality! Fraternity!" was the _____ of the French Revolution.

C Match each word with the correct definition and write the meaning in Chinese.

1   Bronze Age   _____ ☐

2   Fertile Crescent   _____ ☐

3   polytheism   _____ ☐

4   cuneiform   _____ ☐

5   tribune   _____ ☐

6   indulgence   _____ ☐

7   divine right   _____ ☐

8   thesis   _____ ☐

9   Three Estates   _____ ☐

10   Mecca   _____ ☐

a. forgiveness for one's sins

b. a proposal; an argument

c. the belief in many gods and goddesses

d. a writing system created by the Sumerians

e. the birthplace of Muhammad; the holiest city of Islam

f. the three classes of people in eighteenth-century France

g. the concept that the king's right to rule comes from God

h. the period when humans learned to work with copper and tin

i. a plebeian who took part in the government during the Roman Republic

j. an ancient region located between the Tigris and Euphrates rivers

D Write the meanings of the words in Chinese.

1   Ice Age   _____

2   sewage system   _____

3   Hinduism   _____

4   Indus Valley Civilization   _____

5   Indus script   _____

6   Peloponnesian War   _____

7   oligarchy   _____

8   veto power   _____

9   Punic Wars   _____

10   caliph   _____

11   crusade   _____

12   holy book   _____

13   feudalism   _____

14   Black Death   _____

15   Protestant Reformation   _____

16   heliocentric   _____

17   Enlightenment   _____

18   reason   _____

19   primitive   _____

20   prehistoric   _____

21   domesticate   _____

22   irrigate   _____

23   triumvirate   _____

24   triumphant   _____

25   sweep over   _____

26   prophet   _____

27   movable type   _____

28   sect   _____

29   Estates General   _____

30   drive away   _____

2

● Science

Unit 09 The Characteristics of Living Things

What can cells form?

Animals are multi-cellular organisms that are made up of trillions of cells.

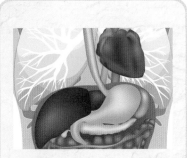

In the body, some similar cells come together to form organs such as the heart and liver.

Cells reproduce by either mitosis or meiosis.

Vocabulary Preview | Write the correct word and the meaning in Chinese next to its meaning.

recessive   mitosis   meiosis   heredity   mutation

1 _____ : a method of cellular reproduction in which a cell divides itself in half

2 _____ : the method in which reproductive cells are created

3 _____ : only appearing in a child if both parents supply the controlling gene

4 _____ : a permanent change in an organism's gene

5 _____ : the passing down of characteristics from parents to offspring

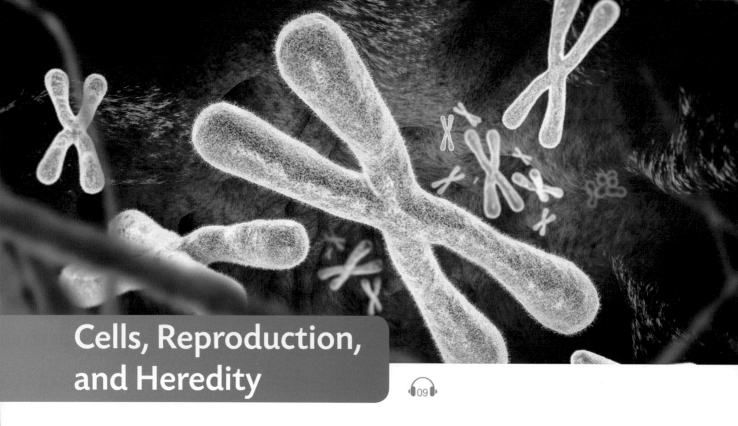

Cells, Reproduction, and Heredity

🎧 09

The basic unit of life is the cell. All living things are made up of at least more than one cell. One-celled, or single-celled, organisms are **microorganisms**. They include bacteria and viruses. However, the majority of life contains more than one cell. These are called multi-cellular,

▲ microorganism

or multi-celled, organisms. Multi-cellular organisms, such as complex animals and plants, are made of different kinds of cells. Similar cells that have the same function form tissue. Tissues of different kinds come together to form an organ, such as the stomach or lungs. A group of organs makes up an organ system, such as the digestive or respiratory systems.

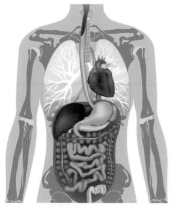

▲ Organs of the body are made up of different kinds of tissues.

All life processes, such as growth and reproduction, **take place** in cells. All organisms start life as one cell. Growth begins when the cell divides and becomes two cells. Both cells divide and become four cells. At the eight-cell stage, cells divide at different rates and continue to divide over their lifetimes.

There are two different ways that cells reproduce: **mitosis** and **meiosis**. Body cells make more body cells by mitosis. In mitosis, the cell merely copies its genetic material, and then it divides itself in half. Reproductive cells are produced by meiosis. Reproductive cells are responsible for reproduction. **Genetic variation** is a result of meiosis.

When babies are born, they often resemble their parents in many ways. For example, a baby and its mother may have the same eye or hair color. Or perhaps the baby and its father may have similar body shapes. This is called **heredity**. Heredity is the passing down of various characteristics, or traits, from parents to their children.

Genes are what determine heredity. Genes have information on how an organism should grow. When a sperm cell and an egg cell join, genes **get transferred** from both the father and the mother. As a result, half of the offspring's genetic material comes from its father while the other half comes from its mother. This is why children have characteristics of both parents.

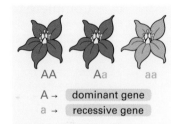

$A \rightarrow$ dominant gene
$a \rightarrow$ recessive gene

▲ Dominant genes are stronger than recessive genes.

There are both **dominant** and **recessive** genes. Dominant genes are ones that are expressed physically or visually. They are stronger than recessive genes, which are present in the body but are overshadowed by dominant genes. Recessive genes can, however, be passed onto offspring and then become dominant genes in the offspring.

While organisms **inherit** their genes from their parents, some organisms are born with **mutations**. A mutation is a permanent change in a gene. Some mutations can be harmful, but others may be helpful to the organism.

white crocodile

▲ mutation

Quick Check Check T (True) or F (False).

1   Genetic variation is caused by mitosis. ☐T ☐F

2   Organisms inherit their genes from their parents. ☐T ☐F

3   Recessive genes are not as strong as dominant genes. ☐T ☐F

1   **What is the main idea of the passage?**
   a. All life processes occur because of cells.
   b. There are dominant genes and recessive genes in a body.
   c. Genes get transferred from both the father and the mother.

2   **Offspring get the characteristics of their parents because of _____.**
   a. mutations   **b.** heredity   **c.** mitosis

3   **What is a mutation?**
   a. A recessive gene in a body.
   b. A permanent change in a gene.
   c. A dominant gene inherited from a parent.

4   **What does overshadowed mean?**
   a. Removed.   **b.** Destroyed.   **c.** Surpassed.

5   **Complete the sentences.**
   a. _____ are the basic unit of life.
   b. Species get genetic variation because of _____.
   c. _____ get transferred from the parents to the offspring.

6   **Complete the outline.**

Cells	Cells Reproduction	Genes

• Are the basic unit of life
• One-celled organisms
  = ᵃ_____
• Multi-cellular organisms
  = most life
• All life processes take
  place in cells.
	Mitosis
	• Is how ᵇ_____ _____ are created
	• A cell copies its genetic material and splits in half.
	Meiosis
	• Is how reproductive cells are created
	• Is responsible for genetic ᶜ_____
		• Determine heredity
		• ᵈ_____ _____
		  are expressed visually
		  or physically.
		• Recessive genes are
		  ᵉ_____ by
		  dominant genes.

Complete each sentence. Change the form if necessary.

take place   get transferred   recessive   inherit   genetic variation

1   Mitosis _____ _____ when a cell divides itself into two parts.

2   The boy _____ his brown eyes from his mother, not his father.

3   _____ _____ comes from meiosis.

4   _____ genes do not get expressed physically in a person.

5   Physical characteristics _____ _____ from parents to offspring thanks to heredity.

Unit 10 The Earth's Oceans

Visual Preview What are some characteristics of the ocean?

Ocean currents affect the land's climate.

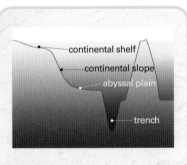

The ocean floor is as varied as the land above water.

Oceans contain countless organisms with different types of ecosystems.

Vocabulary Preview Write the correct word and the meaning in Chinese next to its meaning.

| abyssal plain | intertidal zone | current | continental shelf | continental slope |

1 _____ : the area between the land and sea that is covered by water at high tide and uncovered at low tide

2 _____ : a stream of water that flows through an ocean like a river

3 _____ : the area from the shore to a depth of 200 meters of the ocean floor

4 _____ : the vast, flat floor of the deep ocean

5 _____ : the ocean floor between the continental shelf and the abyssal plain

Oceans and Ocean Life

🎧10

Oceans cover nearly 70% of Earth's surface. These oceans often appear calm and nonmoving. However, this is not actually the case. In fact, the oceans' waters are in constant motion.

The water level of the ocean is constantly changing. One of these changes is caused by **tides**. Tides are the regular rising and falling of an ocean's surface. Tides result mostly from the moon's **gravitational pull** on Earth. When the water is at its highest point, it is called high tide. The water at its lowest point is called low tide.

Ocean waters are also constantly pushed around the land by **currents**. A current is a large stream of water that flows through the ocean. Currents are caused by many factors. Surface currents are produced by global winds. Earth's rotation also affects surface currents. Currents form **due to** differences in water temperatures as well. Cold water near the North and South poles sinks and begins moving toward the equator. Warm water from the equator rises to the surface and heads toward both poles to replace the cold water that is moving away. When the cold and warm waters mix, currents form.

Ocean currents affect the land's climate. Warm-water currents, such

▼ **Earth's ocean currents**

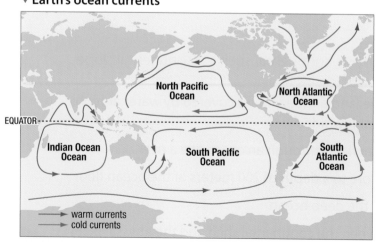

50

as the Gulf Stream, begin near the equator. The Gulf Stream brings warm water across the North Atlantic Ocean toward Europe. During the winter, the warm Gulf Stream keeps Europe's climate mild. The currents are also responsible for ocean circulation. Ocean circulation helps replenish the supply of oxygen in the water.

The **ocean floor** is as varied as the land above water. It contains mountains, deep valleys, plains, and other features. However, all ocean floors can be divided into three major regions. The first region is the **continental shelf**. It extends from the shore to a depth of about 200 meters. It has a gentle slope that is made of continental crust. The **continental slope** is at the edge of the continent between the continental shelf and the **abyssal plain**. It is steeper and deeper than the continental shelf. At the end of the continental slope, there is one of the flattest places on Earth—the abyssal plain. The abyssal plain is the vast, flat floor of the deep ocean. It covers almost half of the ocean floor.

Oceans contain countless organisms with different types of ecosystems, called ocean zones. Each ocean zone has unique types of plant and animal communities. The shallowest ocean zone is the **intertidal zone**. It covers the area that gets exposed when the ocean is at low tide, so intertidal organisms should be able to handle changes in their environments. The **nearshore zone** includes most of the continental shelf. It is fairly shallow water and gets lots of sunlight. It often has abundant life and is much more stable than the intertidal zone. The final zone is the **open-ocean zone**. This is the deepwater area that comprises the largest regions in the oceans. Because of the depth of the open-ocean zone, this area gets little or no sunlight. So most of the animals in the open-ocean zone live near the surface to obtain food.

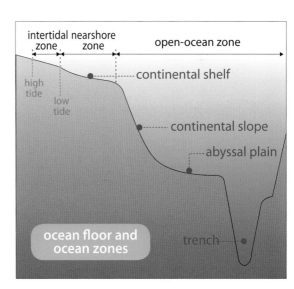

Quick Check Check T (True) or F (False).

1   Both the sun and the moon have an effect on Earth's tides.   T   F

2   The Gulf Stream begins in Europe and flows south toward the equator.   T   F

3   The largest part of Earth's oceans is the intertidal zone.   T   F

1 **What is the passage mainly about?**
    a. The features of Earth's oceans.
    b. The causes of tides and currents.
    c. The zones and regions in the oceans.

2 **Europe has a mild climate in winter because of an ocean _____.**
    a. tide   **b.** circulation   **c.** current

3 **What is the lowest part of the ocean called?**
    a. The abyssal plain.   **b.** The continental shelf.   **c.** The continental slope.

4 **What does replenish mean?**
    a. Refill.   **b.** Create.   **c.** Circulate.

5 **According to the passage, which statement is true?**
    a. Oceans cover approximately half of Earth's surface.
    b. Cold water moves toward the equator while warm water moves toward the poles.
    c. The smallest region is the intertidal zone, and the largest is the near-shore zone.

6 **Complete the outline.**

The Oceans

- Cover 70% of Earth's surface

Tides
- Caused by the moon's ᵃ_____ pull

Currents
- Caused by ᵇ_____ _____, Earth's rotation, and differences in water temperatures
- Affect the land's ᶜ_____

The Ocean Floor and Zones

- ᵈ_____ _____ = from the shore to a depth of 200 meters
- Continental slope = between the continental shelf and the abyssal plain
- Abyssal plain = the vast, flat floor of the deep ocean
- ᵉ_____ _____ = the area exposed at low tide
- Near-shore zone = most of the continental shelf
- Open-ocean zone = the deepwater parts of the oceans

Complete each sentence. Change the form if necessary.

gravitational pull   due to   ocean floor   intertidal zone   open-ocean zone

1 _____ the Gulf Stream, Europe's climate is mild during the winter.

2 The moon's _____ _____ on Earth creates tides.

3 Organisms in the _____ _____ get exposed at low tide, so they have to find shelter.

4 Most of the organisms in the _____ _____ live near the surface.

5 The _____ _____ has mountain ranges and extensive plains on it.

Unit 11 Fossils

What parts of organisms get preserved as fossils?

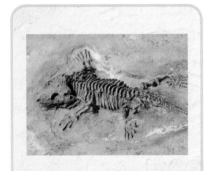

The bones of many animals often get fossilized.

Sometimes, imprints of leaves or other plant parts get preserved in stone.

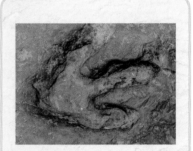

Dinosaur eggs and even footprints are sometimes found by paleontologists.

Vocabulary Preview Write the correct word and the meaning in Chinese next to its meaning.

| vanish | ammonite | paleontologist | fossil record | index fossil |

1 _____ : a fossil of an ancient type of mollusk (= sea animal with a soft body and a hard shell)

2 _____ : a person who studies fossils

3 _____ : a fossil of an organism that lived at a specific time in the past

4 _____ : to stop existing completely

5 _____ : all of the information that people have learned from fossils

What We Can Learn From Fossils

🎧 11

About 65 million years ago, dinosaurs lived on Earth. However, no one has ever seen a living dinosaur because they **went extinct** a long time ago. But how do we know a lot about them, such as what they were like or how many kinds of them lived? We know these things thanks to **fossils**.

Fossils are the **remains** or imprints of living things that died long ago. The remains of dead organisms were often covered with mud, sand, or other sediment. Over time, the sediment and the remains hardened into rock. Almost all fossils are found in sedimentary rocks.

Sometimes, a complete body **gets fossilized**. However, more often, parts of the organism are preserved. The organism's soft parts may often decay quickly, and the hard parts, such as shells and bones, are left behind. Some fossils are not parts of organisms but are only footprints or impressions of an organism's body. They appear in the form of a mold or a cast.

Scientists study fossils to learn about extinct organisms

▲ various fossils

and the environments of the past on Earth. Fossils show dinosaurs, reptiles, plants, insects, and fish that **vanished** a long time ago.

Paleontologists—scientists who study fossils—take great care in unearthing fossils and preserving them. They often **piece together** the individual bones of an animal to show what it once looked like. They can figure out how big it was, how much it weighed, how long it lived, where it lived, and even what kind of food it ate.

Fossils can also tell us about Earth's history. Paleontologists have learned that some fossils are only found in certain layers of rocks. They have assembled a record called the **fossil record**. The fossil record is used to study Earth's history. **Index fossils** are important in determining the fossil record. Index fossils are fossils of organisms that only lived during specific times in the past. They tell the age of the rock in which it is found. When scientists find an index fossil in a certain rock layer, they can know how old the ground is and how Earth's surface has changed over time.

One well-known index fossil is the **ammonite**. It was a cephalopod—a shelled underwater creature—that lived during the time of the dinosaurs. Trilobites are another commonly found index fossil that lived before the dinosaurs.

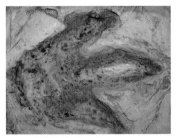

▲ dinosaur footprint

▲ lizard impression

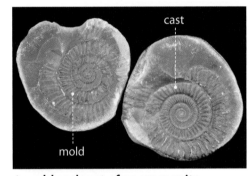

▲ mold and cast of an ammonite

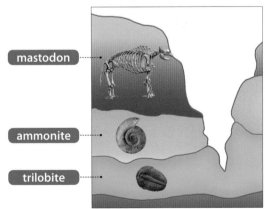

▲ Index fossils can tell us about Earth's history.

Quick Check Check T (True) or F (False).

1	Most fossils are found in sedimentary rocks.	T	F
2	The soft parts of an animal are often found in fossils.	T	F
3	Ammonites and trilobites are important index fossils.	T	F

1 What is the main idea of the passage?
   a. The fossil record tells us many things about Earth.
   b. Index fossils are very important to teach people about the past.
   c. Fossils help us learn about the life and the environments of the past.

2 A fossil is the preserved _____ of a dead organism.
   a. remains   b. sediment   c. blood

3 What can scientists learn when they find an index fossil?
   a. Where they should search to find more fossils.
   b. How old the ground that they found the fossil in is.
   c. How quickly the organism got fossilized.

4 What does decay mean?
   a. Destroy.   b. Smell.   c. Rot.

5 Answer the questions.
   a. When did the dinosaurs become extinct? _____
   b. Why do scientists study fossils?

   _____

   c. When did ammonites live? _____

6 Complete the outline.

Fossils
• Are the ª _____ or imprints of organisms that died long ago
• Are almost always found in ᵇ _____ rocks
• Complete bodies or parts of bodies get fossilized.
• May only be ᶜ _____ or impressions of an organism's body

What We Can Learn From Fossils
• Can learn about extinct organisms and the ᵈ _____ in the past
• Can also learn about Earth's history
• Fossil record = all the information we know from fossils
• ᵉ _____ _____ = fossils of organisms that only lived at specific times in the past

Complete each sentence. Change the form if necessary.

remains   get fossilized   vanish   piece together   ammonite

1 The paleontologists are trying to _____ _____ the bones into a complete dinosaur.

2 _____ are small shelled creatures that lived millions of years ago.

3 Many species of animals have completely _____ from Earth.

4 It can take millions of years for an organism to _____ _____.

5 They discovered the fossilized _____ of some animals while digging.

12 Force and Motion

What were some of the scientific accomplishments of Isaac Newton?

Newton discovered the Law of Universal Gravitation.

The state of motion of an object does not change until a force is applied to it.

For every action, there is an equal and opposite reaction.

Vocabulary Preview Write the correct word and the meaning in Chinese next to its meaning.

| acceleration | gravity | at rest | inertia | reaction |

1 _____ : the tendency of a moving object to keep moving in a straight line

2 _____ : an increase in velocity

3 _____ : a response to an action

4 _____ : the force that pulls all objects toward Earth

5 _____ : inactive; not in motion

Newton's Laws

🎧 12

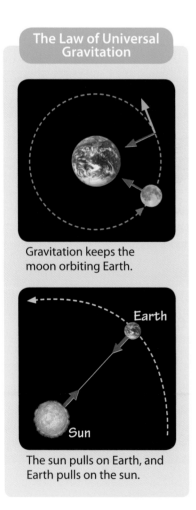

The Law of Universal Gravitation

Gravitation keeps the moon orbiting Earth.

Earth

Sun

The sun pulls on Earth, and Earth pulls on the sun.

Have you ever seen **skydivers** float in a circle in the sky? The skydivers are actually in freefall before their parachutes open. They are falling toward Earth with the **acceleration** caused by a force pulling them toward the center of Earth. What force pulls them toward the center of Earth? It is **gravity**. All objects are pulled to the ground by gravity.

Isaac Newton, one of the world's greatest scientists, discovered that everything is pulled to the ground and that it is the same force that keeps the planets **orbiting** the sun. This is Newton's Law of Universal **Gravitation**. Gravitation is the force that acts between any two objects and makes them **attract** one another. Gravity—the force that acts between Earth and objects—is an effect of gravitation. Gravitation keeps the moon in a circular path around Earth. It pulls the moon and Earth toward each other. This pull prevents the moon from **flying off** away from Earth. Gravitation also holds Earth and the other planets in their orbits around the sun.

Isaac Newton, an Englishman, lived from 1643 to 1727. During his life, he worked in many fields of science and mathematics. But, most of all, he is known for his work in physics. In addition to discovering the Law of Universal Gravitation, he also discovered the three laws of motion.

The first law of motion states that an object **at rest** will stay at rest and an object in motion will not change its velocity unless an outside force acts on it. One of the main outside forces is gravity. For instance, you may throw a ball up in the air. Without the force of gravity affecting it, the ball would continue going straight forever. However, because gravity—an outside force—acts on it, the ball falls back down to the ground. Newton's first law of motion is often called the Law of **Inertia**.

▲ Roller coasters use gravity.

The second law of motion is called the Law of **Acceleration**. This law states that the greater the force on an object, the greater its acceleration. It is often written as a formula: $a = F \div m$. a is acceleration, F is force, and m is mass. So an object's acceleration equals the force divided by the object's mass. This law also states that objects with a greater mass require more force to move than objects with a lesser mass. For instance, it requires much more force to throw a brick than to throw a tennis ball since a brick has more mass than a tennis ball.

The third law of motion is called the Law of **Action and Reaction**. For every action, there is an equal and opposite reaction. One object pushing on another will receive a push in return. For instance, crews on a racing boat push on the water with their oars. The water, in turn, pushes back on the oars and propels the boat forward.

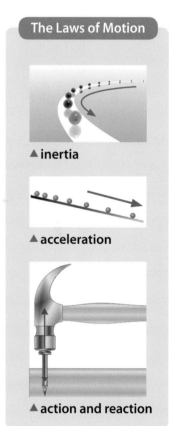

The Laws of Motion

▲ inertia

▲ acceleration

▲ action and reaction

Quick Check Check T (True) or F (False).

1 Gravitation is the force that keeps the planets orbiting the sun.   T   F
2 The only work that Newton did was in the field of physics.   T   F
3 The second law of motion is called the Law of Inertia.   T   F

1 **What is the passage mainly about?**
   a. The three laws of motion.
   b. The scientific discoveries of Isaac Newton.
   c. The reason why objects fall to the ground.

2 **According to the Law of Inertia, an object at rest _____.**
   a. begins to move after being acted upon by gravity
   b. will remain in motion when another force acts on it
   c. stays at rest unless acted upon by an outside force

3 **Which force keeps a planet in orbit around the sun?**
   a. Gravitation.   **b.** Acceleration.   **c.** Freefall.

4 **What does propels mean?**
   a. Accelerates.   **b.** Moves.   **c.** Slows.

5 **Complete the sentences.**
   a. All objects are pulled back to Earth because of the force of _____.
   b. The first law of motion is often known as the Law of _____.
   c. For every _____, there is an equal and opposite reaction.

6 **Complete the outline.**

Law of Motion

Law of Universal Gravitation

- The force that acts between any two ᵃ_____ and makes them attract one another
- Gravity is an ᵇ_____ of gravitation.

First Law of Motion
- The Law of ᶜ_____
- The state of motion of an object does not change unless an outside force acts on it.

Second Law of Motion
- The Law of ᵈ_____
- The greater the force on an object, the greater its acceleration

Third Law of Motion
- The Law of ᵉ_____ and Reaction
- For every action, there is an equal and opposite reaction.

Complete each sentence. Change the form if necessary.

skydiver	attract	fly off	at rest	gravitation

1 An object _____ will stay unmoving unless an outside force affects it.

2 The force that makes two objects _____ one another is called gravitation.

3 _____ acts between any two objects, such as Earth and the sun.

4 _____ will eventually fall to the ground because of gravity.

5 Without gravitation, Earth would _____ in a straight line into deep space.

Visual Preview **What are some features of light energy?**

Light has various wavelengths.

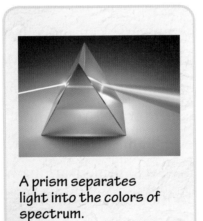

A prism separates light into the colors of spectrum.

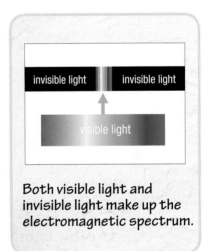

Both visible light and invisible light make up the electromagnetic spectrum.

Vocabulary Preview **Write the correct word and the meaning in Chinese next to its meaning.**

| photon | concave lens | prism | vacuum | infrared light |

1 _____ : a tiny particle that makes up light

2 _____ : a transparent block of glass that breaks up white light into seven colors

3 _____ : a space that has had all the air and any other gases removed from it

4 _____ : a lens such that a parallel beam of light passing through it is caused to diverge or spread out

5 _____ : invisible light next to red on the electromagnetic spectrum

Light Energy

🎧 13

Light is a type of energy that the human eye can see. Light is comprised of billions of very tiny particles called **photons**. These photons travel in waves. Nothing in the universe can move faster than light. It travels at approximately 300,000 kilometers per second. Most waves need some kind of medium to travel through. For instance, sound waves need matter, such as solids, liquids, and gases, to travel. You cannot hear in a **vacuum** because there is no matter. However, light can move anywhere, even in a vacuum.

Since light moves in waves, it has various **wavelengths**. Not all of its wavelengths are visible to the human eye. The light that humans can see is called **visible light**. All of the colors that humans can see—called the colors of the spectrum—are found in a rainbow, which has seven colors: red, orange, yellow, green, blue, indigo, and violet. The light waves that have the longest wavelengths appear red. The light waves with the shortest wavelengths appear violet.

▲ Isaac Newton using a prism to break white light into a spectrum

A simple way to see all of the colors of the spectrum is to use a **prism**. There was an experiment first conducted by Isaac Newton hundreds of years ago. He sent a beam of sunlight through a prism and noticed that it spread out into a band of the colors of the rainbow. Then, he passed that same light through another prism, and it returned to being white light. What happens is that a prism refracts light when light passes through it. White light is actually a combination of an entire spectrum of colors.

Something else that can bend light through refraction is a lens. There are both convex and concave lenses. A **convex lens** collects light onto one spot, called the focal point. A **concave lens** works in the opposite manner. It collects light and then spreads it out. We can use lenses for many different purposes. Convex lenses are used in glasses, contact lenses, telescopes, and binoculars. Concave lenses are often used for equipment such as television projectors.

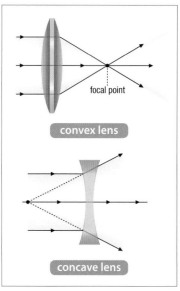

▲ light and lenses

Some light waves have wavelengths that are either too long or too short for humans to see. The light that humans cannot see is called **invisible light**. Both visible light and invisible light make up the **electromagnetic** spectrum. It includes everything that travels in waves. For instance, red has the longest wavelength of visible light. But **infrared light** has a longer wavelength. And microwaves—like the ones we use to cook with in microwave ovens—and radio waves have even longer wavelengths. On the other side of the spectrum, **ultraviolet light** has a shorter wavelength than visible violet light. But X-rays and gamma rays have even shorter wavelengths than ultraviolet light.

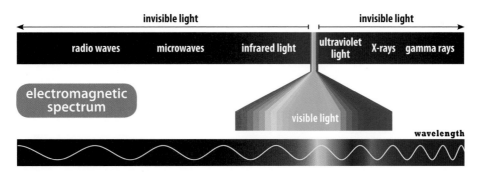

1   There are eight colors in a rainbow.   T   F

2   The color red has a longer wavelength than the color green.   T   F

3   Convex and concave lenses work in different manners.   T   F

1 **What is the main idea of the passage?**

a. Light is made of billions of photons.

b. There are many types of light on the electromagnetic spectrum.

c. A person can use a prism to see the colors of the spectrum.

2 **Isaac Newton used a _____ to separate the colors of the spectrum.**

a. microscope   b. magnifying glass   c. prism

3 **Which has wavelengths longer than red light?**

a. Violet light.   b. Infrared light.   c. Ultraviolet light.

4 **What does refracts mean?**

a. Shapes.   b. Bends.   c. Pushes.

5 **According to the passage, which statement is true?**

a. Light travels faster than everything else in the universe.

b. Concave lenses are used for glasses and telescopes.

c. Infrared light has a shorter wavelength than ultraviolet light.

6 **Complete the outline.**

Light
• Is made of billions of [a]_____
• Moves in waves
• Is faster than everything else in the universe
• Can travel anywhere, even in a [b]_____
• Has different wavelengths
• Visible light makes up the colors of the [c]_____.

Electromagnetic Spectrum
• Is made up of [d]_____ and invisible light
• Visible light = the colors of the spectrum
• Invisible light = light with wavelengths too long or too short to be seen
• Radio waves, microwaves, and infrared light = long wavelengths
• Gamma rays, [e]_____, and ultraviolet lights = short wavelengths

Complete each sentence. Change the form if necessary.

in a vacuum   convex lens   concave lens   electromagnetic   ultraviolet light

1 Telescopes and contact lenses both use _____ _____.

2 A _____ _____ collects light but then spreads it out widely.

3 The _____ spectrum covers everything that travels in waves.

4 Light, unlike sound, can even travel _____ _____ _____.

5 _____ _____ has a wavelength similar to that of visible violet light.

Visual Preview What are some interactions between Earth, the moon, and the sun?

Earth, like all of the planets, orbits the sun.

While Earth orbits the sun, at the same time, the moon orbits Earth.

The interaction of Earth, the moon, and the sun sometimes causes eclipses to happen.

Vocabulary Preview Write the correct word and the meaning in Chinese next to its meaning.

| lunar eclipse | solar eclipse | solar corona | partial lunar eclipse | umbra |

1 _____ : an event caused when the moon moves between Earth and the sun

2 _____ : an event caused when the moon moves into Earth's shadow

3 _____ : an eclipse in which the moon is not completely immersed in the umbra of the earth's shadow

4 _____ : the darker shadow cast by the moon or Earth during an eclipse

5 _____ : the white glow around the moon during a solar eclipse

Eclipses

▲ annular eclipse

▲ partial eclipse

▲ solar corona

▲ the "diamond ring" effect

Have you ever seen the moon slowly begin to darken and turn a red color for a few hours? You may have seen a **lunar eclipse**. An eclipse occurs because of the moon's revolving around Earth. There are two types of eclipses. According to the locations of the moon, Earth, and the sun, an eclipse can be either a lunar eclipse or a **solar eclipse**.

As the moon orbits Earth, it sometimes passes right between the sun and Earth. Then, the moon **blocks** sunlight from reaching parts of Earth and casts a shadow on Earth. This is a solar eclipse.

During a **partial solar eclipse**, the moon blocks only part of the sun's light. During a **total solar eclipse**, you can only see a white glow around the dark moon. This is called the **solar corona**. Sometimes you can see a "diamond ring" effect as well. A solar eclipse usually lasts for only a few minutes. When the moon moves out of its position between Earth and the sun, the sky brightens again.

A lunar eclipse occurs when the moon moves into Earth's shadow. A **total lunar eclipse** occurs when the moon passes through Earth's darker, or inner, shadow, called the **umbra**. As the moon passes

▲ lunar eclipse

through the umbra, Earth blocks all sunlight from reaching the moon and casts a shadow on the moon. Then, the moon becomes totally dark because it does not make its own light but just **reflects** light from the sun. When only

a part of the moon is in the shadow, it is called a **partial lunar eclipse**. A lunar eclipse may last a few hours.

During a solar eclipse, you should never look directly at the sun. You could damage your eyes permanently or even blind yourself.

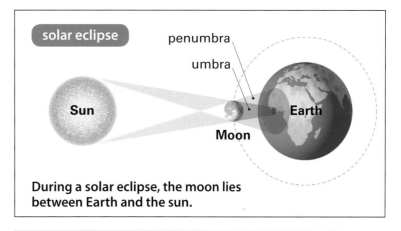

During a solar eclipse, the moon lies between Earth and the sun.

▲ total lunar eclipse

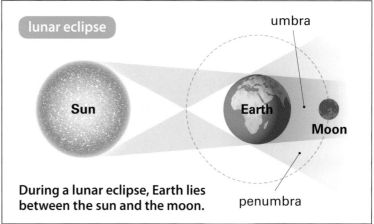

During a lunar eclipse, Earth lies between the sun and the moon.

Quick Check   Check T (True) or F (False).

1	Solar eclipses often last for more than an hour.	T	F
2	Earth's shadow is known as the corona.	T	F
3	It is dangerous to look at the sun during a solar eclipse.	T	F

1 **What is the passage mainly about?**
  a. Solar and lunar eclipses.
  b. Earth's umbra and the sun's corona.
  c. Why looking at an eclipse is dangerous.

2 **The solar corona appears during** _____.
  a. a total solar eclipse   b. a total lunar eclipse   c. a partial solar eclipse

3 **What causes an eclipse?**
  a. Earth's revolving around the sun.
  b. The moon's revolving around Earth.
  c. The location of the moon.

4 **What does revolving mean?**
  a. Rotation.   b. Moving.   c. Orbiting.

5 **Answer the questions.**
  a. What are the two types of eclipses? _____
  b. When does the "diamond ring" effect sometimes appear? _____
  c. Up to how long may a lunar eclipse last? _____

6 **Complete the outline.**

Solar Eclipse
• Happens when the moon ª_____ the sun's light and casts a shadow on Earth
• Can be a ᵇ_____ solar eclipse or a total solar eclipse
• Solar corona = the white glow of the sun around the moon
• Usually lasts for a few ᶜ_____

Lunar Eclipse
• Happens when the ᵈ_____ moves into Earth's shadow
• Umbra = Earth's darker shadow
• Sunlight is prevented from reaching the moon.
• Can be a partial lunar eclipse or a ᵉ_____ lunar eclipse
• May last a few hours

Vocabulary Review **Complete each sentence. Change the form if necessary.**

partial solar eclipse   block   total solar eclipse   reflect   partial lunar eclipse

1   During a _____ _____ _____, only a part of the moon is in Earth's shadow.

2   A _____ _____ _____ can cause a solar corona to be created.

3   During a lunar eclipse, light from the sun is _____ by Earth and cannot reach the moon.

4   The moon cannot make its own light but _____ the sun's light instead.

5   The moon only blocks part of the sun's light during a _____ _____ _____.

The Human Body

What are some parts of the body that protect it from diseases?

The skin serves as the body's first line of defense to protect it from diseases.

Tears help keep germs and bacteria from entering the body through the eyes.

White blood cells help repair the body and fight infections as well.

Write the correct word and the meaning in Chinese next to its meaning.

| gland   communicable   contagious   antibody   immune system |

1 _____ : catching; communicable; infectious

2 _____ : the integrated system that protects a body from diseases

3 _____ : a substance that your body produces in your blood to fight illnesses and infections

4 _____ : able to be transferred from one person to another

5 _____ : a part of your body that produces a chemical substance that your body needs

Diseases and the Immune System

🎧 15

▲ Lung cancer is a noncommunicable disease.

▲ The flu is a communicable disease.

Every once in a while, a person may catch a disease and become sick. There are two kinds of diseases: **noncommunicable** and **communicable** diseases.

Noncommunicable diseases cannot be passed from one person to another. Many of these diseases result from a person's lifestyle. For instance, smoking, drinking, eating too much, and not exercising enough can cause a person to get diseases such as lung cancer or heart disease. Fortunately, other people cannot catch these diseases from an **infected** person.

Communicable diseases, on the other hand, can be passed from one person to another. The common cold and the flu are two types of communicable diseases. Human contact frequently results in one person catching these diseases from another. Communicable diseases are said to be **contagious**. Occasionally, a large number of people in an area catch a certain disease at the same time. This results in an **epidemic**.

Fortunately, the human body has many defenses to fight all kinds of diseases. We call these defenses the **immune system**. The first line of defense is the skin. The skin helps prevent many types of germs and bacteria from entering the body, where they can do harm. The skin also contains some **glands** that can kill germs and bacteria when they touch the body.

Germs and bacteria frequently attempt to enter the body through the nose, eyes, and mouth. But these parts of the body all have their own defenses. Mucus in the nose acts like skin to stop foreign bodies from entering. Tears in the eyes and saliva in the mouth do the same thing. And, for germs and bacteria that enter the body when a person eats food, there are acids in the stomach that kill them.

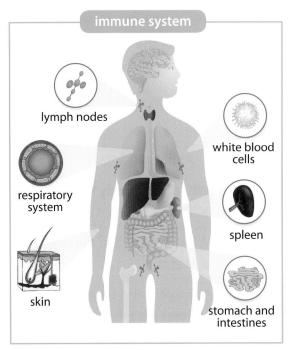

immune system

lymph nodes

respiratory system

skin

white blood cells

spleen

stomach and intestines

However, some foreign bodies still manage to enter the body and cause harm. When that happens, the body's **lymphatic system** goes to work. The body has lymph nodes, or glands, that can destroy bacteria, germs, and viruses. Also, **white blood cells** help fight infections. There are several types of white blood cells. Many of them clean the body and help repair any damaged parts. Other white blood cells create **antibodies** that attack germs and viruses and then kill them.

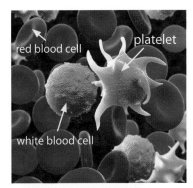

red blood cell

platelet

white blood cell

▲ White blood cells protect the body from infections.

Sometimes, the human body cannot fight certain foreign invaders. This is often true of viruses. So humans have developed vaccines to fight viruses. When a vaccine is injected into a body, it stimulates the production of antibodies that will fight a specific virus. Thanks to vaccines, people can become immune to deadly diseases such as malaria, cholera, yellow fever, and even influenza, the flu.

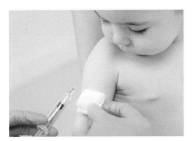

▲ Vaccinations make people immune to various diseases.

Quick Check Check T (True) or F (False).

1 Lifestyle choices are often what cause noncommunicable diseases. T F

2 The cold and the flu are both communicable diseases. T F

3 Red blood cells in the body fight infections. T F

1 **What is the main idea of the passage?**
   a. White blood cells are an important part of the immune system.
   b. The body has many defenses to protect it against infections.
   c. Vaccines can help a person become immune to certain viruses.

2 _____ **are created by some white blood cells to fight germs and viruses.**
   a. Antibodies   **b.** Vaccines   **c.** Mucus and saliva

3 **What is the body's defense system to fight diseases called?**
   a. The lymphatic system.   **b.** The immune system.   **c.** Antibodies.

4 **What does saliva mean?**
   a. Water.   **b.** Acid.   **c.** Spit.

5 **Complete the sentences.**
   a. Smoking and drinking are often two causes of _____ diseases.
   b. Lymph nodes are _____ that can kill bacteria in the body.
   c. _____ make people immune to diseases such as malaria and yellow fever.

6 **Complete the outline.**

Diseases
Noncommunicable diseases   • Cannot be passed from one person to another   • Are often caused by a person's a_____   **Communicable diseases**   • Are b_____ diseases   • Can affect many people and cause epidemics

Immune System
• Fights diseases   • Skin = keeps germs and bacteria from entering the body   • Mucus and c_____ = protect the nose and mouth   • Stomach d_____ = kills bacteria in the stomach   • Lymphatic system = uses lymph nodes to kill invaders   • e_____ _____ _____ = clean the body, repair damaged parts, and create antibodies

Complete each sentence. Change the form if necessary.

infect   gland   lymphatic system   white blood cell   antibody

1 When your _____ are swollen, it means your body is fighting an infection.

2 When a vaccine is injected into the body, it creates _____ to fight a virus.

3 A person who is _____ by a disease needs to see a doctor.

4 Some _____ _____ _____ clean the body, and others repair damaged parts of it.

5 The _____ _____ uses lymph nodes to fight infections in the body.

A Complete each sentence with the correct word. Change the form if necessary.

| heredity | continental shelf | take place | footprint | divide |
| imprint | get exposed | index fossil | meiosis | surface |

1 All life processes, such as growth and reproduction, _____ _____ in cells.

2 Growth begins when the cell _____ and becomes two cells.

3 There are two different ways that cells reproduce: mitosis and _____.

4 _____ is the passing down of various characteristics from parents to their children.

5 Tides are the regular rising and falling of an ocean's _____.

6 The _____ _____ extends from the shore to a depth of about 200 meters.

7 The intertidal zone covers the area that _____ _____ when the ocean is at low tide.

8 Fossils are the remains or _____ of living things that died long ago.

9 Some fossils are not parts of organisms but are only _____ or impressions of an organism's body.

10 _____ _____ are fossils of organisms that only lived during specific times in the past.

B Complete each sentence with the correct word. Change the form if necessary.

| attempt | attract | vaccine | comprise | electromagnetic |
| eclipse | umbra | motion | communicable | noncommunicable |

1 Gravitation is the force that acts between any two objects and makes them _____ one another.

2 Newton's first law of _____ is often called the *Law of Inertia*.

3 Light is _____ of billions of very tiny particles called photons.

4 Both visible light and invisible light make up the _____ spectrum.

5 An _____ occurs because of the moon's revolving around Earth.

6 A total lunar eclipse occurs when the moon passes through Earth's darker shadow, called the _____.

7 Many of _____ diseases result from a person's lifestyle.

8 The common cold and the flu are two types of _____ diseases.

9 Germs and bacteria frequently _____ to enter the body through the nose, eyes, and mouth.

10 When a _____ is injected into a body, it stimulates the production of antibodies.

C

Match each word with the correct definition and write the meaning in Chinese.

1 mitosis _____ ☐

2 meiosis _____ ☐

3 mutation _____ ☐

4 abyssal plain _____ ☐

5 paleontologist _____ ☐

6 inertia _____ ☐

7 wavelength _____ ☐

8 solar corona _____ ☐

9 contagious _____ ☐

10 immune system _____ ☐

a. a person who studies fossils
b. catching; communicable; infectious
c. the vast, flat floor of the deep ocean
d. a permanent change in an organism's gene
e. the white glow around the moon during a solar eclipse
f. the tendency of a moving object to keep moving in a straight line
g. the method in which reproductive cells are created
h. the integrated system that protects a body from diseases
i. the distance between one peak of a wave and the next peak
j. a method of cellular reproduction in which a cell divides itself in half

D

Write the meanings of the words in Chinese.

1 microorganism _____

2 heredity _____

3 tide _____

4 current _____

5 continental shelf _____

6 continental slope _____

7 index fossil _____

8 go extinct _____

9 acceleration _____

10 reaction _____

11 gravity _____

12 photon _____

13 prism _____

14 invisible light _____

15 infrared light _____

16 solar eclipse _____

17 lunar eclipse _____

18 umbra _____

19 epidemic _____

20 recessive _____

21 ocean floor _____

22 intertidal zone _____

23 get fossilized _____

24 fly off _____

25 at rest _____

26 gravitation _____

27 convex lens _____

28 electromagnetic _____

29 ultraviolet light _____

30 lymphatic system _____

3

- **Mathematics**
- **Language**
- **Visual Arts**
- **Music**

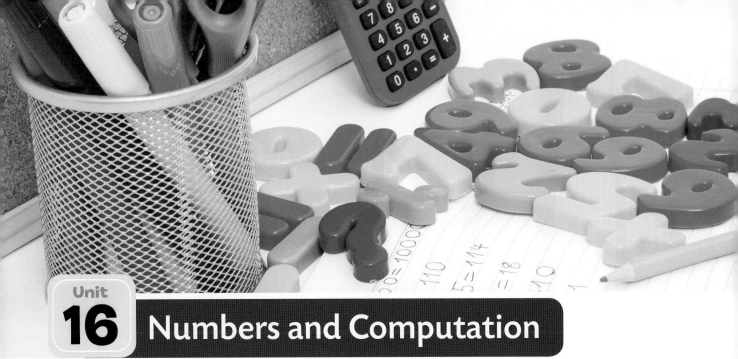

Visual Preview **What are some different ways to express numbers?**

$$10 = 2 \times 5$$

composite number — prime factors

Any composite number can be broken down into several prime factors.

$$10^3$$
$$= 10 \times 10 \times 10$$
$$= 1,000$$

Larger numbers can be expressed by using exponents, which tell you how many times a number is used as a factor.

$$\sqrt{100} = 10$$

The number 100 can be expressed by using the symbol for square root. The square root of 100 is 10.

Vocabulary Preview **Write the correct word and the meaning in Chinese next to its meaning.**

| exponent | square root | prime number | composite number | perfect square |

1 _____ : a number that can only be divided evenly by itself and 1

2 _____ : a number with more than two factors

3 _____ : a number which produces a specified quantity when multiplied by itself

4 _____ : a raised number showing how many times a number is used as a factor

5 _____ : a number that is the square of another number

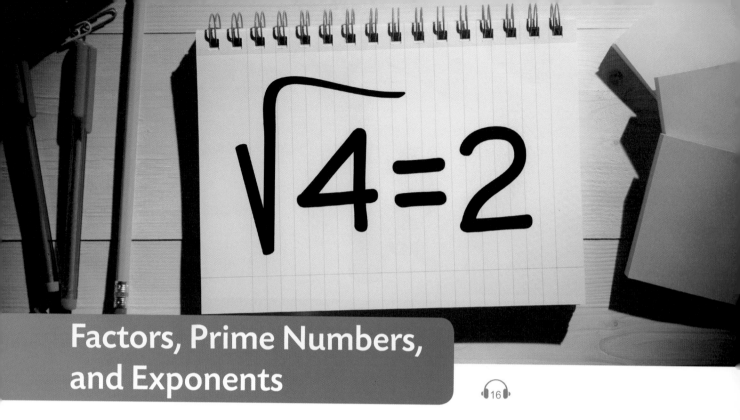

$$\sqrt{4} = 2$$

Factors, Prime Numbers, and Exponents

16

Every whole number greater than 1 has at least two factors. A factor is a number that divides another number **evenly** without a remainder. Many numbers can be broken into factors in different ways. What are the factors of 6?

$6 \div 1 = 6$ $6 \div 2 = 3$ $6 \div 3 = 2$

$6 \div 4 = $ does not divide evenly

$6 \div 5 = $ does not divide evenly $6 \div 6 = 1$

So, the factors of 6 are 1, 2, 3, and 6.

prime numbers

2, 3, 5, 7, 11, 13, 17 …

4, 6, 8, 9, 10, 12, 14 …

composite numbers

Some numbers, such as 3 and 5, can only be divided by 1 and themselves. If a number has only two factors, it is called a **prime number**. Numbers such as 3, 5, and 7 are prime numbers. A number that has more than two factors is called a **composite number**. So numbers such as 4 and 6 are composite numbers. Every whole number greater than 1 is either a prime or composite number. But the number 1 is neither prime nor composite since it only has one factor, the number 1 itself.

Any composite number can be **broken down** into several **prime factors**. Prime factors are the prime numbers that, when multiplied together, result in a composite number. For example, the number 10 can be broken down into the prime factors 2 and 5. When 2 and 5 are multiplied, they make the composite number 10. $10 = 2 \times 5$. What about a number such as 16? You can break it down into 4×4. But 4 is not a prime number since it can be broken down further into 2×2. So if you want to break down 16 to its prime factors, it should be like this: $16 = 2 \times 2 \times 2 \times 2$.

We can write the expression $16 = 2 \times 2 \times 2 \times 2$ by using an **exponent**: $16 = 2^4$. An exponent is a raised number that tells you how many times a number is used as a factor in multiplication. In other words, 2^4 means that 2 is used as a factor four times. You read 2^4 as "two to the fourth power." Also, the number 2 is called the *base* while the number 4 is the *exponent* or *power*.

Sometimes, we multiply a number by itself. In this case, we square the number. For example, 3×3 is expressed as 3^2. 3^2 is read "three **squared**" or "three to the second power." When the exponent is 3, then the number is "**cubed**." So 5^3 is "five cubed" or "five to the third power."

There are some numbers that are called **perfect squares**. A perfect square is a number that is the square of a number. For instance, 25 is a perfect square because $5 \times 5 = 25$. Also, 64 and 100 are perfect squares because $8 \times 8 = 64$, and $10 \times 10 = 100$. These numbers can also be expressed using the term **square root**. For example, $5^2 = 5 \times 5 = 25$, or we can use the symbol for square root, $\sqrt{25} = 5$. We say that the square root of 25 is 5.

composite numbers

$$10 = 2 \times 5$$
$$16 = 2 \times 2 \times 2 \times 2$$

prime factors

exponent/power

$$16 = 2^4$$

base

$$3^2 = \text{three squared}$$
$$3^3 = \text{three cubed}$$

perfect square

$$25 = 5^2$$
$$\sqrt{25} = 5$$

square root

Quick Check Check T (True) or F (False).

1 The factors of 6 are 1, 2, 3, 4, and 6. ☐ T ☐ F
2 An exponent is a raised number beside another number. ☐ T ☐ F
3 A number with an exponent of 3 is squared. ☐ T ☐ F

1 **What is the main idea of the passage?**
　　a. There are many different ways to express numbers.
　　b. Exponents are easy ways to write large numbers.
　　c. Every number has factors and prime numbers.

2 **The exponent 4^2 equals _____.**
　　a. 8　　　　**b.** 16　　　**c.** 32

3 **Which of the following numbers is a perfect square?**
　　a. 15.　　　**b.** 20.　　　**c.** 25.

4 **What does result in mean?**
　　a. Solve.　　**b.** Cause.　　**c.** Equal.

5 **According to the passage, which statement is true?**
　　a. A composite number has only one or two factors.
　　b. The prime factors of 10 are 2 and 5.
　　c. Three cubed equals 3×3.

6 **Complete the outline.**

Factors
• Factor = a number that divides another number a_____
• Prime number = a number that can only be divided by b____ and itself
• Composite number = a number with more than two factors
• Prime factors = prime numbers that equal a c_____ _____ when multiplied together

Exponents
• Exponent = a raised number that shows how many times a number is used as a d_____ in multiplication
• Square = multiplying a number by itself
• Cube = multiplying a number by itself three times
• Perfect square = a number that is the e_____ of a number
• Square root = the square root of 25 is 5

Complete each sentence. Change the form if necessary.

evenly　　break down　　cubed　　squared　　square root

1 The _____ _____ of 64 is 8.

2 It is possible to _____ _____ a composite number into more than two factors.

3 The number 6 can be divided _____ by 1, 2, 3, and 6.

4 Four _____ is equal to 16.

5 When three is _____, then it equals 27.

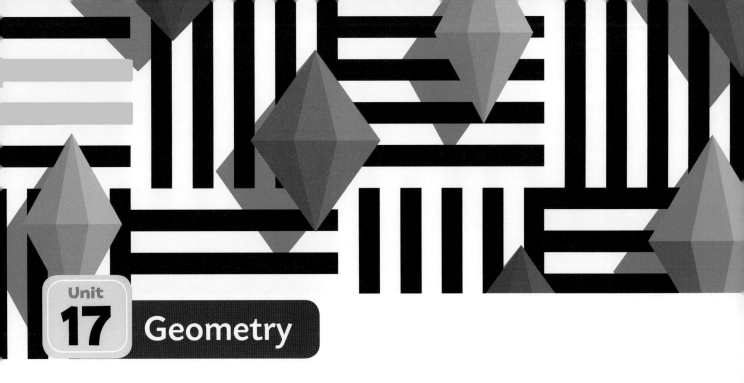

Unit 17 Geometry

Visual Preview

What are the three dimensions?

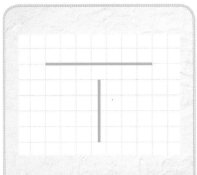

Length is the first dimension and can be expressed by a straight line.

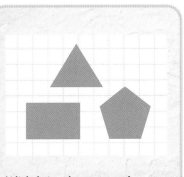

Width is the second dimension and can be expressed by a plane figure.

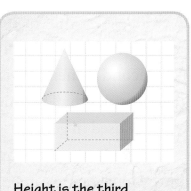

Height is the third dimension and can be expressed by a solid figure.

Vocabulary Preview

Write the correct word and the meaning in Chinese next to its meaning.

| congruent | infinite | one-dimensional figure | two-dimensional figure | three-dimensional figure |

1 _____ : a line or line segment

2 _____ : a plane figure

3 _____ : a solid figure

4 _____ : exactly alike in shape and size

5 _____ : without any end or limit

Dimensions

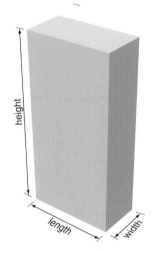

A dimension is a measurement along a straight line of the length, width, or height of a figure. In **geometry**, three dimensions are commonly used. The first dimension is length. The second dimension is width. And the third dimension is height or depth. The fourth dimension is time, but it is not typically used in geometry.

A **one-dimensional figure** is a line or a line segment. A one-dimensional figure can be measured in only one direction, such as length. It lacks both width and height.

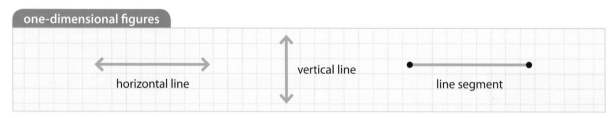

one-dimensional figures

horizontal line   vertical line   line segment

A **two-dimensional figure** is measured in two directions, such as length and width. Two-dimensional figures are called plane figures. Figures with two dimensions can be drawn on a **plane**. Some of the most common two-dimensional figures are polygons. A polygon is a closed shape that is formed by three or more line segments that do not intersect one another. A triangle is a two-dimensional figure that is composed of three line segments. Squares, rectangles, parallelograms, trapezoids, and rhombuses are all two-dimensional figures that have four sides. Pentagons have five sides, and hexagons have six sides. Polygons can actually have an

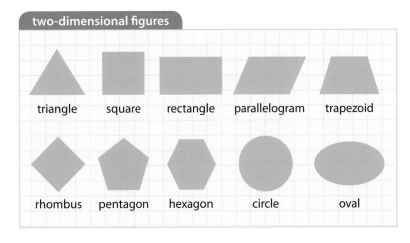

two-dimensional figures

triangle   square   rectangle   parallelogram   trapezoid

rhombus   pentagon   hexagon   circle   oval

infinite number of sides. In addition, circles and ovals are two more kinds of two-dimensional figures.

Three-dimensional figures are called solid figures. They have length, width, and height. Solid figures can be classified by the shape and the number of their **bases**, faces, vertices, and edges. Prisms have two **congruent** and parallel bases, but pyramids only have one base. Solid figures also often **correspond with** plane figures. For instance, while a triangle has two dimensions, a pyramid, which is shaped like a triangle, has three. A square has two dimensions, yet a cube, which is shaped like a square, has three. Some solid figures have **curved** surfaces. A cylinder has two circular bases. A cone has one circular base.

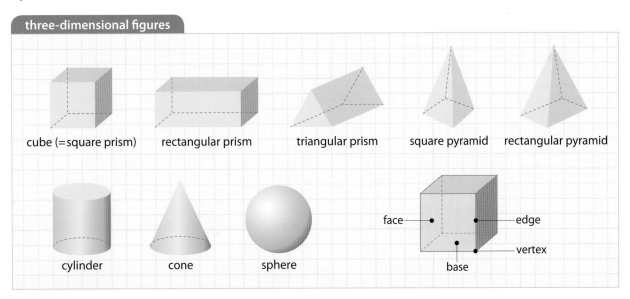

three-dimensional figures

cube (=square prism)   rectangular prism   triangular prism   square pyramid   rectangular pyramid

cylinder   cone   sphere   face — edge — vertex — base

Quick Check Check T (True) or F (False).

1   The third dimension is not frequently used in geometry.   T   F

2   A polygon is a two-dimensional figure.   T   F

3   Solid figures are either two-dimensional or three-dimensional figures.   T   F

1 **What is the passage mainly about?**
  a. How to make three-dimensional figures.
  b. The differences between plane figures and solid figures.
  c. Various dimensional figures that are commonly used in geometry.

2 **A _____ is a polygon that has five sides.**
  a. pentagon   **b.** hexagon   **c.** square

3 **What is a three-dimensional figure shaped like a triangle?**
  a. A cube.   **b.** A cylinder.   **c.** A pyramid.

4 **What does intersect mean?**
  a. Pass.   **b.** Cross.   **c.** Approach.

5 **Answer the questions.**
  a. What are the three dimensions? _____
  b. What is a one-dimensional figure? _____
  c. How are solid figures classified?
  _____

6 **Complete the outline.**

One-Dimensional Figures	Two-Dimensional Figures	Three-Dimensional Figures
• Have only ª_____ • Lack width and height • Are lines or line segments	• Have length and width • Lack height • Are ᵇ_____ figures • Can have an ᶜ_____ number of sides	• Have length, width, and ᵈ_____ • Are ᵉ_____ figures • Can be prisms, pyramids, cones, and cylinders

Complete each sentence. Change the form if necessary.

plane	infinite	base	curved	correspond with

1 It is possible to draw two-dimensional figures on a _____.

2 The _____ of a solid figure is its bottom part.

3 Many solid figures _____ _____ similarly shaped plane figures.

4 A cylinder and a sphere are two solid figures that have _____ surfaces.

5 There may be an _____ number of sides in a polygon.

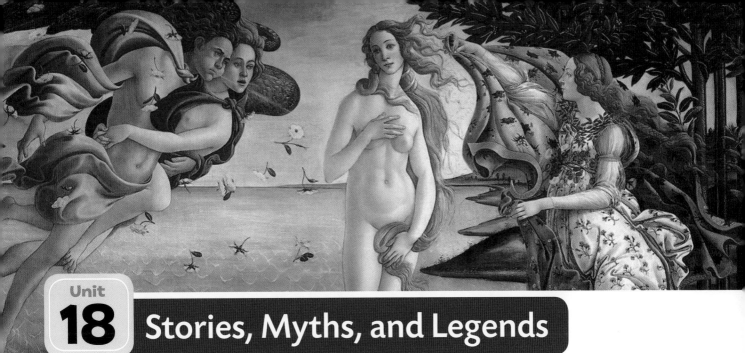

Stories, Myths, and Legends

Visual Preview Who were some of the characters in the story of Pygmalion?

Pygmalion was a brilliant sculptor from the island of Cyprus.

Galatea was the beautiful sculpture that was made by Pygmalion.

Aphrodite was the goddess of love in Greek mythology.

Vocabulary Preview Write the correct word and the meaning in Chinese next to its meaning.

| Pygmalion | captivate | longing | grant | come to life |

1 _____ : a sculptor who fell in love with a statue he had sculpted

2 _____ : become active

3 _____ : to attract or interest someone very much

4 _____ : to consent to perform or fulfill

5 _____ : a desire for someone or something

Pygmalion

🎧 18

There once lived a sculptor named **Pygmalion**. He was a man from the island of Cyprus. According to some stories, he was a king of Cyprus. According to other stories, he was **merely** a sculptor.

Anyhow, Pygmalion was a brilliant sculptor. He was able to make **statues** that looked as if they were alive. But Pygmalion had a problem. He was not interested in women. No woman that he saw could ever please him. So he had no wife.

One day, Pygmalion decided to create a statue of a woman. He set to work on a statue made out of **ivory**. He worked on and on and finally completed a perfect statue. He had sculpted a statue of a woman more beautiful than any living woman. Pygmalion was **captivated** by the statue's beauty and immediately fell in love with the statue. He loved his statue like other men love women. She **seemed** to be so real to him. He spent a lot of time staring at his statue and even spoke to her. But, of course, she gave no answer. Pygmalion grew weak and thin because of his hopeless **longing**.

Sometime later, there was a festival held in Cyprus in honor of Aphrodite. Pygmalion went to the festival, **made an offering** to the goddess of love, and then made a wish. "I sincerely wish that my ivory sculpture will change into a real woman." Aphrodite heard his prayer and **granted** his wish. When Pygmalion returned home, Cupid, who was sent by Aphrodite, kissed the ivory sculpture on the hand. This caused the statue to **come to life** as a beautiful young woman. A ring was put on her finger. It was Cupid's ring, which made love achieved.

Pygmalion could not have been happier. He named the young woman Galatea. Aphrodite blessed the marriage of Pygmalion and Galatea. And they later had a son named Paphos.

Over the years, many writers wrote stories that were based on Pygmalion. One of the most famous was a play called "Pygmalion" that was written by George Bernard Shaw. This gave rise to something called the Pygmalion effect. According to the Pygmalion effect, if you believe that someone is capable of achieving greatness, then that person will indeed achieve greatness.

▲ **Aphrodite (= Venus),** the goddess of love and beauty

▲ **Cupid (= Eros),** the god of love

▲ **Pygmalion and Galatea**

Quick Check Check T (True) or F (False).

1   Pygmalion fell in love with the statue of a woman that he had sculpted.   T   F

2   Pygmalion prayed to Cupid to make his statue come to life.   T   F

3   Pygmalion and Galatea got married and had a son named Paphos.   T   F

1 **What is the passage mainly about?**
   a. The Pygmalion effect.
   b. Pygmalion and Galatea.
   c. Aphrodite and Cupid.

2 **When Cupid _____, it came to life.**
   a. kissed the statue's hand
   b. put a ring on the statue's finger
   c. breathed on the statue

3 **Where did Pygmalion make an offering to Aphrodite?**
   a. At her temple.   **b.** At a festival.   **c.** At his workshop.

4 **What does achieved mean?**
   a. Offered.   **b.** Believed.   **c.** Accomplished.

5 **Complete the sentences.**
   a. Pygmalion was not married because he was not _____ in women.
   b. After Pygmalion made his statue, he fell in _____ with it.
   c. Aphrodite _____ Pygmalion's wish that his statue come to life.

6 **Complete the outline.**

Pygmalion
• Was a sculptor from ᵃ_____
• Created a beautiful ivory statue and then fell in love with it
• Stared at his statue all the time
• Went to a festival for ᵇ_____ and prayed to her to give his statue life

Galatea
• Was the statue made by ᶜ_____
• Was given life by Aphrodite
• Came alive when Cupid ᵈ_____ her hand
• Was able to love when Cupid put a ᵉ_____ on her finger
• Married Pygmalion
• Had a son named Paphos

Complete each sentence. Change the form if necessary.

merely   captivated by   seem   make an offering   come to life

1 The statue that Pygmalion made was so good that it _____ real.

2 Aphrodite sent Cupid to make the statue _____ _____ _____.

3 Pygmalion was _____ _____ the beauty of the statue he had made.

4 Galatea was _____ a statue before she was given life by Aphrodite.

5 Pygmalion _____ _____ _____ to Aphrodite, so she granted his wish.

Grammar and Usage

What are some different types of sentences?

"My brother is a doctor."

A simple sentence has one independent clause.

"I like apples, but she likes oranges."

A compound sentence has two independent clauses.

"Because it is raining, I will take my umbrella."

A complex sentence has one independent clause and at least one dependent clause.

Write the correct word and the meaning in Chinese next to its meaning.

| passive voice | interrogative sentence | subordinate clause | imperative sentence | clause |

1 _____ : an order

2 _____ : a question

3 _____ : the voice used to indicate that the grammatical subject of the verb is the recipient of the action denoted by the verb

4 _____ : a clause in a complex sentence that cannot stand alone as a complete sentence

5 _____ : a sentence with a subject and a predicate

Sentences

🎧 19

When we speak and write, we express our thoughts in sentences. A sentence has both a subject and a predicate. The subject is often a noun or noun phrase while the predicate includes the verb and any other words in the sentence.

There are four kinds of sentences. The most common sentence is the **declarative sentence**. A declarative sentence is a sentence that makes a statement about something. It always ends with a period (.). An **interrogative sentence** is a question. It always ends with a question mark (?). An **exclamatory sentence** is a sentence that expresses a strong emotion. It always ends with an exclamation point (!). An **imperative sentence** is an order. The subject of an imperative sentence is "you," but "you" is **omitted**. In other words, do not say or write "you" in an imperative sentence. An imperative sentence may end with a period or an exclamation point. Look at the following sentences:

Declarative Sentences:	The sun is shining.	My brother likes music.
Interrogative Sentences:	What's that?	Where are you going?
Exclamatory Sentences:	That's incredible!	What a beautiful day!
Imperative Sentences:	Open the door.	Be quiet!

Many times, we speak and write with simple sentences. A simple sentence contains one **independent clause**. A **clause** is a sentence with a subject and a predicate. An independent clause is a clause that can express a complete thought and stand alone as a sentence. It has both a subject and a predicate.

Sometimes, we combine two independent clauses by using **conjunctions** such as *and*, *but*, *so*, and *or*. This creates a compound sentence. A compound sentence is a sentence with two or more independent clauses.

Other times, we combine an independent clause and a dependent clause, also called a **subordinate clause**. A dependent clause cannot express a complete thought and cannot function as a sentence by itself. It must be connected to an independent clause with a subordinate conjunction such as *because*, *since*, *if*, *even though*, and *although*. This creates a complex sentence. A complex sentence has one independent clause and at least one dependent clause. Look at the following sentences:

Simple Sentence:	The dog is chasing the cat.
Compound Sentence:	I like pizza, but my sister does not like it.
Complex Sentence:	If you go to the game with me, we will have fun.

We also use different voices when we speak and write. We use the **active voice** to say what the subject does. We use the **passive voice** to say what happens to the subject. Look at the following sentences:

Active Voice:	David lives in a house.
	They practice the piano every day.
Passive Voice:	That hotel was made by Mr. Jones.
	I was confused by the answer.

Quick Check Check T (True) or F (False).

1 An exclamatory sentence always ends with a question mark.   T   F
2 A compound sentence needs a conjunction like *and*, *but*, or *so*.   T   F
3 Two different voices are the active and passive voices.   T   F

1 **What is the main idea of the passage?**
   a. Most people use simple sentences when speaking.
   b. There are many different types of sentences.
   c. The active voice is more common than the passive voice.

2 **Conjunctions like *because*, *since*, and *if* are used in** _____.
   a. compound sentences   **b.** simple sentences   **c.** complex sentences

3 **What is a dependent clause?**
   a. A clause that can express a complete thought.
   b. A clause that can stand alone as a sentence.
   c. A clause that cannot function as a sentence by itself.

4 **What does connected to mean?**
   a. Joined with.   **b.** Compared to.   **c.** Replaced by.

5 **According to the passage, which statement is true?**
   a. Interrogative sentences ask questions.
   b. Declarative sentences give orders.
   c. Imperative sentences make statements.

6 **Complete the outline.**

Kinds of Sentences
• Declarative sentence = a statement
• Interrogative sentence = a ᵃ_____
• Exclamatory sentence = an exclamation
• Imperative sentence = an ᵇ_____

Sentence Types and Voices
• Simple sentence = one independent clause
• Compound sentence = two ᶜ_____ clauses
• Complex sentence = one independent clause and at least one ᵈ_____ clause
• ᵉ_____ _____ = says what the subject does
• Passive voice = says what happens to the subject

Complete each sentence. Change the form if necessary.

omit   independent clause   conjunction   subordinate clause   passive voice

1 An _____ _____ contains both a subject and a predicate.

2 A _____ _____ is a dependent clause, so it is not a complete sentence.

3 Do not _____ the question mark at the end of an interrogative sentence.

4 We use the _____ _____ to say what happens to the subject.

5 *And*, *but*, *because*, and *since* are all _____.

Visual Preview **What are some art movements since the Renaissance?**

Baroque Art focused on both emotional and dramatic scenes.

Cubism was formed by using geometric shapes when painting figures.

Pop Art, like the art that Andy Warhol created, used all sorts of materials.

Vocabulary Preview **Write the correct word and the meaning in Chinese next to its meaning.**

Neoclassicism   revive   Rococo Art   Realism   evoke

1 _____ : to make something become active, successful, or popular again

2 _____ : to bring a particular emotion, idea, or memory into your mind

3 _____ : an art movement that was decorative and lighthearted

4 _____ : an art movement that revived classical art

5 _____ : an art movement in which painters focused on everyday scenes

From Baroque Art to Pop Art

▲ **Baroque Art**
by Rembrandt

▲ **Rococo Art**
by Jean-Honoré Fragonard

▲ **Neoclassical Art**
by Jacques-Louis David

After the Renaissance, a period involving the "rebirth" of the classical world, there have been many **art movements** that have had their own unique characteristics.

One of the first art movements to follow the Renaissance was **Baroque Art**. This was not just an art movement, but it also influenced architecture, music, and literature. The Baroque Period lasted from around 1600 to 1750. Some of the major artists in this period were Caravaggio, Rembrandt, and Rubens. Compared with the classicism of the Renaissance, Baroque Art is **characterized by** the dramatic contrast of light and shadow as well as vivid emotional expressions. Baroque Art often **evokes** an emotional and dramatic feeling in the viewer.

A period that **emerged** as the Baroque Period was ending was the Rococo Period. It started in France around 1750. **Rococo Art** is characterized by its decorative and lighthearted look that uses delicate pastel colors. *The Swing*, by Jean-Honoré Fragonard, and *The Pleasures of Life*, by Jean-Antoine Watteau, are good examples of the Rococo style.

However, in the late eighteenth and nineteenth centuries, many artists started to **turn away** from the dramatic Baroque and flashy Rococo styles. The ideas of the Enlightenment, with its emphasis on reason, swept over Europe and affected the visual arts. Eventually, it led to a new style of art called the Neoclassical Movement. **Neoclassicism** lasted from the middle of the eighteenth century to the early nineteenth century. The artists in this period **revived** classical forms from ancient Greece and Rome just like the artists of the Renaissance had done. Jacques-Louis David, a French painter, is a famous artist from this period.

During the late eighteenth century, the Romantic Movement, or Romanticism, began. During this period, artists had an interest in nature scenes and focused on both emotion and imagination. They turned away from the orderly style of Neoclassicism. Blake, Delacroix, and Goya are some of the representative artists from this period.

Romanticism later gave way to **Realism**, which dominated art from around 1850 to 1890. Artists like Jean Millet and Gustave Courbet tried to paint their subjects exactly as they saw them. They focused especially on everyday scenes and lives of poor ordinary people.

Realism was replaced by Modern Art. In Modern Art, there have been many unique movements. One of the most important was Impressionism. This was an abstract form of art, so the artists did not paint their subjects exactly as they looked. Monet, Manet, Van Gogh, and Cézanne were all Impressionists. Later, artists such as Picasso painted in the Cubist style. The objects in their paintings were made in the shapes of geometric figures. In the twentieth century, Dadaism and Pop Art were two more well-known art movements. Andy Warhol was the most famous member of the Pop Art Movement.

▲ **Romantic Art**
by William Blake

▲ **Realist Art**
by Gustave Courbet

▲ **Impressionist Art**
by Van Gogh

▲ **Pop Art**

Quick Check   Check T (True) or F (False).

1   Rococo Period was the period that immediately followed the Baroque Period.   T   F
2   Jacques-Louis David was a painter in the Neoclassical Movement.   T   F
3   Monet and Manet were both Realist painters.   T   F

1 **What is the passage mainly about?**
   a. The most famous artists since the Renaissance.
   b. The styles that artists used since the Renaissance.
   c. The various art movements from the Baroque Period to the present.

2 **Goya was a painter in the** _____.
   a. Neoclassical Movement   **b.** Baroque Period   **c.** Romantic Movement

3 **What kind of art did painters of Impressionism make?**
   a. Abstract Art.   **b.** Pop Art.   **c.** Realistic Art.

4 **What does imagination mean?**
   a. Realism.   **b.** Creativity.   **c.** Color.

5 **Answer the questions.**
   a. When did the Baroque Period begin and end? _____
   b. What are the characteristics of Rococo Art? _____
   _____
   c. Who were two famous Realist artists? _____

6 **Complete the outline.**

From Baroque to Realism

- a_____ = contrasted light and shadows and used vivid emotions
- Rococo = decorative and lighthearted with pastel colors
- b_____ = revived Greek and Roman classical forms
- Romanticism = focused on emotion and imagination
- c_____ = focused on everyday scenes of regular people

Modern Art

- Impressionism = abstract art by Monet, Manet, Van Gogh, and Cézanne
- d_____ = used shapes of geometric figures
- Dadaism = well-known art movement
- e_____ _____ = was done by Andy Warhol

Complete each sentence. Change the form if necessary.

| characterized by   evoke   emerge   revive   turn away |

1 Rococo Art _____ as Baroque Art was ending.

2 Abstract artists _____ _____ from Realism and painted in a different style.

3 Baroque paintings _____ strong feelings in viewers.

4 Romanticism is _____ _____ its emphasis on imagination.

5 Neoclassicism _____ classical forms and subjects.

The Music of the Middle Ages

Visual Preview

What are some types of music sung during the Middle Ages and Renaissance?

Christian monks often sang Gregorian Chants.

A canon and a round are two types of polyphonic music.

Row, Row, Row Your Boat is a common round that people still sing.

Vocabulary Preview

Write the correct word and the meaning in Chinese next to its meaning.

| Gregorian Chant   a cappella   monotonous   polyphonic music   round |

1 _____ : a composition for two or more voices in which each voice enters at a different time with the same melody

2 _____ : a type of singing done by monks in Christian monasteries

3 _____ : music in which many voices sing at different pitches

4 _____ : having the same tone; not changing in tone

5 _____ : a song that is sung with no music accompanying it

Gregorian Chants and Polyphonic Music

🎧 21

▲ Pope Gregory the Great

▼ monastery

The Middle Ages lasted from around 500 to 1400. During this time, the Church had a tremendous influence on society. Many young men wanted to serve the Church, so a lot of them entered **monasteries**. The men who lived in these monasteries were called **monks**. The monks' lives were very structured. They spent much of the day reading the Bible, praying, or working. Many people believe that life in a monastery was **dreary**. But the monks also had time to enliven their days by singing.

However, the singing that medieval monks did was not like modern-day singing. Instead, the monks **chanted**. Their songs were called **Gregorian Chants** after Pope Gregory the Great.

Gregorian Chants were typically verses from the Bible or other religious books. The songs were sung in Latin, so they sound unfamiliar to modern people. In addition, the monks did not have any musical instruments to accompany them. They merely sang. This kind of music is called **a cappella**. The individual voices of the monks sounded **monotonous**. However, they blended together and harmonized. In fact, monks in monasteries all around the world still sing Gregorian Chants today.

After the Middle Ages, the Renaissance began. During the Renaissance, **polyphonic music** gained popularity. *Polyphony* means "many voices" in Greek. This was unlike Gregorian Chants. When the monks chanted, their voices all had the same tone or inflection. In polyphonic music, however, different voices sing different melodies or even different words at the same time.

A **canon** is one type of polyphonic music. In this style, one voice begins singing. After some time, another voice joins and sings the same melody but at either a higher or lower pitch. Throughout the melody, more voices join in as each person sings in a slightly different way.

A **round** is another type of polyphonic music. As the name implies, this is a song that goes around in a circle. In a round, everyone sings the same melody and the same words. However, each person starts singing at a different time. For instance, the first person begins to sing. Once that person completes the first line, another person starts from the beginning. When that person completes the first line, a third person joins in. As a result, all of the voices overlap with one another, yet they still harmonize. *Dona Nobis Pacem*—"give us peace"—was a popular round from the Renaissance. The only three words in the song are *dona*, *nobis*, and *pacem*. Today, *Frère Jacques—Are You Sleeping?*—and *Row, Row, Row Your Boat* are two common rounds that people still sing.

▲ A round is a song in which several people sing the same words and melodies at different times.

Quick Check Check T (True) or F (False).

1   Monks no longer sing any Gregorian Chants.   T   F

2   "Polyphony" is a word that has Greek origins.   T   F

3   *Row, Row, Row Your Boat* was a canon from the Middle Ages.   T   F

1   **What is the passage mainly about?**
   a. The ways that medieval monks sang songs.
   b. Some of the most popular songs in the Middle Ages.
   c. The type of singing in the Middle Ages and Renaissance.

2   **Gregorian Chants are named after** _____.
   a. Pope Gregory the Great   b. King Gregory the Great
   c. Emperor Gregory the Great

3   **What is "a cappella" music?**
   a. Music with many voices.   b. Music with no instruments.
   c. Music that has several tones.

4   **What does enliven mean?**
   a. lengthen   b. abandon   c. brighten

5   **Complete the sentences.**
   a. The men who lived in and worked at monasteries were called _____.
   b. A _____ and a round are both types of polyphonic music.
   c. There are only three _____ in the song *Dona Nobis Pacem*.

6   **Complete the outline.**

Gregorian Chants	Polyphonic Music
• Were sung by medieval ᵃ_____ • Were made of verses from the Bible • Were sung in Latin • Were "a cappella" music • Sounded monotonous • Blended together and ᵇ_____ • Are still sung today	• Means "many ᶜ_____" in Greek • Different voices sing different melodies or words at the same time. • Canon = one voice sings while others join in and sing at different pitches • ᵈ_____ = goes around in a circle

Complete each sentence. Change the form if necessary.

monastery   monk   dreary   chant   round

1   A _____ is a man who belongs to a monastery.

2   Life in a medieval _____ involved working, praying, and reading the Bible.

3   Life was not always _____ for monks because they often got to sing.

4   *Row, Row, Row Your Boat* is a popular _____ that people still sing today.

5   Monks _____ their songs instead of actually singing them.

A Complete each sentence with the correct word. Change the form if necessary.

solid figure	evenly	factor	prime number	perfect square
broken down	direction	base	line segment	exponent

1 Every whole number greater than 1 has at least two _____.

2 A factor is a number that divides another number _____ without a remainder.

3 If a number has only two factors, it is called a _____ _____.

4 Any composite number can be _____ _____ into several prime factors.

5 We can write the expression $16 = 2 \times 2 \times 2 \times 2$ by using an _____ : $16 = 2^4$.

6 A _____ _____ is a number that is the square of a number.

7 A one-dimensional figure is a line or a _____ _____.

8 A two-dimensional figure is measured in two _____, such as length and width.

9 Three-dimensional figures are called _____ _____.

10 Solid figures can be classified by the shape and the number of their _____, faces, vertices, and edges.

B Complete each sentence with the correct word. Change the form if necessary.

statue	contrast	sculptor	passive voice	independent clause
statement	sculpt	melody	dominate	complex sentence

1 Pygmalion was a brilliant _____ from the island of Cyprus.

2 One day, Pygmalion _____ a statue of a woman more beautiful than any living woman.

3 Pygmalion was captivated by the statue's beauty and immediately fell in love with the _____.

4 A declarative sentence is a sentence that makes a _____ about something.

5 An _____ _____ is a clause that can express a complete thought and stand alone as a sentence.

6 A _____ _____ has one independent clause and at least one dependent clause.

7 We use the _____ _____ to say what happens to the subject.

8 Baroque Art is characterized by the dramatic _____ of light and shadow as well as vivid emotional expressions.

9 Romanticism later gave way to Realism, which _____ art from around 1850 to 1890.

10 In polyphonic music, different voices sing different _____ or even different words at the same time.

C Match each word with the correct definition and write the meaning in Chinese.

1 prime number _____ ☐

2 prime factors _____ ☐

3 composite number _____ ☐

4 two-dimensional figure _____ ☐

5 three-dimensional figure _____ ☐

6 ivory _____ ☐

7 statue _____ ☐

8 grant _____ ☐

9 clause _____ ☐

10 monotonous _____ ☐

a. a solid figure
b. a plane figure
c. to consent to perform or fulfill
d. a number with more than two factors
e. a sentence with a subject and predicate
f. having the same tone; not changing in tone
g. a hard cream-colored substance from an elephant's tooth
h. a number that can only be divided evenly by itself and 1
i. the prime numbers that equal a composite number when multiplied together
j. a large stone or metal sculpture of a person or an animal

D Write the meanings of the words in Chinese.

1 exponent _____

2 perfect square _____

3 congruent _____

4 one-dimensional figure _____

5 geometry _____

6 longing _____

7 polyphonic music _____

8 Gregorian Chant _____

9 canon _____

10 a cappella _____

11 art movement _____

12 Baroque Art _____

13 Rococo Art _____

14 Neoclassicism _____

15 Realism _____

16 imperative sentence _____

17 interrogative sentence _____

18 declarative sentence _____

19 exclamatory sentence _____

20 square root _____

21 squared _____

22 cubed _____

23 infinite _____

24 merely _____

25 be captivated by _____

26 come to life _____

27 omit _____

28 independent clause _____

29 subordinate clause _____

30 monastery _____

- Word List
- Answers and Translations

Word List

01 Early People and Civilizations – Early People

1	**primitive** (a.)	原始的
2	**simplistic** (a.)	過分簡單化的
3	**share . . . with . . .**	和……共有……
4	**ape** (n.)	猿猴
5	**extremely** (adv.)	極度地
6	**endure** (v.)	歷經
7	**the Ice Age**	冰河時期
8	**sheets of ice**	冰層
9	**glacier** (n.)	冰河
10	**recede** (v.)	退去
11	**evolve** (v.)	演化
12	**spread out**	散佈
13	**become civilized**	文明化
14	**archaeologist** (n.)	考古學家
15	**three-age system**	三時代系統
16	**prehistoric** (a.)	史前的
17	**the Stone Age**	石器時代
18	**the Bronze Age**	青銅時代
19	**the Iron Age**	鐵器時代
20	**the Old Stone Age**	舊石器時代
21	**the New Stone Age**	新石器時代
22	**hunter-gatherer** (n.)	採獵者
23	**improvement** (n.)	改進
24	**farm the land**	耕田
25	**domesticate** (v.)	馴養
26	**raise** (v.)	飼養
27	**nomad** (n.)	游牧者
28	**copper** (n.)	銅
29	**tin** (n.)	錫
30	**weapon** (n.)	武器
31	**pottery** (n.)	陶器
32	**commonplace** (a.)	普遍的；司空見慣的

02 Rivers and Civilizations – The Fertile Crescent and the Kingdoms of Egypt

1	**the Fertile Crescent**	新月沃土；肥沃月彎
2	**lie** (v.)	位於
3	**the Tigris River**	底格里斯河
4	**the Euphrates River**	幼發拉底河
5	**Mesopotamia**	美索不達米亞
6	**the Middle East**	中東
7	**arise** (v.)	出現；形成
8	**advantage** (n.)	有利條件；優勢
9	**irrigate** (v.)	灌溉
10	**canal** (n.)	灌溉渠
11	**pipe** (n.)	水管
12	**dam** (n.)	水壩
13	**artificial lake**	人工湖
14	**eventually** (adv.)	最終
15	**city-state** (n.)	城邦
16	**Sumer** (n.)	蘇美
17	**Sumerian** (n.)	蘇美人
18	**cuneiform** (n.)	楔形文字
19	**hieroglyphics** (n.)	象形文字
20	**practice** (v.)	信奉（某宗教）
21	**polytheism** (n.)	多神教；多神論
22	**ziggurat** (n.)	金字形神塔
23	**calendar** (n.)	曆法
24	**Babylonia** (n.)	巴比倫王國（或稱巴比倫尼亞，首都為巴比倫 Babylon）
25	**Assyria** (n.)	亞述
26	**Hittite** (n.)	西臺
27	**Israel** (n.)	以色列
28	**settle down**	定居
29	**be centered on**	以……為中心；集中於
30	**the Old Kingdom**	古王國時期
31	**the Middle Kingdom**	中王國時期
32	**the New Kingdom**	新王國時期
33	**pharaoh** (n.)	法老
34	**god-king** (n.)	神王
35	**flourish** (v.)	興盛
36	**territory** (n.)	領土

03 Asian Civilizations – The Indus Civilization

1	the Indus River	印度河
2	modern-day (a.)	現今的
3	the Indus Valley Civilization	印度河流域文明
4	the Harappan Civilization	哈拉帕文明
5	gain access to	可接觸到
6	unearth (v.)	挖掘
7	settlement (n.)	定居地
8	artifact (n.)	手工藝品
9	well organized	組織良好的
10	lay out	設計；規畫
11	grid pattern	棋盤狀；網格狀
12	granary (n.)	穀倉
13	bathhouse (n.)	公共浴池
14	paved street	鋪設的道路
15	sewage system	污水系統；下水道系統
16	monsoon (n.)	季風
17	seasonal wind	季風
18	take advantage of	利用
19	surplus (a.)	剩餘的
20	in case of	以防
21	drought (n.)	乾旱
22	engage in	參與
23	Indus script	印度河文字
24	decline (v.)	衰敗
25	the Ganges River	恆河
26	Aryan (n.)	阿利安人
27	Hinduism (n.)	印度教
28	Hindus (n.)	印度教徒

04 The Ancient World – Ancient Greece

1	peninsula (n.)	半島
2	Mediterranean Sea	地中海
3	mainland (n.)	本土；大陸
4	be suitable for	適合
5	depend on	依賴
6	influence (v.)	影響
7	Minoan (n.)	米諾斯人
8	Crete (n.)	克里特島
9	Mycenaean (n.)	邁錫尼人
10	Phoenician (n.)	腓尼基人
11	trader (n.)	貿易商
12	trade goods	交易商品
13	the basis for	……的根基
14	government system	政府體系
15	independent (a.)	獨立的
16	be ruled by	由……統治
17	monarchy (n.)	君主政體
18	oligarchy (n.)	寡頭政治
19	democracy (n.)	民主政體
20	take part in	參與
21	Athenian (n.)	雅典人
22	lead the way	先行；帶頭
23	birthplace (n.)	發源地
24	sea power	海上強權
25	Spartan (n.)	斯巴達人
26	the Peloponnesian War	伯羅奔尼撒戰爭
27	cease (v.)	停止
28	be involved in	涉入；加入
29	Macedon (n.)	馬其頓王國
30	be murdered	被謀殺
31	ambitious (a.)	野心勃勃的
32	Alexander the Great	亞歷山大大帝

05 The Ancient World – The Roman Empire

1	be founded by	由……所建立
2	the Tiber River	台伯河
3	at its height	在全盛時期
4	Etruscan (a.)	伊特拉斯坎人的
5	drive away	驅逐
6	republic (n.)	共和政體；共和國
7	representative (n.)	代表

8	patrician (n.)	貴族
9	consul (n.)	執政官
10	senator (n.)	元老院議員
11	concerning (prep.)	關於
12	plebeian (n.)	平民
13	plebeian assembly	公民大會
14	tribune (n.)	護民官
15	veto power	否決權
16	defend (v.)	保衛
17	plebeians' rights	平民權利
18	Carthage (n.)	迦太基
19	the Punic Wars	布匿戰爭
20	master (n.)	霸主
21	take over	接管
22	civil war	內戰
23	erupt (v.)	爆發
24	Julius Caesar	凱撒
25	triumvirate (n.)	三頭政治
26	decade (n.)	十年
27	emerge triumphant	獲得勝利
28	be assassinated	被暗殺
29	Roman Senate	羅馬元老院
30	Octavian (n.)	屋大維
31	Augustus (n.)	奧古斯都
32	Pax Romana	羅馬治世；羅馬和平
33	split . . . into . . .	將……分成……
34	Constantine I (= Constantine the Great)	君士坦丁一世
35	rename (v.)	重新命名
36	Byzantine Empire	拜占庭帝國

06　The Arab World – The Rise of Islam

1	the Arabian Peninsula	阿拉伯半島
2	Arab (n.)	阿拉伯人
3	Islam (n.)	伊斯蘭教
4	Muhammad (= Mohammad)	穆罕默德
5	founder (n.)	創立者
6	Mecca (= Makkah)	麥加

7	Muslim (n.)	穆斯林；伊斯蘭教徒
8	the angel Gabriel	天使加百列
9	Allah (n.)	阿拉
10	Arabic word	阿拉伯文字
11	vision (n.)	看見；所見事物
12	preach (v.)	傳教
13	Koran (n.)	可蘭經
14	Five Pillars of Islam	五功；信仰五柱
15	testify (v.)	證實
16	prophet (n.)	先知；傳遞神旨之人
17	make a prayer	禱告
18	face (v.)	面向
19	give charity	施捨；捐贈
20	the poor	窮人
21	the needy	貧困的人
22	fast (v.)	齋戒；禁食
23	Ramadan (n.)	齋月
24	make a Hajj	朝聖
25	pilgrimage	朝聖之旅
26	caliph (n.)	哈里發
27	govern (v.)	管理
28	successor (n.)	繼承者
29	Jerusalem (n.)	耶路撒冷
30	up to	直到
31	be pushed back	被擊退
32	alarm (v.)	使驚慌不安
33	urge (v.)	極力主張
34	Holy Land	聖地
35	the Crusades (n.)	十字軍東征
36	the Crusaders (n.)	十字軍
37	recapture (v.)	收復
38	the Ottoman Empire (= the Osman Turk Empire)	鄂圖曼帝國

07　The Renaissance and the Reformation – From the Middle Ages to the Reformation

1	collapse (v.)	瓦解
2	suffer (v.)	遭受

3	Medieval (a.)	中世紀的
4	feudalism (n.)	封建制度
5	peasant (n.)	農民
6	serf (n.)	農奴
7	the Age of Faith	信仰時代
8	plague (n.)	瘟疫
9	Black Death	黑死病
10	speed up	加速
11	the Renaissance (n.)	文藝復興
12	rebirth (n.)	重生
13	rediscover (v.)	重新發現
14	value (v.)	重視
15	humanist (n.)	人文主義者
16	Renaissance Man	文藝復興人
17	curiosity (n.)	好奇心
18	printing press	印刷術
19	Johannes Gutenberg	古騰堡
20	movable type	活字印刷術
21	accessible (a.)	可（或易）得到的
22	previously (adv.)	先前
23	come up with	想出
24	interpretation (n.)	解釋
25	the Protestant Reformation	宗教改革
26	pope (n.)	教宗
27	bishop (n.)	主教
28	Martin Luther	馬丁‧路德
29	corrupt (a.)	腐敗的
30	indulgence (n.)	贖罪券
31	nail (v.)	釘上
32	thesis (n.)	論點
33	reform (v.)	改革
34	sect (n.)	教派
35	Anglican Church	（英國）聖公會
36	Lutheran sect	路德教派
37	Presbyterian sect	長老教派
38	Anabaptist sect	重浸教派

08 The Enlightenment: The Age of Reason – The Enlightenment and the French Revolution

1	sweep over	橫掃
2	the Enlightenment (n.)	啟蒙運動
3	the Age of Reason	理性時代
4	process (n.)	過程
5	scientific method	科學方法
6	remarkable (a.)	傑出的
7	Galileo Galilei	伽利略
8	telescope (n.)	望遠鏡
9	solar system	太陽系
10	Nicolaus Copernicus	哥白尼
11	heliocentric theory	日心說；太陽中心說
12	sun-centered (a.)	以太陽為中心的
13	calculus (n.)	微積分
14	gravity (n.)	重力；地心吸力
15	the laws of motion	運動定律
16	René Descartes	笛卡兒
17	logic (n.)	邏輯
18	reason (n.)	理性
19	expound (v.)	闡述
20	revolution (n.)	革命
21	divine right	君權神授
22	in any way	以任何方式
23	concept (n.)	觀念
24	Parliament (n.)	國會
25	be forced to	被強迫
26	the American Revolution	美國革命
27	pay off	付清
28	the American Founding Fathers	美國的建國元老
29	the French Revolution	法國大革命
30	estate (n.)	階級
31	clergy (n.)	神職人員
32	nobility (n.)	貴族階級
33	the Three Estates	三等級（指法國大革命以前法國社會的三個等級：教士、貴族和庶民）

34	the Estates General	三級會議
35	**bankruptcy** (n.)	破產
36	**levy** (v.)	徵收
37	**rebel** (v.)	反抗
38	**National Assembly**	國民議會
39	**storm** (v.)	猛攻
40	**Bastille** (n.)	巴士底監獄
41	**fraternity** (n.)	博愛
42	**National Convention**	國民公會

09 The Characteristics of Living Things – Cells, Reproduction, and Heredity

1	**cell** (n.)	細胞
2	**one-celled** (a.)	單細胞的
3	**microorganism** (n.)	微生物
4	**multi-cellular** (a.)	多細胞的
5	**complex** (a.)	高等的
6	**tissue** (n.)	組織
7	**come together**	組合
8	**organ** (n.)	器官
9	**organ system**	器官系統
10	**digestive system**	消化系統
11	**respiratory system**	呼吸系統
12	**reproduction** (n.)	再生；繁殖
13	**take place**	發生
14	**mitosis** (n.)	有絲分裂
15	**meiosis** (n.)	減數分裂
16	**body cell**	身體細胞
17	**genetic material**	遺傳物質
18	**in half**	分半
19	**reproductive cell**	生殖細胞
20	**be responsible for**	承擔……的責任
21	**genetic variation**	遺傳變異
22	**heredity** (n.)	遺傳
23	**gene** (n.)	基因
24	**determine** (v.)	決定
25	**get transferred**	被轉移
26	**offspring** (n.)	下一代

27	**dominant gene**	顯性基因
28	**recessive gene**	隱性基因
29	**present** (a.)	存在的
30	**be overshadowed by**	被……遮蔽
31	**inherit** (v.)	遺傳；繼承
32	**mutation** (n.)	突變；變種

10 The Earth's Oceans – Oceans and Ocean Life

1	**calm** (a.)	平靜的
2	**constant** (a.)	經常的
3	**in motion**	運動中
4	**water level**	水平面
5	**constantly** (adv.)	經常地
6	**be caused by**	由……造成
7	**tide** (n.)	潮汐
8	**result from**	起因於……
9	**gravitational pull**	萬有引力
10	**highest point**	最高點
11	**high tide**	滿潮
12	**lowest point**	最低點
13	**low tide**	乾潮
14	**current** (n.)	洋流
15	**stream of water**	水流
16	**factor** (n.)	因素
17	**global winds**	全球風系
18	**Earth's rotation**	地球自轉
19	**due to**	由於
20	**equator** (n.)	赤道
21	**move away**	離開
22	**Gulf Stream**	墨西哥灣暖流
23	**ocean circulation**	海洋環流
24	**replenish** (v.)	補給
25	**ocean floor**	海床
26	**as varied as**	和……一樣多變
27	**continental shelf**	大陸棚
28	**gentle slope**	緩坡
29	**continental crust**	大陸地殼

30	continental slope	大陸坡
31	abyssal plain	深海平原
32	ocean zone	海洋帶
33	shallowest (a.)	最淺的
34	the intertidal zone	潮間帶
35	get exposed	暴露
36	the nearshore zone	近岸區；近濱帶
37	abundant (a.)	豐富的
38	the open-ocean zone	遠洋帶

11 Fossils – What We Can Learn From Fossils

1	dinosaur (n.)	恐龍
2	go extinct	絕種
3	thanks to	歸功於……
4	fossil (n.)	化石
5	remains (n.)	遺骸
6	imprint (n.)	痕跡
7	sediment (n.)	沉積物
8	harden (v.)	硬化
9	sedimentary rock	沉積岩
10	get fossilized	成為化石
11	be preserved	被保存
12	decay (v.)	腐爛
13	shell (n.)	殼
14	be left behind	被遺留下來
15	footprint (n.)	足跡
16	impression (n.)	印記
17	in the form of	以……形式
18	mold (n.)	模子；模具
19	cast (n.)	鑄型
20	extinct (a.)	絕種的
21	vanish (v.)	絕跡
22	paleontologist (n.)	古生物學家
23	unearth (v.)	挖掘
24	piece together	拼湊
25	figure out	得知
26	weigh (v.)	有多少重量

27	assemble (v.)	組合
28	fossil record	化石紀錄
29	index fossil	標準化石；指標化石
30	specific (a.)	特定的
31	rock layer	岩層
32	ammonite (n.)	菊石（鸚鵡螺的化石）
33	cephalopod (n.)	頭足動物
34	trilobite (n.)	三葉蟲

12 Force and Motion – Newton's Laws

1	skydiver (n.)	跳傘選手
2	float (v.)	飄浮
3	freefall (n.)	自由落體
4	parachute (n.)	降落傘
5	acceleration (n.)	加速度
6	gravity (n.)	重力；地心引力
7	Newton's Law of Universal Gravitation	牛頓萬有引力定律
8	gravitation (n.)	萬有引力
9	attract (v.)	吸引
10	effect (n.)	作用
11	in a circular path	繞行
12	prevent . . . from . . .	防止……做……
13	fly off	飛離
14	physics (n.)	物理學
15	the first law of motion	第一運動定律
16	at rest	靜止
17	in motion	運動中
18	velocity (n.)	速率
19	unless (conj.)	除非……
20	outside force	外力
21	act on	作用於……
22	fall back down	往回落下
23	the Law of Inertia	慣性定律
24	the second law of motion	第二運動定律
25	the Law of Acceleration	加速度定律
26	formula (n.)	公式；方程式
27	the third law of motion	第三運動定律

28	the Law of Action and Reaction	作用力與反作用力
29	in return	以……回應；回報
30	propel (v.)	推進

13 Light Energy – Light Energy

1	be comprised of	由……組成
2	billions of	數十億的
3	particle (n.)	粒子
4	photon (n.)	光子
5	in waves	以波的形式
6	approximately (adv.)	大約
7	medium (n.)	媒介
8	in a vacuum	在真空中
9	wavelength (n.)	波長
10	visible light	可見光
11	the colors of the spectrum	光譜色
12	prism (n.)	稜鏡
13	be conducted by	由……執行
14	beam of sunlight	太陽光束
15	refract (v.)	折射
16	combination (n.)	結合
17	bend (v.)	彎曲
18	refraction (n.)	折射
19	convex lens	凸透鏡
20	concave lens	凹透鏡
21	focal point	焦點
22	binoculars (n.)	雙目望遠鏡
23	television projector	電視投影機
24	invisible light	不可見光
25	electromagnetic spectrum	電磁光譜；電磁波譜
26	infrared light	紅外線
27	microwave (n.)	微波
28	ultraviolet light	紫外線
29	X-ray (n.)	X 光
30	gamma ray	伽瑪射線

14 The Universe – Eclipses

1	darken (v.)	使變暗
2	lunar eclipse	月蝕
3	eclipse (n.)	天蝕
4	moon's revolving	月球沿軌道繞行
5	location (n.)	位置
6	solar eclipse	日蝕
7	block . . . from . . .	阻擋……使其無法……
8	cast a shadow	投下陰影
9	partial solar eclipse	日偏蝕
10	total solar eclipse	日全蝕
11	glow (n.)	光芒
12	solar corona	日冕
13	diamond ring effect	鑽石環現象
14	last for	持續……之久
15	brighten (v.)	變明亮
16	Earth's shadow	地球陰影
17	total lunar eclipse	月全蝕
18	inner (a.)	內部的
19	umbra (n.)	地球本影
20	reflect (v.)	反射
21	partial lunar eclipse	月偏蝕
22	directly (adv.)	直接地
23	permanently (adv.)	永久地
24	blind oneself	使自己失明

15 The Human Body – Diseases and the Immune System

1	(every) once in a while	有時；偶而
2	catch a disease	罹患疾病
3	noncommunicable disease	非傳染病
4	communicable disease	傳染病
5	lung cancer	肺癌
6	heart disease	心臟病
7	infected (a.)	受感染的
8	(common) cold (n.)	（一般）感冒
9	the flu (n.)	流行性感冒

10	contagious (a.)	接觸傳染的
11	epidemic (n.)	流行病；傳染病
12	defense (n.)	防禦
13	the immune system	免疫系統
14	the first line of defense	第一道防線
15	prevent . . . from . . .	保護……免於……
16	germ (n.)	病菌
17	gland (n.)	腺體
18	attempt to	企圖要……
19	mucus (n.)	黏液
20	foreign body	異物
21	saliva (n.)	口水；唾液
22	acid (n.)	酸
23	manage to	成功做到……
24	the lymphatic system	淋巴系統
25	lymph node	淋巴結
26	lymph gland	淋巴腺
27	white blood cell	白血球
28	infection (n.)	感染
29	antibody (n.)	抗體
30	foreign invader	外來入侵者
31	vaccine (n.)	疫苗
32	inject (v.)	注射
33	stimulate (v.)	刺激
34	deadly (a.)	致命的
35	yellow fever	黃熱病
36	influenza (n.)	流行性感冒

16 Numbers and Computation – Factors, Prime Numbers, and Exponents

1	whole number	整數
2	factor (n.)	因數
3	evenly (adv.)	平均地
4	remainder (n.)	餘數
5	be broken into	被分解成
6	divide evenly	整除
7	prime number	質數
8	composite number	合數

9	prime factor	質因數
10	result in	形成；造成
11	expression (n.)	算式
12	exponent (= power) (n.)	指數（＝次方）
13	the fourth power	四次方
14	base (n.)	底數
15	square (v.)	使成平方
16	the second power	二次方
17	cube (v.)	使成立方
18	the third power	三次方
19	perfect square	完全平方數
20	square root	平方根

17 Geometry – Dimensions

1	dimension (n.)	維度
2	straight line	直線
3	length (n.)	長度
4	width (n.)	寬度
5	height (n.)	高度
6	geometry (n.)	幾何學
7	the first dimension	一度空間
8	the second dimension	二度空間
9	the third dimension	三度空間
10	depth (n.)	深度
11	the fourth dimension	四度空間
12	typically (adv.)	傳統上
13	one-dimensional figure	一度空間圖形
14	lack (v.)	缺少
15	two-dimensional figure	二度空間圖形
16	plane figure	平面圖形
17	plane (n.)	平面
18	polygon (n.)	多邊形
19	intersect (v.)	相交；交叉
20	infinite (a.)	無限的
21	three-dimensional figure	三度空間圖形
22	solid figure	立體圖形
23	base (n.)	底

24	**face** (n.)	面
25	**vertex** (n.)	頂點
26	**edge** (n.)	邊
27	**congruent** (a.)	全等的
28	**parallel** (a.)	平行的
29	**correspond with**	和……相呼應
30	**curved** (a.)	弧形的
31	**cube (= square prism)**	正方體
32	**rectangular prism**	長方體
33	**triangular prism**	三角柱
34	**square pyramid**	正四角錐
35	**rectangular pyramid**	長方錐
36	**cylinder** (n.)	圓柱
37	**cone** (n.)	圓錐
38	**sphere** (n.)	球體

18 Stories, Myths, and Legends – Pygmalion

1	**sculptor** (n.)	雕刻師
2	**name** (v.)	給……命名
3	**Pygmalion** (n.)	皮革馬利翁
4	**Cyprus** (n.)	塞浦路斯
5	**merely** (adv.)	只是
6	**brilliant** (a.)	聰穎的
7	**statue** (n.)	雕像
8	**as if**	彷彿
9	**set to**	開始；著手
10	**ivory** (n.)	象牙
11	**be captivated by**	被……所迷倒
12	**fall in love with**	愛上……
13	**stare at**	凝視……
14	**longing** (n.)	渴望；熱望
15	**in honor of**	向……致敬
16	**Aphrodite** (n.)	阿芙羅黛蒂
17	**make an offering**	獻上供品
18	**the goddess of love**	愛之女神
19	**make a wish**	許願
20	**sincerely** (adv.)	誠摯地

21	**grant** (v.)	應允
22	**come to life**	甦醒過來；活過來
23	**achieve** (v.)	達成
24	**marriage** (n.)	婚姻
25	**George Bernard Shaw**	蕭伯納
26	**give rise to**	引起……
27	**the Pygmalion effect**	期待效應；皮革馬利翁效應
28	**be capable of**	能夠……
29	**achieve greatness**	有所成就
30	**indeed** (adv.)	的確

19 Grammar and Usage – Sentences

1	**subject** (n.)	主詞
2	**predicate** (n.)	述語
3	**declarative sentence**	直述句
4	**make a statement**	陳述事實
5	**end with**	以……結尾
6	**interrogative sentence**	疑問句
7	**question mark**	問號
8	**exclamatory sentence**	感嘆句
9	**exclamation point**	驚嘆號
10	**imperative sentence**	祈使句
11	**be omitted**	被省略
12	**in other words**	換句話說
13	**incredible** (a.)	不可思議的
14	**simple sentence**	簡單句
15	**independent clause**	獨立子句
16	**clause** (n.)	子句
17	**stand alone**	獨立存在
18	**conjunction** (n.)	連接詞
19	**compound sentence**	並列句
20	**dependent clause**	非獨立子句
21	**subordinate clause**	附屬子句
22	**function** (v.)	起作用
23	**by itself**	靠自己
24	**be connected to**	和……連接

25	subordinate conjunction	從屬連接詞
26	complex sentence	複合句
27	the active voice	主動語氣
28	the passive voice	被動語氣

20 Art Movements – From Baroque Art to Realism

1	art movement	藝術運動
2	unique (a.)	獨特的
3	the Baroque Art	巴洛克藝術
4	architecture (n.)	建築
5	compared with	和⋯⋯比較
6	classicism (n.)	古典主義
7	be characterized by	具有⋯⋯的特徵
8	dramatic (a.)	戲劇性的
9	contrast of	和⋯⋯的對比
10	vivid (a.)	活潑的；鮮明的
11	emotional expression	情感表達
12	evoke (v.)	喚起
13	emerge (v.)	興起
14	the Rococo Period	洛可可時期
15	decorative (a.)	裝飾的
16	lighthearted (a.)	輕快的
17	delicate (a.)	精緻的
18	pastel color	柔和、淡雅的顏色
19	turn away from	背棄⋯⋯；厭惡⋯⋯
20	flashy (a.)	俗艷的
21	emphasis on	對⋯⋯的重視
22	lead to	造成⋯⋯
23	the Neoclassical Movement	新古典主義運動
24	Neoclassicism (n.)	新古典主義
25	revive (v.)	復興；復甦
26	the Romantic Movement	浪漫主義運動
27	Romanticism (n.)	浪漫主義
28	imagination (n.)	想像力
29	orderly (a.)	制式的；規矩的
30	give way to	讓位給⋯⋯
31	Realism (n.)	寫實主義

32	be replaced by	被⋯⋯取代
33	Impressionism (n.)	印象派
34	abstract (a.)	抽象的
35	Impressionist (n.)	印象派畫家
36	Cubist (n.)	立體派藝術家
37	Dadaism (n.)	達達主義
38	Pop Art	普普藝術

21 The Music of the Middle Ages – Gregorian Chants and Polyphonic Music

1	the Middle Ages	中世紀
2	tremendous (a.)	極度的；巨大的
3	monastery (n.)	修道院
4	monk (n.)	修道士
5	be structured	有組織的
6	dreary (a.)	枯燥的
7	enliven (v.)	使活躍
8	medieval (a.)	中世紀的
9	chant (n.)	吟唱；吟誦
10	Gregorian Chants	格雷果聖歌
11	Pope Gregory the Great	教宗格雷果
12	verse (n.)	（《聖經》的）經節；詩句
13	in Latin	以拉丁文呈現
14	unfamiliar (a.)	不熟悉的
15	accompany (v.)	為⋯⋯伴奏
16	a cappella	阿卡貝拉（無伴奏合唱）
17	monotonous (a.)	單調的
18	harmonize (v.)	和諧
19	polyphonic music	多聲部合唱
20	gain popularity	受到歡迎
21	inflection (n.)	語調抑揚變化
22	canon (n.)	卡農
23	slightly (adv.)	稍微地
24	round (n.)	輪唱
25	imply (v.)	暗示
26	overlap (v.)	重疊

01 Early People 早期的人類

數百萬年前，原始人和現代人截然不同。他們是簡化的生物，同時具有人類和猿猴的特性。在這段時期，地球長時間處於嚴寒，歷經了漫長的冰河時期。在冰河時期，大部分的地表被稱為冰河的巨大冰層覆蓋。而約在一萬兩千五百年前，冰河時期結束，冰塊與冰河從地表退去。之後人類開始演化與遷徙，並逐漸開化。

考古學家採用三時代系統為史前文化分期，分別是「石器時代」、「青銅器時代」和「鐵器時代」。

「石器時代」通常分為「舊石器時代」和「新石器時代」。舊石器時代是石器時代的早期階段，約始於西元前兩百萬年，而新石器時代則是晚期階段，約始於西元前一萬年。

舊石器時代的人類過著狩獵與採集的生活。他們獵捕動物，並採集野生植物為食。在此階段的人類只能用石頭製作簡單的工具，不過已經懂得如何生火。火的發現使人類生活產生巨變。人類使用火來照明和取暖，最重要的是，得以烹煮食物。

新石器時代的生活更加進步。人類學會耕作，並且馴養像是狗、綿羊和山羊等野生動物。有些人開始在一些土壤肥沃、適合耕種的村落定居。由於可以種植自己的作物和畜牧，他們毋須再過著游牧的生活。不過他們仍然使用石器，所以此階段被稱為新石器時代。

大約在西元前三千年，有些地區開始進入「青銅器時代」。這個時期人類開始使用銅和錫這類的軟金屬，並學會用青銅來製造工具和武器。陶製品也在此階段變得更加普遍。

大約在西元前一千五百年，歐洲進入「鐵器時代」，當然有些地方開始得早，有些地方比較晚。在鐵器時代，人們開始使用鐵器工作。最早的一些真正的城市也開始出現，城市之間的貿易變得更加普遍。人類文明在這個階段以前所未有的速度蓬勃發展。

- **Vocabulary Preview**

1 **Ice Age** 冰河時期　　2 **domesticate** 馴養（動物）；馴化
3 **Bronze Age** 青銅時代　　4 **primitive** 原始的；早期的
5 **hunter-gatherer** 採獵者

- **Quick Check**

1 **(T)**　　2 **(T)**　　3 **(F)**

- **Main Idea and Details**

1 **(a)**　　2 **(b)**　　3 **(b)**　　4 **(c)**
5 a. **glaciers**　　b. **Bronze Age**　　c. **Iron Age**
6 a. **stone**　　b. **domesticate**　　c. **copper**　　d. **Pottery**
　　e. **iron**

- **Vocabulary Review**

1 **fertile soil**　　2 **nomads**　　3 **prehistoric**
4 **domesticate**　　5 **Primitive**

02 The Fertile Crescent and the Kingdoms of Egypt 新月沃土與埃及王國

世界最早的文明之一發源於西南亞的「新月沃土」，位於底格里斯河和幼發拉底河之間。後人將此區稱為「美索不達米亞」，意思是「兩河之間的土地」。今日，我們稱這個地方為中東地區。

這兩條河流對於美索不達米亞的居民來說十分重要。每當河流氾濫時，會帶來有利耕種的肥沃土壤，因此這個地區很早就發展出農業文明。美索不達米亞的居民也懂得利用地理環境和資源，這裡的農民運用灌溉渠和水管，自底格里斯河和幼發拉底河引水灌溉乾地。他們也建造水庫，用人工湖來儲水。他們在河裡捕魚，並飼養動物作為食物和衣料的來源。到了西元前三千年，美索不達米亞的村莊已經成長為較大的城市，最終發展為城邦。位於美索不達米亞南部的諸多城邦，後來成為我們所知的「蘇美文明」。

蘇美人擁有高度的文明，他們發展出的書寫系統稱為「楔形文字」，甚至比古埃及的象形文字還要早。他們是多神信仰，每個城市都有一座為神明所建的宏偉金字形神廟。他們也發展出基礎數學，並創造了我們今日使用的十二月曆法。在蘇美文明殞落之後，美索不達米亞地區歷經許多帝國的興衰，包括巴比倫、亞述、西臺和古以色列都曾在這裡建立文明。

大約於此同時，非洲也發展出另一個偉大的文明。約莫西元前四千年，人們開始在埃及的尼羅河畔定居，並且在此地建立村莊與城鎮，形成「古埃及文明」。

古埃及的生活以尼羅河為中心。就像美索不達米亞的兩河一樣，尼羅河每年夏天氾濫，為周圍地區帶來肥沃的土壤。當尼羅河氾濫之後，沿岸的土壤充滿了礦物質和其他養分，有利於許多農作物生長。沒過多久埃及便聚集了大量人口，建立起強大的農業經濟。

古埃及文明大約始於西元前 3100 年，結束於西元前 332 年，被亞歷山大大帝征服。古埃及歷史常被分為三個時期：「古王國時期」、「中王國時期」與「新王國時期」。

古王國時期約從西元前 3100 年到西元前 2200 年。大約在西元前 3100 年時，上埃及的統治者曼尼斯征服了下埃及，統一了埃及全境，成為埃及的第一位法老。古王國時期的法老權高勢重，被奉為現世的神王，金字塔是石砌的法老陵墓，就是在當時所建造。中王國時期約從西元前 2100 年到西元前 1700 年，通常被視為古埃及的輝煌時期。此時期的貿易興盛，在藝術、數學和科學方面也都有長足的進展。新王國時期則約從西元前 1500 年到西元前 1000 年。法老阿曼和闐二世和拉曼西斯二世都曾於此時期統治王朝。這個時期的埃及拓展領土，國威達於鼎盛。

- **Vocabulary Preview**

1 **irrigate** 灌溉　　2 **Mesopotamia** 美索不達米亞
3 **ziggurat** 金字形神塔　　4 **polytheism** 多神論
5 **cuneiform** 楔形文字

- **Quick Check**

1 **(T)**　　2 **(T)**　　3 **(F)**

- **Main Idea and Details**

1 **(c)**　　2 **(a)**　　3 **(b)**　　4 **(c)**　　5 **(b)**
6 a. **Tigris**　　b. **irrigated**　　c. **polytheism**　　d. **calendar**
　　e. **pyramids**　　f. **New Kingdom**

- **Vocabulary Review**

1 **ziggurat**　　2 **irrigate**　　3 **god-king**
4 **writing systems**　　5 **flourished**

03　The Indus Civilization 古印度文明

約在西元前 2500 年，印度河流域也就是現今的印度和巴基斯坦地區，誕生了另一個偉大的文明。我們現在稱之為「印度河流域文明」或是「哈拉帕文明」。

就像其他建立於河岸的偉大文明一樣，印度河流域的居民也沿著印度河興建村鎮和城市，這樣方便他們取水，以供飲用、耕種和飼養動物之用。其中兩個河岸城市現在被稱為哈拉帕和摩亨佐達羅。

考古學家已經挖掘出一千多個來自印度河流域文明的村落。他們透過研究當時的手工藝品，得知印度河流域文明相當有組織。舉例來說，它的城市規畫為長方形，街道呈網格狀分布，城市內有宮殿、寺廟、糧倉和公共浴池，鋪設了寬廣的街道，甚至還建有污水系統。

印度河流域文明的居民通曉農業。印度河和季風——會在夏季帶來豪雨的季節風——左右著印度人的生活。哈拉帕的農民懂得善用天氣，種植各種作物，剩餘的穀物就儲存起來供旱災時使用。他們也馴養牛羊和豬隻，用黏土和銅製作鍋壺和工具。當地居民甚至和其他像是美索不達米亞等地區的人進行貿易。他們的書寫系統稱為印度河文字，但歷史學家尚無法解讀。

古印度文明持續了一千多年之久，歷史學家無法確認此文明的衰敗原因。原本的居民基於某種理由陸續離開印度河沿岸的城市，新文明在位於印度另一處的恆河展開。接著來自西北方的新種族阿利安人在此定居，征服並統治了印度人。阿利安人多年的統治改變了印度人民的生活，其中最大的改變就是印度教的誕生。阿利安人結合自己和印度人所崇拜的神祇，創立了印度教，是現今世界最古老的宗教之一。今日的印度有八億五千多萬人是印度教徒。

- **Vocabulary Preview**

1 **sewage system** 污水系統　　2 **decline** 衰退；衰落
3 **Indus Valley Civilization** 印度河流域文明
4 **Indus script** 印度河文字　　5 **monsoon** 季風

- **Quick Check**

1 **(T)**　　2 **(F)**　　3 **(F)**

- **Main Idea and Details**

1 **(c)**　　2 **(c)**　　3 **(b)**　　4 **(b)**
5 a. **It is called Indus script.**
　 b. **They domesticated sheep, cattle, and pigs.**
　 c. **It lasted more than 1,000 years.**
6 a. **Indus River**　　b. **sewage**　　c. **monsoons**
　 d. **northwest**　　e. **Hinduism**

- **Vocabulary Review**

1 **engaged in**　　2 **decline**　　3 **laid out**　　4 **monsoon**
5 **in case of**

04　Ancient Greece 古希臘文明

古希臘由地中海的兩個半島「阿緹卡」和「伯羅奔尼撒」組成，而地中海沿岸還有超過四百座島嶼。希臘沒有如尼羅河般會氾濫的河流，本土大陸多為丘陵和山脈所覆蓋。多岩乾燥的土壤並不適合耕種，所以古希臘人以海為生，並透過航海進行貿易。

古希臘文明受到三個早期的地中海文明影響，分別是克里特島的米諾斯人、來自中亞征服米諾斯的邁錫尼人、地中海東岸的腓尼基人。他們航越地中海經商，在進行貨品貿易之際，也傳播自己的文化和觀念。腓尼基人發明的字母系統，後來成為我們今日使用的字母原型。

希臘人實踐許多新想法，並實施各種不同的政府體系。希臘人住在不同的城邦中，這些城邦各自獨立，但所有居民都統一說希臘語。

有些城邦由國王統治，稱作「君主政體」；有些城邦由多位富人統治，稱作「寡頭政治」；少數城邦施行「民主政治」，由全體公民參與政治並選出領袖，雅典人便首開民主先例。不過只有男性才能成為公民，女性和奴隸都被排除在外，無法投票。雖然雅典的民主制度未臻完美，卻仍影響了後世的許多國家。今日，我們稱雅典為「民主的發源地」。

大約在西元前 500 年，雅典和斯巴達是希臘勢力最強大的兩個城邦，他們的價值觀和文化大相逕庭。雅典人施行民主，握有海上霸權；斯巴達人則是驍勇善戰，擁有強大的軍隊。西元前 431 到 404 年間，雅典和斯巴達在「伯羅奔尼撒戰役」中對峙，最後由斯巴達獲得勝利，雅典的強權時代就此告終。

希臘的許多城邦也參與了伯羅奔尼撒戰役。戰爭結束後，這些城邦元氣大傷。馬其頓位於希臘北部，由腓力國王領導，陸續征服包含雅典在內的希臘城邦。西元前 336 年，腓力國王遭到謀殺，由其子亞歷山大繼任王位。亞歷山大迅速擊敗了希臘半島的其他城邦後，這位野心勃勃的年輕人繼續帶兵東征。亞歷山大大帝在西元前 323 年過世時，已經擊潰波斯帝國，並征服了大半的西亞和北非。他在辭世之際，已是當時世界最大帝國的統治者。

- **Vocabulary Preview**

1 **Peloponnesian War** 伯羅奔尼撒戰役
2 **ambitious** 野心勃勃的　　3 **oligarchy** 寡頭政治
4 **monarchy** 君主政體　　5 **city-state** 城邦

- **Quick Check**

1 **(F)**　　2 **(F)**　　3 **(T)**

- **Main Idea and Details**

1 **(b)**　　2 **(c)**　　3 **(a)**　　4 **(b)**
5 a. **peninsulas**　　b. **citizens**　　c. **Peloponnesian**
6 a. **Phoenician**　　b. **kings**　　c. **democracies**
　 d. **Athens**　　e. **Alexander**

- **Vocabulary Review**

1 **practiced**　　2 **ambitious**　　3 **birthplace**
4 **influenced**　　5 **suitable for**

05　The Roman Empire　古羅馬帝國

傳說中，羅馬是在西元前 753 年，由羅木勒斯和雷木斯兄弟於義大利半島上所建立。原本只是坐落在台伯河畔七座山丘上的小城市，卻日漸擴展成為龐大帝國的中心。羅馬帝國在全盛時期的版圖，橫跨了今日大半的歐洲、部分的非洲和中東地區。

早期羅馬被伊特拉斯坎國王統治了 250 年。西元前 510 年，羅馬人驅逐了這些國王，建立了一個新形態的共和政府，羅馬共和國於焉誕生。在共和制度裡，人民可以選出自己的代表，來為人民制訂政治決策。共和國內的富人，也就是貴族，可以選出兩位領導人作為執政官，並且選出元老院議員擔任執政官的顧問，為元老院服務。執政官和元老院同心協力治理羅馬，執行羅馬城的重要決策。後來，貧窮的農商人民等平民被賦予召開平民大會的權力，以選出十位護民官。護民官擁有否決權，以捍衛平民的權利。

羅馬的勢力逐年擴張。到了西元前 300 年，羅馬已經掌控了大半個義大利半島，成為地中海強權。但是地中海對岸卻有迦太基與羅馬爭奪霸權。自西元前 275 年起，羅馬與迦太基分別在三場「布匿戰爭」中交手。第三場布匿戰爭結束於西元前 146 年，羅馬在取得勝利之後成為地中海地區的霸主。

羅馬繼續擴張版圖，拿下歐洲、亞洲和非洲的多數土地。但在布匿戰爭之後，富裕的羅馬貴族和擁權的將領之間爆發了數次內戰。最後由龐培、克拉蘇和凱撒成立三頭政治共同治理羅馬，維持了約十年光景，三人就互相開戰。凱撒獲得了勝利，卻在西元前 44 年於元老院遭到暗殺。

凱撒去世後，戰火頻仍，直到西元前 31 年屋大維打敗安東尼和克麗奧佩脫拉後，戰爭才結束。屋大維在戰勝之後成為皇帝。羅馬共和國結束，帝國興起，屋大維是羅馬帝國的第一位皇帝，現被稱為「奧古斯都」。奧古斯都執政後，開啟了「羅馬治世」，也就是「羅馬和平」，維持了將近兩百年的承平時期。

羅馬帝國日漸龐大，單憑一人之力難以治理。西元 293 年，戴克里先為了治國方便，將羅馬分為東羅馬和西羅馬，然而此舉造成了帝國日後在君士坦丁一世手中徹底分裂。西元 324 年，君士坦丁一世將權力中心轉移到拜占庭，並重新命名為君士坦丁堡，成為日後的「拜占庭帝國」。

西羅馬帝國於分裂後日趨衰落，羅馬城最終被日耳曼的入侵者所征服，而拜占庭帝國則繼續存在了一千多年。.

- **Vocabulary Preview**

1 **triumvirate** 三頭政治　　2 **tribune**（古羅馬的）護民官
3 **triumphant** 勝利的；成功的　　4 **Punic Wars** 布匿戰爭
5 **Pax Romana** 羅馬治世

- **Quick Check**

1 **(F)**　　2 **(T)**　　3 **(F)**

- **Main Idea and Details**

1 **(b)**　　2 **(c)**　　3 **(a)**　　4 **(a)**　　5 **(b)**
6 a. **consuls**　　b. **tribunes**　　c. **eastern**
　　d. **Byzantine Empire**　　e. **Germanic**

- **Vocabulary Review**

1 **drive away**　　2 **Senators**　　3 **civil war**
4 **triumvirate**　　5 **emerged triumphant**

06　The Rise of Islam
伊斯蘭教的崛起

世界上最大的一些沙漠地帶位於阿拉伯半島，大部分的地區十分乾燥炎熱。然而人們已經在此居住了數千年，並孕育出璀璨的文明。這些在阿拉伯半島上住了三千多年的人，我們稱之為阿拉伯人。

「伊斯蘭教」發源於阿拉伯半島，自西元 610 年創立後便快速發展。穆罕默德為伊斯蘭教創始人，於西元 570 年左右誕生在阿拉伯半島的麥加城。伊斯蘭教的信徒穆斯林堅信，阿拉於 610 年派了天使加百列傳遞訊息給穆罕默德。「阿拉」這個字在阿拉伯語中是「神」的意思。

根據伊斯蘭教的傳說，穆罕默德見過天使加百列之後就開始向其他阿拉伯人傳教。他要求信徒們只能信奉阿拉為唯一真神，倡導眾生平等，富人應照顧窮人。穆罕默德去世後，他的門徒將其教誨撰寫下來，成為伊斯蘭的聖典《可蘭經》。伊斯蘭教中有五項基本戒律，稱為「五功」，分別是：

1. 證言阿拉是唯一的神，穆罕默德是阿拉的使者。
2. 每天朝麥加方向祈禱五次。
3. 將財富捐贈給貧困之人。
4. 齋戒：在神聖的「齋月」期間，白日不可飲食。
5. 一生至少到麥加朝聖一次。

穆罕默德於 632 年逝世後，穆斯林領袖選出「哈里發」來管理穆斯林世界。哈里發是被選中的穆罕默德繼承者，是穆斯林的政治和宗教領袖。西元 632 年到 661 年間總共有四位哈里發，在他們的帶領下，伊斯蘭世界迅速擴張。穆斯林軍隊征服了亞歷山大城、耶路撒冷和大馬士革等基督教城市，攻佔了西亞、北非和西班牙的領土；他們繼續北征法國，但在 732 年被查理·馬特擊退；往東則遠叩拜占庭帝國首都君士坦丁堡的大門，不過一樣戰敗而返。

伊斯蘭教的擴張驚動了西方世界。11 世紀下半葉，教宗號召西歐的基督徒派遣軍隊前往耶路撒冷解放聖地，此舉開啟了「十字軍東征」。西元 1099 年，第一次十字軍東征奪回聖地耶路撒冷。接下來的兩百年間，陸續經歷了數次的十字軍東征。然而，十字軍最後仍被擊潰，穆斯林收復了十字軍東征期間的失土。

爾後，鄂圖曼帝國於 13 世紀崛起，成為當時的強權，並在 1453 年攻下君士坦丁堡，終結了拜占庭帝國。鄂圖曼帝國一直到第一次世界大戰結束才瓦解。

- **Vocabulary Preview**

1 **caliph** 哈里發（伊斯蘭教中穆罕默德的繼承人）
2 **crusade** 聖戰　　3 **prophet** 先知　　4 **holy book** 聖典
5 **fast** 禁食；齋戒

- **Quick Check**

1 **(F)**　　2 **(T)**　　3 **(T)**

- **Main Idea and Details**

1 **(a)**　　2 **(b)**　　3 **(b)**　　4 **(a)**
5 a. **A Hajj is a pilgrimage to Mecca.**
　b. **Charles Martel defeated the Muslims in France in 732.**
　c. **In 1453, the Ottoman Empire captured Constantinople and destroyed the Byzantine Empire.**
6 a. **Muhammad**　　b. **prophet**　　c. **Ramadan**
　d. **Islam**　　e. **Ottoman Empire**

1 **captured**　2 **testify**　3 **giving charity**　4 **prophet**
5 **fast**

07　From the Middle Ages to the Reformation　從中世紀到宗教改革

羅馬帝國時期幅員廣及地中海沿岸各地以及大部分的歐洲。在羅馬治世下，羅馬士兵維持了數百年的和平。龐大的羅馬帝國於 476 年瓦解後，歐洲就戰事不斷。從羅馬滅亡到十五世紀這段期間稱為「中世紀」。

對大多數的歐洲人而言，中世紀的生活很困苦。在封建制度下，中世紀的社會是金字塔結構：國王與貴族在最上層，往下一層是騎士，最底層則是農奴。人民飽受戰爭與飢餓的摧殘，無數人死於惡疾。科學、文學、藝術或其他領域都沒有什麼進展。

但對基督教會而言，中世紀是成長茁壯的時期。西元 313 年，基督教成為羅馬帝國的合法宗教。教會不斷擴張，甚至在西羅馬帝國崩潰之後仍然持續。到了西元 1000 年，多數的歐洲人都成為基督徒，教會更是掌控了人民的日常生活。因此中世紀有時又被稱為「信仰時代」。

14 世紀時，名為黑死病的瘟疫肆虐歐洲，造成數百萬人喪命。人口的大量死亡改變了歐洲的經濟，並加速封建制度的瓦解。許多農奴死亡，貴族只好付錢請工人來照顧莊園。

中世紀在 1400 年左右結束，「文藝復興」在義大利興起。Renaissance 這個字意味著「重生」。在這段期間，人們重新發現和重視藝術、科學、文學，以及古希臘羅馬的思想，也引領他們產生自己的新發現。首先是人文主義者，他們探討古希臘羅馬的著作，將重心放在人而非宗教上。此時在科學、藝術、文學、音樂等各個領域都有卓越的進步。達文西和米開朗基羅這樣的人成為「文藝復興人」，此頭銜代表充滿好奇心且精通多項領域的通才。

文藝復興傳遍歐洲各地，在這期間出現了一項重要發明，即印刷術，大大地改變了社會。15 世紀中葉，約翰尼斯·古騰堡發明了活字印刷術，使得書籍更加普及。書籍製作變得便宜且容易，更多人學會認字，也使得更多人可以自己閱讀《聖經》。以前只有神父和有錢人能識字，但現在普羅大眾皆可閱讀《聖經》，並且可做出自己的詮釋，這導致了後來的「宗教改革」。

天主教會在文藝復興時期仍握有大權，有些教宗和主教成為權高位重的政治領袖。但是德國神父馬丁路德認為教會過於腐敗，他尤其不滿的是教會出售贖罪券來重建羅馬的聖彼得教堂。1517 年，馬丁路德來到一所教堂，將《九十五條論證》釘在門上，就此揭開了宗教改革的序幕。

許多人和馬丁路德的想法一樣，認為教會需要改革。宗教改革的思潮迅速從德國擴展到瑞士、荷蘭、法國和英國。許多人脫離天主教會，建立起自己的基督教派。英國國王亨利八世也於 1530 年代脫離天主教會，建立英國國教。路德教派、長老會和重浸教派都創立於這個時期。

• **Vocabulary Preview**
1 **sect** 教派（分裂出來的教派）
2 **Protestant Reformation** 宗教改革　3 **thesis** 論點
4 **Black Death** 黑死病
5 **indulgence**（天主教的）特赦；豁免

1 **(F)**　2 **(T)**　3 **(T)**
• **Main Idea and Details**
1 **(c)**　2 **(b)**　3 **(b)**　4 **(a)**
5 a. **feudalism**　b. **humanists**　c. **Germany**
6 a. **Italy**　b. **humanists**　c. **Renaissance Men**
　d. **theses**　e. **Anglican Church**　f. **sects**
• **Vocabulary Review**
1 **movable type**　2 **nailed**　3 **speed up**　4 **sects**
5 **humanists**

08　The Enlightenment and the French Revolution　啟蒙運動與法國大革命

在 17、18 世紀期間，關於世界和科學發現的新思維席捲全歐洲，是為「啟蒙運動」，也稱為「理性時代」。

啟蒙時代的科學家發展出一套稱為「科學方法」的步驟，開始對萬物提問，因此有了許多驚人的科學發現。伽利略改良了早期的望遠鏡，並且研究太陽系，他也支持哥白尼的「日心說」。牛頓發明了微積分，這是一門新的數學，並提出萬有引力與運動定律。醫生們用新的概念和方法來改良醫藥。法國哲學家笛卡兒發展出以邏輯和理性為基礎的哲學。霍布斯、洛克、孟德斯鳩等哲學家，闡述了政府與人民的基本權利。

啟蒙運動的思想改變了人們對社會和政府的理解方式，這些思維最後也在英國、美國和法國各地引發戰爭與革命。

在 17 世紀，歐洲的國王擁有至高無上的權力，他們主張君權神授，堅稱上帝遴選他們為王，因此可以為所欲為地統治國家。但人民對政府已有新的認知，再加上平權思想，君權神授的說法不再為世人所接受。結果，英王查理一世與議會之間的嫌隙，使英國在 1642 年爆發內戰。1649 年，查理一世戰敗，英國國王被迫遵從國會所通過的法律。

啟蒙運動的思維也對 1775 年爆發的美國革命有深遠影響。1763 年，英國政府要求美洲殖民地幫忙償還與法國交戰所花費的巨債，遭到殖民地居民的抗議。1776 年，美洲殖民者脫離英國，隨後建立了美利堅合眾國。而美國建國元老們的自由思想，就是奠基於啟蒙運動學者的著作。

幾年後，法國大革命於 1789 年爆發，同樣是受到啟蒙運動影響。當時的法蘭西王國分為三級，第一級是天主教會裡的神職人員，第二級是貴族，第三級是不含上述階級的其他人。第三級占了總人口約 98%，大多是貧苦的農民，他們負擔大部分的稅金，在政府內卻無一席之地。

根據法蘭西法律，三級的人民都有權推派代表參加「三級會議」。然而從 1614 年起，沒有法國國王召開三級會議。到了 1789 年，法國瀕臨破產，法王路易十六召開三級會議，欲徵收更多稅金，引發第三級的民怨。他們群起反抗，成立「國民議會」。群眾攻占巴黎的巴士底監獄，奪取武器捍衛人民的權利。「自由！平等！博愛！」是當時法國大革命的口號。1792 年，「國民公會」結束君主專制，創立了共和國。

- **Vocabulary Preview**

1 **heliocentric** 日心的；以太陽為中心的

2 **Enlightenment** 啟蒙運動　　3 **Three Estates** 三級制度

4 **remarkable** 非凡的；卓越的　　5 **divine right** 君權神授

- **Quick Check**

1 **(T)**　　2 **(T)**　　3 **(F)**

- **Main Idea and Details**

1 **(c)**　2 **(a)**　3 **(b)**　4 **(a)**　5 **(b)**

6 a. **philosophers**　b. **divine right**　c. **Enlightenment**
　d. **Bastille**　e. **monarchy**

- **Vocabulary Review**

1 **remarkable**　2 **clergy**　3 **influential**　4 **swept over**

5 **Estates General**

Wrap-Up Test 1

A

1 **three-age**	2 **hunter-gatherers**
3 **New Stone Age**	4 **lies**
5 **ziggurat**	6 **Old Kingdom**
7 **artifacts**	8 **worshipped**
9 **influenced**	10 **practiced**

B

1 **height**	2 **Mediterranean**
3 **Pax Romana**	4 **Arabian**
5 **Muhammad**	6 **captured**
7 **knights**	8 **nailed**
9 **swept over**	10 **slogan**

C

1 青銅時代	h	2 新月沃土；肥沃月彎	j
3 多神教；多神論	c	4 楔形文字	d
5 護民官	i	6 特赦；豁免	a
7 君權神授	g	8 論點	b
9 三級制度	f	10 麥加	e

D

1 冰河時期	2 污水系統
3 印度教	4 印度河流域文明
5 印度河文字	6 伯羅奔尼撒戰役
7 寡頭政治	8 否決權
9 布匿戰爭	10 哈里發
11 聖戰；十字軍東征	12 聖典
13 封建制度	14 黑死病
15 宗教改革	16 日心的；以太陽為中心的
17 啟蒙運動	18 理性
19 原始的	20 史前的
21 馴養	22 灌溉
23 三頭政治	24 勝利的
25 橫掃	26 先知
27 活字印刷術	28 教派
29 三級會議	30 驅逐

09　Cells, Reproduction, and Heredity
細胞、繁殖、遺傳

生命的基本單位是細胞，所有的生物都由至少一個以上的細胞所組成。單細胞生物是微生物，包括細菌和病毒。而大部分的生物含有一個以上的細胞，稱為多細胞生物，例如高等動植物，是由各種不同的細胞組成。功能相同的類似細胞會形成「組織」，不同的組織一起構成「器官」，例如胃或肺臟。一組器官組成「器官系統」，例如消化系統或呼吸系統。

所有的生命程序，如生長和繁殖，都是在細胞中發生。所有生物的生命都是由單一細胞開始，當細胞一分為二，就開始成長。一分為二的細胞會繼續分裂成四個，在分裂為八個細胞時，細胞的分裂速度各有不同，並且會在一生中不斷分裂。

細胞繁殖的方式有兩種：「有絲分裂」和「減數分裂」。身體的細胞透過有絲分裂增加，在有絲分裂的過程中，細胞只會複製遺傳物質，然後分裂成兩個子細胞。生殖細胞則透過「減數分裂」產生，生殖細胞負責生命的繁衍。「遺傳變異」就是減數分裂的結果。

剛出生的嬰兒通常會在許多方面與父母親相似，例如，有的嬰兒的眼珠或頭髮顏色會與母親相同，或是體型和父親相似，這就是「遺傳」，父母親會將各種性格或特徵遺傳給下一代。

遺傳由「基因」決定，基因上面有生物該如何成長的訊息。當精子與卵子結合，來自父母雙方的基因就會傳送到下一代，因此下一代的遺傳物質有一半來自父親，一半來自母親，所以小孩會擁有父母雙方的特徵。

基因有「顯性」和「隱性」之分。顯性基因表現在身體或外觀上，比隱性基因強大。隱性基因存在於體內，卻被顯性基因所遮蓋。然而，隱性基因可以遺傳給下一代，並且可能在下一代身上變成顯性。

雖說生物是遺傳父母的基因，但有些生物是天生的「突變」。突變是一種基因的永久改變。有些突變可能有害，有些則可能對生物有利。

- **Vocabulary Preview**

1 **mitosis** 有絲分裂　　2 **meiosis** 減數分裂

3 **recessive** 隱性的　　4 **mutation** 變種；突變

5 **heredity** 遺傳

- **Quick Check**

1 **(F)**　　2 **(T)**　　3 **(T)**

- **Main Idea and Details**

1 **(a)**　2 **(b)**　3 **(b)**　4 **(c)**

5 a. **Cells**　b. **meiosis**　c. **Genes**

6 a. **microorganisms**　b. **body cells**　c. **variation**
　d. **Dominant genes**　e. **overshadowed**

- **Vocabulary Review**

1 **takes place**　2 **inherited**　3 **Genetic variation**

4 **Recessive**　5 **get transferred**

10 Oceans and Ocean Life
海洋與海洋生物

海洋的總面積占了地球表面的 70%。海洋經常看來平靜不動，但實際上並非如此，海洋的水體始終在流動。

海洋的水位不斷在變化，其中一個變化是由潮汐引起。潮汐是海床表面規律的潮起潮落，主要是由月球對地球的引力所造成。水位到達最高點時稱為「滿潮」，最低點時稱為「乾潮」。

海水也受洋流影響，不停沿著陸地邊緣流動。「洋流」是穿過海洋的龐大水流，成因有很多。表層洋流是由地球風力造成；地球自轉也會影響表層洋流；海水的溫度變化也是洋流的成因之一，靠近北極和南極的冰冷海水下沉，開始往赤道移動，赤道的溫暖海水上升到表面，往兩極移動，取代該處流失的冰冷海水，冷暖海水相交時就產生了洋流。

洋流會影響陸地氣候。例如墨西哥灣等暖流，在赤道附近生成，挾帶溫暖的海水橫越北大西洋到達歐洲，使歐洲的冬天氣候溫和。洋流也是海洋環流的成因，海洋環流可以協助補給海水中的氧氣。

海床和陸地一樣有許多地形變化，有高山、深谷、平原等各種地貌。不過，所有的海床都可分為三大區：第一區稱為「大陸棚」，從海岸延伸到水深約兩百公尺處。此處的坡度較緩，由大陸地殼所組成。「大陸坡」位於大陸邊緣，介於大陸棚與深海平原之間，地勢比大陸棚陡峭。大陸坡的外緣是地球上最平坦的地勢之一，也就是「深海平原」。此處廣闊平坦，占了海床幾乎一半的面積。

海洋蘊含了無數的生物，有各種不同的生態體系，稱為「海洋帶」。每個海洋帶都有獨特的動植物群。最淺的海洋帶為「潮間帶」，這個區域在乾潮時會暴露在海水之外，因此潮間帶生物必須能夠適應環境的改變。「近濱帶」幾乎涵蓋了整個大陸棚，此處水淺而陽光充足，往往有大量的生物，環境也比潮間帶穩定。最後是「遠洋帶」，這是海洋中面積最廣的深海區，由於深不見底，陽光很少甚至不見陽光，因此遠洋帶的大多數生物會靠近海面生活，以獲取食物。

- **Vocabulary Preview**

1 **intertidal zone** 潮間帶　　2 **current** 洋流

3 **continental shelf** 大陸棚　　4 **abyssal plain** 深海平原

5 **continental slope** 大陸坡

- **Quick Check**

1 **(T)**　　2 **(F)**　　3 **(F)**

- **Main Idea and Details**

1 **(a)**　　2 **(c)**　　3 **(a)**　　4 **(a)**　　5 **(b)**

6 a. **gravitational**　　b. **global winds**　　c. **climate**

　　d. **Continental shelf**　　e. **Intertidal zone**

- **Vocabulary Review**

1 **Due to**　　2 **gravitational pull**　　3 **intertidal zone**

4 **open-ocean zone**　　5 **ocean floor**

11 What We Can Learn From Fossils 化石告訴我們的事

大約在六千五百萬年前，恐龍曾棲息在地球上，不過沒有人看過真正的恐龍，因為牠們很久以前就絕種了。那我們是如何得知這麼多恐龍的事情的呢？比如恐龍長什麼樣子？牠們有多少種類？這都得歸功於「化石」。

化石是古老的生物死亡後留下的遺骸或是活動痕跡。生物的遺骸常會被掩埋在泥土、沙子或其他沉積物裡。隨著時間推移，這些沉積物和遺骸硬化成岩石。幾乎所有的化石都是在沉積岩中找到的。

有些化石的形體完整，但是大多數時候只有部分軀體被保留下來。生物柔軟的部位通常腐爛得很快，但是像外殼和骨骼這類堅硬的部位會被留下。有些化石並不是生物的軀體，而是足跡或身體的印記，以鑄模的形式保存下來。

科學家藉由研究化石來認識絕種的生物和地球過去的環境。化石能夠顯示出很久以前絕跡的恐龍、爬蟲類、植物、昆蟲和魚類。

研究化石的「古生物學家」專門從事化石挖掘和保存的工作。他們常會將動物分散的骨頭加以拼湊，還原其原本的面貌。古生物學家們能藉此得知生物的體型、重量、壽命、棲息地，甚至可以知道牠們吃什麼食物。

化石還可以讓我們了解地球的歷史。古生物學家發現，有些化石只會在特定的岩層中出現。他們整理出一套稱為「化石紀錄」的資料，用來研究地球的歷史。「標準化石」對於確立化石紀錄很重要。標準化石是只存在於過去某個特定年代的化石，可以藉此判定該岩層的年代。當古生物學家在某個岩層中找到標準化石，就可以得知該地層的年代和地表歷年來的變化。

「菊石」是知名的標準化石，屬於「頭足類動物」，是一種帶殼的海中生物，和恐龍同一時代。「三葉蟲」是另一種常見的標準化石，比恐龍的年代更早。

- **Vocabulary Preview**

1 **ammonite** 菊石（鸚鵡螺的化石）

2 **paleontologist** 古生物學者　　3 **index fossil** 標準化石

4 **vanish** 消逝；絕跡　　5 **fossil record** 化石記錄

- **Quick Check**

1 **(T)**　　2 **(F)**　　3 **(T)**

- **Main Idea and Details**

1 **(c)**　　2 **(a)**　　3 **(b)**　　4 **(c)**

5 a. **They became extinct about 65 million years ago.**

　b. **Scientists study fossils to learn about extinct organisms and the environments of the past on Earth.**

　c. **Ammonites lived during the time of the dinosaurs.**

6 a. **remains**　　b. **sedimentary**　　c. **footprints**

　　d. **environments** e. **Index fossil**

- **Vocabulary Review**

1 **piece together**　　2 **Ammonites**　　3 **vanished**

4 **get fossilized**　　5 **remains**

12 Newton's Laws 牛頓定律

你看過跳傘選手圍成一圈飄浮在空中嗎？在他們的降落傘打開之前，這些選手其實處於自由落體的狀態。一股力量將他們拉向地心，以加速度落向地球。是什麼力量呢？就是「重力」。所有物體都被重力拉向地面。

艾薩克·牛頓是世界上最偉大的科學家之一，他發現萬物都會被拉向地面，這股力量也是行星繞行太陽的原因，這就是牛頓的「萬有引力定律」。萬有引力作用於任何兩個物體之間，使它們互相吸引。地心引力作用於地球和其他物體之間，也是萬有引力的效應。萬有引力使月球繞著地球旋轉，讓地球和月球互相吸引，這股拉力讓月球不會飛離地球。萬有引力也讓地球和其他行星得以沿著各自的軌道繞行太陽。

牛頓是英國人，生於 1643 年，卒於 1727 年。他一生中涉獵科學和數學的諸多領域，但他最為人所知的還是他在物理學上的成就。除了發現萬有引力定律，他也發現三大運動定律。

「第一運動定律」指出，物體「靜者恆靜，動者恆動」，除非受外力作用，否則移動中的物體會以等速前進。其中一個主要外力就是重力。舉例來說，你可以把球往上拋向空中，缺乏重力影響的情況下，這顆球會一直往上走。然而由於重力這個外力的作用，這顆球會落回地面。牛頓第一運動定律又稱為「慣性定律」。

「第二運動定律」稱為「加速度定律」，是指物體的受力越大，加速度就越快。常以公式表達為「a＝F÷m」，a 為「加速度」，F 為「作用力」，m 為「質量」。物體的加速度等於作用力除以物體質量。此定律還指出物體質量較大時，移動所需的作用力較大；質量較小時，所需作用力較小。比方說，投擲一塊磚頭比投擲一顆網球更費力，因為磚頭的質量大於網球。

「第三運動定律」稱為「作用力與反作用力」。凡是有一個「作用力」產生時，必定有一大小相等、方向相反的「反作用力」。一物體推向另一物體時，必會受到回推力。比方說，當划船比賽的選手以船槳划水時，水也會回推船槳，將船向前推進。

- **Vocabulary Preview**

1 **inertia** 慣性　　2 **acceleration** 加速度
3 **reaction** 反作用力　　4 **gravity** 重力；地心引力
5 **at rest** 靜止

- **Quick Check**

1 (T)　　2 (F)　　3 (F)

- **Main Idea and Details**

1 (b)　　2 (c)　　3 (a)　　4 (b)
5 a. **gravity**　　b. **Inertia**　　c. **action**
6 a. **objects**　　b. **effect**　　c. **Inertia**　　d. **Acceleration**
　 e. **Action**

- **Vocabulary Review**

1 **at rest**　　2 **attract**　　3 **Gravitation**　　4 **Skydivers**
5 **fly off**

13 Light Energy 光能

「光」是人類肉眼可見的一種能量。光由數十億的微小粒子「光子」所組成，並以「波」的形式傳遞。宇宙中沒有比光移動得更快的物質，光速每秒可達約三十萬公里。大多數的波需要某種介質才能傳播，比方說，聲波需要透過物質傳播，像是固體、液體和氣體。真空中沒有物質，所以我們聽不到聲音。然而，即使在真空中，光也可以自由移動。

光以波的形式移動，因此有各種不同波長。但肉眼無法看到所有的波長，肉眼看得見的波長稱為「可見光」。人類看得見的顏色稱為「光譜色」，也就是彩虹的七個顏色：紅、橙、黃、綠、藍、靛、紫。最長的光波為紅光，最短的為紫光。

要一窺光譜的所有色彩，最簡單的方式就是透過「三稜鏡」。牛頓在數百年前首度進行了這項實驗。他讓太陽光束穿透一面三稜鏡，看到光四向成一道七色彩虹。接著他又讓同一道光束穿透另一個三稜鏡，光束又變回白光。原理是三稜鏡在光線通過時將光線折射，而白光其實就是所有光譜色的組合。

另外一種可以折射光線的是透鏡，分為「凸透鏡」和「凹透鏡」。凸透鏡將光線聚焦於一點，稱為「焦點」，凹透鏡的作用相反，它接收了光線之後會放射出去。透鏡的運用十分廣泛。凸透鏡可用於眼鏡、隱形眼鏡、望遠鏡和雙目望遠鏡等；凹透鏡則常運用在電視投影機這類器材上。

有些光波因為過長或過短，所以肉眼無法看見。肉眼看不見的光稱為「不可見光」。可見光與不可見光組成「電磁光譜」，涵蓋所有以波傳遞的光能。舉例來說，紅光是波長最長的可見光，但是紅外線的波長又更長。微波，例如我們平常用來烹煮食物的微波爐，和無線電波的波長又更長。至於在光譜另一端，紫外線的波長比可見光的紫光短，而 X 光和伽瑪射線的波長又比紫外線短。

- **Vocabulary Preview**

1 **photon** 光子　　2 **prism** 稜鏡　　3 **vacuum** 真空
4 **concave lens** 凹透鏡　　5 **infrared light** 紅外線

- **Quick Check**

1 (F)　　2 (T)　　3 (T)

- **Main Idea and Details**

1 (b)　　2 (c)　　3 (b)　　4 (b)　　5 (a)
6 a. **photons**　　b. **vacuum**　　c. **spectrum**　　d. **visible**
　 e. **X-rays**

- **Vocabulary Review**

1 **convex lenses**　　2 **concave lens**　　3 **electromagnetic**
4 **in a vacuum**　　5 **Ultraviolet light**

14 Eclipses 天蝕

你看過月亮慢慢變暗，接著轉為紅色達幾個小時嗎？你可能看到了月蝕。「天蝕」是由月球繞行地球所發生的現象，分為兩種。根據月球、地球和太陽的位置，可分為「月蝕」或「日蝕」。

當月球繞行地球，有時會剛好經過太陽與地球之間。此時月球會遮蔽太陽的光線，使部分的地球照不到陽光，被月球的陰影覆蓋，這就是「日蝕」。

「日偏蝕」發生時，月球只遮蔽了太陽部分的光線。「日全蝕」時，你只看得到暗月周圍透出的白光，稱為「日冕」。有時你還可以看到「鑽石環」的現象。日蝕通常只持續幾分鐘，當月球離開了地球和太陽之間，天空就會恢復明亮。

當月球進入地球的陰影時，就會產生「月蝕」。當月球進入地球內側較深的陰影，也就是本影時，稱為「月全蝕」。月球通過地球本影時，地球遮蔽了所有照向月球的陽光，使月球沒入地球的陰影中。月球不會自己發光，只能反射太陽光，因此這時候月球是一片黑暗。如果只有部分的月球被陰影遮蔽，稱為「月偏蝕」。月蝕可達數小時之久。

日蝕發生時，絕對不可直視太陽，會對眼睛造成永久傷害，甚至導致失明。

- **Vocabulary Preview**

1 **solar eclipse** 日蝕　　2 **lunar eclipse** 月蝕

3 **partial lunar eclipse** 月偏蝕　　4 **umbra** 本影

5 **solar corona** 日冕

- **Quick Check**

1 **(F)**　　2 **(F)**　　3 **(T)**

- **Main Idea and Details**

1 **(a)**　　2 **(a)**　　3 **(b)**　　4 **(c)**

5 a. **They are solar eclipses and lunar eclipses.**

　　b. **It sometimes appears during a total solar eclipse.**

　　c. **It may last a few hours.**

6 a. **blocks**　　b. **partial**　　c. **minutes**　　d. **moon**　　e. **total**

- **Vocabulary Review**

1 **partial lunar eclipse**　　2 **total solar eclipse**

3 **blocked**　　4 **reflects**　　5 **partial solar eclipse**

15 Diseases and the Immune System 疾病與免疫系統

人多少會罹患疾病，導致身體不適。疾病分為兩種：「非傳染性疾病」與「傳染性疾病」。

「非傳染性疾病」不會互相傳染。許多這類型的疾病都是由個人生活型態造成，例如抽菸、飲酒、暴食、缺乏運動等，會讓人罹患肺癌或心臟病等疾病。幸好別人並不會被患者傳染這類疾病。

反之，「傳染性疾病」會互相傳染。一般感冒和流行性感冒是兩種典型的傳染病。人體接觸頻繁是這類疾病傳播的主因。傳染病可以透過接觸傳染。有時候，一個地區大量人口同時感染某種疾病，就造成了「流行病」。

還好人體有許多防禦機制可抵抗各種疾病。我們把這樣的防禦機制稱為「免疫系統」。第一道防線是皮膚，可以阻擋多種病菌和細菌進入人體、危害健康。皮膚上有一些腺體，可將接觸人體的病菌和細菌殺死。

病菌與細菌常企圖從眼、鼻、口腔進入人體，但這些器官都有自己的防禦系統。鼻涕的功用就像皮膚，可以阻止異物進入人體，眼淚和唾液的功用也相同。還有，人在進食時，如果吃進病菌和細菌，也會被胃酸消滅。

不過有些異物仍然成功進入人體作怪，這時體內的淋巴系統就會開始作用。人體有淋巴結，或稱淋巴腺，可以消滅病菌、細菌和病毒。白血球細胞也會幫忙抵抗感染。白血球分為很多

種，大部分像是身體的清道夫，並協助修復受損的組織。另外有些白血球細胞負責製造抗體，攻擊並殺死各種病菌和細菌。

人體有時無法抵抗某些外來的入侵者，尤其是病毒。因此人類發明了疫苗來對抗病毒。注射到人體的疫苗會刺激抗體生成，以抵禦特定病毒。有了疫苗，人類得以對瘧疾、霍亂、黃熱病甚至流感等致命疾病免疫。

- **Vocabulary Preview**

1 **contagious** 接觸傳染性的　　2 **immune system** 免疫系統

3 **antibody** 抗體　　4 **communicable** 會傳染的　　5 **gland** 腺

- **Quick Check**

1 **(T)**　　2 **(T)**　　3 **(F)**

- **Main Idea and Details**

1 **(b)**　　2 **(a)**　　3 **(b)**　　4 **(c)**

5 a. **noncommunicable**　　b. **glands**　　c. **Vaccines**

6 a. **lifestyle**　　b. **contagious**　　c. **saliva**　　d. **acid**

　　e. **White blood cells**

- **Vocabulary Review**

1 **glands**　　2 **antibodies**　　3 **infected**

4 **white blood cells**　　5 **lymphatic system**

Wrap-Up Test 2

A

1	take place	2	divides
3	meiosis	4	Heredity
5	surface	6	continental shelf
7	gets exposed	8	imprints
9	footprints	10	Index fossils

B

1	attract	2	motion
3	comprised	4	electromagnetic
5	eclipse	6	umbra
7	noncommunicable	8	communicable
9	attempt	10	vaccine

C

1	有絲分裂	j	2	減數分裂	g
3	變種；突變	d	4	深海平原	c
5	古生物學家	a	6	慣性	f
7	波長	i	8	日冕	e
9	傳染的	b	10	免疫系統	h

D

1	微生物	2	遺傳
3	潮汐	4	洋流
5	大陸棚	6	大陸坡
7	標準化石	8	絕種
9	加速度	10	反作用力
11	地心引力	12	光子
13	稜鏡	14	不可見光
15	紅外線	16	日蝕
17	月蝕	18	地球本影
19	流行病	20	隱性的
21	海床	22	潮間帶
23	成為化石	24	飛離

- **Vocabulary Review**

1 **square root**　　2 **break down**　　3 **evenly**
4 **squared**　　5 **cubed**

16　Factors, Prime Numbers, and Exponents　因數、質數、指數

任何一個大於 1 的整數，都至少有兩個因數。「因數」是可以整除其他數字而沒有餘數的數字。許多數字可用不同的方式分解出因數。看看數字 6 的因數有哪些？

$6 \div 1 = 6$　　　$6 \div 2 = 3$　　　$6 \div 3 = 2$
$6 \div 4 \rightarrow$ 無法整除　　　$6 \div 5 \rightarrow$ 無法整除
$6 \div 6 = 1$

以上得出，6 的因數為 1、2、3、6。

有些數字只能被數字 1 和自己整除，例如 3 和 5，像這種只有兩個因數的數字，稱為「質數」，3、5、7 是質數。有兩個以上因數的數字，稱為「合數」，因此 4 和 6 是合數。所有大於 1 的整數不是質數就是合數。但數字 1 既非質數，也非合數，因為它只有 1 這個因數。

所有合數都可分解成數個「質因數」。質因數是質數，相乘後形成合數。舉例來說，10 可以分解成質因數 2 和 5，2 和 5 相乘得出合數 10，$10 = 2 \times 5$。那麼數字 16 呢？它可以被分解成「4×4」，但 4 不是質數，因為它可以進一步分解「2×2」。所以如果你要將 16 分解成質因數的話，應該是：$16 = 2 \times 2 \times 2 \times 2$。

我們可以把算式「$16 = 2 \times 2 \times 2 \times 2$」寫成指數「$16 = 2^4$」。「指數」是上標數字，說明某個因數需被連乘幾次。換句話說，「2^4」表示 2 這個因數被連乘 4 次，讀作「2 的 4 次方」。另外數字 2 被稱為「底數」，數字 4 則被稱為「指數」或「次方」。

有時我們會將數字自乘，此時稱作某數的「平方」。比方說，「3×3」寫成 3^2，讀作「3 的平方」或「3 的 2 次方」。當指數為 3 時，稱作某數的「立方」。5^3 讀作「5 的立方」或「5 的 3 次方」。

有些數字被稱為「完全平方數」，這些數字是某數的平方。比方說，25 是完全平方數，因為「$5 \times 5 = 25$」。另外 64 和 100 也是完全平方數，因為「$8 \times 8 = 64$」，「$10 \times 10 = 100$」。這些數字也可以用「平方根」的形式表現。比方說，「$5^2 = 5 \times 5 = 25$」，我們可以用根號表示「$\sqrt{25} = 5$」，讀作「25 的平方根為 5」。

- **Vocabulary Preview**

1 **prime number** 質數　　2 **composite number** 合數
3 **square root** 平方根　　4 **exponent** 指數
5 **perfect square** 完全平方數

- **Quick Check**

1 (F)　　2 (T)　　3 (F)

- **Main Idea and Details**

1 (a)　　2 (b)　　3 (c)　　4 (c)　　5 (b)
6 a. **evenly**　　b. **1**　　c. **composite number**
　 d. **factor**　　e. **square**

17　Dimensions　維度

維度是用來說明物體長、寬、高的直線距離的方式。幾何學中常常使用到三個維度。「一度空間」是長度，「二度空間」是寬度，「三度空間」是高度或深度。「四度空間」是時間，一般不屬於幾何學範疇。

「一度空間」是線或線段，一度空間圖形只有一個方向，例如長度，缺少寬度和高度。

「二度空間」有兩個方向，例如長和寬。二度空間圖形又稱為「平面圖形」，可以畫在平面上。多邊形是常見的二度空間圖形，是由三條以上互不交叉的線段組成的閉鎖圖形。三角形是由三條線段組成的二度空間圖形。正方形、長方形、平行四邊形、梯形和菱形都是有四個邊的二度空間圖形。五邊形有五個邊，六邊形有六個邊。多邊形其實可以有無限個邊。此外，圓形和橢圓形也是二度空間圖形。

「三度空間」的圖形被稱為「立體圖形」，由長、寬、高組成。立體圖形可依照「底」、「面」、「頂點」、「邊」的形狀和數量來分類。「角柱」有兩個全等且平行的底，而「角錐」只有一個底。立體圖形常和平面圖形相呼應，舉例來說，三角形只有二度空間，形狀像三角形的「角錐」卻有三度。正方形有二度空間，形狀像正方形的「正方體」卻有三度。有些立體圖形有弧面。「圓柱體」有兩個圓底，而「圓錐體」只有一個。

- **Vocabulary Preview**

1 **one-dimensional figure** 一度空間圖形
2 **two-dimensional figure** 二度空間圖形
3 **three-dimensional figure** 三度空間圖形
4 **congruent** 全等的　　5 **infinite** 無限的

- **Quick Check**

1 (F)　　2 (T)　　3. (F)

- **Main Idea and Details**

1 (c)　　2 (a)　　3 (c)　　4 (b)
5 a. **The three dimensions are length, width, and height.**
　 b. **A one-dimensional figure is a line or a line segment.**
　 c. **They are classified by the shape and the number of their bases, faces, vertices, and edges.**
6 a. **length**　　b. **plane**　　c. **infinite**　　d. **height**　　e. **solid**

- **Vocabulary Review**

1 **plane**　　2 **base**　　3 **correspond with**　　4 **curved**
5 **infinite**

18　Pygmalion　皮格馬利翁

很有以前有一位名叫「皮格馬利翁」的雕刻師，他來自塞浦路斯島。有些故事版本說他是塞浦路斯的國王，有些則說他只是一名雕刻師。

不管怎麼說，皮格馬利翁是位天資聰穎的雕刻師，他製作的雕像栩栩如生。不過他有個毛病，就是不愛女色。他所見過的女人無一能取悅他，所以一直沒有娶妻。

有一天，皮格馬利翁決定要創作一個女子雕像。他以象牙為材料開始雕刻。他不停地雕著，終於完成了完美的雕像。他雕出一個舉世無雙的絕美女子。皮格馬利翁拜倒於雕像之美，很快就墜入愛河。他對雕像的愛，就像其他男人對女人的愛一樣，這座雕像對他而言無比真實。他大多時候皆凝望著雕像，甚至還對她說話。不過雕像當然無法回應他。皮格馬利翁因為求愛不得，日漸憔悴消瘦。

不久後，塞浦路斯為女神「阿芙羅黛蒂」舉辦了一場慶典。皮格馬利翁參與了盛宴，向這位愛之女神獻上供品並許下心願，他說：「我誠摯地希望我的象牙雕刻可以變成一名真正的女子。」阿芙羅黛蒂聽見了他的祈求並應允了他。當皮格馬利翁回到家中，阿芙羅黛蒂派遣來的邱比特親吻了象牙雕像的玉手，雕像因此活了過來，幻化為美麗的少女。邱比特將一枚戒指套到少女手指上，少女因而有了愛人的能力。

皮格馬利翁歡欣無比，將少女命名為「葛拉蒂亞」。阿芙羅黛蒂還為倆人的婚姻賜福，他們後來生下兒子「佩佛斯」。

多年來，許多作家以皮格馬利翁為原型，發展出各種故事。其中最知名的是蕭伯納所創作的戲劇《賣花女》。此劇引發了所謂的「皮格馬利翁效應」（期待效應），指的是當你賦予他人較高的期望時，對方真的會有所成就。

• **Vocabulary Preview**

1 **Pygmalion** 皮格馬利翁　　2 **come to life** 甦醒過來；活過來
3 **captivate** 使著迷　4 **grant** 同意；准予　5 **longing** 渴望

• **Quick Check**

1 (T)　　2 (F)　　3 (T)

• **Main Idea and Details**

1 (b)　　2 (a)　　3 (b)　　4 (c)
5 a. **interested**　b. **love**　c. **granted**
6 a. **Cyprus**　b. **Aphrodite**　c. **Pygmalion**
　d. **kissed**　e. **ring**

• **Vocabulary Review**

1 **seemed**　2 **come to life**　3 **captivated by**
4 **merely**　5 **made an offering**

19　Sentences 句子

我們說話或寫作時會使用「句子」來表達想法。句子包含了「主詞」和「述語」。主詞通常為名詞或名詞片語，述語則包含動詞和句子裡的其他字。

句子可分為四大類。最常見的是「直述句」，用來陳述一件事，必須以句號結尾。「疑問句」用來提問，必須以問號結尾。「感嘆句」用來表達強烈的情感，以驚嘆號結尾。「祈使句」表示命令，在英文中主詞為 you，但會被省略。也就是說，祈使句不需要說出或寫出 you。「祈使句」可以用句號或驚嘆號結尾。看看下列句子：

直述句	陽光燦爛。	我弟弟喜歡音樂。
疑問句	那是什麼？	你要去哪裡？
感嘆句	真是不可思議！	多麼美好的一天！
祈使句	把門打開。	安靜！

很多時候我們說寫用的是簡單句，簡單句包含一個獨立子句。子句是由一個主詞和一個述詞構成的句子。獨立子句是表達完整概念並可獨立存在的句子，其中有主詞也有述詞。

我們有時會用連接詞 and、but、so、or 連接兩個獨立子句，成為「並列句」。並列句由兩個以上的獨立子句構成。

有時我們會將一個獨立子句和一個非獨立子句結合，非獨立子句又稱為附屬子句。附屬子句無法表達完整的概念，無法單獨執行句子的功用，必須以從屬連接詞 because、since、if、even though、although 連接獨立子句，形成「複合句」。複合句包含一個獨立子句和至少一個附屬子句。看看下列句子：

簡單句	這隻狗正在追那隻貓。
並列句	我喜歡披薩，但我妹妹不喜歡。
複合句	你和我一起參加比賽的話，我們會玩得很愉快。

我們說話或寫字的時候也會用不同的語氣。我們用「主動語氣」表示主詞在做什麼，用「被動語氣」表示主詞發生了什麼事。看看下列句子：

主動語氣	大衛住在一棟房子裡。
	他們每天練習彈鋼琴。
被動語氣	那間飯店是瓊斯先生蓋的。
	我被這個答案搞糊塗了。

• **Vocabulary Preview**

1 **imperative sentence** 祈使句
2 **interrogative sentence** 疑問句
3 **passive voice** 被動語氣
4 **subordinate clause** 附屬子句
5 **clause** 子句

• **Quick Check**

1 (F)　　2 (T)　　3 (T)

• **Main Idea and Details**

1 (b)　　2 (c)　　3 (c)　　4 (a)　　5 (a)
6 a. **question**　b. **order**　c. **independent**
　d. **dependent**　e. **Active voice**

• **Vocabulary Review**

1 **independent clause**　2 **subordinate clause**
3 **omit**　4 **passive voice**　5 **conjunctions**

20　From Baroque Art to Pop Art
從巴洛克藝術到普普藝術

在歷經「文藝復興」這個古典藝術的重生年代之後，許多獨特的藝術運動紛紛崛起。

文藝復興之後，首先出現的藝術運動為「巴洛克藝術」。巴洛克不只是一項藝術運動，也影響到建築、音樂和文學等層面。巴洛克時期從 1600 年發展至 1750 年，期間主要的藝術家有卡拉瓦喬、林布蘭、魯本斯。相較於文藝復興的古典主義，巴洛克藝術的特色是光影的強烈對比和鮮明的情感表現。巴洛克藝術常會喚起觀賞者內心澎湃洶湧的情緒。

巴洛克時期結束後，緊接著興起的是「洛可可時期」，約始於 1750 年的法國。洛可可藝術的風格帶有裝飾與輕快的元素，用色淡雅細緻。尚–奧諾雷·弗拉戈納爾的作品《鞦韆》與尚–安東尼·華鐸的《甜美的生活》是洛可可風格的代表作。

123

然而到了十八世紀晚期及十九世紀，許多藝術家厭倦了戲劇化的巴洛克風和俗艷的洛可可風。「啟蒙運動」興起，強調理性的思潮席捲歐洲，也影響到視覺藝術，促成了「新古典運動」的新藝術風格。新古典主義從十八世紀中期延續到十九世紀前期，這時期的藝術家仿效文藝復興大師，重現古希臘羅馬的古典形式。法國畫家賈克–路易·大衛是此時期的知名畫家。

十八世紀晚期，開始了「浪漫主義運動」。此時的藝術家對大自然景色產生興趣，重視情感與想像力，不再遵循新古典主義的制式風格。布雷克、德拉克洛瓦、哥雅是此時期的代表性畫家。

浪漫主義式微後，「寫實主義」興起，主宰了 1850 到 1890 年左右的藝術風格。米勒和庫爾貝等畫家追求所畫即所見，主題圍繞著日常場景和貧苦百姓的生活。

而後寫實主義被「現代藝術」所取代。現代主義有許多獨特的流派，其中最重要的是「印象派」。印象派屬於抽象藝術，畫家們並不精確描繪物體的外貌。莫內、馬內、梵谷和塞尚都是知名的印象派大師。之後，「立體主義」畫家如畢卡索出現在藝壇，他們以幾何圖形描繪物體。二十世紀的另外兩項知名藝術運動則是「達達主義」和「普普藝術」。安迪·沃荷是最知名的普普藝術運動代表人物。

- **Vocabulary Preview**

1 **revive** 使復興　　2 **evoke** 喚起；引起

3 **Rococo Art** 洛可可藝術　　4 **Neoclassicism** 新古典主義

5 **Realism** 寫實主義

- **Quick Check**

1 **(T)**　　2 **(T)**　　3 **(F)**

- **Main Idea and Details**

1 **(c)**　　2 **(c)**　　3 **(a)**　　4 **(b)**

5 a. **The Baroque Period lasted from around 1600 to 1750.**
  b. **Rococo Art is characterized by its decorative and lighthearted look that uses delicate pastel colors.**
  c. **They were Jean Millet and Gustave Courbet.**

6 a. **Baroque**　b. **Neoclassical**　c. **Realism**　d. **Cubism**
  e. **Pop Art**

- **Vocabulary Review**

1 **emerged**　　2 **turned away**　　3 **evoke**

4 **characterized by**　　5 **revived**

21　Gregorian Chants and Polyphonic Music
格雷果聖歌與多聲部合唱

西元 500 年到 1400 年為中世紀，這段期間教會在社會中扮演了舉足輕重的角色。許多年輕男性想在教會服務，於是很多選擇進入修道院，這些居住在修道院的男性被稱為修道士。修道士的生活十分有序，他們每天花很多時間閱讀聖經、禱告或工作。許多人認為修道院的生活十分枯燥，不過這些修道士們會利用時間唱歌，讓生活充滿朝氣。

這些中世紀的修道士唱歌的方式和現代不同，他們其實是吟唱。這些歌曲以教宗格雷果命名，因此被稱為「格雷果聖歌」。

格雷果聖歌一般是出自《聖經》或其他基督教典籍的詩偈。歌曲以拉丁文吟唱，故對現代人而言很陌生。此外，修道士在吟唱時也沒有樂器伴奏，只有清唱，這種音樂稱為「阿卡貝拉」。修道士們各自的聲音固然單調，合唱起來卻能交融和諧。事實上，今日世界各地修道院中的修道士仍吟唱著格雷果聖歌。

中世紀之後開始了文藝復興運動，這時期流行「多聲部合唱」。polyphony 在希臘文中表示「多聲的」。多聲部合唱和格雷果聖歌不同，修道士們吟唱時，音調或抑揚頓挫都相同，但在多聲部合唱中，每個聲部會同時唱不同的旋律，甚至不同的歌詞。

「卡農」是一種多聲部合唱，這種音樂是先由一人獨唱，接著第二人開始升調或降調吟唱同樣的旋律。整首歌曲有越來越多合聲加入，每個人的唱法都稍有不同。

「輪唱」則是另一種多聲部合唱，如同字面所述，就是一首歌一直循環。在輪唱中，每個人唱相同的旋律和歌詞，但是在不同的時間開始唱。比方說，第一個人開始唱，他唱完第一句歌詞後，第二個人從頭開始唱，等他唱完第一句歌詞後，第三個人再加入。結果所有的聲音互相重疊，卻依然和諧。歌曲《願主賜我們平安》便是文藝復興時期流傳下來的知名輪唱曲。這首歌曲從頭到尾就重複著 dona、nobis、pacem 三個字。而《雅克弟兄》──英文版為《你睡了嗎？》（譯註：中文版即我們熟知的《兩隻老虎》）──和《划船歌》則是至今仍傳唱的輪唱曲。

- **Vocabulary Preview**

1 **polyphonic music** 多聲部合唱

2 **Gregorian Chant** 格雷果聖歌

3 **round** 輪唱　　4 **monotonous** 單調的

5 **a cappella** 阿卡貝拉（無伴奏合唱）

- **Quick Check**

1 **(F)**　　2 **(T)**　　3 **(F)**

- **Main Idea and Details**

1 **(c)**　　2 **(a)**　　3 **(b)**　　4 **(c)**

5 a. **monks**　b. **canon**　c. **words**

6 a. **monks**　b. **harmonized**　c. **voices**　d. **Round**

- **Vocabulary Review**

1 **monk**　2 **monastery**　3 **dreary**　4 **round**　5 **chant**

Wrap-Up Test 3

A

1 factors	2 evenly
3 prime number	4 broken down
5 exponent	6 perfect square
7 line segment	8 directions
9 solid figures	10 bases

B

1 sculptor	2 sculpted
3 statue	4 statement
5 independent clause	6 complex sentence
7 passive voice	8 contrast
9 dominated	10 melodies

C

1	質數	h	2	質因數	i
3	合數	d	4	二度空間圖形	b
5	三度空間圖形	a	6	象牙	g
7	雕像	j	8	應允	c
9	子句	e	10	單調的	f

D

1	指數	2	完全平方數
3	全等的	4	一度空間圖形
5	幾何學	6	渴望
7	多聲部合唱	8	格雷果聖歌
9	卡農	10	阿卡貝拉（無伴奏合唱）
11	藝術運動	12	巴洛克藝術
13	洛可可藝術	14	新古典主義
15	寫實主義	16	祈使句
17	疑問句	18	直述句
19	感嘆句	20	平方根
21	成平方	22	成立方
23	無限的	24	只是
25	被……所迷倒	26	甦醒過來；活過來
27	省略	28	獨立子句
29	附屬子句	30	修道院

FUN學 美國英語閱讀課本 9
各學科實用課文

Authors

Michael A. Putlack
Michael A. Putlack graduated from Tufts University in Medford, Massachusetts, USA, where he got his B.A. in History and English and his M.A. in History. He has written a number of books for children, teenagers, and adults.

e-Creative Contents
A creative group that develops English contents and products for ESL and EFL students.

作者	Michael A. Putlack & e-Creative Contents
翻譯	邱佳皇
編輯	丁宥榆／黃鈺云
校對	申文怡
製程管理	洪巧玲
發行人	周均亮
出版者	寂天文化事業股份有限公司
電話	+886-(0)2-2365-9739
傳真	+886-(0)2-2365-9835
網址	www.icosmos.com.tw
讀者服務	onlineservice@icosmos.com.tw
出版日期	2017 年 7 月 二版一刷 (080201)

國家圖書館出版品預行編目 (CIP) 資料

FUN 學美國英語閱讀課本：各學科實用課文 / Michael
A. Putlack, e-Creative Contents 著；丁宥暄, 鄭玉瑋譯.
-- 二版 . -- [臺北市]：寂天文化, 2017.02- 冊 ; 公分

ISBN 978-986-318-552-9 (第 1 冊：平裝附光碟片)
ISBN 978-986-318-554-3 (第 2 冊：平裝附光碟片)
ISBN 978-986-318-559-8 (第 3 冊：平裝附光碟片)
ISBN 978-986-318-566-6 (第 4 冊：平裝附光碟片)
ISBN 978-986-318-567-3 (第 5 冊：平裝附光碟片)
ISBN 978-986-318-578-9 (第 6 冊：平裝附光碟片)
ISBN 978-986-318-581-9 (第 7 冊：平裝附光碟片)
ISBN 978-986-318-584-0 (第 8 冊：平裝附光碟片)
ISBN 978-986-318-597-0 (第 9 冊：平裝附光碟片)

1. 英語 2. 讀本

805.18   106001668

FUN學
美國英語閱讀課本

各學科實用課文 二版

9

Workbook

AMERICAN
SCHOOL
TEXTBOOK

READING KEY

作者 Michael A. Putlack & e-Creative Contents　　譯者 邱佳皇

🎧 22

A Listen to the passage and fill in the blanks.

1. A couple of million years ago, _____ humans were nothing like the modern humans of today. They were _____ creatures that shared characteristics with both humans and _____. For much of this time, the earth was _____ cold. It _____ a very long Ice Age. During the Ice Age, much of the earth's surface was covered by huge sheets of ice called _____. However, around 12,500 years ago, the _____ _____ ended. The ice and glaciers _____. And humans began to _____, to spread out, and to become more civilized.

2. Archaeologists have created a three-age system to describe _____ cultures. They are the Stone Age, the Bronze Age, and the _____ _____.

3. The Stone Age is often divided into the _____ _____ _____ and the New Stone Age. The Old Stone Age was the first part of the Stone Age and began around _____ B.C. The New Stone Age was the last part of the Stone Age and began around _____ B.C.

4. During the Old Stone Age, humans lived as _____. They hunted animals and _____ wild plants for food. People could only make simple _____ out of stone. Yet people learned how to _____ _____ during this age. Having fire changed _____ _____ a lot. Fire provided light and helped people _____ _____. Most of all, people could _____ their food.

5. In the New Stone Age, there began to be some more _____. People learned to farm the land. People also learned to _____ wild animals such as dogs, sheep, and goats. Some people began to settle in villages where there was _____ _____ for farming. Since they could grow their own crops and _____ their own animals, they no longer had to live as _____. However, they still used stone tools, so this time is called the _____ _____ _____.

6. Around 3000 B.C., the _____ _____ began in some parts of the world. During it, humans started working with soft _____ such as copper and tin. They learned how to create tools and _____ out of bronze. And pottery became more common during this time.

7. Around _____ _____, the Iron Age began in Europe. Of course, it started _____ in some places and later in other places. During the Iron Age, humans began working with _____. Also, the first real cities began to appear, and trade between cities became more _____. It was during this age that human _____ started to develop much more quickly than ever before.

B Complete each sentence with the correct word. Change the form if necessary.

Ice Age	fertile soil	three-age	Iron Age	copper

1 During the _____ _____, much of the earth's surface was covered by glaciers.

2 Archaeologists have created a _____ system to describe prehistoric cultures.

3 In the New Stone Age, some people had settled in villages where there was _____ _____ for farming.

4 Around 3000 B.C., humans started working with soft metals such as _____ and tin.

5 During the _____ _____, the first real cities began to appear.

C Write the meaning of each word and phrase from Word List (main book p.104) in English.

1 原始的 _____
2 過分簡單化的 _____
3 和……共有…… _____
4 猿猴 _____
5 極度地 _____
6 歷經 _____
7 冰河時期 _____
8 冰層 _____
9 冰河 _____
10 退去 _____
11 演化 _____
12 散佈 _____
13 文明化 _____
14 考古學家 _____
15 三時代系統 _____
16 史前的 _____

17 石器時代 _____
18 青銅時代 _____
19 鐵器時代 _____
20 舊石器時代 _____
21 新石器時代 _____
22 採獵者 _____
23 改進 _____
24 耕田 _____
25 馴養 _____
26 飼養 _____
27 游牧者 _____
28 銅 _____
29 錫 _____
30 武器 _____
31 陶器 _____
32 普遍的；司空見慣的 _____

▶ A、C大題解答請參照主冊課文及Word List（主冊 p. 104）
B大題解答請見本書p. 44 Answer Key

02 Rivers and Civilizations
The Fertile Crescent and the Kingdoms of Egypt

∩ 23

A   Listen to the passage and fill in the blanks.

1. One of the world's first civilizations began in the _____ _____ in Southwest Asia. The Fertile Crescent region _____ between the Tigris and Euphrates rivers. Later, people called this area _____, which means "the land between two rivers." Today, we call this area the _____ _____.

2. The two rivers were _____ important to the people of Mesopotamia. When these rivers _____, they left rich soil that was good for farming. It led an early farming civilization to _____ in this region. The Mesopotamians also used their _____ and resources to their advantage. Mesopotamian farmers learned to use the waters of the _____ and Euphrates to _____ dry fields by using canals and pipes. They also constructed _____ to store water in artificial lakes. They _____ fish in the rivers and raised animals for food and clothing as well. By _____ _____, Mesopotamia's villages had grown into larger cities and _____ developed into city-states. Many of these city-states in southern Mesopotamia became known as _____.

3. The _____ had a very advanced civilization. They developed a writing system called _____ even before the ancient Egyptians created _____. They practiced _____ and built a massive _____ for their gods and goddesses in each city. They also developed basic _____ and created the 12-month calendar that we use today. After the fall of Sumer, many empires _____ and _____ in Mesopotamia. Babylonia, Assyria, Hittite, and ancient _____ were all civilizations that were established there.

4. Around the same time, another great _____ was being developed in Africa. Sometime around 4000 B.C., people started to _____ _____ and found villages and towns in areas alongside the _____ _____ in Egypt. This was _____ Egypt.

5. Life in ancient Egypt was _____ on the Nile River. Like the rivers in Mesopotamia, the land around the Nile was very _____ because the river flooded every summer. After the Nile flooded, the soil along the river was full of minerals and other _____ that helped many crops grow. Soon, Egypt had a large _____ and a strong farming economy.

6. Ancient Egypt lasted from around _____ B.C. until it was conquered by Alexander the Great in 332 B.C. Egyptian history is often divided into three _____ _____: the Old Kingdom, the Middle Kingdom, and the New Kingdom.

7. The _____ _____ lasted from around 3100 B.C. to 2200 B.C. About 3100 B.C., the _____ of Upper Egypt, Menes, conquered Lower Egypt and _____ it. He became the first _____ of Egypt. The Old Kingdom was the age when the pharaohs became very powerful and were worshipped as living _____. The pyramids, stone _____ for the pharaohs, were built then. The _____ _____ lasted from around 2100 B.C. to about 1700 B.C. Many people consider this the _____ _____ of ancient Egypt. Trade _____ during this period. And there were great _____ made in art, mathematics, and science. As for the _____ _____, it lasted from around 1500 B.C. to _____ _____ The pharaohs Amenhotep II and Ramses II both _____ during the New Kingdom. Egypt expanded its _____ and reached the peak of its power during this period.

Complete each sentence with the correct word. Change the form if necessary.

| Sumerian | Mesopotamia | irrigate | peak of | unite |

1 _____ means "the land between two rivers."

2 Mesopotamian farmers learned to use the waters of the Tigris and Euphrates to _____ dry fields.

3 The _____ practiced polytheism and built a massive ziggurat for their gods and goddesses.

4 The ruler of Upper Egypt, Menes, conquered Lower Egypt and _____ it.

5 Egypt expanded its territory and reached the _____ _____ its power during the New Kingdom.

C Write the meaning of each word and phrase from Word List in English.

1 新月沃土；肥沃月彎 _____

2 位於 _____

3 底格里斯河 _____

4 幼發拉底河 _____

5 美索不達米亞 _____

6 中東 _____

7 出現；形成 _____

8 有利條件；優勢 _____

9 灌溉 _____

10 灌溉渠 _____

11 水管 _____

12 水壩 _____

13 人工湖 _____

14 最終 _____

15 城邦 _____

16 蘇美 _____

17 蘇美人 _____

18 楔形文字 _____

19 象形文字 _____

20 信奉（某宗教） _____

21 多神教；多神論 _____

22 金字形神塔 _____

23 曆法 _____

24 巴比倫王國 _____

25 亞述 _____

26 西臺 _____

27 以色列 _____

28 定居 _____

29 以……為中心；集中於 _____

30 古王國時期 _____

31 中王國時期 _____

32 新王國時期 _____

33 法老 _____

34 神王 _____

35 興盛 _____

36 領土 _____

⌒ 24

A Listen to the passage and fill in the blanks.

1 Around 2500 B.C., there was another great _____ rising in the Indus River region, which is in modern-day India and _____. Today, it is known as the _____ _____ Civilization. It is also called the _____ Civilization.

2 Much like the other great civilizations were _____ beside rivers, the Indus Valley people built their villages, towns, and cities _____ the Indus River. In doing so, they gained easy _____ to water for drinking, farming, and raising animals. Today, two of these cities are called Harappa and _____.

3 Archaeologists have _____ more than 1,000 different settlements from the Indus Valley Civilization. By studying _____, archaeologists have learned that the Indus Valley Civilization was well organized. For instance, its cities were _____ _____ in a grid pattern in the shape of a rectangle. Within the cities were palaces, temples, _____, bathhouses, and wide paved streets. They even had _____ systems.

4 The Indus Valley people knew about _____. The Indus River and _____—seasonal winds that cause heavy rains during summer—influenced Indian life. Harappan farmers learned to _____ _____ of this weather, so they grew a variety of crops. _____ grain was stored in case of droughts. They also _____ sheep, cattle, and pigs. They made _____ and tools from clay and copper. They even _____ _____ trade with other places such as Mesopotamia. While they had a writing system called _____ _____, historians have not been able to read it yet.

5 The Indus Civilization lasted more than _____ years. Historians are not sure why the Indus Civilization _____. But, for some reason, the people began to leave the cities along the _____ _____. A new civilization developed along the _____ _____ in another part of India. But then new people, called Aryans, came from the _____ and settled in the region. They conquered and ruled the _____ people. Over many years, the _____ changed the way that the Indian people lived. One of the biggest changes was the birth of _____. The Aryans combined their gods with the gods _____ by the Indian people. Hinduism is now one of the world's oldest _____. Today, more than 850 million people in India are _____.

B Complete each sentence with the correct word. Change the form if necessary.

| Indus Valley | Ganges River | organize | combine | take advantage |

1 The _____ _____ people built their villages, towns, and cities along the Indus River.

2 Archaeologists have learned that the Indus Valley Civilization was well _____.

3 Harappan farmers learned to _____ _____ of monsoons, so they grew a variety of crops.

4 A new civilization developed along the _____ _____ in another part of India.

5 The Aryans _____ their gods with the gods worshipped by the Indian people.

C Write the meaning of each word and phrase from Word List in English.

1 印度河	_____	15 污水系統；下水道系統	_____
2 現今的	_____	16 季風	m_____
3 印度河流域文明	_____	17 季風	s_____
4 哈拉帕文明	_____	18 利用	_____
5 可接觸到	_____	19 剩餘的	_____
6 挖掘	_____	20 以防	_____
7 定居地	_____	21 乾旱	_____
8 手工藝品	_____	22 參與	_____
9 組織良好的	_____	23 印度河文字	_____
10 設計；規畫	_____	24 衰敗	_____
11 棋盤狀；網格狀	_____	25 恆河	_____
12 穀倉	_____	26 阿利安人	_____
13 公共浴池	_____	27 印度教	_____
14 鋪設的道路	_____	28 印度教徒	_____

04 The Ancient World
Ancient Greece

🎧 25

A Listen to the passage and fill in the blanks.

1. Ancient Greece was made up of two _____ in the Mediterranean Sea: Attica and Peloponnesus. There were also more than 400 islands along the coast of the _____ Sea. Greece had no flooding river like the Nile, and much of its _____ was covered with hills and mountains. Its rocky, dry soil was not _____ _____ farming, so the ancient Greeks _____ _____ the sea for food and trade.

2. Three earlier Mediterranean civilizations _____ the ancient Greek culture. They were the _____ of the island of Crete, the Mycenaeans, who came from central Asia and conquered the Minoans, and the _____ of the eastern Mediterranean. They sailed across the Mediterranean as traders and spread their cultures and ideas along with their _____ _____. The Phoenicians invented the _____ which became the basis for the alphabet we use today.

3. The Greeks practiced many new ideas and _____ government systems. The Greeks lived in separate _____. These city-states remained _____ of each other, but the people living in them all spoke the same _____ language.

4. Some city-states were _____ _____ a king. This kind of government is called a _____. Other city-states were ruled by groups of _____ _____. This kind of government is called an _____. A few city-states practiced _____, in which all of the citizens took part in the government and chose their leaders. The _____ led the way. But only _____ could be citizens. _____ and slaves were not citizens, so they could not vote. _____ _____ democracy in Athens was not perfect, it still influenced many nations in _____ _____. Today, we call Athens the _____ of democracy.

5. By about _____ _____, the two most powerful city-states in Greece were Athens and _____. They had different _____ and cultures. Athens practiced democracy and was a great _____ _____. The Spartans were _____ warriors and had a powerful army. From 431 B.C. to 404 B.C., Athens and Sparta fought one another in the _____ _____. Eventually, Sparta won, and Athens _____ to be a great power.

6. Many other Greek city-states were also _____ _____ the Peloponnesian War. After it ended, these city-states were all _____. North of Greece was _____. It was _____ by King Philip. He began to _____ many Greek city-states, including Athens. Philip was _____ in 336 B.C., and his son Alexander became the king. _____ quickly defeated the rest of the Greek peninsula. However, he was an _____ young man. Alexander took his army _____. By the time Alexander the Great died in _____ _____, he had destroyed the _____ Empire and conquered much of Western Asia and Northern Africa. He was the ruler of the largest _____ in the world when he died.

B Complete each sentence with the correct word. Change the form if necessary.

| monarchy | independent | depend on | Persian | Peloponnesian War |

1 The ancient Greeks _____ _____ the sea for food and trade.

2 The Greek city-states remained _____ of each other.

3 Athens and Sparta fought one another in the _____ _____.

4 A _____ is a kind of government that is ruled by a king.

5 Alexander the Great destroyed the _____ Empire and conquered much of Western Asia and Northern Africa.

C Write the meaning of each word and phrase from Word List in English.

1 半島 _____

2 地中海 _____

3 本土；大陸 _____

4 適合 _____

5 依賴 _____

6 影響 _____

7 米諾斯人 _____

8 克里特島 _____

9 邁錫尼人 _____

10 腓尼基人 _____

11 貿易商 _____

12 交易商品 _____

13 ……的根基 _____

14 政府體系 _____

15 獨立的 _____

16 由……統治 _____

17 君主政體 _____

18 寡頭政治 _____

19 民主政體 _____

20 參與 _____

21 雅典人 _____

22 先行；帶頭 _____

23 發源地 _____

24 海上強權 _____

25 斯巴達人 _____

26 伯羅奔尼撒戰爭 _____

27 停止 _____

28 涉入；加入 _____

29 馬其頓王國 _____

30 被謀殺 _____

31 野心勃勃的 _____

32 亞歷山大大帝 _____

05 The Roman Empire

🎧 26

A Listen to the passage and fill in the blanks.

1 According to legend, Rome was founded by the brothers Romulus and Remus on the _____ peninsula in 753 B.C. It was a small city _____ on seven hills along the Tiber River, but, as it grew, Rome became the center of a _____ empire. At its _____, the Roman Empire included most of modern-day Europe and some of _____ and the Middle East.

2 Early in its history, Rome was ruled by Etruscan kings for _____ years. In 510 B.C., the Romans _____ _____ these kings and founded a new form of government called a republic. Thus, the Roman _____ was born. In a republic, people choose _____, who make political decisions for them. Every year, the wealthy men in the Roman Republic, known as _____, selected two leaders, called _____. They also elected _____, who advised the consuls and served in the Roman Senate. Together, they ruled Rome and made important decisions _____ the city. Later, the _____—the poor farmers and shopkeepers— were given a plebeian assembly to elect 10 plebeian _____. These tribunes had _____ _____ and defended the plebeians' rights.

3 Over the years, _____ power grew. By 300 B.C., Rome controlled most of the Italian peninsula and was a _____ _____ on the Mediterranean Sea. But Rome had a _____ across the Mediterranean: the city of Carthage. Beginning in 275 B.C., the Romans battled _____ in three separate wars, called the _____ _____. The Third Punic War ended in _____ B.C. After winning the Punic Wars, the Romans became the _____ of the Mediterranean region.

4 Rome continued _____ its territory. It _____ _____ very much land in Europe, Asia, and Africa. But after the Punic Wars ended, several _____ _____ erupted between wealthy Romans and powerful generals. Eventually, Pompey, Crassus, and Julius Caesar formed a _____ to rule Rome. This lasted for around a _____ until the three men started fighting. Julius Caesar emerged _____, but he was assassinated in the Roman _____ in 44 B.C.

5 After _____ death, there was more fighting until 31 B.C., when Octavian _____ Anthony and Cleopatra. After his victory, _____ became emperor. The Roman Republic _____, and the Roman Empire began with Octavian, now called _____, as the first emperor. Augustus's rule began the _____ _____, the "Roman Peace." This peace lasted nearly _____ years.

6 Over time, the empire _____ too big for one man to rule. In _____ A.D., Diocletian _____ the empire into eastern and western parts. His goal was to make _____ the empire easier. However, this led to the complete split of the Roman Empire under _____ ____. In 324, Constantine I moved the center of power to Byzantium and _____ the city Constantinople. This would become the _____ Empire.

7 The Western Roman Empire grew _____ after the split. Finally, in _____, Germanic _____ conquered the city of Rome. But the Byzantine Empire lasted for almost one _____ more years.

B Complete each sentence with the correct word. Change the form if necessary.

| triumvirate | peninsula | representative | Punic Wars | Byzantium |

1 Rome was founded by Romulus and Remus on the Italian _____ in 753 B.C.
2 In a republic, people choose _____, who make political decisions for them.
3 The Romans battled Carthage in three separate wars, called the _____ _____.
4 Eventually, Pompey, Crassus, and Julius Caesar formed a _____ to rule Rome.
5 Constantine I moved the center of power to _____ and renamed the city Constantinople.

C Write the meaning of each word and phrase from Word List in English.

1 由……所建立　_____
2 台伯河　_____
3 在全盛時期　_____
4 伊特拉斯坎人的　_____
5 驅逐　_____
6 共和政體；共和國　_____
7 代表　_____
8 貴族　_____
9 執政官　_____
10 元老院議員　_____
11 關於　_____
12 平民　_____
13 公民大會　_____
14 護民官　_____
15 否決權　_____
16 保衛　_____
17 平民權利　_____
18 迦太基　_____
19 布匿戰爭　_____
20 霸主　_____
21 接管　_____
22 內戰　_____
23 爆發　_____
24 凱撒　_____
25 三頭政治　_____
26 十年　_____
27 獲得勝利　_____
28 被暗殺　_____
29 羅馬元老院　_____
30 屋大維　_____
31 奧古斯都　_____
32 羅馬治世；羅馬和平　_____
33 將……分成……　_____
34 君士坦丁一世　_____
35 重新命名　_____
36 拜占庭帝國　_____

🎧 27

A Listen to the passage and fill in the blanks.

1. The _____ Peninsula has some of the world's largest desert areas. Much of the region is very _____ and hot. Yet people have lived on the Arabian Peninsula for _____ of years, and wonderful civilizations have _____ there. We call the people who have lived there for more than 3,000 years _____.

2. _____ developed on the Arabian Peninsula starting in _____ and grew rapidly. Muhammad (= Mohammad), the _____ of Islam, was born in the city of _____ (= Makkah) in the Arabian Peninsula around 570. Muslims, Islam's followers, believe that _____ was visited by the angel _____ with a message from Allah in 610. _____ is the Arabic word for God.

3. According to Islamic tradition, after Muhammad had a _____ of the angel Gabriel, he began _____ to other Arabs. He preached that they should _____ only one god: Allah. He _____ that all people are _____ and that the rich should take care of the poor. After Muhammad's death, his teachings were written down by his _____, and they became the _____ _____ of Islam, called the Koran (= Quran). There are five basic _____ in Islam. These are called the Five _____ of Islam. They are:

   1. _____ that there is no god but Allah and that Muhammad is Allah's _____.
   2. Make _____ five times a day while facing Mecca.
   3. Give _____ to the poor and the needy.
   4. _____, which means not to eat or drink anything, during the daytime in the holy month of _____.
   5. Make a _____, which means to make a _____ to Mecca, during one's lifetime.

4. After Muhammad died in _____, Muslim leaders selected _____ to govern the Muslim community. A caliph was a _____ political and religious leader who was selected as a _____ of Muhammad. From _____ to _____, there were four caliphs. Under them, Islam spread _____. Muslim armies conquered Christian cities such as Alexandria, _____, and Damascus. They took over land in western Asia, North Africa, and _____. They went north up to _____, but they were defeated by Charles Martel in 732. In the east, they reached the gates of Constantinople, the _____ of the Byzantine Empire, before they were _____ back.

5. The spread of Islam _____ many people in the West. So, in the late eleventh century, the pope _____ Christians in Western Europe to send armies to Jerusalem to free the Holy Land. This began the _____. In 1099, during the First Crusade, the _____ captured Jerusalem. For the next _____ years, there were several Crusades. In the end, though, the crusaders were _____, and the Muslims _____ all of the lands that they had lost during the Crusades.

6. Later, the _____ _____ arose during the 1200s. It became _____ powerful. In _____, the Ottoman Empire captured Constantinople and _____ the Byzantine Empire. The Ottoman Empire _____ _____ until the end of World War I.

12

B Complete each sentence with the correct word. Change the form if necessary.

| successor | Crusade | Muhammad | Arabian Peninsula | Five Pillars |

1 Islam developed on the _____ _____ starting in 610 and grew rapidly.

2 Muslims believe that _____ was visited by the angel Gabriel with a message from Allah.

3 There are five basic duties in Islam, called the _____ _____ of Islam.

4 A caliph was a Muslim political and religious leader who was selected as a _____ of Muhammad.

5 During the First _____, the crusaders captured Jerusalem.

C Write the meaning of each word and phrase from Word List in English.

1 阿拉伯半島 _____

2 阿拉伯人 _____

3 伊斯蘭教 _____

4 穆罕默德 _____

5 創立者 _____

6 麥加 _____

7 穆斯林；伊斯蘭教徒 _____

8 天使加百列 _____

9 阿拉 _____

10 阿拉伯文字 _____

11 看見；所見事物 _____

12 傳教 _____

13 可蘭經 _____

14 五功；信仰五柱 _____

15 證實 _____

16 先知；傳遞神旨之人 _____

17 禱告 _____

18 面向 _____

19 施捨；捐贈 _____

20 窮人 _____

21 有需要的人 _____

22 齋戒；禁食 _____

23 齋月 _____

24 朝聖 _____

25 朝聖之旅 _____

26 哈里發 _____

27 管理 _____

28 繼承者 _____

29 耶路撒冷 _____

30 直到 _____

31 被擊退 _____

32 使驚慌不安 _____

33 極力主張 _____

34 聖地 _____

35 十字軍東征 _____

36 十字軍 _____

37 收復 _____

38 鄂圖曼帝國 _____

From the Middle Ages to the Reformation

🎧 28

A Listen to the passage and fill in the blanks.

1. The Roman Empire had controlled _____ _____ the land along the coast of the _____ Sea and most places in Europe. Under the *Pax Romana*, Rome's _____ had _____ the peace for centuries. After the vast Roman Empire _____ in 476, Europe suffered almost _____ war. The period between _____ _____ _____ Rome and the 1400s is called the Middle Ages.

2. For most Europeans, life was hard during the _____ _____. Medieval society was like a pyramid based on _____: the kings and lords were on top, the knights were below them, and the _____, or serfs, were on the bottom. People suffered from _____ wars and hunger, and diseases killed thousands of people. There were few _____ in science, literature, art, and other fields.

3. However, for the Christian Church, the Middle Ages were _____ _____ _____ growth. Since Christianity became the official _____ of the Roman Empire in 313, the Church continued to expand _____ _____ the Western Roman Empire collapsed. By the year 1000, most Europeans were _____, and the Church dominated people's daily lives. This is why the Middle Ages is sometimes called _____ _____ _____ _____.

4. In the 1300s, a _____, called the _____ _____, struck Europe. It killed _____ _____ people. The _____ _____ so many people changed Europe's economy and _____ _____ the end of feudalism in Europe. So many serfs died that _____ had to pay workers on their manors.

5. Around _____, the Middle Ages came to _____ _____, and the Renaissance began in Italy. The word Renaissance means "_____." During this period, people began to _____ and value art, science, literature, and the ideas of ancient Greece and Rome. This led them to make new _____ of their own. _____ led the way. They studied ancient Greek and Roman writings and _____ _____ humans more than religion. There were _____ advances made in science, art, literature, music, and other _____. People like Leonardo da Vinci and _____ became Renaissance Men—men with curiosity and talents in many fields.

6. The _____ spread throughout Europe. During it, there was one important invention that greatly _____ society. It was the _____ _____. Johannes Gutenberg invented _____ _____ in the 1450s. His invention made books more _____. Books became _____ and easier to make, so more people learned to read. This let more people read the _____ for themselves. _____, only priests and the rich could read it. But, now, common people could read the Bible and _____ _____ _____ their own _____ of it. This helped _____ _____ the Protestant Reformation.

7. During the Renaissance, the _____ Church still had great power. Some _____ and _____ became powerful political rulers. But Martin Luther, a German _____, thought that the Church was too corrupt. He was especially upset that the Church sold _____ to rebuild St. Peter's Church in Rome. In 1517, he went to a church and _____ a paper with ninety-five _____ on it. His actions resulted in the _____ _____.

8. Many others felt the same as _____. They thought the Church needed to be _____. The ideas of the Reformation rapidly spread from Germany to _____, the Netherlands, France, and England. More people left the Catholic Church and founded their own Christian _____. Even King Henry VIII of _____ split with the Catholic Church and established the _____ Church in the 1530s. The Lutheran, _____, and Anabaptist sects were all founded during this time.

B Complete each sentence with the correct word. Change the form if necessary.

corrupt	Black Death	Middle Ages	Christian sect	movable type

1 During the _____ _____, people suffered from terrible wars, hunger, and diseases.

2 The _____ _____ changed Europe's economy and sped up the end of feudalism in Europe.

3 Johannes Gutenberg's invention of _____ _____ made books more accessible.

4 Martin Luther thought that the Church was too _____.

5 More people left the Catholic Church and founded their own _____ _____.

C Write the meaning of each word and phrase from Word List in English.

1 瓦解 _____

2 遭受 _____

3 中世紀的 _____

4 封建制度 _____

5 農民 _____

6 農奴 _____

7 信仰時代 _____

8 瘟疫 _____

9 黑死病 _____

10 加速 _____

11 文藝復興 _____

12 重生 _____

13 重新發現 _____

14 重視 _____

15 人文主義者 _____

16 文藝復興人 _____

17 好奇心 _____

18 印刷術 _____

19 古騰堡 _____

20 活字印刷術 _____

21 可（或易）得到的 _____

22 先前 _____

23 想出 _____

24 解釋 _____

25 宗教改革 _____

26 教宗 _____

27 主教 _____

28 馬丁・路德 _____

29 腐敗的 _____

30 贖罪券 _____

31 釘上 _____

32 論點 _____

33 改革 _____

34 教派 _____

35 （英國）聖公會 _____

36 路德教派 _____

37 長老教派 _____

38 重浸教派 _____

08 The Enlightenment and the French Revolution

🎧 29

A Listen to the passage and fill in the blanks.

1 During the 1600s and _____, new ideas about the world and scientific discoveries _____ _____ Europe. This was the _____. It is also called the Age of _____.

2 During the Enlightenment, scientists developed a _____ called the scientific _____ and began to ask questions about everything. As a result, there were many _____ scientific discoveries. Galileo Galilei improved the early _____ and studied the solar system. He supported Nicolaus Copernicus's _____, sun-centered theory. Isaac Newton invented _____, a new kind of mathematics, and discovered _____ and the laws of motion. Doctors improved _____ with new ideas and methods. The French philosopher René Descartes developed a _____ based on logic and reason. Philosophers such as Thomas Hobbes, John Locke, and Baron Montesquieu _____ on governments and people's basic _____.

3 The ideas of the Enlightenment changed how people _____ society and government. Eventually, these ideas would lead to war and _____ in England, the United States, and France.

4 In the 1600s, _____ kings were very powerful. They claimed that they ruled by _____ _____. They insisted that God had _____ them to be kings, so they had the right to rule the country _____ _____ _____ they wanted. But the new ideas about the government and _____ no longer accepted the _____ of divine right. As a result, the _____ between the English King Charles I and Parliament _____ _____ a civil war in England in 1642. In 1649, Charles I was defeated, and the English kings were _____ _____ respect the laws passed by _____.

5 The ideas of the Enlightenment were also very _____ to the American Revolution, which began in _____. In 1763, the English government wanted the American colonies to _____ _____ the debt _____ _____ an expensive war with France. But the colonists _____. In 1776, the colonists separated from Great Britain and later _____ the United States of America. The American Founding Fathers _____ their ideas _____ freedom on the works of Enlightenment _____.

6 A few years later, in 1789, the French _____ began. It too was _____ _____ the Enlightenment. The kingdom of France was divided into three "_____," or classes. The First Estate was the _____ in the Catholic Church. The Second Estate was the _____. The Third Estate was _____ _____. The Third Estate included about 98 percent of _____. Most of these people were poor _____. They paid the _____ _____ the taxes but had no role in the government.

7 According to French law, each of the _____ had the right to elect representatives to send to the _____, an assembly. However, no _____ king had called a meeting of the Estates General since _____. By 1789, France was nearing _____. King Louis XVI called the Estates General in order to _____ more taxes. The Third Estate was _____. They _____ and formed a National Assembly. They _____ the Bastille, a prison in Paris, and took weapons that were there to _____ their rights. "_____! Equality! Fraternity!" was the _____ of the French Revolution. In _____, the National Convention ended the _____ and established a republic.

Complete each sentence with the correct word. Change the form if necessary.

Estates General	revolution	Enlightenment	slogan	influence

1 During the _____, there were many remarkable scientific discoveries.

2 The ideas of the Enlightenment led to war and _____ in England, the United States, and France.

3 The French Revolution was _____ by the Enlightenment.

4 King Louis XVI called the _____ _____ in order to levy more taxes.

5 "Liberty! Equality! Fraternity!" was the _____ of the French Revolution.

C Write the meaning of each word and phrase from Word List in English.

1 橫掃   _____

2 啟蒙運動   _____

3 理性時代   _____

4 過程   _____

5 科學方法   _____

6 傑出的   _____

7 伽利略   _____

8 望遠鏡   _____

9 太陽系   _____

10 哥白尼   _____

11 日心說；太陽中心說 _____

12 以太陽為中心的 _____

13 微積分   _____

14 重力；地心吸力 _____

15 運動定律   _____

16 笛卡兒   _____

17 邏輯   _____

18 理性   _____

19 闡述   _____

20 革命   _____

21 君權神授   _____

22 以任何方式   _____

23 觀念   _____

24 國會   _____

25 被強迫   _____

26 美國革命   _____

27 付清   _____

28 美國的建國元老 _____

29 法國大革命   _____

30 階級   _____

31 神職人員   _____

32 貴族階級   _____

33 三級（指法國大革命以前法國社會的三個等級：教士、貴族和庶民） _____

34 三級會議   _____

35 破產   _____

36 徵收   _____

37 反抗   _____

38 國民議會   _____

39 猛攻   _____

40 巴士底監獄   _____

41 博愛   _____

42 國民公會   _____

Cells, Reproduction, and Heredity

🎧 30

A Listen to the passage and fill in the blanks.

1. The basic unit of life is the _____. All living things are made up of _____ _____
more than one cell. One-celled, or single-celled, organisms are _____.
They include bacteria and _____. However, the _____ _____ life contains
more than one cell. These are called _____, or multi-celled, organisms.
Multi-cellular organisms, such as _____ animals and plants, are made of different
kinds of cells. Similar cells that have the same function form _____. Tissues of
different kinds _____ _____ to form an organ, such as the _____ or
lungs. A group of organs makes up an _____ _____, such as the digestive or
_____ systems.

2. All life _____, such as growth and reproduction, _____ _____ in cells.
All organisms start _____ as one cell. Growth begins when the cell _____ and
becomes two cells. _____ cells divide and become four cells. At the eight-cell stage,
cells divide at _____ _____ and continue to divide over their lifetimes.

3. There are two different ways that cells _____: mitosis and meiosis. Body cells
make more body cells by _____. In mitosis, the cell merely _____ its genetic
material, and then it divides itself _____ _____. Reproductive cells are produced by
_____. Reproductive cells are _____ _____ reproduction.
_____ _____ is a result of meiosis.

4. When babies are born, they often _____ their parents in many ways. For
example, a baby and its mother may have the same eye or _____ _____. Or
perhaps the baby and its father may have _____ body shapes. This is called
_____. Heredity is the passing down of various characteristics, or _____,
from parents to their children.

5. Genes are what _____ heredity. Genes have information on how an organism
should grow. When a sperm cell and an egg cell join, genes _____ _____
from both the father and the mother. As a result, half of the _____ genetic
material comes from its father _____ the other half comes from its mother. This is
why children have _____ of both parents.

6. There are both _____ and recessive genes. Dominant genes are ones that are
expressed _____ or visually. They are stronger than _____ genes, which
are present in the body but are _____ by dominant genes. Recessive genes
can, however, be _____ _____ offspring and then become dominant genes in
the offspring.

7. While organisms _____ their genes from their parents, some organisms are born
with _____. A mutation is a _____ change in a gene. Some mutations
can be harmful, but others may be _____ to the organism.

Complete each sentence with the correct word. Change the form if necessary.

| overshadow | cell | take place | dominant | mitosis |

1. All living things are made of at least more than one _____.
2. All life processes, such as growth and reproduction, _____ _____ in cells.
3. Body cells make more body cells by _____.
4. _____ genes are ones that are expressed physically or visually.
5. Recessive genes are present in the body but are _____ by dominant genes.

C Write the meaning of each word and phrase from Word List in English.

1. 細胞 _____
2. 單細胞的 _____
3. 微生物 _____
4. 多細胞的 _____
5. 高等的 _____
6. 組織 _____
7. 組合 _____
8. 器官 _____
9. 器官系統 _____
10. 消化系統 _____
11. 呼吸系統 _____
12. 再生；繁殖 _____
13. 發生 _____
14. 有絲分裂 _____
15. 減數分裂 _____
16. 身體細胞 _____

17. 遺傳物質 _____
18. 分半 _____
19. 生殖細胞 _____
20. 承擔……的責任 _____
21. 遺傳變異 _____
22. 遺傳 _____
23. 基因 _____
24. 決定 _____
25. 被轉移 _____
26. 下一代 _____
27. 顯性基因 _____
28. 隱性基因 _____
29. 存在的 _____
30. 被……遮蔽 _____
31. 遺傳；繼承 _____
32. 突變；變種 _____

10 Oceans and Ocean Life

The Earth's Oceans

🎧 31

Listen to the passage and fill in the blanks.

1 Oceans cover nearly _____ of Earth's surface. These oceans often appear _____ and _____. However, this is not actually _____ _____. In fact, the oceans' waters are in _____ motion.

2 The water level of the ocean is _____ changing. One of these changes is caused by _____. Tides are the regular _____ and _____ of an ocean's surface. Tides result mostly from the moon's _____ _____ on Earth. When the water is at its _____ _____, it is called high tide. The water at its lowest point is called _____ _____.

3 Ocean waters are also constantly _____ around the land by _____. A current is a large _____ of water that flows through the ocean. Currents are caused by many _____. Surface currents are produced by _____ _____. Earth's rotation also _____ surface currents. Currents form _____ _____ differences in water temperatures as well. Cold water near the North and South poles _____ and begins moving toward the _____. Warm water from the equator rises to the surface and _____ _____ both poles to replace the cold water that is _____ _____. When the cold and warm waters _____, currents form.

4 Ocean currents affect the land's _____. Warm-water currents, such as the _____ _____, begin near the equator. The Gulf Stream brings warm water across the North _____ _____ toward Europe. During the winter, the warm Gulf Stream keeps Europe's climate _____. The currents are also responsible for ocean _____. Ocean circulation helps _____ the supply of oxygen in the water.

5 The _____ _____ is as varied as the land above water. It contains mountains, deep valleys, plains, and other _____. However, all ocean floors can be divided into three _____ regions. The first region is the _____ _____. It extends from the _____ to a depth of about 200 meters. It has a _____ _____ that is made of continental crust. The _____ _____ is at the edge of the continent between the continental shelf and the _____ _____. It is _____ and deeper than the continental shelf. At the end of the continental slope, there is one of the _____ places on Earth—the abyssal plain. The _____ _____ is the vast, flat floor of the deep ocean. It covers almost _____ _____ the ocean floor.

6 Oceans contain _____ organisms with different types of ecosystems, called _____ _____. Each ocean zone has _____ types of plant and animal communities. The _____ ocean zone is the _____ _____. It covers the area that _____ _____ when the ocean is at low tide, so intertidal organisms should be able to _____ changes in their environments. The _____ _____ zone includes most of the continental shelf. It is fairly _____ water and gets lots of sunlight. It often has _____ life and is much more stable than the intertidal zone. The final zone is the _____ zone. This is the deepwater area that _____ the largest regions in the oceans. Because of the _____ of the open-ocean zone, this area _____ little or no sunlight. So most of the animals in the open-ocean zone _____ near the surface to _____ food.

B Complete each sentence with the correct word. Change the form if necessary.

| continental shelf | tide | current | intertidal zone | abyssal plain |

1 _____ are the regular rising and falling of an ocean's surface.

2 A _____ is a large stream of water that flows through the ocean.

3 The _____ _____ extends from the shore to a depth of about 200 meters.

4 The _____ _____ is the vast, flat floor of the deep ocean which covers almost half of the ocean floor.

5 The shallowest ocean zone is the _____ _____.

C Write the meaning of each word and phrase from Word List in English.

1 平靜的 _____

2 經常的 _____

3 運動中 _____

4 水平面 _____

5 經常地 _____

6 由……造成 _____

7 潮汐 _____

8 起因於…… _____

9 萬有引力 _____

10 最高點 _____

11 滿潮 _____

12 最低點 _____

13 乾潮 _____

14 洋流 _____

15 水流 _____

16 因素 _____

17 全球風系 _____

18 地球自轉 _____

19 由於 _____

20 赤道 _____

21 離開 _____

22 墨西哥灣暖流 _____

23 海洋環流 _____

24 補給 _____

25 海床 _____

26 和……一樣多變 _____

27 大陸棚 _____

28 緩坡 _____

29 大陸地殼 _____

30 大陸坡 _____

31 深海平原 _____

32 海洋帶 _____

33 最淺的 _____

34 潮間帶 _____

35 暴露 _____

36 近岸區；近濱帶 _____

37 豐富的 _____

38 遠洋帶 _____

Fossils

11 What We Can Learn from Fossils

🎧 32

Listen to the passage and fill in the blanks.

1 About 65 million years ago, _____ lived on Earth. However, no one has ever seen a living dinosaur because they _____ _____ a long time ago. But how do we know a lot about them, such as what they were _____ or how many kinds of them lived? We know these things _____ _____ fossils.

2 Fossils are the _____ or imprints of living things that died long ago. The remains of dead organisms were often covered with _____, sand, or other _____. Over time, the sediment and the remains _____ into rock. Almost all fossils are found in _____ rocks.

3 Sometimes, a complete body _____ _____. However, more often, parts of the organism are _____. The organism's soft parts may often _____ quickly, and the hard parts, such as _____ and bones, are _____ behind. Some fossils are not parts of organisms but are only footprints or _____ of an organism's body. They appear in the form of a _____ or a cast.

4 Scientists study fossils to learn about _____ organisms and the environments of the past on Earth. Fossils show dinosaurs, _____, plants, insects, and fish that _____ a long time ago.

5 _____—scientists who study fossils—take great care in _____ fossils and preserving them. They often _____ _____ the individual bones of an animal to show what it once looked like. They can _____ _____ how big it was, how much it _____, how long it lived, where it lived, and even what kind of food it ate.

6 Fossils can also tell us about _____ history. Paleontologists have learned that some fossils are only found in certain _____ of rocks. They have _____ a record called the fossil record. The _____ _____ is used to study Earth's history. _____ _____ are important in determining the fossil record. Index fossils are fossils of organisms that only lived during _____ times in the past. They tell the age of the rock _____ _____ it is found. When scientists find an index fossil in a _____ rock layer, they can know how old the _____ is and how Earth's surface has changed _____ _____.

7 One well-known index fossil is the _____. It was a _____—a shelled underwater creature—that lived during the time of the dinosaurs. _____ are another commonly found index fossil that lived before the dinosaurs.

B Complete each sentence with the correct word. Change the form if necessary.

impression   remains   unearth   ammonite   index fossil

1 Fossils are the _____ or imprints of living things that died long ago.

2 Some fossils are only footprints or _____ of an organism's body.

3 Paleontologists take great care in _____ fossils and preserving them.

4 _____ _____ are fossils of organisms that only lived during specific times in the past.

5 One well-known index fossil is the _____.

C Write the meaning of each word and phrase from Word List in English.

1	恐龍	_____	18	模子；模具	_____

1 恐龍 _____

2 絕種 _____

3 歸功於…… _____

4 化石 _____

5 遺骸 _____

6 痕跡 _____

7 沉積物 _____

8 硬化 _____

9 沉積岩 _____

10 成為化石 _____

11 被保存 _____

12 腐爛 _____

13 殼 _____

14 被遺留下來 _____

15 足跡 _____

16 印記 _____

17 以……形式 _____

18 模子；模具 _____

19 鑄型 _____

20 絕種的 _____

21 絕跡 _____

22 古生物學家 _____

23 挖掘 _____

24 拼湊 _____

25 得知 _____

26 有多少重量 _____

27 組合 _____

28 化石紀錄 _____

29 標準化石；指標化石 _____

30 特定的 _____

31 岩層 _____

32 菊石（鸚鵡螺的化石） _____

33 頭足動物 _____

34 三葉蟲 _____

🎧 33

A Listen to the passage and fill in the blanks.

1. Have you ever seen _____ float in a circle in the sky? The skydivers are actually in _____ before their parachutes open. They are falling toward Earth with the _____ caused by a force _____ them toward the center of Earth. What force pulls them _____ the center of Earth? It is _____. All objects are pulled to the ground by _____.

2. Isaac Newton, one of the world's greatest _____, discovered that everything is pulled to the ground and that it is the same _____ that keeps the planets _____ the sun. This is Newton's Law of Universal _____. Gravitation is the force that acts _____ any two objects and makes them _____ one another. Gravity—the force that acts between Earth and objects—is an _____ of gravitation. Gravitation keeps the moon in a _____ path around Earth. It _____ the moon and Earth toward each other. This pull prevents the moon from _____ _____ away from Earth. Gravitation also _____ Earth and the other planets in their orbits around the sun.

3. Isaac Newton, an Englishman, lived from 1643 to _____. During his life, he worked in many _____ _____ science and mathematics. But, most of all, he is known for his work in _____. In addition to discovering the Law of Universal Gravitation, he also discovered the three _____ _____ _____.

4. The first law of motion states that an object _____ _____ will stay at rest and an object in motion will not change its _____ unless an outside force acts on it. One of the main _____ forces is gravity. For instance, you may _____ a ball _____ in the air. Without the force of gravity affecting it, the ball would continue going _____ forever. However, because gravity—an outside force—acts on it, the ball _____ back down to the ground. Newton's first law of motion is often called the Law of _____.

5. The second law of motion is called the Law of _____. This law states that _____ _____ the force on an object, the greater its acceleration. It is often written as a _____: $a = F \div m$. a is acceleration, F is force, and m is _____. So an object's acceleration _____ the force divided by the object's mass. This law also states that objects with a _____ mass require more force to move than objects with a _____ mass. For instance, it requires much more force to _____ a brick than to throw a tennis ball since a _____ has more mass than a tennis ball.

6. The third law of motion is called the Law of _____ and _____. For every action, there is an equal and _____ reaction. One object pushing on another will receive a push _____ _____. For instance, crews on a _____ _____ push on the water with their _____. The water, in turn, pushes back on the oars and _____ the boat forward.

B Complete each sentence with the correct word. Change the form if necessary.

| gravitation | Action | gravity | Reaction | Inertia | Acceleration |

1 All objects are pulled to the ground by _____.

2 _____ is the force that acts between any two objects and makes them attract one another.

3 Newton's first law of motion is often called the Law of _____.

4 The second law of motion is called the Law of _____.

5 The third law of motion is called the Law of _____ and _____.

C Write the meaning of each word and phrase from Word List in English.

1 跳傘選手 _____

2 飄浮 _____

3 自由落體 _____

4 降落傘 _____

5 加速度 _____

6 重力；地心引力 _____

7 牛頓萬有引力定律 _____

8 萬有引力 _____

9 吸引 _____

10 作用 _____

11 繞行 _____

12 防止……做…… _____

13 飛離 _____

14 物理學 _____

15 第一運動定律 _____

16 靜止 _____

17 運動中 _____

18 速率 _____

19 除非…… _____

20 外力 _____

21 作用於…… _____

22 往回落下 _____

23 慣性定律 _____

24 第二運動定律 _____

25 加速度定律 _____

26 公式；方程式 _____

27 第三運動定律 _____

28 作用力與反作用力 _____

29 以……回應；回報 _____

30 推進 _____

13 Light Energy

Light Energy

🎧 34

A Listen to the passage and fill in the blanks.

1. Light is _____ _____ _____ energy that the human eye can see. Light is comprised of _____ of very tiny particles called _____. These photons travel _____ _____. Nothing in the universe can move _____ than light. It travels at _____ 300,000 kilometers per second. Most waves need some kind of _____ to travel through. For instance, sound waves need matter, such as solids, liquids, and _____, to travel. You cannot hear _____ _____ _____ because there is no matter. However, light can move _____, even in a vacuum.

2. Since light moves in waves, it has various _____. Not all of its wavelengths are visible to the _____ _____. The light that humans can see is called _____ _____. All of the colors that humans can see—called the colors of the _____—are found in a rainbow, which has seven colors: red, orange, yellow, green, blue, _____, and violet. The light waves that have the longest wavelengths _____ red. The light waves with the shortest wavelengths appear _____.

3. A simple way to see all of the _____ of the spectrum is to use a _____. There was an experiment first _____ by Isaac Newton hundreds of years ago. He sent a _____ of sunlight through a prism and noticed that it spread out into a _____ _____ the colors of the rainbow. Then, he _____ that same light _____ another prism, and it returned to being white light. What happens is that a prism _____ light when light passes through it. White light is actually a _____ of an _____ spectrum of colors.

4. Something else that can _____ light through refraction is a _____. There are both convex and concave _____. A _____ _____ collects light onto one spot, called the focal point. A _____ _____ works in the opposite manner. It collects light and then _____ it _____. We can use lenses for many different _____. Convex lenses are used in _____, contact lenses, telescopes, and _____. Concave lenses are often used for _____ such as television projectors.

5. Some _____ _____ have wavelengths that are _____ too long or too short for humans to see. The light that humans cannot see is called _____ light. Both visible light and invisible light make up the _____ spectrum. It _____ everything that travels in waves. For instance, _____ has the longest wavelength of visible light. But _____ _____ has a longer wavelength. And _____—like the ones we use to cook with in microwave ovens—and radio waves have even longer wavelengths. On the other side of the spectrum, _____ _____ has a shorter wavelength than visible violet light. But _____ and gamma rays have even shorter wavelengths than ultraviolet light.

B Complete each sentence with the correct word. Change the form if necessary.

wavelength	comprise	prism	electromagnetic	invisible light

1 Light is _____ of billions of very tiny particles called photons.

2 Light has various _____, but not all of its wavelengths are visible to the human eye.

3 A simple way to see all of the colors of the spectrum is to use a _____.

4 The light that humans cannot see is called _____ _____.

5 Both visible light and invisible light make up the _____ spectrum.

C Write the meaning of each word and phrase from Word List in English.

1 由……組成 _____

2 數十億的 _____

3 粒子 _____

4 光子 _____

5 以波的形式 _____

6 大約 _____

7 媒介 _____

8 在真空中 _____

9 波長 _____

10 可見光 _____

11 光譜色 _____

12 稜鏡 _____

13 由……執行 _____

14 太陽光束 _____

15 折射 _____

16 結合 _____

17 彎曲 _____

18 折射 _____

19 凸透鏡 _____

20 凹透鏡 _____

21 焦點 _____

22 雙目望遠鏡 _____

23 電視投影機 _____

24 不可見光 _____

25 電磁光譜；電磁波譜 _____

26 紅外線 _____

27 微波 _____

28 紫外線 _____

29 X 光 _____

30 伽瑪射線 _____

14 The Universe Eclipses

🎧 35

1 Have you ever seen the moon slowly begin to _____ and turn a red color for a few hours? You may have seen a _____ _____. An eclipse occurs because of the moon's _____ around Earth. There are two types of _____. According to the _____ of the moon, Earth, and the sun, an eclipse can be _____ a lunar eclipse or a solar eclipse.

2 As the moon _____ Earth, it sometimes passes right between the sun and Earth. Then, the moon _____ sunlight from reaching parts of Earth and _____ a shadow on Earth. This is a _____ _____.

3 During a _____ solar eclipse, the moon blocks only _____ _____ the sun's light. During a _____ solar eclipse, you can only see a _____ _____ around the dark moon. This is called the _____ _____. Sometimes you can see a "diamond ring" _____ as well. A solar eclipse usually _____ _____ only a few minutes. When the moon _____ _____ of its position between Earth and the sun, the sky brightens again.

4 A lunar eclipse occurs when the moon moves into Earth's _____. A total lunar eclipse occurs when the moon passes through Earth's _____, or inner, shadow, called the _____. As the moon passes through the umbra, Earth _____ all sunlight _____ reaching the moon and casts a shadow on the moon. Then, the moon becomes totally dark because it does not make its own light but just _____ light from the sun. When only a part of the moon is in the shadow, it is called a _____ _____ _____. A lunar eclipse may last _____ _____ hours.

5 During a solar eclipse, you should never look _____ at the sun. You could damage your eyes _____ or even blind yourself.

B Complete each sentence with the correct word. Change the form if necessary.

> partial solar eclipse   partial lunar eclipse   umbra   revolving   location

1 An eclipse occurs because of the moon's _____ around Earth.

2 According to the _____ of the moon, Earth, and sun, an eclipse can be either a lunar eclipse or a solar eclipse.

3 During a _____ _____ _____, the moon blocks only part of the sun's light.

4 A total lunar eclipse occurs when the moon passes through Earth's darker shadow, called the _____.

5 When only a part of the moon is in the shadow, it is called a _____ _____ _____.

C Write the meaning of each word and phrase from Word List in English.

1 使變暗   _____
2 月蝕   _____
3 天蝕   _____
4 月球沿軌道繞行 _____
5 位置   _____
6 日蝕   _____
7 阻擋⋯⋯使其無法⋯⋯ _____
8 投下陰影   _____
9 日偏蝕   _____
10 日全蝕   _____
11 光芒   _____
12 日冕   _____

13 鑽石環現象   _____
14 持續⋯⋯之久   _____
15 變明亮   _____
16 地球陰影   _____
17 月全蝕   _____
18 內部的   _____
19 地球本影   _____
20 反射   _____
21 月偏蝕   _____
22 直接地   _____
23 永久地   _____
24 使自己失明   _____

29

15 The Human Body
Diseases and the Immune System

🎧 36

A Listen to the passage and fill in the blanks.

1 Every _____ _____ _____ _____ , a person may catch a disease and become sick. There are two kinds of _____ : noncommunicable and communicable diseases.

2 _____ diseases cannot be _____ from one person to another. Many of these diseases result from a person's _____ . For instance, smoking, drinking, eating too much, and not _____ enough can cause a person to get diseases such as _____ _____ or heart disease. Fortunately, other people cannot catch these diseases from an _____ person.

3 _____ diseases, on the other hand, can be passed from one person to another. The common cold and _____ _____ are two types of communicable diseases. Human contact frequently results in one person _____ these diseases from another. Communicable diseases are said to be _____ . Occasionally, a large number of people in an area catch a _____ disease at the same time. This results in an _____ .

4 Fortunately, the human body has many _____ to fight all kinds of diseases. We call these defenses the _____ system. The first line of defense is the _____ . The skin helps prevent many types of _____ and bacteria from entering the body, where they can do _____ . The skin also contains some _____ that can kill germs and bacteria when they touch the body.

5 Germs and bacteria _____ attempt to enter the body through the nose, eyes, and mouth. But these parts of the body all have their own _____ . Mucus in the nose acts like skin to stop _____ _____ from entering. Tears in the eyes and _____ in the mouth do the same thing. And, for germs and _____ that enter the body when a person eats food, there are _____ in the stomach that kill them.

6 However, some foreign bodies still _____ _____ enter the body and cause harm. When that happens, the body's _____ _____ goes to work. The body has _____ _____ , or glands, that can destroy bacteria, germs, and _____ . Also, _____ _____ _____ help fight infections. There are _____ types of white blood cells. Many of them clean the body and help _____ any damaged parts. Other white blood cells create _____ that attack germs and viruses and then kill them.

7 Sometimes, the human body cannot fight certain foreign _____ . This is often _____ _____ viruses. So humans have developed _____ to fight viruses. When a vaccine is _____ into a body, it _____ the production of antibodies that will fight a specific virus. Thanks to vaccines, people can become immune to _____ diseases such as malaria, _____ , yellow fever, and even _____ , the flu.

Complete each sentence with the correct word. Change the form if necessary.

| vaccine | communicable | noncommunicable | immune system | lymph node |

1 _____ diseases cannot be passed from one person to another.

2 The common cold and the flu are two types of _____ diseases.

3 Fortunately, the human body has the _____ _____ to fight all kinds of diseases.

4 The body has _____ _____, or glands, that can destroy bacteria, germs, and viruses.

5 When a _____ is injected into a body, it stimulates the production of antibodies.

C Write the meaning of each word and phrase from Word List in English.

1 有時;偶而 _____

2 罹患疾病 _____

3 非傳染病 _____

4 傳染病 _____

5 肺癌 _____

6 心臟病 _____

7 受感染的 _____

8 （一般）感冒 _____

9 流行性感冒 _____

10 接觸傳染的 _____

11 流行病;傳染病 _____

12 防禦 _____

13 免疫系統 _____

14 第一道防線 _____

15 保護……免於…… _____

16 病菌 _____

17 腺體 _____

18 企圖要…… _____

19 黏液 _____

20 異物 _____

21 口水;唾液 _____

22 酸 _____

23 成功做到…… _____

24 淋巴系統 _____

25 淋巴結 _____

26 淋巴腺 _____

27 白血球 _____

28 感染 _____

29 抗體 _____

30 外來入侵者 _____

31 疫苗 _____

32 注射 _____

33 刺激 _____

34 致命的 _____

35 黃熱病 _____

36 流行性感冒 _____

16 Factors, Prime Numbers, and Exponents

Numbers and Computation

🎧 37

A Listen to the passage and fill in the blanks.

1 Every _____ _____ greater than 1 has at least two factors. A _____ is a number that divides another number _____ without a _____. Many numbers can be _____ _____ factors in different ways. What are the _____ of 6?

$6 \div 1 = 6$ $6 \div 2 = 3$ $6 \div 3 = 2$

$6 \div 4 =$ does not divide evenly

$6 \div 5 =$ _____ _____ divide evenly $6 \div 6 = 1$

So, the factors of _____ are 1, 2, 3, and 6.

2 Some numbers, such as 3 and 5, can only be _____ _____ 1 and themselves. If a number has only two factors, it is called a _____ _____. Numbers such as 3, 5, and _____ are prime numbers. A number that has more than two factors is called a _____ _____. So numbers _____ _____ 4 and 6 are composite numbers. Every whole number greater than 1 is _____ a prime or composite number. But the number 1 is _____ prime nor composite since it only has one factor, the number 1 _____.

3 _____ composite number can be broken down into _____ prime factors. Prime factors are the prime numbers that, when _____ together, _____ _____ a composite number. For example, the number _____ can be broken down into the prime factors 2 and 5. When 2 and 5 are multiplied, they _____ the composite number 10. $10 =$ _____. What about a number such as _____? You can break it down into _____. But 4 is not a prime number since it can be broken down _____ into 2×2. So if you want to break down _____ to its prime factors, it should be like this: $16 = 2 \times 2 \times 2 \times 2$.

4 We can write the _____ $16 = 2 \times 2 \times 2 \times 2$ by using an _____: $16 = 2^4$. An exponent is a _____ _____ that tells you how many times a number is used as a factor in multiplication. In other words, 2^4 means that 2 is used as a factor _____ _____. You read _____ as "two to the fourth power." Also, the number 2 is called the _____ while the number 4 is the *exponent* or *power*.

5 Sometimes, we multiply a number _____ _____. In this case, we _____ the number. For example, 3×3 is expressed as _____. 3^2 is read "three _____" or "three to the second power." When the exponent is 3, then the number is "_____." So 5^3 is "five cubed" or "five to the _____ _____."

6 There are some numbers that are called _____ _____. A perfect square is a number that is the _____ of a number. For instance, _____ is a perfect square because $5 \times 5 = 25$. Also, 64 and _____ are perfect squares because $8 \times 8 = 64$, and _____ $= 100$. These numbers can also be expressed using the term _____ _____. For example, $5^2 = 5 \times 5 = 25$, or we can use the symbol for _____ _____, $\sqrt{25} = 5$. We say that the square root of _____ is 5.

B Complete each sentence with the correct word. Change the form if necessary.

| remainder | composite number | prime number | perfect square | raised number |

1 A factor is a number that divides another number evenly without a _____.

2 If a number has only two factors, it is called a _____ _____.

3 A number that has more than two factors is called a _____ _____.

4 An exponent is a _____ _____ that tells you how many times a number is used as a factor in multiplication.

5 A _____ _____ is a number that is the square of a number.

C Write the meaning of each word and phrase from Word List in English.

1 整數　　　_____

2 因數　　　_____

3 平均地　　_____

4 餘數　　　_____

5 被分解成　_____

6 整除　　　_____

7 質數　　　_____

8 合數　　　_____

9 質因數　　_____

10 形成；造成 _____

11 算式　　　　_____

12 指數（＝次方）_____

13 四次方　　　_____

14 底數　　　　_____

15 使成平方　　_____

16 二次方　　　_____

17 使成立方　　_____

18 三次方　　　_____

19 完全平方數　_____

20 平方根　　　_____

17 Geometry Dimensions

A **Listen to the passage and fill in the blanks.**

☐1 A dimension is a measurement along a _____ _____ of the length, width, or height of a figure. In _____, three dimensions are commonly used. The first dimension is _____. The second dimension is _____. And the third dimension is _____ or depth. The fourth dimension is _____, but it is not typically used in geometry.

☐2 A _____ figure is a line or a line segment. A one-dimensional figure can be measured in only one _____, such as length. It _____ both width and height.

☐3 A _____ figure is measured in two directions, such as length and width. Two-dimensional figures are called _____ _____. Figures with two dimensions can be _____ on a _____. Some of the most common two-dimensional figures are _____. A polygon is a closed shape that is formed by three or more _____ _____ that do not _____ one another. A triangle is a two-dimensional figure that is _____ _____ three line segments. Squares, rectangles, _____, trapezoids, and rhombuses are all two-dimensional figures that have four sides. Pentagons have five sides, and _____ have six sides. Polygons can actually have an _____ number of sides. In addition, circles and _____ are two more kinds of two-dimensional figures.

☐4 _____ figures are called _____ _____. They have length, width, and height. Solid figures can be _____ _____ the shape and the number of their _____, faces, vertices, and edges. Prisms have two congruent and _____ bases, but pyramids only have one base. Solid figures also often _____ _____ plane figures. For instance, while a triangle has two dimensions, a _____, which is shaped like a triangle, has three. A square has two dimensions, yet a _____, which is shaped like a square, has three. Some solid figures have _____ surfaces. A _____ has two circular bases. A cone has one _____ base.

Complete each sentence with the correct word. Change the form if necessary.

infinite	line segment	two-dimensional	solid figure	vertex

1 A one-dimensional figure is a line or a _____ _____ .

2 A _____ figure is measured in two directions, such as length and width.

3 Polygons can actually have an _____ number of sides.

4 Three-dimensional figures are called _____ _____ .

5 Solid figures can be classified by the shape and the number of their bases, faces, _____ , and edges.

C Write the meaning of each word and phrase from Word List in English.

1 維度   _____

2 直線   _____

3 長度   _____

4 寬度   _____

5 高度   _____

6 幾何學   _____

7 一度空間   _____

8 二度空間   _____

9 三度空間   _____

10 深度   _____

11 四度空間   _____

12 傳統上   _____

13 一度空間圖形 _____

14 缺少   _____

15 二度空間圖形 _____

16 平面圖形   _____

17 平面   _____

18 多邊形   _____

19 相交；交叉 _____

20 無限的   _____

21 三度空間圖形 _____

22 立體圖形   _____

23 底   _____

24 面   _____

25 頂點   _____

26 邊   _____

27 全等的   _____

28 平行的   _____

29 和……相呼應 _____

30 弧形的   _____

31 正方體   _____

32 長方體   _____

33 三角柱   _____

34 正四角錐   _____

35 長方錐   _____

36 圓柱   _____

37 圓錐   _____

38 球體   _____

18 Pygmalion

🎧 39

A **Listen to the passage and fill in the blanks.**

1 There once lived a _____ named Pygmalion. He was a man from the island of _____. According to some stories, he was a _____ of Cyprus. According to other stories, he was _____ a sculptor.

2 Anyhow, Pygmalion was a _____ sculptor. He was able to make _____ that looked _____ _____ they were alive. But Pygmalion had a _____. He was not _____ _____ women. No woman that he saw could ever _____ him. So he had no _____.

3 One day, _____ decided to create a statue of a woman. He set to work on a statue made out of _____. He worked on and on and finally completed a _____ statue. He had sculpted a statue of a woman more beautiful than any _____ _____. Pygmalion was _____ _____ the statue's beauty and immediately fell in love with the statue. He loved his statue like other men love _____. She _____ _____ be so real to him. He spent a lot of time _____ _____ his statue and even spoke to her. But, of course, she gave _____ _____. Pygmalion grew weak and thin because of his hopeless _____.

4 Sometime later, there was a _____ held in Cyprus in honor of Aphrodite. Pygmalion went to the festival, _____ _____ _____ to the goddess of love, and then made a wish. "I _____ wish that my ivory sculpture will change into a real woman." Aphrodite heard his prayer and _____ his wish. When Pygmalion _____ home, Cupid, who was sent by Aphrodite, _____ the ivory sculpture on the hand. This caused the statue to _____ _____ _____ as a beautiful young woman. A ring was put on her _____. It was Cupid's ring, which made love _____.

5 Pygmalion could not have been _____. He _____ the young woman Galatea. Aphrodite blessed the _____ of Pygmalion and Galatea. And they later had a _____ named Paphos.

6 Over the years, many writers wrote stories that were _____ _____ Pygmalion. One of the most famous was a _____ called "Pygmalion" that was written by George Bernard Shaw. This _____ _____ _____ something called the Pygmalion effect. According to the _____ _____, if you believe that someone is _____ _____ achieving greatness, then that person will _____ achieve greatness.

B Complete each sentence with the correct word. Change the form if necessary.

> sculptor   captivated by   Pygmalion effect   Aphrodite   make a wish

1 There once lived a _____ named Pygmalion, who was a man from the island of Cyprus.

2 Pygmalion was _____ _____ the statue's beauty and immediately fell in love with the statue.

3 There was a festival held in Cyprus in honor of _____.

4 Pygmalion went to the festival, made an offering to the goddess of love, and then _____ _____ _____.

5 According to the _____ _____, if you believe that someone is capable of achieving greatness, then that person will indeed achieve greatness.

C Write the meaning of each word and phrase from Word List in English.

1	雕刻師	_____	16	阿芙羅黛蒂	_____
2	給……命名	_____	17	獻上供品	_____
3	皮革馬利翁	_____	18	愛之女神	_____
4	塞浦路斯	_____	19	許願	_____
5	只是	_____	20	誠摯地	_____
6	聰穎的	_____	21	應允	_____
7	雕像	_____	22	甦醒過來；活過來	_____
8	彷彿	_____	23	達成	_____
9	開始；著手	_____	24	婚姻	_____
10	象牙	_____	25	蕭伯納	_____
11	被……所迷倒	_____	26	引起……	_____
12	愛上……	_____	27	期待效應；皮革馬利翁效應	
13	凝視……	_____			_____
14	渴望；熱望	_____	28	能夠……	_____
15	向……致敬	_____	29	有所成就	_____
			30	的確	_____

🎧 40

1. When we speak and write, we express our _____ in sentences. A sentence has both a subject and a _____. The subject is often a noun or noun _____ while the predicate includes the verb and any other words in the _____.

2. There are four _____ _____ sentences. The most common sentence is the _____ sentence. A declarative sentence is a sentence that makes a _____ about something. It always ends with a _____ (.). An _____ sentence is a question. It always ends with a _____ _____ (?). An _____ sentence is a sentence that expresses a strong emotion. It always ends with an _____ _____ (!). An _____ sentence is an order. The subject of an imperative sentence is "you," but "you" is _____. In other words, _____ _____ _____ or write "you" in an imperative sentence. An imperative sentence may _____ _____ a period or an exclamation point. Look at the _____ sentences:

Declarative Sentences:	The sun is _____.	My brother likes music.
Interrogative Sentences:	What's that?	Where are you going?
Exclamatory Sentences:	That's _____!	What a beautiful day!
Imperative Sentences:	Open the door.	_____ _____!

3. Many times, we speak and write with _____ sentences. A simple sentence contains one _____ clause. A _____ is a sentence with a subject and a predicate. An independent clause is a clause that can express a complete thought and _____ _____ as a sentence. It has both a _____ and a predicate.

4. Sometimes, we _____ two independent clauses by using _____ such as *and*, *but*, *so*, and *or*. This creates a _____ sentence. A compound sentence is a sentence with two or more independent _____.

5. Other times, we combine an independent clause and a _____ clause, also called a _____ _____. A dependent clause cannot express a complete thought and cannot _____ as a sentence by itself. It must be _____ _____ an independent clause with a _____ conjunction such as *because, since, if, even though*, and *although*. This creates a _____ sentence. A complex sentence has one independent clause and _____ _____ one dependent clause. _____ _____ the following sentences:

Simple Sentence:	The dog is _____ the cat.
Compound Sentence:	I like pizza, but my sister does not like it.
Complex Sentence:	If you go to _____ _____ with me, we will have fun.

6. We also use different _____ when we speak and write. We use the _____ _____ to say what the subject does. We use the _____ _____ to say what happens to the subject. Look at the following sentences:

Active Voice:	David lives in a house.
	They _____ the piano every day.
Passive Voice:	That hotel was _____ _____ Mr. Jones.
	I was _____ _____ the answer.

B Complete each sentence with the correct word. Change the form if necessary.

> interrogative   conjunction   declarative   complex sentence   dependent clause

1 A _____ sentence is a sentence that makes a statement about something.

2 An _____ sentence is a question.

3 Sometimes, we combine two independent clauses by using _____ such as *and*, *but*, *so*, and *or*.

4 A _____ _____ cannot express a complete thought and cannot function as a sentence by itself.

5 A _____ _____ has one independent clause and at least one dependent clause.

C Write the meaning of each word and phrase from Word List in English.

1 主詞　_____

2 述語　_____

3 直述句　_____

4 陳述事實　_____

5 以……結尾　_____

6 疑問句　_____

7 問號　_____

8 感嘆句　_____

9 驚嘆號　_____

10 祈使句　_____

11 被省略　_____

12 換句話說　_____

13 不可思議的　_____

14 簡單句　_____

15 獨立子句　_____

16 子句　_____

17 獨立存在　_____

18 連接詞　_____

19 並列句　_____

20 非獨立子句　_____

21 附屬子句　_____

22 起作用　_____

23 靠自己　_____

24 和……連接　_____

25 從屬連接詞　_____

26 複合句　_____

27 主動語氣　_____

28 被動語氣　_____

20 From Baroque Art to Pop Art

Art Movements

🎧 41

A Listen to the passage and fill in the blanks.

1 After the Renaissance, a period _____ the "rebirth" of the classical world, there have been many _____ _____ that have had their own unique characteristics.

2 One of the first art movements to follow the _____ was Baroque Art. This was not just an art movement, but it also influenced _____, music, and literature. The _____ Period lasted from around 1600 to 1750. Some of the major _____ in this period were Caravaggio, Rembrandt, and Rubens. Compared with the _____ of the Renaissance, Baroque Art is _____ _____ the dramatic contrast of light and shadow as well as vivid emotional expressions. Baroque Art often _____ an emotional and dramatic feeling in the viewer.

3 A period that _____ as the Baroque Period was ending was the Rococo Period. It started in France around _____. Rococo Art is characterized by its decorative and _____ look that uses delicate _____ colors. The Swing, by Jean-Honoré Fragonard, and The Pleasures of Life, by Jean-Antoine Watteau, are good examples of the _____ _____.

4 However, in the late eighteenth and nineteenth _____, many artists started to _____ _____ from the dramatic Baroque and _____ Rococo styles. The ideas of the Enlightenment, with its _____ on reason, swept over Europe and affected the visual arts. Eventually, it _____ _____ a new style of art called the Neoclassical Movement. _____ lasted from the middle of the eighteenth century to the early nineteenth century. The artists in this period _____ classical forms from ancient Greece and Rome _____ _____ the artists of the Renaissance had done. Jacques-Louis David, a French _____, is a famous artist from this _____.

5 During the late eighteenth century, the Romantic Movement, or _____, began. During this period, artists had an interest in _____ _____ and focused on both emotion and _____. They turned away from the _____ style of Neoclassicism. Blake, Delacroix, and Goya are some of the _____ artists from this period.

6 Romanticism later gave way to _____, which dominated art from around 1850 to 1890. Artists like Jean Millet and Gustave Courbet tried to _____ their subjects _____ as they saw them. They _____ especially on everyday scenes and lives of poor _____ people.

7 Realism was _____ by Modern Art. In Modern Art, there have been many _____ movements. One of the most important was _____. This was an _____ form of art, so the artists did not paint their subjects exactly as they looked. Monet, Manet, Van Gogh, and Cézanne were all _____. Later, artists such as Picasso painted in the _____ style. The objects in their paintings were made in the shapes of _____ figures. In the twentieth century, _____ and Pop Art were two more _____ art movements. Andy Warhol was the most famous member of the _____ _____ Movement.

Complete each sentence with the correct word. Change the form if necessary.

| Dadaism | art movement | Rococo | Impressionist | Realism |

1 After the Renaissance, there have been many _____ _____ that have had their own unique characteristics.

2 A period that emerged as the Baroque Period was ending was the _____ Movement.

3 _____ focused especially on everyday scenes and lives of poor ordinary people.

4 Monet, Manet, Van Gogh, and Cézanne were all _____.

5 In the twentieth century, _____ and Pop Art were two more well-known art movements.

C Write the meaning of each word and phrase from Word List in English.

1 藝術運動	_____	20 俗艷的	_____
2 獨特的	_____	21 對⋯⋯的重視	_____
3 巴洛克藝術	_____	22 造成⋯⋯	_____
4 建築	_____	23 新古典主義運動	_____
5 和⋯⋯比較	_____	24 新古典主義	_____
6 古典主義	_____	25 復興；復甦	_____
7 具有⋯⋯的特徵	_____	26 浪漫主義運動	_____
8 戲劇性的	_____	27 浪漫主義	_____
9 和⋯⋯的對比	_____	28 想像力	_____
10 活潑的；鮮明的	_____	29 制式的；規矩的	_____
11 情感表達	_____	30 讓位給⋯⋯	_____
12 喚起	_____	31 寫實主義	_____
13 興起	_____	32 被⋯⋯取代	_____
14 洛可可時期	_____	33 印象派	_____
15 裝飾的	_____	34 抽象的	_____
16 輕快的	_____	35 印象派畫家	_____
17 精緻的	_____	36 立體派藝術家	_____
18 柔和、淡雅的顏色	_____	37 達達主義	_____
19 背棄⋯⋯；厭惡⋯⋯	_____	38 普普藝術	_____

21 The Music of the Middle Ages
Gregorian Chants and Polyphonic Music

🎧 42

A Listen to the passage and fill in the blanks.

1. The Middle Ages lasted from around 500 to _____. During this time, the Church had a _____ influence on society. Many young men wanted to _____ the Church, so a lot of them entered _____. The men who lived in these monasteries were called _____. The monks' lives were very _____. They spent much of the day reading the Bible, _____, or working. Many people believe that life in a monastery was _____. But the monks also had time to _____ their days by singing.

2. However, the singing that _____ monks did was not like modern-day singing. Instead, the monks _____. Their songs were called _____ _____ after Pope Gregory the Great.

3. Gregorian Chants were typically _____ from the Bible or other _____ books. The songs were _____ in Latin, so they sound _____ to modern people. In addition, the monks did not have any musical instruments to _____ them. They _____ sang. This kind of music is called ____ _____. The individual voices of the monks sounded _____. However, they _____ together and harmonized. In fact, monks in _____ all around the world still sing Gregorian Chants today.

4. After the _____ _____, the Renaissance began. During the Renaissance, _____ _____ gained popularity. *Polyphony* means "many voices" _____ _____. This was _____ Gregorian Chants. When the monks chanted, their voices all had the same tone or _____. In polyphonic music, however, different voices sing different _____ or even different words at the same time.

5. A _____ is one type of polyphonic music. In this style, one _____ begins singing. After some time, another voice _____ and sings the same melody but at either a higher or _____ _____. Throughout the melody, more voices join in as each person sings in a _____ different way.

6. A _____ is another type of _____ music. As the name _____, this is a song that goes around in a circle. In a round, everyone sings the same melody and the same _____. However, each person starts singing at _____ _____ _____. For instance, the first person _____ to sing. Once that person _____ the first line, another person starts from the beginning. When that person completes the first line, a third person _____ _____. As a result, all of the voices _____ with one another, yet they still harmonize. *Dona Nobis Pacem*—"give us peace"—was a _____ round from the Renaissance. The only three words in the _____ are *dona*, *nobis*, and *pacem*. Today, *Frère Jacques—Are You Sleeping?—* and *Row, Row, _____ Your Boat* are two common rounds that people still _____.

B Complete each sentence with the correct word. Change the form if necessary.

polyphonic monk round word Gregorian Chant

1 _____ _____ were typically verses from the Bible or other religious books.

2 When the _____ chanted, their voices all had the same tone or inflection.

3 During the Renaissance, _____ music gained popularity.

4 In polyphonic music, different voices sing different melodies or even different _____ at the same time.

5 In a _____, everyone sings the same melody and the same words.

C Write the meaning of each word and phrase from Word List in English.

1 中世紀 _____

2 極度的；巨大的 _____

3 修道院 _____

4 修道士 _____

5 有組織的 _____

6 枯燥的 _____

7 使活躍 _____

8 中世紀的 _____

9 吟唱；吟誦 _____

10 格雷果聖歌 _____

11 教宗格雷果 _____

12 （《聖經》的）經節；詩句 _____

13 以拉丁文呈現 _____

14 不熟悉的 _____

15 為……伴奏 _____

16 阿卡貝拉（無伴奏合唱）_____

17 單調的 _____

18 和諧 _____

19 多聲部合唱 _____

20 受到歡迎 _____

21 語調抑揚變化 _____

22 卡農 _____

23 稍微地 _____

24 輪唱 _____

25 暗示 _____

26 重疊 _____

Answer Key

Daily Test 01

B 1 Ice Age 2 three-age 3 fertile soil
4 copper 5 Iron Age

Daily Test 02

B 1 Mesopotamia 2 irrigate 3 Sumerians
4 united 5 peak of

Daily Test 03

B 1 Indus Valley 2 organized
3 take advantage 4 Ganges River
5 combined

Daily Test 04

B 1 depended on 2 independent
3 Peloponnesian War 4 monarchy
5 Persian

Daily Test 05

B 1 peninsula 2 representatives
3 Punic Wars 4 triumvirate 5 Byzantium

Daily Test 06

B 1 Arabian Peninsula 2 Muhammad
3 Five Pillars 4 successor 5 Crusade

Daily Test 07

B 1 Middle Ages 2 Black Death
3 movable type 4 corrupt
5 Christian sects

Daily Test 08

B 1 Enlightenment 2 revolution
3 influenced 4 Estates General 5 slogan

Daily Test 09

B 1 cell 2 take place 3 mitosis
4 Dominant 5 overshadowed

Daily Test 10

B 1 Tides 2 current 3 continental shelf
4 abyssal plain 5 intertidal zone

Daily Test 11

B 1 remains 2 impressions 3 unearthing
4 Index fossils 5 ammonite

Daily Test 12

B 1 gravity 2 Gravitation 3 Inertia
4 Acceleration 5 Action, Reaction

Daily Test 13

B 1 comprised 2 wavelengths
3 prism 4 invisible light
5 electromagnetic

Daily Test 14

B 1 revolving 2 locations
3 partial solar eclipse 4 umbra
5 partial lunar eclipse

Daily Test 15

B 1 Noncommunicable 2 communicable
3 immune system 4 lymph nodes
5 vaccine

Daily Test 16

B 1 remainder 2 prime number
3 composite number 4 raised number
5 perfect square

Daily Test 17

B 1 line segment 2 two-dimensional
3 infinite 4 solid figures 5 vertices

Daily Test 18

B 1 sculptor 2 captivated by 3 Aphrodite
4 made a wish 5 Pygmalion effect

Daily Test 19

B 1 declarative 2 interrogative
3 conjunctions 4 dependent clause
5 complex sentence

Daily Test 20

B 1 art movements 2 Rococo 3 Realism
4 Impressionists 5 Dadaism

Daily Test 21

B 1 Gregorian Chants 2 monks
3 polyphonic 4 words 5 round

❗ 在上述用法的情況下，現在進行式常搭配副詞或時間用語，例如：

now or right now ｜ at the moment ｜ at present

現在進行式還可用在以下情況：

❸ 已經開始但尚未結束的行為，即使在講話當下還沒發生也沒關係：
- She's taking a course in business and administration.

❹ 暫時性的活動，有別於例常行為的事：
- I'm working at the school cafeteria this month.

❺ 屢次出現、讓講者很受不了的動作：
- He's always playing video games and not doing anything else and that annoys me.

❻ 在不久的將來安排好的事：
- We're leaving tomorrow at 5 p.m.

❗ 表達將於**未來進行**的事項時，現在進行式通常會搭配：

❶ 副詞和時間用語，例如：
tonight ｜ tomorrow ｜ next week/month/summer

❷ 確切時間點，如：tomorrow at four o'clock。

9 請配對每個句子和用法。

1 We're meeting the counselor tomorrow morning at ten.

2 Two people are walking in the rain. They're holding a big umbrella.

3 Mark is attending a painting course this term.

4 Sorry, Fran. I'm driving. I'll call you back later.

5 This week Rebecca is standing in for a colleague in the new office in Marlowe Road.

6 He's always looking at his cell phone, even when we're having lunch together.

A Speaking on the phone

B Speaking about a temporary activity, different to what we usually do

C Describing a picture

D Talking about an annoying action

E Talking about an action in progress at this time

F Talking about a definite arrangement in the near future

1 .....　**2** .....　**3** .....　**4** .....　**5** .....　**6** .....

10 請使用以下單字來完成句子。

tonight　right　these　next　tomorrow　this　always　nowadays

1 Laura is .... chatting with Ann during the lessons. It's so annoying.

2 "Are you going to the movies ....?" "Yes, we're meeting at 8:30 p.m. outside the movies."

3 We're really working hard .... days.

4 They're spending their vacations in Spain .... summer.

5 I'm going out .... now. Can you call me later?

6 Alice is only working in the mornings .... week, so she's free in the afternoons.

7 Technology is changing rapidly ....

8 Our friends are leaving for Sardinia ....

11 偵探正在觀察飯店大廳的訪客,希望能找到嫌犯。請運用以下動詞搭配正確時態來完成他的思路。

sit	talk	wait	drink	hail
carry	run	not walk	walk	

So . . . someone tall . . . Look at that man near the elevator. He's tall. He [1]........................ probably .... for someone, maybe the elegant lady who [2]........................... to the receptionist. Could he be the thief? But there's another tall man. He [3]........................... in that armchair and [4]........................... a cup of tea. He looks like a businessman, but who knows . . . The young man who [5]........................... a heavy suitcase is the porter, but he isn't tall. And who's that lady [6]........................... towards the door? She [7]........................... simply .... She [8]........................... to the door! She seems to be in a hurry. Wait a minute. The message says that a tall person is the thief, not a tall man. She [9]........................... a taxi right now. I must stop her!

LESSON 3 現在進行式 vs. 簡單現在式
Present continuous vs. present simple

簡單現在式用於表達以下事物	現在進行式用於表達以下事物
1 經常重複的習慣行為: I **do** yoga from six to seven on Friday evenings.	**1** 在講話當下發生的行為: I'**m doing** yoga right now.
2 日常例行行為: She usually **wakes** up at seven.	**2** 與例常行為不同的暫時行為: She'**s waking** up at five today because she'**s getting** the 6:15 train to Washington.
3 固定或永久狀態: Ben **is** an architect. He **works** for a big building company.	**3** 暫時的情況: He'**s working** in Dubai this winter. They'**re building** a luxury hotel there.
4 永遠屬實的科學事實: Water **boils** at 100°C.	**4** 現在在發生的行為: The water'**s boiling**. Add the spaghetti, please.

1 請圈出正確的時態。

1 **I'm spending** / **I spend** my holidays in France this year.

2 **Do you collect** / **Are you collecting** ancient coins?

3 **You're always making** / **You make always** a mess when you cook! It's so annoying!

4 Darren **does not go** / **is not going** home this weekend.

5 We **visit** / **are visiting** St. Paul's Cathedral today.

6 They **are usually eating** / **usually eat** a packed lunch.

7 Lily **works** / **is working** for a big company. She's got a permanent job as an assistant manager.

8 David **watches** / **is watching** cartoons now.

2 請以下列動詞的簡單現在式或現在進行式，來完成句子。

cook   read (x2)   cycle   do   drive   shine   set   rain

1 I usually .... historical novels, but I .... a great thriller at the moment.

2 Mom usually .... the cooking, but it's her birthday today, so Dad .... her a special dinner.

3 John generally .... to work, but today it .... a lot, so he .... to the office.

4 The sun always .... on this island.

5 Look! The sun .... behind the mountains. How lovely!

3 請運用括號裡動詞的簡單現在式或現在進行式，來完成對話。

Steve Hello, Helen. Nice to see you!

Helen Hello, Steve. Nice to see you, too!

Steve [1]................ you still .... in that nice little apartment in the town center? (live)

Helen Well, no. I [2]........................ in the country now. (live)

Steve In the country? What [3]........................ there? (you, do)

Helen Well, my husband and I [4]........................ a farm. We [5]........................ crops — wheat, oats, rye — and we have fruit trees. (run, grow)

Steve So you're a farmer now. That's a big change from before, isn't it?

Helen Yes, but this month I [6]........................ in town because we [7]........................ a farm stand near the station. (stay, open)

Steve Great! Are you free tomorrow evening?

Helen Yes, I think so. Why?

Steve You [8]........................ dinner with me and my family so you can tell us everything about your new life! (have)

Helen Okay, Steve, that sounds great! Can I invite my husband, too?

Steve Of course!

行為動詞與狀態動詞

❶ **行為動詞** 如 read、swim、drive 等，可用於 **簡單現在式** 和 **現在進行式**。
- I always **read** in the evenings before I go to sleep.
- We **are reading** Shakespeare's tragedies at school this term.

❷ **狀態動詞**並非表達行為的動詞，所以通常**沒有**現在進行式的用法。包括第 80 頁所列的動詞（Unit 5 Lesson 2），都是類似 **see** 或 **hear** 等生理本能類的感官動詞，通常會搭配情態助動詞 **can**：

- **Can** you **see** those people over there?
- **Can** you **hear** this noise?

❸ 而 **feel** 或 **hope** 等表達感受和情緒的動詞，簡單式和進行式的用法都有：

- I don't **feel** very well.
- **I'm** not feeling very well today.
- I **hope** you like my cake.
- Doctors **are hoping** to find a better cure for cancer.

❹ 有些動詞的意義會因為時態不同而改變。作為**進行式**的時候，具有表達**該行為**的意思；作為**簡單式**的時候，則是表達**心理狀態**的意思：

❶ **think**（表達看法）：I think it's a good idea.
thinking（反思）：I'm thinking about his suggestions.

❷ **enjoy**（喜歡）：We enjoy skiing.
enjoying（自娛、樂在其中）：I'm enjoying this party.

❸ **see**（理解）：I see what you mean.
seeing（要預約時間見到某人）：I'm seeing the dentist tomorrow morning at nine.

❹ **remember**（記得某事）：I remember the house where I lived as a child.
remembering（回想）：We are remembering our early school days.

請圈出正確的用字。

1 I **can't hear / am not hearing** what you're saying. Can you speak more clearly, please?

2 Sarah **enjoys / is enjoying** her vacation in Spain.

3 He **doesn't mind / is not minding** doing the dishes.

4 We **see / are seeing** Dan tomorrow morning to organize our work schedule.

5 **Do you like / Are you liking** this movie?

6 **Do you think / Are you thinking** study tour are a good way to improve your English?

7 Dad **is having / has** a shower right now.

8 Kim **knows / is knowing** everything about her favorite group.

9 **Do you want / Are you wanting** a new mobile phone?

10 **Are you remembering / Do you remember** John? He was at primary school with us.

11 **I enjoy / I'm enjoying** swimming in the sea, but I don't like swimming in a pool.

12 "What **do you think / are you thinking** about?" "My exam tomorrow. I'm quite anxious."

請運用括號裡動詞的「簡單現在式」或「現在進行式」，來完成對話。

A What ¹.. of? (you, think)

B My old school mates.

A Why?

B Well, ².. Mark Robson? (you, remember)

A No, I ³.. him. (not know)

B Mark is one of my old schoolmates. He ⁴.. in Dubai (live) and we ⁵.. on a new project now after 20 years. (cooperate)

A ⁶..with Edward? (not, usually work)

B Yes, but now he ⁷.. his honeymoon on the French Riviera. (enjoy)

現在式的時態

簡單現在式與現在進行式的用法整理

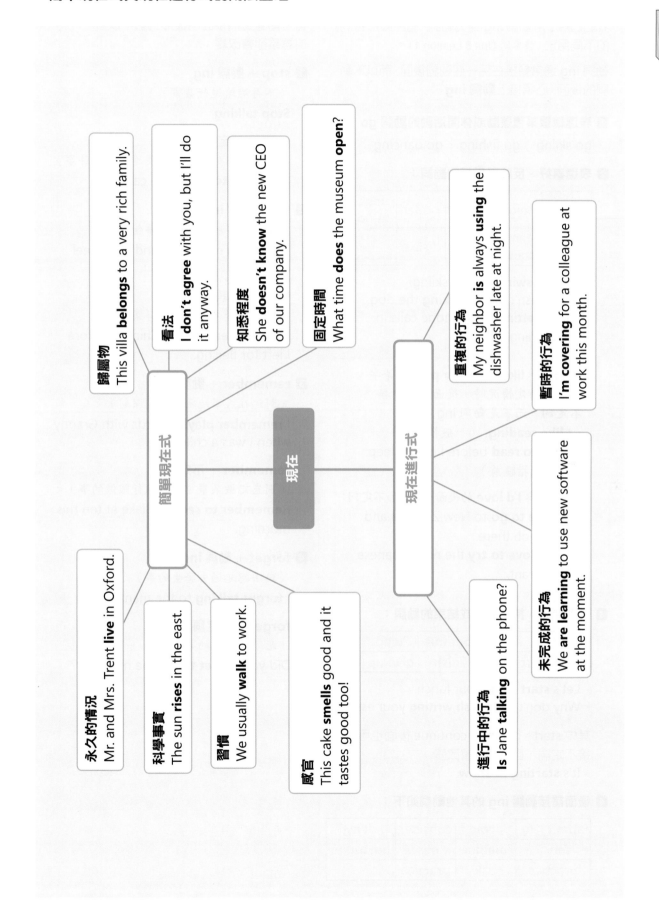

現在

簡單現在式

歸屬物
This villa **belongs** to a very rich family.

看法
I **don't agree** with you, but I'll do it anyway.

知悉程度
She **doesn't know** the new CEO of our company.

固定時間
What time **does** the museum **open**?

永久的情況
Mr. and Mrs. Trent **live** in Oxford.

科學事實
The sun **rises** in the east.

習慣
We usually **walk** to work.

感官
This cake **smells** good and it tastes good too!

現在進行式

重複的行為
My neighbor **is** always **using** the dishwasher late at night.

暫時的行為
I'**m covering** for a colleague at work this month.

未完成的行為
We **are learning** to use new software at the moment.

進行中的行為
Is Jane **talking** on the phone?

LESSON 4 動詞 ing 與不定詞 *V–ing* and verbs + infinitive

我們已經了解動詞 ing 作為動詞、名詞與形容詞的不同用法（請參閱 Unit 6 Lesson 1）。

動詞 ing 通常會接在另一個動詞後面，而以下動詞的後面，必須接上**動詞 ing**：

1 表達練習某種運動或休閒活動的動詞 go：

go skiing | go fishing | go dancing

2 表達喜好、反感與偏好的動詞：

like	enjoy	love	prefer	don't mind
hate	can't stand	loathe	dislike	

- I **prefer swimming** to skiing.
- She doesn't **mind walking** the dog.
- I **hate getting** work phone calls in the evening.

> **!** 像 **love**、**like**、**hate** 和 **prefer** 等字，當論及**特定情況**時，後面通常會接**不定詞**，而不是動詞 ing：
> - I **like reading**.（一般情況下）
> - I **like to read** before I go to sleep.（特別指睡前）
>
> **I'd like** 與 **I'd love** 的後面一定要加**不定詞**：
> - **I'd like to go** to New Zealand and find a job there.
> - **We'd love to try** the new Japanese restaurant.

3 表達開始、持續進行或結束的動詞：

begin	start	continue	keep	stop
keep on	go on	finish	give up	

- Let's **start eating** our lunch.
- Why don't you **finish writing** your essay?

其中 start、begin 和 continue 後面也可以接不定詞，且意義不會改變：
- It's **starting to snow**.

4 後面需接動詞 ing 的其他動詞如下：

admit (to)	avoid	consider	deny
fancy	imagine	miss	postpone
practice	risk	practice	

有些動詞雖然後面兩種形式都可以接，但意義卻會改變：

1 stop + 動詞 ing
（不再繼續進行某事）：
Stop talking.

stop + 不定詞
（停止原本的活動，以便進行另一件事）：
Let's **stop to fill up** the car.

2 try + 動詞 ing
（第一次實驗、嘗試某事物）：
Try eating more fruit and you'll feel better.

try + 不定詞
（試圖或努力進行或獲得某事物）：
I **tried to learn** some Chinese before I left for Beijing.

3 remember + 動詞 ing
（對過往人事地物的記憶深刻）：
I **remember playing** cards with Granny when I was a child.

remember + 不定詞
（別忘記做某事、實際執行該做的事）：
Remember to see Mr. Blake at ten this morning.

4 forget + 動詞 ing
（無法想起過去發生的事）：
I **forgot talking** to the manager.

forget + 不定詞
（忘了做該做的事）：
Did you **forget to see** the manager?

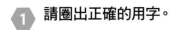

1 請圈出正確的用字。

1 We'd like **to eat** / **eating** out from time to time.
2 Try to give up **smoking** / **to smoke**. You'll feel much better.
3 Avoid **getting** / **to get** into trouble this year!
4 Please, go on **to talk** / **talking** about the history of this town. It's interesting.
5 Can't you consider **moving** / **to move** to another country?
6 They tried **eating** / **to eat** chicken feet when they were in China!
7 Do you miss **to work** / **working** at the bank now that you've retired?
8 I want to stop **having** / **to have** some lunch. I'm so hungry.
9 She admitted to **drive** / **driving** without a license.
10 They don't mind **helping** / **to help** their parents with the dishes.

2 請以「不定詞」或「動詞 ing」來完成句子。

> meet (x2)   drink   have   eat   learn   watch   ski   sing   wash

1 Stop .... so much junk food and you'll feel better.
2 Can't we stop here .... some lunch?
3 I must remember .... Jack at the café after work.
4 I forgot .... Jack yesterday. I should have seen him at three.
5 They hate .... romantic movies.
6 I can't stand .... the dishes.
7 Why don't we go .... in the Alps in December?
8 Try .... some Spanish before your vacation in Ibiza.
9 Please, keep .... , Diana. You have a wonderful voice.
10 Why don't you finish .... your milk?

3 以下每個句子都有一個錯誤。請標出底線，並訂正為正確句子。

1 Keep to work hard and you'll get a promotion.   ....
2 I'd love touring the Australian outback.   ....
3 He denied to steal the gold necklace.   ....
4 I'd like talking to the manager, please.   ....
5 My son always avoids to help with the housework!   ....
6 Don't forget buying some bread for tonight.   ....
7 Do you miss to live in a big city?   ....
8 I always stop buying the newspaper on my way to work.   ....
9 I often fancy to tour Iceland in the summer.   ....
10 Why don't we stop here having breakfast?   ....

4 請以「不定詞」或「動詞 ing」來完成短文。

> wake up   be   tell   say   run (x2)   do   avoid

All of my friends keep [1]........................... me that I have to do some exercise. They say that
I shouldn't be so lazy and I should try [2]........................... early and go [3]........................... . But
I hate [4]........................... , especially in the early morning. I'd like [5]........................... more active, but
I am in my late fifties and I must remember [6]........................... doing too many aerobic activities.
I don't mind [7]........................... some gardening in good weather, but my friends say that watering
the plants is not enough to keep fit. They forget [8]........................... how tiring things such as
weeding the garden or cutting the grass can be.

ROUND UP 6

延伸補充

不定詞的其他用法

我們已經了解表達意願的動詞（want、would like）與其他動詞（decide、hope、try），後面接不定詞（to + 原形動詞）的用法。

不定詞還可用於以下情況：

❶ 表達目的或出發點：
- I went there <u>to meet</u> them.
- I'm going <u>to tell</u> you a story.
- His aim was <u>to earn</u> as much money as possible.

❷ 放 too + 形容詞或形容詞 + enough 後面，表達某事物的結果：
- It's **too cold** <u>to go</u> out.
- I wasn't close **enough** <u>to hear</u> what they said.

❸ 放在 where、how、what 的後面：
- She has no idea **where** <u>to go</u>.
- Do you know **how** <u>to fix</u> this bike?
- He didn't know **what** <u>to say</u>.

❹ 放在 determined、sorry、free、happy、glad、 pleased、sad 等形容詞的後面：
- I'm **sorry** <u>to hear</u> that.
- I'm **determined** <u>to finish</u> this job.
- Feel **free** <u>to call</u> me any time.
- I'm **glad** <u>to be</u> here!

❺ 非人稱的表達方式，例如：
- It's time to . . .
- It's good/nice/great to . . . ,
- It's a good idea to . . . / It's too late to . . .
- It's never too late to . . . / It's important to . . .

❻ 作為句子的主詞或受詞，用法和動詞 ing 雷同：
- <u>To err</u> is human; <u>to forgive</u>, divine. (Alexander Pope)
- I like <u>to paint</u> flowers.

! 在動詞已知或易於理解的情況下，也可以單獨使用 **to**：
- He asked me to join them, but I said I didn't want **to**. （後句可理解為「I didn't want to join him.」）
- "Would you like to go?" "Yes, I'd love **to**!" （後句可理解為「I'd love to go.」）

---

1 請使用以下動詞的「不定詞」形式，來完成句子。

talk	abandon	play	become	find	give
leave	go	get up	see	buy	do

1 He wants .... a job abroad.

2 They were so angry they refused .... to us.

3 They threatened .... the conference.

4 We can't afford .... on vacation this summer.

5 I decided not .... a diesel car.

6 I'm learning .... the guitar.

7 What are you planning .... next weekend?

8 He offered .... me a lift in his new car.

9 They were so sad .... !

10 He's determined .... the mayor.

11 It's seven o'clock. It's time .... !

12 It's nice .... you again.

動詞ing的用法整理

動詞ing

動名詞

1 句子的主詞：
Living alone is not too bad after all.

2 句子的直接受詞：
I love **meeting** up with old friends.

3 句子的間接受詞
（放在介系詞後面）：
She dreams of **going** to live in the USA.
（請參閱 Unit 7 Lesson 4）

現在分詞

1 作為形容詞：
Complete the **following** sentences.

2 替代關係子句：
There are three roads **leading** off the traffic circle.

3 放在動詞後面，表達執行後續動作的方式：
She looked up, **smiling** at you.

4 搭配 **be** 動詞而形成進行式：
The baby is **crying.**

FAQ

Q: 為什麼快上映的電影都會說「coming soon」？

A: 因為大家能意會沒有說出來的部分。這句話的原句應為「The movie is coming soon.」，coming soon 這種現在進行式片語是用來表示「某事預計於不久的將來會發生」。

2 請運用以下動詞 + ing 來完成句子。

> act   cook   rise   smoke   bully   talk   cry   raise   dance

1 She failed the exam and came home ....

2 I hope .... will be banned everywhere! It really harms our health.

3 The syllabus offers .... and .... as optional activities. Lots of students take them.

4 .... is becoming a more and more popular hobby. Lots of TV programs teach you how to make really tasty meal.

5 Cases of depression are .... among young adults.

6 We need to take some kind of action against .... It has become a big problem in our school.

7 They are .... funds for their campaign. They need $50,000.

8 I saw him .... on the phone.

3 強森太太有個從不幫忙家務事的兒子。請閱讀下文，使用括號提示的動詞，以「不定詞」或「動詞 ing」來完成短文。

Mrs. Johnson is a busy woman. She's a nurse and she never stops
[1] .... (work), either in the hospital or in her home. She doesn't
mind [2] .... (cook), but she doesn't like [3] .... (clean)
at all, so she would like her teenage son, David, [4] .... (help) her
sometimes. But David always avoids [5] .... (help) with the cleaning. He stays in his
room and promises [6] .... (help) later, but he never does. To make David help, she has
to threaten [7] .... (stop) his pocket money.
Mrs. Johnson's husband doesn't help much in the house either. He sometimes offers
[8] .... (employ) someone [9] .... (help) with the housework, but she says she
doesn't like to have a stranger in the house. "I can't imagine [10] .... (pay) someone to
do the jobs you boys should be doing," she says.

4 請閱讀以下電子郵件，圈出正確的用字。

Dear Jack,

How are you? I'm on vacation in sunny California. I [1] **am staying / stay** in a great hotel in Santa Barbara. I [2] **am going / go** to the beach every morning and I [3] **lie / am lying** in the sun for hours. I [4] **don't swim / swim not** a lot though, because the water of the ocean is quite cold. But tomorrow I [5] **go / am going** surfing for the first time in my life. I [6] **am looking / look** forward to it. What [7] **do you do / are you doing** in cold and foggy England? [8] **Do you study / Are you studying** hard?

Let me know!

Carol

5 請運用括號裡動詞的「簡單現在式」或「現在進行式」，來完成短文。

Mr. Robson is 55 years old. He ¹............................ (live) in Brentwood and he ²............................ (work) for a big company in the area. He's the sales manager. He ³............................ (get) to work in his car, driving about half an hour. He ⁴............................ (start) work at nine in the morning and usually ⁵............................ (finish) at 5 p.m. Before he ⁶............................ (get) home, he usually ⁷............................ (go) to a pub near his house where he ⁸............................ (meet) his friends every evening. He's married to Sylvia and they have a son, Peter.

Peter is 25 and is unemployed at the moment. He ⁹............................ (look) for a job, but it isn't easy to find a good one. He ¹⁰............................ (stay) at a friend's house in Manhattan at the moment because there are more job opportunities there. He ¹¹............................ (not have) a routine because every day is different. Tomorrow he ¹²............................ (have) an interview at 11 a.m. in the City, so he ¹³............................ (get up) quite late. After the interview, he ¹⁴............................ (go) to eat in a Thai restaurant in the area with a couple of friends. He isn't married, but he ¹⁵............................ (date) a girl called Jennifer. This weekend they ¹⁶............................ (go back) to Brentwood because he ¹⁷............................ (want) to introduce Jennifer to his parents.

6 請分析以下句子來判斷動詞 ing 的用法。如為現在分詞，請寫 **PP**；如為動名詞，請寫 **G**。

.... **1** Playing rugby has become more popular in our country.
.... **2** After doing the housework, Sheila often goes out for a coffee with her friends.
.... **3** There are a few people sitting in the waiting room.
.... **4** They aren't walking home. They are taking the bus.
.... **5** Please answer the following questions.
.... **6** Jane entertained the guests, speaking about her journeys around Africa.

Reflecting on grammar

請研讀文法規則，再判斷以下說法是否正確。

		True	False
1	動詞 try 的 ing 形式是 trying。		
2	動詞 ing 具有名詞、現在分詞或動名詞的用法。		
3	現在進行式是以助動詞 have + 主動詞 ing 所構成。		
4	現在進行式用於表達日常例行行為。		
5	已經預計在將來執行的某行為／事物，可以用現在進行式來表達。		
6	我們通常以簡單現在式表達暫時的行為。		
7	簡單現在式用以表達宇宙或科學方面的真理法則。		
8	狀態動詞通常沒有進行式的用法。		
9	love、like 和 hate 的後面永遠不能接不定詞		
10	「I miss talking to you.」是正確句子。		

Revision and Exams 2 (UNITS 4 – 5 – 6)

1 請運用以下動詞，搭配第二人稱單數祈使句來完成短文。

ride admire discover not forget observe rent finish

Greece
The Thessaloniki Waterlands

¹............................. the beautiful waterlands of Thessaloniki, just a few kilometers away from the city center. Start from Chalastra and go along the Coastal Bank up to the Lighthouse of the Axios Delta. ²............................. a bike and ³............................. the beautiful rice fields which are everywhere. ⁴............................. by the salt marshes and ⁵............................. the rare species of birds you can see. ⁶............................. your trip at the Lighthouse of the naval Army of the Thermalikos Gulf and ⁷............................. to try the local food along the way!

2 請運用以下動詞，搭配肯定或否定祈使句，來完成公告內容。

take keep use put remember leave smoke forget

Park Rules

- ¹........................... our park clean!
- ²........................... plastic bags on the ground after picnics. ³...........................! They take ten to twenty years to decompose.
- ⁴........................... recyclable containers and ⁵........................... them home with you.
- ⁶........................... your food leftovers into the special bins for organic materials. We use them to fertilize the soil.
- ⁷........................... in the park. ⁸........................... that cigarette butts take up to five years to decompose!

3 請運用括號裡動詞的「簡單現在式」、「現在進行式」或「祈使句」，來完成對話。

Teacher [1].......................... a few problems with your grammar, Kate? (have)

Kate Yes, I [2].......................... making the same mistakes. I never [3]..........................
the rules. (keep, remember)

Teacher When you [4].......................... a new rule, [5].......................... some sentences with it.
[6].......................... about yourself: This [7].......................... you to remember it better.
(learn, write, write, help)

Kate Okay. I [8].......................... that now. I [9].......................... sentences with the imperative,
the present simple and the present continuous. I [10].......................... about my habits
and about what I [11].......................... on weekends. (try, write, talk, do)

Teacher You see, you [12].......................... the tenses correctly now because you
[13].......................... interested in what you [14].......................... . (use, be, say) Well done!

4 派翠西亞（**Patricia**）和瑪麗文（**Marion**）在不同場所從事相同工作，請閱讀相關短文，
並使用下列動詞的「簡單現在式」來完成

| work | live | send | organize | sleep | do | pass | start | have | go **(x2)** | meet |

Patricia lives in London, and Marion [1].......................... in Chicago.
They [2].......................... from their homes for the same firm,
an Italian shoe manufacturing company. They [3]..........................
the orders, [4].......................... the invoices and [5]..........................
shipments for the European and American markets.
They often [6].......................... the same things but not at the same
moment. Local time in London is six hours ahead of Chicago, so
when Patricia [7].......................... work in London in the morning,
it's night in Chicago and Marion [8]..........................

When Patricia [9].......................... lunch, Marion starts work
In Chicago. In the afternoon London time, which is morning in
Chicago, they are both on their computers and sometimes they have video conferences. And
when Patricia [10].......................... to bed, Marion is sometimes still on her computer or has just
finished working. Patricia and Marion
[11].......................... once a year, in June, when they [12].......................... to Italy for the
annual conference at their company's headquarters.

5 請再閱讀一次第 **4** 大題的短文，並運用括號裡動詞的「現在進行式」，寫出兩人在不同時段所做的事。

1 It's seven o'clock London time. Patricia .... while Marion .... still .... (get up / sleep)

2 It's 1:30 p.m. London time. Patricia .... lunch while Marion .... work. (have / start)

3 It's four o'clock London time. Patricia and Marion .... both .... Patricia .... some invoices and Marion .... a big shipment to San Diego, California. (work / pass / organize)

4 It's five o'clock London time. Today they .... a video conference. (have)

5 It's 11 p.m. London time. Patricia .... to bed, while Marion .... still .... on the latest orders (go / work).

6 This year, Patricia and Marion .... on June 9th at the company's headquarters in Milan. They .... forward to it! (meet / look)

6 下方是倫敦維多利亞與艾伯特博物館的部分導覽手冊內容。請運用括號裡動詞的「簡單現在式」、「現在進行式」或「祈使句」，來完成短文。

The Victoria and Albert Museum is the world's leading museum of art and design. Its collections [1] .... (span) two thousand years of art in virtually every medium, from every part of the world. Besides the permanent collections on show, the museum [2] .... (offer) a number of temporary exhibitions on every aspect of applied arts. Presently, you can visit a very interesting exhibition about footwear and another one about Indian jewelry. The V&A is also a very active educational center. It [3] .... (offer) courses, workshops and evening events, as well as free tours and lesson-planning resources for schools and colleges.

On one of the current courses, professional goldsmiths [4] .... (teach) how to make jewelry. If you are interested, [5] .... (enroll) now because the course will only last till the end of March.

The museum [6] .... (open) at 10 a.m. and [7] .... (close) at 5:45 p.m. with a late evening on Fridays till 10 p.m.

As they [8] .... (carry out) repairs at the main entrance this month, the main information desk is closed. Also the Members Desk [9] .... (be) located in Room 50 in this period.

[10] .... (visit) the V&A website for any information you need.

7 這是你的網友傳給你的部分電子郵件內容。

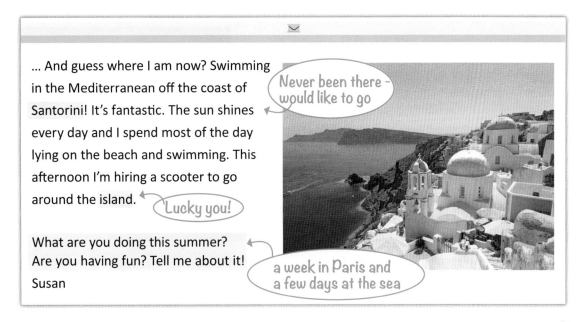

... And guess where I am now? Swimming in the Mediterranean off the coast of Santorini! It's fantastic. The sun shines every day and I spend most of the day lying on the beach and swimming. This afternoon I'm hiring a scooter to go around the island.

Never been there – would like to go

Lucky you!

What are you doing this summer? Are you having fun? Tell me about it!
Susan

a week in Paris and a few days at the sea

請以大約一百字的篇幅，回信答覆你朋友的問題。

8 閱讀下方短文，使用最貼切的單字來完成本篇克漏字。每一格僅能填入一個單字，可參考短文第 **0** 格的示範。

0 ....Do........... you know what most European teenagers have in common? They all own a smartphone. They use it for a number of purposes, 1 .... they hardly ever make phone calls. They chat with friends on social networks, surf the Internet, 2 .... photos, and make selfies.

Teenagers don't have many technological gadgets now 3 .... they use their smartphones for everything. They 4 .... write many text messages either because they are always connected via their 4G or 5G Internet connection.

Thirty-five percent of European teenagers also own a tablet and study or 5 ....
homework with it. But when they write a lot, they still prefer using a computer with a keyboard 6 .... it is much easier.

Only about 20 percent of teenagers own a digital camera; they are amateur photographers, 7 .... they want to have the best equipment possible.

When it comes to playing video games, nearly 90 percent declare they have a console 8 .... 50 percent of them also play video games on their computers.

Towards Competences

你所居住地區的當地觀光局要求你準備一份該區簡介手冊。內容必須說明一日遊行程，包括主要景點以及特色小吃。別忘了行程表裡也要寫出起迄時間、行程地圖和主要景點的照片。

可使用右圖所示的範本，並參考第 106 頁第 1 大題的介紹格式。

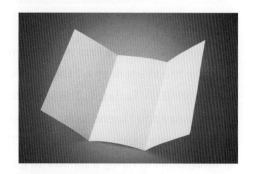

Self Check 2

請選出答案，再至解答頁核對正確與否。

1 What .... for breakfast?
  Ⓐ have you usually got
  Ⓑ do you usually have
  Ⓒ have you usually

2 Tom and Sheila .... a nice cottage in the country.
  Ⓐ has got   Ⓑ have   Ⓒ 've got

3 Sonia .... a snack in the afternoon.
  Ⓐ don't have
  Ⓑ hasn't got
  Ⓒ doesn't have

4 "Do you have a cat?" "Yes, ..."
  Ⓐ I do   Ⓑ I've got   Ⓒ I've

5 I .... right. This is not Baileys & Co's invoice.
  Ⓐ do   Ⓑ am   Ⓒ do

6 "......... hungry?" "No, not really."
  Ⓐ Are you   Ⓑ Have you
  Ⓒ Do you have

7 "Whose bag is this?" "It's ...."
  Ⓐ my   Ⓑ mine   Ⓒ the mine

8 "Is that Mike's cell phone?" "No, it isn't ...."
  Ⓐ his   Ⓑ his's   Ⓒ hers

9 These are .... bicycles.
  Ⓐ the children's   Ⓑ the childrens'
  Ⓒ the children

10 I'll have .... next month.
  Ⓐ a holiday of week
  Ⓑ a weeks' holiday
  Ⓒ a week's holiday

11 .... is coming to New York next week.
  Ⓐ One Daniel's friend
  Ⓑ One of Daniel's friends
  Ⓒ One friend of Daniel

12 Carol Sheer is the new sales manager. .... office is on the top floor.
  Ⓐ She's   Ⓑ Hers   Ⓒ Her

13 .... are on my desk.
  Ⓐ Some your documents
  Ⓑ Some of your documents
  Ⓒ Some of the your documents

14 .... some salad. It's good for you.
  Ⓐ You have   Ⓑ Have you   Ⓒ Have

15 .... go out now. It's too hot!
  Ⓐ Don't let's   Ⓑ Let's not   Ⓒ Let not

16 Gloria and I always .... to work every day to keep fit.
  Ⓐ cycles   Ⓑ are cycling   Ⓒ cycle

17 .... the late show start at 10 p.m.?
  Ⓐ Does   Ⓑ Is   Ⓒ Do

18 .... a break in the afternoon.
  Ⓐ We haven't often got
  Ⓑ We don't have often
  Ⓒ We don't often have

19 Where .... your shoes?

Ⓐ do you buy usually

Ⓑ do you usually buy

Ⓒ you usually buy

20 .... skiing in winter?

Ⓐ Are you usually going

Ⓑ Do you go usually

Ⓒ Do you usually go

21 "How often .... your emails?"

"Once a day."

Ⓐ do you check   Ⓑ are you checking

Ⓒ check you

22 Stop! The sign says "......... entry." We can't drive in there.

Ⓐ Don't   Ⓑ No   Ⓒ Mustn't

23 Luke and I are going shopping. Do you want to come with ....?

Ⓐ me   Ⓑ our   Ⓒ us

24 Ruth wants to try paragliding .... she is going to the mountains this weekend.

Ⓐ because   Ⓑ so   Ⓒ but

25 I love .... in the sun on the beach.

Ⓐ lying   Ⓑ lieying   Ⓒ lieing

26 Most of my friends are constantly .... their smartphones when we are in a restaurant together. It's so annoying!

Ⓐ checking   Ⓑ check   Ⓒ checked

27 Why .... so loud? I'm not deaf.

Ⓐ do you talk   Ⓑ are you talking

Ⓒ don't you talk

28 Water .... at 0°C.

Ⓐ freezes   Ⓑ is always freezing

Ⓒ freeze

29 Start .... without me. I'll be home late from work today.

Ⓐ eat   Ⓑ to eating   Ⓒ eating

30 I'm here .... the Personnel Manager. I have an appointment at ten.

Ⓐ meeting   Ⓑ for meet   Ⓒ to meet

31 We have no idea what .... tonight. Any suggestions?

Ⓐ doing   Ⓑ to do   Ⓒ do

32 "Do you fancy .... to the swimming pool this afternoon?" "Yes, good idea."

Ⓐ going   Ⓑ to go   Ⓒ go

33 We .... at home in the winter.

Ⓐ are often staying   Ⓑ often stay

Ⓒ stay often

34 "Are you free tomorrow afternoon?" "No, it's Friday and .... yoga on Friday afternoons."

Ⓐ I always do   Ⓑ I'm always doing

Ⓒ I'm always having

35 "What's that noise? .... video games?" "Yes, as usual."

Ⓐ Do the kids play

Ⓑ Don't the kids play

Ⓒ Are the kids playing

36 "......... sleep in on Sundays ?" "No, my mom always gets up before eight."

Ⓐ Do you all

Ⓑ Have you all got

Ⓒ Are you all having

37 She .... dancing.

Ⓐ don't like   Ⓑ doesn't likes

Ⓒ doesn't like

38 .... to music is so relaxing!

Ⓐ Listen   Ⓑ Listening   Ⓒ To listening

39 "Let's play squash tomorrow evening." "No, I don't want .... Let's go for a walk and relax."

Ⓐ it   Ⓑ playing   Ⓒ to

40 We're all so happy .... you here again.

Ⓐ seeing   Ⓑ to see   Ⓒ for seeing

Assess yourself!

☐ 0 - 10   還要多加用功。

☐ 11 - 20   尚可。

☐ 21 - 30   不錯。

☐ 31 - 40   非常好！

LESSON 1 表達時間的介系詞 Prepositions of time

固定時間	一段期間	開始~結束	開始	結束	之前／之後
at on in	over for during between . . . and	from . . . to	since	until till in within by	before after

介系詞 in、on、at 均放在用以表達固定時間的受詞前面：

"When?" "**In** December. / **On** Monday."

"**At** what time?" "**At** three o'clock."

❶ in 具以下功能：

  ❶ 表達年分：

    in 2015 | **in** the year 34 BC

  ❷ 表達世紀：**in** the 20th/21st century

  ❸ 表達季節：**in** winter | **in** the summer

  ❹ 表達月分：**in** January | **in** March

  ❺ 表達一天之中的某時段：

    in the morning | **in** the afternoon |
    in the evening | **in** the middle of
    the day

❷ on 具以下功能：

  ❶ 表達星期幾：**on** Monday | **on** Sunday

    （包括：on Monday morning/afternoon...）

  ❷ 表達日期：

    on June 7th | **on** December 9th, 2016

  ❸ 表達特殊日子：

    on my birthday | **on** Christmas Day

  ❹ 一天之中的某時段，前面如有形容詞，
    就要使用 on：

    on a cold morning | **on** a dark rainy night

❸ at 具以下功能：

  ❶ 表達時間：

    at eight o'clock | **at** half past ten |
    at lunchtime | **at** dinnertime

  ❷ 表達會延續幾天的假期：**at** Christmas

  ❸ 表達一天中的某時段：

    at night | **at** dawn | **at** sunset

❶ 請圈出正確的用字。

1 The Industrial Revolution started **in** / **on** the 18th century.

2 I often read **in the** / **at** night. The house is so quiet then.

3 I like having a lie-in **on** / **in** cold rainy mornings.

4 Do they often go for a walk **at** / **in the** afternoon?

5 **In** / **At** summer, we often wake up **at** / **on** dawn and go running in the park.

6 Why don't we meet **on** / **at** lunchtime?

7 We generally stay at home **in** / **on** the weekend and relax in our garden.

8 I love sitting on the beach **at** / **on** sunset watching the seagulls.

❷ 請填入正確的介系詞來完成句子。

1 The exams start ...... June 18th this year.

2 We usually go on a skiing holiday ...... Christmas.

3 My sister's birthday's ...... April 4th.

4 Naomi was born ...... the year 2000.

5 They sometimes go to Spain ...... summer.

6 I often play video games ...... the evening.

7 Shall we meet ...... four o'clock at my house?

8 Where are you going ...... New Year's Day?

9 Are you meeting Mrs. Ferns ...... Monday?

10 I don't like getting up early ...... the morning.

11 Mozart was born ...... the 18th century in Salzburg, Austria.

12 I was born ...... the summer — my birthday is ...... July.

4 **for** 用以表達時間的長短："How long did you walk **for**?" "We walked **for** two hours."
但請注意以下用法："How long have you been walking?" "We've been walking for two hours."
→ 因為是仍在進行中的行為，所以會使用現在完成式（請參閱 Unit 9 Lesson 3）

5 **during/over** 和 **between . . . and . . .**
用以表達經歷的一段時間：
- **during** the day/night/week
- **over** the weekend
- **between** the 3rd and the 5th of August

6 **from . . . to . . .** 表示某行為事件的開始和結束
時間：
- **from** 2 **to** 4 p.m.
- **from** Monday **to** Friday
- **from** 2010 **to** 2013

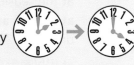

7 **since** 用以表達開始某行為的時間，且行為通常
會延續到現在：
- "How long have you lived in England?"
  "We've lived in England **since** 1999."（因為是
  依然持續到現在的行為，所以使用現在完成式）

8 **until** 或 **till** 用以表達行為結束以前的
時間：I waited **till** dawn.

9 **in** 或 **within**（較正式）用以表達行為
會在某時間範圍內結束：
- I'm coming back **in** a week.
- You have to hand in your project
  within three days.

10 **by** 用以表達必須完成某行為的精準時
間範圍（幾點、哪個日期）：
- Please deliver the goods **by** 16th
  May.

11 **before/after** 表示之前或之後的時間：
- Come back **before** midnight. Don't
  come back **after** midnight.

3 請圈出正確的用字。

1 **In** / **On** July, 2015, we were in Milan **for** / **since** a couple of days to visit Expo.

2 I usually read the newspaper **after** / **within** lunch.

3 "He should be here **in** / **by** an hour or so." "Oh I see. **By** / **Between** five o'clock, then."

4 My son stayed with an American family **from** / **between** January to June last year.

5 I couldn't put this book down. I kept reading it **for** / **since** hours, **until** / **after** I finished it.

6 He sleeps **before** / **during** the day and works **in** / **at** night.

7 Please try to be here **by** / **from** eight o'clock, when we open the shop.

8 Where have you been **over** / **within** the weekend?

9 The goods should arrive **till** / **within** two weeks.

10 I waited **by** / **until** four o'clock but he didn't turn up.

4 請選出正確的介系詞來完成句子。

| from . . . to | since | for | between | by | during | before | in |

1 Have you been working .... long?

2 We're going to have a vacation sometime .... June and August.

3 They work .... Monday .... Thursday and have a long weekend.

4 I never wake up .... the night. I sleep like a log.

5 John has been picking fruit .... seven o'clock this morning. He's dead tired.

6 You have to hand in your essay .... Thursday April 13th at the latest.

7 Mr. Jackson is not here. He'll be back to work .... a week.

8 The theater opens half an hour .... the show.

5 請找出句中的錯誤並訂正。

1 I often study in night. ....
2 Are you free on Monday to five from six? ....
3 What do you usually do at Christmas Day? ....
4 We have to hand in our essays within next Monday. ....
5 We like sleeping until late at Sundays. ....

LESSON 2 表達地點的介系詞 Prepositions of place

表示地點和位置的介系詞

表示地點和位置的介系詞能交代出某物或某人的所在位置，此類介系詞會放在 **be、stay、live、stop、lie、stand、sit、land** 和 **arrive** 等狀態動詞的後面。

此類介系詞主要有：

1 in：此介系詞通常後接定冠詞 **the**，如 in the mountains、in the garden 等；但 in bed、in hospital、in town 等表達方式除外。

in 的意義如下：

① 表示某物或某人在某處裡面：
It's **in** the box.
② 表示某人的居住地：I live **in** Seattle.
③ 表示某地點的地理位置：
Penzance is **in** Cornwall, **in** the southwest of England.

2 at：此介系詞通常後接定冠詞 **the**，如 **at** the seaside、**at** the theater 等，但 **at** home、**at** work、**at** school/college/university 等其他表達方式除外。

at 用以表示某物或某人位在**特定的地理位置**，或是**開放式的露天空間**：
She's **at** the bus stop.

> **!** 我們會以 **at** 表達地址裡的**門牌號碼**：
> I live **at** 25 Brompton Road.
> 但注意是 I live **on** Brompton Road.

3 on：此介系詞用以表示**某物站立或平放在某表面**，或**面朝某物**：
It's **on** the table/lake/coast

4 under/below：表示**較低矮的位置**

5 over/above：表示在**沒有接觸的情況下**，位置高於某物

FAQ

Q: 我聽過有人說「They live on a farm.」，為什麼是用「on」而不是「in」呢？

A: 這裡的 **on** 意指**居住**和**工作地點**都在農場，進行的活動均與此地息息相關。其他例子像是「The students live on a campus.」、「Most Native Americans live on reservations.」。

1 請使用 **on、in、at** 或 **over** 等介系詞來完成句子。

1 The icon of the file you're looking for is .... the desktop.
2 The Statue of Liberty stands .... Liberty Island, ... the entrance of New York harbor.
3 The Hawaiian Islands lie .... the Pacific Ocean.
4 We live .... Pearson Street, ... number 19.
5 Edinburgh castle is .... top of a hill.
6 There's an LED lamp .... my desk and another one .... my bed.
7 We're spending a week's holiday .... the mountains .... Wales.

如需表達某物位置與其他事物或參考點的關係，我們會採用以下介系詞：

1 near / close to / next to / beside（表示彼此相距不遠）

2 far from/off（表示偏遠與相隔兩地）

3 from（表達距離）

4 in front of（在前方，例如排隊的人潮）

5 opposite（面向某物，或在某物對面）

6 behind（在某物的後面）

7 between . . . and（在兩者之間）

8 among（超過兩者以上的人事物之間）

9 around/round（像圈圈一樣，環繞在某物外圍）

10 along（從某物的某端到另一端，通常是指漫長的某物）

11 ahead of（在空間上超前某事物）

2 請使用下方介系詞來完成句子

from next between opposite around off along in front behind among

1 I usually sit .... to my friend Nora in the science class.

2 There are lots of shops .... the main road.

3 The village where I live is not far .... Nottingham.

4 The children are walking in a line, one .... of the other.

5 The Roman wall is all .... the town of York.

6 Great Keppel Island lies .... the coast of Queensland, near the Tropic of Cancer.

7 The travel agency is .... Lloyd's Bank and a restaurant.

8 They're our new neighbors. They've just bought the house .... ours.

9 The photographer made Sara stand .... me in the school photo because she's much taller than me.

10 He wandered .... the other guests at the party, feeling shy as he didn't know anyone.

表示移動性質的介系詞

此類介系詞能表示從某參考點移動、或移動至某參考點的情況。一般會放在 **go**、**come**、**walk**、 **drive**、**cycle**、**return** 或 **come back** 等移動類動詞的後面。

主要的此類介系詞如下：

1 to（某地點移動）：
- We're going <u>to</u> school / the park.
- Have you ever been <u>to</u> France?

❗ **home** 此單字不需搭配介系詞 to：
We're going home.
方位同樣不需搭配介系詞 to：
Go west/north/south/east.

2 into（進入到一個密閉場所或轉進某街道）：
- We're going <u>into</u> the supermarket.
- Turn left <u>into</u> that street.

3 from（從某地點、某起點或源頭開始移動）：
We're coming back <u>from</u> the office.

4 out of（離開）：
Get <u>out of</u> here.

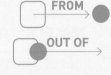

5 away from（兩物相隔）：
Go <u>away from</u> here.

6 past（穿越）：
Go <u>past</u> the flower shop.

7 over（越過）：
He climbed <u>over</u> the wall.

115

FAQ

Q: 哪些介系詞用於搭乘交通工具呢？為什麼 get on the bus 和 get into the car 使用不同的介系詞？

A: **get on** 用於表達搭乘**火車**、**飛機**、**公車**與**兩輪交通工具**，因為我們必須「**往上走**」或跨上此類交通工具。但搭乘房車的時候，是「**坐進去**」密閉空間的動作，因此使用 **get into**。

另一方面，我們從房車下車時，會使用 **get out of** 的說法，從其他交通工具下來則是使用 **get off**，例如「We're getting off the plane just now.」。

其他表示移動性質的介系詞如下：

8 towards（朝向）   TOWARDS →

9 along（沿著）   ALONG

10 across/through（穿過）   ACROSS   THROUGH

11 as far as / up to（到某處前）   AS FAR AS ...   UP TO...

12 up / down（上升 / 下降）   UP↑   ↓DOWN

抵達與離開

1 抵達
get to / arrive at / arrive in（特別用在城鎮）：
- How are you <u>getting to</u> the station?
- He <u>arrived at</u> the airport by taxi.
- They <u>arrived in</u> London yesterday.

2 離開
leave + 直接受詞：
They're <u>leaving the USA</u> tomorrow.
（離開紐約）**NOT** ~~leaving from the USA~~

3 離開當地，前往某處
leave for：
They're <u>leaving for Paris</u> in an hour.
（前往巴黎）

---

3 請圈出正確的用字。

1 Would you like to go **to / into** the office by bus or by subway?

2 Let's get **into / on** this bus. It goes straight **to / at** the station.

3 My brother is going **to / in** France on business.

4 Go **past / over** the drugstore and turn right. The flower shop is on your left.

5 Sam is leaving **for / to** New York in an hour.

6 Are you leaving **from / ---** Edinburgh tomorrow?

7 Let's go for a walk **along / past** the riverbank.

8 Get **out of / off** the bus at the next stop.

4 請使用下方介系詞來完成句子。

out of	from	along	at	up to	into	away from	to	through	for	as far as

1 My friend Ally comes .... Edinburgh.

2 My grandparents arrived .... my house this morning.

3 When are you leaving .... Greece?

4 Let's go for a stroll .... the beach. It's a nice walk.

5 The robbers got .... the house .... the window.

6 Read this survey .... page ten.

7 Move .... that crane. It may be dangerous.

8 This is not your room. Get .... here!

9 Have you ever been .... Scotland for your holidays?

10 Drive .... the next traffic circle.

5 表達地點的介系詞經常用於指引方向。請圈選正確的報路說法。

1 Go **towards** / **down** this road **as far as** / **until** the traffic circle.

2 Turn right **into** / **from** Sutton Lane and take the first **at** / **on** the left.

3 Stop **to** / **at** the traffic lights and go **across** / **along** the square.

4 Get **off** / **out of** the bus **in** / **at** the next stop and walk **along** / **through** the main road.

5 Go **past** / **up** the bank and you'll see the post office **in** / **on** your left.

6 Excuse me. How do I get **at** / **to** the stadium, please?

7 Go **up** / **down** a hundred steps and you'll get a great view **for** / **from** the top.

8 Could you take me **in** / **to** my hotel, please? It's **on** / **into** Fairbank Avenue.

9 Drive **along** / **away** this road and you'll find the hospital at the end, on the right.

10 You should go **towards** / **onto** the station if you want to find a flower shop.

LESSON 3 其他介系詞／有兩個受詞的動詞
Other prepositions; verbs with two objects

以下是引導間接受詞的常見介系詞：

1 **with** + 人物（和）：
I usually walk to school **with** <u>Sara</u>.

with + 方法（用）：
Sign the form **with** <u>a black pen</u>, please.

2 **without**（沒有，**with** 的反義詞）：
I can't see **without** my glasses.

3 **by** + 交通工具（藉由）：
I go to work **by** <u>train/subway/car</u>.
但交通工具是放在所有格的後面：
on my bike / in my mother's car
另外，注意是 on foot/horseback。

by + 被動語態裡當受詞的主事者（由）：
The movie is directed **by** <u>Spielberg</u>.
（請參閱 Unit 17 被動語態的內容）

5 **of** + 材質（從）：
It's made **of** <u>cotton</u>.

of + 指定細節（……的）：
The frame **of** <u>my glasses</u> is light and flexible.
但如果是**某人**持有某物，我們會說 Maria's
house（請參閱第 68 頁的所有格說明）

6 **like**（像）：
- My smartphone is just **like** yours.
- What's the weather **like**?
- She looks **like** her sister.

7 **about** + 主題（關於）：
The novel is **about** <u>a young girl</u>.

8 **except/but (for)**（除了……之外，都）：
All the food was great **except for** the cake,
which was not very nice. They all left quite

1 請以合適的介系詞完成句子。

1 Mom usually goes to work .... bus, but sometimes she goes .... foot.

2 "What's this old table made .... ?" "It's made .... oak."

3 "Isn't Jack at home?" "No, he's out .... his motorbike."

4 Here's an article you should read. It's .... job opportunities in Australia.

5 Look at you in this photo. You really look .... your mother.

6 The study .... rocks is called geology.

7 My class is going on a school trip .... the history teacher tomorrow.

8 The Shard, designed .... architect Renzo Piano, is the tallest building in London.

9 You're the person I want to be with. I can't live .... you.

10 Is this .... me? Wow! Thank you so much.

介系詞 to 搭配雙重受詞的用法

❶ 介系詞 to 用以引導被某行為影響的人事物：
- You'd better talk **to** <u>him</u>.
- What have you done **to** <u>your hair</u>?

❷ 某些動詞後面會有兩個受詞，一個是**直接受詞**，另一個是**被該行為影響的人物**，例如「把某物交給某人」。

最常見的此類動詞包括 **give**、**offer**、**lend**、**show**、**bring**（往講者的方向送去）、**take**（往講者的相反方向拿走）、**send**、**tell**、**ask** 等。

在此情況下，可使用以下兩種句型：

> **❶ 主詞 + 動詞 + 受詞 + 介系詞 to + 人物 →**
> I gave the keys to Brian.
> **❷ 主詞 + 動詞 + 人物 + 受詞 →**
> I gave Brian the keys.

上方的句型 **❷** 中，我們先將受到行為影響的人物（**Brain**）放在句子前半段，將直接受詞或物品（**keys**）放在人物後面。由於句子裡沒有介系詞，因此看似有兩個受詞。

❸ 如果是以一個**代名詞**來表達句子的**受詞**、以**名詞**表達人物，或者有**兩個代名詞**，我們會偏好使用句型 **❶**：
- I haven't got the keys. I gave <u>them</u> **to** Brian / I gave <u>them</u> **to** <u>him</u>.

❹ 但如果是以**代名詞**來表達**人物**，我們偏好使用句型 **❷**：I gave <u>him</u> <u>the keys</u>.。

❺ 其他動詞沒有雙重受詞的用法，只有單一受詞，句型為：

> **動詞 + 受詞 + to + 人物**

此類動詞有 explain/introduce/dictate/report/deliver/suggest/propose/say：
- She reported <u>the news</u> **to** <u>everybody</u>.
- He's introduced <u>his girlfriend</u> **to** <u>his parents</u>.

  NOT He's introduced ~~his parents his girlfriend~~.

FAQ

Q: 在英文文法裡，object 這個字只有直接受詞的意思嗎？

A: 不是的，object 是**受詞種類**的統稱。直接受詞通常不需搭配介系詞。需要搭配介系詞（to、for 等）的受詞，稱為間接受詞。精確來說，雙重受詞的用法應該要稱為「直接雙重受詞」。

2 請在正確的句子後打勾，並且訂正錯誤句子。

1 Show me your notebook, will you? ☐ ....
2 Can you lend to me your credit card, Dad? ☐ ....
3 Dave gave a present to each of his nephews. ☐ ....
4 Samantha explained me her plans. ☐ ....
5 "Take this basket to your grandmother," said Little Red Riding Hood's mother to her daughter.
   ☐ ....
6 She introduced the new assistant to the manager. ☐ ....
7 Can you give him this document, please? ☐ ....
8 They offered to us a very good meal. ☐ ....
9 Why don't you dictate this letter to your secretary? ☐ ....
10 We will deliver our customers the goods in two weeks. ☐ ....
11 We must report the manager the theft. ☐ ....
12 Could you bring me a glass of water, please? ☐ ....

3 請改寫句子在筆記本上，以雙重受詞取代畫底線單字。注意其中有兩個句子無法改寫，找出無法改寫的句子為何。

1 Can you give a lift to my friend, please?
2 Can you lend this book to me? I'd like to read it.
3 The teacher explained the new rule to the students.
4 Give this paper to your sister, please.
5 If you like, I'll show my photos to you.
6 They offered a red rose to all the ladies.
7 He said something to the teacher.
8 Have you sent an email to Mr. Wayne yet?
9 My neighbor told the news to everybody.
10 The coach asked their names to the players.

LESSON 4 後接介系詞的形容詞與動詞
Adjectives and verbs followed by prepositions

形容詞後面經常需要接介系詞，再接上名詞、代名詞或動詞 ing（請參閱第 91 頁）。

形容詞 + 介系詞 + 名詞或代名詞 → I'm good at math. / I'm good at it.	形容詞 + 介系詞 + 動詞 ing → I'm tired of listening to the same old story!

以下列出需要後接介系詞的常見形容詞：

sorry	about	I'm **sorry about** the mistake.
worried		Are you **worried about** tomorrow's test?
surprised	at	He was **surprised at** seeing her there.
good		I'm not very **good at** swimming.
disappointed	by/at/with	We were **disappointed by/at/with** the quality of the food.
qualified	for	James is not **qualified for** this job.
responsible		Who's **responsible for** this mess?
different	from/to	The hotel was quite **different from/to** what I expected.
interested	in	I'm not really **interested in** politics.
fond		She's very **fond of** her aunt.
afraid		I'm **afraid of** the dark.
scared	of	She's **scared of** spiders.
tired		Aren't you **tired of** moving to different places every year?
aware		She's not **aware of** the importance of her new position.
keen	on	My brother's **keen on** parachuting.
married	to	He isn't **married to** Elisa. He's just **engaged to** her.
engaged		
angry		Don't be **angry with** him!
happy		I'm really **happy with** the exam results.
bored	with	I'm getting **bored with** being at home.
popular		Paul is very **popular with** his classmates.
satisfied		Are you really **satisfied with** this piece of writing?

1 請以下方的形容詞完成句子。

1 I'm not really .... on going to this concert.

2 .... about the wait! I hope it wasn't too long!

3 He was .... at hearing the news.

4 "Are you .... with me?" "No, why should I be?"

5 The lead singer is very .... with girls!

6 I wish we didn't have to read this textbook.
I'm really .... with it.

7 I'm not .... of spiders, but I'm
.... of bats!

8 "Aren't you ....
in sport?" "Well, not really."

9 I'm not very ....
at skiing. I'm better at
snowboarding.

10 The teachers are not
.... with your
behavior at school.

2 請以合適的介系詞完成短文。

Your problem is that you're always worried [1] .... silly things. You should be happier [2] ....
your life. You're married [3] .... a good-looking man who's clever and keen [4] .... sports like
you. You have an interesting job and are very popular [5] .... your colleagues. Your days are very
different [6] .... the dull routine lots of people have. So don't make me angry [7] .... you. Stop
complaining. Your father and I are both getting bored [8] .... your behavior.

3 請找出句中錯誤並訂正。

1 Aren't you surprised see me here? ....

2 My father is interested at learn how to surf the Internet. ....

3 Mr. Higgins is really angry to his son because he has just broken the kitchen window. ....

4 I am very keen at English. ....

5 I am quite worried for the Spanish test. I haven't studied much. ....

6 I'm not very happy for my job. I would like a change. ....

7 Is she married with the new doctor? ....

8 Come on! You can't be scared with bugs. They're harmless. ....

9 She's always been very fond with her grandmother. She visits her every day. ....

10 We are really disappointed for the quality of this project. ....

11 Are you aware with all the risks involved in using chemicals? ....

12 He's responsible of the whole marketing department. ....

後接介系詞的動詞

與形容詞一樣，許多動詞後面也會接上介系詞，來引導一個間接受詞。
可使用的句型如下：

❶ 主詞 + 動詞 + 介系詞 + 名詞或代名詞 →
They're talking about their friend. / They're talking about her.

❷ 主詞 + 動詞 + 介系詞 + 動詞 ing（動名詞）→
I'm thinking of changing my job.

FAQ

Q: 我查詢動詞 **ask** 時，發現以下三種用法：
❶ ask sth ❷ ask sb sth
❸ ask sb about sth
這些 **sb**、**sth** 的縮寫是什麼意思？

A: **sth** 是 **something** 的簡寫，**sb** 則是 **somebody** 的意思。
ask 的用法例句如下：
❶ I asked a question（直接受詞）
❷ I asked John a question.（雙重受詞）
❸ I asked John about the weather（直接受詞＋間接受詞）
每種動詞通常都有不同句構或句型的用法。如果還是有疑問，可以查找編排比較優良的字典。

以下列出後接一或多種介系詞的常見動詞：

- **agree with sb about/on sth** （贊同）
  We agreed with them about the price.
- **apologize to sb for sth**（道歉）
  They apologized to the teacher for being late.
- **apply for sth**（申請、應徵）
  I applied for the job but I didn't get it.
- **approve of sth**（核准）
  I don't approve of his decisions.
- **argue with sb about sth**（爭論）
  They're always arguing with him about money.
- **believe in sb/sth**（相信）
  Do you believe in our friendship?
- **borrow sth from sb/sth**（借入）
  I borrowed two books from the library.
- **care about sb/sth**（關心）
  I do care about the future of our planet.
- **complain to sb about sth**（抱怨）
  He complained to the boss about his wage cut.
- **depend on sb/sth**（視情況而定）
  It depends on the weather.
- **get used to sth**（習慣）
  I'll never get used to waking up so early.
- **hear from sb**（聽到消息）
  Have you heard from them yet?
- **hear of sb**（聽過）
  Have you heard of that famous singer?
- **laugh at sb/sth**（嘲笑）
  Are you laughing at me?
- **listen to sb/sth**（傾聽）
  I enjoy listening to the pop music.

- **look after sb/sth**（照顧）
  Who's going to look after the puppy?
- **look at sb/sth**（看著）Don't look at me!
- **look for sb/sth**（尋找）
  We're looking for a new apartment.
- **look forward to sth**（期待）
  We're looking forward to meeting you.
- **pay for sth**（支付某事物的款項）
  I'll pay for the bill!
- **prepare for sth**（為某事做準備）
  Sue can't go out tonight because she has to prepare for her exam tomorrow.
- **protect sb/sth from sb/sth**（保護）
  This spray can protect you from UV rays.
- **rely on sb**（依賴）We all rely on you, Paul.
- **shout at sb**（喊叫）Stop shouting at me!
- **succeed in sth / in doing sth**（成功）
  She succeeded in having her first novel published.
- **suffer from sth**（受苦）
  My sister suffers from headaches.
- **talk/speak to sb about sth**（談論）
  Did you talk to him about your plan?
- **thank sb for sth/for doing sth**（感謝）
  I thanked them for their nice present.
- **think of/about sb/sth**（想到／思念）
  I'm thinking about my girlfriend.
- **wait for sb/sth**（等待）
  Come on! We're waiting for you.
- **worry about sb/sth**（擔心）
  Don't worry about me.

4 請將 **1–10** 與 **A–J** 配對成完整的句子。

..... **1** Everybody is looking
..... **2** You should think
..... **3** What are you thinking
..... **4** Who have you been
..... **5** Talk to me later. I'm listening
..... **6** I haven't heard
..... **7** I'm getting used
..... **8** You should apologize
..... **9** My sister suffers
..... **10** I really don't approve

A about other people a bit more.
B waiting for?
C to working the night shift.
D to the news.
E from my cousin for ages.
F of doing now?
G to your friend.
H for something better in life.
I of the way she dresses.
J from asthma caused by an allergy to cats.

請圈出正確的用字。

1 I think we all agree **with / on / in** the importance of learning a foreign language.
2 We don't approve **for / about / of** your behavior, Kate.
3 Have you heard **of / from / by** Tina recently?
4 I don't think Tom cares **about / with / of** anything except eating.
5 They finally succeeded **at / about / in** fulfilling their dream: Going on vacation to New Zealand.
6 Why do you keep worrying **with / of / about** silly things?
7 Can you please thank your mom **of / for / to** the cake she made?
8 Do I have to pay **for / about / with** the excursion?
9 Are you waiting **to / for / with** the bus?
10 Who is looking **at / up / after** the children this afternoon?

請使用正確的介系詞來完成句子。

1 Do you promise to think .... my proposal?
2 Do you know what they're talking ....?
3 Jenny usually looks .... her sister in the afternoon.
4 Do you agree .... me .... the importance of a healthy diet?
5 I hope I succeed .... getting my doctorate.

6 I borrowed this dictionary .... a friend.
7 He keeps worrying .... things that don't really matter.
8 Who paid .... the train tickets?
9 Don't ask me .... money. I haven't got any.
10 The hotel guests complained .... the manager .... the rooms.

請運用以下動詞的正確形式來完成句子。

ask agree get used apologize complain shout argue thank look borrow

1 We want to .... the teacher about the arrangements for the exam.
2 I would like to .... to you for what I said yesterday.
3 I don't .... with you about the causes of the problem.
4 I can't .... to American coffee. It's too watery.
5 We are going to .... to the manager about our room. It's so dirty.
6 He always .... money from his sister.
7 Our neighbors are always .... about something. They keep shouting!
8 We are .... forward to receiving your initial order.
9 Why are you .... at me? I'm not deaf. You can speak quietly.
10 I'd like to .... you for hosting me. You have been very kind.

請使用以下 look 相關的片語動詞，來取代句子裡的粗體字動詞。

look around look at look for look after look into look up

1 We're going to **visit** an interesting archaeological site this afternoon. ....
2 We have to **care for** my daughter's dog while she's away. ....
3 I must **find** the meaning of this word in the dictionary. ....
4 The local police said they are **investigating** the problem. ....
5 We **examined** the paintings for a long time. ....
6 We **searched for** her lost bracelet everywhere. ....

介系詞 to 與不定詞 to 的用法

❶ **to** 是最常用的英文單字。to 作為**介系詞**的用法如下：

❶ 用來後接移動至某處的受詞：・go <u>to</u> work　・get <u>to</u> the office

❷ 用以引導被某行為影響的人事物：・talk <u>to</u> sb　・give sth <u>to</u> sb

❸ 用於「from . . . to . . .」的表達方式：
   ・<u>from</u> beginning <u>to</u> end　・<u>from</u> London <u>to</u> Manchester

❹ 表達分數：・They won by three goals <u>to</u> two.

❺ 搭配動詞 prefer 時，後接不是那麼偏好的事物：・I prefer cycling <u>to</u> walking.

❻ 放在 devoted、married、engaged、used/accustomed（較正式的用法）等形容詞的後面：
   ・He's devoted <u>to</u> his family.　・We aren't used <u>to</u> this muggy weather.

❷ **to** 放在原形動詞前面，可稱為「不定詞標誌」，目的在於強調**不定詞**的用法。
不定詞特別會放在具有未來時態意味的動詞後面，例如：

❶ 意願動詞：want/would like/decide/refuse
   ・I want <u>to go</u> home.　・He decided <u>to leave</u> earlier.
   ・Would you like <u>to join</u> us for dinner?　・They refused <u>to talk</u> to us.

❷ 表達未來願景或計畫的動詞：
hope/plan/manage/learn/afford/need/arrange/expect/mean/agree/threaten/
offer/promise
   ・She hopes <u>to start</u> university in November.
   ・He expected <u>to get</u> a reward.
   ・I didn't mean <u>to hurt</u> you.　・We agreed <u>to meet</u> in the afternoon.
   ・We managed <u>to arrive</u> on time.　・I learned <u>to swim</u> when I was three years old.

❸ 不定詞的否定用法是 **not** + **to** + **原形動詞**：He promised <u>not to say</u> anything.

FAQ

Q: 為什麼大家都說「I used to get up early.」，而不是使用動詞 ing 來說「I'm used to getting up early.」？

A: 第一句裡的動詞 used，代表的是**過去的習慣**，後面接的是**不定詞**意義的 to。第二句裡的 used 則是**形容詞**，後面接的是**介系詞**意義的 to。
我們已學過，放在介系詞（to、of、about、at）後面的動詞都要加上 ing。以下再列出介系詞 to 後接動詞 ing 的例句:
「I'm looking forward **to going** to New York.」。

9 請圈出正確的用字。

1　I'm getting used to **have** / **having** five hours' sleep a night.
2　I can't wait to **get** / **getting** the exam results.
3　He's tired of **waiting** / **wait** for her.
4　I'm thinking about **go** / **going** abroad next year.
5　We're looking forward to **see** / **seeing** you soon.
6　I'd like to **be** / **being** an engineer when I grow up.
7　Have you arranged to **meeting** / **meet** him?
8　I need to **find** / **finding** a little bit of courage.
9　I used to **be** / **being** very shy when I was little.

10　They're going to **play** / **playing** football tonight.
11　I can't afford to **go** / **going** on vacation this year.
12　I'm used to **work** / **working** the night shift now, but I found it very hard when I started.
13　She threatened to **tell** / **telling** his boss what he'd done.
14　I'm not accustomed to **be** / **being** spoken to like that.

ROUND UP 7

1 請謹記介系詞 **in** 的以下表達方式：
- to be **in** prison/hospital/bed
- **in** the rain/sun
- **in** the middle/center of →
  While exploring Alaska I we found ourselves **in the middle of** nowhere.

2 介系詞 **on** 的表達方式：
- **on** the right/left | **on** the way home | **on** the way back | **on** top of the hill
- **on** vacation | **on** a trip | **on** a cruise | **on** a diet | **on** TV

3 請同樣謹記以下用法：

1 **in/on** the corner | **at/on** the corner **of**：
- Write your name **in the top left-hand corner**.
- Let's meet **at the corner of** Kearny and Grant Street.

2 **at** the front | **at/on** the back （ **BUT** **in** the front/back **of the car/bus**）：
- There's a garden **at the back** of the house.
- She was sitting **in the front of the car**.

1 請使用正確的介系詞來完成句子。

1 There's a newsdealer .... the corner of Columbus and Ocean Road.

2 I don't like sitting .... the front of the car. If I'm not driving, I prefer to sit .... the back.

3 There's a warehouse .... the back of the factory.

4 Your jacket is hanging .... the back of the chair near your desk.

5 I always meet Peter .... the way back from my office.

6 Are you going .... a school trip this year?

7 Mr. Smith is .... vacation in Morocco.

8 Are you still .... bed? Come on! Get up! We can have a nice walk .... the sun this morning.

9 Did you know John is .... hospital? He fell off a ladder yesterday.

10 Look at that castle .... top of the hill! Isn't it beautiful?

2 請使用正確的介系詞來完成句子。

1 I will go, with or .... you!

2 I often go to school .... foot, even though it's quite a long way .... my house.

3 Today's history lesson was .... the Napoleonic wars.

4 Here's a little present .... the children.

5 This novel was written .... Stephen King.

6 Do you like going .... parties?

7 You'll never guess what happened .... me last night!

8 I can play badminton, but I'm not very good .... it.

9 There's a lovely park .... the center of the town.

10 Fiona's not here — she's gone .... a Caribbean cruise.

3 下方某些句子的介系詞用法有錯誤，請<u>畫底線</u>並訂正。

1 I was born in October 8th, 2005. ....

2 I don't like being home alone in the night. ....

3 We usually go in the mountains for a week on August. ....

4 I'm having a party at my house on Sunday. ....

5 I usually have a quick breakfast before I go to school. ....

6 I will be at home between four to five in the afternoon tomorrow. ....

7 We live at 16 Queen Victoria Road. ....

8 Go until the traffic lights and then turn to left. ....

9 A solar-powered plane landed in Hawaii after a five-day journey across the Pacific Ocean from Japan. ....

10 Do you often go jogging at morning? ....

4 請依照例句來改寫句子，以「雙重受格」取代 **to** 的用法。

0 They offered a cup of tea to their guest.
   They offered their guest a cup of tea.
   ....

1 He lent his cell phone to his son.
   ....

2 Can you bring that magazine to me, please?
   ....

3 Give your email address to my secretary, will you?
   ....

4 They sent a lot of photos to us when they were in Australia.
   ....

5 Will you please give this book to your teacher?
   ....

6 We showed our new car to our friends.
   ....

7 He sent a beautiful present to his girlfriend for her birthday.
   ....

8 Take some money to the beggar.
   ....

延伸補充

後接介系詞的其他形容詞

• **proud of**（驕傲）
I'm really <u>proud of</u> my son for winning the race.

• **ashamed of**（不好意思）
Don't be <u>ashamed of</u> asking for help.

• **bad/hopeless at**（不擅長）
I'm really <u>hopeless at</u> playing the piano!

• **embarrassed at/about**（尷尬）
You mustn't feel <u>embarrassed at</u> standing up and speaking out.

後接介系詞的其他動詞：

• **forgive sb for doing sth**（原諒）
Please <u>forgive</u> me <u>for</u> being late.

• **suspect sb of doing sth**（懷疑）
The math teacher <u>suspects</u> one of his students <u>of</u> copying an exam paper.

• **dream of/about doing sth**（夢想）
I <u>dream of</u> going to live in New York.

• **accuse sb of doing sth**（指控）
Maggie <u>accused</u> one <u>of</u> her classmates of bullying her.

• **congratulate sb on doing sth**（恭喜）
I want to <u>congratulate</u> you <u>on</u> working so hard this year.

• **insist on doing sth**（堅持）
He always <u>insists on</u> paying for the taxi.
（但注意是 He insists on me paying for the taxi.）

• **prevent sb from doing sth**（防止）
My parents <u>prevented</u> me <u>from</u> having a tattoo.

• **feel like doing sth**（想要）
I don't <u>feel like</u> going shopping today.

• **warn sb against doing sth**（警告）
He <u>warned</u> me <u>against</u> driving too fast.

125

!
> **❶ It's worth / It isn't worth doing sth** 意指「做了某事是有用或重要的／沒用的不重要的」：
>   • **It isn't worth working** so hard.
> **❷ for + 動詞 ing**，表示原因或行為的動機：
>   • He felt bad **for hurting** her.（等同於 . . . because he had hurt her.）
> **❸ by + 動詞 ing**，表示進行某行為的方式，或某行為該有的態度：
>   • Delete the word **by putting** a cross through it.
>   • You'll always be respected **by respecting** the others.
>   （等同於 . . . if you respect the others.）

5 請閱讀以下短文，選出正確的選項來完成克漏字。

Whether you like it or not, adults are examples to young people. If you are a teacher or a parent, it is really important ¹...... your children ²...... succeeding in the things they do. If they feel you are proud ³...... them, they will want to achieve new things. If they are ⁴...... on doing something, however small or simple it is, it is important to show that you recognize it. If they are bad at ⁵...... something, they may feel embarrassed, and

Look, Mom! I can swim!

you must be prepared for them not succeeding ⁶...... everything. For example, my son is really bad at soccer, but I would not dream ⁷...... to force him to practice. None of us is good at doing everything, and we must forgive our children ⁸...... perfect. As Albert Einstein said, "Everybody is a genius, but if you judge a fish by its ability ⁹...... a tree, it will live its whole life ¹⁰...... that it is stupid."

1	Ⓐ to congratulate	Ⓑ to congratulating	Ⓒ congratulate	Ⓓ congratulates
2	Ⓐ at	Ⓑ with	Ⓒ of	Ⓓ on
3	Ⓐ with	Ⓑ of	Ⓒ to	Ⓓ at
4	Ⓐ fond	Ⓑ keen	Ⓒ able	Ⓓ good
5	Ⓐ do	Ⓑ to do	Ⓒ doing	Ⓓ done
6	Ⓐ on	Ⓑ with	Ⓒ for	Ⓓ in
7	Ⓐ of try	Ⓑ to try	Ⓒ to trying	Ⓓ of trying
8	Ⓐ for not being	Ⓑ for being not	Ⓒ not to be	Ⓓ to be not
9	Ⓐ to climb	Ⓑ of climbing	Ⓒ to climbing	Ⓓ in climbing
10	Ⓐ to believe	Ⓑ believes	Ⓒ believing	Ⓓ for believing

6 請使用以下介系詞來完成句子。

> about　for (x2)　of (x2)　to　at　like　by　on　with

1 He was sorry .... causing me trouble.

2 You'll never get anywhere .... being so rude to others!

3 He thanked me .... helping him.

4 I would never dream .... lying to you!

5 He insisted .... us going to stay with them.

6 John talked .... the manager .... employing more staff.

7 My cat is bad .... chasing birds. He's a lazy cat!

8 I don't feel .... cooking tonight. Let's go to a restaurant.

9 Are you aware .... the problems you're causing?

10 They weren't satisfied .... the accommodation they had found.

7 請使用正確的動詞或介系詞來完成句子。

1 Why are you .... me of hiding your school bag? Isn't it the one under your desk?

2 I must congratulate Mr. Berenson, the sales manager, ... achieving great results this year.

3 Jason always feels .... at speaking to an audience — he's very shy.

4 Do you .... like going to the movie theater tonight?

5 You shouldn't insist so much .... always being the group leader.

6 I'm really proud .... my students. They did a great project.

7 Ask .... help while doing group work. Don't be ashamed!

8 I often dream .... living by the sea.

9 Who is responsible .... quality control in this company?

10 This lotion should .... you from mosquitoes.

Reflecting on grammar

請研讀文法規則，再判斷以下說法是否正確。

		True	False
1	介系詞 on 必須放在月分和季節的前面。		
2	till 和 until 屬於表達時間的介系詞，且意義相同。		
3	before 的意思與 after 相反。		
4	「I'm going to home with the bus.」是正確的句子。		
5	介系詞後面可接名詞、代名詞或動詞 ing。		
6	give、offer 與 show 等動詞可用於雙重受詞的句型。		
7	「The teacher explained us the lesson.」是正確的句子。		
8	在雙重受格的句子裡，必須先有受詞，再接人物的單字。		
9	to 身兼介系詞和不定詞標誌的用法。		
10	「I'm tired of studying.」是正確的句子。		

LESSON 1 簡單過去式：be 動詞 Verb *be* – past simple

→ 圖解請見P. 410

肯定句

be 動詞有 **was** 和 **were** 這兩種簡單過去式。簡單過去式只有完整形式，沒有縮讀形式。

I	was
he/she/it	was
we/you/they	were

- I **was** at home this morning.
- We **were** at school yesterday.

否定句

完整形式：
I/he/she/it **was not**
we/you/they **were not**

縮讀形式：
I/he/she/it **wasn't**
we/you/they **weren't**

縮讀形式屬於最為常見的用法：

- It **wasn't** a good idea.
- They **weren't** at the stadium.

疑問句與簡答句

簡單過去式的 be 動詞的問句：
Was I/he/she/it . . . ?
Were we/you/they . . . ?

否定問句：
Wasn't I/he/she/it . . . ?
Weren't we/you/they . . . ?

簡答句：
Yes, + 主格代名詞 + was/were.
No, + 主格代名詞 + wasn't/weren't.

- "**Were** the prices good?"
  "Yes, they were. The sales were on."
- "**Wasn't** Luke at the party?"
  "No, he wasn't."

Wh 問句：
- **What was** the weather like?
- **Why were** you late?
- **When was** your wedding anniversary?

There+be 動詞的過去式句型則為：
There was / There were . . .
There wasn't / There weren't . . .
Was there . . . ? / Were there . . . ?

- **There were** lots of people at the ceremony.
- **There wasn't** enough time.
- **Was there** a tennis court near the hotel?

Focus

簡單過去式的 be 動詞可用來描述**在過去某特定時間完成**的事件：
- He **was** at the restaurant when they called from the office.
- They **were** at a party last night.

FAQ

Q: 為什麼要用「I was born . . .」來表達自己的生日和出生地？

A: **to be born** 只能用**被動語態**表達，意思是「從媽媽肚子裡被生出」，所以很明顯必須使用**簡單過去式**。而問句「Where and when were you born?」一樣須使用簡單過去式的 be 動詞。

1 請根據提示用字，使用過去式寫出完整的句子。

0 a / mini-market

    There was a mini-market.

1 not / a / restaurant

....

2 two / playground

....

3 a / beach

....

4 lots of / tourist

....

2 請使用正確的簡單過去式 be 動詞來完成句子。

1 Don't put the blame on me. It .... my fault!

2 It .... a very exciting basketball game. The final score .... 86 to 84.

3 The weather .... very good, but we had a good time anyway.

4 There .... any good prizes in the raffle.

5 "........................... it a good weekend?" "Yes, it .... fantastic."

6 There .... a pool in the hotel, but there .... a beauty center. I couldn't have a massage.

7 The wedding .... fabulous. There .... hundreds of guests. The location and the food .... just perfect.

8 "...................... you on the Continental flight to New York?" "Yes, we ...."

3 請將 1–8 與 A–H 配對成完整的句子。

..... **1** The bus drivers were on strike yesterday,

..... **2** There were some interesting statistics in yesterday's paper

..... **3** There were so many good movies on at the Multiplex last weekend

..... **4** There was a terrible storm last night

..... **5** The winner of "America's Got Talent" last year

..... **6** The weather was really good last weekend,

..... **7** The cave was dark and damp

..... **8** There was a spectacular view

A that we couldn't make up our minds which one to see!

B was a young girl with a beautiful voice.

C so we decided to go to the lake.

D so there was a long queue for taxis.

E and there were long stalactites hanging from the roof.

F with strong wind, hail and thunder.

G from the top of Taipei 101.

H about unemployment figures in Spain.

LESSON 2 簡單過去式：規則動詞和不規則動詞
Regular and irregular verbs – past simple

➜ 圖解請見 P. 410–411

肯定句

英文裡有分規則動詞和不規則動詞。

❶ **規則動詞**只要在原形動詞後面加上 **ed**，即可成為簡單過去式：

listen → listen**ed** | play → play**ed** | wait → wait**ed** | They **waited** an hour.

❷ **不規則動詞**的簡單過去式則有不同變化，必須用背的，例如：

go → **went** | write → **wrote** | begin → **began** | have → **had**

She had an important meeting yesterday.

❸ 有些動詞的原形和簡單過去式均相同，例如 put → put。

許多常見動詞均為不規則動詞，大家可查看第 427 至 428 頁的表格。

❹ **簡單過去式**適用於所有人稱，所以無論是規則動詞或不規則動詞，都不用因人稱不同而有所變化。

在字尾加上 ed 時，要留意以下的拼字規則。

1 如果動詞字尾有 **e**，僅需加上 **d**：like → like**d** | live → live**d**

2 以下情況則需重複一次子音字尾：

① 字尾為**一個母音 + 一個子音**的單音節動詞：
clap → clap**ped** | rob → rob**bed**
BUT clean → clean**ed**（字中兩個母音） | rent → rent**ed**（字尾兩個子音）

② 重音在**第二音節**的雙音節動詞，且字尾為**一個母音 + 一個子音**：
prefer → prefer**red** | omit → omit**ted**
BUT offer → offer**ed**（重音在第一音節）
repeat → repeat**ed**（第二音節有兩個母音）
adopt → adopt**ed**（字尾有兩個子音）

③ 字尾是 **el** 的動詞，且前面有**單一母音**（此為英式英文用法）：
travel → travel**led**（美式英文用法：travel**ed**）**BUT** peel → peel**ed**（兩個母音）

3 字尾是**子音 + y** 的動詞，要先將 y 改成 **i**，再加上 **ed**：
cry → cr**ied** | study → stud**ied** **BUT** stay → stay**ed**（母音 + y）

1 請到第 **427** 至 **428** 頁查找不規則動詞的表格，並在下方寫出各動詞的簡單過去式。

規則動詞		不規則動詞	
原形	過去式	原形	過去式
stop		have	
help		know	
play		leave	
shout		meet	
work		go	
try		tell	
refer		take	
quarrel (Br.E.)		read	
submit		come	
move		speak	

2 請使用第 **1** 大題的簡單過去式動詞，來完成下方句子。

1 Sam .... basketball when he was at college and was quite good.

2 I .... my old friend Dave on my way to work this morning.

3 My neighbors .... so loudly last night that I was going to call the police!

4 I .... for a transport company in London until May, then I .... to work in New York.

5 I .... a lot of books when I was on vacation in July.

6 I .... and I .... again, but I couldn't solve the problem. It was way too difficult for me.

7 They .... the 54 bus to the stadium last Saturday.

8 We .... a big breakfast this morning, so we aren't hungry now.

9 My teacher .... me a lot when I was having problems with my exam preparation.

10 He .... his application and CV to the Human Resources Manager.

3 請使用括號裡的動詞完成一篇在部落格發表的家庭遊記。請將動詞改為簡單過去式，並找出文中唯一的規則動詞。

We [1].......................... a fantastic holiday in Australia last summer. (have) We [2].......................... a flight to Sydney via Singapore, where we [3].......................... a six-hour stopover. (take, have) We [4].......................... to Sydney at 11 a.m. local time and we [5].......................... a bit strange for the first few days because of jet lag. (get, feel) We [6]..........................

five days in Sydney and [7].......................... the Opera House, the Harbor Bridge and all the beautiful sights of the bay. (spend, see) After that, we [8].......................... north in a minivan and [9].......................... the fantastic beaches of Queensland, past Brisbane then up to the Capricorn Islands. (drive, see) Then we [10].......................... to Darwin, on the north coast, and [11].......................... the outback in a jeep, stopping at Ayers Rock, or Uluru, as the Aborigines call it. (fly, cross over) We [12].......................... lots of unusual animals on our trip — dingoes, kangaroos, wombats and snakes. (come across) It [13].......................... really an unforgettable journey. (be)

否定句

簡單過去式的否定句具有完整形式和縮讀形式，但後者較為常用：

完整形式：
主詞 + **did** + **not** + 原形動詞

- I **did not** know the answer.

縮讀形式：
主詞 + **didn't** + 原形動詞

- We **didn't** go to the theater.

疑問句

簡單過去式的問句如下：
Did + 主詞 + 原形動詞 + . . . ?

否定問句：
Didn't + 主詞 + 原形動詞 + . . . ?

簡答句：
Yes, + 主格代名詞 + did.
No, + 主格代名詞 + didn't.

- "**Did** you like the show?" "Yes, I did."
- "**Didn't** they give you an answer?" "No, they didn't."

以疑問詞開頭的 Wh 問句：
Wh 疑問詞 + **did** + 主詞 + 原形動詞 + . . . ?

- **What did** you do on the weekend?
- **Where did** you see him?

4 **a** 史提爾夫婦昨天在家度過寧靜的一晚。請以第一個動詞是肯定形式、第二個動詞是否定形式的方式，來完成句子。

1 Mr. and Mrs. Steel .... at home last night, they .... their friends. (stay, meet)

2 They .... dinner at home, they .... to a restaurant. (have, go)

3 They .... a movie on TV, they .... to the movie theater. (watch, go)

4 They .... to bed early, they .... late. (go, stay up)

b 史提爾夫婦有天晚上和朋友外出。請將上一大題的句子，以第一個動詞是否定形式、第二個動詞是肯定形式的方式，來改寫句子。

1 ....

2 ....

3 ....

4 ....

5 請使用括號裡的動詞，來完成簡單過去式的問句和簡答句。

1 "........................ you .... the concert?" "Yes, ... It was great." (enjoy)

2 "........................ Tom .... in the last cricket match?" "No, ... He was ill." (play)

3 "........................ they .... by bus?" "No, ... They went on the train." (travel)

4 "........................ she .... last Saturday?" "Yes, ... , but only in the morning." (work)

5 "........................ you .... a good time at summer camp?" "No, ... It was a bit boring." (have)

6 "........................ Rob .... home late last night?" "Yes, ... He came home at 9:30 p.m." (come)

6 請重新排序單字，來寫出簡單過去式的問句或否定句。

1 didn't / We / at all / the / movie / like / .
....

2 buy / Did / you/a / train ticket / return / ?
....

3 this morning / you / emails / check / Didn't / your / ?
....

4 didn't / go out / last night / with / She / Thomas / .
....

5 she / get up / Sunday / Did / late / on / ?
....

6 do / didn't / yesterday / our homework / We / .
....

7 the / same story / he / repeat / over and over / Did / again / ?
....

8 so early / They / didn't / to leave / want / the party / .
....

7 請以合適的 Wh 問句搭配 you 來完成對話。

1 **A** .... that lovely bag?

B I bought it at Kensington market last week.

A .... for it?

B You won't believe it . . . I only paid £3!

2 **A** .... on the weekend, Dave?

B I went to Brighton, on the south coast of England.

A .... with?

B I went with my wife and the kids, and a friend of mine.

A .... get there?

B We took the car. It was a couple of hours.

3 **A** Hi, Simon. How nice to see you!
....?

B I got here yesterday morning. And I'm leaving tonight.

A Really? It's just for a short stay, then.

4 **A** .... in the USA?

B I studied at Stanford University.

A .... there?

B I studied politics and economics, then I got a Master's in business administration.

5 **A** So you were in Paris last week.
.... there?

B Oh, I visited the Louvre for a whole day. I went up the Eiffel Tower and I saw the Tour de France on Sunday.

A That was lucky!
.... your trip?

B I booked it online — the flight, the hotel and everything. I found a very good last-minute offer.

LESSON 3 簡單過去式 / 時間用語與順序 / used to 用法
Use of the past simple, time expressions and time sequencing, *used to* . . .

簡單過去式

1 簡單過去式是描述**過去事件**的時態，用以表達在過去開始與結束的情況。適用範圍如下：

❶ 過去的經驗：
- I **got** a good grade in yesterday's math test.

❷ 歷史事件：
- The Normans **came** to England in 1066.

❸ 自傳：
- William Shakespeare **was born** in 1564 in Stratford-upon-Avon and **died** in the same place in 1616, on the same day of his birth, April 23rd.

❹ 故事和寓言：
- Cinderella **had** two wicked stepsisters.

❺ 新聞報導：
- The car **didn't stop** at the red light and **crashed** into a van coming the other way.

❻ 詢問某事發生的時間、地點等問題：
- When **did** you **go** to the bank?
- What time **did** you **get** up this morning?

2 除非事件發生的時間點非常明確，否則簡單過去式的句子裡都會提及**時間**。句中可使用以下時間用語或時間子句：
- this morning/afternoon
- yesterday/the day before yesterday
- last night
- last week/month/year
- two hours/days ago
- a long/short time ago
- in December
- in 2013
- on June 4th
- at two o'clock
- in the 20th century
- when I was young / a child / six years old

3 此類**時間用語**或**時間子句**通常會放在**句尾**：
- I started reading this book **three hours ago**.
- I got up early **this morning**.

但也可放在**句首**：
- **When I was young**, I lived in Russia.

> **!** 注意「The last time I saw her was in March.」此句也可用**副詞** last 來表達：
> I <u>last</u> saw her in March.
> = I saw her <u>last</u> in March.

---

1 請留意下方各句中的動詞時態與時間用語，並圈出正確的用字。

1 I went to Taipei on business **next** / **last** Friday.

2 Our teachers **give** / **gave** us a lot of homework every weekend.

3 The club usually **opens** / **opened** at nine, but it **opens** / **opened** at ten last Sunday.

4 Some of my classmates play basketball **on** / **last** Wednesdays.

5 They spent the evening in a pub **last** / **every** Saturday.

6 Sam phoned me at 12 **yesterday** / **last** night.

7 We had an English test three days **long** / **ago**.

8 I didn't see him in his office **this** / **last** morning.

9 Ken left for Sydney the day **before yesterday** / **yesterday before**.

10 I finished work very early **last night** / **yesterday night**.

2 請以符合邏輯的時間用語來完成句子。

1 It last rained heavily ....

2 The last time I went on a trip was ....

3 I saw a really good movie ....

4 I got a present ....

5 I bought some new clothes ....

6 I got a Tweet or an SMS ....

7 I had a haircut ....

8 The last time I got a bad score was ....

9 I last sent a postcard ....

10 The last time I took a train was ....

時間順序

❶ 就像食譜列出步驟依序說明，我們通常也會**照時間發生順序**來描述事件。副詞或片語會用來指示時間順序，而且這些詞常放在文章段落的**開頭**。

順序用詞
- First / First of all
- Then
- After that
- Next
- Finally / In the end

> ❗ 請注意 before/after 與 first/then 的差異。
> **before/after** 是介系詞，可後接名詞或代名詞；
> **first/then** 則是副詞，需要加連接詞來連接**兩個子句**：
> - I went out **after dinner**.
> - He helped me fix my bike. **After that**, he mowed the lawn and cleaned my garage.
> - I did my homework, and **then** I went out with my friends.
> - I went shopping **before lunch**.
> - **First** I went shopping, and **then** I had lunch. (NOT Before I went shopping, after I had lunch.)

❷ **after** 和 **before** 亦可作為引導從屬子句（主詞 + 動詞）或動詞 ing 的連接詞：

- We started eating dinner only <u>after my father arrived</u>.
- We waited for my father to arrive <u>before we started eating dinner</u>.
- <u>After giving</u> him the prize, we had a little party.
- I went jogging in the park <u>before having</u> breakfast this morning.

---

3 請以 **then**、**finally**、**first**、**after** 等時間順序用詞，來完成短文。

Last Monday was a busy day for me. I got up very early. ¹.............. having a quick breakfast, I left home in a hurry. ².............. I went to the bank to get some cash, and ³.............. I met George at the train station and we took a train to O'Hare International Airport. We waited for our German colleague Hans, who was arriving from Frankfurt, there. ⁴.............. saying hello to him, we helped him with his luggage and ⁵.............. we set off for the center of Chicago. Hans had a lot of bags, so we took him to his hotel ⁶.............. . ⁷.............. he left his luggage at the concierge, we drove to the Malcolm X College where our meeting was scheduled. We stayed there till 7 p.m. ⁸.............. , we all went for dinner in a good restaurant in the area.

4 請以 **first**、**then**、**after that**、**next**、**finally** 搭配以下動詞的簡單過去式，
來描述遊記經歷的順序。

> visit the cathedral   have lunch in a fast food restaurant
> go around the shops and buy gifts   have coffee and drive back home

Last Saturday, we went on a trip to Canterbury. ....

....

....

....

5 請重新排序此食譜的步驟說明。你可從指示順序的單字和片語中得到線索。

To make good chocolate-chip cookies, follow this simple recipe.
You need: 125 g butter, 50 g sugar, 150 g self-raising flour,
175 g plain chocolate, one egg.
After weighing all the ingredients, put them on the table and start working.

☐ Then bake in the oven for 15 to 20 minutes until the cookies are golden brown.

☐ Finally, put them on a wire rack to cool.

☐ Then break up the chocolate into small pieces and put them into the mixture.

☐ After greasing a baking sheet, put about 20 teaspoonfuls of the mixture onto it.

☐ When the butter and sugar mixture is light and fluffy, beat in the egg and slowly add the flour.

☐ First preheat the oven to 180°C.

☐ To make the dough, mix the butter and sugar together.

Used to

我們使用 **used to + 原形動詞**
來說明**過去的習慣**，尤其是指**過去會做**，但**現在已不做**的事情。

所有人稱的 used to 用法均相同。

- I **used to** go sailing when I was your age.
- We **used to** go camping every summer.
- There **used to** be a statue in the square.

used to 的否定句和問句用法，與其他簡單過去式相同：

> **否定句：**
> 主詞 + **didn't** + **use to** + 原形動詞

- My mother **didn't use to** put on make-up when she was my age.

> **疑問句：**
> **Did/Didn't** + 主詞 + **use to** + 原形動詞 + ...?

- "**Didn't** he **use to** work abroad?"
  "Yes, he did. But he's retired now."

> **Wh 問句：**
> Wh疑問詞 + **did/didn't** + 主詞 + **use to** + 原形動詞？

- "**Where did** they **use to** go fishing?"
  "In the little lake near their farmhouse."

6 請重新排序單字來造句。

1 your / Did / brother / use to / a boy scout / be / ?

2 dye / Jane / her hair / used to / red / she / when / was / younger / .

3 used to / long hours / I / study / when / was / at college / I / .

4 cell phones or / didn't / use to / MP3 players / We / have / .

5 a youth hostel / used / My family / to run/the / town center / in / .

6 you / did / use to / Where / go dancing / in / old days / the / ?

7 請以肯定或否定的 **used to** 來完成句子。

Christmas is always a festive time, but lots of things have changed since I was a child. When I was little, I remember we ¹........................... (have) a real Christmas tree in the living room — now we have an artificial one. We ²........................... (not buy) Christmas cakes or puddings, my grandmother ³........................... (make) them. My sister and I ⁴........................... (hang up) a stocking where Santa Claus could put our presents. We ⁵........................... (not sleep) much on Christmas Eve because we were always very excited. We ⁶........................... (not have) a party at school, but we ⁷........................... (act) in a Nativity play and we ⁸........................... (sing) Christmas carols at church.

8 請完成意義相近的句子。

1 There was a fountain in this park.

There used ....
....

2 We wore a uniform in primary school.

We used ....

when we ....

3 Before I went out, I closed all the windows and switched off the lights.

I went out after ....
....

4 First I helped my grandma with the shopping, then I went skateboarding in the park.

Before going ....,

I helped ....

5 After driving five hours, my husband stopped at a service area.

My husband drove ....

before ....

6 When I was little, my father always helped me with my homework.

My father used ....

when ....

7 I last missed a day's work two years ago.

The last time ....
....

8 The last time I was in bed with flu was during the Christmas holidays three years ago.

I was last ....
....

LESSON 4 過去進行式 / 以 When 與 While 構成的時間子句
Past continuous, time clauses with *When/While*

❶ 過去進行式是以過去**簡單式的 be 動詞**後接**動詞 ing** 所組成。

肯定句：主詞 + **was/were** + **動詞 ing**

• I **was practicing** for my piano exam.

否定句：主詞 + **wasn't/weren't** + **動詞 ing**

• The baby **wasn't sleeping**.

疑問句：Was/Were + 主詞 + **動詞 ing** + . . . ?

• **Were** you **having** a good time at the party?

否定問句：
Wasn't/Weren't + 主詞 + **動詞 ing** + . . . ?

• **Wasn't** she **dating** Rob at that time?

簡答句：
Yes, + 主詞 + was/were.
No, + 主詞 + wasn't/weren't.

• "Was it snowing?"
  "Yes, it was."

• "Were they wearing uniforms?"
  "No, they weren't."

Wh 問句：
Wh 疑問詞 + **was/were** + 主詞 + **動詞 ing** + . . . ?

• **What were** you **doing**?
• **Where was** she **going**?
• **Why were** you **crying**?

❷ 過去進行式用在表達以下情況：

  ❶ 說明在**過去特定時間**發生且**持續一陣子**的行為：
- I **was watching** a movie at nine o'clock last night.

  ❷ 說明**過去逐漸發展**的行為。在此情況下，我們會使用 **get + 形容詞**的表達方式：
- It was **getting dark**.   • I was **getting tired**.

  ❸ 說明**過去重複發生一段時間**且**令人不悅**的行為，通常會搭配副詞 **always**：
- They were **always** talking nonsense.

  ❹ 鋪陳故事的場景或來龍去脈：
- The wind **was blowing** and not a soul **was walking** in the street.

❸ 過去進行式主要搭配行為動詞，但有時亦可搭配 **feel**、**hope**、**enjoy** 等動詞：
- I **wasn't feeling** very well.   • We **were enjoying** our meal.

1 下方句中的人物昨天下午都在哪裡？都在做什麼事？請將 **1–10** 的句子與 **A–J** 的句子配對。

1 Patrick was at a club in Tokyo.
2 Gerald was in the Sahara desert.
3 Mark was on a train to Seoul.
4 Clare was on a golf course in Stratford.
5 Kate was at a street market in Osaka.
6 Mario was at a language school in Oxford.
7 Sarah was at home with her grandmother.
8 Peter was at the stadium with his dad.
9 Sheila was on a cruise on the Baltic Sea.
10 Agnes was behind the counter in her cafe.

A She was teaching her how to surf the Internet.
B She was making coffees and teas for her customers.
C She was buying some secondhand clothes.
D They were watching a great rugby match.
E He was riding on a camel among the dunes.
F She was learning how to play with her instructor.
G He was taking the Preliminary exam.
H He was having a party with his friends.
I He was reading the newspaper.
J She was lying in the sun on the upper deck.

1 .....   **2** .....   **3** .....   **4** .....   **5** .....   **6** .....   **7** .....   **8** .....   **9** .....   **10** .....

2 請運用括號內動詞的「過去進行式」來完成對話。

1 A .... you .... your blue dress at the wedding? (wear)

  B No, I wasn't. I .... my long black skirt and pink top. (wear)

2 A .... your brother .... your car around town yesterday morning? (drive)

  B No, I don't think it was him. He .... at home. (study)

3 A What .... you .... on Sunday at around ten o'clock, Tom? (do)

  B At ten? Er . . . I .... in the garden, I guess. (work)

4 A Why .... the kids ....? (argue)

  B Because Mark .... a lot of noise while Jim
        .... TV. (make, watch)

5 A I .... fast, Officer. (not drive)

  B Oh yes, you were. You .... at nearly 80 miles per
        hour. And the limit is 60 miles on this road. (go)

以 when 和 while 構成的時間子句

when 和 **while** 屬於引導時間子句的連接詞。

1 **when** 能用來引導一個已經發生的行為（使用簡單過去式），與在過去同時間內另一個進行中的行為（使用過去進行式）：

主詞 1 + 過去進行式 + **when** + 主詞 2 + 簡單過去式
↓ ↓
主要子句 **從屬子句**

- My mother was reading in her room **when** her friend from France called her on Skype.
- I was making a cake **when** somebody rang at the door.

2 也可以用 **while** 或 **when** 來引導某事件發生時（使用簡單過去式），仍在進行中的行為（使用過去進行式）：

主詞 1 + 簡單過去式 + **while/when** + 主詞 2 + 過去進行式

- I entered the conference room **while/when** the delegates were debating an important issue.
- The cars stopped **while** all the runners in the marathon were leaving the stadium.

3 **while** 還可以說明兩種以上同時進行中的行為，此時的主要子句和從屬子句均為過去進行式。

主詞 1 + 過去進行式 + **while** + 主詞 2 + 過去進行式

- Peter was listening to music **while** his brother was playing video games.
  Also Peter was listening to music **and** his brother was playing video games.

> **1** when 比 while 更常使用。我們會以 **when** 來說明已完成的**簡短**行為和**進行中**的行為；**while** 則只會用來描述**進行較久**的行為。
>
> **2** 注意，子句的順序可以倒裝。也就是可以先表達從屬子句，接著表達主要子句，但在此情況下，**主要子句**的前面必須加上**逗號**。
> - When my sister arrived, we were all watching a football match on TV.
> - While I was working on my computer, the light suddenly went off.

FAQ

Q: 有一首兒歌的歌詞是這樣的：
As I was going to St. Ives,
I met a man with seven wives,
Each wife had seven sacks,
Each sack had seven cats,
Each cat had seven kits:
Kits, cats, sacks and wives,
How many were going to St. Ives?
為什麼句首是 as？
不是應該用 while 或 when 嗎？

A: 在此情況下，連接詞 as 的意義和 while 相同。

順帶一提，你知道最後這句「How many were going to St. Ives?」的答案是什麼嗎？如果你不曉得，答案是 one：因為只有講話的這個人要去 St. Ives，其他人都要往反方向走！

3 請閱讀以下知名的美國歷史事件，並將 **A–G** 的句子填入空格。

> **A** She was sitting there
> **B** was the beginning of a long struggle
> **C** and he was standing.
> **D** She was going home after a day's work.
> **E** no one took the bus
> **F** but she refused.
> **G** everybody walked to work

On the evening of December 1st, 1955, an Afro-American woman called Rosa Parks got on a bus in Montgomery, Alabama. ¹☐ All the seats at the back of the bus were taken, so she took a seat in the front, which was reserved for white people. ²☐ when a white passenger got on the bus. He couldn't find a free seat ³☐ . The bus driver asked Rosa to give her seat to the white man ⁴☐ . So the driver called the police and she was arrested. This episode ⁵☐ called "The bus boycott." From that day, all the Afro-Americans living in Montgomery stopped using the bus as a form of protest against the segregation laws between black and white people. Every day, for 12 months, ⁶☐ and ⁷☐ any more. Finally, in December, 1956, the Supreme Court in Washington stated that segregation on buses was illegal. It was the first great victory for the civil rights movement in the USA and for its leader, Reverend Martin Luther King.

4 請以 **while** 為句首來改寫句子，但意思仍需與原句相同。

1 I was walking in the street when I saw a bad accident.

....

2 We were all cheering when a group of hooligans invaded the football pitch.

....

3 They were going home when they saw an old friend getting off the bus.

....

4 The actors were getting ready for the shoot when the director suddenly left.

....

5 I was doing my homework while my friend was waiting for me in the hall.

....

6 I was talking to the English teacher when the principal came into the library.

....

7 We were having a drink when a band started playing folk music.

....

8 The exam students were still writing when the final bell rang.

....

5 請判斷句子應為簡單過去式還是過去進行式，並用括號裡動詞的正確形式來完成句子。

1 When I .... down a country road, I .... two deer behind a bush. (cycle, see)

2 A delicious smell .... from the kitchen where Dad's apple pie .... (come, bake)

3 The burglar .... to break the lock when the alarm .... (try, go off)

4 When I .... the front door, I .... a strange noise coming from the garden. (open, hear)

5 She .... when her cat .... on her bed and .... her .... (dream, jump, wake up)

6 Rick .... very well and .... the match when it .... to rain and they had to leave the court. (play, win, start)

ROUND UP 8

1 請使用 **be** 動詞的簡單過去式來完成以下短文：

Most people lived in small villages in the countryside in the 15th century, either in farmhouses or in cottages. A typical cottage of Tudor times
¹ .... very small. The walls ² ....
made of wood, mud and straw. The roof ³ ....
often made of straw too, it ⁴ .... called
"thatched" roof. The windows ⁵ .... small and
sometimes there ⁶ .... any windows at all, just
a door. There ⁷ .... a kitchen downstairs and
one or two bedrooms upstairs. The beds ⁸ ....
quite short because people ⁹ .... very tall
then. There ¹⁰ .... always a fireplace in the kitchen with a spit to roast meat. There
¹¹ .... a toilet — people washed themselves and their clothes outside in a stream
or in a big basin in the kitchen when it ¹² .... cold. People often lived together with
their animals—chicken, sheep and goats—so the floor ¹³ .... very clean. In fact, there
¹⁴ .... a tiled floor, just dried mud covered with straw.

2 請以下列動詞的簡單過去式，完成莎士比亞的生平。

| study | be | not go | become | have | be born | retire |
| leave | found | write | buy | die | start | marry |

William Shakespeare, often called the English national
poet, is considered the greatest dramatist of all time.
He ¹ .... in Stratford-upon-Avon in 1564. He
² .... in Stratford at the local grammar school, but
he probably ³ .... to university. In 1582, when he
⁴ .... only 18 years old, he ⁵ .... Anne
Hathaway, who was 26. They ⁶ .... three children:
a daughter and twins.
In 1586, Shakespeare ⁷ .... his native town to go to
London, where he ⁸ .... an actor with the Company
of the Lord Chamberlain's Men. In London, he ⁹ ....
writing plays. He ¹⁰ .... many historical plays,
tragedies, comedies and also sonnets.

With the Lord Chamberlain's Men, he ¹¹ .... the Globe Theater, where his works were
performed. When he was rich and famous, he ¹² .... a large house in Stratford where
he ¹³ .... in 1611.
Shakespeare ¹⁴ .... in 1616, on the same day of his birth, April 23rd, and was buried in
the churchyard of Stratford Parish Church.

延伸補充

過去的習慣

我們可用 **used to** 或 **would + 原形動詞**，來說明**過去的習慣**。

- I **used to travel** a lot when I worked as a sales rep.
  = I **would travel** a lot, when I worked as a sales rep.

3 請使用 **would** 或 **used to** 來寫出意義相同的句子。

0 The children used to drink a lot of orange juice. ...The children would drink a lot of orange juice.......

1 I used to cycle to my grandma's every Sunday.

....

2 We would learn nursery rhymes by heart when we were in primary school.

....

3 He used to work six days a week for his former company.

....

4 My mother used to cook fresh vegetables every day.

....

5 They would go to an organic market to buy local cheeses when they lived in Lincoln.

....

6 I used to walk a lot when I was younger.

....

7 She didn't use to take her sister with her.

....

8 My brother would ride a big red motorcycle when he was young.

....

4 請排序以下的時間用語，最近發生的寫 **1**，最久以前發生的寫 **7**。

- ☐ Two months ago
- ☐ Last night
- ☐ Last week
- ☐ Three hours ago
- ☐ Five minutes ago
- ☐ Last year
- ☐ Yesterday morning

5 請以「簡單過去式」或「過去進行式」的動詞，來填空完成對話。

Adam Hi, Jack. What were you doing when we ⁰.....had.... (have) the blackout last night?

Jack I was at home with my wife. We ¹... (watch TV).
What about you?

Adam I ².. (go back home) in my car. I ³................................ (wait) at the
traffic lights when all of a sudden all the lights ⁴.................................... (go out).

Jack It ⁵...................................... (be) really bad. It ⁶.. (last) so long!

Adam Yes, nearly four hours. When I ⁷.. (get back home),
I just ⁸.. (go to bed).

Jack Yes, so did I. With no electricity, there's nothing much you can do!

6 請運用括號裡動詞的簡單過去式來完成短文。

The origin of coffee is lost in the timeless legends of the Middle East. What we know for sure is that coffee beans [1].......................... (spread) from Ethiopia to Yemen around 1400 and [2].......................... (not reach) Europe until the 17th century. At that time, all the coffee [3].......................... (come) from Arabia. However, thanks to the Dutch merchants, coffee cultivation [4].......................... (begin) in the Americas. It [5].......................... (spread) quickly to the West Indies, but the country where it [6].......................... (grow) best was Brazil. Between 1850 and 1900, other Latin American countries [7].......................... (develop) extensive coffee plantations. Around 1900, commercial coffee growing [8].......................... (start) in central Africa thanks to the British, but the area only [9].......................... (become) a major source of coffee after World War II.

7 請運用以下動詞的「簡單過去式」或「過去進行式」來完成對話。

do	check	have	get (x2)	hear	meet (x2)
sleep	walk	be (x3)	enjoy	leave see	know

John Have I called you at a bad time? [1].............. you ....?

Irene No, I [2].............................. my emails. When [3].............. you .... back from London?

John I [4].............. back two days ago.

Irene [5].............. you .... your business trip?

John Well, yes. I [6].............. various interesting meetings. And there's something more. Guess who I [7].............. in London!

Irene How should I know? Who [8].............. you ....?

John While I [9]............................... to the hotel, I [10].............. somebody I [11].............. sure I [12].............. It [13].............. Peter. Do you remember him? He [14].............. at university with us, but then he [15].............. with his family and we never [16].............. of him again.

Irene Peter? Yes, I remember him. What [17].............. he .... in London?

John Well, he lives there. He's a journalist with *The Guardian*.

8 請以合適的單字來完成短文。每一格僅能填入一個單字。

I went [1].......................... Neil's party last Saturday. There [2].......................... about 30 people there and we [3].......................... a great time. The party [4].......................... in the garden of his parents' house, the same place where we [5].......................... to play when we were children. There were a [6].......................... of tables with the food, while the drinks were in big buckets full of ice. Before dinner, we all chatted with one another because most of us hadn't seen each other for a long time. [7].......................... Neil was grilling steaks on the barbecue, his wife was frying chips in a huge deep fat fryer. Not the healthiest food ever, but we all enjoyed it when it was ready.

[8].......................... dinner, Jason got his old guitar out of his car and started playing and singing old songs. [9].......................... the party was getting a bit too nostalgic, Neil put on some lively music and we all [10].......................... till dawn.

9 請完成短文。將括號裡動詞改為「簡單過去式」或「過去進行式」，有時需要使用否定形式。

What a terrible night! I ¹............................. (sleep) in my bed, when the telephone ²............................. (ring). I ³............................. (answer) immediately, but I ⁴............................. (hear) anything on the other side, just a strange sound, like a cat mewing.

I ⁵............................. (put) the telephone down and I ⁶............................. (try) to go to sleep again, but it ⁷............................. (ring) again and again and again.

I could only hear the same strange sound and nothing else. After an hour like this, I ⁸............................. (decide) to call the police. While I ⁹............................. (dial) the number, I ¹⁰............................. (see) a light in my garden. Someone ¹¹............................. (walk) there and ¹²............................. (search) the garden with a torch.

At that point, I was really scared. When the police officer ¹³............................. (answer) the phone I ¹⁴............................. (whisper), so as not to be heard by the person in the garden and I ¹⁵............................. (try) to explain what ¹⁶............................. (happen).

While I ¹⁷............................. (wait) for the police to come I ¹⁸............................. (hide) behind the curtains of my bedroom window to watch what the person ¹⁹............................. (do). While the reassuring sound of the police siren ²⁰............................. (get) nearer, I ²¹............................. (hear) a banging at the door. . . .

10 現在請自行編寫故事的結局。

Reflecting on grammar
請研讀文法規則，再判斷以下說法是否正確。

		True	False
1	be 動詞的簡單過去式有兩種形式。		
2	I was 並沒有縮讀形式。		
3	不規則動詞字尾加上 ed 即可形成簡單過去式。		
4	「She didn't learnt anything.」是正確的句子。		
5	簡單過去式是用來說明講話當下仍在進行的行為。		
6	used to 是用來說明過去的習慣。		
7	時間順序的表達方式，通常最後會搭配副詞 then。		
8	「First I had breakfast, after I read the newspaper.」是正確的句子。		
9	過去進行式是用來說明，在過去特定時間持續進行的行為。		
10	我們不能在 when 開頭的子句裡使用過去進行式。		

UNIT 9 現在完成式和過去完成式
Present Perfect and Past Perfect

LESSON 1 簡單現在完成式 /ever、never、recently、today等用法
Present perfect simple: ever, never, recently, today . . .

→ 圖解請見P. 412–413

簡單現在完成式（之後簡稱為「現在完成式」）是以**助動詞 have + 主動詞的過去分詞**所構成。

過去分詞的形式：

規則動詞	不規則動詞
和簡單過去式相同，在字尾加上 **ed** 即可，如 finish**ed**、start**ed**、paint**ed** 等。	每種動詞都有自己的變化。有時候過去分詞會和原形動詞或是簡單過去式相同，像 come、found、cut 等。但通常都是不同的形式，如 been、spoken、written 等。大家可在第472–428 頁查找不規則動詞表第三欄的過去分詞。

肯定句、否定句和疑問句

肯定句
完整形式：主詞 + **have/has** + **過去分詞**
縮讀形式：主詞 + **'ve/'s** + **過去分詞**（主詞是代名詞時常使用此形式）

- We **have finished** (We've finished) at last.
- She **has arrived**! (She's arrived!)
- The children **have had** their lunch.

否定句：主詞 + **have not (haven't) / has not (hasn't)** + **過去分詞**

- I **haven't been** very well.
- He **hasn't bought** a newspaper today.

疑問句：**Have/Has** + 主詞 + **過去分詞** . . . +?
否定疑問句：**Haven't/Hasn't** + 主詞 + **過去分詞** . . . +?

簡答句：Yes, + 主詞 + have/has.　　No, + 主詞 + haven't/hasn't.

- "**Have** you **seen** Dad anywhere?" "No, I haven't."
- "**Hasn't** she **passed** her driving test?" "Yes, she has."

Wh 問句：Wh 疑問詞 + **have/has** + 主詞 + **過去分詞** . . . +?

- **Where have** you **been**?　　• **What have** you **bought**?

Focus

現在完成式一定要加上助動詞 have/has，所以 be 動詞的現在完成式要改作：

| I/you/we/they **have been** | he/she/it **has been** |

- I**'ve been** here for two hours.
- She**'s been** our general manager for ten years.

Q: 有時候會聽到「He's been to . . .」或「He's gone to . . .」這類「某人曾到過某地」的說法，這兩者有差異嗎？還是都通用？

A: 兩者的確不同，若說「He's **been to** South Africa.」，意思是此人**曾**去過南非，但現在已經回家了；而如果說「He's **gone to** South Africa.」，則是此人**還在**南非的意思。

---

1 請運用括號裡動詞的現在完成式，搭配縮讀形式來完成句子。

1 Oh no! I .... my wallet with all my credit cards. (lose)

2 We .... any new shrubs in our garden this year. (not plant)

3 I .... skiing a few times, but I'm just hopeless at it! (try)

4 Emma .... to a new apartment near the city center. (move)

5 I'm sorry, Miss Trevor. I .... my English homework today. (not do)

6 Stop being silly. I .... enough of your stupid antics. (have)

7 You .... the plants. Look — their leaves are all dried up. (not water)

8 We .... always .... this band. They play great music. (like)

9 Josh, you .... the dishes! They're all in the sink where they were last night! (not wash)

10 "........................... , sir?"
"No, you .... the menu yet."
(order, not bring)

---

2 請以現在完成式的動詞完成 **1–6** 的問句，並與 **A–F** 的答句配對。

..... **1** .... you .... your emails? (check)

..... **2** Your bag's heavy! What .... you ....? (buy)

..... **3** .... the new teacher ....? (arrive)

..... **4** .... they .... any new houses here? (build)

..... **5** .... you .... Kate? (see)

..... **6** Why .... Mom .... all this food? (cook)

A No. What happened to her?

B Yes, I have.

C Lots of fruit and veggies.

D No, he hasn't.

E We're having a dinner party tonight.

F Yes, at the end of the street.

---

3 請圈出正確的用字。

1 Sally, you look wonderful! Have you **been** / **gone** to the hairdresser's?

2 Where have you **been** / **gone**? You're 15 minutes late and the lesson's started.

3 Do you know where Bill's **gone** / **been**? His motorcycle isn't in the garage.

4 My friend Julie has just **been** / **gone** to India. She brought me back this beautiful silk sari.

5 Liza's **gone** / **been** to the doctor's. I hope she feels better when she comes back.

6 The boys have **been** / **gone** camping. They'll be back on Sunday.

7 Beth? She's **been** / **gone** to the mountains like every weekend. You know she's mad about trekking.

8 My husband's **been** / **gone** to the bank. There's something strange on our statement. I hope it's just a mistake and he can sort it out.

9 What a beautiful suntan! Where have you **been** / **gone**?

10 Haven't you **been** / **gone** to the gym this afternoon? The instructor has just called.

現在完成式的部分用法

現在完成式用來形容較特定的語境，可看作「銜接」現在式與過去式的時態、「截至目前為止」的時態或「現今」時態。

現在完成式通常用來說明以下情況：

❶ 在**過去**某時間點發生的行為，尤其該行為的**結果延續至今**，或與現在有關：

We **have run** out of gasoline.

John **has broken** his arm.

Dad **has painted** the front door.

再看看其他例子：

- I**'ve sold** my car and I**'ve bought** this one. Do you like it? (意指「現在」可看到新車)
- The Millers **have moved** into the apartment next to ours. (雖然沒有說這件事發生的時間點，但有點出米勒一家「現在」住在這裡的事實)

❷ 說明**經驗**、**詢問**與**表示**某事件是否曾發生；經常需要搭配副詞 ever/never/always：

- "**Have** you **ever tried** paragliding?" "I**'ve never tried** it, but I'd like to."

有時句尾會有副詞 before 或 so far：

- I**'ve** never **been** on a plane before. This is my first flight.
- Nothing **has happened** so far.

❸ 說明**最近剛發生的事**，常搭配副詞 recently 或 lately：

- We**'ve had** quite a lot of rain recently.

❹ 說明在**進行中的時間點**所發生的事，如 today、this week、in the last few days 等：

- I**'ve been** very busy in the last few days.

> **!** 但如果事件發生在 yesterday、last week 等**過去特定時間範圍**，就一定要用**簡單過去式**來表達，而不是現在完成式（請參閱第 133 頁）：
> - I **was** very busy last week.

---

4 請以 ever 或 never 來完成句子。

1 "Have you .... been to Berlin?" "Yes, quite a lot. My aunt lives there."

2 Has anyone here .... had a part in a musical?

3 This is the best party I've .... been to.

4 We've .... stayed in a five-star hotel.

5 I've .... slept in a treehouse, but I'd like to.

6 I've .... heard anything like that. It's a very strange story.

5 請重新排序單字來造句。

1 son / has / My / never / lived / before / on his own / .

....

2 ever / Have / thought / moving / you / of / abroad / ?

....

3 picture / never / such a / I've / seen / beautiful / !

....

4 you / any / done / so far / research / Have / ?

....

5 all day / It's / today / been / hot and / sunny / .

....

6 have / never / there / been / We / .

....

7 your / Has / match / team / this / won / a / so / far / year / ?

....

8 worked / restaurant / She / never / in / has / a / before / !

....

6 請將 **1–8** 的句子與 **A–H** 的句子配對。

1 I haven't seen the weather forecast today.

2 The children haven't put their toys away.

3 Matt has posted some photos of the baby today.

4 I've been to Rome many times in the last few years.

5 My parents have never been on a cruise.

6 I've eaten a lot in the last few months.

7 I haven't been very well lately.

8 Lily has gone to New York on a business trip.

A Do you want to see them on my cell phone?

B I'm putting on some weight, I'm afraid.

C She's coming back tomorrow.

D They're still all over the living room floor.

E They're going on one next week for their 20th wedding anniversary.

F I don't know what the weather's going to be like.

G I'm going again in April.

H I'm going to hospital for a check-up tomorrow.

1 .....   2 .....   3 .....   4 .....   5 .....   6 .....   7 .....   8 .....

LESSON 2 簡單現在完成式 / just、already、yet 用法 / 簡單現在完成式 vs. 簡單過去式
Present perfect simple: just, already, yet / comparison between the present perfect and the past simple

現在完成式還能用在對「**現在**」造成影響的事件。
尤其是以下情況：

❶ 表達**剛剛發生的事**，此時在助動詞 have 和主動詞的過去分詞之間常使用副詞 **just**：

• They**'ve just come** home from school.
• They**'ve just got** married.

147

❷ 詢問是否完成某事，例如下列旅遊前的待辦事項：

> · turn off heating　　· water plants　　· get passports　　· weigh hand luggage

Have you **turned** off the heating?　Yes, I have.

Have you **watered** the plants?　Yes, I have.

Have you **got** the passports?　Yes, I have.

And **have** you **weighed** the hand luggage? We're flying low cost.　　No, I haven't. You do it!

此類問句通常會搭配副詞 **yet**（放在句尾）或 **already**（放在主詞後面）：

- **Have** you **had** lunch **yet**?（中立語氣的問句）
- **Have** you **already had** lunch?（帶驚訝語氣的問句）

❸ 在助動詞 have 和過去分詞之間，使用副詞 **already** 來說明**已經完成**的事項；或在句尾使用 **yet**，來說明**尚未完成**的事項：

- I**'ve already fed** the dog. I **haven't taken** him for a walk **yet**.

而否定句裡，我們會用 **still . . . not**，而不是 not . . . yet。
still 用以暗示早就要執行、卻還沒執行的情況（語氣會像是「What? Haven't you done it yet?」的感覺）：

- You **still haven't taken** your medicine. Do it now, you must keep to the times.

請再閱讀以下例句：

- I **haven't read** this book **yet**.（中立語氣）
- I **still haven't read** this book.（意指「我想讀這本書，但還沒設法做到這件事」）

> **!** 在美式口語英文裡，**just**、**already** 和 **yet** 等單字搭配的時態常是**簡單過去式**。
>
> | 口語用法 | 書面用法 |
> | --- | --- |
> | · I **just saw** her. | · I**'ve just seen** her. |
> | · I **already did** everything, | · I**'ve already done** everything. |
> | · **Did** you **hear** from her **yet**? | · **Have** you **heard** from her **yet**? |

1 請以 just、already、yet、still 完成克漏字。

1 "Hi. Am I calling at a bad time?"　"No, I'm at home. I've .... come back from work."

2 He's been away ten days and I .... haven't received a message from him.

3 James has .... found a new job in the bank. He's starting next week.

4 "Have the boys come back from the gym .... ?"　"No, not ...."

5 The bus has .... stopped at a highway service area and everyone is getting out.

6 Oh no! The baby has .... woken up and his milk isn't ready ....

7 The teacher hasn't given us back our tests ....
   (Two days later) She .... hasn't given them back to us!

8 No, thanks. I don't need your dictionary, I've .... done the translation.

9 Have you .... finished your homework? I can't believe it.

2 請從每一欄選出一項單字，搭配現在完成式，造出六個句子。

主詞	助動詞	副詞	過去分詞	受詞
We		just	written	this movie.
They	have		read	a flight to New York.
I		already	seen	bungee jumping.
My sister			played	the xylophone.
He	has	never	booked	my history project.
She			tried	this novel.

3 芬瑞準備幫兒子在花園辦場派對。請看一下她的筆記，打勾的項目是她已經完成的，打叉的則是尚未完成的。請依照例句的形式，用 **already** 或 **not . . . yet** 來造句。

* call Steve's mom to see if he's coming ☑
* buy some bags of sweets for the kids ☑
* decorate the birthday cake ☒
* put the play tent up in the garden ☒
* organize some games ☑
* ask Martha for some more chairs ☒
* buy some balloons and party hats ☑

0 ..Fran has already called Steve's mom to see if he's coming...

1 ....

2 ....

3 ....

4 ....

5 ....

6 ....

UNIT
9
現在完成式和過去完成式

4 請將 **1–10** 的問句和 **A–J** 的答句配對。

1 What a lot of washing-up! Let me help!

2 Have you told your mom about your exam results yet?

3 Has John already gone to the airport?

4 Where have you been? Shopping?

5 Now, where have I put the car keys?

6 Have you seen my glasses anywhere?

7 Haven't you done your homework yet?

8 Has Diana got back from Spain yet?

9 Who did you say you've just seen?

10 It's only eight o'clock. Have the kids already gone to bed?

A Yes, and I've just bought this dress.

B Yes, they were tired!

C Yes, I've just put them on your bedside table.

D No, not yet. She'll be angry with me when she hears I've failed.

E Yes, she's just arrived. She said she loved Barcelona!

F Jude Law, that famous actor. He was sitting next to me on the subway!

G Don't worry. I've already put a lot of it in the dishwasher.

H No, I'm going to do it now, I promise.

I You've probably left them on the kitchen table.

J Yes, he wanted to get there a bit ahead of time.

1 .....　**2** .....　**3** .....　**4** .....　**5** .....　**6** .....　**7** .....　**8** .....　**9** .....　**10** .....

FAQ

Q: 我該如何判斷使用現在完成式和簡單過去式的時機呢？

A: 你可以試試將你想說的事想像成**電腦裡的檔案**。如果檔案是**關閉且歸檔**在資料夾的狀態，就用**簡單過去式**；但如果檔案仍為**開啟**或**放在桌面**的狀態，就用**現在完成式**。

也就是說：

在過去特定時間所發生且已完成的經驗（等同已歸檔文件）
➡ **簡單過去式**

仍與現在有關的經驗、或在過去發生但尚未完成的經驗
（等同電腦文件仍開啟的狀態）➡ **現在完成式**。

---

5 請圈出正確的時態。

1 My family **lived** / **have lived** in Wales before they **came** / **have come** to London over two years ago.

2 We **were** / **have been** in San Francisco for a week now. We're enjoying it!

3 I **have got up** / **got up** later than usual yesterday morning. I **have had** / **didn't have** anything important to do.

4 We **have lived** / **lived** on this farm for a long time. We really like living in the country.

5 I **have read** / **read** three books so far this week. This one is my favorite.

6 She **hasn't been** / **wasn't** very well recently. She should talk to the doctor.

7 I **have had** / **had** a lot of interviews, but I still **haven't found** / **didn't find** a good job.

8 I **stayed** / **have stayed** at a very good hotel when I was in Tokyo.

9 We **haven't had** / **didn't have** time to meet Peter when we **were** / **have been** in London on business.

10 **Have you ever been** / **Were you ever** to Kenya?

---

6 請重新排序單字來造句。如果是簡單過去式（**Past Simple**）的句子，請寫 **PS**；如果是現在完成式（**Present Perfect**）的句子，請寫 **PP**。

1 tidied / haven't / I / yet / bedroom / my / .
☐ ....

2 tidied / She / bedroom / Saturday / her / last / .
☐ ....

3 Louise / from / France / yet / back / got / Has / ?
☐ ....

4 did / Louise / back / get / France / When / from / ?
☐ ....

5 just / who / Guess / seen / have / I / town / in / !
☐ ....

6 saw / an / friend / mine / I / old / of / last / theater / at / night / the / .
☐ ....

7 brother / has / My / already / graduated / from / school / high / .
☐ ....

8 graduated / I / year / from / high / last / school / .
☐ ....

7 請完成句子，將括號裡動詞改為現在完成式或簡單過去式。可利用粗體字的副詞或時間用語幫助判斷時態。

1 We .... (have) dinner at a Mexican restaurant **last night**. The food .... (be) excellent. .... (**ever** / try) tacos?

2 We are in London! We .... (**already** / do) lots of things: **yesterday** we .... (go) to the National Gallery and we .... (see) the Changing of the Guard. We .... (not visit) the British Museum **yet**. We're going today.

3 We .... (**just** / get back) from summer camp. We had a great time there.

4 "........................ (book) the flight **yet**?" "Yes, I .... (do) it **last night**."

5 I .... (**already** / buy) the presents for most people, but I .... (**still** / not buy) one for my sister.

6 **Last year**, I .... (not go) on vacation, but **this year** I .... (**already** / be) to the seaside twice.

7 I .... (**never** / be) to the stadium to watch a football match.

8 Mark .... (**just** / phone). He .... (arrive) at the hotel **two hours ago**.

8 請以括號內的提示用詞完成以下對話。

1 Mark ....? (visited the Tate Modern)
   Julie .... (Yes)
   Mark ....? (When / go)
   Julie .... (yesterday afternoon)
2 Adam ....? (been camping)
   Rick .... (Yes)
   Adam ....? (like)
   Rick .... (Yes / great experience)
3 Brad ....? (been to Australia)
   Frances .... (twice)
   Brad ....? (stay long)
   Frances ....
   (two weeks the first time / three weeks the second time)
   Brad .... (cities / visit)
   Frances .... (Sydney and Melbourne)

LESSON 3 簡單現在完成式／現在完成進行式／How long 問句／for 與 since 用法
Present perfect simple and continuous / How long . . . ? / for / since

現在完成式

❶ 現在完成式具有「**從過去持續到現在**」的意思。
此時態用以說明行為發生於過去，且仍維持到現在，表示此行為尚未結束。

❷ 我們會以介系詞 **for** + **一段時間**或介系詞 **since** + **開始該行為的時間點**，來表達行為的**持續狀態**：
   • I've lived in India **for** three years.
   • I've lived here **since** December, 2015.

1 請將下方各時間用語填入正確的分類。

| ten minutes | yesterday | March 2015 | two years | last month | an hour |
| last week | five o'clock | 1998 | centuries | a long time | ages |

FOR	SINCE

FAQ

Q: 我曾寫過「I've lived in this town since when I was born.」，老師卻說我寫錯了。我的句子哪裡有問題呢？

A: since when 的用法是錯誤的。**since** 可作為連接詞，意指「**從某時間點的那個當下開始**」（from the time when），因此**不需再加上 when**。另外，由 since 引導的子句，使用簡單過去式的動詞，這個是寫對的。

2 請使用現在完成式的動詞，搭配 **for** 或 **since** 來完成句子。

1 The Wilsons .... (live) next door to us .... the summer of 2010. They're a nice family.

2 Kylie .... (be) in Greece .... last Monday. She says she's having a great time there.

3 I .... (know) my music teacher .... years .... I started playing the guitar.

4 I .... (want) to see the mountains in Nepal .... I saw a documentary about Everest on TV when I was a child.

5 We .... (live) in this house .... we got married in 2003.

6 Bill .... (own) this shop .... a long time. He's doing good business.

7 I .... (be) a teacher of English .... 1980. I .... (teach) generations of students .... nearly forty years.

8 Claire and Tom .... (work) together in the same office .... ten years now, ... Tom moved to Chicago from Los Angeles.

---

❶ 行為動詞又稱為**動態動詞**，指的是具有**實際動作**（如 run）或**描述狀態改變**（如 change）的動詞。

❷ 當句子中的動詞不是行為動詞時，就要使用**現在完成式**來表示持續狀態。搭配的動詞如下：

　❶ 狀態動詞，如 **be**、**live**、**stay** 等：I've **been** here for an hour.

　❷ 具「持有」意義的動詞，如 **have**、**own**：→They**'ve owned** the shop for two years.

　❸ 表達心理狀態或感受的動詞，如 **know**、**want**、**love** 等：
　　She**'s known** him for a long time.

❸ 而句中主動詞若是**行為動詞**，通常會用**現在完成進行式**來表示持續狀態（請參閱第 154 頁）。

- "How long **have** you **been playing** video games?"
  "I**'ve been playing** for an hour."

持續狀態的否定句和疑問句否定句

否定句

現在完成式的狀續時態中，如果是在表達**某時間點尚未發生的情況或行為**，即可搭配行為動詞和狀態動詞來表達否定句：

> 主詞 + **haven't/hasn't** + **過去分詞** + **for/since . . .**

- I **haven't been** to New York **for** ten years.
- She **hasn't played** the piano **for** a long time.

疑問句

Yes/No 問句，用以詢問某情況是否已持續一段時間：

> **Have/Has** + 主詞 + **過去分詞** + **for/since . . .** + ?

- "**Have** you **been** here **for** a long time?"
  "No, I haven't. I**'ve** just **been** here **for** a couple of weeks."

How long 與 Since when 問句：

> **How long/Since when** + **have/has** + 主詞 + **過去分詞 . . .** + ?

- "**How long have** you **had** this car?"
  "I've had it for a long time. It's quite old."
- "**Since when have** you **known** Jennifer?"
  "Since last Saturday. I met her at a party."

> ❗ 另外，如果想詢問某事件發生的**時間點**（如 When 問句），一定要使用**簡單過去式**，因為我們詢問的是過去某特定時間的事：
> - "When **did** you **meet** Jennifer?"
>   "I **met** her last Saturday."

UNIT
9
現在完成式和過去完成式

---

❸ 請完成對話，將括號裡的動詞改成「現在完成式」或「簡單過去式」。

A How long ¹............................ Bruce for? (know)

B Bruce? I ²............................ (know) him since we were at primary school together, so that means about 20 years. We've been close friends ever since.

A And when ³............................ last .... him? (see)

B Well, I ⁴............................ (see) him a couple of weeks ago. He ⁵............................ (come) to my house with his wife.

A Really? I didn't know he was married. When
⁶... ? (get married)

B He got married in June. Ellen, his wife, is really nice.

A How long ⁷... each other? (they, know)

B Not that long. They ⁸............................ (meet) in January and decided to get married six months later. He says they ⁹............................ (be) in love since they first met!

A It was love at first sight, then!

B By the way, ¹⁰... (hear) from Sara? I ¹¹................................... (not hear) from her for ages.

A Yes, she's just emailed me from Tanzania. She ¹²............................ (be) there for six months working with a charity.

B How interesting!

請完成意義相近的句子。

1 The last time I was in New York was ten years ago.

   I haven't been to ....

2 We last had dinner in a restaurant on my birthday.

   We haven't ....

3 I haven't had a long holiday since the summer of 2020.

   The last time ....

4 I have owned this Harley Davidson for three years.

   I bought ....

5 I started being a Manchester City fan when I was five years old.

   I've been ....

6 They've been best friends for a long, long time.

   They became ....ago.

7 He went to a club at 11 last night and stayed there until 2 a.m.

   He was .... for .... last night, from .... to ....

8 We last had a heavy snowfall in the winter of 2014.

   We haven't ....

9 Carol met Richard in 2019 and they got married a year later.

   Carol and Richard .... 2019 and .... 2020.

10 The last time they played tennis together was last year.

   They .... last year.

現在完成進行式

英文裡所有時態都有簡單式和進行式此兩種形式。英文時態系統具有結合「時間」和「狀態」特性，因此可讓讀的人知道，某行為是重複發生，還是只發生在單一時間點；是已完成還是仍在進行中。

複習一下之前學過的時態：

簡單現在式（參閱第 80 頁）：
表達習慣、重複多次的行為以及固定情況

現在進行式（參閱第 95 頁）：
表達進行中或暫時的行為

簡單過去式（參閱第 133 頁）：
表達過去已完成的行為

過去進行式（參閱第 137 頁）：
表達過去一段特定時間發生的行為

我們有學過，進行式是以 be 動詞加上現在分詞或主動詞 ing 所構成：

現在進行式

| 簡單現在式的 be 動詞 + 動詞 ing |

I'm waiting.（現在在等候）

過去進行式

| 簡單過去式的 be 動詞 + 動詞 ing |

• I was waiting.（過去在等候）

因此，現在完成進行式的句子，必須採用**現在完成式的 be 動詞**，變成「**I've been** waiting.」（持續等候到現在）

| 肯定句：主詞 + **have/has been** + 動詞 ing |
| 疑問句：（Wh 疑問詞）+ **have/has** + 主詞 + **been** + 動詞 ing + ? |
| 否定句：主詞 + **haven't/hasn't been** + 動詞 ing（較不常見）|

此時態用以表達**持續進行、延續至現在的行為**，通常會與 all day / all day long、all night、all week 等副詞片語搭配使用。

• "What have you been doing today?"
   "We've **been studying** all day."

現在完成進行式代表的是某種**過程**，
現在完成式則是突顯該行為的**最終結果**：

- He**'s been chopping** wood all morning.
- Look! He**'s chopped** over twenty large trunks.

5 學校師生整個早上都在進行不同的活動，且各有不同結果。
請瀏覽下表，依照例句的方式來造句。

	過程	結果
students in Class 4	work in groups	make a PowerPoint presentation about bioenergy
Mr. Reed	teach Class 3	design a school web page
students in Class 2	read their study notes	revise things for their exams
the ICT teacher	tutor a small group	learn InDesign
our English class	look at the present perfect	do this exercise
the headmaster	write end-of-term reports	nearly finish all the reports
Mrs. Seath	revise French irregular verbs	read out a list of difficult verbs

0 The students in Class 4 have been working in groups. They have made a PowerPoint presentation about bioenergy.

1 ....

2 ....

3 ....

4 ....

5 ....

6 ....

現在完成進行式的持續時態

1 依照第 152 頁所說明的規則，現在完成進行式經常搭配 **for** 或 **since**，
用以表達**某行為持續了多久時間**：
"How long have you been running?"
"I**'ve been running** for a couple of hours."

2 現在完成進行式適用於以下情況：

1 有行為動詞時　　**2** 肯定句或疑問句　　**3** 行為仍在進行中，或者剛結束且能當下看到結果

6 請選出正確的句子。

1 Ⓐ How long have you been in this school?
　 Ⓑ How long have you being in this school?

2 Ⓐ I've been in this school for two years.
　 Ⓑ I've been in this school since two years.

3 Ⓐ He's been slept since three o'clock.
　 Ⓑ He's been sleeping since three o'clock.

4 Ⓐ I've lived in Dallas for five years before I moved to New York.
　 Ⓑ I lived in Dallas for five years before I moved to New York.

5 Ⓐ My brother hasn't driven a pickup since he was in the army.
　 Ⓑ My brother hasn't been driving a pickup since he was in the army.

6 Ⓐ We have been working for this firm since 2013.
　 Ⓑ We are working for this firm since 2013.

7 Ⓐ I've been having this bicycle for ten years.
　 Ⓑ I've had this bicycle for ten years.

8 Ⓐ I haven't been seeing her for ages.
　 Ⓑ I haven't seen her for ages.

7 請以括號裡動詞的現在完成進行式完成 **1–8** 的句子。
再將 **1–8** 的句子和 **A–H** 的句子配對。

..... **1** I .... French for two years, (learn)

..... **2** I .... since seven o'clock. (work)

..... **3** We .... for you for ages. (wait)

..... **4** We .... for hours. (walk)

..... **5** Mr. Simmons .... math in my school since 2005. (teach)

..... **6** I .... to find a job for months, (try)

..... **7** She .... the harp in this orchestra for three years. (play)

..... **8** I .... for my piano exam for weeks. (practice)

A Why are you always late?

B He's a really good teacher.

C but I still haven't got one!

D but I still don't speak it fluently.

E She plays very well!

F I'm really tired.

G I'm ready now.

H Let's have a rest now.

8 請根據答句內容寫出合適的問句。

1 Since when .... ?
I've been singing in the school choir since the beginning of the year.

2 Has .... there?
Yes, it's been raining all afternoon. And it's been raining hard!

3 How long .... the kids .... ?
They've been playing all afternoon.

4 .... you .... chemistry?
No, I've been studying physics actually. We have a test tomorrow.

5 How long .... for?
We've been eating since 2 p.m. — it's a big dinner!

6 What kind of music .... you .... to ?
I've been listening to a live concert of The Rolling Stones!

7 What .... this afternoon?
I've been cleaning the house.

8 Since when .... on your computer?
I've been working since nine this morning and I'm quite tired now.

9 請完成意義相近的句子。

1 I started working on this project five days ago and still haven't finished.

I've ....

for ....

2 It's seven o'clock now. Peter has been working out in the gym since five.

Peter ....

for ....

3 I have told you many times how to behave!

I've been ....

over and over again ....

4 It started snowing at 9 p.m. It's midnight now and it's still snowing.

It's been ....

for ....

since ....

5 The boys started swimming an hour ago and are still in the pool. They've been training for their next event.

The boys have ....

for ....

for their next event.

10 請完成對話，將括號裡動詞改為「現在完成式」或「現在完成進行式」。

1 A .... you already .... , Ben? (order)

B Yes, I have actually.

A You didn't wait for me? Oh well, what .... you .... ? (order)

B Lasagne. It's great here.

A OK. I'll have the same.

2 A What .... you .... at home all day? (do)

B I .... and .... and .... TV. It's been a lazy day! (sleep, read, watch)

A What .... on TV? (watch)

B I .... my favorite series — *Dr. Martin*! (watch) I love watching TV on a rainy day like this.

3 A Mom's in a cooking mood today, she .... all afternoon! (cook)

B What .... she .... ? (cook)

A She .... some really nice things: chocolate muffins, fruit tarts and shortcake! (make)

B Yum!

4 A You .... from that book for hours. (not look up) What .... you .... about? (read)

B An international spy ring. I .... nearly .... it now. (finish)

5 A .... you ever .... white-water rafting, Rachel? (try)

B No, never! And nor would I like to. Have you?

A Yes, I go rafting on the river with an instructor every Sunday. It's good fun!

B Very adventurous!

現在完成式

簡單現在完成式與現在完成進行式的用法整理

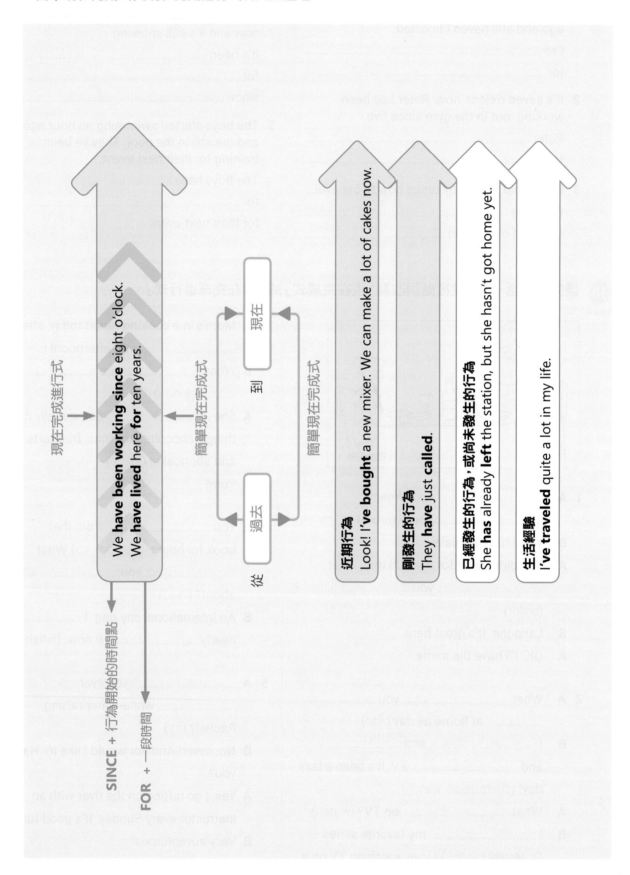

現在完成進行式

We **have been working since** eight o'clock.
We **have lived** here **for** ten years.

SINCE + 行為開始的時間點
FOR + 一段時間

簡單現在完成式

從　到　現在　過去

簡單現在完成式

近期行為
Look! I'**ve bought** a new mixer. We can make a lot of cakes now.

剛發生的行為
They **have just called**.

已經發生的行為，或尚未發生的行為
She **has** already **left** the station, but she hasn't got home yet.

生活經驗
I'**ve traveled** quite a lot in my life.

LESSON 4 簡單過去完成式／過去完成進行式
Past perfect simple and continuous

簡單過去完成式

簡單過去完成式(我們之後簡稱為「過去完成式」)是以助動詞 **had** + **主動詞**的過去分詞所構成，且適用於所有人稱。

肯定句、否定句和疑問句

肯定句：
完整形式：主詞 + **had** + **過去分詞**
（規則動詞的字尾加 ed，或是參考不規則動詞表的第三欄）
縮讀形式：主詞 + **'d** + **過去分詞**
（此為最不常見的用法）

- They **had** already **left** when we got there.

否定句：
主詞 + **had not(hadn't)** + **過去分詞**

- We **hadn't been** there before.

疑問句：
Had + 主詞 + **過去分詞** + ... + ?
否定疑問句：
Had + 主詞 + **not** + **過去分詞** + ... + ?
Hadn't + 主詞 + **過去分詞** ... + ?

簡答句：
Yes, + 主詞 + had.
No, + 主詞 + hadn't.

- "**Had** she **made** a mistake?" "No, she hadn't."
- "**Hadn't** he **passed** his final exam?" "Yes, he had."

Wh 問句：
Wh 疑問詞 + **had** + 主詞 + **過去分詞** + ... + ?

- **Where had** they **been**?
- **What had** she **said**?
- **How long had** he **had** that job?

Focus

英文的過去完成式裡，助動詞只能用 **had**，如 I had had、I had gone、they had arrived：

be 動詞的過去完成式：I/You/He/She/It/We/They **had been**

have 動詞的過去完成式：I/You/He/She/It/We/They **had had**

過去完成式的部分用法

❶ 過去完成式用於說明**某事在過去發生**，且發生在其他以**簡單過去式**表達的行為**之前**。
過去完成式也具有「**以前已經發生過**」的意義。此時態常與副詞 **already** 搭配使用：

- The police **arrived** quickly, but the robber **had already escaped**.
（意指「歹徒在警察抵達前早已逃離」→ 逃離比抵達早發生）

❷ **過去完成式常見的特性：**

❶ 用在**主要子句**，且前有連接詞 **when**、**before** 或片語 **by the time** 引導的附屬時間子句。
而從屬子句的動詞需使用簡單過去式：

- **When** he **called** her, she **had already crossed** the road and couldn't hear him.

　　↑ 從屬子句：　　　　↑ 主要子句：
　　用簡單過去式　　　　用過去完成式

- **Before** it **got** dark, they **had mowed** the lawn and watered the garden.
- **By the time** my parents **got** home, we **had cleaned** the house.

❷ 用於以 after 或 till/until 引導的從屬子句。在此情況下，主要子句的動詞需使用簡單過去式：

• **After** he **had spoken** to the students, the principal **turned** to the door and **left** the class.

      ↑ 從屬子句：   ↑ 主要子句：

      用過去完成式   用簡單過去式

• She **didn't want** to leave **until** everybody **had finished** eating.

    ↑ 主要子句：   ↑ 從屬子句：

    用簡單過去式   用過去完成式

❸ 用在轉述句中，且當句中動詞是簡單過去式（say 或 tell），而被轉述的事件早已發生時（請參閱第 351 頁）：

• They **said** they **had** already **bought** everything we needed.
• I **told** her I **had been** there before.

---

1 請勾選與原句意義相同的句子。

1 My friend tried to ring my phone soon after I had switched it off.
- [ ] **Ⓐ** I switched off my phone before my friend tried to ring.
- [ ] **Ⓑ** My friend tried to ring before I switched my phone off.

2 Mr. Connelly couldn't ring my phone because he had lost my phone number.
- [ ] **Ⓐ** Mr. Connelly couldn't find my phone number so he didn't ring me.
- [ ] **Ⓑ** I had never given Mr. Connelly my phone number so he couldn't ring.

3 My daughter had learned to read before she started primary school.
- [ ] **Ⓐ** My daughter learned to read soon after she started primary school.
- [ ] **Ⓑ** My daughter learned to read, then she went to primary school.

4 By the time all the students were seated, the teacher had already handed out all the test papers.
- [ ] **Ⓐ** The teacher had started handing out the test papers before all the students were seated.
- [ ] **Ⓑ** The teacher waited for all the students to be seated, then handed out all the test papers.

5 Matthew went to work for a non-profit organization as soon as he had finished university.
- [ ] **Ⓐ** After finishing university, Matthew went to work for a non-profit organization.
- [ ] **Ⓑ** Matthew started working for a non-profit organization, then finished university.

6 By the time Jack finished his homework, he had already eaten two sandwiches.
- [ ] **Ⓐ** Jack finished his homework, then ate two sandwiches.
- [ ] **Ⓑ** Jack ate two sandwiches while he was doing his homework.

---

2 請以「簡單過去式」或「過去完成式」的動詞，來完成克漏字。

1 I arrived late at the venue and the conference .... already .... (begin)

2 The traffic on the highway was so bad last night that I .... home at half past eleven, when everybody .... already .... to bed. (get, go)

3 After Mary .... her breakfast, she met her friend and .... to school. (eat, walk)

4 When I .... the fridge, I found out that someone .... all the beer. (open, drink)

5 Fiona's birthday was in July, but her mom .... already .... her a present three months before. (buy)

6 Our cousins .... to see us in Italy last summer. We .... them since they left for Buenos Aires in 1998. (come, not see)

7 I was so happy! I .... never .... an A in a math test before. (get)

8 As soon as Jim read the exam questions, he knew that he .... enough. (not study)

過去完成進行式

1 過去完成進行式是以**過去完成式的 be 動詞**後接**動詞 ing** 所組成，如「I had been waiting.」。

> 肯定句：主詞 + **had been** + **動詞 ing**
> 否定句：主詞 + **hadn't been** + **動詞 ing**（較少見）
> 疑問句：（Wh 疑問詞） + **had** + 主詞 + **been** + **動詞 ing** + ... + ?

2 **過去完成進行式**用於表達某一行為，**過去持續過一段特定時間且現在仍進行中**，或**剛在過去某時間點結束**。此時態尤其適用說明**曾持續發生的過往事件**，此時會搭配 **all day**、
all afternoon 等時間用語：

- It **had been raining** all day and we were looking forward to a little bit of sunshine.
- My uncle arrived at last. We **had been waiting** for him all morning.

請依照邏輯，先將 **1–10** 與 **A–J** 配對，然後將括號裡的動詞改為「過去完成式」或「過去完成進行式」，來完成句子。

UNIT

現在完成式和過去完成式

1 Yesterday I found the book I .... (look for).

2 Tom started doing his homework at ten o'clock.

3 Tina started working in a shop when she was 18.

4 My father .... retired for a couple of years (be)

5 When Miss Bradshaw said her name,

6 Before my daughter took her final exam,

7 Ben .... cartoons for two hours (watch)

8 We .... for hours without a break (drive)

9 They .... the house for hours (tidy)

10 The party .... (already / finish)

A By 11, he .... half of it. (do)

B when he decided to start a new business.

C she .... an advanced ICT course. (attend)

D It was in a drawer.

E when his mom told him to switch off the TV.

F when we finally stopped at a highway service area.

G I remembered I .... her before. (meet)

H By the age of 20, she .... a promotion. (have)

I when Philip turned up.

J because their parents were about to come home from their holidays.

1 ..... 2 ..... 3 ..... 4 ..... 5 ..... 6 ..... 7 ..... 8 ..... 9 ..... 10 .....

過去完成式和過去完成進行式的持續狀態

1 現在完成式是用來表達某行為從過去持續到現在（請參閱第 151 頁），而**過去完成式**也一樣，是用來表達**某行為從更久以前持續到過去某個時間點**。

2 過去完成式更特別表示**某行為在過去持續一段時間**，或在**過去特定時間點結束**。句子裡通常會搭配介系詞 since 表示此段時間從何開始，或搭配介系詞 for 表示期間範圍。

3 過去完成式會**搭配行為動詞以外的動詞**，或是否定句下的所有類型的動詞：

- He **had been** mayor **for** two years when he was ousted in a bribery scandal.

- The tenor **hadn't sung for** some time because his voice was a little hoarse.

4 過去完成進行式則僅用於**肯定句**和**疑問句**，且搭配**行為動詞**：

- When I entered the theater in the evening, the actors told me they **had been rehearsing** since one o'clock. They were exhausted.
- How long **had** you **been training** when I saw you on the track the other day?
- We **had been training** for a few minutes.

---

4 請圈出正確的用字。

1 Sara found the glasses she **was / had been** looking for all morning.

2 The gold medalist **had been / was been** training for months before she won the event.

3 As soon as he had finished writing emails, he **went / had gone** for a run in the park.

4 His wife was exhausted because she **had / has** been doing household chores all day.

5 A group of teenagers **had been shouting / had shouted** in the street when the police arrived.

6 Jane **had been hoping / used to be hoping** to get a job interview for months — when she finally did, it was for a job she really hated.

7 What **have / had** you been doing here? What's all this mess?

8 Joanne fell asleep during the lecture because she **had been / was** walking all day to visit as much as she could of the city.

9 When their parents **got / had got** home, the kids had already tidied up after the party.

10 Lucy **was / had been** studying for months for her anatomy exam and she got a top score in the end.

---

5 請運用括號裡動詞的「簡單過去式」、「過去完成式」或「過去完成進行式」，來完成短文。

Jessica, my grandmother's helper, [1].......................... (not be) to her native country, Ecuador, for four years when she finally [2].......................... (have) a chance to go back last summer. She [3].......................... (look forward) to it for a long time. As soon as she got there, she [4].......................... (visit) her parents and all of her relations, including a new nephew and a niece she [5].......................... (never meet) before. Her family [6].......................... (organize) a welcome party for her. She [7].......................... (stay) with her parents for a whole month and, when it was time for her to go, everybody [8].......................... (be) upset. My grandmother was happy when Jessica got back. She [9].......................... (miss) her when she [10].......................... (be) away.

過去式

過去式的用法整理

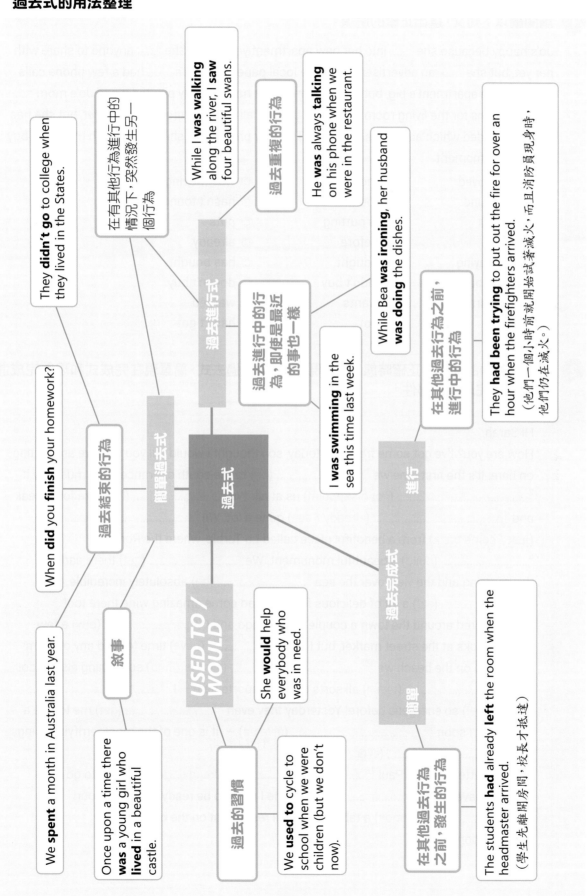

They **didn't go** to college when they lived in the States.

在有其他行為進行中的情況下，突然發生另一個行為

While I **was walking** along the river, I **saw** four beautiful swans.

過去重複的行為

He **was** always **talking** on his phone when we were in the restaurant.

過去進行式

過去進行中的行為，即使是最近的事也一樣

I **was swimming** in the sea this time last week.

While Bea **was ironing**, her husband **was doing** the dishes.

在其他過去行為之前，進行中的行為

They **had been trying** to put out the fire for over an hour when the firefighters arrived.

（他們一個小時前就開始試著滅火，而且消防員現身時，他們仍在滅火。）

When **did** you **finish** your homework?

過去結束的行為

簡單過去式

過去式

進行

過去完成式

簡單

The students **had** already **left** the room when the headmaster arrived.

（學生先離開房間，校長才抵達）

We **spent** a month in Australia last year.

敘事

Once upon a time there **was** a young girl who **lived** in a beautiful castle.

USED TO / WOULD

She **would** help everybody who was in need.

過去的習慣

We **used to** cycle to school when we were children (but we don't now).

在其他過去行為之前，發生的行為

163

ROUND UP 9

1 請閱讀以下短文，選出正確的選項。

Jo's happy because she ¹...... into her new apartment yesterday. She ²...... anyone to share with her yet, but she ³...... an advertisement in the local paper and she's ⁴...... had a few phone calls about it. The apartment's big, but Jo and her brother have already painted it and Jo's mom ⁵...... some curtains for the living room last week. Jo ⁶...... all the furniture she needs yet, but she has already decided which armchairs she ⁷...... . The only problem is, she ⁸...... enough money to buy them at the moment.

1	Ⓐ has moved	Ⓑ moved	Ⓒ was moving
2	Ⓐ has found	Ⓑ found	Ⓒ hasn't found
3	Ⓐ has put	Ⓑ is putting	Ⓒ puts
4	Ⓐ yet	Ⓑ before	Ⓒ already
5	Ⓐ was buying	Ⓑ bought	Ⓒ has bought
6	Ⓐ hasn't bought	Ⓑ didn't buy	Ⓒ doesn't buy
7	Ⓐ has wanted	Ⓑ wants	Ⓒ wanted
8	Ⓐ get	Ⓑ got	Ⓒ hasn't got

2 請將括號內的動詞用正確時態（簡單現在式、簡單過去式、簡單現在完成式和現在完成進行式），以完成電子郵件。

Hi Sarah,

How are you? I've got some free time today, so I thought I would tell you how we are getting on here. It's the first time we ¹........................... (be) to the south of France and I must say it ²........................... (not disappoint) us at all. We ³........................... (be) here for a week and ⁴........................... (already / see) quite a lot. We ⁵........................... (just / come back) from a beautiful place called La Turbie, where the Romans ⁶........................... (build) a beautiful monument. We ⁷........................... (get) there early this morning and the view over the sea ⁸........................... (be) absolutely incredible. We ⁹........................... (eat) a lot of delicious fish and had some amazing wine there too! We wandered around the town a couple of days ago and I ¹⁰........................... (buy) a few French books at the street market, but I ¹¹........................... (have) time to read any of them yet — even on the beach we ¹²........................... (always / find) something else to do! They ¹³........................... (teach) all sorts of water sports here — I ¹⁴........................... (never / feel) so energetic before! Yesterday they even ¹⁵........................... (get) me to ride a jet-ski, but I soon ¹⁶........................... (give up) — it is one of the most terrifying things I ¹⁷........................... (ever / do).

Well, I'd better go now. Paul ¹⁸........................... (already / get) dressed to go out, but I still have to. He ¹⁹........................... (tell) me I need to be ready in half an hour! We ²⁰........................... (book) a table at a small restaurant on the beach.

See you soon!

Emma

3 請使用下列動詞的「簡單過去式」、「過去進行式」和「過去完成式」，來完成短文。

look   find   live (x2)   come   ask   can   break   throw   imagine

When I was a child, I ¹............................ in an old house in the country. One summer, while
I ²............................ around the attic for old things, I ³............................ across a big old wooden
box under a pile of curtains. I immediately imagined I ⁴............................ the treasure from some
famous robbers who ⁵............................ in the house centuries ago. The box was locked.
I ⁶............................ open it, so I ⁷............................ my elder brother to come and help and he tried
to open it with a screwdriver.
He tried and tried, and we heard the sound of metal objects rattling around inside. We
⁸............................ all the jewels inside the box: long pearl necklaces, diamond rings, golden coins.
Suddenly, the lock ⁹............................ and the box sprung open . . . Inside were the old, battered
pots and pans used by our great-grandparents that my mother ¹⁰............................ away because
they were too old.

延伸補充

現在完成進行式**鮮少用於否定句**，因為若行為或事件根本沒有發生，就也不會有持續進行的發展。
然而，有些否定句仍會使用現在完成進行式，但這種句子通常用肯定句也能表達相同的句意：

The kids **haven't been playing** for <u>long</u>. → The kids **have been playing** for <u>a short time</u>.

4 請使用提示用詞完成意義相近的句子，請勿變更提示用詞。

1 He has been studying for three hours and he's beginning to feel tired.

   STARTED He .... ago and he's beginning to
   feel tired.

2 We were standing talking when the robbery happened.

   WHILE .... talking, the robbery happened.

3 I've never walked farther than I did yesterday.

   EVER Yesterday it was the farthest ....

4 Marion started her project at the beginning of the week and she hasn't finished yet.

   SINCE Marion .... the beginning of the week.

5 The shops opened before we got to the shopping center.

   WHEN .... to the shopping center,
   the shops ....

6 The performance started before we got to the theater.

   ALREADY When .... , the performance
   ....

7 Henry hasn't been waiting for long. Why is he complaining?

   SHORT Henry .... Why is he complaining?

8 We haven't been working out much this week.

   LITTLE We .... this week.

5 請運用括號裡動詞的簡單過去式或過去完成式，來完成短文。

As soon as I [1]........................... (get) home last night, I [2]........................... (realize) that something strange [3]........................... (happen). I was sure someone [4]........................... (break) into my apartment. I [5]........................... (open) the living-room door and immediately I saw that things [6]........................... (move). I [7]........................... (leave) my laptop on the table and, when I looked, it [8]........................... (be) on the floor! I [9]........................... (clear up) everything in the kitchen before I [10]........................... (leave) for the weekend, but now there were dirty plates and glasses in the sink. I [11]........................... (phone) my sister because I thought maybe she [12]........................... (be) there while I was away . . . but, no, she hadn't. It's a complete mystery!

6 請運用括號裡動詞的正確過去式，來完成短文。

I [1]........................... (decide) to go to London for the day. I [2]........................... (not have) much money. I [3]........................... (go) to the ticket office and [4]........................... (buy) a day return to London. Since I [5]........................... (have) 40 minutes to wait for the train, I [6]........................... (decide) to buy a newspaper and have a coffee. Then I [7]........................... (go) to the platform, where the ticket inspector [8]........................... (ask) to see my ticket. I [9]........................... (can not) find it anywhere. I [10]........................... (search) everywhere for it. "I'm sorry, Inspector," I [11]........................... (say), "but I [12]........................... (lose) my ticket." "That's too bad," he [13]........................... (say), "you can't get on the train without a valid ticket." The train [14]........................... (come) and the train [15]........................... (leave) without me. Eventually, I [16]........................... (find) my ticket in my inside jacket pocket, so I [17]........................... (catch) the next train. On the train, I [18]........................... (go) to the buffet car, where I met an old friend. He [19]........................... (ask) me how I [20]........................... (be) and I [21]........................... (tell) him that I [22]........................... (lose) my ticket and [23]........................... (miss) the last train. "But," I [24]........................... (say), showing it to him, "I [25]........................... (find) it now!"

7 請完成短文，寫出括號裡的動詞的正確時態（如簡單過去式、過去完成式、過去完成進行式、簡單現在完成式、現在完成進行式）。

I remember my first day at work quite clearly. I [1]........................... (have) a job interview two weeks before for the position of Digital Manager. I had mixed feelings about whether I would get the job, as I felt the guy who [2]........................... (interview) me didn't like me that much. He was very serious. However, a week later I [3]........................... (receive) a letter saying that the job was mine. I was happy. I [4]........................... (look) for a job for over three months and I knew I had the right qualifications and skills.

On my first day, I [5]........................... (arrive) in good time and they [6]........................... (take) me to see the director of the company. He was quite a serious, intimidating man who [7]........................... (not show) much emotion, but he was welcoming and professional.

My team were hardworking and I [8]........................... (feel) very at ease with them.

And now? I'm still working here. I [9]........................... (work) here for over 25 years and I [10]........................... (be) very happy all that time.

8 請運用括號裡動詞的正確過去式來完成短文。

When I [1]............................... (arrive), the post office [2]............................... (already / close). Shame, because I [3]............................... (have) to send an urgent parcel. It [4]............................... (be) the new model of our famous mixer, and our clients in Spain [5]............................... (wait) for it. It [6]................... (be) a Friday evening and the post office would only reopen on Monday morning. While I [7]............................... (go) back home, I was quite upset. My boss [8]............................... (tell) me to hurry up and deliver the parcel just two hours earlier, but I [9]............................... (want) to finish writing some urgent emails. And now I had to explain to him that the parcel still [10]............................... (not leave).

9 請運用括號裡動詞的正確過去式來完成短文。

Last week, Luke and Alice [1]............................... (dance) in a Latin American dance competition. They [2]............................... (practice) for six months before they [3]............................... (take part) in the competition. They [4]............................... (be) very good. While they [5]............................... (wait) for their turn, they [6]........................... (talk) to their friend Mathilda, who [7]............................... (be) in the audience. She [8]............................... (never / see) them dance before. In fact, Luke and Alice [9]............................... (never / dance) in front of anyone before the competition.
After everyone [10]............................... (perform), the judges [11]............................... (announce) the winners. Luke and Alice [12]............................... (win)! Alice said she [13]............................... (never / be) so happy before.

Reflecting on grammar
請研讀文法規則，再判斷以下說法是否正確。

		True	False
1	現在完成式是以助動詞 have 或 be 動詞所構成。		
2	現在完成式用於表達過去所完成、且不會影響現在的行為。		
3	英式英文和美式英文的現在完成式規則均相同。		
4	「I have just washed the dishes.」是正確的句子。		
5	「We have moved to our new house last week.」是錯誤的句子。		
6	簡單現在完成式和現在完成進行式，均有持續時態的表達方式。		
7	「We've been here since yesterday.」是正確的句子。		
8	「How long . . . ?」與「Since when . . . ?」的意思完全相同。		
9	「He's been waiting for us since three days.」是正確的句子。		
10	從屬子句以 when、before 或 by the time 引導時，主要子句經常會使用過去完成式。		

1 請圈出正確的用字。

Jim Emma!

Emma Yes, Jim. What's the matter?

Jim Can you give me a lift? Mark's not going to work and I don't want to get the bus.

Emma Alright, get ¹ **on / into** the car. Are you going ² **to / in** the university?

Jim Yes, I'm going to a different department to my usual one, but I'll tell you where to go. Drive ³ **down / from** this road. Not so fast. Slow down!

Emma What shall I do when I get ⁴ **in / to** the crossroads?

Jim Turn left ⁵ **into / in** Darwin Street. Darwin was a famous . . .

Emma I know who Darwin was . . .

Jim Well, the applied physics department is ⁶ **on / at** the end of the street ⁷ **on / at** the left. It's next ⁸ **of / to** the astrophysics department . . .

Emma Okay, now can you get ⁹ **off / out of** the car, Jim? I'm really late for work.

2 美國商人羅伊‧布魯克斯（**Roy Brooks**）和女友失蹤了。警官正在撰寫報告，描述羅伊最後被人發現行蹤的情況。請運用合適的時態，將現在式的文字改寫為過去式，並且進行必要的更改（例如 **this** 換成 **that** 等等）。

Roy Brooks gets up at 9:00 on Monday, May 11th, 2015, and has breakfast on the terrace of his penthouse overlooking the bay. He usually has a big breakfast, but this morning he only has a cup of green tea.

He feeds his dogs, two giant black Schnauzers, and plays with them for half an hour. After washing and getting dressed, he leaves home at about 11:00 and drives to his office downtown. At 11:30, he parks his car in his office parking lot and takes the elevator to the 27th floor, where his secretary greets him with a cup of coffee.

He doesn't have any lunch today. At 3:00, a South American man goes into Roy's office and they talk for about an hour. Just before the man leaves the office, Roy is shouting some words in Spanish. When the man leaves, Roy is visibly upset and makes a few telephone calls.

At 6:00, he takes a taxi to The Fox and Hunter, a fashionable bar on Columbus Avenue, where his girlfriend Linda is waiting for him. They have a Martini, leave the bar and walk to a nearby Chinese restaurant, Chow Mei. They have dinner there and Roy talks to the Chinese restaurant manager for quite a long time. At 10:30, a driver they have never seen before picks them up and drives them towards the harbor.

3 請圈出正確的用字。

When we saw Debbie, she ¹ **had been sitting** / **sat** on the same chair in the same café for over an hour. She ² **had** / **has** been waiting for Mark, but he hadn't turned up. She ³ **was** / **has been** half worried and half furious with him. She ⁴ **was** / **had been** calling him on his phone for the last 20 minutes, but it was switched off.

"You know, he used to be late most of the time in the past, but lately he ⁵ **has always been** / **always was** on time," she said.

We ⁶ **reminded** / **used to remind** her that he often forgot to recharge the battery of his phone, so he was probably stuck somewhere and was not able to call her.

We sat at Debbie's table and waited with her. While we ⁷ **had been chatting** / **were chatting**, Debbie's phone rang. It was Mark, at last! But where was he?

4 請運用括號裡動詞的簡單過去式來完成短文。

A SHORT HISTORY OF YORK

York ¹......................... (become) important during Roman times when the Romans ²......................... (establish) a permanent fortress in AD 71. The fortress was the largest military garrison in the north and ³......................... (house) 6,000 soldiers.

When the Romans ⁴......................... (withdraw) from Britain, the fort and the town ⁵......................... (fall) under Anglo-Saxon rule and York ⁶......................... (become) the capital of the independent Kingdom of Northumbria. The Vikings ⁷......................... (be) the next group to rule the city in 866 and ⁸......................... (give) it the name of "Jorvik."

When the Normans ⁹......................... (invade) Britain in 1066, William the Conqueror soon ¹⁰......................... (establish) a presence in York, and over the next 300 years, the city ¹¹......................... (flourish), becoming the capital of the north and the second largest city in the country.

Between the 15th and the 17th centuries, the importance of the city ¹²......................... (decline), but with the restoration of the English monarchy, York ¹³......................... (enter) the period of Enlightenment with elegant new buildings, such as the Assembly Rooms, Assize Courts and numerous hospitals.

During the Industrial Revolution, York ¹⁴......................... (become) a major railway center and this ¹⁵......................... (help) expand the manufacturing industry.

Today, although traditional manufacturing has declined, new industries have sprung up in the city and with nearly four million visitors a year, the tourist industry now plays a major role in the local economy.

5 請先看看關於英國布萊頓皇家行宮的敘述，再閱讀下方短文。敘述說明正確請勾選 **A**，不正確請勾選 **B**。

		A	B
1	Marine Pavilion is the name of a neo-classical villa next to the Royal Pavilion.	☐	☐
2	George became king before they finished building the Pavilion.	☐	☐
3	Everybody liked the Pavilion when it was built.	☐	☐
4	The king liked hosting people at his Brighton residence.	☐	☐
5	Queen Victoria fell in love with the building at first sight.	☐	☐
6	She spent some time there alone with her husband.	☐	☐
7	The Royal Pavilion is closed three days a year.	☐	☐
8	In summer, visitors have one more hour to see the Pavilion.	☐	☐
9	The ticket office closes at 4:30 in October.	☐	☐
10	Groups don't need a reservation if they visit the Pavilion in winter.	☐	☐

Experience the extraordinary at the **Royal Pavilion**, an exotic palace in the center of Brighton. Built as a seaside pleasure palace for George IV, this historic house mixes Regency grandeur with the visual style of India and China.

The Royal Pavilion started as a modest 18th-century lodging house. Architect Henry Holland helped George, Prince of Wales, turn his house into a neo-classical villa — known as the Marine Pavilion.

In 1815, George hired architect John Nash to redesign the building in Indian style. By the time the work was completed in 1823, George had become the king. Though largely criticized at the time, today this building is the symbol of Brighton.

George enjoyed entertaining society guests. At the Royal Pavilion, he hosted gastronomic feasts in the Banqueting Room, and balls and concerts in the Music Room.

Queen Victoria first visited the Royal Pavilion in 1837 and felt it was a "strange, odd, Chinese-looking place, both outside and inside." She returned for a longer stay with her husband Albert and two children in 1842, and the upstairs chamber floor was adapted to accommodate the Queen and her family.

Today, the Royal Pavilion is open daily with the exception of Christmas Eve, Christmas Day and Boxing Day. From October to March, the visiting times are between 10 a.m. and 5:15 p.m., while they start half an hour earlier and finish half an hour later from April to September. Remember that in both periods, the last tickets are sold three-quarters of an hour before closing time.

As the Royal Pavilion is very busy in July and August, especially at weekends, they do not admit unbooked groups. Call this number for group bookings — 03000 290901 — and our booking team will give you a time slot for entry. Or visit the groups page on their website for more information.

6 請閱讀以下短文，選出正確的答案。

Mirella has never ^{0} .B.. to England, but she ^{1} ...... writing to a young man called Tom, from Margate in the south of England. He ^{2} ...... Italian for five years now and really loves it. Last year, Tom ^{3} ...... three weeks in Verona, in the north-east of Italy, and ^{4} ...... a full-immersion course where no English was spoken.

Mirella and Tom ^{5} ...... emails almost every day ^{6} ...... the past two months. Mirella is going to England ^{7} ...... and she ^{8} ..... a low-cost flight from Bergamo to Stansted, one of the London airports. She'll then get the train to Margate. It ^{9} ...... Mirella's first time abroad. When she was a child, she ^{10} ...... spend every summer in the French Riviera.

0 Ⓐ gone	Ⓑ been	Ⓒ got	Ⓓ went
1 Ⓐ has recently started	Ⓑ started recently	Ⓒ did recently start	Ⓓ have recently started
2 Ⓐ studies	Ⓑ studied	Ⓒ has been studying	Ⓓ has studied
3 Ⓐ has spent	Ⓑ spent	Ⓒ has been spending	Ⓓ have spent
4 Ⓐ attended	Ⓑ has attended	Ⓒ did attend	Ⓓ attend
5 Ⓐ exchange	Ⓑ exchanges	Ⓒ are exchanging	Ⓓ have been exchanging
6 Ⓐ for	Ⓑ since	Ⓒ from	Ⓓ after
7 Ⓐ at July	Ⓑ next July	Ⓒ last July	Ⓓ on July
8 Ⓐ has booked	Ⓑ has been booking	Ⓒ books	Ⓓ is booking
9 Ⓐ hasn't been	Ⓑ won't be	Ⓒ wasn't	Ⓓ will be
10 Ⓐ used	Ⓑ has used to	Ⓒ used to	Ⓓ did use to

7 請使用提示用詞完成意義相近的句子，請勿變更提示用詞，如例句所示，務必使用包括提示用詞在內的二至五個單字來完成句子。

0 It's ten o'clock and Maggie rang the dentist a few minutes ago.

JUST   It's ten o'clock and Maggie ....has just rung.......... the dentist.

1 We have lived near the Griffins for ten years.

BEEN   The Griffins .... neighbors for ten years.

2 Dan and Brian were golf champions years ago.

USED   Dan and Brian .... golf champions years ago.

3 I sat down at my desk as soon as I got into the office at 9 a.m. It's 1 p.m. and I'm still sitting here.

HAVE   I .... at my desk for four hours.

4 Sam started cooking at ten and he was still cooking at 12.

HAD   By 12 o'clock, Sam .... two hours.

5 Luke started watching his favorite cartoons hours ago and he's still watching them.

FOR   Luke has been watching ....

6 We met Susan ten years ago.

KNOWN   We .... years.

7 I tidied my room earlier, Mom.

ALREADY   I .... room, Mom.

8 I saw your sister a few minutes ago.

JUST   I ....

Towards Competences

受當地旅行社之託，你的學校要負責編寫旅行社官網的英文版當地資訊。你要用約 250 字寫出介紹所處城市歷史的短文，並搭配照片或繪圖。

Self Check 3

請選出答案，再至解答頁核對正確與否。

1 They used to have a family reunion once a year, usually .... Christmas.
Ⓐ on   Ⓑ at   Ⓒ in

2 I usually switch my mobile off .... night.
Ⓐ during   Ⓑ at   Ⓒ in

3 We would like to receive the goods .... May 20th.
Ⓐ within   Ⓑ in   Ⓒ by

4 He lives .... 10 Ramsay Lane, not far from my mother's house.
Ⓐ on   Ⓑ at   Ⓒ in

5 She generally goes to work .... her colleague's car.
Ⓐ by   Ⓑ on   Ⓒ in

6 Hurry up! I'm waiting here .... the rain and I haven't got an umbrella with me!
Ⓐ at   Ⓑ under   Ⓒ in

7 The President was sitting .... the back of the car next to his wife.
Ⓐ in   Ⓑ on   Ⓒ at

8 The police warned us .... driving along the mountain road in the snow.
Ⓐ by   Ⓑ from   Ⓒ against

9 Why don't you offer .... in your restaurant?
Ⓐ to him a job   Ⓑ him a job
Ⓒ a job him

10 We got bored .... staying at home and decided to go for a walk.
Ⓐ by   Ⓑ at   Ⓒ with

11 I remember .... to the park every afternoon when I was a child.
Ⓐ to walk   Ⓑ walking   Ⓒ walk

12 "What are you looking ....?" "My wallet. I may have left it at Helen's house."
Ⓐ for   Ⓑ after   Ⓒ at

13 .... you stay at home last weekend?
Ⓐ Have   Ⓑ Are   Ⓒ Did

14 My cousin .... his leg last Sunday while skiing.
Ⓐ breaks   Ⓑ broke   Ⓒ broken

15 "What .... at the party last night?" "My new red dress."
Ⓐ were you wearing
Ⓑ have you worn
Ⓒ have you been wearing

16 Tom .... a meal at the restaurant when he got an urgent phone call.
Ⓐ ordered   Ⓑ has been ordering
Ⓒ was ordering

17 She .... why her son was always late for dinner.
Ⓐ didn't understood
Ⓑ didn't understand
Ⓒ understood not

18 Dad .... to work when we lived in Hastings.
Ⓐ used to walk
Ⓑ used to walking
Ⓒ would to walk

19 They .... their summers in Wales when they were younger.
Ⓐ used to spending
Ⓑ would spend
Ⓒ would to spend

20 .... "No, but I'll finish it tomorrow."
Ⓐ "Have you finished your project yet?"
Ⓑ "Have you ever finish your project?"
Ⓒ "When will you finish your project?"

21 Tess .... here for ten years now.
Ⓐ lived   Ⓑ lives   Ⓒ has lived

22 Our team .... a match recently.
Ⓐ has never win   Ⓑ has won
Ⓒ never won

23 My brother .... a new apartment in the town center.
Ⓐ has bought   Ⓑ have bought
Ⓒ has buyed

24 Dad has .... arrived home from work. He's having dinner now.
Ⓐ never   Ⓑ just   Ⓒ yet

25 "Have they had breakfast ....?" "No, they are waiting for us. We're having breakfast together."
Ⓐ already   Ⓑ yet   Ⓒ still

26 "Where's Benjamin?" "He .... to the bank."
Ⓐ has been   Ⓑ has gone
Ⓒ has been going

27 Where have you ....? The movie started ten minutes ago.
Ⓐ been   Ⓑ gone   Ⓒ stayed

28 We're really worried. Ann hasn't ....
Ⓐ got home yet.
Ⓑ already got home.
Ⓒ ever got home.

29 "......... did you arrive in Italy?" "Two years ago."
Ⓐ How long   Ⓑ Since when   Ⓒ When

30 Miles has been driving .... six hours and he's feeling quite tired now.
Ⓐ since   Ⓑ from   Ⓒ for

31 "........ have you had this computer?" "For three years."
Ⓐ Since long   Ⓑ How much time
Ⓒ How long

32 "Have you .... tried free climbing?" "Are you joking? I'm terrified of heights."
Ⓐ just   Ⓑ ever   Ⓒ yet

33 "What's the matter with you? You look exhausted." "........ for over an hour."
Ⓐ I've been run   Ⓑ I've been running
Ⓒ I ran

34 Poor Paula! She .... the dishes for an hour. She should buy a dishwasher.
Ⓐ has been washing
Ⓑ has washed
Ⓒ washed

35 "........ have they lived in this village?" "Since last August."
Ⓐ Since long   Ⓑ Since when
Ⓒ How often

36 When I got there, the library ....
Ⓐ had closed just
Ⓑ had already been closing
Ⓒ had already closed

37 Dan .... all afternoon, but a dog got into the flower beds and destroyed all of his work!
Ⓐ gardens
Ⓑ had been gardening
Ⓒ was gardening

38 We were very late. .... we got to the airport, the boarding gate had closed and we had to wait for another flight.
Ⓐ As soon as   Ⓑ After
Ⓒ By the time

39 The guests arrived before I .... cooking the dinner.
Ⓐ had finished   Ⓑ was finishing
Ⓒ had been finishing

40 By the time the train got into the station, the passengers .... and moved towards the doors.
Ⓐ stood up   Ⓑ were standing up
Ⓒ had already stood up

Assess yourself!

☐ **0 - 10** 還要多加用功。

☐ **11 - 20** 尚可。

☐ **21 - 30** 不錯。

☐ **31 - 40** 非常好！

LESSON **1** 情態副詞與其他副詞 Adverbs of manner and other adverbs

❶ 情態副詞是用來**表達某事物發生、進行的情形、狀態、方式或程度**：

• "How does she speak English?"
  "She speaks **fluently**."

❷ 通常在形容詞後面加上 **ly** 即可形成副詞。

• Will you please listen careful**ly**?

形容詞	副詞
quick	quick**ly**
slow	slow**ly**
clear	clear**ly**
short	short**ly**

看看下方的拼字規則：

字尾為 **y** 的形容詞	**y → i**	lucky happy	luck**ily** happ**ily**

但注意是 shy → shyly NOT shily

字尾為 **ple**、**ble**、**tle** 的形容詞	**–ply, –bly, –tly**	simple, irritable, gentle	sim**ply**, irritab**ly**, gent**ly**
字尾為 **al**、**ul** 的形容詞	**–ally, –ully**	central careful	central**ly** careful**ly**
單音節且字尾為不發音 **e** 的形容詞	**去掉 e**	true	tru**ly**

但注意是　pure → pure**ly**　｜　safe → safe**ly**　｜　rude → rude**ly**

> ❗ 某些形容詞的字尾一樣是 ly，如 lovely、friendly、silly。
> 在此情況下，就會以 **in a . . . way** 來表達副詞句型：
> • She talked to me **in a** friendly **way**.
> • Don't behave **in a** silly **way**.

1 請將以下形容詞改為副詞，並寫在正確的欄位裡。

angry possible easy soft comfortable lazy probable quick lucky political
beautiful cheap free honorable idle social impressive practical incredible whole

smartly	hungrily	notably	ideally	truly

副詞和形容詞

情態副詞雖然通常放在動詞後面，但也能修飾**形容詞**、**過去分詞**或**另一個副詞**：

副詞 + 形容詞	This beach is **really** beautiful.
副詞 + 過去分詞	I'm **absolutely** overwhelmed by its beauty.
副詞 + 副詞	Tourism is developing **incredibly** slowly in this area.

當感官動詞（look、smell、sound、feel 等）為不及物用法的時候，後面必須接**形容詞**，而不是副詞：
- This cake smells **delicious**! NOT deliciously
- It sounds **good**. NOT well

並非所有副詞字尾都是 ly，有些副詞的形式和形容詞相同：

	形容詞	副詞
hard	It's **hard** work.	He works **hard**.
fast	He's a **fast** runner.	He runs very **fast**.
straight	She's got **straight**, blonde hair.	Go **straight** on along this road.
early	I had an **early** start this morning.	I woke up **early** this morning.

請留意不規則變化 **good** → **well**：
He's a **good** cook. He cooks very **well**.

並非所有字尾 ly 的副詞均為情態副詞，有些是**頻率副詞**，例如常見的 rarely 和 usually，以及 generally、especially、mainly 等；還有些是**程度副詞**，如 fairly 和 extremely。

UNIT
10
副詞和量詞

FAQ

Q: 如果 hard 可同時作為副詞和形容詞，那麼我常聽到的 hardly 是什麼意思？

A: **hardly** 是從 hard 衍生出來的副詞，但意思是「**幾乎不是**」或「**幾乎沒有**」，如：
She has <u>hardly</u> any free time these days.
She's very busy.

有兩種形式且意義不同的副詞

還有其他副詞和 hard/hardly 一樣，擁有兩種形式，意思卻完全不同：

high（高） Look at that kite. It's flying really **high**!	**highly**（非常、極為） Business in this country is **highly** competitive.
late（遲到） Sorry for being **late**.	**lately**（最近） Have you seen David **lately**?
near（附近） The exam date is drawing **near**.	**nearly**（將近） It's **nearly** ten o'clock.
fine（安好） Good job! You're doing **fine**.	**finely**（精細） Chop the herbs **finely**.

2 請判斷該使用形容詞或副詞，並圈出正確的用字。

1 James can't type very **good** / **well**. For this position we need a person who types **quick** / **quickly**.

2 "Have I spelled your name **correctly** / **correct**?" "Yes, it's **perfect** / **perfectly**."

3 The assistant did a very **good** / **well** job.

4 Her essay is too **simple** / **simply**. I don't think she will get a good grade.

5 She looked **beautiful** / **beautifully** in that evening dress.

6 This coffee smells **deliciously** / **delicious**. Can I have some?

7 It's been a **hard** / **hardly** week. I've **hardly** / **hard** slept more than five hours.

8 Andrea Bocelli sang **wonderful** / **wonderfully** during his latest concert.

3 請將副詞放在正確位置來改寫句子。

totally terribly seriously happily highly incredibly carefully

0 Everything has been planned for the trip. ......Everything has been carefully planned for the trip.......

1 The computer system was damaged by a virus. ....

2 Harrison Ford is unrecognizable in this movie. ....

3 Your lasagna is good. You always cook it well. ....

4 It's improbable that they will be here tomorrow. ....

5 Dear me! It's late. I must hurry up. ....

6 They have been married for over 20 years. ....

4 請根據以下形容詞，改寫為對應的副詞來完成句子。

early fast hard quiet careful easy

1 The manager left the room .... , without saying anything else.

2 Ian studied very .... for his final exam.

3 The editor checked the essay .... before publishing it.

4 Nicole woke up very .... this morning and made breakfast for herself.

5 Irene understood everything quite ....

6 He had an accident because he was driving too ....

5 請運用以下形容詞或對應的副詞來完成句子。

late lucky correct easy delicious different angry careful hard friendly good

1 .... nobody was badly hurt in the accident.

2 Sally looks very .... I .... recognized her at the supermarket yesterday.

3 I don't know why, but James talked to us ....

4 .... I haven't been feeling ....

5 Our new neighbors are very nice and we often have a .... chat over the garden fence.

6 I .... get bored. I need something new every day.

7 Listen .... , please.

8 Most students answered the test questions ....

9 That cake you made tasted really .... Can you make another one soon?

LESSON 2 程度副詞 Adverbs of degree

性狀形容詞用來形容事物的性質或狀態，而**程度副詞**則是用來修飾性狀形容詞或副詞，達到**加強或減弱字意程度**的效果。程度副詞通常會放在要修飾的形容詞或副詞**前面**。

以下程度副詞依強弱程度排序：

+ +	**too** old
+	**very/really** old
+ −	**fairly/quite/rather** old
−	**not very** old
− −	**not** old **at all**

❶ **強化副詞**能夠**加強形容詞**的程度，常見的有 **too**、**very**、**really**、**extremely** 和 **absolutely**；**definitely** 搭配的則是動詞：

- The movie was **too** long.
- It's a **very** interesting book.
- It was a **really** nice day.
- She's **extremely** patient.
- You're **absolutely** right.
- I **definitely** remember texting him about the meeting.

too 可搭配 **much**、**way** 或 **far** 來進一步加強語氣：

- It's **much** too late to ring him up.
- They spend **way** too much money on clothes.
- This silk shirt is **far** too expensive for me.

❷ **弱化副詞**則能**降低形容詞**的程度，常見的有 **fairly**、**quite**、**rather**、**pretty**、**enough**、**not very**、**not at all**。

　❶ **fairly** 常搭配正面意義的形容詞和副詞來表達肯定：

　　Today's test was **fairly** easy.（意指「我對於這種情況感到開心」）

　❷ **quite** 可搭配形容詞、副詞和動詞：

- Her new hairstyle is **quite** nice.
- **Quite** surprisingly, they didn't finish before midnight.
- They **quite** enjoyed the show.

　❸ **rather** 帶有一點**批評或失望**的意味，但也能表示超乎尋常或**出乎意料之外地好**：

- Yesterday's training session was **rather** hard.（意指「連我都覺得太難」）
- The band's new concert was **rather** long.（意指「我不喜歡拖這麼久」）
- He's just got his license but he drives **rather** well.
  （意指「開車技術意外好到令我驚訝」）

　rather 亦可放在**動詞前面**，如 I **rather** like it.

　請觀察句子裡有名詞時，不定冠詞 **a** 的位置：

- A lot of people thought it was **rather a** success, but not me.（只有名詞時，放在名詞前）
- It's **a rather** difficult question. / It's **rather a** difficult question.（有形容詞＋名詞時，放在副詞前後皆可）

Focus

觀察下句，當句子裡有名詞時，不定冠詞 **a** 會放在副詞與形容詞**之間**：

It was **quite a good** concert. NOT ~~a quite good concert.~~

④ **pretty** 僅能搭配形容詞和副詞，通常是用在**非正式的會話**中：
- We had a **pretty** good time at the party.
- She can sing **pretty** well.

⑤ **enough** 可搭配形容詞、副詞和動詞，且一般放在此類詞的後面：
- You aren't old **enough** to drive a car.
- He doesn't speak fluently **enough**.
- We haven't trained **enough** for the match.

但如果句子裡有名詞，enough 就要放在名詞的**前面** → We don't have **enough tables**.

> **!** 請看看以下例子：
> We don't have enough big tables.（enough 修飾 tables）→ 我們的大桌子不夠多
> We don't have big enough tables.（enough 修飾 big）→ 我們的桌子不夠大

⑥ **not very** 和 **not at all** 均用於**否定句**：
- What you said is **not very** interesting.
- I'm **not** happy about it **at all**. (Also I'm **not at all** happy about it.)

FAQ

Q: 我曾聽過有人問「Are you sure?」，並得到回答「Yes, definitely.」。這個回答是什麼意思呢？

A: **definitely** 意指「**無庸置疑、絕對**」，所以有人問你「是否確定」時，回答 definitely 代表「十分確定」。我們再舉另一個例句：「You look tired, you definitely need a break.」，這句話是告訴對方，他看起來很累，**絕對**需要休息一下。

1 請重新排序單字，寫出邏輯通順的句子。

1 quite / I / had / a / in / good / yesterday's / result / test / .

....

2 perfect / performance / absolutely / was / Their / .

....

3 We / quite / last / watched / an / movie / night / enjoyable / .

....

4 but / It's / late / the / still / shop / is / rather / open / .

....

5 pretty / can / They / well / dance / .

....

6 everybody / there / for / chairs / Were / enough / ?

....

7 The / was / fairly / a / building / hotel / modern / .

....

8 what / This / holiday / is / expensive / way / package / for / it / too / offers / .

....

2 請以正確的程度副詞，來完成句子。

| not at all   not very   enough   rather   fairly   too (x2)   extremely |

1 After they won the lottery, they bought an .... huge house near the beach.

2 Our elementary school teacher was .... patient with us. She often lost her temper.

3 The boss is .... satisfied .... with their work. They will have to do it all over again.

4 Her latest novel is .... good—much better than her previous one, I must say.

5 This movie is .... violent. I'm not going to watch it to the end.

6 I knew her .... well, but we were not really close friends.

7 I can't believe it! It's .... good to be true.

8 This room isn't big .... for all these people.

「極端」形容詞

「極端」形容詞本身已經具有**最高級**的意思，因此**不能**再使用 **very**、**fairly**、**rather** 和 **too** 等**程度副詞**來修飾，而是要使用 **really**、**absolutely** 或 **quite** 等副詞，表達「**完全地**」的意思。

極端形容詞有 huge、awful、wonderful、amazing、great、impossible、essential 等，看看例句：

• The party was **absolutely great**. NOT very great

• The food was **really awful**. NOT fairly awful

• You're **quite right**. NOT very right

3 請將各形容詞填入正確的欄位。

| ugly   happy   excited   marvelous   scared   nice   astonishing   sad   furious |
| cold   freezing   fantastic   nervous   angry   frantic   afraid   horrible |

普通形容詞	極端形容詞

修飾動詞的程度複詞

某些程度副詞能修飾後方動詞的意思，如：

❶ almost/nearly（幾乎）

• She **almost/nearly** fainted when she saw him.

❷ hardly/scarcely/ barely（幾乎不）

• It was so foggy that we could **hardly/scarcely/barely** see the road.

• He was so tired he could **hardly/scarcely/barely** keep his eyes open.

❸ just（只）

• They **just** sat down without saying a word.

❹ only（只）

• We **only** need a few more glasses.

❺ very much 和 **a lot** 要接在動詞或動詞 + 受詞的後面：

• I like reading **a lot**.

• I like reading detective stories **very much**.

❻ so 和 **such a** 能加強感嘆句的意思，請看以下的句型用法：

❶ so + 形容詞或副詞
It's **so cold** today!

❷ such a/an + 形容詞 + 名詞
It's **such a cold day**!

連續子句若表現結果，通常會以 **that** 引導，並接在此類加強副詞後面：

• It was **so** cold / **such** a cold day **that** we couldn't even go skiing.

179

4 請圈出正確的用字。

1 The English test was **so** / **such** difficult that nearly all the students failed it.
2 Hardwell's music was **very** / **really** fantastic.
3 I **quite** / **fairly** like drawing and painting.
4 It was **quite a hard** / **a quite hard** match, but we won in the end.
5 It sounds **absolutely** / **too** incredible, but George Clooney is shooting a movie in my town.
6 That horse was **really** / **very** amazing—he won every race!
7 What a goal! He's **such a** / **so** great player!
8 I'm two meters tall and the hotel bed is not **enough long** / **long enough** for me.

5 請重新排序單字，寫出邏輯通順的句子。

1 had / We / really / a / holiday / nice / summer / last / . ...
2 The / was / big / so / we / got / that / lost / palace / . ...
3 quite / He / good / is / a / actor/. ....
4 It / enough / warm / to / isn't / the / swim / lake/in / . ...
5 such / It's / a / dog / cute / little / . ...
6 rather / day / It's / dull / a / autumn /. ....

6 以下句子均有一個錯誤。請以<u>底線</u>標出錯誤，並訂正為正確句子。

1 He's enough old to cook his own meals.
....

2 It's a so exciting thriller. It keeps you on edge until the end.
....

3 I could hard understand what she was saying.
....

4 The view from the hotel terrace is very amazing.
....

5 We bought a quite cheap dishwasher but it broke after a couple of years.
....

6 My son likes a lot cooking.
....

7 請使用以下副詞來完成句子。

much quite hardly too so really

1 Are you sure that the show tickets aren't .... expensive?
2 I was .... moved during the ceremony that I could .... speak.
3 Mark was .... embarrassed when he got his award.
4 It was .... late when we got to the restaurant, but it was still open.
5 He got good results in the test. I'm surprised, because he doesn't usually study ....

LESSON 3 表達大量的不定形容詞與代名詞
Indefinite adjectives and pronouns to express large quantities

描述大數量

a lot of / lots of / plenty of	放在複數可數名詞和不可數名詞的前面	多用於肯定句
much	放在不可數名詞的前面	多用於否定句和疑問句
many	放在複數可數名詞的前面	

請參閱第 14 頁，了解可數名詞和不可數名詞的定義。
上表所列各詞皆可用來表達龐大數量的概念，其中 many 和 much 可作不定代名詞和形容詞。

1 **a lot of** 在非正式語境中，可用於肯定句、否定句和疑問句：

- There's **a lot of** noise in this room.
- **A lot of** people visit the museum every weekend.
- There aren't **a lot of** people in the line.

  1 我們會以 **a lot** 與 **plenty** 作為代名詞，此時後面不接 **of**：
  - "How many stamps have you got?" "I've got **a lot**."

  2 **lots of** 和 **plenty of** 均為比較口語的表達方式：
  - There's **lots of / plenty of** room for everyone.

  3 更非正式的口語用法則有 **a load of / loads of**：
  - I've got **loads of** homework for tomorrow.

2 **much** 和 **many** 主要用於問句和否定句：

- We haven't got **much** money. Let's get some from the ATM.
- Have we got **many** eggs?

我們通常會以 **many** 來搭配 **times**，即使是肯定句也是一樣的用法：

- I've been there **many** times.

3 想表達某物數量龐大時，可使用副詞 **too**：

too + 形容詞	It's **too hot** today.
too much + 不可數名詞	There's **too much traffic** on the highway today.
too many + 複數可數名詞	There are **too many cars** in the town center.

too much 和 **too many** 亦可作為代名詞：

- That's **too much**!　　• There are **too many**.

UNIT
10
副詞和量詞

---

1 請以 **a lot of**、**much** 或 **many** 來完成句子。

1 There are .... new apps coming out tomorrow.

2 There aren't .... tomatoes, but there's .... lettuce there to make a salad.

3 I haven't got .... money with me. Let's go to the bank first.

4 "Have you got .... CDs?" "No, I haven't got .... now."

5 You need .... cocoa to make these cookies—about 300 grams.

6 This fruit loaf isn't fattening because there isn't .... butter in it.

詢問數量

詢問數量或某物品的件數時，我們會使用以下表達方式：

How much + 不可數名詞	**How much luggage** have you got?
How many + 複數可數名詞	**How many seats** do we need for the meeting?

How much 和 How many 亦可作為代名詞：
How much / How many do you need?（雖然名詞沒有寫出來，但大家能意會這裡問的是什麼東西）

請圈出正確的用字。

1 It's true. **Too** / **How** many cooks spoil the broth.

2 It's **much** / **too** cold in here. Let's close the windows.

3 The police officer wants to know how **many** / **much** people live in this building.

4 Don't buy too **much** / **many** bread. We're all on a diet!

5 The streets are **too** / **too much** busy today. I'll take my bike.

6 Don't give the kids too **many** / **much** sweets. They'll spoil their teeth.

7 Don't tell me! It's **too** / **too much** good to be true.

8 How **many** / **much** money do you need for the school trip?

9 Don't put all that flour in the bowl. That's way too **much** / **many**!

10 How **much** / **many** information can you fit on that memory stick?

11 It's **too much busy** / **too busy** in town today. Let's come back another day.

12 Are you **too** / **too many** tired to help me?

表達數量的其他形容詞和代名詞

可表達數量的其他形容詞與代名詞如下：

enough	There's **enough** paper in the printer. （指紙張數量足夠）
most	**Most** students live in this area. （意同「大多數的學生……」）
all	• **All** the seats were taken. （指完全沒有空位） • "Anything else?" "No, that's **all**, thanks." （指不需要其他東西。）

FAQ

Q: 「Most plants in this garden are tropical.」與「Most of the plants in this garden are tropical.」，這兩句話都對嗎？

A: 兩句話的句型都正確。不過一般而言，在**不詳細討論**的情況下，僅使用 **most** 就好，如「She likes most vegetables.」；但如果句中有**代名詞**，就一定要使用 **most of**，如「As most of you know, we have a new colleague.」。

! 請留意使用 **enough** 時的句型：

enough + 名詞	There were **enough handouts** for everyone.
形容詞 + enough	The room was **big enough** for all the participants.
動詞 + enough	I **have enough** to do today.

FAQ

Q: 我聽過「I've had plenty.」或「We saw plenty of him.」的說法，但我覺得這裡的 plenty，應該不是 **a lot**（很多）的意思。

A: 事實上，**plenty** 在**非正式**用法裡也有 **enough** 的意思，因此符合這兩句的邏輯。第一句的意思是「我受夠了」，第二句的意思是「我們太常看到他，以致於看膩了」。這兩句亦可寫作：「I've had enough.」跟「We saw enough of him.」。

3 請圈出正確的用字。

1 Does Sam have **many** / **much** / **lots** CDs by Jason Derulo?

2 We haven't got **lots** / **many** / **plenty of** new Facebook friends.

3 Have you got **much** / **many** / **loads** free time in the evening?

4 I can't speak **lot of** / **much** / **many** languages, only English and Italian.

5 There's **plenty of** / **too many** / **most** food for ten people.

6 **All** / **Most** / **Plenty** the candidates are ready for the exam to start.

7 **Lot** / **Most** / **Much** of the class want to do a cultural exchange with a German school.

8 We don't have **plenty** / **enough** / **many** money for a meal in that posh restaurant.

9 Let's book that hotel—there are **much** / **loads of** / **plenty** things to do there.

10 Do you have **plenty** / **much** / **enough** money to buy a new car yet?

4 請重新排序單字，寫出邏輯通順的句子。請留意 **enough** 在句子裡的位置。

1 aren't / There / enough / for / sandwiches / these / all / people / .

....

2 enough / The / room / isn't / big / the / party / for / .

....

3 have / movie / seen / enough / of / this / We / .

....

4 studied / He / enough / pass / hasn't / this / to / test / .

....

5 Harry / enough / isn't / to / his own / old / credit card / have / .

....

5 請以合適的形容詞或副詞完成句子。

1 There aren't .... restaurants in this area.

2 I'm new in this school and I don't know .... of my colleagues.

3 In the conference hall there aren't .... chairs for all the participants.

4 How .... money do you have on your credit card?

5 There are too .... car parks in this town, but not .... playgrounds.

6 I know .... of the songs on this album, but not .... of them.

LESSON 4 表達少量的不定形容詞和代名詞
Indefinite adjectives and pronouns to express small quantities

描述少量

a little	放在不可數名詞的前面	little	放在不可數名詞的前面（具負面含意）
a few	放在複數可數名詞的前面	few	放在複數可數名詞的前面（具負面含意）

上表所列的字可用來表達少量概念，其中 little 和 few 可作**不定形容詞**和**代名詞**：

• I'm sorry but I've got <u>little</u> information about this topic.

• There are <u>few</u> folders left. We must buy some.

• Here's <u>a little</u> money.

請注意 little 與 a little、few 與 a few 的差異。

1 **little** 的意思是 not much，用在不可數的名詞前，**few** 的意思是 not many，用在可數的名詞前，兩者都指**不夠多**、**很稀少**，帶有**負面**含意：
- There's **little** milk. I can't make a milkshake.
- She feels lonely because she knows **few** people here.

2 **a little** 與 **a few** 則表示 some、a small number，指**還有一些**，帶有**正面**含意：
- There's **a little** milk. We can make a milkshake.
- She moved here only last month but she's already got **a few** friends.

3 **A bit (of) / a little bit (of)** 經常取代 a little，是較**口語**的表達方式：
- Can I have **a bit of** sugar in my tea, please?
- "Would you like some milk too?" "Just **a little bit**."

1 請以 little、a little、few 或 a few 完成句子。

1 She works a lot, even on the weekend, so she has .... time for her family.

2 She never works on the weekend because she wants to have .... time for her family.

3 Have a sandwich. There are .... on the table.

4 I can't make an apple pie. There are just .... apples.

5 Look! There are .... people in the garden. What are they doing?

6 Hurry up! We have .... minutes left before the train leaves.

7 I've already put .... salt in the soup but maybe it's not enough.

8 You'll get .... help from her. She's such a selfish girl.

若要表達**少量**或**完全沒有**，則有以下用法：

1 表達**少量**，可使用 **not much** 和 **not many**，或者在 **a little** 或 **a few** 前面搭配副詞 **only** 或 **just**：
I didn't have **many** chances. = I **only** had **a few** chances.

2 表達**極少數量**，可使用 **very little**、**very few** 和 **hardly any**：
- I know **very little** about New Zealand.
- We have **hardly any** gas in the tank. Let's stop to fill up.
- **Very few** people live in this village.

3 表達「零數量」的概念，可使用身兼形容詞和代名詞的 **not any**，或是形容詞 **no** 及代名詞 **none**（請參閱第 45 頁）：
- "Have you got any more tickets for tonight's show?"
  "I'm afraid we've got **no tickets** left. / . . . we've got **none** left."

2 請圈出正確的用字。

1 "Do you have **a few / a little** coins in your pocket?" "No, **any / none** at all."

2 The President doesn't have **many / much** power in my country.

3 In Italy, there's **few / hardly any** interest in cricket.

4 Very **few / little** English students learn ancient Greek today.

5 I only have **a few / a little** money left. Let's get some from the ATM.

6 There are **a lot of / a little** stars in the sky tonight. It'll be a beautiful day tomorrow.

7 Just **a little / a few** people have a lot of responsibility in our company.

8 **Not many / Not a few** tourists visit this museum even though it's really worth it!

9 There are **very little / hardly any** tea bags left. Can you put some on the shopping list, please?

10 I wanted to buy a ticket for the Rihanna concert, but there were **none / no** left.

3 請圈出正確的答案。

1 Oh dear! Let's stop at the service station. We've got ...... gasoline left.
Ⓐ much　Ⓑ little　Ⓒ few　Ⓓ a lot of

2 I'm working hard. I don't have ...... time to go out with my friends.
Ⓐ a lot　Ⓑ many　Ⓒ little　Ⓓ much

3 We can't make a cheesecake. There isn't ...... cottage cheese in the fridge.
Ⓐ many　Ⓑ any　Ⓒ few　Ⓓ some

4 Venice is a unique city so ...... tourists visit it every year.
Ⓐ very　Ⓑ a lot　Ⓒ lots of　Ⓓ few

5 I'm quite happy to live in this town. People are friendly and I have already made quite ...... friends here.
Ⓐ a little　Ⓑ a few　Ⓒ much　Ⓓ lots

6 Jim doesn't like living in Los Angeles. He only has ...... few friends there.
Ⓐ much　Ⓑ any　Ⓒ a　Ⓓ many

7 We have hardly ...... time.
Ⓐ some　Ⓑ any　Ⓒ little　Ⓓ much

8 I've taken ...... of photos!
Ⓐ many　Ⓑ loads　Ⓒ lot　Ⓓ much

4 請完成意義相近的句子。

1 We have little information about the facilities in this town.
We haven't got .... about the facilities in this town.

2 There are two little lakes outside the town, but at this time of year the water is too cold to swim in.
There are two little lakes outside the town, but at this time of year the water isn't .... to swim in.

3 I know there aren't many ethnic restaurants.
I know there are only ....

4 There's little traffic except for the rush hour.
There isn't .... except for the rush hour.

5 It's a quiet town so there is hardly any traffic at this time.
It's a quiet town so there isn't .... at this time.

6 I don't want you to take any risks while you're diving.
I want you to .... while you're diving.

7 The rhythm of the music was so irresistible that everyone started to dance.
The music had ....that everyone started to dance.

5 請用填入合適的詞來完成句子。

| very little　few　a little (x2)　much　many (x2)　no　a few |

1 He can speak English, French, Japanese, and .... German.

2 There were very .... people at the conference. Pity, because it was very interesting.

3 There's still .... ink in the printer.

4 When we got back home from our holidays, there was .... to eat in the fridge so we ordered a meal from the Chinese takeout.

5 We didn't visit .... museums when we were in Paris.

6 There isn't .... sugar in my coffee.

7 There weren't .... supporters at the stadium last Saturday.

8 There were .... flowers in the garden, but not many.

9 There was .... point in continuing, as nobody was listening.

強化副詞   延伸補充

❶ 我們學過的 very 和 really 是用來強調形容詞或副詞的意義；口語裡還有其他功能相同的單字，
例如 **just**、**awfully**、**amazingly**、**terribly**、**totally** 和 **incredibly**：
  • Everything's **just** fine!   • She was **terribly** late.   • It's **totally** useless!

❷ 我們也可以使用較為正式的 **thoroughly** 和 **utterly**：
  • I'm **thoroughly** confused.   • You look **utterly** exhausted!

弱化副詞

我們可以使用 **slightly**、**a bit / a little**、**fairly**、**rather**、**quite** 與 **pretty** 等副詞，來減弱形容詞或
副詞的程度：   • It's **slightly** different.   • He was **a bit** worried.

1 請使用下方的程度副詞來完成句子。某些句子可能適用多個副詞。

very	quite	too	absolutely	such	really	so	at all	a bit	rather	slightly	just

1 This coffee is .... strong! I can't possibly drink it.

2 You're .... good at chess! You always beat me.

3 They're .... right! There's nothing we can say.

4 The test was .... easy. I think I got it right.

5 Yesterday was .... a lovely day! We had a .... nice walk.

6 She was not .... lucky this time!

7 They weren't successful .... !

8 This problem is just .... more difficult than the other one.

9 She's just .... overweight, but not very.

10 My new shoes are nice, but they're .... uncomfortable.

11 You're .... hopeless! How can you play .... badly?

2 請使用下方的情態副詞來完成句子。

quietly	fluently	unfortunately	luckily	well
enthusiastically	straight	beautifully	hard	

1 Sit down .... and concentrate on your work.

2 Go .... ahead and then turn right.

3 My father speaks German ....

4 She's a great dancer. She dances ....

5 .... we still have plenty of time!

6 My son is doing incredibly .... in his new school.

7 They're studying really .... this term.

8 The math teacher didn't speak very .... about her class.

9 I'm sorry to tell you that .... you have failed the test again.

不定量化形容詞與代名詞

1 little 身兼不定形容詞、代名詞與性狀形容詞。

① **a little** 若後接**不可數名詞**，意指「**少量**」：I have **a little** <u>money</u>.
② **a little** 若後接**單數可數**名詞，意指「**一個小型的**」：I have **a little** <u>dog</u>.

> small 和 little 的意思略有不同。**small** 用於形容體型嬌小的人物、動物和物品；
> **little** 則是用於形容**還會長大**的年幼動物或人物 →
> I have a little brother. He's two years old.   My sister is a small girl.

2 不定形容詞 several 較為正式，但用法與 many 和 a lot of 一樣，是來表達大數量的人事物：
• There are **several** foreign students this year.

3 口語上常將 quite 放在 a few 和 a lot 的前面：
• **Quite** <u>a few</u> people were waiting at the bus stop.
• He used to spend **quite** <u>a lot of</u> time in France.

4 all 需搭配**不可數**名詞、**複數**名詞和**時間用語**，如 all day、all night long、all week：
• They've lost **all** their money.   • I like **all kinds** of music.   • I worked **all day**.

① 如果**子句**以性狀形容詞說明**更多細節**，我們會在**複數**名詞前面使用 **all the** 或 **all of the**：
• We liked **all (of) the** songs they sang last night.

② all 亦可作為**代名詞**：• They've **all** worked hard. / **All** of them have worked hard.
• She bought tickets for us **all**.

5 the whole 意指「**所有、全部**」，一般會搭配**單數可數**名詞：They ate **the whole** cake!

3 請以 all、all of、all the 及 the whole 來完成句子。

1 Not .... people you invited are coming.
2 He didn't want to hear .... story. It was long and boring.
3 There are people going in .... directions.
4 Please be quiet! .... you!
5 Do you really know .... these people?
6 I stayed at home .... day yesterday because I wasn't very well.
7 I love this album—I know .... the songs on it by heart.
8 .... class is going on the trip—no one is staying behind.

4 請重新排序單字，寫出邏輯通順的句子。

1 too / It's / true / good / to / be / . ...
2 salt / too / There's / much / in / soup / the / . ...
3 coffee / There / sugar / in / enough / isn't / my / . ...
4 too / noise / in / much / room / this / There's / . ...
5 The / are / on / too / shops / the / first / day / of / the / sales / crowded / .
....
6 here / are / too / There / people / many / today / . ...
7 got / money / I / enough / haven't / ticket / the / for / . ...
8 enough / table / isn't / This / large / . ...

5 請使用以下單字來完成對話。

How many	finely	How much	gently	enough
delicious	some (x3)	a little	any	slowly

Fiona What are you doing, Mom?

Mom I'm making [1].......................... chocolate-chip cookies.

Fiona Cookies? Great! Can I help you?

Mom Sure. Get [2].......................... chocolate, please.

Fiona [3].......................... do you need?

Mom 175 grams.

Fiona We've got whole 200 grams, so that's
[4].......................... . Do you need
[5].......................... butter?

Mom Yes, 125 grams. And now eggs . . .

Fiona [6].......................... eggs do you need?

Mom Just one. And 150 grams of flour.

Fiona One egg and [7].......................... flour. Here you are. Anything else?

Mom Yes, I need [8].......................... sugar, about 50 grams.

Fiona Here. What should I do now?

Mom Chop the chocolate [9].......................... while I'm creaming the butter and sugar.

Fiona Okay. What next?

Mom Beat in the egg. And now add the flour [10].......................... . Mix [11].......................... .

[30 minutes later]

Mom You can take the cookies out of the oven now, Fiona. They're ready.

Fiona Mmmm . . . They smell and look [12].......................... .

6 請使用以下副詞或量詞來完成短文；詞彙可重複使用。

a few	a little	very	much
very much	any	actually	fairly

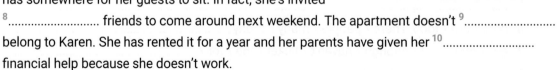

Karen is [1].......................... pleased because she has just
moved into her new apartment in San Francisco. It hasn't got
[2].......................... furniture, but she has brought [3]..........................
essential things from her parents' house. She's got a bed and a
[4].......................... big table, but she hasn't got [5]..........................
chairs yet, so she has to sit on the bed. She has already painted
the walls because she didn't like the old color [6]..........................
and she has hung a few pictures up. She's [7]..........................
optimistic and she's planning to have a party when she
has somewhere for her guests to sit. In fact, she's invited
[8].......................... friends to come around next weekend. The apartment doesn't [9]..........................
belong to Karen. She has rented it for a year and her parents have given her [10]..........................
financial help because she doesn't work.

7 請運用以下單字和片語來完成短文。

especially	quite a	a few	all	quite	all of us	completely
the most	rather	a bit	definitely	whole	slightly	so few

Have you ever been on vacation in February? I'm spending [1]........................... days in the French Riviera because a friend of mine has [2]........................... big house in the hills and has invited me for her birthday. There are five of us, and we all come from different European countries. [3]........................... are French teachers and we are making [4]........................... of this opportunity to speak French [5]........................... day long. The village where we are is [6]........................... small, but it's always [7]........................... crowded in summer, whereas at this time of year there are [8]........................... visitors that it looks quite different. It's [9]........................... sad sometimes, [10]........................... in the late afternoon when the sun starts setting and the [11]........................... atmosphere changes [12]........................... . We are often the only people walking along the silent streets and lanes, which makes us feel [13]........................... uneasy. In spite of the amazing beauty of the landscape, we all [14]........................... prefer a holiday in the summer.

8 請閱讀下文，將行末的大寫提示用詞改為合適詞性，來完成該行的克漏字。

The natural display of varying colors in the Arctic sky is one of Iceland's biggest tourist sights. [1]........................... it's rather   FORTUNATE

[2]........................... , so visitors should try a few times to be sure   PREDICT

they can see the Northern Lights. But what are they? The Northern Lights refer to one of the most [3]........................... wonders of   AMAZE

the world, the aurora borealis, a [4]........................... and flickering   GLOW

display of colors most [5]........................... seen in the northern   COMMON

hemisphere. The colors you see are caused by gases in the air,

[6]........................... a mixture of oxygen and nitrogen.   MAIN

Reflecting on grammar

請研讀文法規則，再判斷以下說法是否正確。

		True	False
1	字尾是 ly 的所有單字都是副詞。		
2	所有情態副詞的字尾都是 ly。		
3	我們會在 smell、sound、look、feel 等動詞後面，接 great 等類的形容詞，而不是副詞。		
4	「There were hardly any people at the conference.」這句話是說會議室裡有很多人。		
5	too 需放在形容詞或副詞的前面。		
6	enough 需放在形容詞前面或名詞的後面。		
7	「It's a very fabulous landscape.」是正確的句子。		
8	little 和 few 在描述少量概念方面，具有負面意思。		
9	「We haven't got much time.」是正確的句子。		
10	「How many passengers were on the bus?」是正確的問句。		

11 各種比較級 Comparisons

LESSON 1 比較級形容詞 Comparative adjectives

➜ 圖解請見 P. 418

比較級形容詞用來**比較人事物的特性**，表示甲比乙還重要、有趣等，也就是擁有較高程度的某特質。
比較級形容詞的結構各有不同，需視形容詞的**音節數**而定。

more + 形容詞	❶ **三個音節以上的形容詞** more difficult | more popular | more expensive ❷ **雙音節形容詞** more famous | more recent | more careful
形容詞 + er	❶ **單音節的形容詞** older | smaller | colder 注意 ❶ 字尾是 e 的形容詞，僅加上 r： nice → nicer | large → larger ❷ 字尾是「一個單母音 + 一個子音」時，要重複最後一個子音： hot → hotter | thin → thinner BUT cheap → cheaper（有兩個母音） ❷ **字尾為 y 的雙音節形容詞，且要先將 y 改成 i，再加上 er：** easy → easier | happy → happier

有些雙音節形容詞適用**兩種**比較級的表達方式，例如字尾 **ow**、**er**、**le** 的形容詞，以及 **quiet**、
friendly、**polite**、**common**、**stupid** 等形容詞：

- narrow → more narrow / narrower
- gentle → more gentle / gentler
- friendly → more friendly / friendlier
- clever → more clever / cleverer
- quiet → more quiet / quieter

1 請將下方形容詞改為比較級，並填入正確的類別。
請小心，某些形容詞的字尾必須重複最後一個子音。

healthy tall intelligent slim dry smart dangerous heavy cheap interesting
hot happy successful bright important lucky beautiful pretty

形容詞 + er	形容詞 + ier	more + 形容詞

2 請依照例句，運用第 **1** 大題中的原級和比較級形容詞，來描述圖片。

0 <u>This diamond is bright. The other one is brighter.</u>

1 ....

....

2 ....

....

3 ....

....

4 ....

....

5 ....

....

6 ....

....

比較級的句型

> 主詞 + **be 動詞** + **比較級形容詞** + **than** + 被比較的名詞

1 比較級句子中，要用 **than** 來引導兩者之中被拿來比較的後者：

• Exercise 1 is easier **than** exercise 2.

2 **than** 的後面可接：

❶ 名詞或代名詞：My cousin is younger **than** <u>me</u>.

請小心，受格代名詞（如 me、him、her 等詞，請參閱第 83 頁）更常用於口語英文，較正式的用法
則是以主詞代名詞加上 be 動詞或助動詞：My cousin is younger **than** <u>I am</u>.

❷ 次要比較級子句：The exam was harder **than** <u>I thought</u>.

3 比較級形容詞亦可用於表達屬性，這時一定要放在**名詞前面**，就和原級形容詞一樣
（請參閱第 46 頁）：

• Manchester is a big city. It's a <u>bigger</u> city than New York.

1 表達**同時產生變化的兩件事**：

> **The** + 第一個比較級（+ 主詞 + 動詞），
> **the** + 第二個比較級（+ 主詞 + 動詞）

- **The richer** he gets, **the meaner** (he gets).
- **The greater** the challenge, **the greater** the reward.
- **The older** this wine gets, **the better** it is.

2 如果比較的是兩種**行為**，那**第一個比較級**會以**不定詞 to + 原形動詞**的方式表達，**第二個比較級**則僅需使用**原形動詞**：
Sometimes it's quicker **to cycle** than **go** by car.

3 還可用**比較兩者**的方式，來表達**最高級**的概念：

> **the + 比較級 + of**

- I bought **the cheaper of** the two dresses.
- They took **the shorter of** the two roads.

3 請以比較級形容詞來完成句子，並於必要位置加上 **than**。

1 The flight was .... we expected—it cost only £60. (cheap)

2 He isn't .... you. You can do just as well. (clever)

3 This test is .... the one we had last week. (difficult)

4 Try to be .... when writing in English. You've made a lot of spelling mistakes. (careful)

5 His second novel has been .... the first one. (successful)

6 The .... the food you eat, the .... you are. (healthy)

7 Today is a .... day .... yesterday. (warm)

8 I think it's .... to travel with a friend .... travel on your own. (nice)

9 I'll take the "0915 express," it's the .... of the two trains. (fast)

10 The .... you are to people, the .... people will be to you. (kind)

Much more / A little more / Get more and more

我們已經了解運用 very、quite 和其他相似詞來加強原級形容詞的方法（請參閱 Unit 10 Lesson 2）。

1 如需**加強**比較級形容詞的意思，我們會使用 **much、a lot、far、way**（美式英文用法）等副詞：
- "Their room is very large."
  "Yes, it's **much bigger** than ours."
- Tom is a **far smarter** guy than Rick.

2 如果要**減弱**比較級的程度，則會使用 **a little / a bit** 或 **slightly**：
- My dad is **a bit more patient** than my mom.

3 而**增加**比較級程度的另一個方式，就是以連接詞 **and** 搭配**兩個一樣的比較級形容詞**，來表示**逐漸增加**的意思：
- It's getting **warmer and warmer**.
- Gasoline is getting **more and more expensive**.

4 請以比較級形容詞來完成句子，並視情況，自行在形容詞前面加上 **much、a lot** 或 **far** 等加強副詞。

0 Today's English lesson was ....*much more interesting*.... than yesterday's. (interesting)

1 His latest movie was .... than his previous ones. (exciting)

2 Christina is .... than the other girls in her class. (quiet)

3 It's getting .... and .... We'll soon be able to see the stars. (dark)

4 These sneakers are .... but they're also .... than the others. (expensive, comfortable)

5 This summer has been .... than all the other ones I can remember. (hot)

6 She's on a strict diet. She's getting .... and ....
every day. (thin)

不規則比較級

有些形容詞具有不規則的比較級和最高級變化（請參閱第 198 頁）：

good bad	**better** **worse**

far	**farther** (指距離上較遠) **further** (指程度上較多)

old	**older**
	elder (指手足中年齡較長的)

看下方的例句：

- I have to admit that my wife is a **better** skier than I am.
- Yesterday the weather was bad, but today it is even **worse**.
- Saturn is **farther** from the Sun than Venus.
- For **further** information, call 0369382662.
- Rachel is my **elder** sister. She's three years **older** than me.

5 請依照例句，選用 good、healthy、relaxing、exciting、tiring、boring、expensive、cheap、nice、easy 等形容詞，寫出比較兩者的句子。
由於這是你自己的看法，因此句子請都用「I think . . .」來開頭。

0 salad / French fries
~~I think salad is healthier than French fries,~~
~~but French fries are much nicer!~~

1 living in a big city / living in the country
....
....

2 adventure movies / comedies
....
....

3 cycling / walking
....
....

4 traveling by train / traveling by car
....
....

5 working in an office / working in the open air
....
....

6 doing yoga / going jogging
....
....

7 golf / football
....
....

UNIT
11

各種比較級

193

LESSON 2 「less . . . than」和「not as . . . as」搭配形容詞的比較級用法
Comparative structures using *less . . . than* and *not as . . . as* with adjectives

less . . . than 的比較級句型

❶ 要表達**某特質程度較低**時，我們會將一個事物與另一個較不重要、不實用的事物比較，並會使用 less than 這個比較級。

❷ 副詞 **less** 需放在所有形容詞的前面（包含單音節和雙音節以上的形容詞）。
和 **more** 的句型一樣，比較級句子會以 **than** 來引導兩者之中被拿來比較的後者：

> **less** + 形容詞 + **than** + 被比較的後者（名詞或代名詞）

• The sequel was <u>less interesting than</u> the first movie.

❸ **than** 也能用來引導次要比較級**子句**：
Our holiday in the Bahamas was less exciting <u>than we thought</u>.

---

1 請依照例句，以 **less** 搭配括號內的形容詞，來寫出意義相近的句子。

0 My car is an older model than yours. (recent)
<u>My car is a less recent model than yours.</u>

1 Mr. Johnson's lessons are usually more interesting than Mr. Riley's. (boring)
....
....

2 The blue coat is cheaper than the brown one. (expensive)
....
....

3 My suitcase is lighter than yours. (heavy)
....
....

4 This building is a more classical style than the other one. (modern)
....
....

5 Today it's cooler than yesterday. (warm)
....
....

6 This TV series is more boring than the one on Channel 4. (exciting)
....
....

7 It's unlikely to rain this afternoon. (likely)
....
....

---

as . . . as 的比較級

❶ 另一種比較人事物的方式，是在表達某個人事物和另一個人事物一樣有趣、重要等等，也就是兩者的**特質程度相同**。
句型如下：

> **as** + 形容詞 + **as** + 被比較的後者（名詞或代名詞）

• Houses in this area are as **expensive** as those in my town.

❷ 我們也可以在 **as + 形容詞**前面加上副詞 **just**，來加強語氣：
• John is **just** as clever as his brother.

這種所謂的「**同等比較**」，經常用於**否定句**，來作為減弱程度的另一種比較級表達方式。
在此情況下，第一個 **as** 可用 **so** 來代替：
• Today it isn't as cold as yesterday.
• The prices here are **not** so high as in the other supermarket.

2 請運用括號裡的單字和 **as . . . as** 來完成比較級句子。

1 (just / beautiful) She's .... her sister.

2 (busy) Luckily I'm not .... today .... I was yesterday.

3 (famous) Bob Dylan is .... Bruce Springsteen.

4 (interesting) This article is not .... the one in *TIME* magazine.

5 (exciting) The show was .... a cold rice pudding!

6 (just / good) Their latest concert was .... last year's.

7 (popular) The Rolling Stones were .... The Beatles in the 1960s.

3 請搭配 **(not) as . . . as** 和括號裡的形容詞，來寫出比較級肯定句或否定句。

0 Joe: 1.70 m / Marion: 1.70 m (tall)
Joe is as tall as Marion.

1 Claire: 60 years old / Karen: 60 years old (old)
....
....

2 Today: 38 °C / Yesterday: 38°C (hot)
....
....

3 Blue jacket: $65.00 / Black jacket: $80.00 (expensive)
....
....

4 Their apartment: 70 sq.m / Our apartment: 100 sq.m (large)
....
....

5 The history book: 250 pages / The grammar book: 300 pages (big)
....
....

6 The Ohio river: 1,579 km / The Mississippi: 3,730 km (long)
....
....

7 The Breithorn: 4,164 m / Mont Blanc: 4,810 m (high)
....
....

8 Phoenix: about 570 km from here / Los Angeles: about 190 km from here (far)
....
....

4 請使用 **not as . . . as** 的句型，來寫出意義相同的句子。

0 The oral exam was less difficult than the written one.
The oral exam wasn't as difficult as the written one.

1 Cross-country skiing is less risky than alpine skiing or snowboarding.
....

2 A small tent is less comfortable than a campervan.
....

3 This song is less famous than the others on her latest album.
....

4 Baseball is less popular in Italy than football.
....

5 She's been less successful in her career than her sister.
....

6 My scooter is less sporty than your motorcycle.
....

最高級形容詞

如果要將某人事物和另一群人事物的特性做比較，我們就需要使用最高級形容詞。

最高級形容詞用以表達某特定事物最重要、最有趣等等，也就是與群體中其他事物相比，此事物具有最高等級的特質。最高級的變化需取決於形容詞的音節數量，就和之前學到的比較級一樣。

most + 形容詞	❶ **三個音節以上的形容詞** the **most** dangerous ｜ the **most** important ｜ the **most** expensive ❷ **雙音節形容詞** the **most** frequent ｜ the **most** careful ｜ the **most** secure
形容詞 + est	❶ **單音節的形容詞** the small**est** ｜ the tall**est** ｜ the young**est** **注意** ❶ 字尾是 e 的形容詞，僅加上 st 　wide → the wid**est** ｜ safe → the saf**est** ❷ 字尾是單母音加上單子音的形容詞，要先重複最後一個子音， 　再加上 **est**： 　fat → the fat**t**est ｜ thin → the thin**n**est 　**BUT** cheap → the cheap**est**（有兩個母音） ❷ **字尾為 y 的雙音節形容詞，且要先將 y 改成 i，再加上 est：** heavy → the heav**i**est ｜ funny → the funn**i**est

有些雙音節形容詞適用**兩種**最高級的表達方式，例如字尾 **ow**、**er**、**le** 的形容詞，以及 **quiet**、**friendly**、**polite**、**common**、**stupid** 等形容詞：

- narrow → the most narrow / the narrowest　• stupid → the most stupid / the stupidest
- clever → the most clever / the cleverest

Focus

❶ 最高級前面幾乎都要加上定冠詞 **the**：
- This is **the** <u>most important</u> event of the year.

❷ 「**one of the** + 最高級」的形式亦十分常見：
- Basketball is **one of the** <u>most popular</u> sports in the United States.

1 請將括號內的形容詞改為「**the + 最高級**」的形式，並完成句子。
請注意，其中有一個句子不能使用冠詞 **the**。

1 New York's Central Park is one of .... urban parks in the USA. (large)

2 Yellowstone is .... National Park in the USA. (old)

3 One of America's .... national monuments is Waco Mammoth in Texas. (new)

4 Rotterdam is one of .... ports in Europe. (busy)

5 Robert is .... driver I know. He's never had an accident. (careful)

6 The Hilton is one of .... hotels in London. (exclusive)

7 Last summer I went to Jamaica. It was .... holiday of my life. (exciting)

8 The atom used to be considered .... particle which matter is made up of. (small)

最高級句型

最高級形容詞的後面，通常會出現以下句型：

1 如果是指**場所**，通常會有 in 引導的受詞：
- The Nile is one of **the longest** rivers **in** the world.

2 如果是以下情況，則會由 **of** 來引導受詞，例如：

① 表示時間
It's one of **the best** novels **of** all time.
Also It's one of the best novels ever.

② 表示與某群體的關聯
He's **the most generous of** all my friends.

3 最高級的句型裡，還可搭配現在完成式動詞，並接上**關係子句**（關係代名詞 that 可有可無），另外也可使用副詞 ever：
- It's one of **the funniest** movies (that) I've **ever** seen.

如果主要子句的動詞是**簡單過去式**，那注意，後接的關係子句要使用**過去完成式**的動詞：She <u>was</u> **the kindest** person I <u>had</u> <u>ever</u> <u>met</u>.

4 如需強調最高級，還可以加上 **by far**：
- Today is **by far the hottest** day of the month. The temperature has reached 42° C.

UNIT
11

各種比較級

FAQ

Q: 英文文法裡的最高級都是「相對最高級」的意思，也就是和特定群組比較下的相對關係。我從沒聽過英文有「絕對的最高級」，有這種用法嗎？

A: 事實上，英文並沒有特定的最高級形式。如果要加強形容詞的意思，我們通常會使用副詞 **very**，甚至會重複兩次，或者是美式口語英文裡的 **way**：
very, very tall / way tall
我們還可使用 **most + 形容詞**來表示最高級：
It's most annoying.

2 請以介系詞 **of** 或 **in** 來完成句子。

1 Aconcagua is the highest peak .... South America.

2 January is usually the coldest month .... the year.

3 Which is the biggest city .... India?

4 He was one of the greatest actors .... all time.

5 This is the most important event .... the musical season.

6 Bill Gates is one of the richest people .... the world.

7 He's the most talented student .... his school.

8 This is going to be the best day .... my life.

9 This is the most expensive house .... the whole city.

3 請重新排序單字，寫出邏輯通順的句子。

1 most / This / is / exciting / one/of / the / matches / we / have / football / seen / ever / .
....

2 most / Mrs. Ray / is/the / teacher / I've / ever / competent / met / .
....

3 This / best / is / the / ever / career / opportunity / by far / Jack / has / had / .
....

4 It's / moving / of / most / stories / one / I've / ever / the / read / .
....

197

4 請依照例句，將動詞改為「現在完成式」或「過去完成式」，並將兩組句子配對。

0	My friend, Pat, is the most intuitive person	**A**	they / ever / grow
1	Last night's fireworks display was the most spectacular	**B**	I / ever / hear
2	This is the biggest pumpkin	**C**	we / ever / walk up
3	This is the most comfortable armchair	**D**	I / ever / meet
4	It's one of the funniest stories	**E**	I / ever / have
5	That was the steepest path	**F**	I / ever / try
6	I'm having fun in Ibiza. It's the most exciting holiday	**G**	we / ever / see
7	George thought that was the hardest exam	**H**	he / ever / take

0 <u>My friend Pat is the most intuitive person I've ever met.</u> **(D)**
1 ....
2 ....
3 ....
4 ....
5 ....
6 ....
7 ....

不規則最高級

! 我們有學過，某些形容詞（請參閱第 193 頁）會有不規則的比較級和最高級變化，某些形容詞則只有最高級有不規則變化。

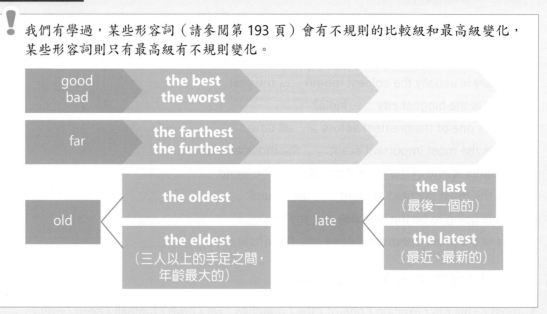

- Anne and I are **best** friends.
- This is **the worst** experience I've had in my entire life.
- Since Pluto was named a "dwarf planet," Neptune has been considered **the farthest** planet from the Sun.
- John is our **eldest** brother. He's 24 years old.
- *The Tempest* is Shakespeare's **last** work.
- I read an interesting article in **the latest** issue of *National Geographic*.

5 請以 good、bad、far、old、late 等形容詞的不規則最高級形式來完成句子。

1 This is one of the .... restaurants I've ever been to—great food and excellent service.

2 Martin is the .... singer I know. He has no sense of rhythm and his voice is terrible!

3 Simon is Brian's .... friend. They've been good friends for a long time.

4 I think we should go to a beach that is nearer. Golden Beach is the .... from here.

5 My friend Lawrence is a good athlete. His .... time for the 100 meters is just over ten seconds.

6 You don't like this singer. Why do you have his .... CD?

7 My mother has three sisters who are younger than her. She's the .... in her family.

8 I'm leaving tomorrow. This is my .... day in New York.

9 This is the .... car I've ever had. It keeps breaking down, and repairing it has already cost me a fortune.

10 The Shetland Islands are .... north you can go in the UK.

最高級 least 的用法

最高級 least 用於表達特定事物最不重要、最不有趣等等，也就是與其他事物比較下，具有的特質**程度最弱**。句子中 the least 必須放在**形容詞的前面**：

- Flying with a low-cost company is **the least** <u>expensive</u> way to travel abroad.

6 請運用括號裡的單字，搭配「**the least** + 形容詞 + 名詞」來完成句子。

1 (useful / thing) This is .... you've ever bought!

2 (exciting / match) This is .... I've ever watched.

3 (amusing / program) It's .... we've ever seen.

4 (complicated / person) He's .... I've ever met.

5 (interesting / place) This is .... we have ever been to.

6 (popular / resort) This must be .... in the region.

7 (expensive / bag) This is .... they have in this shop.

8 (relevant / thing) It's .... I've ever heard.

9 (flattering / outfit) That's .... you've ever worn!

10 (impressive / attempt) His last jump was .... at clearing two meters in the high jump.

FAQ

Q: 我常聽見 last but not least 的說法，這到底是什麼意思呢？

A: 這是在告訴他人「某人事物最後出現，並不是因為最不重要」，也就是在說，雖然是最後出現，但與前面幾項事件同等重要。

Q: 什麼時候可以用 more or less？

A: more or less 的意思是**將近、大約**。用法如以下例句：
It weighs ten kilos, **more or less**.（這大約十公斤重）

LESSON 4 副詞的比較級和最高級／修飾名詞數量和動詞程度的比較級
Comparative and superlative of adverbs, comparatives with nouns and verbs

副詞的比較級

副詞的比較級句型和形容詞類似（請參閱第 190 頁和第 194 頁），有以下規則與用法：

1 在單音節副詞最後加上 **er**，尤其是形式與形容詞相同的副詞，例如：
late/fast/high/long/hard →
lat**er**/fast**er**/high**er**/long**er**/hard**er**

2 使用 **more**，當字尾是 ly 的副詞時 →
more slowly｜**more** quickly

3 使用 **less**，當字尾是 ly 的副詞時 →
less carefully｜**less** fluently

上方三種用法均以 **than** 來引導被比較的後者，或是次要子句：
- It took much longer **than** I thought.

4 如需表達同時變化的兩件事時，則使用以下句型：

> **The** + 第一個比較級副詞 + 主詞 + 動詞，
> **the** + 第二個比較級副詞 + 主詞 + 動詞

- **The harder** you study, **the sooner** you'll get your diploma.

5 使用 **as . . . as**，用法就和搭配形容詞相同：
This morning I didn't get up **as** early **as** I did yesterday.

副詞的最高級

副詞的最高級規則和形容詞的規則相同（請參閱第 196 頁）：

1 單音節副詞前面要加上 **the**，並於字尾加上 **est**：the longest
- The turtle is one of the animals that lives **the longest**.

2 字尾是 **ly** 的副詞，則搭配 **the most** 來表達最高級：the most quickly
- I work **the most quickly** when I'm not under pressure.

most 前方沒有冠詞 the 時，是用在強調副詞的語氣，具有「**極為**」、「**大量地**」意思：
- You behaved **most** stupidly!

不規則比較級和最高級的副詞

well	better	best
badly	worse	worst

- You dance **better** than he does. Actually, you dance the **best** of all.
- I usually play **badly**, but yesterday I played **worse** than ever!

FAQ

Q: 我看過句子使用 as well as，但意思卻不是「和……一樣好」。這個用法還有其他意思嗎？

A: 有，as well as 具「和、也有、還有」的意思，例如：「You can use my laptop <u>as well as</u> my tablet.」（你可以用我的筆電和平板）。

1 請圈出正確的用字。

1 Tonight we're going to bed just as late **than** / **as** yesterday.

2 *Les Miserables* is one of the **longest** / **longer** running musicals ever.

3 You can get the floor cleaned **most** / **more** quickly if you use a robot.

4 The **later** / **latest** you arrive, the **longest** / **longer** the line you'll find at the ticket office.

5 You can eat your lunch **more** / **most** slowly, we're not in a hurry.

6 "What time shall I come?" "The sooner, the **best** / **better**."

7 He jumped **higher** / **more high** than ever before. He broke his own record.

8 My father drives **less** / **least** carefully **than** / **as** my mother.

9 The **more** / **most** you tease him, the **more** / **most** likely he is to cry.

10 The **farther** / **more far** you get from an object, the **smaller** / **smallest** it looks.

2 請重新排序單字來造句。

1 as you / sure / I / run / I'm / as fast / can / .

....

2 I / This term / studied / as hard / last term / as / haven't / .

....

3 than / always / Paula / harder / everyone else / works / .

....

4 later / festival / this year / started / The movie / .

....

5 higher / They / than / ever / climbed / before / .

....

6 longer / journey / usual / took/us / The last / than / .

....

7 quickly / speaks / the most / He / nervous / he's / when / .

....

8 you / The / earlier / leave / the less / you'll / find / traffic / much / many a lot

....

修飾名詞數量的比較級和最高級

much/many a lot	more	the most

little few	less few	the least the fewest

1 **more / the most + 不可數**名詞或**複數**名詞：

• I've had **more free time** since I retired from work.
• In the summer I have **the most free time**.
• I have **more friends** here than I had where I lived before.
• This is where I've had **the most friends** ever.

2 less / the least + 不可數名詞：

- I've got **less money** than you.
- No one has got much, but I've got **the least money** of all.

3 fewer / the fewest + 複數可數名詞：

- You've made **fewer mistakes** than usual.
- In this test you've made **the fewest mistakes** ever. Well done!

4 as much + 不可數名詞 + as：

- This week I haven't got **as much time** to train **as** last week.

5 as many + 複數可數名詞 + as：

- There aren't **as many people** on the beach today **as** there were yesterday.

修飾動詞程度的比較級用法

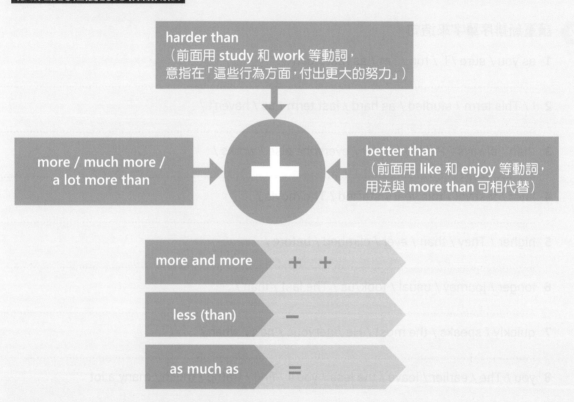

- He used to be very reserved, but he talks **a lot more** now.
- I'm working **much** harder this month.
- I like this song **better than** the other one.
- You're eating **more and more** every day. Isn't that too much?
- She looks sad. She's smiling **less than** usual.
- I'm not spending **as much as** I used to. I'm trying to save some money.

切記！否定句裡的 **any more** 意指「不會再有」：

- I can't play **any more**. 〔意思等同「I can play no longer.」〔我不能再玩了〕〕
- The hooligans got an ASBO. They can't cause **any more** trouble now.
  〔意同「They can no longer cause trouble.」〔他們不能再捅婁子了〕〕

3 請依照例句，使用 **as much as** 或 **as many as** 來改寫句子。

0 Both the Robsons and the Wilsons have four children, two sons and two daughters.

The Robsons have as many children as the Wilsons, two sons and two daughters.

1 Yesterday we had 20 guests in our restaurant. Today we have 20 guests too.

....

2 We spent a lot of time to clean the house and a lot of time to prepare dinner.

....

3 There are 50 seats in the conference room on the second floor and 50 in the one on the first floor.

....

4 There are 12 fish in the aquarium and 12 fish in the pond.

....

5 Both Italy and Belarus got ten gold medals in the Baku 2015 European Games.

....

6 Both Paul and Lawrence collect elephant statuettes and they have 550 each.

....

4 請根據句尾的符號，使用比較級 **more**（+）、最高級 **the most**（++）、比較級 **less**（−）、最高級 **the least**（− −）或比較級 **as . . . as**（=）來完成句子。

1 People should be a bit more relaxed; there should be .... competition. (−)

2 I like this T-shirt .... the other one (+), but I like the blue one .... of all. (++)

3 The English teacher has .... patience .... the PE teacher. (−) The math teacher has the .... patience of all. (− −)

4 I can't spend a lot! I don't have .... money with me .... you have. (=)

5 In my class there are .... students .... in your class this year. (=)

6 Today I have .... homework .... usual. That's great! (−)

7 You've got a lot of luggage, but I've got .... you. (+)

8 These cookies contain .... sugar and .... fat .... most others. (−)

9 I'm not spending .... you this month (=). I'm saving .... (+)

10 This year my son is getting .... rewarding marks .... he did last year. (+)

11 I have .... students this year in my courses .... I did last year (+), but my colleague Albert has got .... in the whole school. (++)

12 He has always got .... baggage of all, only a small backpack. (− −)

5 請使用合適的比較級來完成克漏字。

1 I enjoy eating out .... cooking—I hate doing the dishes!

2 The .... time I spend with Tim, the .... I like him.

3 My holiday to Kos cost much .... my friend's holiday to the Caribbean, so I saved money.

4 There are .... reasons to shop around for your car insurance these days.

5 Karen studied .... Michelle all year, so it wasn't surprising when she got a better mark in the exam.

6 We like Italian food .... Chinese food. It's always really hard to choose!

ROUND UP 11

修飾名詞數量的比較級和最高級整理

	a lot of	more	the most
搭配肯定句裡的複數可數名詞和不可數名詞	• We had **a lot of** guests last summer. • Annie earns **a lot of** money.	• We had **more** guests than usual. • Simon earns **more** money than her.	• Last year we had **the most** guests ever. • Jessica earns **the most** money of all.
	many	**more**	**the most**
搭配否定句和疑問句裡的複數可數名詞	• I didn't have **many** friends then. • Did you have **many** problems at the customs?	• I don't have **more** friends than you. • Did you have **more** problems than last year?	• Which student had **the most** friends of all? • When did you have **the most** problems?
	much	**more**	**the most**
搭配否定句和疑問句裡的不可數名詞	• Pete didn't have **much** time to train. • Did they have **much** money?	• Sam didn't have **more** time than Pete. • Did they have more **money** than you?	• Which player had **the most** time of all? • Who had **the most** money?
	few / a few	**fewer**	**the fewest**
搭配複數可數名詞	• There were **few** seats available. • There are only **a few** cookies left.	• There will be **fewer** seats tomorrow night. • And there are even **fewer** sandwiches.	• This stadium has got **the fewest** seats of all. • Who ate **the fewest** sandwiches?
	little / a little	**less**	**the least**
搭配不可數名詞	• Arlene has **little** patience with the children. • We'll have **a little** time to go shopping.	• I have got even **less** patience than Arlene. • We'll have **less** time for shopping today.	• Charlie has got **the least** patience of all. • We had **the least** time for shopping last week.

1 請圈出正確的用字。如果不確定答案，可查看上一頁的表格內容。

1 Our new restaurant is doing very well. There are **many** / **much** customers every night, but tonight we've had **the most** / **the more** customers since we opened.

2 My little daughter usually gets **lots of** / **lot of** presents at Christmas, but this year she's got **the much** / **the most**!

3 There are only **a few** / **a little** tickets left for the concert. If you wait till tomorrow, there will be even **fewer** / **fewest** or none at all.

4 We can't buy all these things. We have very **little** / **less** money.

5 I like doing different things every day. I agree with the saying "**The less** / **The least** routine, **the more** / **the most** life."

6 **More and more** / **Many and many** people are gathering in Trafalgar Square in London to celebrate the New Year.

7 It took me **less** / **fewer** than one hour to get to York.

8 Who signed **the most** / **the many** autographs? The movie director or the main actor?

9 There are very **few** / **little** people who can play the piano as well as Margot.

10 If you have **fewer** / **less** than £100 in your account, you won't earn any interest.

延伸補充

❶ 某些所謂「**強烈**」或「**不可分級**」的形容詞，因為本身已具有**絕對**意義，所以**沒有比較級**或**最高級**的變化。例如：

| full / empty | right / wrong | correct / incorrect | freezing / boiling | equal / unequal |

❷ 但嘲諷的表達方式例外，如喬治‧歐威爾著名小說《動物農莊》的這句話：
- All animals are equal, but some animals are more equal than others.
  （所有動物都是平等的，但某些動物比其他的更平等）

❸ 另外，在下列情況中，此類形容詞和**多音節形容詞**一樣，需搭配 **more** 來表達比較級，搭配 **most** 來表達最高級：

❶ 形容詞是過去分詞時：
- more bent | the most drunk | the most hidden   **BUT** the best known

❷ 形容詞字尾有 less 或 ful 的字尾：
- harmless → more harmless → the most harmless
- hopeful → more hopeful → the most hopeful

---

2 請以下方形容詞的比較級或最高級形式，來完成句子。

| hidden   bent   known   harmless   hopeless   helpful   renowned   shaken |

1 The tall pine tree was the .... by the strong wind.

2 This type of snake is the .... It isn't poisonous at all.

3 This is the .... place in the wood. Nobody will ever find you there!

4 That spoon is .... than ever! It was quite straight before you started messing with it.

5 This is one of the .... novels by this author.

6 This is her .... poem. We have all read it in school.

7 You're the .... football player I've ever seen! You never score a goal!

8 He's usually .... than his sister. He usually offers to do the dishes.

3 請閱讀以下短文，選出正確答案。

Some people think that the quality of life in a small quiet town like the one where I live is ¹...... than in a big city. There aren't ²...... as ³...... go to work or school by bike, so the center is quiet. A small town is generally ⁴...... than a big one, which is another reason why ⁵...... ten percent of the people living in cities have now chosen to move to ⁶...... . None of the people we've interviewed complain about the lack of opportunities in a town with ⁷...... 50,000 inhabitants. They all say that they can find whatever they want and they can easily reach ⁸...... big city if they want to see a new movie release or theater show.

1	Ⓐ much better	Ⓑ much best	Ⓒ as good
2	Ⓐ much cars	Ⓑ many cars	Ⓒ any cars
3	Ⓐ few of the people	Ⓑ more of the people	Ⓒ most of the people
4	Ⓐ less polluted	Ⓑ not so polluted	Ⓒ least polluted
5	Ⓐ at last	Ⓑ at least	Ⓒ at most
6	Ⓐ smallest places	Ⓑ more small places	Ⓒ smaller places
7	Ⓐ no more than	Ⓑ any more than	Ⓒ none more than
8	Ⓐ the nearer	Ⓑ the most near	Ⓒ the nearest

4 下方所有句子都有一個錯誤，請標出錯誤並訂正。

1 Who jumped the farther in the last event? ....

2 Your girlfriend was the most elegant in all the girls at last night's party. ....

3 The most people communicate through social networks these days. ....

4 Please drive more carefuller than usual. There's a baby in the car. ....

5 Why didn't you study as hard than usual? ....

6 Always try to do your better. ....

7 I like this song as than the other one. ....

8 Their later CD is much better than the previous one. ....

9 Which was the worse experience you've ever had, if I may ask? ....

10 Don't go any farthest. It could be dangerous. ....

11 The more people there are, the loudest you'll have to shout. ....

12 As harder as it seems, it will be worth it in the end. ....

5 請使用以下形容詞與副詞的最高級或比較級，來完成克漏字。

late (x2)   good   long   old   young

Come to the concert tomorrow night. There will be ¹........................ rock and hip-hop bands of our town with their ²................. songs. My ³................. brother is coming too when he finishes work, but not my ⁴........................ brother because he's got a basketball match after school. Let's meet at 8:00. Don't be late as usual. The ⁵................. you get there, the ⁶................. we will have to line up for the tickets.

6 請閱讀以下短文，選出正確的答案。

These are the outcomes of a survey which was carried out by a group of famous psychologists a few months ago. According to them, life is much ¹...... when people are ²...... and behave ³...... to each other. But too often people become ⁴...... when their life gets ⁵...... than before. The pace of life is getting ⁶...... every day and few people seem to be able to live ⁷...... these days. Even children don't seem to be ⁸...... they were. They watch ⁹...... television and eat ¹⁰...... food than previous generations, and generally live ¹¹...... . In their report, the psychologists underline the need to find a way to make everyone ¹²...... .

1	Ⓐ nicer	Ⓑ nicest	Ⓒ nice	Ⓓ nicely
2	Ⓐ less happy	Ⓑ happy	Ⓒ more happy	Ⓓ happily
3	Ⓐ kind	Ⓑ kindly	Ⓒ less kind	Ⓓ more kind
4	Ⓐ more aggressive	Ⓑ aggressiver	Ⓒ aggressively	Ⓓ most aggressive
5	Ⓐ difficult	Ⓑ difficulter	Ⓒ difficulty	Ⓓ more difficult
6	Ⓐ fast	Ⓑ faster	Ⓒ fastly	Ⓓ more fast
7	Ⓐ calm	Ⓑ calmer	Ⓒ calmly	Ⓓ calmest
8	Ⓐ so carefree than	Ⓑ carefreer than	Ⓒ carefreest as	Ⓓ as carefree as
9	Ⓐ most	Ⓑ much	Ⓒ more	Ⓓ the most
10	Ⓐ badder	Ⓑ worse	Ⓒ worst	Ⓓ baddest
11	Ⓐ unhealthy	Ⓑ unhealthiest	Ⓒ unhealthier	Ⓓ unhealthily
12	Ⓐ more contented	Ⓑ less contented	Ⓒ as contented as	Ⓓ much contented

Reflecting on grammar
請研讀文法規則，再判斷以下說法是否正確。

		True	False
1	所有雙音節形容詞的比較級均需搭配 more。		
2	搭配 more 或 less 的比較級句子，會以 then 來引導兩者之中被拿來比較的後者。		
3	「He's very younger than me.」是正確的句子。		
4	bad 的比較級是 worse，最高級是 worst。		
5	「She is as old as me but looks much younger.」是正確的句子。		
6	電視影集出現完結篇時，我們會說「This is the latest episode of the series.」。		
7	far 的最高級是 the farthest 。		
8	三音節的形容詞，字尾加上 est 就是最高級。		
9	「He's the eldest of two brothers.」是正確的句子。		
10	「This book is less interesting than the other one.」的意思和「This book is not so interesting as the other one.」相同。		

12 形容詞和代名詞 Adjectives and Pronouns

LESSON 1 以 some、any 和 no 構成的不定代名詞

Indefinite pronouns made with some, any and no

→ 圖解請見 P. 417

以 some、any 和 no 構成的不定代名詞如下：

	–THING	–BODY	–ONE	–WHERE
SOME–	something (+/?)	somebody (+/?)	someone (+/?)	somewhere (+/?)
ANY–	anything (+/?/–)	anybody (+/?/–)	anyone (+/?/–)	anywhere (+/?/–)
NO–	nothing (+)	nobody (+)	no one (+)	nowhere (+)

結合 **thing**，就成為**事物**的複合代名詞。

something 的用法如下：

❶ 肯定句：I have **something** to tell you.

❷ 主動示意的問句：
Would you like **something** to eat?

❸ 提出要求的句子：
Can I have **something** to drink, please?

❹ 希望聽到肯定回應的問句：
So, did you learn **something**?（意指「我真的認為且希望你有得到收穫」）

anything 的用法如下：

❶ 詢問資訊的「中立」問句：
Did you buy **anything** in the sales?

❷ 在肯定句裡，意指「眾多東西中的任一個」、「哪一個都可以」：
You can have **anything** you like.

❸ 搭配動詞的否定句：
I don't know **anything** about that.

nothing 的用法如下：

❶ 以肯定形式的動詞來表達否定意思的句子：
We had **nothing** to eat.

❷ 作為句子的主詞：**Nothing** happened.

Focus

一個英文句子裡僅能使用**一種否定意義**的用詞，因此共有兩種否定句型：

❶ 否定動詞 + 結合 **any** 的複合代名詞：I don't know **anything**.

❷ 肯定動詞 + 結合 **no** 的複合代名詞：I **know nothing**. **NOT** ~~I don't know nothing.~~

1 請使用 something、 anything 或 nothing 來完成句子。

1 "Didn't they tell you ....?" "No, they didn't."

2 "Do you want .... to eat?" "Yes, please."
"What would you like?" ".......................... you have in the fridge, I don't mind."

3 There's .... to watch on TV this evening. Let's go out!

4 There's .... good and .... bad in all of us.

5 We have .... to do here now. Why don't we go somewhere else?

6 "Could we have .... to drink, please?" "Yes, sure. Here's a glass of water."

7 I can't eat .... late at night because I'm on diet.

8 Do you have .... to tell me? Like how this window got broken?

9 There's .... better than spending the day puttering around at home.

10 I couldn't find .... about the news story on the Internet.

結合 **body** 和 **one**，即成為**人物**的複合代名詞。兩者意義相同，因此可互換使用，例如：

Did you see **anybody**? / Did you see **anyone**?

結合 body 和 one 產生的代名詞，使用規則和 thing 一樣。

> some 具有肯定意義，no 具有否定意義，any 則具有「中立」意義（請參閱第 44 頁）。

下方是一些例句：

- You must tell **someone**.（肯定句）
- Did you meet **anyone** from the management?（中立句，詢問資訊）
- It's so easy that **anybody** can do it!（肯定句，意指「不管是誰，任何人都能做到」）
- I did**n't** know **anybody**. = I knew **nobody**.（只用單一否定用詞，來表達否定意義）
- **Nobody** knows. = **No one** knows.（以 nobody/no one 為主詞，帶有否定意義）

2 請圈選正確的代名詞。

1 I've found **someone** / **anyone** / **something** who can help me with my homework.
2 Can **nothing** / **anyone** / **anything** here play a musical instrument?
3 There's **somebody** / **nobody** / **something** at the door. Go and see who it is.
4 When I got back home, the lights were on but **no one** / **anyone** / **someone** was there.
5 There isn't **anyone** / **someone** / **somebody** who knows how to fix my computer.
6 Did you meet **somebody** / **anybody** / **anything** you knew at the concert?
7 Is there **anything** / **anybody** / **nobody** I can do for you?
8 **Nobody** / **Nothing** / **Anything** is as important as good education.
9 **Something** / **Somebody** / **No one** must have seen **anything** / **nothing** / **something** — the robbery happened in broad daylight!
10 There's **nobody** / **no one** / **nothing** that can be done to improve the situation, unfortunately.
11 "Is there **anybody** / **no one** / **anything** I can do to help?"
   "No, **something** / **nothing** / **anything**, thanks."
12 That's **anything** / **nothing** / **something** that I've been wanting to learn for ages.

結合 **where** 即成為**地點**的複合代名詞，且用法和上述的規則相同。

- Let's go **somewhere** this afternoon.（肯定句）
- Did you go **anywhere** last weekend?（中立問句）
- Put your bag **anywhere** you like.（肯定句，表示「放在你喜歡的任何地方」）
- I did**n't** go **anywhere**. = I went **nowhere**.（有否定意義的句子）
- **Nowhere** is like home.（nowhere 是這句的主詞）

Focus

❶ 不定代名詞後面常會接**形容詞**，如 something/nothing/anything + 形容詞：
  - At your wedding you must wear **something old**, **something new**, **something borrowed** and **something blue**.
  - There's **nothing interesting** on TV tonight.

❷ 不定代名詞後面也會接副詞 **else**，如 something/nothing/nobody/somewhere + else：
  - "Do you need **anything else**, madam?" "No, **nothing else**, thank you."

3 請依照例句，使用括號裡的不定代名詞來完成意義相近的句子。

0 There wasn't anyone in the hall. (no one) ....There was no one in the hall....

1 John told me nothing about what had happened last night. (anything)

....

2 There was no one who knew the right answer. (anybody)

....

3 If we don't have a car, there isn't anywhere we can go. (nowhere)

....

4 We haven't bought anything for Emily's birthday yet. (nothing)

....

5 I have nothing new to tell you. (anything)

....

6 I saw nobody in town yesterday. (anybody)

....

7 We went nowhere on the weekend, we stayed at home. (anywhere)

....

8 Sorry, there isn't anything else I can do for you. (nothing)

....

4 請參考第 **208** 頁的表格，選出代表事物、人物或地點的正確代名詞來完成句子。

1 .... is as important to me as my wedding ring.

2 Is there .... special you want to go tonight?

3 .... can dance as well as Kim. She's such a great dancer!

4 There is .... at the airport where you can leave your bags, so keep them with you.

5 Look! .... is walking down the street in a clown costume!

6 My brother is going to work .... in Australia soon.

7 Oh no! The fridge is empty. There isn't .... left.

8 We didn't know .... in this town when we came to live here.

9 I can't find my keys .... They must be .... in the house.

10 I hope there's .... nice to eat tonight. My husband has been cooking all day.

11 Jane was so unhappy. .... called her on her birthday.

12 "Is .... absent today?" "No, Miss. We're all here." "Good. Let's start then."

5 每個句子都有一個錯誤。請在錯誤處標出底線，並寫出正確句子。

1 There must be something of wrong with the dishwasher. It doesn't work properly.

....

2 We aren't doing nothing special tomorrow night.

....

3 There wasn't someone waiting for us at the station. We had to take a taxi.

....

4 "Are you reading anywhere interesting these days?" "Yes, a very good novel."

....

5 "Is anything going to buy the food for the picnic?" "Yes, I am."

....

6 "Some cheese . . . some ham . . . Anything other?" "No, thanks, that's all."

....

7 Let's go anywhere tonight. I don't want to stay at home.

....

8 No, thanks. I don't want nothing to eat. I'm not hungry.

....

LESSON 2 分配形容詞與代名詞
both、most、all、everybody、everything等
Distributive adjectives and pronouns; *both, most, all; everybody, everything . . .*

分配形容詞意指群體裡的**每一獨立個體**，通常後接**單數名詞**和**單數動詞**。分配形容詞有以下幾個：

each 每一個	**Each** test has the same level of difficulty. （指每個測驗難度都相同）	every 和 each 的意思雷同，但 every 只能當作形容詞，each 則可身兼形容詞與代名詞，兩者通常都會後接**「of + 複數名詞或代名詞」**。 • Each student / Every student / Each of the students NOT ~~Every of the students~~ • Each of us NOT ~~Every of us.~~
every 每一個	**Every** student on this course gets a tablet to work on. （指修課的每位學生都有拿到平板電腦）	
either 任一個	Come on Friday or Saturday. **Either** day is fine. （指哪一天都可以）	either 和 neither 都可作為代名詞，或後接**「of + 複數名詞或代名詞」**。 • **Either of these books / Either of them** is available in the library. • **Neither of us** went to Jane's party.
neither 任一個（都不）	**Neither** answer is correct. （指哪個答案都不對）	要表示「兩者皆非」，可用**「neither + 肯定動詞」**或**「either + 否定動詞」**的句型，注意一個句子中僅能使用一種否定用詞： • "Did you pass both exams?" "Actually, I **passed neither** of them. / I **didn't pass either** of them."

上述所有詞均可後接 **one**，來加強每一個體在群體裡的**獨立**概念，如 each **one** of us、every **one** of the students、either **one** of you、neither **one** of them 等。

both、most 與 all

英文裡還有其他形容詞可表示將各個體視為**一體**，且這些詞通常會後接**複數名詞**和**複數動詞**。主要的此類形容詞如下：

both 兩者都	**Both** novels are very good. （意同「This novel and that novel . . .」〔這本小說和那本小說……〕）	both、most 和 all 亦可作為代名詞，後接「of + 複數名詞或代名詞」： • **Most of the candidates** passed their exams. • **Most of them** soon found a good job. • **All of my friends** joined the music club.
most 大部分 （請參閱第182頁）	**Most** children go to kindergarten when they're three or four years old. （意同「Almost all . . .」〔幾乎所有……〕請注意，動詞均為複數！）	
all 全部都 （請參閱第182頁）	**All** the people in the room were well dressed.（意指沒有人被排除在外）	

1 請圈出正確的用字。

1 You can borrow **either** / **each** of my two bikes.

2 **Most of** / **Most** the people in the audience **was** / **were** journalists.

3 He gave me **all** / **every** the latest news about his family business.

4 You can't visit **both** / **either** exhibition. You don't have time.

5 "Where shall we go for our holidays? Malta or Greece?" "**Either** / **Neither**. I'd rather go to Sardinia."

6 The two dogs are similar: they're **both** / **all** Labradors.

7 I can't remember **neither** / **either** song. I'm not very musical.

8 They studied **all** / **every** day yesterday. They have an exam soon.

9 You can **both** / **all** come in the car with us. There's room for two more.

10 "Do you want strawberry or vanilla ice cream?" "**Neither** / **Either**, I don't mind."

11 Don't be greedy—you can't have **both** / **all** the cakes.

12 Don't take **each** / **all** day about it—we're waiting for you!

2 請使用 both、each、either 或 neither 來完成句子。

1 The school band had a lot of performances this year and .... one of them was a success.

2 If you like this skirt and the other one, why don't you buy them .... ?

3 .... candidate presented his/her CV and was interviewed by the human resources manager.

4 .... of the men is trustworthy. I can't really trust .... of them.

5 "Which movie shall we see? This one or the other one?"
"..................... is fine. They're .... good."

6 "Which of these two books would you suggest for my 12-year-old son?"
"They're .... good, but this one's probably more popular with boys."

7 You can't park on .... side of the road. This is a no-parking zone.

8 "Shall we go to the pub or the movies?" "..................... . I'm too tired to go out tonight."

9 "Can .... of you speak Spanish?" "No, we can't."

10 "Shall we meet on Saturday or Sunday?" "..................... I'm afraid. I'm busy all weekend."

結合 every 的複合代名詞與複合副詞

everybody/everyone 每個人（代名詞）	**Everyone** said it was a great match. It's a shame I wasn't there!
everything 每件事（代名詞）	**Everything** was ready for the party.
everywhere 每個地方（副詞）	There are people **everywhere**.

注意以下幾個使用重點：

❶ 使用 **everybody/everyone/everything** 時一定要搭配**單數動詞**：
- Everybody **likes** this cake. It's delicious.

❷ 以**口語英文**而言，對應的所有格通常是**複數**，如：
- Everybody must have **their** money ready before getting on the bus.

（也可以說 . . . his/her money ready . . . ，但此用法較少見）

❸ 要表示「我們所有人」時不能說 everybody of us，而該說 **all of us/you/them**。

3 請以 every、everybody/everyone、everything 或 everywhere 完成句子。

1 I go to work at seven o'clock .... day, including Saturdays.

2 Come on, ... ! It's time to go. Aren't you ready yet?

3 .... said the food was excellent.

4 We haven't seen .... yet—there are a few more places we want to go to.

5 Get organized! A place for .... and .... in its place.

6 I knew most people at the party, but I didn't talk to ....

7 I'd like to buy .... in this shop. They have such fabulous clothes!

8 Ever since global warming, natural disasters can be seen .... on earth. We really need to take actions immediately!

9 .... employee attended the presentation of the company outcomes.

10 .... in the class was working hard when the principal opened the door.

4 下方部分句子有誤。 句子如正確請打勾，錯誤請打叉並訂正。

1 Everyone I know like reading. ....

2 My friend is a shopaholic. He would buy everything he sees! ....

3 Everybody of them went to the same place for their holidays. ....

4 These souvenirs cost five dollars each. ....

5 There's free WiFi in every rooms of the hostel. ....

6 If you want everything, you may end up with nobody. ....

7 Everyone wants to have a good job and be well paid. ....

8 Money is not everything! ....

5 請改寫句子，使用代名詞或副詞片語來取代畫底線的單字，但意思須與原句相同。

1 We went to all the possible places when we were travelling in Argentina.

....

2 They interviewed all the people who had attended the course.

....

3 I did all the possible things to avoid him getting angry.

....

4 I'd like to play this game and that game.

....

5 80% of the students passed their entrance exams.

....

6 100% of the passengers said they enjoyed the journey.

....

7 Not you or me can make any difference.

....

8 You can't go to any place.

....

9 The sales manager and the purchasing manager spoke to the CEO yesterday morning.

....

10 Not the doctor or the nurse had seen the patient leave his room.

....

LESSON 3 相互代名詞 each other 與 one another / 相關連接詞 「both ...and ...」與「either ...or ...」/ 結合 ever 的複合詞
Reciprocal pronouns each other / one another; correlative conjunctions *both . . . and . . . / either . . . or . . . ; compound words with –ever*

相互代名詞

❶ 相互代名詞是表示「**兩人以上的群體對彼此進行相同的事**」。**each other** 和 **one another** 均為相互代名詞，兩者具有類似的意義。
- They love and respect **each other**.
  = He loves and respects her, she loves and respects him.
- During the debate, everyone talked to **one another** at the same time. It was very confusing!

❷ 相互代名詞也具**所有格**的形式，寫成 **each other's** 與 **one another's**：
- We sometimes spend the weekend at **one another's** houses.

FAQ

Q. 我在酒吧看到一個招牌說：「Yes, we do have free Wi-Fi, but don't forget to talk to each other.」，但這句話不是該用 to one another 嗎？畢竟 each other 是用於「兩個人」的情況，one another 才是泛指多人，我有想錯嗎？

A: 你理解的用法是正確的。但在現今口語英文裡，此界線已經逐漸模糊，口語會話最常出現 each other 的用法。

1 請使用提示用詞搭配 each other 或 one another 來造句。

0 The three brothers / not talk / for a long time
The three brothers haven't talked to one another for a long time.

1 Simon and Rachel / often / help
....
....

2 They / not listen / , all of them just went on talking
....
....

3 Sally and I / send / birthday cards / for many years
....
....

4 My neighbor and I / often / look after / cats / when we're away
....
....

5 Mark and Fiona / be / madly in love
....
....

6 When we met at the airport, we / give / a big hug
....
....

相關連接詞

相關連接詞一定要在**句中成對出現**，先連接甲，再連接乙，而甲乙是一個句子中對等的兩者。
相關連接詞用法如：

❶ both A and B（兩者皆是）
- **Both** my mom **and** my dad came to the college Open Day last week.

❷ not only A but also B（不只有 A，還有 B）
- She had **not only** a dessert **but also** a cup of hot chocolate.

❸ either A or B（不是 A 就是 B）
- You can come to my house **either** now **or** later.

❹ neither A nor B（兩者皆非）
- This color is **neither** green **nor** blue.

在一個句子裡，我們可使用此類相關連接詞，
以連接不同子句：

- You can **either** have lunch at home **or**
  grab a sandwich in the canteen.

我們在比較級的單元（請參閱第 194 頁和第 202 頁）
學到的「as . . . as」、「as much . . . as」與
「as many . . . as」，以及之後會學到的「such . . . as」、
「so . . . as」與「rather . . . than」（請參閱第 365 頁），
均為相關連接詞的用法。

> **!** 如果 either . . . or . . . / neither . . . nor . . .
> 是句子的主詞，即需使用**第三人稱單數動詞**：
> Neither the cat nor the dog <u>lives</u> in the house.

---

 2 請將 **1–10** 與 **A–J** 配對成完整的句子。

1 No problem! You can use either

2 The boys both worked hard

3 We enjoyed both the concert

4 Neither the black

5 I went not only to the museum

6 Both the tourists and the guide were late,

7 You can have either the cheesecake

8 The school trip could be either to Barcelona

9 You can eat as much food

10 I answer as many

A nor the blue dress is ready to wear.

B so the tour bus didn't leave on time.

C but also to the theater yesterday.

D and had great fun at the baseball camp.

E as a hundred emails a day.

F "each" or "every" in this sentence.

G as you like for $10.

H or Prague. We'll see which one is more popular.

I or a muffin, but not both!

J and the movie at that night.

1 .....   2 .....   3 .....   4 .....   5 .....   6 .....   7 .....   8 .....   9 .....   10 .....

字首 Wh 結合 ever 的複合單字可作為代名詞、形容詞、副詞或連接詞，來表達「**任何人、事、時、地、物或方法**」。我們通常是以 **who** 或 **what** 等疑問詞（請參閱第 34 頁）銜接 ever。

Wh 結合 ever 的複合字，其用法與肯定句中結合 any 的複合字雷同（請參閱第 208 頁）。

❶ Whoever（任何人）
- **Whoever** said so is a liar.
（也可以說 **Anyone** who said so is a liar.）

❷ Whatever（任何事物）
可當作形容詞和代名詞：
- **Whatever** decision you make, I'll be on your side.
（也可以說 **Any** decision you make . . .）
- You can have **whatever** you like.
（也可以說 You can have **anything** you like.）

❸ Whichever（任何事物，但搭配有限的選擇）
可作為形容詞和代名詞：
- **Whichever** way you look at it, it will never be the right thing to do.

❹ Wherever（任意處、在任何場所、前往任何地方）
- **Wherever** they go, they find new friends.（也可以說 **Anywhere** they go to . . .）

❺ Whenever（任何時間、每一次）
- Come **whenever** you like, I'll be waiting for you.（也可以說 Come **any time** . . .）

❻ However（無論如何、不管是各種可能的方式、用什麼方式）
- **However** hard he tries, he will never please her.
- There's no dress code, you can dress **however** you want.

3 請以下列字首 **Wh** 結合 **ever** 的複合字，來完成句子。

wherever (x2)　whoever (x2)　whatever (x3)　whenever

1 I will find them, ... they are.

2 .... follows me on Twitter is a friend.

3 I will do it, ... the consequences.

4 You can eat .... you like. It's all-inclusive.

5 .... you go, you'll find nice people.

6 Come and see us .... you have time.

7 I don't want to talk to anyone. .... calls me, please say I'm busy.

8 .... will be, will be. We can make no more changes now.

4 請使用以下單字來改寫句子，並且維持原句的意義。

whichever　　anywhere (x2)　　whoever (x2)　　anything
whenever (x2)　whatever (x2)　any time

0 Every time they meet, they have lots of things to talk about.
Whenever they meet, they have lots of things to talk about.
....

1 Wherever you go on this island, you find people enjoying themselves.
....

2 You can go into any bars or restaurants wearing anything you like.
....

3 Just call me whenever you want.
....

4 Whatever I cook, he finds something wrong with it.
....

5 Anyone who touches my computer wouldn't dare do so again.
....

6 Any one of you who wants to work on this project should come to tomorrow's meeting.

....

7 Some cause happiness to every place they go, others anytime they go. (Oscar Wilde)

....

8 I take my tablet with me wherever I go.

....

9 Tell anyone who comes that I'm very busy these days.

....

10 Here's some money for your birthday. Buy anything you like.

....

LESSON 4 反身代名詞 / one 與 ones 用法 Reflexive pronouns; *one/ones*

主格代名詞		受格代名詞		反身代名詞
I	→	me	→	myself
you	→	you	→	yourself
he	→	him	→	himself
she	→	her	→	herself
it	→	it	→	itself
we	→	us	→	ourselves
you	→	you	→	yourselves
they	→	them	→	themselves

反身代名詞是由兩部分構成：**所有格形容詞**（my/your/our）或**受格代名詞**（him/her/it/them），後接**表達單數人稱的 self** 或**表達複數人稱的 selves**。**oneself** 也是反身代名詞，具有不限定或強調意義。

動詞 + 反身代名詞

當**主詞**和**受詞**相同，且動詞的結果會直接**反應到主詞**身上時，就可使用**反身代名詞**。

反身代名詞可作為：

1 某些動詞的**直接受詞**，如：enjoy oneself ｜ hurt oneself ｜ help oneself

2 前面有**介系詞**的**間接受詞**，如：think to oneself ｜ say to oneself ｜ make a fool of oneself

> ! 如果動詞是片語動詞，那反身代名詞需放在**動詞**和**質詞**的**中間**：
> Joan felt she had **let herself down** when she failed her driving test.
> （let down 為片語動詞，其中的 down 是質詞，故在此情況下，反身代名詞 herself 會放在 let 與 down 中間）

FAQ

Q: 我不太會使用動詞 enjoy。enjoy 後不是總是搭反身代名詞嗎？

A: 不是的。只有當用 enjoy 是用來表達「**玩得開心**」時，才要搭配**反身代名詞**，例如「They enjoyed themselves at the party.」。其他情況下，當 enjoy 解釋成「**喜歡**」，後面接**直接受詞**（如名詞、代名詞或動詞 ing）即可，如「They enjoyed the party. / They enjoyed it very much. / They enjoyed dancing at the party.」。

如果句子中的直接受詞是**人體部位**，在英文裡，我們只能使用**所有格代名詞**，而非反身代名詞，如：

• Wash **your** hands. NOT Wash ~~yourself the hands~~.

• She cut **her** finger with a knife.

跟其他語言相比，英文的反身動詞較少。不過，英文會使用「**get + 形容詞**」的句型，來表達其他語言裡反身動詞的意思：get angry、get married、get ready、get dressed、get used、get drunk 等

1 請將 1–8 與 A–H 配對成完整的句子。

..... **1** I cut   **A** cut itself on some glass in the park.

..... **2** The baby cried   **B** look at herself in the mirror before she goes out?

..... **3** Tess and Daniela   **C** myself when chopping onions.

..... **4** The dog   **D** a fool of yourself!

..... **5** Are you   **E** to himself that he wouldn't go.

..... **6** Can't she   **F** enjoyed themselves a lot at karaoke last night.

..... **7** Don't make   **G** washing yourselves, kids?

..... **8** He said   **H** when he saw himself in the mirror.

2 請以合適的反身代名詞完成句子。

1 You can't keep it to .... You should tell someone.

2 I said to .... , "I mustn't get angry this time."

3 Nobody understands how Paula hurt .... the other day.

4 I can't stand people who are always talking about ....

5 We enjoy .... a lot when we have a sleepover at each other's houses.

6 Jason made a fool of .... at the party last night. He got very drunk.

7 The cat meowed when it saw .... in the mirror.

8 Behave .... , girls! Don't be so loud!

9 We washed .... in the lake when we were camping.

10 Help .... to another drink.

3 請使用以下動詞的正確時態，搭配合適的反身代名詞，來完成克漏字。

| cut | cheer up | wash | enjoy | tie | find | ask | scare | buy | hurt |

1 Albert .... with a knife while carving a big piece of meat.

2 Thank you very much! We really .... at the party.

3 The dog .... in the river when we went for a walk.

4 She .... a very nice leather handbag in Florence.

5 Why don't you .... if you really want to go to university?

6 They .... stranded at the airport because of a strike.

7 He got very confused when trying to explain the instructions and ....
up in knots.

8 Fortunately, I didn't .... when I fell off my bike.

9 They .... silly watching a horror movie late at night.

10 Tania .... by eating a big box of chocolates.

以反身代名詞帶出強調意義

要表達「親自做某事」的意思有以下的方法：

1 名詞／代名詞 + 反身代名詞（表示「我自己」、「他自己」）：
- Did you make **it yourself**? • The **President himself** congratulated the Olympic champions.

2 **by + 反身代名詞** = alone（獨自）：
- I'm often at home **by himself**.
- Tom doesn't like working **by himself**. He prefers working in a team.

3 **on + 所有格形容詞 + own**（有「靠自己完成」的意味）：
- My daughter has lived **on her own** since she was 18.
- He doesn't mind being **on his own**.

FAQ

Q: self 到底是什麼意思呢？

A: self 是名詞，意指「**一個人**」。英文裡有許多結合 self 的複合單字，其他語言亦有此用法，例如 self service（自行服務）、self help（自助）、self conscious（自我意識）、self control（自我控制）；另外，由 self 衍生出的形容詞 selfish（自私），則是 generous（慷慨）的反義詞。

4 請填空單字以完成句子。

1 Dear me! Can't you iron your clothes on .... own?

2 When I was young I used to travel around Europe .... myself.

3 I would like my students to learn to think for ....

4 I hate playing video games by .... I like to play with my friends.

5 What? Did you leave little Henry by .... in the house?

6 My son is going to live .... his own next month.

7 She shouldn't always work by .... Working in a team would be easier.

8 Come on! I'm sure you didn't make this amazing cake ....

9 I can't lift this box on my .... Can you help me, please?

10 My mom enjoys having time to .... , but it doesn't happen very often!

5 請以反身代名詞改寫出意義相近的句子。

0 She likes to spend time alone.
She likes to spend time by herself.

1 He was on his own all weekend.
....

2 They did it without any help.
....

3 You can work on your own today.
....

4 I traveled around France alone.
....

5 I have never sung solo before.
....

6 You can't leave a baby alone in the house!
....

7 He was able to run the firm single-handed.
....

8 I don't mind living on my own in my new apartment.
....

9 Don't worry. She's used to staying at home on her own.
....

10 Look at this beautiful cake! I decorated it without any help.
....

代名詞 one/ones

❶ 當要避免重複剛用過的名詞，或是當句子裡有受詞且能明顯了解主題的情況下，我們會使用代名詞 **one/ones**。

one 用以取代**單數**名詞，**ones** 用以取代**複數**名詞：

- I like this **racket**, but I prefer the other **one**.
- I don't like these **shoes**. The other **ones** are much nicer.

❷ one 與 ones 需放在以下用詞的後面：

one/ones	定冠詞 the	I'd like **the one/ones** on the left.
	指示形容詞	I'd like **this one** here / **those ones** over there.
	疑問詞 which	**Which one/ones** would you like?
	the other	Give me **the other one/ones**, please.
one	不定冠詞 a + 形容詞	I want to rent a new apartment. I'd like **a bigger one**.
ones	不限定用詞 (some/any/no) + 形容詞	I'd like some apples. Have you got **any nice ones**?

6 請選出正確的代名詞。

1 I don't like this T-shirt. I prefer the red **one / ones**.

2 "Is this your hat?" "No, it's the other **ones / one**."

3 "Can you please pass me those books?" "Which **one / ones**?"
  "The **one / ones** on the top shelf."

4 Eat this strawberry yogurt because the other **one / ones** has gone bad.

5 Would you like these Italian shoes or the English **one / ones** over there?

6 Which painting do you like? This **one / ones** here or that **one / ones** over there?

7 My car keeps breaking down. I want to buy a more reliable **one / ones**.

8 I just got a new phone. It's **one / ones** of the latest **one / ones**.

7 下方部分句子有誤。請在錯誤的部分<u>畫底線</u>並訂正。

1 Lisa must learn to control himself. ....

2 I don't like that sweater. I prefer the other one. ....

3 "I like those boots." "Which one do you mean?" ....

4 I always tell the children to wash themselves the hands before eating.
  ....

5 Tom convinced himself that he was right. ....

6 You will need to look after yourself! ....

7 We really enjoyed myself at the barbecue party. ....

8 Help yourself, guys! There's food for everyone. ....

9 The twins hurt theirselves when their treehouse fell down. ....

10 We need to ask ourselves if this is the right move for us. ....

8 請看下圖，以 **one** 或 **ones** 與其他單字來完成對話。

1 A: Can I try this ¹.............. on?

B: Which ².............. do you mean?

A: The ³.............. in the middle.

B: This one is too small for you. I'll get you a bigger ⁴.............. .

A: And how much are the ⁵.............. underneath?

B: The blue ⁶.............. ? They're £50. But the ⁷.............. on the right are 30% off. That's a good discount.

2 A: Why don't we buy a ⁸.............. for tonight?

B: Let's buy the small ⁹.............. , the ¹⁰.............. with apples. I'm on a diet.

A: But there are six of us. And Jim doesn't like apples. I would buy the chocolate ¹¹.............. .

9 請使用以下詞語來完成對話，並於必要時加上 **a**、**an** 或 **the**。

| similar one | French one | best one | Which one | new one | another one |

1 A: What do you think of Brad Pitt's latest movie?

B: I think it is .... of his career so far.

2 A: Oh no! The washing machine isn't working!

B: Don't panic! Let's buy .... This one is old anyway.

3 A: What kind of cheese would you recommend?

B: .... They're very good.

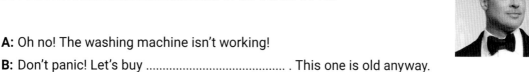

4 A: .... is your toothbrush?

B: The one on the right.

5 A: Have another burger, Jack!

B: Thanks, but I'm full to the brim. I couldn't possibly eat ....

6 A: Do you like this blue purse, madam?

B: No, I've already got ....

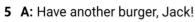

ROUND UP 12

1 請使用下方不定形容詞或代名詞來完成對話。

someone (x2)	everybody	some (x2)	all (x2)	no one	anyone (x3)	any

Drama teacher Hello, class 2D! Listen, please. We're going to put on a musical for the end of the school year and we need ¹........................... help.

Brian What kind of help?

Drama teacher First of ²........................... , we need ³........................... who can help with the costumes. Is ⁴........................... here good at sewing? ⁵...........................? Well, never mind, I'll ask the people from another class. Are there ⁶........................... artists who can help with the scenery maybe?

Thomas I enjoy painting and doing things like that. I think I could help.

Drama teacher Sure, thanks. We also need ⁷........................... who can play a musical instrument.

Marion I play the piano.

Steve And I play the guitar but I'm not very good at it. Can I still help?

Drama teacher Yes, of course. We need ⁸...........................'s help. And is ⁹........................... in the school choir? We need people who are good at singing. One, two, three, four . . . Great. This is a very musical class! And, last but not least, we have to write the invitation cards. Can ¹⁰........................... help with that?

Lisa I could make ¹¹........................... nice cards. I like graphic design.

Drama teacher Fine. Will you please give me ¹²........................... your names? I'll let you know . . .

2 請使用下方單字來完成句子。

both . . . and	most	every	each (x2)
neither . . . nor	something	each other	nothing

1 .... my husband .... I have joined a yoga class. It's very relaxing.

2 .... of the students took part in the school exchange, but not all of them.

3 I've been thinking of you .... single day!

4 .... season has its own fruits.

5 I'm going to .... Greece .... Spain this year. I want to do .... different, so I've booked a trip to Iceland.

6 Come on, shake hands with .... and forget all about it!

7 .... gives you more comfort than a nice cup of hot chocolate.

8 .... of you should have a map of the city.

3 請使用 **either** 或 **neither** 來完成答句。

1 "Do you like these two paintings?" "Actually, I don't like .... of them. They're too dark."

2 "You can have two bottles of shampoo for the price of one. Would you like these two?"
"No, ... of them, thanks. I bought some yesterday."

3 "Could you give me his fax number or his email address, please?" "I'm sorry I can't remember
.... of them at the moment."

4 "Which pub shall we go to? The Courage or the Red Lion?" "........................... of them.
I have to work tonight."

5 "Do you want to watch a comedy or an action movie?" "........................... of them. I want to
finish reading this gripping detective story."

6 "Do you think anybody could help me fix my laptop?" "........................... Paul or Jason.
They're both very good at repairing computers."

4 下方各句都有一個錯誤，請找出錯誤並改寫為正確句子。

1 Every of these sentences contains a mistake. Find and correct it.

....

2 Most of the tourists who visit Juliet's house in Verona leaves a love message.

....

3 He's new here. He doesn't know nobody yet.

....

4 Everybody like this cake. It's very popular with my family.

....

5 All, clap your hands and give our host a warm welcome.

....

6 Either John and Jack must have left his coat behind.

....

7 You can have whenever you like; it's all free.

....

8 Whoever want to join me on my adventure is welcome.

....

5 請使用結合 **ever** 的複合詞來完成句子。

1 I take my laptop with me .... I go.

2 .... wants to meet me, tell them I'm very busy this morning.

3 Come .... you like. I'm free all day.

4 You can eat .... you like. It's an "All you can eat" kind of restaurant.

5 .... I go in this little town I meet somebody I know.

6 I must have this beautiful leather handbag .... much it costs.

6 請將問句和答句配對。

1 Can you pass me those glasses, Ted?   **A** I'm sorry, I haven't got one with me.
2 Which sneakers are the most comfortable?   **B** The warm woolen ones. It'll be cold in the mountains.
3 Could you lend me an umbrella?   **C** It's a French blue one.
4 Which sweaters shall I pack?   **D** Try the ones on that shelf. They're very comfortable.
5 What sort of cheese is that?   **E** The white chocolate one.
6 Which cake would you like, Davina?   **F** The ones on the coffee table?

1 .....   **2** .....   **3** .....   **4** .....   **5** .....   **6** ....

223

請圈出正確的答案。

1 That boy and that girl are madly in love with ....
Ⓐ both   Ⓒ one other
Ⓑ either   Ⓓ each other

2 .... Sam and Ann can help you. They're very good cooks.
Ⓐ Both   Ⓒ Neither
Ⓑ Either   Ⓓ Each

3 Kathleen was so sad. .... of her Irish relatives phoned her on her birthday.
Ⓐ Not   Ⓒ None
Ⓑ Nobody   Ⓓ Either

4 We need .... warm clothes and trekking boots for the excursion.
Ⓐ both   Ⓒ neither
Ⓑ either   Ⓓ none

5 Diana cut .... with a broken glass while washing the dishes.
Ⓐ her   Ⓒ –
Ⓑ herself   Ⓓ her own

6 Good night and thank you. We have really enjoyed .... tonight.
Ⓐ us
Ⓑ our own
Ⓒ one another
Ⓓ ourselves

7 "Where can we buy this brand of perfume?" "......... you see this logo in the shop window."
Ⓐ Whatever   Ⓒ However
Ⓑ Wherever   Ⓓ Whoever

8 Don't be sad! .... happens, I'll be here with you.
Ⓐ Whoever
Ⓑ Whenever
Ⓒ Whatever
Ⓓ However

9 Don't worry. You can call me .... time you like.
Ⓐ whenever   Ⓒ each
Ⓑ any   Ⓓ some

10 "What would you like to eat?" "......... . I'm very hungry."
Ⓐ However
Ⓑ Any
Ⓒ Anything
Ⓓ Whoever

請圈出正確的用字。

[1] **Every / all** time I watch TV after dinner, I tend to fall asleep on the sofa [2] **whatever / anything** the program is. I may sleep for about twenty minutes; then I wake up and keep watching, but I always miss [3] **everything / something**, so I start asking questions to [4] **anything / whoever** is at home with me. I like action movies quite a lot, but I often have to watch them twice because I miss over a quarter of [5] **each / every** of them. Nowadays, with satellite TV, I can rewind to the point when I fell asleep and watch it again, but only if I'm at home on my [6] **own / myself**. The problem is that if I have a nap, then I can't sleep [7] **any more / anyone** until well after midnight, so I'm quite tired when I wake up in the morning.

9

請以合適的單字完成克漏字。

1 I've looked .... , but I can't find my sunglasses. They must be .... , though.

2 .... of the city center is a pedestrian area, so there isn't much traffic.

3 I don't like working on my .... I prefer working in a team.

4 "Don't worry. You'll find your ideal partner one day. There must be .... somewhere who's looking for you." "Yes, but who? And .... ? I'd really like to know."

5 .... you go, you'll find nice and friendly people.

6 Don't be selfish! Help one ....

7 There were only two exercises in the test, but they were .... very difficult. I doubt I'll pass it.

8 I'd like to go .... this afternoon, but I don't know where.

9 "Is there .... I could do for you?" "No, thanks. I'm fine."

10 "Do you need .... else?" "No, ... else, thanks."

10 請閱讀下方雪梨歌劇院網站的網頁內容，並圈出正確的答案。

| Search for ... 🔍 | What's On | Visit Us | Our Story | Give | Backstage | Schools | Login |

Welcome to Sydney Opera House

Around a quarter of Sydney Opera House performances are for kids under 12. Did you know that? Kids and families are welcome here all year round because there is a program for ¹................. season. They can enjoy ²................. classics such as episodes from Alice in Wonderland or classical music shows suitable for introducing toddlers to classical music. ³................. you choose, your kids will find ⁴................. immersed in a unique classical music experience.

Treat ⁵................. and your kids to the Opera Bar or Opera Kitchen, in a quiet and relaxed atmosphere with the best harbor views.

⁶................. adult ticket includes coffee and a slice of cake. Children's tickets include a "babychino," a small cappuccino with no coffee in it, while children under 12 months get free entry.

1	Ⓐ both	Ⓑ all	Ⓒ each	Ⓓ everything
2	Ⓐ –	Ⓑ themselves	Ⓒ themself	Ⓓ them
3	Ⓐ Whoever	Ⓑ Whenever	Ⓒ Whatever	Ⓓ Wherever
4	Ⓐ themselves	Ⓑ theirselves	Ⓒ them	Ⓓ ourselves
5	Ⓐ you	Ⓑ ourselves	Ⓒ –	Ⓓ yourself
6	Ⓐ All	Ⓑ Some	Ⓒ Each	Ⓓ Everyone

Reflecting on grammar

請研讀文法規則，再判斷以下說法是否正確。

		True	False
1	「I don't know nothing about that.」是正確的說法。		
2	anybody 等與 any 結合的複合詞，可用於肯定句、否定句和疑問句。		
3	nothing else 和 nothing other 均為正確片語。		
4	each 和 every 的意思雷同。		
5	both 意指兩者（人事物）。		
6	「most + 複數名詞」後面要接複數動詞。		
7	字尾為 one 的不定代名詞意指事物，字尾為 body 的不定代名詞則意指人物。		
8	「Everybody of us.」是正確的說法。		
9	whatever 的意義近似於肯定句中的 anything。		
10	所有反身代名詞均以所有格形容詞加上 self 或 selves 所構成。		

1 請閱讀以下短文，圈出正確的用字。

When my family moved to Bristol, ¹ **none / any** of us was happy about it. ² **Both / As** my brother
Dave ³ **and / than** I had to leave our friends behind and we missed them.

Our new school was ⁴ **quite / enough** small and there weren't ⁵ **lot of / many** sports facilities, just
a gym and an outdoor tennis court. ⁶ **Neither / Either** Dave ⁷ **or / nor** I enjoyed playing tennis but
it was the only sport available. One day a new PE teacher started working at our school. He was
⁸ **such a / a so** great tennis player that we ⁹ **either / both** became very good and started to train
every day. Now we represent our school in the county championships.

2 瑪莎是個加拿大女孩，請閱讀她描述的義大利生活概況，並視情況使用下方單字的最高
級或比較級來完成短文。請記得於必要時加上 the 和 than。

| far   long   exclusive   hot   good   mild   cold   dark   tasty   few |

I moved to Como from Montreal last year. Why Como?
Because I wanted to meet George Clooney, of course!
Just kidding! I had the opportunity of working in one
of ¹.......................... hotels in the area. I'm an assistant
manager and I really enjoy my job now that I've got used
to living in Italy.
Life is different here. First of all, the weather. Although
Como is in the north of Italy, in summer it is much
².................................. Montreal. The winter is not
³................................. as back home, and it is even ⁴................................. in nearby Milan.
That's because Como is on a lake and the micro-climate here is different from that of other
places which are ⁵................................. away from a big mass of water. What's more, winter days
are ⁶................................. and ⁷................................. in Canada – but I miss the special light of
Canadian spring.
Then the food. Italian food is much ⁸.................................. and more varied than Canadian food.
Our cuisine has certainly ⁹................................. dishes than Italian; still, I think that our poutine is
one of ¹⁰................................. dishes in the world. What is it? French fries topped with fresh cheese
curds and covered with brown gravy. A real treat!

3 請圈出正確的用字。

I know that ¹ **everyone / whoever** always thinks I have a great time ² **everywhere / whenever**
I go to Italy on business, but actually I don't! It's very hard work—one day I find ³ **me / myself** on
a train or plane going ⁴ **somewhere / wherever** or in an office having a meeting. And I can tell you
that there is ⁵ **anything / nothing** more frustrating than discussing work when you know there's
⁶ **something / whatever** beautiful to see in the next street! The problem is that you can't
⁷ **either / both** work and play at the same time. However, there isn't ⁸ **nothing / anything** nicer
than sitting at a café in a nice square after a hard day's work.

4 請使用以下單字來完成對話。

| best | faster | anyone | either | more | very | both | anything (x2) | herself | all |

Alice   Is there [1]............................ here who could win a medal for our school in the town sports competition?

Ben   Well, Mark can run very fast. He could do well in the 100 or 200 meters.

Alice   But he can't win [2]............................ because there are [3]............................ runners in the other schools. What about long jump?

Ben   Julie is [4]............................ good at it. She won last year and she may win again this year.

Alice   You're forgetting Sara. She's the [5]............................ one in town in the long jump. She will win for sure.

Ben   I still think that we have [6]............................ chances in the long jump. Let's ask Julie.

Alice   Hang on, I've just remembered — we can't ask Julie. She hurt [7]............................ last week. She fell off her bike on her way to school.

Ben   Oh no! Poor Julie! Did she break [8]............................ ?

Alice   No, but she hurt [9]............................ her legs quite badly. She's got cuts and grazes [10]............................ over them.

Ben   That's terrible! Is there [11]............................ we can do to help her?

| how much | anything | ones (x2) | much | how many | many |

Produce Seller   Can I help you?

Lady   Yes, please. Could I have those green apples over there?

Produce Seller   Sorry, which [12]............................ ?

Lady   The green [13]............................ next to the pears.

Produce Seller   [14]............................ would you like?

Lady   Four, please . . . er, no, make it six.

Produce Seller   [15]............................ else?

Lady   Yes, four bananas and something else for a fruit salad except pears. We don't like them very [16]............................ .

Produce Seller   What about kiwis? You don't need [17]............................ of them. Three is enough.

Lady   Alright. [18]............................ is it altogether?

Produce Seller $6.50.

5 請使用以下形容詞和代名詞來完成短文。

| himself | lots of | everybody (x2) | neither (x2) | each other (x3) | both |

Bob and Jasmine were madly in love with [1]............................ . [2]............................ thought they would get married soon because they also shared [3]............................ interests. They [4]............................ liked art and going to exhibitions. [5]............................ enjoyed crowded places or loud music, so they never went to discos. They liked the same kind of food. They gave [6]............................ the same kinds of presents. They were always together. [7]............................ of them would go to a party on their own.

Their friends found them boring and stopped going out with them. After a few months, Bob and Jasmine got bored with [8]............................ too, and to [9]............................'s surprise, they broke up. Last time I saw Bob, he was dancing in a crowded disco and seemed to be enjoying [10]............................ very much. Life is strange, isn't it?

6 請閱讀以下短文，選出正確的答案。

I have ⁰...B.. important to do on Monday. I'm meeting ¹...... from the local council to discuss recycling waste ²...... in our company. So far, ³...... has been putting ⁴...... into the same trash can. It makes me cross because I recycle ⁵...... at home.

We want to convince the local council to give us ⁶...... trash cans to put ⁷...... they are needed.

We also need ⁸...... trash cans in the courtyard to collect all the waste from the building.

We have already sent a letter to the council, but ⁹...... has replied. Two days ago, I called the office and asked to meet ¹⁰...... involved with urban waste.

0	Ⓐ someone	Ⓑ something	Ⓒ somewhere	Ⓓ anywhere
1	Ⓐ someone	Ⓑ nobody	Ⓒ anybody	Ⓓ somewhere
2	Ⓐ proper	Ⓑ property	Ⓒ properly	Ⓓ proper way
3	Ⓐ everywhere	Ⓑ everything	Ⓒ everybody	Ⓓ anything
4	Ⓐ everywhere	Ⓑ something	Ⓒ nothing	Ⓓ everything
5	Ⓐ something	Ⓑ everything	Ⓒ everywhere	Ⓓ somewhere
6	Ⓐ any	Ⓑ each other	Ⓒ enough	Ⓓ no
7	Ⓐ everywhere	Ⓑ nowhere	Ⓒ somewhere	Ⓓ anything
8	Ⓐ biggest	Ⓑ more big	Ⓒ bigger	Ⓓ the most big
9	Ⓐ anybody	Ⓑ everybody	Ⓒ everyone	Ⓓ nobody
10	Ⓐ anyone	Ⓑ no one	Ⓒ anywhere	Ⓓ anything

7 請閱讀短文，填入最適合的單字。每一格僅能填入一個單字；可參考第 **0** 格示範。

It was my ⁰........last............... day at the school where I had taught Art for 30 years.

I was retiring the next day. ¹........................... my wife and my daughter came along to help me collect ²........................... of my stuff—books, notes, folders, etc. I was feeling ³........................... sad. Lots of my colleagues had already said goodbye, but I knew I would miss my students ⁴........................... of all. While I was collecting my things, ⁵........................... from the secretary's office turned up to tell me I should drop into the sports hall for a minute before leaving the school. When I got there, all my students were cheering and clapping. ⁶........................... of them wanted to shake my hand and thank me. My wife and daughter were just as touched as me by them. ⁷........................... said something nice—it was the ⁸........................... send-off I could have wished for.

8 請參考例句，使用包括提示用詞在內的二至五個單字，來完成意義相近的句子。
注意不能變更提示用詞。。

0 I have never walked farther than I did yesterday.

   FARTHEST   It was .... the farthest I've ever .... walked.

1 The movie crew is leaving Los Angeles tomorrow.

   LAST   Today is the .... in Los Angeles.

2 Nobody in the class is such a good dancer as Alice.

   BEST   Alice dances ....

3 Nobody in our family drives as fast as he does.

   THE   He is .... in our family.

4 There isn't anything John wouldn't do for us.

   IS   There .... wouldn't do for us.

5 I have nothing suitable to wear to the party.

   DON'T   I .... to wear to the party.

6 We quite like English cheddar and French camembert cheese.

   MIND   We don't .... or French camembert cheese.

7 The theater is almost empty tonight.

   LOT   There are .... seats in the theater tonight.

8 All of the students got their certificates.

   STUDENT   .... got his/her certificate.

9 The elevator was too small for all of us to get into.

   ENOUGH   There .... for all of us to get into the elevator.

10 The movie was so funny that it became a big box-office hit.

   SUCH   It was .... that it became a big box-office hit.

11 He is the fastest runner in his team.

   AS   .... him in his team.

12 There's nobody in the hall. Perhaps the lecture has been put off.

   ISN'T   .... in the hall. Perhaps the lecture has been put off.

Towards Competences

校刊編輯決定出版一期特殊刊物《比比看》，此刊物也會寄給海外的姊妹校。你的任務是撰寫一篇英文文章。可任選影響你人生的兩個人物或兩個地方來做比較，並說明影響你的方式和原因。文章字數需控制在 200 字至 250 字。

Self Check 4

請選出答案，再至解答頁核對正確與否。

1 She looks .... in that dress.
ⓐ beautifully   ⓑ beautiful
ⓒ in a beautiful way

2 I hope Jack will cook tonight. He cooks ....
ⓐ really good   ⓑ really nice
ⓒ really well

3 I .... recognized him when I saw him in hospital last week.
ⓐ hard   ⓑ hardly   ⓒ difficult

4 Everybody thought the movie festival was .... success this year.
ⓐ quite a   ⓑ a quite   ⓒ pretty a

5 There were over 150 people at the meeting and we didn't have ....
ⓐ an enough big room
ⓑ a room big enough
ⓒ a big room enough

6 Oh dear! We're .... late. Let's run!
ⓐ plenty   ⓑ terribly   ⓒ totally

7 Don't ask Tom to sing on stage—he's .... shy.
ⓐ little   ⓑ lot   ⓒ very

8 It was .... freezing this morning.
ⓐ absolutely   ⓑ fairly   ⓒ very

9 I have to file .... documents by the end of the week, Sara. Can you help me?
ⓐ load of   ⓑ plenty   ⓒ loads of

10 .... people wanted to buy tickets. They were all sold out by 2 p.m.
ⓐ Too much   ⓑ Too many
ⓒ Too plenty of

11 .... in the room already knew the speaker, so it was a good talk.
ⓐ Plenty of the people
ⓑ All people
ⓒ Most of the people

12 They only sent out .... invitations, so there weren't many people at the wedding.
ⓐ a few   ⓑ little   ⓒ a little

13 You've eaten .... melon. You're going to feel sick.
ⓐ all   ⓑ the all   ⓒ the whole

14 "Would you like some more cake?" "Yes please, but just ...."
ⓐ little   ⓑ a little bit   ⓒ a few

15 Vegetables are .... than cheese or meat.
ⓐ much healthy
ⓑ much more healthier
ⓒ much healthier

16 The road was getting .... and the bus driver was getting worried.
ⓐ more narrow and more narrow
ⓑ narrower and narrower
ⓒ always more narrow

17 Wear your warm coat. Today it's .... than yesterday.
ⓐ much freezing   ⓑ much colder
ⓒ more freezing

18 This is .... the two villages.
ⓐ the quieter of   ⓑ the quietest of
ⓒ quieter than

19 Dan isn't .... as Steve.
ⓐ as cleverer   ⓑ as clever
ⓒ cleverer

20 A: Isn't this exercise .... difficult than you expected?

B: Yes, it's hard!

Ⓐ more   Ⓑ less   Ⓒ very less

21 The blue whale is .... animal ever known to have existed.

Ⓐ the heavier

Ⓑ the most heavy

Ⓒ the heaviest

22 Mark is the most reliable .... my friends.

Ⓐ of   Ⓑ than   Ⓒ from

23 Look at that man! He's .... renowned surgeon in town.

Ⓐ the most   Ⓑ the more   Ⓒ the best

24 Which was the .... journey of your life?

Ⓐ terriblest   Ⓑ most ugly   Ⓒ worst

25 Did you read the article about Rome in *Time* magazine's .... issue?

Ⓐ last   Ⓑ latest   Ⓒ most late

26 Could I have .... onions, please? I don't like them very much.

Ⓐ less   Ⓑ the less   Ⓒ fewer

27 Dad doesn't drive .... mom.

Ⓐ as fastly as

Ⓑ as fast as

Ⓒ as fastest as

28 Irene lives .... in the middle of the country.

Ⓐ somewhere   Ⓑ anywhere

Ⓒ nowhere

29 We haven't spoken to .... about the new project yet.

Ⓐ nobody   Ⓑ somebody

Ⓒ anybody

30 The people in the room were all talking to .... and weren't paying attention.

Ⓐ each one   Ⓑ anyone else

Ⓒ one another

31 Can I have something .... to eat? I'm still very hungry.

Ⓐ else's   Ⓑ other   Ⓒ else

32 I have lunch in the same restaurant .... day.

Ⓐ every   Ⓑ all   Ⓒ each one

33 Why don't we get a different pizza .... and then we can share?

Ⓐ every   Ⓑ each   Ⓒ both

34 The school wants to give a tablet to .... student in Grade 6.

Ⓐ each   Ⓑ some   Ⓒ any

35 We invited Eric and Fiona, but .... turned up.

Ⓐ either of them

Ⓑ neither of them

Ⓒ both them

36 Are you sure you can't find your jacket? Have you really looked for it .... , even in the car?

Ⓐ somewhere   Ⓑ nowhere

Ⓒ everywhere

37 What's that? It's .... sweet .... sour. It isn't a dessert. Anyway, whatever it is, I don't like it.

Ⓐ either . . . nor   Ⓑ neither . . . nor

Ⓒ neither . . . or

38 .... , tell them I'm out.

Ⓐ Whoever calls   Ⓑ Whoever call

Ⓒ Whenever call

39 Are you sure you don't need any help? You can't always do everything ....

Ⓐ on yourself   Ⓑ by yourself

Ⓒ by your own

40 The kids were really enjoying .... at summer camp.

Ⓐ theirselves   Ⓑ theirself

Ⓒ themselves

Assess yourself!

☐	0 – 10	還要多加用功。
☐	11 – 20	尚可。
☐	21 – 30	不錯。
☐	31 – 40	非常好！

表達能力、可能性與意願的情態助動詞
Modal Verbs to Express Ability, Possibility and Volition

LESSON 1 情態助動詞的特性 / can/could與表達相似概念的動詞
Characteristics of modal verbs; *can/could* and verbs that express similar concepts

情態助動詞會搭配其他動詞，來表達能力、可能性、義務、意願和其他各種情況與狀態。常見的情態助動詞有：

1 **can/could**：表達能力

2 **may/might**：表達可能性

3 **will/would**：表達意願

4 **must、ought to、shall/should**：表達義務

情態助動詞的規則

1 第三人稱單數也不需加 s：
- She **can** speak four languages.

2 後面需要接**原形動詞**：
- You should **try** again.

3 由於是助動詞的性質，因此問句開頭為**「情態助動詞 + 主詞」**，如「Can we stay here?」，否定句型則是**「情態助動詞 + not」**（或縮讀形式 n't），且不需搭配 do/does 或 did，如「You mustn't be late.」。

4 由於情態助動詞沒有現在分詞或過去分詞的形式，因此也**沒有**進行式、現在完成式或過去完成式等**複合時態的用法**，或搭配 will 的未來式或不定詞的用法。若想表達上述的情況，應使用其他動詞，而非情態助動詞。

---

1 每個句子都有一個錯誤，請以底線標出錯誤並訂正。

1 Sam cans ski well because his father is a ski instructor. ....

2 They might to arrive a bit late tonight. ....

3 Does he will go to university after high school? ....

4 You don't should go to bed so late every night! ....

5 Do we may hand in our assignment next week, Miss? ....

6 Joe can drives us to the restaurant. His car's bigger than ours. ....

情態助動詞 can/could 的句型

1 現在式

1 **can** 用於**現在式** → I/You/He/She/It/We/You/They **can** do it.

2 **cannot** 或 **can't**（縮讀形式較為常見）用於現在式否定句 → I/You/He/She/It/We/You/They **can't** do it.

2 過去式／條件句

1 **could** 用於**過去式**和**條件句** → I/You/He/She/It/We/You/They **could** do it.

2 **could not** 或 **couldn't** 用於過去式和條件句的否定句 → I/You/He/She/It/We/You/They **couldn't** do it.

❸ 不同種類的問句和答句

肯定問句 • "**Can** I do it?" "Yes, you can. / No, you can't."
　　　　　 • "**Could** they help him?" "Yes, they could. / No, they couldn't."

- -

否定問句 • "**Can't you** stay a bit longer?" "No, I can't. Sorry."
　　　　　 • "**Couldn't he** come with me?" "Yes, he could. Good idea."

- -

Wh 問句 • "**Where can** I find the key?" "It's in my bag."
　　　　　 • "**What could** you do for her?" "Nothing much, I'm afraid."

情態助動詞 can/could 代表的意義如下：

執行某事的可能性	I **can/could** come and see you tomorrow. （意指「我可能可以過來」）
執行某事的能力	• I **can't/couldn't** pay for everyone. I haven't got enough money. • They **couldn't** solve this problem.
請示以獲得許可 （**could** 比 **can** 還正式）	• "**Can** I have a look at your profile?" "Sure." • "**Could** I ask you a question?" "Yes, of course." （另一種詢問許可的正式說法為「May I ask you a question?」；請參閱第 237 頁）
提出要求或點餐，例如在酒吧或商店裡時	"**Can/Could** we have two of those sandwiches, please?" "Sure. Here you are."
用於否定句，表達對於看似不可能的事物感到不可置信的態度	• Really? It **can't** be true. • She **couldn't** have all that money!
用於條件句，有禮地向他人提出執行某事的要求（**could** 比 **can** 還正式）	**Could** you please sign here?

> ❗「You can . . .」是十分常見的非正式用法，觀光手冊會以這種用法來引導遊客於某處進行活動：
> **You can** go to the top of the tower or **you can** walk along the busy lanes of the town center.

❷ 請以 can、can't、could 或 couldn't 來完成句子。

1 Luke is a good swimmer, but he .... do the backstroke at all.

2 ".............. you ski when you were a child?" "Yes, I .... I started skiing when I was three!"

3 We .... call on Sarah last night because we left the office quite late.

4 ".............. I use your phone, Sam? I forgot mine." "Sorry, you .... The battery's flat."

5 "Excuse me, ... I have a doughnut and an orange juice, please?" "Certainly. Here you are."

6 Are you joking? That white Maserati .... be theirs. They .... afford such an expensive car.

7 ".............. you please fill in this form, sir?" "Yes, of course. .... I have a pen, please?"

8 ".............. you go to the doctor's another day?" "No, I have to go now. I need an urgent prescription."

9 You .... do all that work in one day, it would be impossible for anyone.

10 ".............. we have two cups of tea, please?" "Yes, of course."

11 ".............. you talk to them?" "Well, I tried to, but got no answer."

請根據答句內容寫出問句。

1 .... No, I can't look after your dog today. I'm really busy.

2 .... No, he couldn't. He started walking when he was 15 months old.

3 .... Yes, I can help you paint the kitchen. When?

4 .... Yes, sir. Here's your coffee. And the milk.

5 .... No, you can't. My car is too fast and you aren't a good driver.

6 .... Which door? The garage door? Okay. Shall I lock it too?

7 .... Euston Station? Yes, go straight along this road for about half a mile.

8 .... No, they couldn't go on vacation last summer. They had a lot of work to do.

4 請判斷以下句子的屬性。如果是表達可能性（**possibility**），請寫 **P**；如果是表達懷疑或不可置信（**incredulity**），請寫 **I**；如果是表達要求（**request**），請寫 **R**；如果是表達能力（**ability**），請寫 **A**。

..**P**.. **0** I'm not working, so I can go to Paul's house tomorrow.

...... **1** Come on! Susan can't be 50. She looks so young.

...... **2** Julie can't take part in the race. She's not very well.

...... **3** Could you make a cake for my birthday?

...... **4** They can dance the flamenco really well.

...... **5** Dave, can I have a cheese sandwich, please?

...... **6** I could play squash quite well when I was younger.

...... **7** I couldn't see the exhibition. I was away on business.

...... **8** It can't be Tom! He was so thin when I last saw him.

情態助動詞 can 的替代用詞

情態助動詞 can 無法表達現在完成式、過去完成式、不定詞、ing 形式及未來式等，因此想表示前述時態時，可用下方動詞或名詞化動詞來搭配。

❶ 如果是表達「**可能性**」，可替代為**非人稱用法 be possible**
（It is possible to do sth. / It is possible for sb. to do sth.）：
• **Is it possible to** get to the stadium by train? = **Can** you get to . . . ?
（兩者均適用於現在式）
• It won't **be possible** for you to join in.（僅適用於未來式）

❷ 如果是表達「**能力**」，替代用詞如下：
❶ **be able to**
• The lawn mower is still broken. I haven't **been able to** fix it.（現在完成式）
• Will you **be able to** get there by eight?（will 未來式）
• It was a shame that they **weren't able to** join in!（簡單過去式）
（也可以說 . . . they couldn't join in.）
❷ **manage to**（設法克服複雜的阻礙）
• I thought they had **managed to** qualify for the final!（過去完成式）

❸ 如果是表達「**許可**」，可替代為 **be allowed to / be permitted to**（較正式）
• I haven't **been allowed to** bring my dog in.（現在完成式；意指「我沒有得到此許可」）
• You **are permitted to** carry only one piece of hand luggage on this flight.
（十分正式的現在式）

5 請依據括號裡的時態與替代詞，來改寫句子。

0 Could you see the latest exhibition at MOMA, Emma? (*past simple – manage to*)
Did you manage to see the latest exhibition at MOMA, Emma?

1 I'm sorry I can't come to the conference next week. I'll be away on business. (*will future – be able to*)

....

2 I couldn't get to the top of the mountain. It was too hard for me. (*past simple – manage to*)

....

3 We can't park on this side of the road. (*present simple – be allowed to*)

....

4 Students can't smoke in the school grounds. (*present simple – be permitted to*)

....

5 Could you talk to the manager? (*present perfect – be able to*)

....

6 Can we see the house later this afternoon? (*will future – be possible*)

....

7 We can't enter the club. We aren't dressed properly. (*will future – be allowed to*)

....

LESSON 2 情態助動詞 may/might Modal verb *may/might*

肯定句和否定句

1 現在式

❶ may 用於現在式：
I/you/he/she/it/we/you/they **may** arrive soon.

❷ may not 用於現在式否定句：
I/you/he/she/it/we/you/they **may not** arrive soon.

2 條件句

❶ might 用於條件句：
I/you/he/she/it/we/you/they **might** arrive soon.

❷ might not（或是較少見的 mightn't）用於否定條件句：
I/you/he/she/it/we/you/they **might not** arrive soon.

3 問句和不同類型的答句

may/might 問句不一定只能回答「Yes, you may. / No, you may not.」。看看下方的例子：

- "**May** I use your Internet access, please?"
  "**Yes, of course**. This is the password."

- "**Might** your sister know him?"
  "**Yes, she might**. / **No, I don't think so**."

4 may/might 用於表達**現在或未來發生某事的可能性**：
- My father **may** be here soon.
  （可能會來，但不確定）

❶ 其中 may 代表的可能性較大，might 的可能性則較小。但其實兩者差異非常微小，幾乎同義：
  - "Do you think she **may** like this T-shirt?"
    "Yes, I think she **might** like it."

❷ may not 或 might not 則指某事**可能不會發生**，或我們**不確定是否會發生**。

1 請以 **may**（可能）、**may not**（不確定）或 **might not**（非常不確定）來造句。

0 I'm unsure if Liz will arrive in time for the conference.
Liz may not arrive in time for the conference.

1 It is possible that my favorite basketball team will win the championship this year.

....

2 It is possible that they will arrive any minute now.

....

235

3 It's very unsure that we will go on vacation with our parents next summer.

....

4 I'm unsure that I will be able to come to your graduation next week.

....

5 It's very unsure that the local council will organize a summer festival this year.

....

6 We're unsure that we will join the drama club this year.

....

如果要以其他說法代替 may/might，來表達某事有可能發生，可採用以下方式：

❶ 現在式或未來式的動詞搭配副詞 **perhaps**、**maybe**、**probably**：

- **Perhaps** they are not at home at this time. = They **may** not be at home . . .
- Look at the sky. It **will probably** snow today. = It **may** snow today.
- **Maybe** we **will** go to London for the weekend. = We **might** go . . .

> **!**
> **maybe** 這個副字劃分為二後，就是 **may be**（情態動詞＋動詞原形）。

❷ 非人稱用法「**It's likely / unlikely / not likely that . . .**」：

- **It's not likely** that she will come. =She may not come.
  （也可以說「She's not likely to come.」意思和第三人稱為主詞的句型一樣）
- **It's likely** that it will rain later in the day. =It may rain later in the day.
  （也可以說 It's likely to rain / It will probably rain）

---

2 請使用括號裡的副詞完成意義相近的句子。

0 I may not play the piano at the school concert. (unlikely)

It's unlikely that I will play the piano / I'm unlikely to play the piano at the school concert.

....

1 Your brother may know our new colleague. (maybe)

....

2 They might spend next weekend in Paris. (perhaps)

....

3 Tom may leave early tomorrow morning. (likely)

....

4 Mary may want to go to the zoo next Sunday. (maybe)

....

5 Melanie might not go to John's party if you're not going. (unlikely)

....

6 Jim and I might visit the new museum on Saturday morning. (perhaps)

....

7 We may join the carnival tomorrow if it's sunny. (likely)

....

8 Ben may decide to retire next year. (probably)

....

9 We may not have time to go. (maybe)

....

10 My sister may join the yoga club. (likely)

....

may/might 亦可用於以下情況：

❶ 在正式用法中，用 **I** 或 **we** 為主詞的問句**請求許可**，或是**核准或拒絕該請示**：
- **May I** have your email address, please?（請求他人告知電子郵件地址）
- You **may** go now.（這是具有權威性質的用法，意指「我允許你走」）

❷ 要表達這種句意，還可以用 **be permitted** 或 **be allowed** 來取代 may（請參閱第 234 頁）：
- I'm not **allowed** to go to the party.

❸ **表達祝願**，通常是文書方面的寫法：**May** you live happily together forever and ever.

❹ 搭配副詞 **as well** 或 **just as well**，用以表達「**有意做某事，因為沒別的事可做，或沒有理由不去做**」，類似中文的「**也只好**」：

- It's only 5 a.m., but since he's wide awake, he **may as well** get up.
- It's already nine and she's not coming, so we **might as well** start without her.
- I **might just as well** stay with you one more day. I won't be able to get home before Sunday, anyway.

FAQ

Q: 我媽媽告訴我，她以前上學的時候，如果要離開教室，必須問老師「May I go out please, Miss?」。如果她用「can」而不是「may」，就會顯得沒有禮貌。但是現在大家似乎都會使用「Can I go out?」的說法，難道是語言的用法改變了嗎？

A: may 確實是用於較為正式的情況。以往的師生關係較疏離，現今則不同，所以雖然 can 是較非正式的用詞，但仍是正確用法。不過，千萬別忘了加上 please，因為不論是過去還是現在，please 都是英語人士社交的關鍵字！

❸ 請判讀以下句子的性質。如果表達的是可能性（**probability**），請寫 Pr；如果是許可（**permission**），請寫 Pe；如果是祝願（**wish**），請寫 W；如果是有意做某事（**intention**），請寫 I。

...... **1** We may as well go to the movies if it keeps raining.

..... **2** She might not get to work tomorrow morning. She's not well.

..... **3** Those guys over there might be Susan's friends.

..... **4** I may just as well give up smoking if it's forbidden in so many places.

..... **5** Long may she reign / May she defend our laws . . . (from *God Save the Queen*)

...... **6** You may say I'm a dreamer, but I'm not the only one (from *Imagine* by J. Lennon)

...... **7** May I use your phone for a moment, please? I need to send an urgent message.

...... **8** May all of your dreams come true!

...... **9** My wife is a bit tired of her job, so she might look for a part-time job next year.

...... **10** May your days be merry and bright. (from *White Christmas* by I. Berlin)

4 請使用 **may** 或 **might** 完成意義相近的句子。

0 Maybe I'll watch a new episode of my favorite TV series tonight.
I may watch a new episode of my favorite TV series tonight.

1 Perhaps my friends will organize a barbecue in their garden next Sunday.
....

2 Peter is not likely to marry Jane. They're so different.
....

3 Ted and Sue will probably enjoy their vacation in Florida.
....

4 It's possible that Greg will buy a new suit for the wedding.
....

5 We will probably join our friends in the pub tonight.
....

6 It's unlikely that Lily will leave Marshall. She still loves him.
....

7 It's possible that my father will give me some money to buy a present for Jenny.
....

8 The tourist guide is likely to organize an excursion to the island.
....

9 It's likely that Mr. Ross will put off his lesson to next week.
....

10 It's unlikely that the twins will wear the same clothes at the wedding tomorrow.
....

LESSON 3 情態助動詞 will/would／動詞 want 和 wish
Modal verb *will/would*; verbs *want* and *wish*

情態助動詞 will/would 的句型

❶ 現在式

　❶ **will** 用於**現在式** → I/You/He/She/It/We/You/They **will** go.

　❷ **will not**（或縮讀形式 **won't**）僅能用於**現在式的否定句** →
　　I/You/He/She/It/We/You/They **won't** go.

❷ 過去式／條件句

　❶ **would** 用於**過去式**和**條件句** → I/You/He/She/It/We/You/They **would** go.

　❷ **would not**（或縮讀形式 **wouldn't**）僅能用於**過去式**和**條件句的否定句** →
　　I/You/He/She/It/We/You/They **wouldn't** go.

❸ 不同種類的問句和答句

肯定問句	• "**Will** you dance with me?" "Oh thanks. I'd love to. / No, thanks. I can't dance." • "**Would** you say I'm too thin?" "No, I didn't mean that."
否定問句	• "**Won't** you do what I tell you?" "Well, I'm trying to." • "**Wouldn't** she marry him?" "No, I don't think she would."
Wh 問句	• "**What would** you like with your tea? Cake or cookies?" "A piece of cake, please." • "**When would** you go there?" "In the afternoon."

will/would 主要用於**第二人稱單數和複數**，來表達以下意思：

主動示意	"**Will** you have an ice cream?" "No, thanks."
邀請某人做某事	"**Will** you come to my house this afternoon?" "Okay. What time?"
有禮的提出要求	"**Will** you open the window, please?" "Yes, certainly." （也可以說「Could you open … ?」或用比較正式的 would 取代 will，說「**Would** you open the window, please?」。這句話是所謂的反詰問句，意即我們不是要問對方是否想打開窗戶，而是期望聽到對方回覆願意幫我們打開窗戶；我們亦可運用祈使句說「Open the window, please!」） （請參閱第 233 頁）
強烈意願，尤其是帶有會引起不滿的頑固態度	My son always wants to have his own way. He just won't take my advice. He **wouldn't** listen to me when I told him to find a better job.

但注意，要表達**過去的習慣**時僅能使用 **would**，且通常會搭配副詞 always 或其他 every 類的時間用語（every day/week 等）；此特性類似 **used to** 的用法（請參閱第 135 頁）。

另外，will 屬於未來式的助動詞，would 則適用於搭配所有動詞的條件句（請參閱第 269 與 288 頁）。

1 請根據題目，使用 will 或 would 寫出合適的問句。

1 Invite a friend to have lunch with you today.

....

2 You ask Jack if he wants a sandwich.

....

3 You want the menu. Ask the waiter.

....

4 You want more salt. Ask Susan to pass you some.

....

5 You need some help to make dinner. Ask your son Harry.

....

6 Offer a drink to your friend.

....

2 請將 1–5 的句子和 A–E 的屬性配對。

...... **1** They won't listen to me!

...... **2** We would go for a bike ride every day when we lived in the country.

...... **3** Will you close the door, please?

...... **4** Will you have some tea, Max?

...... **5** Will you go to the movies tomorrow?

A Offer something

B Ask for something politely

C Disapprove

D Talk about habits in the past

E Invite somebody

want 是最常在非正式情境中用於表達**意願**，且 want 並非情態助動詞，而是規則動詞，簡單過去式與過去分詞均為 wanted。

 由於 want 不是情態助動詞，故有以下特性：

① 用於第三人稱單數時，必須加 s → She wants . . .

② 用於否定句時，需搭配 don't/doesn't/didn't →
   I **don't** want / He **doesn't** want / We **didn't** want . . .

③ 用於疑問句時，需搭配 do/does/did →
   Do you want / **Does** she want / **Did** they want . . . ?

④ 後面可接名詞 → He just wanted **some attention**.

⑤ 後面可接不定詞 → He wanted **to get** some attention.

如果需要某人去做某事，我們會採用句型 **want someone to do something**：

主詞 + **want** + 受詞（名詞或代名詞）+ **to** + 動詞

• They **wanted** me **to help**, but I couldn't.
• My parents **want** my sister **to go** to university, but she won't go.

---

3 請依照例句，將動詞 **want** 搭配肯定句或否定句，來改寫句子。

0 Mom: Sarah, will you go to the shops and buy some cheese, please?

Mom wants Sarah to go to the shops to buy
some cheese.

1 Mr. Hanley: Ms. Dell, please make an appointment with Ms. Bradley on Tuesday morning.

....

....

2 Our parents: Tom, Claire, don't get back late tonight!

....

3 John's mother: Don't play video games all afternoon, John!

....

....

4 Tess: Please invite David to your party, Nella.

....

5 My brother: Lend me ten dollars, please.

....

---

wish 不是情態助動詞，而是規則動詞，簡單過去式與過去分詞均為 wished。wish 用以表達**難以成真、無法操之在己的嚮往或渴望之事**。wish 還能表達**夢想**，或表示**對自己與他人的作為感到後悔**的語氣。

wish 的句型很特殊，例如「I wish I were . . .（或較非正式的用法 I wish I was . . .）」、「I wish I had . . .」、「I wish I could . . .」、「I wish I knew . . .」。

① 如果嚮往或渴望之事與**現在的情況有關**，我們可採用以下句型：

主詞 + **wish** + 相同或不同的主詞 + **動詞的簡單過去式**

• We **wish** we **had** more free time.
• I **wish** it **didn't rain** so hard.

或者：

主詞 + **wish** + 相同或不同的主詞 + **could** + 原形動詞

搭配 could 的時候，能強調出**有能力做某事**，或**清楚該如何做某事**的概念：

• Jack **wishes** he **could buy** a motorcycle.
• I **wish** you **could pass** your driving test.

4 請觀察圖片，並完成對話框。

I wish we had some rain.

0 have some rain

1 stop raining

2 not hot

3 lie on a beach

4 have some snow

5 paint better

6 sing like her

---

2 如果我們認為他人應該要**有不一樣的作為**，需採用以下句型：

> 主詞 1 + **wish** + 主詞 2 + **would** + 原形動詞

- I **wish** you **would listen** to me sometimes!
- His parents **wish** he **would give** up smoking. （也可以說「. . . he gave up smoking」，但搭配 would 之後，更強調了「希望將來能更努力達成」的意思）

3 如果是要表達對過往之事感到**後悔**，需採用以下句型：

> 主詞 + **wish** + 相同或不同主詞 + **過去完成式的動詞（had + 過去分詞）**

- I **wish** you **had** never **met** him!
- They **wish** they **had accepted** your offer. （意指「他們對於沒有接受條件而感到後悔，但為時已晚而無計可施」）

4 wish 亦可用於表達**祝願**：
- We **wish** you a Merry Christmas!

5 請使用 **wish** 來造句，表達目前無法成真的嚮往。

0 Laura / go trekking in Nepal
Laura wishes she could go trekking in Nepal.

1 We / our favorite team / win the championship
....

2 I / 10 cm taller
....

3 We / our neighbors / not so noisy
....

4 Dan / have a brand new car
....

5 I / my husband / have more free time
....

6 Our teacher / retire / at the end of this school year
....

6 請使用 **wish** 來造句，以表達失望或後悔。

0 I was so rude to Jack yesterday.
I wish I hadn't been so rude to Jack yesterday.

1 We weren't very lucky!
....

2 Ben and Karen went out trekking in the bad weather.
....
....

3 Dinah was wearing her gold necklace last night and she lost it.
....
....

4 Mike didn't go to university after high school.
....
....

5 I forgot the appointment with an important customer.
....
....

6 They all went to the club without me.
....
....

7 請將 **1–6** 與 **A–F** 配對。

1 My friend Tom would always copy during tests.
2 He would arrive late for classes every day,
3 I wish I could stay here for a few more days,
4 I wish my mother could see me!
5 Would you help me put this bag on the luggage rack, please?
6 Would you join us for lunch?

A saying he had missed the bus.
B I've never looked so good in my life.
C It's too heavy for me to lift.
D He was such a cheat!
E We need to talk about the new office.
F but I have to go back to work tomorrow.

1 ..... **2** ..... **3** ..... **4** ..... **5** ..... **6** .....

8 請判斷以下人物在各情境之中會有的說辭，使用 **wish** 搭配合適時態的動詞並重寫句子。

1 Tom's girlfriend is away and he misses her.
....

2 Sara's friends are going out tonight, but she has to stay at home.
....

3 Diane's feeling sick because she had raw fish last night.
....

4 Hilary regrets she didn't learn to ski when she was young.
....

5 Tina works in a supermarket, but her dream is to be a pop singer.
....

LESSON 4 條件句：would like、would prefer、would rather
Conditional forms *would like, would prefer, would rather*

為了表達**嚮往與喜好**，我們常會使用 I would like、
I would prefer 和 I would rather 等條件句。

Would like

would like 是動詞 like 的**條件句**用法，很像 want
和 wish，但用法不同（請參閱第 240 頁）。
注意，would like 的用法比 want 更**正式**。

❶ 肯定句

只有在主詞是**代名詞**的情況下，would like 才可
以縮讀為 'd like。

- John would like to become a famous
  football player. He**'d like** to play for
  Manchester United.

❷ 否定句

would not like 通常會縮讀為 wouldn't like。

- I **wouldn't like** to be there now!!

❸ 問句和不同類型的答句

問句裡的 would/wouldn't，一定要放在主詞前面：

肯定問句	"**Would** you **like** anything to drink?" "No, thanks. Nothing for me."
否定問句	"**Wouldn't** you **like** to try this restaurant?" "Yes, I'd love to."
Wh 問句	"**What would** you **like** to do tonight?" "I'd like to watch a movie on TV."

請觀察一下 Yes/No 問句的答句。我們通常不會看
到簡答句以 I would / I wouldn't 構成，而是較常用
Yes, please / No, thanks / I'd love to 來表示接
受或拒絕某邀約或提議。

I'd love to（即 I would love to）其實是動詞 love
的條件句用法，我們以此來表達欣然接受某提議或某
邀約。

❹ would like 的用法：

would like 和動詞 want 一樣，
後面可接以下用詞：

❶ 名詞：I'd like **an organic
multi-vitamin juice**, please.

❷ to + 動詞：We'd like **to visit** not
only the museum but also the
temporary exhibition.

> ❗ 請小心，別將「I'd like to」（我想）
> 和「I like + 動詞 ing」（我喜歡）
> 混為一談，例句：I like visiting
> museums.（請參閱第 100 頁）

❺ would like 可用以表示：

❶ 主動示意：

- "**Would** you **like** a milkshake?"
  "Yes, please."

  也可以說「Will/Would you have a
  milkshake?」或更正式地說「Do you
  want a milkshake?」（請參閱第 239
  與 240 頁）

❷ 表達需求或要求，如在餐廳或商店時：

- "So, what **would** you **like** to eat,
  sir?" "**I'd like** some chicken and
  potatoes."

  在此情境下，不適用「What do you
  want . . . ?」，因為會顯得服務生和顧
  客的互動稍嫌失禮。

❸ 表達希望某人幫我們做某事，可使
用與動詞 want 相同的句型，意即
**would like someone to do
something**（請參閱第 240 頁）：

> 主詞 + **would like** + 受詞
> （名詞或代名詞）+ **to** + **動詞**

- We**'d like** our daughter **to become**
  a doctor.
- I**'d like** her **to give** me another
  chance.

FAQ

Q: 「I wish I had a car.」和「I'd like to have a car.」有何差異？

A: 第一句意指講者夢想擁有一部車，且言下之意是他有點後悔沒有買車；這句話就像是後接驚嘆號的感嘆句：「I would like to have a car so much!」

第二句則沒有這種意思，只是單純表達能實現的嚮往之事，表示想要買一部車。

1 請將 1–7 的句子和 A–G 的屬性配對。

...... **1** Our teacher would like us to hand in our projects by Monday.
...... **2** What would you like to drink, sir?
...... **3** I'd like a cup of hot chocolate, please.
...... **4** Would you like to join us at the club tonight?
...... **5** I wish I had a house by the sea.
...... **6** I'd like to have a motorcycle.
...... **7** Would you like some chips, Liz?

A Expressing wants that can be fulfilled
B Expressing wishes
C Offering
D Inviting
E Making a request
F Collecting an order
G Asking somebody to do something

2 請使用 would like 或 like 來完成句子。

1 We .... going to the movies. We often go there on Friday night.

2 I .... to go to the movies tomorrow. Will you come with me?

3 "........................... you .... to play a game of cards?" "Yes, why not?"

4 He .... me to help him with his project, but I really can't this week.

5 We .... vegetables and we eat a lot of them, even though we aren't vegetarian.

6 "........................... you .... cartoons?" "Not really, I prefer watching movies."

Would prefer to / Would rather

條件用語「I would prefer to」或「I would rather」，用來表達**在兩件事物之間做偏好的選擇**。

❶ I would prefer（縮讀形式 I'd prefer）是動詞 prefer 的條件句用法，句型如下：

| 主詞 + **would prefer** + **to** + 原形動詞 |

• My wife would like to go on a cruise, but I**'d prefer to go** on a car trip.

❷ 如果是以相同的主詞，表達在兩種事物之間做偏好的選擇，句型則如下：

| 主詞 + **would prefer** + **to** + 原形動詞 + **rather than** + 原形動詞 |

• I**'d prefer to travel** in a campervan **rather than go** by plane.

❸ I would rather（縮讀形式為 I'd rather）是以 would 搭配副詞 rather（請參閱第 178 頁），來產生以下句型：

| 主詞 + **would rather** + 原形動詞 |

• I**'d rather take** a taxi than go by bus to the airport.
• **Would** you **rather have** tea or coffee?
• What **would** you **rather do**? Stay at home or go for a walk?

3 請使用 would rather 或 would prefer 來完成句子。

1 I .... to stay at home tonight. It's so cold and miserable out.

2 "What shall I cook for dinner?" "Fish. Erik .... eat fish than meat."

3 My parents .... go on a cruise this summer. They're fed up with the mountains.

4 Alan is tired. He .... not play five-a-side football this Saturday.

5 Mom .... to wear a suit to the wedding rather than a long dress.

6 I .... to take you to a good restaurant than have dinner at home.

7 We .... go to London this weekend.

8 I .... to work today and have a day off tomorrow.

4 請將 1–8 的問句與 A–H 的答句配對。

1 Where would you like to go on the weekend?

2 What would you like for breakfast?

3 Would you like to go for a bike ride?

4 What would you like to be when you grow up?

5 Which way would you prefer to go?

6 Would you rather go home now or stay a bit longer?

7 Would you like some cake?

8 If you don't want to play tennis, what would you rather do?

A I'd like to be a chef.

B I'd like to go the country way.

C No, thanks. Just a cup of tea.

D I don't mind. Where would you like to go?

E I'd like to go for a walk on the seafront.

F I'd like some coffee and a blueberry muffin.

G Yes. Let's hire a couple of mountain bikes.

H I'd like to go home, please.

1 .....   2 .....   3 .....   4 .....   5 .....   6 .....   7 .....   8 .....

5 下方每個句子都有一處錯誤，請在錯誤處標出底線，並訂正為正確句子。

1 I'd like that James washes my car. It's so dirty!

....

2 They would rather spending the weekend in London than at home doing gardening.

....

3 He would prefer go to a rock concert. He doesn't like house music very much.

....

4 Would you like coming to my birthday party next week?

....

5 "What would you like to drink" "I like a soft drink."

....

6 Do we really have to go out with Ben and Louise? I had rather eat out with you alone.

....

7 Our instructor would like we trained three times a week.

....

8 It's so cold that I had prefer stay at home tonight.

....

9 "Would you like sitting on the terrace?" "Oh yes, that would be nice."

....

10 "Do you want to drink some water?" "Well, er . . . , I'd rather to have some juice."

....

表達能力、可能性與意願的情態助動詞

ROUND UP 13

1 請以情態助動詞 **can**、**could**、**can't**、**couldn't** 來完成句子。

1 All your dreams .... come true — you only have to work hard to make it happen.

2 They .... join us on the trip, they had work to do.

3 I .... stand all this noise any more. It's so annoying!

4 You .... believe all that he says. He often makes up his stories.

5 It .... cost all that money! It looks like an ordinary bag.

6 My daughter .... read and add up at an early age.

7 I just .... remember what Mom told me to do. I'll have to call her.

8 She .... sing beautifully. She has a fantastic voice.

9 I .... help you with your project if you need me to.

10 He .... do judo very well; he has a brown belt.

延伸補充

「**can't + have + 過去分詞**」的句型，用來表達講話當下假設、以邏輯推論，在過去所發生的事件；
「**may + have + 過去分詞**」的用法和此句型相同。請看以下例句：

- The girl in the club **can't have been** Sara. She hates dancing.
  （意指「於現在推測之前在夜店的那個女孩絕對不是莎拉」）

- They **may have arrived** by now.（意指「於現在推測他們很有可能已經到場了」）

---

2 請使用下方動詞搭配情態助動詞 **can't** 或 **may**，來完成與過去事件有關的推論。

go	hand in	be (x4)	finish	run	have	arrive

1 You .... that hungry at lunch time after all you had for breakfast.

2 They .... to the beach. The weather is gorgeous today.

3 That boy you saw in the pub .... Tom's brother.
Tom's brother left for New York two days ago.

4 The car you saw in the accident .... Jason's car.
His is blue and it's smaller.

5 My father .... in Boston by now.

6 The story they told you .... true. There are too many
strange coincidences.

7 The conference .... , but let's try and go into the room anyway.

8 He .... some problems at work because he hasn't arrived yet.

9 Sara .... so fast. She must have cheated somehow.

10 Judith .... her written exam by now. I hope she passes
because she's really worked hard.

延伸補充

請注意 **I can't help + 動詞 ing** 與 **I can't help but + 原形動詞**，意思是「我**無法不**做某事」。

- **I can't help thinking** he's not being honest with me.

- **I couldn't help laughing**. / **I couldn't help but laugh**. (= I couldn't stop laughing.)

3 請使用提示用詞來完成意義相近的句子，注意勿改變提示用詞。

1 The movie was so moving that I couldn't help crying most of the time.

BUT The movie was so moving that .... most of the time.

2 He couldn't help but tell her, although it was a secret.

TELLING He .... her, although it was a secret.

3 It's possible that they can help you, but I'm not sure.

MIGHT They .... you, but I'm not sure.

4 Perhaps I'll visit my American cousins next summer.

MAY I .... my American cousins next summer.

5 It's unlikely that the witness recognized the thieves. They were wearing masks.

CAN'T The witness .... the thieves. They were wearing masks.

6 Dinah would prefer to buy a notebook instead of a tablet.

RATHER Dinah .... a notebook instead of a tablet.

7 If only I could have more money!

WISH I .... more money!

8 Jane regrets that she didn't learn to play an instrument when she was young.

WISHES Jane .... an instrument when she was young.

9 It's likely that Terry is at home. That's her car over there.

MAY Terry .... at home. That's her car over there.

10 Lucy would rather call a wedding planner to organize the ceremony.

PREFER Lucy .... a wedding planner to organize the ceremony.

4 請重新排序單字來造句。

1 do / you / Will / able / be / to / it / ?

....

2 won't / You / midnight / allowed / to / be / after / come back / .

....

3 haven't / been / They / to / go / allowed / .

....

4 You / calculator / not / be / allowed / to / may / use / your / .

....

5 has / She / time / to / get / managed / on / here / .

....

6 will / that / it / It's / snow / tonight / likely /.

....

7 I / be / know / if / I / don't / come / will / able / to / .

....

8 late / will / She / be / probably / .

....

9 about / you / Could / behavior / horrible / talk / to / him / his / ?

....

10 might / They / be / help / able / to / the / catering / for / organize / garden / your / party / .

....

5 請依據括號裡的時態與單字，來改寫句子。

1 He can leave early tomorrow because there's a train at 6:30 a.m. (*will* future / able)
....

2 Visitors may only see the rooms on the first floor. (past simple / allowed)
....

3 I could fix my bike on my own eventually. (past simple / able)
....

4 I can't stay out late in the evening. (*will* future / allowed)
....

5 I can't come, I'm sorry. I'm very busy tomorrow. (*will* future / able)
....

6 I see you could make this elaborated chocolate cake. It looks delicious.
(present perfect / manage)
....

7 "Could you talk to Mr. Bailey?" "No, I couldn't." (present perfect / able)
....

8 I can't park my car in front of the restaurant. (*will* future / able)
....

9 We can't go to Sally's wedding next month. (*will* future / able)
....

10 They may go to the Halloween party. (past simple / likely)
....

6 請根據下方題目，搭配非正式的「**Will you . . . ?**」或正式的「**Would you . . . ?**」來提出請求。

0 Your friend Liza / help you clear the garage
Will you help me clear the garage, please, Liza?
....

1 Your friend Ben / dig the garden
....

2 A passerby / tell you where Castle Street is
....

3 A man at the post office / wait in the line
....

4 Passengers / fasten their seat belts
....

5 Hotel guest / follow you to the elevator
....

6 Your brother Steve / go to the football match with you
....

7 Your art teacher / go to the art exhibition with you
....

8 Customer / sign at the bottom of the form
....

7 請依照例句改寫句子。

0 I'd like a new bike. (Dad / give me)
I'd like Dad to give me a new bike.

1 She wants a big chocolate cake for her birthday. (her mom / make her)

2 I'd like to go on a cruise. (my parents / book me)

3 Bill wants a fancy-dress party. (his friends / organize)

4 My son would like a grant to study in Berlin. (the university / give him)

5 My brother wants my new laptop. (me / lend him)

6 The citizens want a new indoor swimming pool. (the city council / build)

ROUND UP 13

FAQ

Q: 我常聽到歌詞出現 wanna 這個詞，它和動詞 want 有關係嗎？

A: 確實有關。**wanna** 是 **want to** 的縮讀形式，常用於美式口語英文，如「I wanna go.」，應避免用於書寫語言。非正式用語裡還有一個名詞叫 **wannabe**（由 **wants to be** 轉化而來），指的是想變成他人的人，如「She's a pop singer wannabe!」。

Reflecting on grammar

請研讀文法規則，再判斷以下說法是否正確。

		True	False
1	所有雙音節形容詞的比較級均需搭配 more。		
2	搭配 more 或 less 的比較級句子，會以 than 來引導兩者之中被拿來比較的後者。		
3	「He's very younger than I.」是正確的句子。		
4	bad 的比較級是 worse，最高級是 worst。		
5	「She is as old as me but looks much younger.」是正確的句子。		
6	電視影集出現完結篇時，我們會說「This is the latest episode of the series.」。		
7	far 的最高級是 the farthest。		
8	三音節的形容詞，字尾加上 est 就是最高級。		
9	「He's the eldest of two brothers.」是正確的句子。		
10	「This book is less interesting than the other one.」的意思和「This book is not so interesting as the other one.」相同。		

UNIT 14 表達義務和必要性的情態助動詞
Modal Verbs to Express Obligation and Necessity

LESSON 1 情態助動詞 must / 動詞 have to
Modal verb *must* and verb *have to*

情態助動詞 must

❶ 情態助動詞 must 用以表達**義務**、**必要性**與**禁令**。must 只有**現在式**的用法，搭配所有人稱時均不會產生任何變化。

❷ must 的否定句是 **must not** 或 **mustn't**，使用問句時，則是將 must 放在主詞的前面。與所有情態助動詞一樣，must 後面一定要接另一個原形動詞。

> I/you/he/she/it/we/you/they **must**
> I/you/he/she/it/we/you/they **mustn't**
> **Must** I/you/he/she/it/we/you/they . . . ?

❸ 第一人稱的問句（Must I/we . . . ?），是用在**確認**是否真的需要執行**不太想**做的事。
- **Must I** really tidy my room?
- **Must we** really work next Sunday?

❹ 第二人稱或第三人稱主詞的問句（Must you . . . ?），會有**請對方停止**某些令人不悅或不合適行為的意思。
- **Must you** keep talking?
- **Must they** play such a violent video game?

must/mustn't 用在以下狀況：

❶ 他人叮嚀的義務：
- I **must** take these tablets twice a day. The doctor said so.

❷ 需要盡本分的事：
- I **must** be punctual.
- I **must** do my homework today.

❸ 提出建議、強烈推薦做某事：
- You **must** see that musical. It's really fabulous!
- You **must** visit the new interactive museum. It's so interesting!

❹ 表達被禁止或不建議做的行為（用否定句）
- You **mustn't** smoke in here. See the sign?
- You **mustn't** miss the latest episode of the series. It's the best so far.

❺ 設立規定（常以 You must/mustn't 開頭）：
- **You must** wear a uniform in this school.
- **You mustn't** wear shorts or sleeveless shirts to your classes.

（You can't 比 You mustn't 更常見於非正式用法）

❻ 依證據來進行推論、表達某人事物的可能情況

現在式：

> **must + 原形動詞**

- He **must be** a New Zealander. You can tell from his accent.
- This **must be** Jenny's bag. There's her cell phone in it.

過去式：

> **must + have + 過去分詞**

- It **must have been** an easy test. Everybody finished well before the given time.
- She **must have forgotten** her cell phone at home. It rings but nobody answers it.

Have to / Have got to

動詞 have to 或 have got to 可取代現在式的 must，尤其適用於以下情況：

❶ 例行本分：
I **have to** / I**'ve got to**. be at the office by nine every morning.

❷ 他人叮嚀我們該盡的義務：
You **have to** / You**'ve got to** pay in advance.

❸ have to（不需搭配 got）還可替代 must，用**在因不願做某事而提問**的情況：
- Do I **have to** come with you? Can't I stay at home?

❹ 由於 must 只有現在式，因此我們會使用 have to 來表達其他時態的部分，例如：

❶ 簡單過去式：
- I **had to** wait for an hour.
- I **didn't have to** wait long.

❷ will 未來式：
- You**'ll have to** work hard next year.
- You **won't have to** work very hard.

❸ 現在完成式：
- I**'ve had to** do a lot of work this morning.
- She**'s had to** help her mom tidy the kitchen.

> ⚠ have to 不是助動詞，因此用於問句或否定句時，必須搭配 **do**、**does** 或 **did**。

Mustn't / Don't have to

have to 的否定句（don't/doesn't have to）與 mustn't 的意義不同：

❶ mustn't 帶有「**禁令**」的意思：
- You **mustn't** walk on the flower beds.

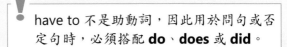

❷ don't have to 則是「**不一定**」的意思，等於 It's not necessary 的用法：
- You **don't have to** water the flowers every day. It's not very hot.
（意指「雖然不是要禁止澆花，但澆花也不是必然要做的事」）

看看下方兩句有何不同：
- You **mustn't** run in the school corridors!（禁止在學校走廊奔跑）
- You **don't have to** run. You still have plenty of time to catch the train.
（你不用跑，還有足夠的時間趕上火車）

---

1 請將 1–6 的句子與 A–F 的句子配對。

1 You mustn't cross the street here.
2 You must get off at the stop after the bus station.
3 It must have been a hard exam.
4 The sea must be very rough.
5 The project needs to be finished by May 8.
6 We have to be home by five.

A Look at that boat – it's being tossed around a lot.
B It's dangerous.
C My parents are arriving.
D The museum's right there. You can't miss it!
E Only a few candidates passed.
F You've got to finish it for that deadline.

1 .....　2 .....　3 .....　4 .....　5 .....　6 .....

2 請根據提示用詞來完成句子。注意不能更改提示用詞。

0 You mustn't park your car here. It's a restricted zone.
　　CAN　　You ...can't park your car... here. It's a restricted zone.

1 He can't stay in bed late in the mornings.
　　GET UP　　He has .... in the mornings.

2 Talking in the library is prohibited.
　　MUST　　You ....

3 Are you going to Greece with that heavy coat? You won't need it.

BRING   You .... that heavy coat to Greece.

4 I already know about that. It's not necessary for you to tell me.

HAVE   You .... me. I already know about that.

5 Dictionaries must be available in each classroom.

HAVE   Students .... dictionaries in each classroom.

6 You must hand in your essays on Friday.

HAVE   You .... on Friday.

③ 請使用括號裡的時態來改寫句子。

0 Mom mustn't cook tonight. We're going to take her out. (will- *future*)

Mom won't have to cook tonight. ....

1 We have to carry a lot of books to classes. (*past simple*)

....

2 They don't have to hurry to catch their train. (*past simple*)

....

3 She has to work very hard to prepare for the exam. (will- *future*)

....

4 I have to buy a new car; mine is very old now. (will- *future*)

....

5 It must be love! (*past perfect*)

....

6 He has to study all the irregular verbs for the test. (*present perfect*)

....

7 I have to mow the lawn every week. (*present perfect*)

....

④ 請將 1–7 的句子與 A–G 的屬性配對。

1 You must see the exhibition in the castle. It's great!

2 You mustn't take photos in the museum.

3 Must we really write this essay for tomorrow morning?

4 I have to make coffee for my boss every morning at ten.

5 I must help them.

6 It must be late. All the shops are closing.

7 You must switch off your phones during the lectures.

A Ask for confirmation of something that you wouldn't do

B Oblige/order somebody to do something

C Express an obligation that you feel as a duty

D Make a supposition

E Say that something is forbidden

F Give a piece of advice

G Speak about routine commitments

1 .....   **2** .....   **3** .....   **4** .....   **5** .....   **6** .....   **7** .....

⑤ 請根據答句內容，寫出合適的問句。

1 ....? No, I don't have to. I only work from Monday to Friday.

2 ....? Yes, you must. The grass is too high.

3 ....? At work? No, I don't have to wear a uniform.

4 ....? You must hand in your project by Friday afternoon.

5 ....? No, sorry, you can't sit on these sofas.

6 ....? Yes, I have to. My old computer is not working any longer and I need a new one.

LESSON 2 Need to / don't need to / needn't / be to用法
Need to / don't need to / needn't ; be to

除了動詞 have to，我們還能用 **need** 表達相同的「必要性」概念。不過 need 屬於奇特的混用動詞，在否定句和疑問句中，可作為主動詞和情態助動詞。

❶ 在**肯定句**裡，need 作為**主動詞**，因此：

　❶ 搭配第三人稱單數時，必須加上 **s** 且後接 **to + 原形動詞**：
　　• She **needs to be** there by ten o'clock sharp.（意指「她有必要到場」）

　❷ 加上 ed 即成為過去式：
　　• He **needed** to have his own car for the job as a sales rep.（意指「他必須具備」）

❷ 在**否定句**裡，則會同「**don't have to**」，有「**不一定**」的意思，此時 need 可作為**主動詞**和**情態助動詞**。請看以下兩種用法：

　現在式　• I don't need to go. = I **needn't** go.（needn't 較常用於英式英文）
　　　　　　• He doesn't need to go. = He **needn't** go.

　- -

　過去式　• "Did you go there?" "No, I **didn't need** to go."
　　　　　　• "Did you go there?" "Yes, but I **needn't** have gone."

在此情況下，兩句的意義並不同。第一個例句的意思是「因為非必要，所以我沒有去」；第二個例句的意思則是「因為非必要，所以我原本可以不去」（同時表示講者已經去了）。

❸ 如果要用於表達「**某事必須被完成**」的被動語態，動詞 need 的後面可以接 **to + 原形動詞**，或直接接**動詞 ing** → Your car **needs to be repaired**. / Your car **needs repairing**.

UNIT
14
表達義務和必要性的情態助動詞

FAQ

Q: need 後面也能接名詞或代名詞嗎？

A: 當然可以。當 need 表示某物很有用時，後面可接名詞，如「I need your help.」或代名詞，如「I need you.」。在此情況下，need 是主動詞，因此否定句和疑問句的句型如下：
I don't need . . . / Do you need . . . ?
→ I don't need your help. / Does he need my help?

1 請使用動詞 **need** 搭配肯定句、否定句或疑問句，來完成句子。

1 Everybody .... to love and to be loved.

2 Thanks for lending me your book, I .... it any more now.

3 "........................... you still .... my pen?" "No, thanks, I've just found mine."

4 We .... to carry some heavy bags, so we'd better go in the car.

5 Janet .... to write her essay today. The deadline is tomorrow.

6 You .... have worried. Everything was okay in the end. *(modal)*

7 I .... to give him the good news. He had already heard about it.

8 She .... to rent a car, but she couldn't find her credit card.

9 "........................... you really .... to buy a new dress?" "Not really, but this one's lovely."

10 You .... work so hard. Get some rest and relax.

11 They .... some warm clothes when they go to Alaska.

12 Do you think the children .... some help with their science project?

2 請使用 **need** 來改寫句子。

0 No booking is required.

You *don't need to book* .

1 It may be necessary for you to reserve a table.

You .

2 It doesn't seem necessary for them to go.

They .

3 It is necessary to dry-clean this coat.

This coat .

4 You don't have to be there before nine o'clock.

You

5 All passengers have to be informed about the safety rules.

All passengers

6 It wasn't necessary to call the doctor for our mother.

We

動詞 be to

我們可在以下情況，使用 **be to** 來替代 **have to**：

表達法律或政府機關所規定的應盡義務（正式用法，較常見於書寫的）	• Each participant **is to** pay a \$10 fee for insurance. （若寫 has to pay 或 needs to pay 則較不正式） • Mr. Johnson's will **is to** be read in the presence of all the heirs.
表達官方事務、固定行程與協議事項（較常見於新聞媒體）	• The US President **is to** arrive in Rio de Janeiro tonight. • He **is to** continue his journey to Uruguay in the following days.

---

3 請使用 **be to** 和以下動詞，來完成句子。

| meet be signed talk vote show get out |

1 All passengers .... their passports at the check-in desk.

2 The British Prime Minister .... to the United Nations on Thursday.

3 The contract .... before tomorrow morning.

4 Senators .... on the new tax bill in tomorrow's session.

5 The First Lady .... a group of children during her charity campaign.

6 .... I .... of the car, Officer?

4 請以 **have to**、**need**、**be to**、**must** 搭配肯定或否定來完成句子。

1 I .... feed the hamster every day. My brother .... clean the cage.

2 You .... to pay in advance. You can pay later.

3 The British Prime Minister .... come back from Brussel today.

4 You .... to read the contract before signing it.

5 Candidates .... leave the room as soon as they finish the test.

6 He .... some more money. He hasn't got enough.

LESSON 3 Shall / should / ought to / had better 用法
Shall/should; ought to; had better

情態助動詞 shall

shall/should 是情態助動詞，主要用於**請教**與**給予指示、建議和提議**。

shall（否定型 shall not 或 shan't）是口語英文裡最少用到的情態助動詞，美式英文裡幾乎聽不到此用法，英式英文一樣很少聽到。

❶ 傳統上，大家用 **shall** 搭配**第一人稱 I** 和 **we** 來**預期未來可能發生的事**：
- This time tomorrow I **shall** be in London.

但現代英文中，若要表示相同情境，我們會以適用所有人稱的 **will** 未來式與縮讀形式：
- This time tomorrow I **will** be / I**'ll** be in London.（請參閱第 269 頁）

❷ shall 的另一個正式用法，則是**下達命令**或**給予指示**，但此用法同樣過時：
- All passengers **shall** remain seated until the sign has been switched off.

情態助動詞 should

should 是 shall 的條件句用法，較常出現在現代英文中：

❶ 肯定句和否定句

I/you/he/she/it/we/you/they **should try**.

I/you/he/she/it/we/you/they **shouldn't try**.

❷ 不同種類的問句和答句

肯定問句	"**Should** I wait for them?" "No, you don't need to. They can go by themselves."
否定問句	"**Shouldn't** you be studying at the moment?" "Yes, Dad, you're right. I'll start now."
Wh 問句	"I'm in trouble. **What should** I do?" "I really don't know!"

❸ should 比 shall 更被廣為使用，其適用情況如下：

給予或請教建議	• You **shouldn't** drink alcohol – certainly not at your age! • "What do you think? **Should** I go for it?" "Yes, I think you **should**."
表達該做的正當之事	We **should** recycle as much waste as we can.
根據已知事實來表達可能發生的情況，與 **must** 的推論用法相似（請參閱第 250 頁）	• They left three hours ago. They **should** be here by now. • We've just passed Slough. We **shouldn't** be far from Windsor.

❹ should 還可替代用於問句的 shall，來表示：

請教指示	**Should** we turn left now?
主動示意執行認為有幫助的事	**Should** I get you some food?
提議	**Should** we go to the movies tonight?

1 請將 1–5 的句子和 A–E 的問句配對。

..... **1** It's a bit cold in here.

..... **2** Come to dinner at 8 p.m.

..... **3** The baby's asleep on the sofa.

..... **4** I'd like to know what the weather will be like tomorrow.

..... **5** I'm quite hungry.

A Shall I switch off the radio?

B Shall I make you a sandwich?

C Shall I check for you on my smartphone?

D Shall I close the window?

E Shall I bring a dessert?

2 請將問句與答句配對。注意答句選項比問句多出兩句。

Let's get some drinks and snacks.	Would three o'clock be okay?
Let's go to the Multiplex.	No, it's cold today.
Take the number 15. It's quicker.	You needn't cook tonight. I'll get pizza.
Would that blue coat suit you?	No, I've got some. Get some chips.

1 Shall I take the bus or the subway? ....

2 What shall we buy for the party? ....

3 Shall I buy some popcorn? ....

4 Where shall we go tonight? ....

5 What time shall we meet? ....

6 What shall I make for dinner? ....

3 請使用 **shall** 或 **should** 來完成意義相近的句子。

0 What about meeting for a chat and a coffee, Bridget?

Shall we meet for a chat and a coffee, Bridget?
....?

1 You're supposed to be working at the moment.

....?

2 Do you think I need to bring a large bag?

....?

3 Why don't we watch this DVD?

....?

4 Do you think it's a good idea to give her some flowers?

....?

5 Why don't we ask Mark to our party?

....?

6 Do you think it is better for them to walk or take the bus?

....?

Ought to

❶ **ought** 是唯一後接 **to** + **原形動詞**的奇特情態助動詞，且僅有一種時態以及條件句的用法：

肯定句	I/you/he/she/it/we/you/they **ought to try**
否定句	I/you/he/she/it/we/you/they **ought not to / oughtn't to try.**
疑問句	**Ought** I/you/he/she/it/we/you/they try? (少用)

2 ought to 與 should 的用法相同，用在：

給予建議	• You **oughtn't to** eat so many sweets. Sugar is bad for your teeth. • You **ought to** eat more vegetables.
表達應為何種情況、原本應會怎樣，或表達該做的正事	• She **ought to** apologize.（現在式） • She **ought to** have apologized.（過去式）
提議	You **ought to** save some money for your next trip.
表達可能發生的情況	It's 11 o'clock. He **ought to** have finished by now.

Had better

had better 可以替代 should 和 ought to，來**給予建議或推薦做法**。但注意此為非正式用法。

肯定句	主詞 + **had ('d) better** + 原形動詞
否定句	主詞 + **had ('d) better not** + 原形動詞

• You**'d better** hurry or you'll be late.
• You**'d better not** say a word. (= It would be a better idea if you didn't say a word.)

FAQ

Q. 我在小說看到「You'd better marry him.」，我以為這是以「'd」當作「would」縮讀形式的條件句，就像「I'd rather . . .」，是這樣嗎？

A: 不是的。**You'd better** 的意思是 **You had better**。我們有點難以文法角度來解釋此用法，但 have 的簡單過去式在此是條件句的意思。這就是英文比較奇特的部分！

4 請圈出正確的用字。

1 I **had better / ought / shall** to give up smoking.

2 You **should / ought / have better** be more careful when driving.

3 You **ought / 'd better / 've better** tell him or he'll be very angry with you.

4 She **shouldn't / not ought / not shall** answer his emails.

5 They **have better / should / ought** study more if they want to pass their exams.

6 "**Shall I / Have I better / Ought I** switch off the lights?" "Yes, please."

5 請以 had better / had better not 或 ought / ought not，來完成句子。

1 You .... wear a warm sweater. It's really cold out today.

2 You .... get up, Mark. It's late!

3 She .... to be more careful. She's always falling over.

4 You .... go out. There's a really bad storm!

5 We .... go skiing this weekend. There are warnings about avalanches.

6 You .... take your umbrella. It's going to rain.

7 They .... to go home until it stops snowing.

8 You .... apologize to your friend. Your behavior has been awful!

LESSON 4 Be obliged/compelled/forced to / be due / be bound / 動詞 owe 用法
Be obliged/compelled/forced to; be due; be bound to; verb owe

❶ Be obliged/compelled/forced to

must 與 have to 有**強硬規定應盡義務**的意思，要表達相同概念，還可以用較正式的 **be + obliged**（oblige 的過去分詞）與 **be + compelled**（compel 的過去分詞），而如果要表達**更強烈的限制**，我們可使用 **be forced**，這幾種用法較常見於書寫中。

> **!** be obliged/compelled/forced 後面必須先接 **to**，再接動詞。
> 這種用法下，只要改變 be 動詞的三態，就有所有動詞時態的變化。例如：
>
> | 現在式 | Thousands of people **are forced to** leave their countries every day because of war and persecution.（語意比 must have 還要強烈） |
> | --- | --- |
> | 過去式 | One of the ministers **was compelled to** resign from office following a bribery scandal.（語意比 had to resign 還要強烈） |
> | 未來式 | They **will be obliged to** accept the agreement.（語意比 They will have to accept 還要強烈） |
> | 現在完成式 | My husband has lost his job so we **have been obliged to** sell our house. |

❷ Be due

be due 用於表達**某情況會在預定時間發生**，尤其適用於說明**交通工具、宅配**等類似事物的抵達時間；**後方動詞**通常因為可以意會而**省略不寫**。

- The train from Lancaster **is due** (to arrive) in 15 minutes.
- Delivery **is due** to arrive within the next few days.
- The flight from Madrid **was due** (to land) at 4:50 p.m., but it is delayed.

❸ Be bound

be bound 用於表達**某情況注定會發生**或**無法避免於將來發生**；後面必須先接 **to**，再接**動詞**。

- It**'s bound to be** so!（意指「我很確定就是這樣，不可能有其他情況」）
- With her talent, she**'s bound to be** successful.（也可以說 she's sure/certain to be successful）
- He's drinking and driving every night—sooner or later he**'s bound to have** an accident.

FAQ

Q: 我家裡有「賽門和葛芬柯」（Simon and Garfunkel）的專輯 CD，其中一首《Homeward Bound》我很喜歡，但這個歌名到底是什麼意思呢？

A: bound 此時的意思是「往……方向」，所以此歌名的直譯是「往家的方向出發」（directed towards home），有歸心似箭的感覺。

其實仔細觀察，會發現「導往」（directed）與「注定」（destined for）兩者之間有其關聯性。想想看，神話英雄尤利西斯（Ulysses）一樣歸心似箭，注定要返回故鄉綺色加（Ithaca）！

4 **To owe**

to owe（簡單過去式和過去分詞皆為 owed）是用來表達**欠錢**，或是比喻**欠人情**的情況：

- He **owes** me a lot of money, which I lent him a long time ago.
- "How much do I **owe** you?" "Fifty pounds."
- You've been of great help to me. I **owe** you a lot!（也可以說 I'm very grateful to you!）

1 請使用 be obliged/forced/due 的正確時態，來完成句子。

1 Yesterday's train delay .... to the storm.

2 He .... to learn Chinese for his job. He's having the first lesson today.

3 Last month Francine .... to resign and look for another job.

4 The bus .... in five minutes. Let's run!

5 Our plane .... to land in New York at 5 p.m.

6 It's a sunny day, but I .... to stay in and study for the test.

2 請運用 be bound 或 owe 的正確時態來完成句子。

1 I .... you all I've ever had. You have been such a good friend!

2 She .... her classmate $15 for the movie ticket.

3 He studied so hard that he .... to pass his science test.

4 How much do I .... you for the pizza and coke?

5 Things .... to go wrong if you don't listen to me!

6 They .... to win. They play so much better than the other team.

3 請使用下方單字來完成短文，注意有多一個單字。

| alerted | due | will be obliged | been forced | compelled to | take off | owing |

The hurricane is ¹................................. to hit the eastern coast of the United States on the weekend. The population has already been ²................................. . All people living within five kilometers of the sea are ³................................. leave their houses by Saturday morning. Airlines have ⁴................................. to cancel all weekend flights that were due to land or ⁵................................. from airports in the area. People traveling in the area ⁶................................. to leave the coastal roads and drive along the highways.

4 請將 1–8 與 A–H 配對成完整句子。

..... **1** We were forced to abandon our house   **A** in two minutes. Hurry up!

..... **2** They owe me   **B** a great actor!

..... **3** I was compelled to   **C** his offer for the house.

..... **4** Their flight is due to land   **D** at Heathrow Airport at 3 p.m.

..... **5** You are bound to become   **E** five euros for the taxi.

..... **6** We'll be obliged to accept   **F** after the earthquake.

..... **7** The train is due   **G** a career in politics.

..... **8** Peter's bound to have   **H** tell him the truth.

表達義務和必要性的情態助動詞

ROUND UP 14

1 請參閱第 **280** 頁的表格，寫下以下句意的性質。

0 Shall we try the new Japanese restaurant?
suggestions and proposals
....

1 You needn't bring your device. There'll be computers in the room.
....

2 They must be at home. The lights are on.
....

3 Can I leave earlier today, Ms. Spencer?
....

4 Shall I go ahead along this road?
....

5 You ought to tell your father about your plans.
....

6 I'd like Jack to cut the grass.
....

7 We have to meet the manager every Monday morning.
....

8 They mustn't touch the old books on that shelf.
....

9 Could we have the menu, please?
....

2 請使用情態助動詞 **must/mustn't** 搭配以下動詞來完成句子。

| forget | fasten | leave | win | tell | tidy | drive | book | be | hurry |

1 You .... lies!

2 Passengers .... their seat belts.

3 We .... this important match.

4 You .... your passport.

5 You .... slowly when it's foggy.

6 You .... your seats in advance.

7 I .... in the office by eight o'clock.

8 Students .... the school building without permission.

9 Emma .... her room. It's a real mess!

10 We're terribly late. We .... !

3 請以 **have to** 搭配正確時態的肯定句、否定句和疑問句，來完成句子。

1 She .... buy a new bike. Hers has been stolen.

2 We .... do a lot of work yesterday. We were really tired in the end.

3 I .... wait long. She arrived after five minutes.

4 .... you really .... get up at five o'clock every morning?

5 We .... sign all the documents before we could leave.

6 Everybody could speak English, so they .... use an interpreter in the meeting.

7 I .... find a new job. My firm has closed down.

8 We .... answer hundreds of emails today.

4 請使用 **must**、**don't have** 或 **should** 來完成句子，然後將 **1–6** 與 **A–F** 配對。

..... **1** We .... buy some food.

..... **2** Tomorrow's my day off.

..... **3** There's been an accident.

..... **4** You .... see this musical.

..... **5** I really .... clean the kitchen.

..... **6** You .... to worry.

A It's fantastic!

B Everything's alright.

C I .... to go to work.

D The fridge is nearly empty.

E I haven't cleaned it for a week.

F We .... call an ambulance.

5 以下是語言學校的校規，請圈出正確的用字。

1 You **can** / **have to** drive to the school, but you **mustn't** / **don't have to** park your car in the teachers' car park.

2 You **mustn't** / **don't have to** eat in the multimedia lab, but you **can** / **can't** have a sandwich in the students' room.

3 You **can** / **must** buy your own books, but you **can't** / **don't have to** buy your own CDs.

6 請使用 mustn't 或 don't/doesn't have to 搭配括號裡的動詞，來完成句子。

1 Your husband .... me to the station, I can take a taxi. (drive)

2 You .... on the ice, you could fall into the lake. (walk)

3 He .... a uniform for his job, but he must dress smartly. (wear)

4 Students .... school before the end of the lessons. (leave)

5 You .... the dishes tonight. I can do it tomorrow morning. (wash)

7 請使用 must/mustn't 和以下動詞，來完成與過去有關的推論。

win	have	cost	be	get up	be

1 Look how happy he is. He .... the competition.

2 They're still together. She .... his partner for at least ten years.

3 They .... a lot of money in the bank to buy that mansion.

4 Climbing that peak .... very hard. You look exhausted.

5 They're already here. They .... very early this morning.

6 Your ring looks very expensive. It .... at least £800.

8 請使用 must be、must have been、can't be、can't have 等用語完成意義相近的句子。

1 Surely you didn't go on vacation with no money.
  You ....

2 I'm sure there's a report on yesterday's athletics competition in the local newspaper.
  There ....

3 I'm certain that he isn't over 65. He's still working!
  He ....

4 I assume that he is fit, as he is a PE teacher.
  He ....

5 I'm certain that there is some coffee left. I bought it yesterday.
  There ....

6 You definitely didn't recharge the cell phone battery last night; it's off already.
  You ....

7 Surely she isn't her mother; she's far too young.
  She ....

8 I'm sure the person who's just left is the new manager.
  That ....

9 請以合適單字來完成句子。

1 You .... to know what to do before leaving.

2 "I .... you five pounds." "No, you don't .... me anything. Don't worry."

3 I'm always under pressure. I really .... work less.

4 You'd .... not spend all your money, you .... save some.

5 We were .... to go back to work before the end of our vacations.

6 You .... to listen to what I have to tell you.

7 You .... to come in the early morning. You can come later.

8 The train was .... at 9:30 but it was late.

9 You're not .... to go into the theater when the show has started.

10 "What .... we make for dinner tonight?" "Let's make chicken salad."

11 I'm not quite sure. .... I stay a little longer or .... I go straight away?

12 They were .... to abandon their farm because of the hurricane alert.

> **延伸補充**
>
> 在 **recommend**、**suggest**、**insist** 等動詞引導的次要子句裡，我們可以使用情態助動詞 **should**。此為典型的英式英文，且十分正式，口語英文裡則較常**省略 should** 與 **that**，而說：
>
> • Our teacher **suggests** we **take** the exam.
> • He **insisted** I **have** lunch with him.

---

10 請圈出正確的用字。

Glen [1]...... ride his motorbike so fast. And he [2]...... wear his crash helmet all the time. If he [3]...... regulations like that, he [4]...... so many fines.

His parents [5]...... his fines. If I [6]...... his mother, I [7]...... his motorcycle in the garage for a week or two after each fine. I [8]...... him to find some kind of Saturday job too, so that he could pay his fines himself. If he [9]...... use his own money, perhaps he [10]...... learn to be a bit more careful.

	Ⓐ	Ⓑ	Ⓒ
1	had better	wouldn't	shouldn't
2	had better to	hadn't better	ought to
3	didn't ignore	ignored not	wouldn't ignore
4	didn't get	wouldn't have got	ought not get
5	ought not to pay	had better pay	shouldn't to pay
6	were	am	would be
7	had better to lock	would lock	ought to lock
8	had better make	should make	would oblige
9	would be obliged	had better	had to
10	must	would	had

11 請以合適的動詞或情態助動詞，來完成以下短文。

Dear Janine,

I'm writing you from the garden of the Hotel Plaza! What am I doing here? I'm working. I've got a new job as junior receptionist. I started two weeks ago and I [1] .... say I'm enjoying what I'm doing.

I [2] .... work six hours a day five days a week. Twice a month I [3] .... work on the weekend. I [4] .... wear a uniform but luckily I [5] .... wear high-heeled shoes. I wouldn't be able to wear them for six hours, standing most of the time.

Anyway, you [6] .... see the hotel. The hall is huge with wonderful liberty decorations and elegant furniture. The guests [7] .... all be very rich because the rooms are extremely expensive. Yesterday a famous French actress arrived. She was [8] .... to come at about midday and lots of journalists were there but she didn't turn up until late in the evening when most of the journalists had left.

12 請找出錯誤並訂正出正確句子。

1 Our bus is due arriving in the next few minutes. Hurry up!

....

2 They were forced leave their home because of the flood.

....

3 "How much owe I you?" "Eight pounds."

....

4 You'd better to come to work on time if you want to keep your job.

....

5 Tess suggested to have lunch together tomorrow.

....

6 You look tired. Shall I to cook for you tonight?

....

Reflecting on grammar

請研讀文法規則，再判斷以下說法是否正確。

		True	False
1	must 和 have to 的否定句用法，因為意義相同，所以可互換使用。		
2	have to 不是情態助動詞，因此問句和否定句裡均需搭配 do/does/did。		
3	You don't have to、You don't need to、You needn't 的意義均相同。		
4	should 是情態助動詞 shall 的條件句用法。		
5	You'd better 的完整形式是 You would better。		
6	be due 用以表達「欠錢」的意思。		
7	「It's bound to happen any time soon.」是正確的說法。		
8	You'll be obliged to go 與 You'll be allowed to go 的意義相同。		
9	「Their plane is due to land in ten minutes.」是正確的句子。		
10	ought 是唯一需要後接 to + 原形動詞的情態助動詞。		

15 未來式 The Future

LESSON 1 各種未來式 / 現在進行式與簡單現在式表達未來
Different types of future tenses; the future with the present continuous and the present simple

表達未來的三大方法如下：

1 現在進行式   **They're leaving** at 10 p.m.

2 be going to 未來式   **They're going to leave**.

3 will 未來式   I think **they will leave** soon.

三種未來式各有適用的情況及不同的意思，要視講者的出發點和內容而定。
常常在相同情境下，可主觀運用不同未來式來表達。

FAQ

Q: 我總是會混淆這三種未來式的用法，不管怎麼選都會用錯！我要如何判斷該選哪種用法？

A: 一般而論，請在選用未來式之前，思考一下以下問題：

- 是你已記在日誌的預約事項嗎？是早已事先規劃的事項嗎？
  → 現在進行式
- 是你有意想做的事嗎？ → be going to 未來式
- 此將來會發生的情況，是否無法取決於你？是一種臆測嗎？
  → will 未來式

如需了解更詳細的解說，可查看第 275 頁的心智圖，來幫助你根據各種不同情況運用未來式。

1 請從三種未來式中，選出適合各題情境的未來式，答案可能不只一種。

1 The weather forecast says ...... on the weekend. (forecast)

   Ⓐ the sun is shining   Ⓑ it will be sunny   Ⓒ it's going to be sunny

2 I think Chelsea ...... the Cup. (prediction)

   Ⓐ is going to win   Ⓑ is winning   Ⓒ will win

3 ...... a party for my birthday. (intention)

   Ⓐ I will have   Ⓑ I'm going to have   Ⓒ I'm having

4 Grandma ...... on the five o'clock train. (planned action)

   Ⓐ is going to arrive   Ⓑ will arrive   Ⓒ is arriving

5 ...... to the dentist's at 11 o'clock. (appointment)

   Ⓐ I'm going   Ⓑ I'm going to go   Ⓒ I will go

6 ...... a trip to Scotland. (intention)

   Ⓐ I'm going to go on   Ⓑ I will go on   Ⓒ I'm going on

現在進行式表達未來

我們在 Unit 6（請參閱第 95 頁）學到可用現在進行式表達未來，句型如下：

> 主詞 + **am/is/are** + 動詞 ing

這種用法是表示：

1 通常在不久的將來會發生的行為、事實或預先規劃的
事件：We**'re playing** an important match tomorrow.

2 預先安排好的個人承諾、決定等事項，例如購票、
訂位、預約固定時間要做某事等：
- I **'m going** to the U2 concert on September 4th.
  I'm looking forward to it!

在這些情況下，句子裡會出現具有**未來意思**的時間用語，例如：
in ten minutes、at six o'clock、later in the day、tonight、
tomorrow、on the weekend、next week 等，此用法常與
go、**come**、**leave**、**arrive** 等移動動詞搭配：

- "**Are** you **coming** to my house **this afternoon**?"
  "Sorry, I can't. I **'m meeting** my aunt at the airport at **four o'clock**.
  She**'s arriving** from Florida."

---

2 請運用提示用詞，寫出「現在進行式」的句子或問句。

0 you / see / Mr. Randall / after the meeting / .
You are seeing Mr. Randall after the meeting.
....

1 we / visit / the Tate Gallery / at three o'clock / .
....
....

2 you / go shopping / this afternoon / ?
....
....

3 I / have dinner / at a Greek restaurant /
tonight / .
....
....

4 what time / you / go to work / tomorrow / ?
....
....

5 when / you / have / your exam / ?
....
....

6 we / get married / next Saturday / .
....
....

7 I / see / the optician / at half past ten /
tomorrow / .
....
....

8 they / leave / for New York / next week / .
....
....

9 who / you / meet / at ten o'clock / ?
....
....

10 where / he / have lunch / today / ?
....
....

3 請判讀句子，如果是代表現在的行動，請寫 **P**；如果是代表未來的行動，請寫 **F**。

...... **1** I'm not going to school tomorrow.

...... **2** We're having a great time on this island.

...... **3** Are you going to basketball practice this afternoon?

...... **4** Not all of my friends are coming to the party tonight.

...... **5** He isn't reading, he's sleeping. Look, his eyes are closed.

...... **6** The train's arriving. Hurry up!

...... **7** We're having a short break next week.

...... **8** Hey, you two! What are you doing? Copying?

簡單現在式表達未來

簡單現在式有時會用來表達**未來時態**，此情況較罕見，但特別適用於以下情況：

1 已安排的活動，例如旅遊行程。

2 會在固定時間發生的事件，例如交通工具到站與離站時間。

這個用法尤其需要搭配 **leave/arrive**、**open/close**、**start/finish** 這類的動詞與精準時間的描述。

VISITING HOURS
MONDAY- FRIDAY
9 am - 1 pm

SATURDAY - SUNDAY
9 am - 1 pm
4 pm - 6 pm

Tomorrow's Saturday, so visiting hours **start** at four.

---

4 導遊正在向柏林的遊客說明旅遊行程。請使用以下動詞來完成短文。

| meet (x2) get visit walk have (x3) |

"May I have your attention, please? Let me tell you what is happening today. We ¹........................... to the Siegel Hotel tonight at seven and we ²........................... dinner at the hotel. Tomorrow, we ³........................... after breakfast at 9:30 and ⁴........................... to the Pergamon Museum. It's not far from the hotel.

We arrive in Berlin at about 6 and check in at the hotel soon after.

We ⁵........................... the museum in the morning and afterwards ⁶........................... lunch in a restaurant nearby. Then you ⁷........................... a free afternoon. We ⁸........................... again in front of the museum at six to go back to the hotel together. Any questions?"

---

5 請將括號裡提示的動詞改成「簡單現在式」或「現在進行式」，來完成句子。

1 Do you know that the yoga course .... on March 1st? (start)

2 I .... on a trip to Bath next weekend. I want to see the Roman baths. (go)

3 We .... at Victoria Station at 7:50 p.m. Will you be there to meet us? (arrive)

4 "What .... you .... tomorrow?" "I don't know. I don't have any plans." (do)

5 Tomorrow I .... the house at 9 a.m. because the bus .... at quarter past. (leave / leave)

6 Louise .... in the school choir tonight. I'm going to see her! (sing)

7 I .... a party on Saturday. Would you like to come? (have)

8 We .... a couple of days in Brighton next week. We've just booked the hotel. (spend)

LESSON 2 be going to 未來式 The future with *be going to*

另一個表達未來的用法是 be going to，尤其適用於表達我們**有意執行、可操之在己去實現**的事。

❶ 肯定句

| 主詞 + **am/is/are** + **going to** + 動詞 |

I am going to help him.
縮讀形式：**I'm going . . .**

❷ 否定句

| 主詞 + **am/is/are not** + **going to** + 動詞 |

I am not going to help him.
縮讀形式：**I'm not going . . .**

❸ 疑問句

| （**Wh 疑問詞**）+ **am/is/are** + 主詞 + **going to** + 動詞 +? |

❹ 簡答句

| Yes, + 主格代名詞 + am/is/are.
No, + 主格代名詞 + 'm not/isn't/aren't. |

- "Are you going to help him?"
  "**Yes, I am.**"
- "Aren't you going to help him?"
  "**No, I'm not.**"
- "Who are you going to help?"
  "All of them, if I can."

❺ 在肯定句和否定句裡，較常使用縮讀形式：

- **She's going to** talk to him.
- **We aren't going to** read all of these books!

be going to 主要用於表達以下未來情境：

❶ 有意要做、但尚未仔細規劃的事，或尚未訂定行程的事

- I'm going to take courses in economics next year.（意指「我有意要修這門課，但還沒報名」，若說「I'm taking a course in economics in September. I start on the second.」則有「我已經報名、已有確定的課程時間」的意思，所以使用現在進行式）

❷ 長期的人生計畫

- I'm going to be a pilot when I grow up.（也可以說「I want to be a pilot.」；請參閱第 240 頁）
- I'm not going to live in this town forever.（也可以說「I don't want to live in this town forever.」）

在這些情況下，句子裡通常會出現時間用語，例如：this coming spring、in two hours、soon、next year、when I grow up、when I go to England 等相似用語：

- **Are** you **going to** find a job **when you go to London**?
- I'm **going to** be a pilot **when I grow up**.

> ❗ 在口語美式英文裡，常聽到 going to 被縮讀成 **gonna**（It's gonna be hard!），但這不是標準用法，就像 gotta（have got to）和 wanna（want to）一樣。

FAQ

Q: 我可以說「I'm going to go to university.」嗎？聽起來好像不太對。

A: 可以，不過移動動詞較常以現在進行式來表達（I'm going to university.），尤其是 go。

---

❶ 請運用括號裡提示的動詞搭配 be going to 用法，來完成句子。

1 We .... in the same office. (not work)

2 I .... a qualification as a nurse. (get)

3 He .... a Spanish course in the summer. (take)

4 .... you .... her a present? (buy)

5 They .... to a bigger house soon. (move)

6 When .... you .... this movie? (watch)

7 She .... for that job. (not apply)

8 Where .... you .... when you grow up? (live)

2 請將題目的動詞分別以 be going to 未來式和現在進行式，來完成 Ⓐ 句和 Ⓑ 句。

1 get married

Ⓐ We're .... this coming spring. In March maybe, or in April. We'll see.

Ⓑ We're .... on May 8th. We've already sent invitations to everyone.

2 not work

Ⓐ I'm .... this weekend. The boss told me they don't need me to. Good news!

Ⓑ I'm .... on the weekend. The project I'm working on is nearly finished and I need to take a break.

3 bring

Ⓐ I'm .... a packed lunch on tomorrow's trip.

Ⓑ I'm .... sandwiches, chips and a juice. I've already bought them.

---

be going to 未來式還適用於以下情況：

3 **表達不久的將來絕對會發生的事。** 在此情況下，句子裡通常不會有時間用語，因為我們能懂此類句子代表「現在」、「立即」就要發生的意思。

- Shhh . . . The movie's **going to** start.
- Step back. The train's **going to** arrive.

如需表達**即將**發生的事件，我們亦可使用 **be about to** 的說法，但此用法較少見：
My mother **is about to** retire from work.

4 **在課程、會議或類似情境裡將要討論的內容**

- We'**re going to** revise the use of the article.
- Today I'**m going to** deal with the problem of cyberbullying.

5 **根據事實證據進行預測，或很確定事情會以特定方式發生**

- I'm sure it'**s going to** be a great party.
- Things **aren't going to** change; that's for certain.

不過，如果要臆測某事，will 未來式是最常見的時態用法（請參閱第 270 頁）。

---

3 請運用 be going to 搭配以下動詞來完成句子。

| take   not change   be   not do   tell |

Luke Are you ready? The headmaster [1] .... here in a minute.

Debbie Good! I [2] .... him why we aren't happy with the new school rules.

Luke There's no point! He knows and he [3] .... anything about it.

Debbie Isn't he? Well, if nobody speaks up, things [4] ....

Luke I don't think we can do much, anyway.

Debbie You're always so negative. When [5] .... you .... some action?

Luke Alright. I'll be on your side this time. There! He's coming.

4 請使用 **be going to** 來改寫句子。請記得維持原句的意義。

1 He wants to be an engineer when he grows up.

....

2 Get an umbrella. It's about to rain.

....

3 I want to plant some fruit trees in my garden this coming spring.

....

4 We want to clean out the garage on the weekend.

....

5 Stop chatting! The lesson is about to start.

....

6 Look at those grey clouds. I'm sure it will rain soon.

....

7 Today I want you to work in pairs.

....

LESSON 3 will 未來式 The future with *will*

will 未來式（亦稱為簡單未來式），是最廣為運用的未來式。此未來式的句型為情態助動詞 will（適用於所有人稱）加上原形動詞。

❶ 肯定句

| 主詞 + **will**（縮讀形式為 'll）+ 動詞 |

• I **will** be there. / I**'ll** be there.

❷ 否定句

| 主詞 + **will not**（縮讀形式為 won't）+ 動詞 |

• I **will not** be there. / I **won't** be there.

在第一人稱單數和複數的句子裡可用 shall 取代 will：「I/We shall be there.」但注意，這不是現今英文的常見用法。

❸ 疑問句

| **（Wh 疑問詞）** + **will/won't** + 主詞 + 動詞 + ？ |

❹ 簡答句

Yes, + 主格代名詞 + will.
No, + 主格代名詞 + won't.

• "**Will** you be there?" "Yes, I will."
• "**Won't** you be there?" "No, I won't."
• "When **will** you be there?"
  "Tomorrow at 11."

縮讀形式的用法雖然最常看到，但不能用於肯定簡答句：Yes, they will.
NOT Yes, they'll.

❶ 請重新排序單字來造句。

1 get / She / will / by / there / noon / .

....

2 It / not / will / again / happen / .

....

3 will / The / set / sun / 7:30 / at / tonight / .

....

4 with / I / always / be / will / you / .

....

5 will / It / cloudy / be / and / tomorrow / cold / .

....

6 will / We / survive / not / on / money / this / for / whole / a / week / .

....

....

7 ahead / Go / , / I / you / follow / will / .

....

8 ready / Everything / be / o'clock / by / will / three / .

....

2 以下列動詞的 **will** 未來式，完成問句和衍生的答句。

> work   find   win   like   be   make   have   stay

1 "What do you think? .... I .... a good job?" "Yes, I'm sure .... !"

2 "................... she .... on Saturday?" "No, ... Actually, she quit the job."

3 "................... it .... a hot weekend?" "No, ... It will be quite cold."

4 "................... you .... here a bit longer?" "Yes, ... I can stay until five."

5 "................... you .... time to finish everything by Friday?" "No, ... , I'm afraid."

6 "................... she .... this book?" "Yes, I think .... She said she likes fantasy."

7 "................... they .... the Cup Final?" "I'm not sure ...."

8 "................... they .... a sequel of this action movie?" "I hope .... It's fantastic."

---

will 未來式主要適用於以下情況：

1 表達無法操之在己而鐵定會發生的事實：
  • I **will** be 50 next year.   • It **will** soon be winter.

2 進行臆測、提問或表達我們認為事情會如何發展。
  句子內常包含 I think / I don't think、I guess、I expect、I'm sure、I wonder 等類似用語：
  • I **think** we'**ll** win the championship this year. We have a good chance.
  • "What **will** you do now?" "**I guess** I'**ll** just wait and see what happens."

will 後面可搭配表達臆測肯定度的副詞，例如 definitely、certainly、probably：
• This match **will definitely** end in a draw.

> **1** 如果是有證據且十分確定的推測，可使用 be going to 未來式：
>   I'm sure we'll have a great time. = We're going to have a great time.
>
> **2** 如果是有機會或有可能發生的事件，我們亦可使用情態助動詞 may/might：
>   They will probably arrive soon. = They may arrive soon.

---

3 請圈出正確的用字。

1 The weather **probably will / will probably** change soon.

2 I'm **think / sure** you will understand.

3 I don't think I **will / won't** apply for that job.

4 The bank will **be / have** closed tomorrow.

5 I wonder who the new headmaster **will be / was** !

6 My sister will **to start / start** university next week.

7 I **sure / hope** you'll have a nice journey.

8 She will certainly **get / gets** the promotion.

9 How long will **the game last / last the game**?

10 I don't think we'll **have / having** enough time.

---

will 未來式亦可表達：

3 承諾：
  • I'**ll** come and see you next year. I promise.

4 希望：
  • We hope we'**ll** be able to see you before you leave.

5 決心：
  • I know I haven't worked hard enough. I'**ll** try and work harder next term.
  • "What are your New Year resolutions?" "I'**ll** do more physical exercise and I'**ll** eat healthier food."

> 動詞 hope 後面，常使用簡單現在式 →
> I hope you will come. = I hope you **come**.

未來時間用語

採用 will 未來式時，通常會搭配**確切或不確切**的時間用語：

確切的時間用語	不確切時間用語
tomorrow / the day after tomorrow 明天／後天	in the (near) future 不久後的將來
next month / next year 下個月／明年	soon 很快地
in four days 四天內	later 不久後
in three years' time 三年內的時間	sooner or later 早晚
in (the year) 2050 在 2050 年	forever 永遠

4 請將以下各臆測填入正確的欄位。

Unemployment will be higher than now.	There will still be hunger and poverty.
Unemployment will be lower.	There will be no more wars.
Everybody will have enough to eat.	There will be less air pollution.
There will still be wars.	There will be a cure for most illnesses.
Air pollution will be worse.	There will be new diseases.

50 年後……	
樂觀預測	**悲觀預測**

5 請將 **1–10** 與 **A–J** 配對成完整句子。

..... **1** I expect the children   **A** and the days will get longer.

..... **2** It will soon be summer   **B** will be ready at 12 p.m.

..... **3** I hope you will all come   **C** and feed the dog every day!

..... **4** We'll do our best   **D** and I'll phone my sister for a chat.

..... **5** The room you've booked   **E** will behave well.

..... **6** Yes, Mom. I will walk   **F** to our housewarming party.

..... **7** I'll call around nine   **G** to check if there's anything you need.

..... **8** My mother will be 60 in May,   **H** to meet your expectations.

..... **9** In case of emergency   **I** but she looks much younger.

..... **10** I'll have a cup of tea   **J** I will call the police.

6 請圈出句中錯誤，訂正為正確的句子。

1 I'll always am on your side. You can be sure of this.

....

2 I don't think it will to rain today.

....

3 Between five days we'll be at the seaside. I can't wait!

....

4 We'll be best friends for always.

....

5 I'm busy now. I'll talk to you next.

....

6 The climate will get probably warmer in the future.

....

7 I willn't fight with my brother again, I promise!

....

8 Where I will meet Mr. Johnson?

....

9 Don't worry. They'll arrive soon or later.

....

10 Do you think you'll be free the day next tomorrow?

....

will 未來式還可表示：

6 **在講話當下臨時做的決定**：

- "So. Who's driving? You, John?" "Okay. I'**ll** drive as far as the next service station."
  （意指「我本來沒想到要開車，是在講話當下才決定」，而若說「I **am going to** drive tonight. I'm the only one who doesn't drink!」則是指「我事先就決定好了」，所以使用 be going to 未來式；請參閱第 267 頁）

而如果我們決定不做某事，則使用 **won't** → I **won't** go!

7 在第一類條件句的主要子句表達「**如果……將會發生……**」：

- If we have time, we'**ll** visit the British Museum.（可參閱 Unit 16 Lesson 2）

FAQ

Q: 通常我們會在求婚的時候說「Will you marry me?」，然後回答「Yes, I will.」，但這應該不是早就決定要做的事嗎？為什麼大家不說「Are you going to marry me?」？

Will you marry me?

A: 如我們在 Unit 13 Lesson 3 所學到的，情態助動詞 will 可表達意願，因此我們可以把這兩句理解為「Do you want to marry me?」、「Yes, I want to.」。情態助動詞 will 在這裡是表達意願和承諾的概念。

7 請先將 1–8 的句子與 A–H 的句子配對，然後再將句意有「有意執行」的句子**畫藍色底線**；
「講話當下才做決定」的句子**畫紅色底線**。

1 I'm going to help them. They really need it.
2 Hi! Welcome back. I'll help you with your bags.
3 I'm going to buy you all a drink tonight.
4 How much do we have to pay?
5 Are we going to get a taxi to the station tomorrow?
6 Oh dear! We're late for the meeting.
7 We're going to a Japanese restaurant tonight.
8 Here's the menu. What will you have?

A Never mind. I'll pay for everyone.
B We'll get a taxi then.
C Good idea. I'll help too.
D That's great! I'm going to have sushi.
E Really? How come? Is it your birthday?
F Oh, thanks. That's so kind of you.
G Er . . . I think I'll have the fish.
H Yes, I think that's the best thing to do.

1 .....   **2** .....   **3** .....   **4** .....   **5** .....   **6** .....   **7** .....   **8** .....

LESSON 4 未來進行式 / 未來完成式 Future continuous; future perfect

未來式也有漸進狀態，文法上稱為**未來進行式**，且適用於所有人稱：

肯定句	主詞 + **will be** ('ll be) + **動詞 ing**
否定句	主詞 + **will not be** (won't be) + **動詞 ing**
疑問句	（Wh 疑問詞） + **will/won't** + 主詞 + **動詞 ing** + ?

* I**'ll be waiting** for you.
* I **won't be working** at this time tomorrow.
* **Will** you **be waiting** for me when I come home?

1 未來進行式用來表達**即將進行的事**，或在**未來的特定時間點正在進行的事**。承襲進行式的意義，
未來進行式代表**某行為將持續一段時間**：

* You**'ll be traveling** to Spain at this time tomorrow.
* Don't call me between 3 p.m. and 5 p.m. this afternoon. I **will be taking** my exams
  at that time.

2 我們也可用未來進行式取代現在進行式，以表示：

1 已安排好行程的待辦事項：
I**'ll be attending** a conference at nine o'clock tomorrow.
= I**'m attending** a conference at nine o'clock tomorrow.

2 詢問他人的計畫：
* **What will** you **be doing** on the weekend? = **What are** you **doing** on the weekend?
* **Will** you **be studying** tonight? = **Are** you **studying** tonight?

1 你正掛念著住在巴哈馬的朋友。請以「未來進行式」完成短文。

I wish I could go on vacation with my friend Stephanie. Next week she ¹............................ (lie)
on a beach in the Bahamas. She ²................................. (relax) and ³................................. (enjoy)
the sunshine, while I will be here in England in the cold rainy weather. Next week
I ⁴................................. (work) eight hours a day every day including Saturday. And, on Sunday,
I ⁵................................. (clean) the house and ⁶................................. (cook) for the following week
as usual. Who wouldn't want a break?

2 請以下列動詞的「未來進行式」與括號內的詞完成 **1–7** 的問句，再與 **A–G** 的答句配對。

> have do leave go use travel go out

1 .... (you) a night shift this week?

2 .... (you) with your new boyfriend tonight?

3 Where .... (they) to on vacation in the summer?

4 What time .... (you) tomorrow morning?

5 When .... (Robert) his next piano lesson?

6 .... (you) to Leeds by bus?

7 .... (you) the car today, Dad?

1 ..... **2** ..... **3** ..... **4** ..... **5** ..... **6** ..... **7** .....

A We'll be leaving quite early.

B He'll be having it at four this afternoon.

C No, I'll be doing one next week.

D No, I won't be going anywhere in the car today.

E They'll be going to the Lake District as usual.

F No, we'll be going by train.

G No, we'll be having a quiet evening at home.

簡單未來完成式與進行式

簡單未來完成式的句型如下：

肯定句	主詞 + **will have ('ll have)** + 動詞的過去分詞
否定句	主詞 + **will not have (won't have)** + 動詞的過去分詞
疑問句	（**Wh 疑問詞**） + **will /won't** + 主詞 + **have** + 動詞的過去分詞 + ?

❶ 簡單未來完成式用以表達「**會在未來某時間點發生過的事**」：

- By the time you get up, the sun **will have risen**.

❷ 未來完成進行式的句型為 **will have been** + 動詞 **ing**，用以表達「**會在未來特定期間內，持續一陣子且完成的行為**」；此用法並不常見。

- I **will have been watching** three movies by the time we land in Los Angeles.

❸ 未來完成式通常會搭配 **by two o'clock**、**by the time you come back**、**in three weeks' time** 等時間用語。

---

3 請運用括號裡動詞的「簡單未來完成式」，來完成句子。

1 By the time you come back, your parents .... (leave)

2 I hope I .... my degree by this time next year. (take)

3 In ten years' time, I .... very rich! (become)

4 You .... to speak German fluently in two years' time. (learn)

5 I .... making dinner by the time you arrive. (finish)

6 By the time you count to 20 everyone .... ! (disappear)

4 請以下列動詞的「未來進行式」或「未來完成式」，來完成句子。

| read eat recover finish use feel |

1 By six tomorrow morning, I .... my night shift.

2 You .... a bit confused about the state of our relationship, I'm sure.

3 .... you .... the documents later?

4 I'm sure he .... from his cold in a week's time.

5 Nobody .... this computer this morning.

6 I .... certainly .... my lunch by two o'clock.

表達未來的方式

長期的人生計畫
I**'m going to** study biology at university.

有意執行的事
We**'re going to** spend our vacations in Spain.

BE GOING TO

預測（有事實根據）
Watch out! The mirror **is going to** fall on your head.

現在進行式

未來式

簡單現在式

規劃好的未來活動
They**'re meeting** their boss at 10 a.m. tomorrow.

固定時間
Our train **leaves** at 9:15 tomorrow.

WILL

希望
I hope he **will** pass his final exam.

氣象預報
It **will** be foggy in the morning.

未來事實
I**'ll** be 16 on my next birthday.

預測（無事實根據）
We expect the economic crisis **will** last for a couple of years.

承諾／決心
I promise I**'ll** do more work this year.

臨時起意的決定
Don't worry. I**'ll** pick you up at the station.

ROUND UP 15

1 請圈出正確的用字。

1 We think our team **will win** / **is winning** the competition tomorrow.
2 "Mom's case is heavy." "**I'm carrying** / **I'll carry** it for her."
3 The sun **is going to set** / **will set** at 5:37 a.m. tomorrow afternoon.
4 "What time **do you meet** / **are you meeting** Mr. Norton?" "We **meet** / **are meeting** at 9:30 a.m. tomorrow morning."
5 Dan! The buzzer went! **Will you open** / **Are you opening** the door, please?
6 I don't think computers **are going to** / **will** replace teachers in the future.
7 "I haven't got my dictionary with me today." "Don't worry! **I'm going to** / **I'll** give you mine."
8 They **are leaving** / **will leave** at 8 a.m. tomorrow morning.
9 I promise that I **will come** / **am coming** and see you soon.
10 At this time next Sunday, we will **lie** / **be lying** on a beach in Greece.

2 請以 be going to、will 或現在進行式來完成句子。

1 I .... the Christmas shopping tomorrow. (do) [planned]
2 .... at the party tonight? (you, be) [intention]
3 It .... later this evening. (rain) [prediction]
4 I .... here again. (never come) [promise]
5 What .... next weekend? (you, do) [intention]
6 I .... tickets for tomorrow's concert. (buy) [intention]
7 I think Barcelona .... the championship. (win) [prediction]
8 Jane .... to Rio for the vacation. (fly) [planned]
9 I .... you at 5 p.m. (meet) [immediate decision]
10 I .... a haircut tomorrow. (have) [planned]

3 請以括號裡動詞的「簡單未來式」或「未來進行式」，來完成短文。

Tomorrow at this time, Steve and Emma [1] .... (fly) from London to Hong Kong.
It [2] .... (be) the first time that they have been to China. They [3] .... (leave)
Heathrow Airport at 10 a.m. and they [4] .... (fly) for 12 hours. At 11 a.m., they
[5] .... (fly) over Germany. They [6] .... (arrive) in Hong Kong at 10 p.m.

4 請判讀句子，並圈選出正確的時態。

1 Will I **be feeling** / **have felt** better by this time next week?
2 The students will **have used** / **have been using** the computer lab for two hours by ten o'clock.
3 The human resources manager will **have interviewed** / **be interviewing** James right now.
4 "Will you **have finished** / **be finishing** your essay by tomorrow?" "Yes, I'll hand it in tomorrow morning."
5 The kids won't **be eating** / **have eaten** their lunch at 11 a.m. Lunch break starts at 12 p.m.
6 My daughter will **be doing** / **have done** her first exam at university tomorrow at this time.

5 請選出正確的答案。

1 There's no milk left, Paul. .... some when you're in town?

Ⓐ Are you getting   Ⓑ Will you get   Ⓒ Are you going to get

2 Here are the tickets. We have to run. The train .... in two minutes.

Ⓐ will have left   Ⓑ is going to leave   Ⓒ is leaving

3 I've got an appointment with the dentist. I .... him at ten o'clock tomorrow morning.

Ⓐ am going to see   Ⓑ am seeing   Ⓒ will see

4 I talked to the manager last week, and we .... again tomorrow.

Ⓐ talk   Ⓑ will have talked   Ⓒ are going to talk

5 .... to Australia, or haven't they decided yet?

Ⓐ Do they move   Ⓑ They will move   Ⓒ Are they going to move

6 It's nice weather, so I think we .... to the beach next weekend.

Ⓐ will go   Ⓑ would go   Ⓒ are going

7 I must go. The children .... home from school soon.

Ⓐ will have come   Ⓑ are going to come   Ⓒ will be coming

8 I .... some food for you in the fridge.

Ⓐ will leave   Ⓑ will have left   Ⓒ will be left

9 Please call back after 11. He .... before then.

Ⓐ will be back   Ⓑ won't be back   Ⓒ is not being back

10 He needs to go to bed early. He .... for at least 12 hours tomorrow.

Ⓐ will have driven   Ⓑ will be driven   Ⓒ will be driving

6 請依據括號內的指示，寫出你（**You**）與蘇珊（**Susan**）的對話。

You ....
(Ask Susan what she's going to do next summer.)

Susan ....
(Go to Cannes and attend a French course.)

You ....
(Ask how long she's going to stay there.)

Susan ....
(Three weeks. Suggests going too.)

You ....
(You can't. Working this summer.)

Susan ....
(Asks you what you're going to work as and where.)

You ....
(Receptionist in a hotel in Geneva.)

Susan ....
(Says she will bring a present from Cannes.)

過去的未來式：was/were going to　

❶ **肯定句**表達過去有意執行的事，可能是在過去還沒實現，或者是我們不確定過去是否已實現：
- I **was going to** sell my house last year, but then I changed my mind.
- When I last saw you, you **were going to** move to London. Have you moved there yet?

❷ **否定句**（wasn't/weren't going to）表達的是我們過去無意執行某事，或是我們本來不想做某事，但還是在過去發生了這件事：
- I **wasn't going to** see her again, but she insisted on getting together one more time.

❸ 當要問及他人的意圖時，可以使用**否定疑問句**：
- "**Weren't they going to** leave yesterday?"
  "Yes, they were. But they didn't. They're leaving today."

> ❗ 我們亦可在間接敘述句使用 **would ＋ 原形動詞**，來表達過去的未來式。
> They said they **would leave** the next day.
> = They said they **were going to leave** the next day.（請參閱第 351 頁）

---

7 請使用 was/were going to 改寫出意義相近的句子。

1 Sarah wanted to be an actress when she was younger.

....

2 I did not intend to study abroad.

....

3 They wanted to share their apartment with a friend.

....

4 We had an appointment for the next day, but he didn't turn up.

....

5 We wanted to have the party at the local Youth Club, but it was not available.

....

6 It looked as if it would rain last night, but it didn't .

....

8 請閱讀以下短文，圈出正確的用字。

Sometimes I look at my two teenage children and I wonder what they will [1] **do / be doing** in ten years' time. Will they [2] **have worked / be working** or will they [3] **be / being** unemployed? [4] **Will / Are** they still be living in England or will they [5] **have moved / have been moved** to some other country? [6] **Will they be / Are they** married? And [7] **are they having / will they have** any children? In about five years' time, they will [8] **be finishing / have finished** secondary school and they will [9] **be thinking / have thought** about their future. Will they look for a job or will they go to university? I hope at least one of them [10] **will decide / is deciding** to study medicine, but I don't think either will [11] **want / be wanting** to follow their father's example. The important thing is that they [12] **will / want** realize their dreams, whatever they are. And what about me? What will I [13] **be / have doing** in ten years' time? I hope I will [14] **have worked / be working** less than now. And I hope I [15] **will / won't** have time to travel to America, just like I was going to do when I was young. But then I got married and had two children . . . and all the big traveling plans had to be postponed!

Q: 我聽過一句歌詞叫「It's gonna be alright.」，這句話到底是什麼意思呢？

A: **gonna** 是美式英文中取代 **going to** 的非正式用法，所以這句是說「一切都會沒事、一切自然會迎刃而解」。不過，在書寫時應避免使用 gonna、wanna 和 gotta 等縮讀形式。

9 下方有四個句子有誤，請找出錯誤處並訂正。

1 Tomorrow at this time I'll hiking in the Alps.

....

2 You needn't worry. Whatever will be, will be.

....

3 I hope my children will have been leaving in a peaceful world.

....

4 The sea level will be steadily risen in the next fifty years.

....

5 The glaciers will melt if the temperature keeps rising.

....

6 "Are you taking an early train tomorrow morning?" "Yes, I'm leaving at 6:30."

....

7 "What will you have done in ten years' time?" "I hope I'll be working in the marketing field."

....

8 "Are all your students going to study Art next year?" "No, some are going to take up a musical instrument."

....

Reflecting on grammar

請研讀文法規則，再判斷以下說法是否正確。

		True	False
1	現在進行式和簡單現在式，只能在特定情況使用未來式。		
2	要表達有意在未來執行某事時，需使用 be going to + 原形動詞。		
3	「He probably will come with me.」的語序是正確的。		
4	「I will pay.」的否定句是「I willn't pay.」或「I'll not pay.」。		
5	如需表達承諾、我們自己的看法或臆測未來情況，我們通常會使用 will 未來式。		
6	「We will have finished our report between three weeks' time.」是正確的句子。		
7	「I will be having dinner in Madrid tomorrow at this time.」屬於未來完成式的句型。		
8	如果是在講話當下臨時做的決定，我們通常會使用 will 未來式。		
9	「Our bus leaves at 7 tomorrow morning.」是正確的句子。		
10	shall 可取代第三人稱單數未來式的 will，但此用法已少見於現今英文。		

情態助動詞和其他動詞：溝通功能複習表

義務或必要性 obligation or necessity	不一定必要 lack of necessity	禁令 prohibition
• We **must** study hard. • We **have to** study hard. • We**'ve got to** study hard. • We **need to** study hard. • We **had to** study hard last year. • We**'ll have to** study hard next year.	• We **don't have to** study hard. • We **don't need to** study hard. • We **needn't** study hard. • We **didn't have to** study hard last year. • We **won't have to** study hard next year.	• You **mustn't** talk in the library. • You **can't** talk in the library. • **Don't** talk in the library. • **No** talking in the library.

建議 advice	推論 deduction	請求指示 requests for instructions
• You **should** study hard. • You **ought to** study hard. • You **had better** study hard. • You **shouldn't worry about** the exam.	• It **must** be late. • It **can't** be late. • It **should** be easy. • It **ought to** be easy. • It **might** be easy.	• What **shall** I do? • What **should** I do? • What **can** we do? • **Shall** we turn right or left?

主動協助 offers of help	能力 ability	可能性 possibility
• **Shall** I help you? • **Can** I help you? • **Could** I help you? • I**'d like to** help you. • **Do** you **want** me to help you? • **Let** me help you! • I**'ll** help you!	• I **can** ski. • I **could** ski when I was young. • I **can't** ride a horse. • I **couldn't** ride a horse last year. • I **wasn't able to** break his record. • I'm afraid I **won't be able to** break his record.	• I **can** go out tonight. （十分確定） • I **may** go out tonight. （有可能） • I **might** go out tonight. （不確定） • I**'m likely to** go out tonight. （有可能） • **The odds are that** I'm going out tonight. （口語）

許可 permission	提出要求（某物） requests (to have something)	提出要求（請他人做某事） requests (for others to do something)
• **Can** I go now? • **Could** I go now? • **May** I go now? • You **can** go now. • You **may** go now. • I **wasn't allowed to** go. • They **didn't let** me go. • I'm sure I **will be allowed to** go. • I'm sure they **will let** me go.	• **Can** I have a cola, please? • **Could** I have a cola, please? • I**'d like (to have)** a cola. • I **want** a cola.	• **Will** you come here, please? • **Can** you come here? • **Could** you come here? • **Do you mind** coming here? • **Would** you mind coming here? • I**'d like you to** come here. • I **want you to** come here right now!

主動提議 offers	提議與提案 suggestions and proposals	嚮往之事與喜好 wants and preferences
• **Will** you have a cola? • **Would** you have a cola? • **Would** you like a cola? • **Do** you **want** a cola? • **How/What about** a cola? • **Have** a cola!	• **Shall** we go to the park? • **Should** we go to the park? • **Let's** go to the park. • **How/What about** going to the park? • **Why don't we** go to the park? • **Would you like to** go to the park?	• I **want to** go home. • I**'d like to** go home. • I **wish** I **could** go home. • **If only** I **could** go home. • I**'d prefer to** go home. • I**'d rather** go home (than stay here).

情態助動詞和其他動詞：時態複習表

can / could / be able to

簡單現在式	過去簡單式	未來式
• can/can't • am/am not able to • is/isn't able to • are/aren't able to	• could/couldn't • was/wasn't able to • were/weren't able to	• will/won't be able to
現在完成式	**過去完成式**	**未來完成式**
• have/haven't been able to • has/hasn't been able to	• had/hadn't been able to	• will/won't have been able to
條件句	**條件句過去式**	
• could/couldn't • would/wouldn't be able to	• could/couldn't have • would/wouldn't have been able to	

may / might / be allowed to

簡單現在式	過去簡單式	未來式
• may / may not • am / am not allowed to • is/isn't allowed to • are/aren't allowed to	• was/wasn't allowed to • were/weren't allowed to	• will/won't be allowed to
現在完成式	**過去完成式**	**未來完成式**
• have/haven't been allowed to • has/hasn't been allowed to	• had/hadn't been allowed to	• will/won't have been allowed to
條件句	**條件句過去式**	
• might / might not • would/wouldn't be allowed to	• might have / might not have • would/wouldn't have been allowed to	

must / have (got) to / need / be compelled/obliged to / should

簡單現在式	過去簡單式	未來式
• must/mustn't • need/needn't • don't/doesn't need to • have/haven't (got) to • has/hasn't got to • don't/doesn't have to	• had / didn't have to • need / didn't need to • was/wasn't compelled to • was/wasn't obliged to • were/weren't compelled to • were/weren't obliged to	• will/won't have to • will/won't be compelled to • will/won't be obliged to
現在完成式	**過去完成式**	**未來完成式**
• has/hasn't been compelled to • have/haven't been obliged to	• had/hadn't been compelled to • had/hadn't been obliged to	• will/won't have had to • will/won't have been compelled to • will/won't have been obliged to
條件句	**條件句過去式**	
• should/shouldn't • would/wouldn't have to	• should/shouldn't have • would/wouldn't have had to	

Revision and Exams 5 (UNITS 13 – 14 – 15)

1 請使用以下字詞來完成短文。

wouldn't like	studying	needs	would like
be allowed	she's going to apply	has	she's going to learn
would prefer	she'd rather go	would like her	wants to

Jeanine ¹..................................... to work for a charity after university. That's why she's currently ²..................................... at the faculty of International Studies in Aberdeen, Scotland. She's in her second year. This year ³..................................... for a scholarship to spend six months in another country. She ⁴..................................... to go to an English-speaking country because she ⁵..................................... learn a new language; ⁶..................................... to East Asia, possibly Japan, because she loves Japanese culture and ⁷..................................... Japanese. If she can't go to Asia, her second choice is America—she ⁸..................................... to go to South America rather than North America. And if she ⁹..................................... to stay in Europe, she hopes she'll ¹⁰..................................... to study in Greece. Jeanine's parents ¹¹..................................... to continue her studies in Scotland near home, but she really ¹²..................................... to be independent.

2 請運用括號裡的動詞搭配 **will** 或 **be going to** 未來式，來完成對話。

Nick　　Guess what! I ¹..................................... (have) a job interview tomorrow morning at ten.

Lindsey　Really? Where?

Nick　　At Debenhams—you know, the big department store in the center of town.

Lindsey　Great! Have you thought about the questions they ²..................................... (ask) you?

Nick　　Not really, but I ³..................................... (answer) them honestly.

Lindsey　They ⁴..................................... (probably – ask) you why you want the job.

Nick　　Well, that's okay. I ⁵..................................... (tell) them I want the job because I like selling things. I'm the right person for them.

Lindsey　Good! It sounds as if you ⁶..................................... (be) fine.
　　　　　I'm sure you ⁷..................................... (get) the job!

3 這是尼克（**Nick**）的部分面試內容。請依照括號裡的指示與動詞來完成對話。

Manager　You know you ¹..................................... (deal – *will* future continuous) with customers, so you ²..................................... (have to – *will* future simple) be polite and patient with all of them.

Nick　　Sure, I know. ³..................................... (I – have to – *will* future) wear a uniform?

Manager　Yes, you ⁴..................................... (have to – *will* future) wear a suit.

Nick　　⁵..................................... (I – have to – *will* future) buy it myself?

Manager　No, we'll buy it for you, but you will need to try it on.

Nick　　⁶..................................... (I – have to – *will* future) work on weekends?

Manager　You ⁷..................................... (have to – *will* future) work only one weekend per month. ⁸..................................... (you – work – past simple) weekends in your previous job?

Nick　　Yes, I ⁹..................................... (work – past simple) every second Sunday, but I didn't mind it.

4 請閱讀以下兩位同事之間的對話，填入 must、have、need 或 want 的適當變化。

Ryan   ¹............................ you .... to go to Bristol again on Friday, Patricia?

Patricia   No, I ²............................ to relax a bit, so I'm taking Friday off. But Mr. Paisley
³............................ me to go to New York for the annual conference next week,
so I ⁴............................ prepare for that.

Ryan   I've prepared most of the documents. ⁵............................ you .... me to
prepare the slides for you?

Patricia   You ⁶............................ to. The presentation is ready. What I still ⁷............................ to do
is to get some dollars from the bank.

Ryan   And you ⁸............................ forget your passport! Last time you went to the States,
I ⁹............................ to rush to the airport to bring it to you.

Patricia   You're right. And I ¹⁰............................ to get a visa too. By the way, ¹¹............................
I .... to sign the documents before I leave?

Ryan   Yes, but you ¹²............................ to do it now.

5 你和你的瑞典朋友都對海外暑期工作感興趣。你在英格蘭的朋友正好傳了一封電子郵件給你，是美國夏令營的相關資訊，你自己則是找到一則法國南部夏令營的廣告。請閱讀兩篇短文，並運用所有資訊，來寫電子郵件給你的瑞典朋友。請在郵件中說明兩份工作的差異、聊聊你偏好的工作，並詢問朋友的看法。

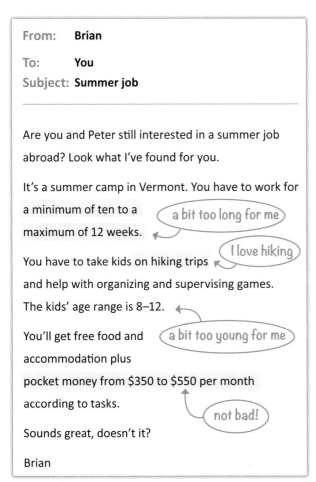

From: **Brian**

To: **You**

Subject: **Summer job**

Are you and Peter still interested in a summer job
abroad? Look what I've found for you.

It's a summer camp in Vermont. You have to work for
a minimum of ten to a ~ a bit too long for me
maximum of 12 weeks.

~ I love hiking
You have to take kids on hiking trips
and help with organizing and supervising games.
The kids' age range is 8–12. ~ a bit too young for me

You'll get free food and
accommodation plus
pocket money from $350 to $550 per month
according to tasks. ~ not bad!

Sounds great, doesn't it?

Brian

Le Pomier – Grenoble

Do you want to work during
the summer and improve
your French?

Do you like life in the open air?
join us and pick fruit for six weeks. ~ shorter period – better for me

You'll get free food and
accommodation on
our farm, plus evening
entertainment. ~ good!

40€ pocket money per week. ~ not much – but there aren't many expenses

Free excursions
on Sundays.

6 請看一下左欄的指示，選出正確的答案。

ALL VISITORS
You must return your headphones to the counter at the end of the tour.

1 Ⓐ Visitors can take the equipment home.
　Ⓑ Visitors have to give the equipment back when they've finished using it.
　Ⓒ Visitors must return to the hall after the tour.

This car park is for use on weekdays only during the bank working hours.

2 Ⓐ Cars can be parked here on Sunday mornings.
　Ⓑ This car park is locked at night.
　Ⓒ This car park can be used only by the bank staff.

ROADWORKS AHEAD
Take the first road on the right and follow the arrows.

3 Ⓐ You must follow the road ahead of you.
　Ⓑ You must keep to the right side of the road.
　Ⓒ You are obliged to make a detour because of roadworks.

The elevator to the roof garden is out of order. Please use the next free one to the 19th floor, then climb the last flight of stairs.

4 Ⓐ You must use the stairs from the first floor to go to the roof garden.
　Ⓑ There's only one elevator going straight to the roof garden and it doesn't work.
　Ⓒ There's only one elevator in this place.

Doug, Peter and I must finish some urgent work tonight. Can we play squash on Saturday? Could you tell Dave too?

Larry

5 Ⓐ Larry can't play squash today, but Peter can.
　Ⓑ Doug would like to play squash on Saturday.
　Ⓒ Larry was supposed to play with Doug and two more people tonight.

7 請閱讀以下短文，選出正確的答案。

From next week, life ⁰..C.. very different for Mark Lampard. On Monday, he ¹...... his new job as a stuntman. Mark's really excited, even if he knows it's ²...... a dangerous job. Mark knows he ³...... nervous at first, but he ⁴...... to it. In a few weeks, he ⁵...... to start work on movie sets—he could soon be the man you ⁶...... flying through a window or jumping from an airplane wearing James Bond's clothes! In September, he ⁷...... in a TV series, so you ⁸...... definitely see him then. Mark has chosen a risky career—but he hopes it ⁹...... challenging and interesting. One thing he can probably be sure of is that the job ¹⁰...... boring.

0 Ⓐ is going to be	Ⓑ is being	Ⓒ will be	Ⓓ is
1 Ⓐ start	Ⓑ is starting	Ⓒ going to start	Ⓓ will starting
2 Ⓐ being	Ⓑ going to be	Ⓒ will be	Ⓓ is going to be
3 Ⓐ feels	Ⓑ is feeling	Ⓒ to feel	Ⓓ will be feeling
4 Ⓐ will be look forward	Ⓑ is looking forward	Ⓒ look forward	Ⓓ is look forward
5 Ⓐ is going	Ⓑ will be	Ⓒ will be going	Ⓓ will
6 Ⓐ going to see	Ⓑ are seeing	Ⓒ see	Ⓓ have seen
7 Ⓐ will appearing	Ⓑ is appearing	Ⓒ is going appear	Ⓓ appear
8 Ⓐ are	Ⓑ do	Ⓒ have	Ⓓ will
9 Ⓐ is being	Ⓑ will have been	Ⓒ will be	Ⓓ will going to be
10 Ⓐ isn't	Ⓑ won't be	Ⓒ doesn't	Ⓓ not

8 請使用提示用詞在內的二至五個單字，來完成意義相近的句子，可看下方例句。

0 The train from Glasgow will arrive in ten minutes.

　　DUE　　The train from Glasgow ....is due to........... arrive in ten minutes.

1 By this time tomorrow, he will be in hospital.

　　GONE　　By this time tomorrow, he .... into hospital.

2 My dentist's appointment is at 11 tomorrow.

　　SEEING　I .... the dentist at 11 tomorrow.

3 Your temperature will have gone down to normal by this evening.

　　HAVE　　You .... a temperature by this evening.

4 You should wear warmer clothes. It's cold today.

　　TO　　You .... wear warmer clothes. It's cold today.

5 Shall I go to the market to buy some fruit, Jenny?

　　WANT　　................................... go to the market to buy some fruit, Jenny?

6 Our bus won't arrive for another 20 minutes. Let's have some coffee while we're waiting.

　　DUE　　Our bus .... for another 20 minutes. Let's have some coffee while we're waiting.

7 You ought not to sunbathe in the middle of the day.

　　BETTER You .... in the middle of the day.

8 Accidents will happen for sure if people drive so fast on icy roads.

　　BOUND Accidents .... if people drive so fast on icy roads.

9 Jason used to organize trips out with his friends when he was a teenager.

　　WOULD Jason .... with his friends when he was a teenager.

10 I would prefer to stay at home tonight because I'm very tired.

　　RATHER　　................................... at home tonight because I'm very tired.

11 There's no need to go to work this coming Sunday.

　　HAVE　　We .... to work this coming Sunday.

12 Perhaps I'll visit my German friends next summer.

　　MIGHT　　................................... my German friends next summer.

13 It's impossible that that girl is Tom's sister. She left for New York two days ago.

　　BE　　That girl .... sister. She left for New York two days ago.

14 That man's very likely to be Ben's father. He looks very much like him.

　　MUST　　That man .... He looks very much like him.

15 Remember that you're seeing Ms. Denver at 3 tomorrow afternoon.

　　APPOINTMENT Remember that .... Ms. Denver is at 3 tomorrow afternoon.

16 We don't have to get up early tomorrow.

　　THERE　　................................... for us to get up early tomorrow.

Towards Competences

1. 你是學生會的幹部，必須負責以 180 字編寫學校網站的國際內容，並於網頁列出英文版的校規摘要。
2. 為了準備交換學生的事務，你必須解說學校必須遵守的環保規定，讓海外姊妹校知道。請製作海報，並列舉環境維護相關的規定，例如列出垃圾分類、節約能源辦法等事項。

Self Check 5

請選出答案，再至解答頁核對正確與否。

1 Students .... park their cars in the teachers' car park.
Ⓐ might not   Ⓑ can't
Ⓒ don't are allowed

2 Jim .... swim when he was four years old.
Ⓐ may have not   Ⓑ could have not
Ⓒ couldn't

3 .... to wear miniskirts at your school?
Ⓐ Are you allowed   Ⓑ Can you
Ⓒ Ought you

4 That woman .... be the new receptionist. They said she was short with brown hair, like her.
Ⓐ can't   Ⓑ must   Ⓒ may not

5 Listen to this song. It .... be an old Rolling Stones' song. This is Mick Jagger's voice.
Ⓐ can't   Ⓑ mustn't   Ⓒ must

6 You look very tired. You .... go to bed earlier, Tom.
Ⓐ ought   Ⓑ should   Ⓒ may

7 This story .... be true. There are too many strange coincidences.
Ⓐ must   Ⓑ may   Ⓒ can't

8 .... we leave the room as soon as we finish the test?
Ⓐ May   Ⓑ Ought   Ⓒ Will

9 Join us for a pizza tonight, ... ?
Ⓐ will you   Ⓑ would you like
Ⓒ you would

10 .... to watch an action movie or the football match?
Ⓐ Would you   Ⓑ Would you like
Ⓒ Will you

11 I wish .... that girl's name.
Ⓐ I remember   Ⓑ I was remembering
Ⓒ I could remember

12 I wish .... so much time in my youth and studied more.
Ⓐ I wasted   Ⓑ I hadn't wasted
Ⓒ I couldn't waste

13 Stop lying, John. You .... tell her the truth!
Ⓐ have   Ⓑ must   Ⓒ will must

14 "What .... for this exam?" "Read ten novels by various authors."
Ⓐ do we have to do
Ⓑ must we have to do
Ⓒ have we got do

15 You .... bring your sleeping bags. There's bed linen at the hostel.
Ⓐ don't have to   Ⓑ need
Ⓒ don't have

16 You .... play video games for such a long time. It's bad for your health.
Ⓐ don't have   Ⓑ needn't to
Ⓒ shouldn't

17 You .... bring so many clothes with you. We'll only be away for three days.
Ⓐ needn't   Ⓑ mustn't
Ⓒ don't need

18 He's .... a great career. He's so clever!
Ⓐ bound to have   Ⓑ due to have
Ⓒ forced to have

19 I .... Karen £20. I must remember to give it back to her.
Ⓐ due   Ⓑ owe   Ⓒ shall

20 You really .... read this novel. It's so gripping.

Ⓐ need　　Ⓑ are bound to　　Ⓒ must

21 The train to Glasgow is .... to arrive in 20 minutes.

Ⓐ owing　　Ⓑ due　　Ⓒ bound

22 The flood has caused a lot of damage. We .... to help the people in the village.

Ⓐ had better　　Ⓑ ought　　Ⓒ should

23 We .... finish this essay by tomorrow. The deadline is next Monday.

Ⓐ mustn't　　Ⓑ don't need　　Ⓒ don't have to

24 Visitors .... answer their phones in the museum.

Ⓐ mustn't　　Ⓑ aren't due to　　Ⓒ don't need

25 Only staff members .... beyond this door.

Ⓐ are bound　　Ⓑ are allowed　　Ⓒ are due

26 My father .... 60 next November.

Ⓐ is going be　　Ⓑ going to be　　Ⓒ will be

27 "......... work abroad after your degree?" "I think so, but I haven't planned anything yet."

Ⓐ Are you going to　　Ⓑ Are you　　Ⓒ Will you be

28 "What time .... the sales manager, Emma?" "At 10:30, Ms Dell."

Ⓐ am I meeting　　Ⓑ will I meeting　　Ⓒ meet I

29 Watch out! That vase .... to fall off the shelf.

Ⓐ will　　Ⓑ ought　　Ⓒ is going

30 "......... early tomorrow?" "Yes, my flight is at eight."

Ⓐ Leave you　　Ⓑ Are you leaving　　Ⓒ Do you leave

31 Look at those black clouds. ....

Ⓐ It will rain.　　Ⓑ It's going to rain.　　Ⓒ It's raining.

32 .... write this essay. It's far too difficult for me.

Ⓐ I'm not going to　　Ⓑ I'm not able　　Ⓒ I won't going to

33 I'm sure .... a great day out. The weather is gorgeous today.

Ⓐ it is being　　Ⓑ it won't be　　Ⓒ it's going to be

34 I think .... record our next album in a couple of weeks.

Ⓐ we'll　　Ⓑ we're　　Ⓒ we'll be

35 We're so happy! Tomorrow at this time .... to the Caribbean.

Ⓐ we'll fly　　Ⓑ we're flying　　Ⓒ we'll be flying

36 Tom .... his degree by this time next year.

Ⓐ will take　　Ⓑ will have taken　　Ⓒ is going to take

37 By the time I finish work tomorrow, the shops ....

Ⓐ will close　　Ⓑ are going to close　　Ⓒ will have closed

38 Next summer .... an English course in Cambridge. I need to improve my speaking.

Ⓐ I'm going to attend　　Ⓑ I'm being attending　　Ⓒ I'll have attended

39 Can you imagine? This time next Saturday, ... my favorite musical in Broadway.

Ⓐ I watch　　Ⓑ I'll be watching　　Ⓒ I'll have watch

40 Coldplay .... on tour in France next summer.

Ⓐ will may be　　Ⓑ are　　Ⓒ will be

Assess yourself!

☐ 0 - 10　還要多加用功。

☐ 11 - 20　尚可。

☐ 21 - 30　不錯。

☐ 31 - 40　非常好！

16 條件句和 if 子句 Conditional Sentences and If-Clauses

LESSON 1 條件句：現在式和過去式 Present and past conditionals

現在式條件句

現在式條件句的句型為情態助動詞 **would + 原形動詞**。

肯定句	I **would talk** / I**'d talk** to him.
否定句	I **would not talk** / I **wouldn't talk** to him.
疑問句與簡答句	"**Would** you **talk** to him?" "Yes, I would. / No, I wouldn't."
Wh 問句	"What **would** you **tell** him?" "I'd tell him to be patient."

1 請重新排序單字，寫出現在式的條件句。

1 you / Would / go / swimming pool / the / me / with / to / ?

....

2 would / It / better / be / to / at / stay / today / home / .

....

3 try / white-water / would / rafting / Jim / not / .

....

4 kayaking / I / go / in / wouldn't / weather / this / .

....

5 lay / you / me / the / table / Would / help / ?

....

6 really / steep / you / climb / Would / a / mountain face / ?

....

2 請使用 would/wouldn't 和下方動詞，並根據括號內的符號來完成句子。
(+) 代表要寫成肯定句，(−) 代表要寫成否定句。

do (x2)　help　be　accept　say

1 .... you .... me with this project? (−)

2 There's nothing I .... for you. (−)

3 I .... it's a good plan. (+)

4 .... you .... that for me? (+)

5 It .... better for you to learn a second language. (+)

6 I .... that job. (−)

過去的未來式

如果主要子句裡用的動詞是簡單過去式，次要子句通常會使用 **would + 原形動詞**，例如：

• I knew (that) he **would come**.

這種句型稱為過去的未來式（請參閱第 351 頁的 Unit 19 Lesson 3）。
比較看看兩者的差異：

現在式 + will（未來式）	過去式 + would（過去的未來式）
I **hope** it **will** be sunny.	I **hoped** it **would** be sunny.
She **says** she **will** help me.	She **said** she **would** help me.
I**'m** sure I**'ll** have a good time.	I **was** sure I **would** have a good time.

也可以參閱第 278 頁，了解同樣用於表達過去的未來式 was/were going to。

• She said she **was going to** help me.

3 請依照例句，將現在式的句子改為過去式。

0 I'm sure Mom will like the idea of eating out.

I was sure Mom would like the idea of eating out.

1 I hope they will arrive for the beginning of the movie.

....

2 They promise they will call around this week.

....

3 Ann thinks she'll take up rowing.

....

4 They know they'll need a lot of training before going trekking in Nepal.

....

5 Tom says he will look for a new job soon.

....

6 We know they will fight for their rights.

....

7 Luke says he will invite us to try kayaking.

....

8 Jim promises he will have a haircut before the wedding.

....

過去式條件句

過去式條件句的句型為情態助動詞 **would + have + 動詞的過去分詞**。

肯定句	I **would have gone**. / I**'d have gone**.
否定句	I **would not have gone**. / I **wouldn't have gone**.
疑問句與簡答句	"**Would** you **have gone**?" "Yes, I would. / No, I wouldn't."
Wh 問句	"Where **would** you **have gone**?" "To your house."

情態助動詞的條件句

情態助動詞的「現在式條件句」與「過去式條件句」的句型如下：

現在式條件句	過去式條件句
could + 原形動詞 • You **could do** better than this.	could have + 過去分詞 • You **could have done** better than this.
might + 原形動詞 • They **might arrive** late.	might have + 過去分詞 • They **might have arrived** late.
should + 原形動詞 • You **should listen** to me.	should have + 過去分詞 • You **should have listened** to me.
would like to + 原形動詞 • I **would like to see** you.	would have liked to + 過去分詞 • I **would have liked** to see you. would like to have + 過去分詞 • I **would like to have** seen you.

4 請使用「過去式條件句」改寫句子。

1 We'd like to go shopping. ....

2 I might attend a German course. ....

3 Would you spend all that money on a pair of shoes? ....

4 You should be more careful. ....

5 They could run faster. ....

6 I wouldn't drive so fast. ....

7 We might buy a new car after the summer. ....

8 They could call after the match. ....

5 請運用下方動詞的正確形式來完成句子。

| tell take like arrive put off rest be go |

1 I think my brother might .... paragliding. I'll tell him about the course.

2 I could have .... part in the tennis tournament because I play quite well.

3 They may .... the conference to next week.

4 You could have .... me that the bank had already closed.

5 I might .... to the beach next Sunday. Would you like to come?

6 You should .... more. You look very tired.

7 They must have .... late. I didn't see them before the show.

8 You should .... quite careful when going horseriding.

情態助動詞 + be + 動詞 ing

我們使用這種像進行式的句型，來表達**可以 (could)**、**可能 (might)**、**一定 (must)**、**應該 (should)** 或**本來會 (would)** 在**現在或未來**的特定時間點執行某事：

- Don't call her now. She **might** be working at this time.
- Why are you standing out here? You **should** be having your history lesson.
- What a noise! My brother **must** be playing the drums again.
- If it weren't so cold, I **would** be swimming in the outdoor pool.

6 請運用括號裡動詞的「進行式」來完成句子。

1 He should .... , not sleeping at this time. (work)

2 If she had taken my advice, she could .... abroad now. (study)

3 What's that you said? You must .... ! (joke)

4 They aren't here yet. That's strange. They should .... for us. (wait)

5 If I didn't have to work today, I would .... to London to meet my girlfriend. (travel)

6 They might .... the match. (win)

7 "Where's Jenny?" "At work. She should .... coffee behind the bar at this time." (serve)

8 There's nobody in the office. They must all .... lunch in the cafeteria. (have)

LESSON 2 條件句：第零類與第一類 Type 0 and Type 1 conditional sentences

條件句是用來表達**「發生什麼事」**(what happens)、**「即將發生什麼事」**(will happen)、**「過去可能會發生什麼事」**(would happen)、**「如果⋯⋯就可能會發生什麼事」**(would have happened, if)。

條件句是由 **if 子句**搭配**主要子句**所構成。我們在 if 子句裡提出假設，然後在主要子句表達該假設的結果。另外，我們可以根據**可能性的程度**，在兩個子句運用不同時態。

FAQ

Q: 上文法課的時候，老師用了一些術語來定義從屬子句和主要子句，但我記不得叫什麼了。

A: 老師說的應該是條件從句（protasis）和結論句（apodosis）。if 子句是條件從句，而主要子句就是結論句。

條件句共分四種，稱為**第零類（Type 0）、第一類（Type 1）、第二類（Type 2）**和**第三類（Type 3）**。

第零類：一定會發生的事實與真理

第零類條件句又稱為零條件句（zero conditional），也就是在某時間點實現某條件後，將有**確定會發生的結果**。在此情況下，兩個子句的時態都是簡單現在式：

if 子句	主要子句
If + 簡單現在式	簡單現在式
If you **book** your flight in advance,	you **get** a discount.

> 如果 if 子句放在主要子句的前面，我們通常會以**逗號**區隔兩個子句 →
> If the "if clause" comes first, you usually insert a comma between the two.

if 子句也能放在主要子句的後面，像「You get a discount **if** you book your flight in advance.」，在此情況下，就不需要使用逗號。

零條件句適用於以下情況：

❶ 表達通則真理和科學原理，且在此情況下 **when** 可取代連接詞 if，因為真理是每次都會發生的常態現象：

- The climate gets colder **if** you go north towards the Arctic Circle.
  = The climate gets colder **when** you go north towards the Arctic Circle.
- **If** you add -ed to a regular verb, you get the past simple.
  = **When** you add -ed to a regular verb, you get the past simple.

❷ 給予假設性質的建議與做法。在此情況下，主要子句的動詞會是祈使句的形式，或是使用情態助動詞 **can** 或 **may**：

- **Get** something to eat if you're hungry.（也可以說 You can/may get something）
- If you see Ben, **give** him this book, please.
- You **may** stay here if you like.

1 請將 **1–8** 與 **A–H** 配對成完整句子。

..... **1** Go to bed early

..... **2** Don't eat too many sweet things

..... **3** Don't stand under a tree

..... **4** Don't behave like that

..... **5** Buy a new squash racket

..... **6** Watch this movie

..... **7** Wear a warm jacket

..... **8** Meet us at 8 p.m. in the bus station

A if you want to lose weight.

B if you want to learn more about the war in Iraq.

C if your old one is broken.

D if you want to go hiking tomorrow morning.

E if you go out. It's cold!

F if you want to go to the movies.

G if you're out in a storm.

H if you want to have a lot of friends.

2 請使用以下動詞的「簡單現在式」來完成句子。

> get　feel　tell　show　improve　buy　like　open

1 If you read a lot, your vocabulary .... and so does your mind!

2 If you cycle fast, the display .... how many calories you are burning.

3 Buy that funny hat if you really .... it.

4 If you .... two large tacos, you get a third one free.

5 If you key in your password, the program ....

6 If you buy the tickets online, you .... a 5% discount.

7 Go to bed if you .... tired.

8 If they ask you, you can .... them what happened.

第一類：未來有可能實現的假設

在第一類條件句亦稱為第一條件句（first conditional），在這類句型中，我們描述的是真的**有可能發生的事件**；也就是在既定條件下，我們可以確定、清楚很有可能會有什麼結果。

在此情況下，if 子句的時態是**簡單現在式**，主要子句則是 **will 未來式**：

if 子句	**主要子句**
If + 簡單現在式	will 未來式
If you **study** hard,	you **will pass** your exam.

以下列舉主要子句放在 if 子句前面和後面的句型：

- If you **listen** to this song, you **will like** it.
- I**'ll go** with him if he **lets** me.

在主要子句中，除了 will 未來式之外，如果某事件很有可能發生，也會搭配情態助動詞 **can**，而如果某事有機會發生，但不太確定，則可使用 **may**：

- You **can** get anything you want if you work hard for it.
- If you go on foot, you **may** arrive late

Focus

第一類條件句中的 **if 子句**一定要使用**現在式**，不能使用 will 未來式。我們通常會採用簡單現在式，有時也會有**現在進行式**的句型：If you**'re staying** overnight, I'll find you a room.

3 請運用括號裡動詞的正確形式來完成句子。

1 If it .... , I .... to the shops. (rain, not go)

2 We .... a barbecue on Sunday if it .... (have, not rain)

3 Okay, I .... my hair cut short if you .... me to. (not have, not want)

4 He .... anything for you if you just .... him. (do, ask)

5 We .... on a cruise next summer if we .... a good offer. (go, find)

6 If you .... all your money on sweets, you .... any left to buy clothes.
(spend, not have)

7 If you .... now, you .... home by ten. (leave, get)

8 If you .... , you .... to pass your test. (not study, not be able)

9 If they .... on time, we .... to the movies together. (come, go)

10 The old apple tree .... on the house if the wind .... blowing like this.
(fall, keep)

4 請判讀下方條件句應為第零類還是第一類。運用括號裡動詞的正確形式來完成句子。

1 If you .... to bully your classmates, I .... to suspend you.
(continue, be obliged)

2 If you .... me by your side, I .... right there! (need, be)

3 If she .... in the next race, I .... and see her. (compete, go)

4 If it .... hard tonight, we .... to school tomorrow. (snow, not go)

5 If you .... blue and yellow, you .... green. (mix, get)

6 Dad .... angry if I .... home late tonight. (be, get)

7 If it .... raining, we .... for a walk in the park. (stop, go)

8 Flowers .... if you .... them enough water. (die, not give)

9 If you .... at the sun without filtering lenses, your eyes ....
damaged. (look, get)

10 You .... into trouble if you .... your homework. (get, not do)

LESSON 3 條件句：第二類與第三類 Type 2 and Type 3 conditional sentences

第二類：不可能發生，或與現況不同的假設

第二類條件句亦稱為第二條件句（second conditional），用以表達**不太可能發生的情況**，
也就是**與現況或事實不同**，而不太可能成真的情況或想像。

在此情況下，if 子句的時態是**簡單過去式**，主要子句則是 **would + 原形動詞**。

if 子句	主要子句
If + 簡單現在式 If we **had** more time,	would + 原形動詞 we **would stop** for a rest.

以上例句意指「現在」沒有多餘的時間，並且如果「現在」有多的時間就能休息，
是對現況不同的假設。

請看以下例句：

- What **would** you **do** if you **won** ten million dollars?
  （因為贏得獎金是非常不可能發生的假設情況，故使用過去式 won）
- Your results **would improve** if you **trained** every day.
  （與實際現況不同，意指「你現在沒有每天訓練自己」，所以使用過去式 trained）

> ❗
> ❶ 第二類條件句裡，所有人稱的 be 動詞只能用 **were**（If I/you/he/she/it/we/you/
> they **were** . . . ）。不過在非正式用法裡，我們可以用 **was** 搭配 I/he/she/it，
> **were** 搭配其他人稱：
> - She would be happier if **she was** at home with her children.
>   （或說 if she were at home）。
> ❷ **If I were you** 的說法，通常用於給予**建議或警告**。
> - **If I were you**, I would accept that job.

1 請圈出正確的用字。

1 What **will / would / do** you do if someone left you in a dangerous situation?

2 You **wouldn't / didn't / hadn't** be happy if you knew the truth.

3 How would you travel to Edinburgh if your car **broke / will break / breaks** down?

4 We **could / will be able / can** invite all our friends if we had a bigger garden.

5 I **won't / wouldn't / didn't** be surprised if Tom got in some kind of trouble.

6 If my husband did more exercise, he **is / would be / will be** fitter.

2 請圈出正確的用字。

1 If you **tries / tried** parkour, I'm sure you'd **enjoy / enjoyed** it.

2 If you **lived / live** nearer London, I **would / had** come and see you more often.

3 Sue **would have / has** problems getting to work if she **wouldn't / didn't** have a car.

4 Mel certainly **didn't / wouldn't** go out with Jack if she **knew / will know** him better.

5 If you didn't **go / went** to bed so late, you **wouldn't be / weren't** so tired in the morning.

6 If they **studied / didn't study** so hard, they **won't / wouldn't** get such good marks.

7 I **wouldn't / didn't** ask the teacher to explain again if I **could / did** understand math better.

8 If it **weren't / wouldn't be** so cold, we **would go / went** out for a walk.

3 請運用括號裡動詞的正確形式來完成句子。

1 Which places would you like to visit if you .... a week's vacation in the USA? (have)

2 I wouldn't have to get up so early if I .... nearer home. (work)

3 If he had a good plan, he .... me. (tell)

4 Would you buy this miniskirt if your mom .... here? (be)

5 Kate would be cross if Tom .... on time. (not turn up)

6 If I had enough money, I .... around the world. (travel)

7 It would be great if we .... go skiing together. (can)

8 Amanda would go to the party if she .... better. (feel)

9 What .... if you found a gold necklace in the street? (you, do)

10 If John .... on time, he could see the presentation from the beginning. (arrive)

4 請運用括號裡動詞的正確時態，來完成第二類條件句。

1 My teacher .... (be) pleased if I .... (get) 10 out of 10 in the test.

2 I .... (dye) my hair green if my parents .... (allow) me to.

3 If you .... (improve) your IT skills, it .... (be) easier for you to find a job.

4 If I .... (not have) an Internet connection, what .... (I, do)?

5 .... (you, buy) these shoes if they .... (not cost) so much?

6 Oliver .... (not go) away on vacation if his neighbor ....
(not look after) his dog.

7 If I .... (know) Simon's phone number, I .... (ring) him.

8 If Chris .... (win) the lottery, he .... certainly .... (give)
some money to charity.

9 If I .... (be) you, I .... (not trust) him.

10 If he .... (find) the tickets, he .... (take) us to the rock concert.

11 I .... (be) disappointed if they .... (not invite) us to their party.

12 He .... (have) a good career if he .... (be) more ambitious.

第三類：完全不可能發生，對過去事件的假設

第三類條件句亦稱為第三條件句（third conditional），用以表達**完全不可能發生的情況**，因為句子指的是**過去的事**，因此**已無法成真**，也就是事情實際上已有不同的發展，我們僅能揣測在假設情況下，也許會演變為不同的情況。

在此情形下，if 子句的時態是**過去完成式**，主要子句則是 **would have ＋ 過去分詞**。

if 子句	**主要子句**
If ＋ 過去完成式（had ＋ 過去分詞） **If** you **had studied** harder,	**would have ＋ 過去分詞** you **would have passed** the exam.

上述例句意指在「過去」沒有認真念書，並且如果「過去」好好念書就會通過考試，是對已過去的事假設。

以下是問句和否定答句的例子：

- "Would you have come to the concert if we had got tickets?"
  "No, I wouldn't have come anyway."

Focus

過去完成進行式可取代第三類條件子句的簡單過去完成式，來強調**該行為延續一段時間**的概念：
- If it hadn't been snowing so hard, I **would** certainly **have gone skiing**.

> ! 我們也會看到「混搭條件句」的用法，也就是 if 子句是用**過去完成式**，主要子句卻用**現在式條件句**（would ＋ 原形動詞），這用在當條件句裡的行為會對「**現在**」造成影響時。
>
> - If I **had followed** his advice, I **wouldn't be** broke **now**.
> - If they **had left** earlier, they **would be** here **by now**.

FAQ

Q: 我在一段短文發現一連串縮讀形式：「If I'd seen her again, I'd have told her I was sorry. It would've been the best thing to do.」，這幾句話的完整形式應該是什麼呢？

A: 是「If I had seen her again, I would have told her I was sorry. It would have been the best thing to do.」。大家可看得出來，had 和 would 的縮讀形式都可以用 **'d**。

要判斷何時是 had、何時是 would，可記得 **had** 的後面只能接**過去分詞**，而 **would** 的後面僅能接**原形動詞**。

5 請將 **1–8** 與 **A–H** 配對成完整的句子，並寫上該句是第一類、第二類還是第三類條件句。

..... **1** If there isn't a bus she can get,
..... **2** If they hadn't told me,
..... **3** If Katie broke up with Charlie,
..... **4** He would have tried bungee jumping
..... **5** If there is some wind,
..... **6** If Jim had had his boots,
..... **7** She would do better at school
..... **8** They would have arrived earlier

A he would easily forget her.
B we'll go sailing today.
C he would have come hiking with us.
D I'll drive her home in the car.
E if they had left on time.
F if he hadn't been so scared!
G I wouldn't have known about the accident.
H if she were more self-confident.

6 請運用以下動詞來完成第三類條件句。

not order	make	wash	tell	make	stay	read	not break	invest	get	wear	know

1 If she .... so many spelling mistakes, she .... a higher mark.

2 I .... casual clothes if you .... me that the party was a barbecue.

3 If we .... the portions were so big, we .... an appetizer.

4 Oh no! My sweater has shrunk. I .... it in cold water if I .... the label first.

5 Ted .... his leg if he .... on the easy ski slopes.

6 If he .... that firm, he .... a great fortune.

7 請依照例句，將句子改寫成條件句。

0 I don't have a smartphone, so I can't send photos to you.
If I had a smartphone, I could send photos to you.

1 I don't want my parents to be angry, so I won't go out tonight.
If I went ....

2 I didn't have my car yesterday, so I couldn't go to the mall.
If I ....

3 I'd love to have a tattoo, but my mom won't let me.
If my mom ....

4 I don't get on with my brother. I never see him.
If I ....

5 I'm not rich, so I can't buy a big house.
If I ....

6 She went to the party and met her future husband.
If she ....

LESSON 4 在條件句運用情態助動詞 Use of modal verbs in conditional sentences

主要子句裡的情態助動詞

❶ 第一類條件句

在第一類條件句裡，使用 **will** 表示很肯定某情況將會發生：If you listen carefully, you **will** understand.

還有其他情態助動詞可用於此類條件句：

❶ may 用以表達某情況有可能發生、但仍不太確定
- You **may** meet Steve if you go to that new restaurant. He often goes there for dinner.

❷ can 意指可以考慮某情況
- If you like Mexican food, you **can** go to the new restaurant in Union Square.

❸ should 意指建議進行某事與否
- If you feel so tired, you **shouldn't** keep on driving, you should stop and relax for a while.

1 請配對兩組句子，然後以 **may** 或 **can** 完成主要子句。

1 You .... have a room overlooking the sea

2 You .... get sunburned

3 You .... see Tom

4 We .... easily find the way

5 I .... be able to join you at the restaurant

6 Mark .... have to work late tonight

A if you lie in the sun too long.

B if we look at Google Maps.

C if the meeting doesn't finish too late.

D if he doesn't finish his presentation this afternoon.

E if you ask for one when you book.

F if you go to the bar on North Street. He works there.

1 ..... **2** ..... **3** ..... **4** ..... **5** ..... **6** .....

❷ 第二類條件句

第二類條件句裡，我們會以 **would** 表達在假設情況下會怎麼做，或會發生什麼事：I **would** wait a bit longer if I were you. She might still turn up.

還有其他情態助動詞可用於此類條件句：

❶ could 用以表達可能性 (possibility)
- If I had a bigger car, I **could** take you all home.

❷ might 用以表達機率 (probability)
- If you tried skiing, you **might** like it.

❸ would have to 用來表達義務 (obligation)
- If I had to work full time, I **would have to** find someone to look after the children.

❹ would like to 用來表達嚮往之事 (desire)
- If I had enough money, I **would like to** buy a new car.

2 請依據括號裡的指示，填入符合的情態助動詞。

1 If we had more time, we .... have one more go on the rides. (possibility)

2 If there was an earthquake, you .... get out of the house. (obligation)

3 If Karen knew about it, she .... decide to give up the idea. (probability)

4 If we rented a bigger apartment, we .... pay more rent. (obligation)

5 If I could retire now, I .... go and live by the sea. (desire)

6 If you trained hard enough, you .... play in the main team. (possibility)

7 If you played an instrument, you .... join the band. (possibility)

8 If my husband tried Japanese food, he .... find that he likes it. (probability)

3 第三類條件句

在第三類條件句裡，我們以 **would have + 過去分詞**表達在過去的假設，我們會怎麼做，或會發什麼事：

I **would have waited** for you if you had told me you were coming.

看看下方的例句，注意 would、could、might 或 should 等情態助動詞的意義和用法：

- If I had brought my racket with me, I **could have played** a match with you.（意指「過去曾有機會做這件事」）

- They **might have got** here on time if they had left earlier.（意指「雖然不確定，但很有可能發生」）

- He **should have warned** us if he knew our flight would be delayed.（表示「對方在過去應該警告我們」；這句話有責備的意思）

- I **would have had** to hire a pair of skis if I hadn't brought mine with me.（表示過去應盡的責任義務）

- I **would have liked** to take a selfie with Bono if I had met him after the concert.（表示過去的渴望或願望）

  Also I would like to have taken a selfie with Bono . . .

---

3 請運用括號裡的動詞搭配第三類條件句，並根據句意，使用 **would**、**could**、**might** 或 **should** 來完成句子。
●●●

1 I .... to go on a cruise if I .... all that money on a new kitchen. (like, not spend)

2 If I .... my wallet at home this morning, I .... lunch in the restaurant! (not leave, have)

3 If we .... for you any longer in the street, we .... frozen! (wait, be)

4 We .... the new museum if there .... fewer people queuing up. (visit, be)

5 They .... the race if they .... harder. (win, train)

6 Carol .... us if she .... that the party had been canceled. (tell, know)

7 I .... your behavior to the headmaster if I .... that you were a bully. (report, know)

8 It .... possible to meet the actors if we .... the theater so soon after the end of the show. (be, not leave)

在 if 子句裡使用情態助動詞

在第二類和第三類條件句裡，我們常在 if 子句裡看到情態助動詞，以及可替代助動詞的同義動詞。

第二類	第三類
If I could . . .	If I could have . . .
If I were able to . . .（能力）	If I had been able to . . .
If I wanted to . . .	If I had wanted to . . .
If I should . . .（可能發生的事）	If I should have . . .
If I had to . . .（義務）	If I had had to . . .

- **If you should** see Tom, please tell him I need to talk to him.
- I wouldn't be very happy **if I had to** go to school in the summer.
- I wouldn't have been very happy **if I had had to** go to school in the summer.

「If you would」表示**有禮地提出正式請求**，尤其用在書寫語言中：

- I would really be grateful **if you would** let me know as soon as possible.

4 請將兩組文字配對。

1 We would be grateful

2 If you should find something wrong with this new appliance,

3 If the company would accept our proposal,

4 If you wanted to start a new business,

5 If he should arrive earlier,

6 We would expand our business a lot

A could you meet him at the airport?

B if we could find a reliable partner in the UK.

C we would be able to give you some financial backing.

D you should report it to our customer service straight away.

E if you could send us your best quotations.

F we could develop an interesting product.

1 ..... **2** ..... **3** ..... **4** ..... **5** ..... **6** .....

5 請依照例句，使用以下單字寫出第三類條件句的問句和答句。

0 you / go / skiing / ?

Yes / if / not / snowing / .

Would you have gone skiing?

Yes, if it hadn't been snowing.

1 he / pass / driving test / ?

yes / if / practice / more often / .

....

....

2 they / enjoy / white-water rafting / ?

yes / if / not be / so scared / .

....

....

3 the team / win / the competition / ?

yes / if / one of them / not hurt / leg / .

....

....

4 you / sail / to the island / yesterday / ?

yes / if / we / know / be windy / .

....

....

5 she / go / to Sally's party / ?

yes / if / she / know / Peter was there / .

....

....

6 請運用括號裡的動詞，以及粗體字標示的條件句類型，填入合適的用字來完成條件句。

1 If I .... talk to him, I .... him not to come. I knew the lecture .... quite boring. (be able to, tell, be) **Type 3**

2 If I .... work on Sundays, I .... this job, but luckily I only occasionally have to work on Saturdays. (have to, not accept) **Type 3**

3 I'm a lazybones. If I .... to do some sport, I think I .... football and I .... as a goalkeeper, so that I wouldn't have to run much! (be obliged, choose, play) **Type 2**

4 If I .... play the violin as well as you do, I .... to find a job in an orchestra. (be able to, try) **Type 3**

5 If I .... harder at school, I .... better marks. Now I realize how important it was. (work, get) **Type 3**

6 If I .... a better-paid job, I .... pay off my mortgage early. (find, be able to) **Type 3**

7 請將每段文字和正確的圖片配對，並寫出適當的回應內容。

1　**A:** Now go and explore! If any of you get lost, you should call me immediately on my phone! ☐

　　B: ....
　　..
　　..

2　**A:** If I could sing, I would enter that talent competition. ☐

　　B: ....
　　..
　　..

3　**A:** If you would ask the manager to see me now, I would appreciate it. ☐

　　B: ....
　　..
　　..

4　**A:** Sorry, Mom! If I could have helped you, I would have, but I had to go to Toby's house. ☐

　　B: ....
　　..
　　..

5　**A:** I wouldn't have bought the dress if I had seen this! ☐

　　B: ....
　　..
　　..

8 請完成下方條件句的重點整理表。

	if 子句	主要子句
第零類	**If** + 簡單現在式	簡單現在式
	If you book the hotel now,	you get a discount.
第一類	**If** + 簡單現在式	**will** 未來式
	If you ^{1}.......................... the hotel now,	you ^{2}.................................... a discount.
第二類	**If** + 過去簡單式	**would** + 原形動詞
	If you ^{3}.......................... the hotel now,	you ^{4}.................................... a discount.
第三類	**If** + 過去完成式	**would have** + 過去分詞
	If you ^{5}.......................... the hotel before,	you ^{6}.................................... a discount.

9 請以情態助動詞 would、wouldn't、should、shouldn't、could、couldn't 來完成句子。

1 If you feel depressed, you .... always stay at home. You .... go out and meet people.

2 We .... be so happy if we .... spend some time with you!

3 You are amazing! If I had done all that work, I .... be exhausted by now.

4 If I were you, I .... go to the Sahara with them. It might be a risky journey.

5 If it .... hail this week, the harvest .... be lost. Let's hope the weather does not change.

6 The situation .... be worse. If we had listened to your advice, we probably .... be in such big trouble now.

7 I .... be so happy if you .... come with me!

10 請將以下第一類條件句，改寫為第二類和第三類條件句。

1 If he goes to the opera, he will certainly enjoy it.

....
....

2 You won't spend too much if you buy things in the sales.

....
....

3 They will talk to him if they see him.

....
....

4 If you have a day off, we will go on a trip to the lake.

....
....

5 If she doesn't turn up on time, we will leave without her.

....
....

6 If you try hard, you will certainly succeed.

....
....

11 請找出句中的錯誤，並改寫為正確句子。

1 You should have tell me that you were not coming.

....

2 If I have brought my packed lunch with me, I would have shared it with you.

....

3 If you like Japanese food, you would try the sushi in this restaurant. It's excellent!

....

4 What do you suggest I might do to improve my English?

....

5 If I had been more time, I would have prepared something special for dinner.

....

6 I was afraid she not might love me any more.

....

7 What would I do if I had been you? I just don't know! You should ask someone else.

....

8 I would had thanked them for their great hospitality if I had seen them.

....

ROUND UP 16

1 請依照例句,將下方句子從現在式,改寫為過去式。

0 You must be joking!
You must have been joking!

1 I wouldn't tell him a lie.
....

2 You should be more careful!
....

3 He could help you.
....

4 They can't be so silly!
....

5 She may know the truth.
....

6 I'd like to see them.
....

7 Which one would you choose?
....

8 They might be lucky.
....

9 It can't be Doug!
....

延伸補充

第一類條件句通常由**「If + 簡單現在式」**的子句,搭配 will 未來式的主要子句而成,
這類條件句還有以下用法:

❶ 使用現在進行式的 if 子句: If she**'s singing**, we'll be there to see her.

❷ 使用其他未來式(be going to 或未來進行式)的主要子句:
- I**'m going to leave** for Thailand if I can find a cheap enough flight.
- Dad **will be painting** the fence if it doesn't rain on Saturday.

❸ 使用非 if 的連接詞,如 provided 或 unless(請參閱第 370 頁):
- You'll have a chance to win, **provided** you train regularly.
- I'm not going to go trekking this time, **unless** they need me as a guide.

---

2 請以下列動詞,搭配 **be going to 未來式**或未來進行式,來完成句子。注意有些題目兩種句型皆適用。

read	leave	book	have	not read	build	melt	stop	not make	watch

1 If the weather gets warmer, the snow .... soon.

2 If the book is boring, I .... it.

3 If you stop the music, we .... dancing!

4 If I can find my glasses, I .... the instructions.

5 If this lecture doesn't finish soon, I ....

6 If the program is interesting, we .... it.

7 If our friends come to see us tomorrow, we .... dinner with them.

8 If I get a pay rise, I .... a vacation straight away!

9 If we go to the beach this afternoon, we .... a huge sand castle.

10 If I don't get a promotion at work this year, I .... a big fuss about it.

3 請運用正確形式的以下動詞，來完成短文：

melt (x2)	continue	become (x2)	rise (x2)	
not limit	be	not be able	increase	not find

Global warming is a very serious problem for our environment. If the temperatures
¹................................. , more land
²................................. desert and the ice of the polar caps ³................................. . And if the ice of the glaciers ⁴................................. , the sea level
⁵................................. and there
⁶................................. more floods. If we
⁷................................. alternative sources of energy and we ⁸................................. traffic in the cities, global warming ⁹.................................
even more. And if global warming ¹⁰................................. , a lot of animal species ¹¹................................. extinct because they ¹²................................. to find any more food or shelter.
Governments must definitely take some action now and we must all do something about it — changing our habits a little bit may be a good start.

延伸補充

如果在第二類與第三類條件句中有用到 **should** 或 **had**，即可**省略連接詞 If**。在此情況下，助動詞需要放在句首，再後接主詞。此用法十分正式，較少用於口語英文：

• **If** anything **should** happen, please call me immediately. → **Should** anything happen . . .
• **If** he **hadn't** known, I would have excused him. → **Had** he **not** known . . .

4 請在不使用 **if** 的情況下改寫出意義相近的句子。

1 If I should arrive late, please save a seat for me.

....

2 If I should decide to go, I'll let you know.

....

3 If we had enough money, we would buy this car.

....

4 If they had any children, they wouldn't be able to go out every evening.

....

5 If it should rain hard, we wouldn't go out.

....

6 If they had traveled more, they would be more open-minded.

....

303

5 請圈出正確的用字。

1 I will be very angry if you **won't** / **don't** come back on time.
2 Okay, do it if you really **want** / **wanted** to!
3 If you **are** / **will be** kind to other people, they will be kind to you.
4 If they hadn't cut down the tree, it **might** / **should** have fallen on the house.
5 It's a perfect moment. If it could only be just like this for ever, I **would** / **will** be the happiest person on earth.
6 If you **open** / **opened** the window, we'll be cold.
7 I was sure it would **be** / **have been** a great vacation!
8 Would you do anything different if you **would** / **could** rewind your life and start again?

6 請根據句意，運用下方動詞的正確型態，來完成 **If** 子句。

be	take	know	not pass	play	sleep	leave	choose

1 If he really wanted to leave, he .... by now!
2 If I could choose between going or staying, I .... staying. I really like being here.
3 If I should find a wallet on the street, I .... it to the police station.
4 If I had a kitten, I .... with it all day!
5 My parents would be very angry if I .... my exams.
6 If I worked in a circus, I .... a clown!
7 If there hadn't been so much noise, we .... much better.
8 If you had paid more attention during the lesson, you .... how to solve the problem now.

7 請運用括號裡的動詞搭配正確時態，來完成文章。

During an advanced course in American history, students were asked a few hypothetical questions, like "What ¹.. (happen) if France ².. (win) the Seven Years' War?" or "³... (American colonies, be) under a more absolutistic power if the kings of France ⁴... (rule) over them?" And again "If North America ⁵.. (be) under French control, what would have happened with the French Revolution?"

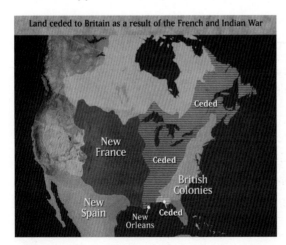

Land ceded to Britain as a result of the French and Indian War

New France
Ceded
Ceded
British Colonies
New Spain
New Orleans
Ceded

Here are some of the students' answers before they actually started a research project on the topic: If France ⁶................................. (win), all of North America ⁷... (speak) French by now. If North America had been under French rule, it ⁸... (back) the revolutionaries and ⁹................................. (gain) independence, but later than they did. ¹⁰... (the French Revolution, break out), without the American Revolution happening first?

The questions and the first answers were just the starting point for a research project that went deeper into the roots of North American history and Europe as well. By trying to answer them, students had to examine lots of aspects of the history of Europe that they ¹¹.. (study) otherwise. The project group is about to publish the results of their research on the university website. It ¹².................................. (be) interesting to read them, don't you think?

8 請根據各題建議的條件句類型，將括號裡的（助）動詞搭配正確時態，來完成各句。

1 Type 0: "All our dreams .... come true if we .... the courage to pursue them." *Walt Disney* (can, have)

2 Type 1: "If you never .... , you .... never ...." *Proverb* (try, know)

3 Type 1: "If you .... a man a fish, he .... hungry tomorrow. If you .... a man to fish, he .... richer forever."
Indian proverb (give, be, teach, be)

4 Type 1: "If you .... an apple and I .... an apple and we exchange these apples, then you and I .... still each .... one apple. But if you .... an idea and I .... an idea and we exchange these ideas, then each of us .... two ideas!" *George Bernard Shaw* (have x6)

5 Type 2: "If I .... a physicist, I .... probably .... a musician. I often think in music." *Albert Einstein* (be x2)

6 Type 2: "Everybody is a genius. But if you .... a fish by its ability to climb a tree, it .... its all life believing it is stupid." *Albert Einstein* (judge, live)

Reflecting on grammar

請研讀文法規則，再判斷以下說法是否正確。

		True	False
1	可縮寫為 'd 的 would 能用於條件句。		
2	我們以 would have + 過去分詞的過去式條件句，來表達「過去的未來」。		
3	「She said she would come.」是正確的句子。		
4	條件句共有三種。		
5	條件句裡的主要子句一定要放在 if 子句前面。		
6	零條件句或第一條件句裡的 if 子句，通常都會使用簡單現式式的動詞。		
7	「Would you have been happy if they had called you on your birthday?」 是正確的句子。		
8	「If I didn't have to work, I would go with them.」是正確的第二類條件句。		
9	第三類條件句的 if 子句，需使用過去完成式。		
10	「If he's on WhatsApp, I would send him our photo.」是正確的句子。		

17 被動語態 Passive Forms

LESSON 1 現在式被動語態 The present passive

被動語態的句型如下：

> 主詞 + **be 動詞** + **動詞的過去分詞**

be 動詞的時態需視情境而定。請參閱下表：

主詞	簡單現在式	現在進行式	簡單過去式	過去進行式	現在完成式	過去完成式	**will** 未來式	過去分詞
I	am	am being	was	was being	have been	had been	will be	called.
he/she/it	is	is being	was	was being	has been	had been	will be	
we/you/they	are	are being	were	were being	have been	had been	will be	

> ❗ 只有及物動詞才能使用被動語態，後接直接受詞。
> 及物動詞例如 make、build、write、use、call 等。

簡單現在式的被動語態

肯定句	It **is made** of glass.
否定句	It **isn't** / It's **not made** of glass.
疑問句	• "**Is** it **made** of glass?" "Yes, it is. / No, it isn't." • "What **is** it **made** of? Glass?" "No, plastic!"

請注意下方主動語態轉換為被動語態的方式：

主動語態		
主詞	動詞	直接受詞
Laura	presents	the new show.

被動語態		
主詞	動詞	主事者
The new show	is presented	by Laura.

❶ 主動語態句裡的直接受詞（the new show），
變成被動語態句的主詞。

❷ 主動語態句的主詞（Laura）成為被動語態句的動作
執行者，且前面必須加上介系詞 **by**。

❸ 被動語態句的 be 動詞時態要和主動語態句的時態
相同（此例句為簡單現在式 is），並且接上動詞的
過去分詞（presented）。

1 請將主動語態句改寫為被動語態句。

1 They sell sports equipment in this store.

....

2 They make designer clothes in this factory.

....

3 They don't produce cars here any more.

....

4 They play the national anthems before each game.

....

....

5 People speak French, German and Italian in Switzerland.

....

....

6 They give prizes to all winners.

....

7 They use computers in the marketing lessons.

....

....

8 A very young woman directs the orchestra.

....

9 They consider him a real math genius!

....

10 Scotland, England, Wales and Northern Ireland make up the United Kingdom.

....

....

UNIT
17

被動語態

2 請根據題目後方的符號指示來改寫句子；若為 **(?)** 則改為問句，**(–)** 則改為否定句。

1 The movie is directed by Steven Spielberg. (?)

....

2 School uniforms are paid for by the families. (?)

....

3 The notice is written in my language. (–)

....

4 Dice are used for this game. (–)

....

5 Spanish is taught in their school. (?)

....

6 These sunglasses are made in Italy. (–)

....

7 The UNO Tower is made of glass and steel. (?)

....

被動語態在以下情況裡，常會**省略動作執行者**：

❶ 表示通知與規定：• Heels are forbidden in the sports hall.
  • A comma is needed after Yes or No in short answers.
❷ 說明生產製程或實驗：
  • Crude oil is pumped into the fractioning column and then it is split into different hydrocarbons.
❸ 想吸引大家注意某事件將要發生，或是希望大家注意結果，而不著墨由何者執行該事件：
  • Oranges are imported to our country from Spain or Morocco.
  （沒有指出由誰來進口橘子，意指「對於誰進口橘子不感興趣」）

3 請將主動語態句改寫為被動語態句。若動作執行者不必出現，可省略不寫。

1 They grind coffee and then they pack it into tins.

....

2 They make these bags in Florence.

....

3 People celebrate Carnival in February.

....

4 Mrs. Jones cleans the rooms every morning.

....

5 Where do they import these tomatoes from?

....

307

現在進行式的被動語態可用來描述**在講話當下**,或大約在講話的時候,所發生的行為、事件與過程,如「Something is being done now / at the moment.」。

肯定句	Lunch **is being served** now.
否定句	Lunch **is not / isn't being served** now.
疑問句	"**Is** lunch **being served** yet?" "Yes, it is. / No, it isn't." "When **is** lunch **being served**?" "It**'s being served** in about ten minutes, at 12:30."

而若說「Lunch is served from 12:30 till 3:00.」,是因為我們描述的是常態事件,
而不是在特定時間點準時發生,也不是會在不久的將來發生的事件。

4 請將括號裡的動詞改為「簡單現在式」或「現在進行式」的被動語態,以完成句子。

1 Rugby .... in both England and Wales. (play)

2 An important match .... tonight between the teams of Wales and England. (play)

3 Prices and conditions .... in our offer. (specify)

4 Some new cottages .... at the end of the road. They will be finished by the end of year. (build)

5 Delivery to your house .... in the price. (include)

6 That old building .... at the moment. It's going to be a four-star hotel. (refurbish)

7 Funds .... to help the people affected by the tsunami. (raise)

8 Breakfast .... in the cafeteria at the moment. (serve)

5 以下描述的消化過程出自一本生物書籍。請以下方動詞的「簡單現在式」被動語態來完成短文。

mix	call	not need	transform	expel	chew	swallow	complete

The food we eat [1]........................... into energy through the process of digestion. Digestion begins in the mouth. Here the food [2]........................... and becomes a bolus, then it [3]........................... and goes down into the stomach, passing through the esophagus. In the stomach, the bolus [4]........................... with gastric juices and forms a thick liquid which goes down into the small intestine. Here, digestion continues. When the process of digestion [5]........................... , the digested food goes into the blood, which carries it to the cells. This process [6]........................... absorption. The substances that [7]........................... by our body get into the large intestine. From here, they pass into the rectum and [8]........................... through the anus in the form of feces.

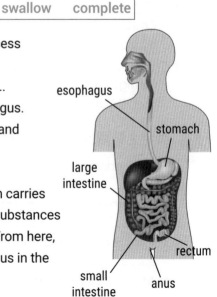

esophagus

stomach

large intestine

rectum

small intestine

anus

6 以下是學校圖書館的規定，請以下方動詞的被動語態來完成句子。

| file | invite | borrow | forbid | fine | ask |

1 Students .... to join the library at the start of term.

2 Students .... to be quiet in the library.

3 Books and periodicals .... alphabetically.

4 It .... to underline or write in books.

5 Books can .... only after filling in a form.

6 Students .... if they lose a book.

LESSON 2 過去式被動語態 The past passive

簡單過去式的被動語態

肯定句	It **was made** in China.
否定句	It **wasn't made** in China.
疑問句	"**Was** it **made** in China?" "Yes, it was. / No, it wasn't." "Where **was** it **made**? In China?" "No, in Korea."

和主動語態一樣（請參閱第 133 頁），過去簡單式的被動語態用以表達「**已經在過去某特定時間點完全結束**」的行為。我們會使用簡單過去式被動語態，來敘述**新發現**與**新發明**等，且記得要在動作執行者前加上介系詞 **by**。

• Johannes Gutenberg introduced the printing press to Europe in 1439.（主動語態）
  = The printing press was introduced to Europe **by** Johannes Gutenberg in 1439.（被動語態）

FAQ

Q: 在收聽英文頻道的節目時，我聽到「He got injured in the crash.」這個句子。我有聽錯嗎？這句聽起來像是被動語態，但為什麼會有 **got**？

A: 你沒有聽錯。在非正式的口語英文裡，**was/were** 等 be 動詞可被 **got** 取代，尤其是在描述**非預料之中的事**。另一個例句像是「He got fined for driving too fast.」。

1 請以下列動詞的簡單過去式來完成句子。

| conquer | name | create | write | design | invent | build | explore | defeat |

1 *Romeo and Juliet* and *Hamlet* .... by William Shakespeare.

2 The capital of the USA .... after president George Washington.

3 Australia and New Zealand .... by Captain James Cook in the 18th century.

4 England .... by the Normans in 1066.

5 Anglo Saxon King Harold .... by William Duke of Normandy in the battle of Hastings.

6 The Shard Tower in London .... by Italian architect Renzo Piano.

7 The television .... by a Scottish engineer, John Logie Baird.

8 The miniskirt .... by Mary Quant in the 1960s in London.

9 The Tower of London .... in the 11th century.

0 Who was the telescope invented by?

The telescope was invented by Galileo Galilei.

1 Who ....

....

The Last Supper was painted by Leonardo da Vinci.

2 When ....

....

The first Liverpool to Manchester railway was opened in 1830.

3 Who ....

....

Mr. Kent was replaced by Miss Ross in the English class yesterday.

4 What ....

....

My first dog was called Sammy.

5 How many languages ....

....

His novel was translated into ten languages.

6 How ....

Where ....

The glasses were packed in boxes and shipped to Africa.

7 Who ....

Brick Lane was written by Monica Ali.

過去進行式的被動語態

過去進行式的被動語態並不常見，是用來表達「**在過去某特定時間點，持續發生一陣子的過程**」：

- Innovative car models **were being produced** by FIAT at the time my father was employed there.

---

3 請將下方被動語態句改為主動語態句。如果被動語態句中沒有主事者，主動語態句的主詞請使用 they。

1 Mickey Mouse and Donald Duck were both created by the Walt Disney Company.

....

2 The light bulb was invented by Thomas Edison.

....

3 The main road was being repaired, so we came by a different route.

....

4 Higher walls were built in New Orleans after Hurricane Katrina destroyed part of the city.

....

5 Lots of cars were damaged by the storm last night.

....

6 The rock star was cheered by his fans all the way to his hotel.

....

7 Rosa Parks was arrested in Montgomery, Alabama, in 1955 because she had sat in a bus seat reserved for white people.

....

8 An ambulance was called immediately after the accident.

....

9 A mistake was made.

....

現在完成式和過去完成式的被動語態

請比較現在完成式裡，主動語態句和被動語態句的差異：

主動語態	The children **have made** this kite.
被動語態	This kite **has been made by** the children.

現在完成式的被動語態適用於以下情況：

❶ 轉述不需交代發生時間的事件：
  • He **has been elected** senator.

❷ 提問某情況是否曾經發生：
  • **Have** you ever **been invited** to one of his parties?

❸ 表達有人剛完成、已經完成或還沒完成某事：
  • The room **has** just/already **been cleaned**.
  • The room **has** not yet **been cleaned**.

以下比較現在完成式與簡單過去式：

• The new leisure center **has just been inaugurated** last Sunday.（句中有副詞 just，但未點出此事何時發生 → 現在完成式）

• The new leisure center **was inaugurated** last Sunday.
  （我們知道此事何時發生 → 簡單過去式）

而**過去完成式**的被動語態是用來表達，**某件在過去的事才剛剛完成、已經完成或尚未完成**：

• When we got to the hotel, our room **had** not **been cleaned** yet.

---

4 請完成句子，將括號裡的動詞寫為簡單過去式被動語態，或現在完成式被動語態。

1 The new library .... by the mayor. (inaugurate)

2 The Modern Art Gallery .... last Saturday. (open)

3 .... to his house? (ever, she, invite)

4 Peter .... as class head last week. (choose)

5 My car .... I can drive you to work now. (repair)

6 Your room .... It is ready for you now! (just, clean)

7 The itinerary for the Italian tour .... yet. (not announce)

8 Their new album .... last week. (release)

9 My bike .... yesterday. (steal)

5 請完成句子，將括號裡的動詞寫為現在完成式被動語態，或過去完成式被動語態。

1 "................................ they ever .... here before?" "No, never. It's the first time I've seen them here." (be)

2 We had already packed our luggage when we heard our flight .... (cancel)

3 Sorry, your car .... yet. It will take a few more hours. (not repair)

4 Unfortunately an agreement .... yet. But they're still talking. (not reach)

5 Harriet .... as leader of the party. (announce)

6 Everything .... already .... by the time we got back: the food .... , the tables .... , and the room .... (do, cook, set, decorate)

7 Two tables .... for you and your family, sir. (reserve)

8 The arrangements for the concert .... before we arrived. (make)

LESSON 3 未來式被動語態 / 搭配情態助動詞的被動語態
The passive form in the future and with modal verbs

未來式被動語態的用法和主動語態一樣（請參閱 Unit 15），我們可以根據情境以及溝通的意圖，來選用 will 或 be going to 未來式。**will** 和 **be going to** 後面均需接上「**be + 動詞的過去分詞**」。

will 未來式的被動語態

肯定句	It **will be done** by tomorrow. （表示承諾）
否定句	It **will not / won't be done** by tomorrow, I'm afraid.（意指「我的臆測」）
疑問句	• "**Will it be done** by tomorrow?" "Yes, it will. / No, it won't." • "When **will it be done**? By tomorrow?" "No . . . in a couple of days."

be going to 未來式的被動語態

肯定句	He**'s going to be rewarded** for what he's done. （意指「即將發生的、預料之中確定會發生的事」）
否定句	He **isn't going to be rewarded**, I'm afraid. （意指「沒有任何跡象會發生這件事」）
疑問句	• "**Is he going to be rewarded**?" "Yes, he is. / No, he isn't." • "How **is** he **going to be rewarded**? With some money?" "No . . . with a smile!"

未來完成式的被動語態

未來完成式用以表達「**某特定行為會在某段時間內被完成**」；此用法十分受限。

will 後面需接上 **have been + 過去分詞**，以及 **by + 時間用語**：

• The winning numbers of the raffle **will have been announced** <u>by this time tomorrow</u>.
• I'm sure Ms. Rubens **will have been appointed** as Home Secretary <u>by next week</u>.

1 請使用下方動詞的被動語態，搭配括號裡指示的未來式來完成句子。

| appoint   choose   ask   take   publish   release   hold   sell |

1 She .... to the committee. She isn't very popular.
(not going to)

2 I don't think his proposal .... seriously by the manager. (will)

3 I'm sure he .... as the new CEO by the end of the week.
(future perfect)

4 You .... lots of questions in the interview. (be going to)

5 Her new novel .... until early next year. (will not)

6 Their next album .... in two months. (will)

7 These beautiful prints .... in all the best art shops.
(going to)

8 The next table tennis tournament .... Dublin. (will)

2 請重新排序單字，寫出未來式被動語態的句子。

1 certainly / You / be / will / innocent / declared / .

....

2 next / His / movie / going / to / New / is / be / in / Zealand / filmed / .

....

3 rooms / old / The / will / mansion / be / the / of / year / next / redecorated / .

....

4 exhibition / going / be / An / opened / this / interesting / month / to / is / later / .

....

5 be / A / will / organized / in / his / concert / memory / .

....

6 This / building / going / old / be / is / to / demolished / .

....

7 to / chosen / Who's / for / the / be / main / role / going / the / in / musical / ?

....

8 names / The / winners / the / of / be / will / tomorrow / announced/ .

....

9 A / with / meal / traditional / wines / local / be / served / will / everyone / to / .

....

10 I / proposal / think / will / be / your / seriously / taken / .

....

搭配情態助動詞的被動語態

情態助動詞（can、could、must、may、would、should 等）後面接的被動語態，其時態不外乎是現在式或過去式。

看看下句，有情態助動詞的主動語態句與被動語態句，轉換中如何保留句意：
You can solve this problem in two different ways. →
This problem can be solved in two different ways.

搭配情態助動詞的被動語態句型如下：

現在式	過去式
主詞 + **情態助動詞** + **be** + **動詞的過去分詞**	主詞 + **情態助動詞** + **have been** + **動詞的過去分詞**
• It **can/could be made** easily.（意指有可能但不確定）	• It **can't/couldn't have been made** by a kid!（表示不相信）
• It **may/might be made** of aluminum.（意指可能性很高）	• Your timetable **may/might have been changed**.（表示很有可能發生，但不太確定）
• It **must be made** now.（具命令意義）	• I **should have been warned** of the delay.（表達不滿）
• It **has to be made** / It **needs to be made** before noon.（意指「有必要這麼做」，注意 have 和 need 的用法和情態助動詞不同，因此必須後接 to）	• This car **must have been used** with very little care.（表示從車子外觀做出的推論）
• It **should be made** by you, not by your mom.（提出建議，但同時也有責備的意味）	
• It **ought to be done** soon.（提出要求，注意 ought 後方要接 to）	
• They said it **would be done** by the next day.	

3 請選用以下最合適的情態助動詞來完成句子，答案可能不只一個。

must	must not	could	would	may	can	couldn't

1 The elevator .... be used by children if not accompanied by an adult.

2 This dish .... be made only with vegetables, but I'm not sure which ones.

3 His latest song .... have been inspired by his new-born baby. It's so sweet.

4 The ball .... be touched with both hands and feet in rugby.

5 Only a monolingual dictionary .... be used in the exam.

6 This work .... have been done much better than this!

7 Treat people as you .... like to be treated.

4 請在情態助動詞保持不變的情況下，將主動語態句改為被動語態句。

1 You should cut the apples into halves.

   ....

2 You need to wash the car today.

   ....

3 You can't touch the ball with the hands in soccer.

   ....

4 You should have informed me!

   ....

5 They might have lost your application form.

   ....

6 They ought to reach an agreement.

   ....

7 They might serve dinner in the garden this evening.

   ....

8 You can't have made it in three minutes!

   ....

5 請根據答句內容，使用情態助動詞和被動語態來寫出問句。

1 ....

   Yes, a boat can be hired for the lake.

2 ....

   No, not all expenses must be paid in advance, luckily!

3 ....

   Yes, a little butter can be added to the sauce if you like.

4 ....

   No, not everyone should be punished. Only those who cause trouble.

5 ....

   Yes, it can be cooked in the microwave. But not in that tin!

6 請將現在式的被動語態句，改為過去式的被動語態句。

1 Your essay should be written more carefully.

   ....

2 We might be invited to his party.

   ....

3 The onions should be chopped more finely.

   ....

4 They might be chosen for the part.

   ....

5 We should be informed about any problems.

   ....

7 請將 1–8 與 A–H 配對成完整的句子。

1 Great photos can be
2 This logo will be
3 A new password has been
4 If your project is really innovative,
5 Earth is called "the blue planet"
6 Pluto was first photographed
7 Not everything can
8 This password is secure. It can't

A be done immediately.
B used on all documents.
C from a short distance in July, 2015.
D downloaded from this site.
E be easily guessed or hacked.
F because it looks like this color when seen from space.
G chosen. Do you know it?
H it might be crowdfunded.

1 .....   2 .....   3 .....   4 .....   5 .....   6 .....   7 .....   8 .....

LESSON 4 人稱與非人稱的被動語態／have/get something done 用法
Personal and impersonal passive form; *have/get something done*

如我們在之前學到的（請參閱第 118 頁），有些動詞可後**接一個直接受詞**和**一個間接受詞**，如 give、lend、send、write 等動詞，此類主動語態句型如下：

> 主詞 + 動詞 + 人物 + 受詞
> They lent John a dictionary.

在被動語態裡，此類動詞通常具有所謂的人稱，也就是句子會以**「人物」來當主詞**，而非「事物」。

> **John** was lent a dictionary.（也可以說「A dictionary was lent to John.」，但較少見）

請再參考以下不同人稱下的被動語態例句：

主動語態句	被動語態句
They **give** young athletes prizes.	Young athletes **are given** prizes.
They **offered** me a big discount.	I **was offered** a big discount.
They **will give** Sharon a present.	Sharon **will be given** a present.

1 請將正確的句子打勾，若句中有錯誤，請訂正在後方的底線上。

☐ 1 The art gallery clients were all give a leaflet of the new exhibition. ....

☐ 2 My friend were given a super new mobile phone for his birthday. ....

☐ 3 On the farm, we were taught how to milk a cow. It was great! ....

☐ 4 Jean was offer a lot of money for her vintage fur coat. ....

☐ 5 They were told to park their car on the other side of the road. ....

☐ 6 I was shown a nice cottage, but the rent was too high. ....

☐ 7 When I had no money on my bank account, I was credit some by my dad. ....

2 請使用被動語態來改寫句子。

1 Somebody sent her red roses.

She was ....

2 They told Susan a nice story.

Susan ....

3 They sent us an invitation to the opening of a new shop.

We ....

4 The shop granted us a 30% discount on last year's clothes.

We ....

5 The bishop showed Paul the cathedral.

Paul ....

6 He asked Caroline to pick him up at the airport.

Caroline ....

7 They gave the children some nice illustrated books.

The children ....

8 Somebody taught me how to model clay.

I ....

---

❶ 敘述動詞或 **believe**、**think**、**consider**、**know**、**find**、**report**、**say**、**suppose**、**warn** 等其他動詞，通常用以表達廣受認同的看法。英文裡會以被動語態表達此類說法，句型如下：

❶ 使用**非人稱代名詞**，搭配**敘述類從屬子句**：It is said (that) he owns a fortune.

❷ 使用**人稱代名詞**，搭配 **to + 原形動詞**：He is said to own a fortune.

❷ 但人稱用法較為常見，看看下方例句：

- **He** is considered to be the best in his category.
- **They** were found to be innocent. **Also** **It** was found that they were innocent.
- **He** was reported to be missing. **Also** **It** was reported that he was missing.

❸ 如果看法或假設與過去有關，我們會使用 **to have + 過去分詞**來表達：

- They are supposed **to have finished** by now.
- She is said **to have won** a big sum on the lottery.

> **!** 請注意以下兩者的差異：
>
> **❶** 針對**過去事實**所發表的**現在看法**：
>
> - People think she was a great dancer. → She is thought to have been a great dancer.
>
> **❷** 針對**過去事實**所發表的**過去看法**：
>
> - People thought she was a great dancer. → She was thought to be a great dancer.

---

3 請使用包括提示用詞在內的二至五個單字，來完成意思相近的句子。
注意不能變更提示用詞。

0 He has always been known to be the greatest poet of his age.

IT ......*It has always been known*...... that he is the greatest poet of his age.

1 We were told a lot of lies.

US .... a lot of lies.

2 It was known that they were good singers.

THEY .... good singers.

3 It is supposed that you should be studying.

ARE .... studying.

4 It was found that he was guilty.

BE .... guilty.

5 This is considered to be an important painting.

IS This .... important.

6 It is said that this villa belongs to a famous billionaire.

TO This .... to a famous billionaire.

4 請判讀句子，如果是和現在（**present**）有關的看法，請寫 **PR**；如果是和過去（**past**）有關的看法，請寫 **PA**。

.... **1** He's thought to have been a genius.

.... **2** They were believed to be the best painters of their time.

.... **3** They are thought to have been robbed during the night.

.... **4** She was considered to be the best fashion designer of the fifties.

.... **5** Some hooligans are thought to have caused serious damage to the sculptures in Rome.

.... **6** He's believed to have spent five years on a little island in the Pacific Ocean.

.... **7** She's thought to be abroad.

.... **8** He was believed to have been the best actor of his time.

5 請使用下方動詞來完成短文。

| was devastated | was | had been taught | has been credited | was given | ran |

10-year-old girl saves lives

A young New Zealand girl
[1] ....
with saving dozens of lives
during last month's Samoan
tsunami. Abby [2] ....
on vacation with her family
in the village of Lalomanu
on Samoa's southern coast
when she noticed the
tsunami warning signs.
She [3] ....
.... about them at school.
She [4] ....
along the beach telling
people to head for higher
ground. Just minutes later,
the entire area [5] ....
.... Her warning
ensured that many people
reached safety in time.
Back home, Abby [6] ....
.... a certificate
of appreciation from the
New Zealand Civil Defense
Director in front of her
impressed classmates in
Wellington.

6 請使用被動語態來改寫句子。

1 People think Martha Miller is an interesting artist.
Martha Miller ....

2 They thought John Landis was a rich art dealer.
John Landis ....

3 The police suppose that someone has already sold the stolen painting.
The stolen painting ....

4 People know that their works are the most expensive in the gallery.
Their works ....

5 Everybody knows that someone gave the painter a new canvas and some watercolors.
The painter ....

6 They suppose that the fakers have moved to South America by now.
The fakers ....

7 Everybody believes the owner of the art gallery is very wealthy.
The owner ....

Have/Get something done

1 如果要表達**他人幫我們完成某事**（通常是某種服務），我們可使用被動語態 have/get something done：I needed a certificate and I **had/got it done** in no time at all!

2 在多數情況下，我們能理解動作執行者是誰，而省略不寫，因為此類人物通常顯而易見或不是重點。
 • My cousin got his arm tattooed with his girlfriend's name.

3 但如果人物有被寫出來，就需要以 **by** 來引導。
 • Rob had his hair shaved **by** the new barber in King Street.

4 有時也會用在我們不情願的情況下發生的事，如：I **had my bag stolen.**

5 **need to / want to / must have something done** 句型亦十分常見：
 • I **need to have my car washed.** It's really filthy!

7 請將 1–6 與 A–F 配對成完整的句子。

..... **1** My sister had her bedroom

..... **2** You've just had your hair cut

..... **3** My husband is getting his computer

..... **4** I'll have my nails

..... **5** I had my wedding dress made

..... **6** We had

A repaired tomorrow.

B manicured one of these days.

C by one of the top designers in London.

D painted white last month.

E our garden landscaped last year.

F —it looks great!

8 請依照例句，使用提示用詞搭配括號裡的動詞來造句。

0 He / get / car / repair / after the accident (need)
He needs to get his car repaired after the accident.

1 I / get / these photos / print (want)
....

2 She / get / her jacket / dry-clean (must)
....

3 I / get / this shirt / iron (need)
....

4 We / get / our computer / repair (need)
....

5 My mom / have / the kitchen / extend (want)
....

6 My parents / have / a new satellite dish / install (want)
....

7 Laura / have / her nails / manicure / before the wedding (must)
....

8 She / have / a hole in her tooth / fill (must)
....

9 I / get / the car / wash (need)
....

10 We / get / the grass / cut / this weekend (must)
....

規則動詞：三態複習表

不定詞 to check	過去分詞 checked	現在分詞 checking

主動語態

簡單現在式 I/You/We/They **check** He/She/It **checks**	**現在進行式** I **am checking** You/We/They **are checking** He/She/It **is checking**
簡單過去式 I/You/He/She/It/We/They **checked**	**過去進行式** I/He/She/It **was checking** You/We/They **were checking**
簡單現在完成式 I/You/We/They **have checked** He/She/It **has checked**	**現在完成進行式** I/You/We/They **have been checking** He/She/It **has been checking**
簡單過去完成式 I/You/He/She/It/We/They **had checked**	**過去完成進行式** I/You/He/She/It/We/They had **been checking**
簡單未來式 I/You/He/She/It/We/They **will check**	**未來進行式** I/You/He/She/It/We/They **will be checking**
簡單未來完成式 I/You/He/She/It/We/They **will have checked**	**未來完成進行式** I/You/He/She/It/We/They **will have been checking**
be going to 未來式 I'm **going to check** You're/We're/They're **going to check** He's/She's/It's **going to check**	**以 be going to 表達過去的未來式** I/He/She/It **was going to check** You/We/They **were going to check**
現在式條件句 I/You/He/She/It/We/They **would check**	**過去式條件句** I/You/He/She/It/We/They **would have checked**

被動語態

簡單現在式 I **am checked** You/We/They **are checked** He/She/It **is checked**	**現在進行式** I **am being checked** You/We/They **are being checked** He/She/It **is being checked**
簡單過去式 I/He/She/It **was checked** You/We/They **were checked**	**過去進行式** I/He/She/It **was being checked** You/We/They **were being checked**
簡單現在完成式 I/You/We/They **have been checked** He/She/It **has been checked**	**簡單過去完成式** I/You/He/She/It/We/They **had been checked**
簡單未來式 I/You/He/She/It/We/They **will be checked**	**簡單未來完成式** I/You/He/She/It/We/They **will have been checked**
be going to 未來式 I'm **going to be checked** You're/We're/They're **going to be checked** He's/She's/It's **going to be checked**	**以 be going to 表達過去的未來式** I/He/She/It **was going to be checked** You/We/They **were going to be checked**
現在式條件句 I/You/He/She/It/We/They **would be checked**	**過去式條件句** I/You/He/She/It/We/They **would have been checked**

回顧上一頁 check 的動詞三態,可觀察出動詞可分為以下三態:

1 語態(form/voice):
主動語態／被動語態(切記:只有及物動詞能使用被動語態!)

2 時態(tense):
現在式／過去式／未來式／現在完成式／過去完成式／未來完成式／現在式條件句／
過去式條件句(切記:「完成式」意指已完成或結束的行為)

3 狀態(aspect):
簡單式／進行式(簡單式意指「永久的情況」;進行式則指「尚未結束且還在進行中、或是暫時的行為」)

1 請依照例句分析**畫底線**的動詞,並寫出所屬的語態、狀態和時態。

0 She <u>was called</u> Mary, after her grandmother. → 被動語態、簡單過去式

1 They <u>were going</u> to school. ....

2 He <u>had been given</u> the house key. ....

3 They <u>will have been flying</u> for ten hours at this time tomorrow.

....

4 We <u>would have accepted</u> their proposal. ....

5 She <u>has been playing</u> since four o'clock. ....

6 They <u>had</u> very good results in their tests. ....

7 They <u>were going to be arrested</u>. ....

8 It <u>will be finished</u> soon. ....

2 下方的動詞有些是規則動詞,有些是不規則動詞。請留意拼字變化,並依照例句寫出動詞的各種時態。

LOOK: looks, looking, looked   DO: does, doing, did, done

1 WASH ....

....

2 CUT ....

....

3 LIVE ....

....

4 WRITE ....

....

5 ENJOY ....

....

6 CRY ....

....

7 COME ....

....

8 SPEND ....

....

9 SEE ....

....

10 SAY ....

....

3 請使用下方動詞搭配括號裡建議的時態，來完成被動語態的句子。

| spend | reward | lose | serve | send | demolish |

1 Lots of money .... by immigrants to their native countries.
(present continuous)

2 My patience .... finally .... —a really big fish started
pulling at my line. (past simple)

3 Everything .... ! We had nothing left. (past perfect)

4 Hopefully more money .... on health care by the government. (*will* future)

5 When we arrived, cocktails .... (past continuous)

6 Many old buildings in the city center .... (present perfect)

4 請在維持相同時態的情況下，將主動語態句改為被動語態句。
若有介系詞，請依照例句將其放在句尾。

0 You don't have to pay <u>for</u> these brochures, they're free.
These brochures don't have to be paid for, they're free.
....

1 We will reply to all your emails.
....

2 A new babysitter will look after the children tonight.
....

3 They have played this song a hundred times on the radio today.
....

4 They might have changed the schedule.
....

5 They are going to sell their car.
....

6 They are building big dams in Venice.
....

7 Students must not use the equipment in the science lab without permission.
....

8 The club members have organized a charity concert.
....

5 請將下列被動語態句從簡單現在式改為簡單過去式。

1 Hot meals are served at all times in the restaurant.
....

2 The cake must be stored in a cool place.
....

3 Very good bargains can be found on Prime Day.
....

4 This dish is prepared in the traditional way.
....

5 All of the carpets are hand-woven in Morocco.
....

6 The sauce needs to be prepared in advance.
....

7 The scarves in the shop window are all hand-painted.
....

8 The bags and belts are made of real leather.
....

6 請依照例句，將所有主動語態句，改為兩種被動語態句。

0 They gave everyone a card.

Everyone was given a card. / A card was given to everyone.
....

1 They offered him a movie contract.
....

2 They will send you two copies of the contract.
....

3 They show new students the syllabus.
....

4 They are going to teach the children a nursery rhyme.
....

5 They have awarded her with an Oscar.
....

6 They passed each council member a folder of documents.
....

7 They have told Sara the story of this strange room.
....

8 They are giving the children some snacks for the break.
....

7 請根據答句內容寫出問句。

1 Can ....

Yes, the oven can be switched off. The muffins are ready.

2 Who ....

Julius Caesar was written by William Shakespeare.

3 Who ....

This song was composed by John Lennon.

4 When ....

She was given the prize last week.

5 What ....

Nothing much can be done now, I'm afraid.

6 Which ....

English, German and Spanish are spoken here.

7 Will ....

Yes, his paintings will be sold at the next auction.

8 Is ....

No, this apartment is not going to be rented.

8 請以下列動詞的過去分詞來完成句子。

| repair | wash | cut | devastate | restyle | do | iron | clean up | dye |

1 It was terrible! They had their shop .... by the flood.

2 We had our car .... last week. It had a problem with the brakes.

3 She got her computer .... after it had caught a virus.

4 I'm going to have my hair .... , ... blond and .... I'm ready for a change!

5 If you use this software, you'll get your work .... in no time.

6 He hasn't got a washing machine so he usually gets his shirts .... and .... at a cleaner's.

9 請找出句中的錯誤並改正。

1 The students were gave some new books. ....

2 Have the stadium gates opened at 6 p.m. for the concert? ....

3 The Sagrada Familia were designed by Antoni Gaudi. ....

4 The movie will be shooted in Central Italy. ....

5 The dog was supposed to missing. ....

6 A radio station has established by Marconi on the Isle of Wight. ....

Reflecting on grammar

請研讀文法規則，再判斷以下說法是否正確。

		True	False
1	被動語態的助動詞一定要用 to have。		
2	所有動詞都有主動語態和被動語態的用法。		
3	被動語態後面通常會以介系詞 from，來引導主事者。		
4	被動語態句如果是現在式，情態助動詞需後接 be + 過去分詞；如果是過去式，就要使用 have been + 過去分詞。		
5	「He should be punished for what he's done.」是正確的句子。		
6	「He is said to have been very rich.」意指對現在所做的判斷。		
7	「I had my hair cut very short.」句中的動詞 have 可被 get 取代：		
8	Wh 問句的介系詞會出現在被動語態句的句尾，就像主動語態句的問句。		
9	「I was given a lot of presents on my birthday.」是錯誤的，正確的寫法應該是「A lot of presents were given to me on my birthday.」。		
10	「She is supposed to have finished by now.」屬於具有人稱的句型；「It is supposed that she has finished by now.」則是非人稱的句型。		

18 關係子句 Relative Clauses

LESSON 1 限定關係子句裡的關係代名詞
Relative pronouns in defining relative clauses

❶ **關係子句**分為「**限定關係子句**」（defining clause）和「**非限定關係子句**」（non-defining clause）。

❷ **限定關係子句**能以**限定話題裡人事物**的方式，來完成句子。

例如我說：「The movie was good.」（這部電影很好看），你也許會問「Which movie?」（是哪一部電影），我則會繼續說「The movie <u>that we saw last night</u>.」（我們昨晚看的那部電影）。這樣靠補充關係子句，就可以指出我說的電影就是 the one we saw last night（我們昨晚看的那部）。如果不使用關係子句，主要子句就會意義不全。

❸ 切記：

① 限定關係子句十分必要，能指出話題裡的人事物。

② 由於限定關係子句與主要子句息息相關，因此千萬**不能以逗號隔開兩個子句**。

❹ 看看下方例子。將兩個子句這樣結合，可避免重複敘述，讓語句更通順流暢。

- Calatrava is the famous Spanish architect. He designed this bridge. → Calatrava is the famous Spanish architect **who** designed this bridge.
- That's the bridge. It was designed by Calatrava. → That's the bridge **which** was designed by Calatrava.
- White is a color. Calatrava prefers this color for his buildings. → White is the color **that** Calatrava prefers for his buildings.

Focus

看看下方**限定子句**中關係代名詞的用法，括號代表可以被省略：

	與人物有關的代名詞	與事物和動物有關的代名詞
主詞	**who** / **that**	**which** / **that**
直接受詞	(**who**) / (**whom**) / (**that**)	(**which**) / (**that**)
間接受詞	(**whom**)	(**which**)
所有格	**whose**	**whose**

關係代名詞可作為句子的主詞、受詞或間接受詞（要搭配介系詞），還可代表所有格。

❶ 關係代名詞作為**限定關係子句**的**主詞**時，一定要寫出來：
- Laura is the girl **who** sits next to me in the science class.
- The turtle is one of the animals **that** live the longest.

❷ 關係代名詞作為**限定關係子句**的**受詞**時，通常因為顯而易見故**可以省略**：
- The blonde girl **(who/whom/that)** you met at the party is my cousin.
- The story **(which/that)** you told me is very interesting.

Q: 代名詞 whom 的使用時機是什麼呢？

A: **whom** 屬於與人物有關的代名詞，具有補語的功能，主要用於搭配**介系詞**，例如「The man **to whom** I was speaking was Mr. Ross.」。但 whom 是正式用法，在口語裡不太常見，在非限定子句才會較常使用（請參閱第 328 頁）。

❸ 當關係代名詞**搭配介系詞**作為**間接受詞**時，有以下三種句型：

  ❶ 將**介系詞**放在 **which 或 whom 的前面**；但如果是 who 或 that 就不能採用此方法：
- Is this the painting **for which** you paid ten thousand dollars?

    NOT . . . for ~~that~~ you paid . . .

  ❷ 將**介系詞**放到**關係子句的句尾**，讓代名詞的位置不變；在此情況下就能使用 **that**：
- The magazine **which/that** you're looking **for** is on your desk.
- The girl **whom/that** you were talking **to** is my sister.

  ❸ 將**介系詞**放到**關係子句的句尾**，並**省略代名詞**；這是口語英文最常見的用法：
- Tonight I'm going out with the boy I talked to you **about**.
- The parcel you were waiting **for** has just arrived.

❹ 如需於關係子句表達**所有格**的意思，我們一定要使用代名詞 **whose**，而且**不能省略**：
- He's an artist. His work has been highly praised. →
  He's the artist **whose** work has been highly praised.

1 請以 **which** 或 **who** 來完成句子。

1 The man .... bought my car works in the same office as my son.

2 That's the cell phone .... I'd like to have for my birthday.

3 The people .... have just come into the shop are from Sweden.

4 That woman .... is writing on her laptop looks like Marilyn Monroe.

5 The elephant .... is in that cage will be moved to a safari park soon.

6 Who is the person .... can fix computers in your company?

7 I like the white laptop .... is in that shop window.

8 The woman .... is responsible for the advertising department is my sister-in-law.

2 請訂正句子裡的錯誤，並寫出正確的句子。

1 That is the lady who she owns the flower shop in the High Street.

....

2 Aren't these the earrings for that you've been looking for ages?

....

3 The doctor for who you're waiting has just arrived.

....

4 I'm sure this is the boy which father works in the bank next to my office.

....

5 Can't you see that car? The one who is parked in front of that gate?

....

6 Isn't he the artist which we met at yesterday's opening in Leo's art gallery?

....

3 請閱讀句子後，用括號標出可以省略的關係代名詞。

1 The guy who I met on the plane was really nice.
2 The guy who was sitting next to me on the plane was very nice.
3 Your carbon footprint is the amount of carbon dioxide that you produce in your daily activities.
4 Emoticons are keyboard symbols that represent the expressions on somebody's face.
5 Emoticons are used in emails and text messages to show the feelings of the person who is sending the message.
6 A stepfamily is the family which is formed when somebody marries a person who already has children.
7 Parkour is a sport which you do in a city, running, jumping and climbing on roofs or walls.
8 The painting that we saw in the museum is a Rembrandt.

4 請以 who、which 或 whose 來完成句子，並以括號標出可以省略的關係代名詞。

1 The guys .... we met on vacation live in Finland.
2 The console .... my parents gave me for Christmas has some great games.
3 The boy .... was running with me in the park is my cousin Philip.
4 The woman .... laptop was stolen on the train is very upset.
5 The hedgehog .... we saw in our garden last night looked really scared.
6 He's the actor .... interpretation of Hamlet was superb.
7 Do you like the electric bike .... is parked outside the shop?
8 The graphic novel .... has just been published is the best I've ever read.

5 請改寫句子，省略關係代名詞，並將介系詞改到關係子句句尾。

0 The vacation to which he was looking forward was canceled.
  The vacation he was looking forward to was canceled.
  ....

1 The friend with whom I usually play tennis has broken his arm falling off his bike.
  ....

2 The colleagues with whom my mother works gave her a necklace on her birthday.
  ....

3 The e-book about which we were talking yesterday got an important award.
  ....

4 The café to which we are going tonight was opened two hundred years ago!
  ....

5 Jack and Beatrix are going to buy the house of which they have been dreaming for a long time.
  ....

6 The document for which I had been looking for two days was in a drawer in my office.
  ....

7 The colleague with whom I travel to work every day is ill this week.
  ....

8 The large order to which we have been looking forward has finally arrived.
  ....

6 請以關係代名詞結合兩個句子，並盡可能省略關係代名詞。

1 That is the boy. His father is a renowned web designer.

....

2 The phone call came too late. I was waiting for it.

....

3 He's the man. You saw him at the pub last night.

....

4 This is the new scanner. I'm going to buy it.

....

5 That's the history teacher. He gives us a lot of homework.

....

6 This is the lady. She gave me her old digital camera.

....

7 The car was found near the park. It's Mr. Beckett's.

....

8 The house is a really smart house. Carol lives in it.

....

UNIT 18 關係子句

7 請使用以下單字和正確的關係代名詞來造句。有些句子可使用兩種不同代名詞。

0 A start-up / company / is just beginning to operate.
A start-up is a company that / which is just beginning to operate.
....

1 Comfort food / kind of food / makes you feel better, like chocolate and cookies.

....

2 Skydiving / sport / you jump from a plane and fall a long way down before opening your parachute.

....

3 A skydiver / person / does skydiving.

....

4 A hoverboard / electric scooter / used in pedestrian areas.

....

5 A drone / aircraft without a pilot / controlled from the ground.

....

6 Paintball / game / people shoot balls of paint at each other.

....

7 A QR Code / type of matrix barcode / consists of black modules arranged in a square grid / can be read by a camera or a scanner.

....

8 A crocoburger / hamburger / made with crocodile meat.

....

LESSON 2 非限定關係子句裡的關係代名詞
Relative pronouns in non-defining relative clauses

非限定關係子句能為主要子句**補充資訊**，但**並非用於指明話題人事物的必要資訊**，因此又稱為「**額外訊息子句**」。請參考以下非限定子句的例子：

• My parents, <u>who have been married for 25 years</u>, are celebrating their wedding anniversary next Sunday.（我父母結婚 25 年，下週日要慶祝結婚週年紀念日）。

就算省略畫底線的部分，我們仍能知道這句話在說的是「my parents」，而且句意仍然符合邏輯：

• My parents are celebrating their wedding anniversary next Sunday.
（我父母下週日要慶祝結婚週年紀念日）

而非限定子句補充的訊息則為「They have been married for 25 years.」。（他們結婚 25 年了）

> 切記：非限定關係子句和主要子句之間，一定要以逗號隔開：
> Yesterday I met my old friend Jack**,** who used to go to my school.

Focus

非限定子句所使用的關係代名詞如下：

	與人物有關的代名詞	與事物和動物有關的代名詞
主詞	**who**	**which**
直接受詞	**who / whom**	**which**
間接受詞	**whom**	**which**
所有格	**whose**	**whose / of which**

注意，非限定子句有以下特性：

1 絕對不能使用代名詞 that；僅能使用與人物有關的 who/whom，以及與事物有關的 which。

2 即使關係代名詞是句子的**受詞**，也一定要說明而**不能省略**：
• Meg and Tom, **who(m)** you met at my house last summer, are living in England now.

3 如果有間接受詞，**介系詞**（with、to、about、for）可放的位置如下：

❶ 放在**關係代名詞的前面**：
This is Mr. Rogers, **with whom** you will work during the next few weeks.

❷ 放在**關係子句的句尾**，但不能省略代名詞：
Yesterday I visited the Tate Modern Gallery, **which** I had never been **to** before.

> 逗號非常重要，因為逗號可改變句子的意思。看看下方的例句：
> **1** 沒有逗號的限定句：
> The students **who** had not received their exam results were feeling very anxious.（意指「只有沒收到成績單的學生很焦慮」）
> **2** 有逗號的非限定句：
> The students, **who** had not received their exam results, were feeling very anxious.（意指「所有學生都沒有收到成績單，而且都很焦慮」）

1 以下部分句子含有非限定關係子句，請找出來並於正確位置標出逗號。

1 The Sullivans who live opposite us have just bought a new car.
2 My washing machine which is quite old keeps breaking down.
3 The cordless phone that we have in our bedroom doesn't always work properly.
4 My son's friends who are often at our house are very pleasant young people.
5 The new app that I have just downloaded is very useful for my job.
6 The dilapidated building which is on the outskirts of the town has been chosen as the set for a movie.
7 Do you know the technician who repairs all the computers in our office?

2 請以關係代名詞 who、whom、which 或 whose 來完成句子。

UNIT
18
關係子句

1 My friend, ... father is a video-game designer, has lots of great video games.
2 Deborah, ... is my next-door neighbor, is a great cook and often invites me to dinner.
3 Steve, meet Dr. Wells, ... works for AT&T.
4 Our French partners, ... we have signed a contract with, will receive the documents next week.
5 This contract, ... we signed last week, must be sent to the buyers immediately.
6 Our rep, ... you met yesterday, is one of the best salesmen in our company.
7 Luke, ... is the best in his class, is also very helpful with all his classmates.
8 *The Big Bang Theory*, ... is a successful TV series, tells the story of four young scientists.

3 請以正確的關係代名詞結合兩個句子，注意部分句子含限定子句。

1 Our French teacher retired last month. We all liked her very much.

....

2 Mr. and Ms. Martin are a married couple. I met them in Spain last summer.

....

3 That is a self-portrait. My father painted it 20 years ago.

....

4 Do you know the name of that model? Her photo was on the front cover of *Vanity Fair* last week.

....

5 I work for Mr. Owen. He's the financial manager of our company.

....

6 I've got two younger sisters. I get on well with them.

....

7 *Cats* is a very famous musical. It has been on in theaters all over the world for years.

....

8 I hate the novels. They tell silly love stories.

....

9 The friends are very good at math and help me a lot. I study with them every day.

....

10 The desk is stacked with books and paper. I work at this desk.

....

LESSON 3 其他關係代名詞和副詞：what、all that、where、when等
Other relative pronouns and adverbs: *what, all that, where, when . . .*

其他代名詞和關係副詞如下：

what	I didn't hear **what** she said.
all/everything	• This is **all** we need. • They could have **everything** they liked. **Also** all that / everything that **NOT** ~~all what~~
which	意指前面一整個句子。由於這是非限定關係子句的用法，因此需要接在主要子句和逗號的後面： We all went to see him off at the station, **which** made him very happy.（指「我們去車站為他送行」這件事讓他很開心）
the reason why / why	I don't know **(the reason) why** she wouldn't tell me. **Also** the reason for which **NOT** ~~the reason because~~
how / the way	This is **how** they make this dish. = This is **the way** they make this dish.
where	The town **where** I was born is in the south of Scotland. = The town **in which** I was born is in the south of Scotland.
when	Youth is the time of life **when** everything seems possible. = Youth is the time of life **in which** everything seems possible.

> 請小心！在使用 **the year**、**the day**、**the time** 等用語時，通常會搭配 **when**、**in which**、**on which**、**at which** 或不使用副詞：
> • 2011 is **the year (when / in which)** we got married.
> • This is **the day (when / on which)** everyone gets their exam results.
> • One o'clock is **the time (when / at which)** we usually meet.

1 請圈出正確的用字。

1 "**All / That** you need is love" is a famous Beatles song.

2 Don't listen to **what / all what** she's saying!

3 I know it isn't much, but that's **all that / how** I can do for you.

4 Why are you so interested in **that / what** I'm doing?

5 There's no reason **how / why** we shouldn't go to that party.

6 You should teach me **all / how** to knit. You always make beautiful sweaters.

7 I like the smell of **how / what** you're cooking. What is it?

8 This is the place **when / where** we usually spend the weekend.

9 This is the year **when / which** Tom will get his degree at last.

10 Let's visit the village **whose / where** my parents met for the first time.

11 He never found out the reason **why / because** she had left him.

12 The office **in which / in where** I work has air conditioning.

2 請以 **when**、**why**、**where**、**that** 或 **how** 來完成句子，若關係代名詞可以省略，請以括號標出。

1 Tell me .... you made these cookies. They're delicious.

2 I'd like to know the reason .... you didn't come.

3 The country .... they come from is quite poor.

4 All .... you say from now on is going to be recorded.

5 This is the time .... they usually leave the office.

6 Tell me all .... you know about them.

7 Prime Day is .... the big sales start in the USA.

8 This is the hotel .... we spent our honeymoon.

9 A proverb says that "Home is .... you belong."

10 He didn't tell me .... he had to leave so early.

3 請使用 **which** 結合兩個句子。

1 Everybody liked the food I had cooked. It was quite surprising.

....

2 Connie passed her driving test. She didn't quite expect it.

....

3 They didn't come to the concert. It was a shame.

....

4 Sam will have to work next Sunday. It's quite unusual.

....

5 A lot of students in our school do voluntary work. It is really admirable.

....

6 Quite a number of start-up companies have opened in our town. This is good news.

....

4 請找出句中錯誤，並改寫出正確句子。

1 Why don't you tell me all which you know?

....

2 Give me one reason because I should help them.

....

3 This is the place on which I saw the accident.

....

4 An Indie Market is a place in where all the traders are independent.

....

5 Why don't you tell me way you solved the problem?

....

6 This is the time at when the ghost is said to appear in the Big Hall.

....

7 I couldn't see that which she was wearing under her coat.

....

LESSON 4 以現在分詞或過去分詞表達的關係子句／感官動詞
Relative clauses expressed by the present or past participle; verbs of perception

1 請觀察右圖，使用動詞 ing 或其他字詞，來寫出符合圖片的完整字句：

1 There's a policeman .... at the gate.

2 There are .... along a path.

3 There are two women .... on a bench.

4 There's a child with .... from a kiosk.

5 There are some boys .... on the grass.

2 請以下方感官動詞的正確形式來完成句子，注意會有一個詞要使用兩次。

hear	smell	taste	feel	watch

1 .... how soft this woolen scarf is!

2 Can't you .... the birds singing?

3 This drink .... so bitter! I don't like it.

4 Yesterday I .... the kids playing football for an hour.

5 I can .... the alcohol on your breath. What have you been drinking?

6 I .... your phone ring a minute ago.

主動行為的感官動詞用法

我們常會看見或聽見某人在做某事，根據不同情境有不同說法：

see/hear someone + 原形動詞	該行為十分短暫， 可以目睹整個過程	I **heard** someone **slam** the door.
see/hear someone + 進行式動詞的關係子句	該行為延續較長時間， 無法目睹整個過程	I **heard** someone **who was crying**.
see/hear someone + 動詞 ing（最常見）		I **heard** someone **crying**.

請參考以下兩個句子的差異：

• I **saw** two people **get** off the train.（有始有終的短暫行為 → **原形動詞**）

• I **saw** two people **waiting** for the train.
（維持較久，且在我停止觀看的當下仍持續中的行為 → **動詞 ing**）

> 在**否定句**或具有 **always**、**never**、**usually** 等頻率副詞的子句裡，
> 我們一般會使用**原形動詞**：
> • I **didn't** hear the phone **ring**. Did you?
> • I **always** hear dad **sing** in the bathroom in the morning.
> • I've **never** seen that girl **smile**.

被動行為的感官動詞用法

see/hear something	+ 過去分詞	該行為十分短暫， 可以目睹整個過程	I **heard** my name **called** out.
	+ 簡單式被動語態 的關係子句		I **heard** my name **that was** **called out**.
	+ 進行式被動語態 的關係子句	該行已發生一段時間， 無法目睹整個過程	I **saw** a cyclist **who was being** **chased by a dog**.
	+ being 過去分詞		I **saw** a cyclist **being chased** by a dog.

Focus

英文常以**過去分詞**取代被動語態的關係子句，例如：

• A fanzine is a magazine **written** and **read** by the fans of a singer or a group.
（取代 which is written and read 的寫法）

• The information **found** on this website needs double-checking.
（取代 that is found 的寫法）

感官動詞的被動語態

當感官動詞用於被動語態時，後面可接以下動詞形式：

to + 原形動詞	短暫的行為	He **was seen to leave** home at about three o'clock.
動詞 ing	持續較久的行為	They **were heard shouting** like mad.

3 請依照例句改寫句子。

0 The crocodile was moving. I saw it. .... *I saw the crocodile moving.* ....
The crocodile moved. I saw it .... *I saw the crocodile move.* ....

1 The kids were laughing. I heard them.

....

2 Something sweet was being baked. I smelled it.

....

3 Two men opened the door of the bank. I saw them.

....

4 A cold wind was blowing in the street. He felt it.

....

5 Two people left the room before the end of the lecture. I noticed them.

....

6 The waiter dropped a pile of plates. We saw him.

....

7 Somebody knocked at the door, but I didn't hear it.

....

8 The girl was playing the violin. I heard her.

....

4 請運用以下動詞的原形或 ing 形式來完成句子。

burn stand crash call wait gossip

1 We heard the sound of the glass .... onto the floor.

2 I saw a young man idly .... next to a lamppost.

3 We overheard two people .... about their colleagues.

4 I can smell something ....

5 Listen! I can hear somebody .... your name.

6 The witness saw the black car .... outside the bank.

5 請重新排序單字，以感官動詞的被動語態來造句。

1 throwing / He / was / stones / seen / .

....

2 heard / She / beautiful / was / a / song / singing / .

....

3 They / opening / were / the / door / heard / late / at / garage / night / .

....

4 noticed / Someone / walking / up / was / street / and / the / down / .

....

5 heard / He / to / was / whistle / .

....

6 been / You / seen / have / exam / during / copying / the / .

....

7 young / were / Some / hanging / people / noticed / late / night / last / around / .

....

8 was / to / Jack / get on / a / seen / the / train / at / station / .

....

9 baby / heard / at / The / was / crying / night / .

....

10 were / like / laughing / They / heard / mad / .

....

6 請依照例句，以「過去分詞」或「現在分詞」來結合兩個句子。

0 The painting was a Gauguin. It was stolen from the art gallery.
The painting stolen from the art gallery was a Gauguin.

1 Draw a picture of one of the animals. The animals are mentioned in the story.

....

2 The news was in an article. The article was published in a local magazine.

....

3 We're going to rent an apartment. The apartment is overlooking the sea.

....

4 The path leads to the waterfall. It's very steep.

....

5 My friend took some notes at the conference. They are very clear.

....

6 Try to explain the words. They are highlighted in the text.

....

7 A lady's sitting in the last row. Do you know her?

....

8 Do you know that girl? She's eating an ice cream.

....

7 請依照例句，將句子中的現在分詞或過去分詞改為「關係子句」。

0 The free WI-FI area was full of people using their laptops.
The free WI-FI area was full of people who were using their laptops.

1 This is the e-book illustrated by my father.

....

2 There were lots of kids playing games on the web.

....

3 There are more and more people using open-source software.

....

4 I met Linda looking for a new digital camera in the store.

....

5 There was a dark spot covering the PC screen.

....

6 He was looking at the images printed in color.

....

7 They usually double-check the information found on Wikipedia.

....

8 This is the new software created by a group of students aged 16.

....

ROUND UP 18

1 請將 1–6 與 A–F 配對成完整的句子。

..... **1** Colin has a computer game
..... **2** This is the girl
..... **3** Mark is the programmer
..... **4** They are the founders of a firm
..... **5** I bought the latest software
..... **6** She's the computer graphics artist

A whose work has been greatly praised.
B which exports hi-tech products.
C which can take days to finish.
D which is on the market.
E who designed my website.
F who lent me her tablet.

2 請以正確的關係代名詞 who、whom、which 或 whose 來完成句子。

1 Mr. Gray, ... is a music teacher, is also a good sportsman.

2 My neighbor, ... I asked for help with my computer, works in an electronics store.

3 Laura, ... is the best at math in our class, is also very good at playing chess.

4 My girlfriend, ... works in a pub, is looking for a better job.

5 This coffee machine, ... I bought last week, doesn't seem to work properly.

6 Your cousin, ... results in the test were outstanding, has joined my class.

7 Mark, ... I often play tennis with, has just bought a new racket.

8 These tennis balls, ... are quite expensive, do not seem to bounce very well.

9 You didn't tell me the truth, ... is quite bad of you.

10 He's the boy .... father is a web designer.

3 請改寫句子，將介系詞放在關係子句句尾，並省略關係代名詞。

0 The vacation to which he was looking forward had to be canceled.
The vacation he was looking forward to had to be canceled.
....

1 The text with which I was working suddenly vanished from the screen.
....

2 Who are the people for whom you are waiting?
....

3 The house in which they live is super technological.
....

4 The people with whom she went to the meeting went home early.
....

5 The e-book about which we were talking got an important award.
....

6 The music to which you are listening is played by the London Symphony Orchestra.
....

7 The kind of life to which they had got used was going to change.
....

8 The baby after whom I looked last summer is now nearly one year old.
....

4 請以 **in/at/on/for + which** 取代 **when/where/why** 來改寫句子。

1 There are moments when I would like to live on a desert island.

....

2 This is the university where both my husband and I studied years ago.

....

3 I don't know the reason why she left her job.

....

4 Last Friday was the day when we moved to the new office.

....

5 Three o'clock is the time when you can meet the sales manager.

....

6 Unfortunately there isn't a place where you can camp near here.

....

7 The country where they speak Urdu is Pakistan.

....

8 Can you give me a good reason why I should have a healthier life?

....

5 你正在把度假時拍的照片給朋友看。請以提示用詞描述照片。

0 alpine star / we saw on a rock   This is an alpine star that we saw on a rock.
1 hut / we stayed there for the night
2 hot chocolate / we drank it to make ourselves warm
3 the view / we had it from the top of the mountain
4 a little lake / we stopped there for a picnic
5 my trekking boots / muddy at the end of the day

6 the mountain peak / we could reach it
7 our friends / they climbed the mountain with us
8 our guide / he led us to the top
9 a marmot / we saw it in a meadow

6 請將下方非限定關係子句填入空格。

| which usually come | who are always directed | which is accompanied |
| which are mostly composed | which are set | which is broadcast |

The New Year's Concert from Vienna, [1].. in most European countries, is a must in my family on New Year's Day. The Wiener Philharmoniker, [2].. by one of the most famous orchestra directors in the world, play waltzes and polkas, [3].. by Johann Strauss father and son. The flowers on the stage, [4].. from Sanremo, Italy, are the most beautiful you've ever seen. The last piece that the orchestra play every year is the Radetzky March, [5].. by the hand clapping of the public. During the concert you can also see fantastic ballets, [6].. in the most amazing villas and parks of Austria.

7 請重新排序單字，寫出邏輯通順的句子。

1 are / Things / always / like / done / not / the way / I / .
....

2 the one / who / I'm / yesterday / to you / on / the / spoke / phone / .
....

3 is / movie / a / "Goodbye Mr. Holland" / good / came out / 1995 / in / which / .
....

4 who / is / A hero / does / day / his / duty / someone / every / .
....

5 is / painter / the / She / whose / girl / famous / mother / is / a / .
....

6 this / Is / the / which / present / for / you / Dad / bought / ?
....

8 請閱讀句子後，用括號標出可以省略的關係代名詞。

1 I've never met the girl who is going out with my brother.

2 It's the kind of game which I really like.

3 He's the man whom we saw at the movies last night.

4 Have you ever visited the art gallery which is in Victoria Road?

5 The MP3 player which I found in the park belongs to my friend Julia.

6 The people who were at your party are really nice.

7 That is the bed which I would like to buy. It looks extremely comfortable.

8 The office which is for rent in this street could be suitable for our start-up.

9 下方句子均有錯誤，請找出錯誤，並改寫出正確的句子。

1 That was all what we could do. ....

2 I'm so curious. Tell me that you know. ....

3 He's the one which I was waiting for. ....

4 We're leaving tomorrow, that makes me very sad. ....

5 My house is the place at which I most like to be. ....

6 Come and see those girls which are dancing so well. ....

7 Cupertino is the town which Apple has its headquarters. ....

8 Tigers are animals who are in danger of extinction. ....

10 請以合適的關係代名詞，來完成以下引述內容。

1 "A gentleman is one .... puts more into the world than he takes out."
George Bernard Shaw, Irish playwright

2 "Thinking is the hardest work there is, ... is probably the reason why so few engage in it." *Henry Ford, American captain of industry*

3 "A soulmate is the one person .... love is powerful enough to motivate you to meet your soul." *Kenny Loggins, American singer and songwriter*

4 "There are people .... , the more you do for them, the less they will do for themselves." *Jane Austen, English author*

5 "The love that lasts the longest is the love .... is never returned."
William Somerset Maugham, English author

11 請以正確的關係代名詞結合兩個句子。

1 Our rep will offer you favorable contracts. You met him last week.

....

2 The technician is really good. He has repaired my computer.

....

3 Tom is a whiz at IT. I'm studying with him today.

....

4 The homepage is updated every week. It was created by one of our programmers.

....

5 The printer is also a scanner and a photocopier. We have it in our office.

....

Reflecting on grammar

請研讀文法規則，再判斷以下說法是否正確。

		True	False
1	非限定子句需以逗號隔開。		
2	限定子句對理解句意十分重要。		
3	我們可以省略代表所有格的關係代名詞 whose。		
4	關係代名詞 that 可以取代限定關係子句裡的 who 或 which。		
5	who 用於表達動物和事物，which 用於表達人物。		
6	「This is the book I told you about.」是錯誤的句子； 「This is the book about which I told you.」才是正確的句子。		
7	我們絕對不能省略和句子受詞有關的關係代名詞。		
8	「This is all I have to tell you.」是正確的句子。		
9	以動詞 ing 形成的現在分詞，可取代關係子句。		
10	如果我們全程目睹某短暫行為，可使用原形動詞。		

1 請運用以下動詞的正確時態來完成短文。

get buy want have pay manage know

When I ^{1}..................................... to have a good laugh, I go to a show in my town. In winter, there are quite a lot of shows with stand-up comedians. I love going and enjoy watching all kinds of shows: musicals, comedies, drama, classical plays. If I had more money and more time, I ^{2}..................................... a season ticket. If you buy a season ticket, you ^{3}..................................... less and you ^{4}..................................... a seat reserved for you. If you buy five tickets for the same show, you ^{5}..................................... a 20% discount. If I ^{6}..................................... about that last year, I would have saved a lot of money because I generally go with four or five friends. If I ^{7}..................................... to save some money, I would have been able to go more often!

2 請將畫底線的片語改為被動語態。

They teach three languages in my school: French, German and Spanish. I'm learning one, German. Ms. Hofer, the German teacher, makes us work very hard: of course, we must speak only German during her lessons. She gives us lots of grammar exercises to do every day. She also asks us to read a new book and write a review of it every month, then we discuss each of our reviews in the class. You can obtain good results with Ms. Hofer only if you study really hard. If you want to learn a language very well, the best thing to do is go to a country where they speak it. But you can learn a language quite well in school too, if you have a teacher like mine!

3 請運用以下動詞的原形或 ing 形式來完成短文。

lead come live say get (x2) look wait sit

Lost and found

Tim Dalton, a six-year-old ^{1}..................................... in a village near Ashdown Forest, disappeared on his way home last Friday afternoon. When his mom didn't see him ^{2}..................................... in at the usual time, she immediately called the local police and a group of friends and they all started searching the area. The boy had been seen ^{3}..................................... on the school bus with his little friends and ^{4}..................................... off at the bus stop near home. Somebody had heard him ^{5}..................................... that he wanted to find the home of Winnie-the-Pooh, a popular fictional bear, in the forest near his house. Tim's mother remembered seeing him ^{6}..................................... out of his bedroom window at the forest, so they all decided to start searching there before it got dark. Along the main path ^{7}..................................... into the forest, the police dogs smelt something and they followed the scent towards a clearing in the wood. Tim was there, ^{8}..................................... in the middle of the clearing, ^{9}..................................... for Winnie to come.

The next day, one of his mom's friends gave Tim a Winnie-the-Pooh bear.

4 請閱讀以下短文，選出正確的答案。

When we think of rice, we imagine south-east Asian landscapes. However, we must remember that rice [0] ..D.. in Europe too, and Italy is the largest European producer. The total Italian production amounts to about 1,200,000 tons, 90% of which [1]...... every autumn in the triangle formed by joining the towns of Novara, Vercelli and Pavia with an imaginary line. Smaller quantities of rice grown in Sardinia and near the Po delta too. Rice [2]...... in April under irrigated conditions in large and highly mechanized farms. Today, less labor is needed than in the past: each hectare, [3]...... in 1939 required an average of 1,028 hours of work, now only needs an average of [4]...... 50 hours. The earliest documents about rice cultivation date back to the late Middle Ages, notably to 1475 when rice [5]...... promoted by Galeazzo Maria Sforza, Duke of Milan. If he [6]...... the Duke of Ferrara one sack of rice which was of such high quality that it enabled the farmer to harvest 12 sacks in return, rice growing [7]...... as quickly in the fertile marshy plains between Piedmont and Lombardy. A system of canals was built and water was brought to flood the rice fields in the month of April [8]...... rice is sown. The Italians have a saying: "Rice grows in water but dies in wine."

The most famous Italian yellow rice dish [9]...... conceived during the construction of the famous Milan cathedral when saffron [10]...... introduced to color the stained-glass windows of the cathedral and was added to rice as a joke.

0 Ⓐ are grown	Ⓑ has been grown	Ⓒ was grown	Ⓓ is grown
1 Ⓐ are harvested	Ⓑ is harvested	Ⓒ harvests	Ⓓ is harvesting
2 Ⓐ are planted	Ⓑ isn't planted	Ⓒ is planted	Ⓓ plants
3 Ⓐ which	Ⓑ who	Ⓒ whose	Ⓓ whom
4 Ⓐ less as	Ⓑ fewer than	Ⓒ as little than	Ⓓ as much as
5 Ⓐ has been	Ⓑ was	Ⓒ is	Ⓓ were
6 Ⓐ didn't give	Ⓑ has given	Ⓒ hadn't given	Ⓓ gave
7 Ⓐ wouldn't have spread	Ⓑ would spread	Ⓒ will have spread	Ⓓ won't spread
8 Ⓐ where	Ⓑ when	Ⓒ on which	Ⓓ which
9 Ⓐ is said to be	Ⓑ says to be	Ⓒ says to have been	Ⓓ is said to have been
10 Ⓐ has been	Ⓑ was	Ⓒ were	Ⓓ will be

5 請完成短文，填入正確的關係代名詞或副詞；可視情況省略非必要的關係代名詞。

Last Saturday, I didn't know [1].................................... to do or [2].................................... to go. My friend Debbie, [3].................................... I had arranged to meet in town, had just rung to say she had to look after her little brother, and so I was on my own. There were two or three things [4].............................. I needed to buy—makeup and some toiletries—so I walked to the shops, [5].................................... I was sure I would find them. But the shop [6].................................... I usually buy these things was closed. A notice, [7].................................... was hung on the front door, said that the shop had moved to Burlington Street, but I didn't know [8].................................... that was. I realized I had left my mobile at home, so I couldn't search the Internet, and I had to do it the old-fashioned way: ask somebody. I walked up to a man [9].................................... was sitting on a bench under a tree and asked him, but he didn't know either, so I decided to walk back home. Suddenly, on my way back and not too far from home, I saw the shop [10].................................... I had been looking for. It was much bigger than it used to be and you should have seen the guy at the cash desk: one of the best-looking young men [11].................................... I have ever seen. And guess what? We are going out together tomorrow, to the restaurant [12].................................... was opened a couple of weeks ago.

6 以下是歐洲海底隧道的說明。請於運用三個以內的單字，完成意義相近的句子。

1 France and Britain began the construction of the Eurotunnel in 1987. It was completed in 1994.

The Eurotunnel construction, ... , was completed in 1994.

2 The Eurotunnel was finished in only seven years.

It took ....

3 Queen Elizabeth II and French President François Mitterand officially opened it on May 6th, 1994.

It was .... on May 6th, 1994.

4 First they started the international freight train in commercial service.

The international freight train ....

5 The passenger shuttle service for cars came later that year. It was started on December 22nd, 1994.

The passenger shuttle service for cars, ..., ... 1994.

6 In March 1999, they named the Eurotunnel "Top Construction Achievement of the 20th Century."

The Eurotunnel ....

EURO TUNNEL

7 請自行思考最貼切的單字，來完成本篇短文。每一格僅能填入一個單字。

I'm so glad that I did that computer course [0] ...... in ...... September. You see, the company was looking for someone [1] .... knew most types of office software. If I hadn't [2] .... good computer skills, I [3] .... have been right for the position I've got now.

When I started the course, I wasn't sure I would [4] .... able to complete it. I had three 90-minute lessons a week, [5] .... is quite a lot when you're working too, and the course lasted four months. On top of that, the lessons, [6] .... were from 7 to 8:30 p.m., weren't always in the same school, so [7] .... I forgot to write the place in my diary, I could easily end up at the wrong school and miss the lesson!

Luckily the teacher was very good. If he [8] .... been, I would have probably given up after a while. He was very clear and patient. We [9] .... taught the most up-to-date versions of the most widely used software and we [10] .... given really challenging tasks, which had to be completed in groups. That way, I also made new friends during the course.

Towards Competences

在以上單元中，我們學到的部分文法都是典型的正式書寫用，尤其是敘述和說明文字的被動語態，以及非限定關係子句。請盡量運用此類文法，完成下方兩個題目。

1 根據學校的交換學生計畫，你的班級需要在科學實驗後，編寫可發表於網站的詳細報告。你是報告負責人，請介紹你在實驗室完成的實驗。

2 學校有專為姊妹校所設計的網站，你的任務是編寫你居住區域的主要活動。請稍微調查，並編寫 300 字左右的內容，附上有趣且實用的照片。

REPORT SHEET

Experiment: [_____]

Date: [_____]

Laboratory: [_____]

Materials used and their quantities:

[_____]

Procedure: [_____]

Self Check 6

請選出答案，再至解答頁核對正確與否。

1. You .... me that the meeting had been canceled.
   Ⓐ could have told   Ⓑ could told
   Ⓒ had told

2. He .... very tired last night. He went to bed at 9:30.
   Ⓐ had to have been   Ⓑ must have been
   Ⓒ must had been

3. If you .... a little milk to the mixture, you get a softer cake.
   Ⓐ will add   Ⓑ added   Ⓒ add

4. Get some bread if you .... to the supermarket.
   Ⓐ will go   Ⓑ go   Ⓒ would go

5. .... too much time watching TV if you want to go out later.
   Ⓐ You won't spend   Ⓑ Don't spend
   Ⓒ Won't spend

6. If my favorite team .... tonight, I'll give up chocolate for a week!
   Ⓐ wins   Ⓑ will win   Ⓒ could win

7. If you book your flight now, ... 30% less.
   Ⓐ you'd pay   Ⓑ you'd paid
   Ⓒ you'll pay

8. If I ...., I wouldn't spend my day watching videos on YouTube.
   Ⓐ were you   Ⓑ be   Ⓒ would be you

9. If Mark .... arrived so late, he could have had lunch with us.
   Ⓐ hadn't   Ⓑ wasn't   Ⓒ didn't

10. .... to work night shifts if they had accepted the job.
    Ⓐ They would had have
    Ⓑ They'd have
    Ⓒ They would have had

11. Would you buy a new suit if they .... you to their New Year's party?
    Ⓐ invited
    Ⓑ had invited
    Ⓒ would invite

12. If Alan Turing .... his data-processing device, we wouldn't have our personal computers today.
    Ⓐ didn't develop
    Ⓑ hadn't developed
    Ⓒ don't develop

13. If he had asked, we .... him.
    Ⓐ could have helped   Ⓑ had helped
    Ⓒ must have helped

14. That vase on the shelf is .... of Bohemian crystal.
    Ⓐ done   Ⓑ built   Ⓒ made

15. The best sports equipment can be .... in the shop in the mall.
    Ⓐ find   Ⓑ found   Ⓒ finding

16. "Who .... ?" "Picasso."
    Ⓐ was Guernica painted by
    Ⓑ by was Guernica painted
    Ⓒ was painted Guernica by

17. The story .... told with background music and photos.
    Ⓐ have been   Ⓑ was   Ⓒ has

18. We discovered our flight .... canceled when we got to the airport.
    Ⓐ is just been   Ⓑ was just been
    Ⓒ had just been

19. The new CEO will .... appointed in a few days.
    Ⓐ have been   Ⓑ be   Ⓒ have be

20. The winners of the competition .... by tomorrow evening.
    Ⓐ will be announcing
    Ⓑ will being announced
    Ⓒ will have been announced

21 Dear me! This project .... before five this afternoon. It's far too long!

Ⓐ may finish   Ⓑ won't be finished
Ⓒ will have finished

22 They .... a wonderful Ferrari, but it was too expensive.

Ⓐ have been shown   Ⓑ are shown
Ⓒ were shown

23 The best students in our school .... a scholarship every year.

Ⓐ are granting   Ⓑ have granted
Ⓒ are granted

24 We .... a very moving story during yesterday's reading meeting at the library.

Ⓐ have been told   Ⓑ were told
Ⓒ would tell

25 Ms. Hogan .... the most skilled financial manager our company has ever had.

Ⓐ say to be   Ⓑ has said being
Ⓒ is said to be

26 This is considered .... one of the most beautiful portraits of our age.

Ⓐ being   Ⓑ to be   Ⓒ be

27 They were supposed .... in the warehouse, but they were actually taking a much longer break.

Ⓐ to be working   Ⓑ work
Ⓒ they will work

28 Karen .... for the end-of-school party.

Ⓐ had her hair dyed blond
Ⓑ did her hair dyed blond
Ⓒ was dyed her hair blond

29 Could you tell me the name of the person .... car is parked next to mine?

Ⓐ which   Ⓑ whom   Ⓒ whose

30 This is the lady .... we met on the train.

Ⓐ which   Ⓑ whose   Ⓒ /

31 The model .... photo was on the cover of Vogue lives next door to my parents.

Ⓐ who her   Ⓑ who's   Ⓒ whose

32 The chair .... is in that corner is very old and valuable.

Ⓐ which   Ⓑ who   Ⓒ what

33 Jane and Tessa, ... are the friends I usually go on vacation with, aren't going to come with us this year.

Ⓐ how   Ⓑ who   Ⓒ that

34 September is the month .... the school year starts in most of Europe.

Ⓐ in which   Ⓑ when   Ⓒ where

35 Tell me the reason .... you gave up your job.

Ⓐ how   Ⓑ because   Ⓒ why

36 Do you know the restaurant .... they serve crocoburgers?

Ⓐ why   Ⓑ on which   Ⓒ where

37 November 15th was the day .... my mother retired.

Ⓐ at when   Ⓑ on which   Ⓒ in which

38 This wine .... off. Throw it away.

Ⓐ tastes   Ⓑ sounds   Ⓒ looks

39 I didn't hear the front door bell .... Are you sure there was somebody there?

Ⓐ rung   Ⓑ is ringing   Ⓒ ring

40 She was seen .... some T-shirts from the market stall.

Ⓐ stolen   Ⓑ stealing   Ⓒ stole

Assess yourself!

0 - 10   還要多加用功。
11 - 20   尚可。
21 - 30   不錯。
31 - 40   非常好！

SELF CHECK 6

LESSON 1 動詞 say 和 tell 的用法 Verbs *say* and *tell*

動詞 say

動詞 say（say–said–said）適用於以下情況：

❶ 在直述句裡，表達「**某人所說的話**」會以引號標出，接著先標逗號，say 則放在最後。

　❶ 講者的名稱通常會放在動詞後面，但也可以放在動詞前面
　　• "Everything's ready," **said Peter / Peter said**.

　❷ 但講者若是**代名詞**，則一定要放在**動詞前面**
　　• "Help me, please!" **he said**.

> ❗ 切記！當我們要寫出說話的**對象**，say 的後面必須接介系詞 **to**：
> "You're right," she said **to** me. NOT she said me.

❷ 引導轉述句當**未指出與我們對話的人物是誰**時：
　• He **said** he would come the following day.

> ❗ 切記！在主要子句和後接的敘述子句之間，連接詞 **that 可被省略**：
> The weather forecast says **(that)** it will rain tomorrow.

❸ **有人稱被動語態**，句型為 **someone is said to be/have**：
　• **She is said to have** a great talent.
　• **He is said to have been** a hero in time of war.

動詞 tell

動詞 tell（tell–told–told）適用於以下情況：

❶ 用來引導轉述句，但只能在**知道講述者名稱**的情況下使用。句中人物、名稱或代名詞，後面均**不需接介系詞**，如：「I told Jane.」、「I told her.」。

　使用動詞 tell 的主要子句，後面可接以下用語：
　❶ 可省略 that 的敘述子句：He told me **(that) he had just arrived**.
　❷ to + 動詞：I told him **to keep** calm.

❷ 用於直述句的引號句子，但只能在引號後**有提及對話人物**時：
　"I'm ready to go," she **told him**.（如果沒有提到對話的人物，只要說 she said 即可）

❸ **有人稱的被動語態**，寫為 **someone was told to do / not to do something**：
　• **He was told to** stay at home.　　• **I was told not to** go.

請參考下方兩種句型的整理表：

直述句	轉述句
" . . . ," he said / said Peter.	He said / Peter said (that) . . .
" . . . ," he said to me / he told me.	He told me (that) . . .
" . . . ," said my father / my father said.	My father told me (that) . . .
" . . . ," my father said to me / my father told me.	My father told me to . . .

say 和 tell 的其他用法

動詞 say 和 tell 亦有以下常用表達用法：

say	tell
say yes/no	tell the truth
say a word	tell a lie
say please	tell the time
say thank you	tell a story
say something, say nothing	tell jokes
say hello/goodbye	tell someone your name
say a poem/prayer	tell someone about something

1 請使用 **say** 或 **tell** 的正確形式來完成句子。

1 .... me about your new school, Simon.

2 Don't .... a word. Someone may be listening.

3 .... thank you to Grandma, Carol.

4 I'm very bad at .... jokes.

5 Why don't you .... me the truth?

6 Did I .... something wrong?

7 .... yes, Mom. Please let me go to the party!

8 Excuse me, can you .... me the time, please?

2 請圈出正確的用字。

1 I told **her** / **to her** it was too late.

2 I said **him** / **to him** that I couldn't come before eight.

3 "Hurry up!" **said she** / **she said**.

4 They were told **not to be late** / **to be not late**.

5 "Wake up, lazybones!" my mother **says** / **tells** every morning.

6 He told **to me** / **me** that it was a lie.

7 They **told** / **said** goodbye and went away.

8 "Don't wait for me. I'll be late," she **told** / **told us**.

3 請將主動語態句改為被動語態句。

1 They told me to wait until they came back.

I was ....

2 They say she's a great artist.

She is ....

3 They told us to reach the conference room before nine.

....

4 They say the lecturer is one of the best in his field.

....

5 They told the Board of Directors to meet in the afternoon.

....

6 They say that Serena Williams is one of the best tennis players ever.

....

LESSON 2 轉述句：下達命令，以及表達至今仍屬實的說辭

Indirect speech: giving orders and expressing statements in the present that are still true

轉述指令或建議

直述句	轉述句
祈使句 My friend said to me: **"Take a break and relax."**	**to / not to + 原形動詞** My friend told me **to take a break and relax.**
	(that) + 主詞 + should/shouldn't + 原形動詞 My friend told me **(that) I should take a break and relax.**

請參考另一個例句：

- "Don't worry, everything will be alright," his mother told him. →
  His mother told him **not to worry / (that) he shouldn't worry.**

除了 tell 和 say，轉述句還能用其他動詞引導子句，例如 order、remind、warn、ask、advise：

- She **reminded** me to lock the door.　• They **warned** us not to drive on the icy road.

1 請依照例句，將句子改寫為兩種句型的轉述句。

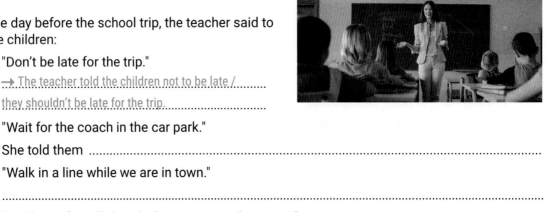

The day before the school trip, the teacher said to the children:

0 "Don't be late for the trip."

　→ The teacher told the children not to be late / they shouldn't be late for the trip.

1 "Wait for the coach in the car park."

She told them ....

2 "Walk in a line while we are in town."

....

3 "Hold your friend's hand when we cross the street."

....

4 "Don't walk around on your own."

....

5 "Bring your packed lunch."

....

6 "Don't forget to bring an anorak and a hat."

....

7 "Wear comfortable shoes."

....

8 "Remind your parents to pick you up at 6 p.m. in front of the school."

....

2 請運用下方動詞的正確形式來完成句子。

| order | warn | remind | ask | advise |

1 "Take some photos of the event, please."

I was .... to take some photos of the event.

2 "Remember to send the photos to the press."

They .... me to send the photos to the press.

3 "You shouldn't drive in this weather!"

They .... us not to drive in that weather.

4 "Three coffees, please."

They .... three coffees.

5 "Keep away from the fire, Jack!"

His mother .... Jack to keep away from the fire.

3 請使用括號裡的動詞，將句子改寫為轉述句。

0 "Don't go out in the cold, Marion," said her mother. (tell)

Marion's mother told her not to go out in the cold.
....

1 "You should use sunscreen in this heat," said Mike. (advise)

....

2 "Don't feed the animals," the ranger said to the visitors. (remind)

....

3 "Stop making so much noise, children," said the teacher. (tell)

....

4 "Don't drive up the mountain in this snow," the police said to the drivers. (warn)

....

5 "Leave your valuables in the hotel safe," said the receptionist to the hotel guests. (advise)

....

轉述現在的說辭：He says that . . .

如果引導動詞是**現在式**，且與當下相比，**所轉述的事實仍未改變**，那在將直述句改為轉述句時，**動詞時態不須改變**。不過，人稱和所有格代名詞卻會有所改變。請看下表：

主格代名詞	I → he/she	you → I/we	we → they
受格代名詞	me → him/her	you → me/us	us → them

主格代名詞	my → his/her	your → my/our	our → their
所有格代名詞	mine → his/hers	yours → mine/ours	ours → theirs

請參考以下例句：

直述句	轉述句
Mom always says, "**I** <u>don't like</u> the way **you** dress. **Your** clothes <u>look</u> so shabby!"	My mother always tells **me** that **she** <u>doesn't like</u> the way **I** dress and that **my** clothes <u>look</u> shabby.

大家可看到，直述句和轉述句均使用簡單現在式，但代名詞和所有格卻有所不同。

> 當引導動詞是**過去式**，且轉述的事實恆為真理，或與當下相比還尚未改變，那麼改為轉述句後，**動詞時態依舊不變**。請看以下例句：
> - "The museum **opens** at nine," said the teacher. → The teacher said that the museum **opens** at nine.（表示博物館 9 點開門，此為確切的事實）
> - "John**'s having** a great time in London," his friend told me. → His friend told me that John**'s having** a great time in London.（意指情況未改變，約翰仍在倫敦玩得很開心）

4 請使用下方動詞來完成句子。

| would like   says (x2)   will be   going   thinks   dates back   look   has passed |

1 A survey .... teenagers .... at their cell phones up to 16 times an hour!

2 James says the exam was very hard, but he .... he .... it.

3 My daughter always says she .... to spend a semester studying abroad.

4 The weather forecast .... it .... overcast in the morning.

5 What does Tom say he's .... to do?

6 Our guide said that the castle .... to the 13th century.

5 請改寫為轉述句。

1 Robert says, "I've just found a part-time job in a pub."

Robert says he .... a part-time job in a pub.

2 Laura always says, "I want to go to the States when I finish studying."

Laura always says .... to go to the States when .... studying.

3 My dad often tells me, "You need to work hard if you want your dreams to come true."

My dad often tells me .... to work hard if .... to come true.

4 Ryan says, "I'm going to the Everglades this afternoon."

Ryan says .... to the Everglades this afternoon.

5 "The next test is on Monday, October 11th," says the teacher.

The teacher says ....

6 a 萊德先生（**Mr. Ryder**）正用 **Skype** 與就讀布萊頓大學的女兒莎拉（**Sarah**）通話。請閱讀以下對話。

Dad So, how is life in Brighton, Sarah?

Sarah I quite like it, Dad. I've made some new friends already. Oh, and I went to see Uncle Jack yesterday in Hove.

Dad Good. What about the weather? Is it cold there?

Sarah Yes, it's quite cold. I've just been out shopping for some winter clothes.

Dad What did you buy?

Sarah I've bought a jumper and an anorak because it's quite windy here.

Dad Are you coming back home next weekend?

Sarah No, I'm not, I'm afraid. I've got to study. I think I'll come back in a fortnight.

Dad Oh, no. I'll be away on business then. But Mom will be home. Well, bye, Sarah! I'll call you again in a couple of days.

Sarah Bye, Dad! And say hello to Mom.

b 萊德先生（**Mr. Ryder**）後來向太太轉述與女兒的對話。請使用與對話相同的動詞來完成以下短文，記得把握時態相同、代名詞不同的原則。

"Sarah says [1] .... life at college. She says that [2] .... some new friends and that [3] .... Uncle Jack yesterday. She says [4] .... just [5] .... shopping for some winter clothes because it's quite cold there. [6] .... a jumper and anorak because [7] .... And she says that [8] .... home next weekend because [9] ....
She thinks [10] .... in a fortnight. Pity, because I [11] .... on business but [12] .... home. Anyway, I [13] .... in a couple of days. Oh, and she says [14] ...."

LESSON 3 轉述句：過去屬實的說辭

Indirect speech: statements that were true in the past

直述句和轉述句

轉述過去屬實的說辭：He said that . . .

如果現在轉述的事實或看法**在過去屬實**，我們就使用**過去式的轉述句**，並依照下表改變動詞時態：

直述句	轉述句
簡單現在式："I like it."	簡單過去式：He said he liked it.
現在進行式："I'm going."	過去進行式：He said he was going.
簡單過去式："I saw John."	過去完成式：He said he had seen John.
現在完成式："I've been there."	過去完成式：He said he had been there.
簡單未來式："I will go."	現在式條件句：He said he would go.

如在第 349 頁所學，在轉述句中許多句子裡的要件會有所改變，看看下方的例子：

指示形容詞	this → **that**	"Take this book!" → **He told me to take that book.**
	these → **those**	"Do you like these paintings?" → **He asked me if I liked those paintings.**
地方副詞	here → **there**	"Come here!"→ **He told me to go there.**
時間副詞和時間用語	now → **then**	"Do it now!" → **He asked me to do it then.**
	today → **that day**	"I'm going shopping today." → **He said he was going shopping that day.**
	tonight → **that night/evening**	"I'm staying home tonight." → **He said he was staying home that night.**
	yesterday → **the day before / the previous day**	"I saw her yesterday." → **He said he had seen her the day before.**
	tomorrow → **the next/following day / the day after**	"I'm leaving tomorrow." → **He said he would leave the next day.**
	last Saturday → **the previous Saturday**	"We arrived last Monday." → **They told me they had arrived the previous Monday.**
	two weeks ago → **two weeks before/earlier**	"We were in Paris two weeks ago." → **They told us they were in Paris two weeks before.**
	next week → **the following week**	"The games start next week." → **They said the games started / would start the following week.**

351

直述句	轉述句
• Ben said, "I **can't** go skating tomorrow because I **have** some work to do."	• Ben said he **couldn't** go skating the following day because he **had** some work to do.
• Danny said, "My friend**'s helping** me a lot with my math homework."	• Danny said his friend **was helping** him a lot with his math homework.
• Emma said, "We **didn't play** the final of the tennis tournament yesterday because it **rained** all day."	• Emma said they **hadn't played** the final of the tennis tournament the day before because it **had rained** all day.
• Alan said, "I**'ve been here** for two months, but I still **don't know** many people."	• Alan said he **had been there** for two months, but he still **didn't know** many people.
• Georgia said, "I**'m going** on a trip to Yosemite National Park next week. I**'m** sure it **will be** a great experience!"	• Georgia said she **was going** on a trip to Yosemite National Park the following week and added (that) she **was** sure it **would be** a great experience.

除了 say 和 tell，轉述句中還能使用其他引導動詞，例如 add、**explain**、**remark**、**claim**、**state**（正式用法）等單字：In 1956, the Supreme Court of the United States **stated** that segregation on buses was illegal.

1 請使用轉述句，來完成句子。

0 "'He's been waiting for an hour," they said.

They said ...he had been waiting.... for an hour.

1 "I won't be back from Chicago till tomorrow," she said.

She said .... from Chicago till ....

2 "Our next school trip will be in two weeks' time. We'll be going to Windsor," said the teacher.

The teacher said .... next school trip .... two weeks later and added .... to Windsor.

3 "I spent my vacation in Oslo three years ago," she said.

She said .... vacation in Oslo three years ....

4 "I'll phone you tomorrow when I arrive," he said.

He said .... when ....

5 "I booked my flight last week," Ted said.

Ted said .... flight ....

2 請使用動詞 say 和 tell 改寫出轉述句。

1 They said to us, "We went to a new Thai restaurant last Saturday. It was really good."

They told us they .... and added it ....

2 Jane said to me, "I always travel by myself. That way I'm more open to meeting new people."

....

3 I said to my secretary, "I'm going to leave earlier tomorrow."

....

4 "We have been to the museum this morning," they said.

....

5 "I'm afraid I won't be able to get seats for tonight's show," the receptionist told us.

....

6 Mom said, "I can't go to bed early tonight. I still have a lot of work to do."

....

3 請運用以下動詞的正確時態來完成短文。

sound write be (x3) say move can live get

When my son [1].......................... in Thailand for the first
time in 2012, he [2].......................... me an email every day.
He [3].......................... enthusiastic about the place. He
[4].......................... the people [5].......................... friendly and
the food was superb. He also said there [6]..........................
fantastic sandy beaches and magnificent plants and flowers.
And he said that if he [7].......................... find a job, he would
like to [8].......................... there. And that's what he did! He
[9].......................... a job as a scuba-diving instructor on the island
of Phuket and [10].......................... there ever since.

4 請使用括號裡的引導動詞，將句子改寫為轉述句。

1 The law in 1865: "Slavery is abolished all over the United States." (state)

....

2 The suspect: "I was at home all day on June 1st. I didn't see anyone except for my wife."
(claim–add)

....

....

3 The physics teacher yesterday: "The speed of a body is the distance it covers over a period
of time." (explain)

....

4 Critics: "The famous composer's new symphony is not very original." (remark)

....

5 運動服飾公司的經理正在開會。請閱讀下方對話，並準備一份會議紀錄報告。

Sales Manager: Some of our customers would like a new, more technological product.
They are asking for an even lighter waterproof jacket.

Purchasing Manager: In that case, we have to buy a different kind of fabric to meet their
requirements.

Production Manager: The machines should be updated too if we want to manufacture a
new product.

Finance Manager: I think we have to draw up a business plan. The costs can't exceed
the benefits.

Sales Manager: We also need to carry out a survey so that we have real data to analyze.

Finance Manager: And the survey must be included in the costs. We can send
questionnaires because interviews will be more expensive.

Now prepare a report about what was discussed.

This is the report of the March 15th meeting.
The Sales Manager stated that some of the customers would like . . .
The Purchasing Manager remarked that . . .

LESSON 4 間接問句 Reported speech: questions

間接問句

1 將直接問句改為間接問句

我們通常使用 **ask** 作為引導問句的動詞。此動詞可用於主動語態（I asked him）和被動語態（He was asked）。

可用其他動詞引導轉述問句，寫成：
I want to know / I'd like to know / I wonder . . .

2 間接問句有下方特性：

❶ 與肯定句的句型相同，也就是**主詞 + 動詞**（不需倒裝）：
"What time is it?"
→ She asked me what time it was.
（ NOT what time ~~was it.~~ ）

❷ 不使用助動詞 **do**：
"What kind of movies do you like?"
→ He asked me what kind of movies I like.

3 Wh 問句

Wh 直接問句裡的 Wh 疑問詞（What、Where、How、How often 等），改為間接問句後仍不變；時態的變化規則則與敘述子句裡的用法相同：

- "How often do you train?" he asked me.
  → He asked me how often I **trained**.
- "Who did you see?" she asked him.
  → She asked him who he **had seen**.

4 Yes/No 問句

❶ 我們使用連接詞 if 來引導 Yes/No 間接問句：
"Do you often go skiing, Trish?" asked Oliver.
→ Oliver asked Trish **if** she often went skiing.

❷ 還可使用連接詞 whether . . . or . . . ：
"Did you do this puzzle by yourself or did someone help you, Julia?"
→ I asked Julia **whether** she had done the puzzle by herself **or (whether)** someone had helped her.

FAQ

Q: 我們常說間接問句，那如果是間接答句呢？

A: 要引導答句，我們可以使用 **answer** 或是更正式的 **reply**。看看下方例句：

- "Do you like the movie?" "Yes, I do."
  → He asked me if I liked the movie and I **answered** that I did.
- "Do you know when we have our next school trip?" "No, I don't."
  → My friend asked me if I knew when we had our next school trip and I **answered** <u>that I didn't</u>。（記住不是說「I answered <u>yes/no</u>。」！）

5 提議與提案

❶ 要轉述有提議或提案意思的問句，如「How/What about . . . ?」、「Why don't you . . . ?」，我們通常使用動詞 **suggest** 或更正式的 **recommend**。看看以下句型：

| **suggest to** + 某人 + **that** + 主詞 + **should/could** + 原形動詞 |

- "Why don't you go for a walk before dinner, Sam?"
- → I **suggested** to Sam that he **could go** for a walk before dinner.

| **suggest that** + 主詞 + 動詞的**簡單過去式** |

- "Why don't you go for a walk?" → I **suggested** that they **went** for a walk.

❷ 當有人提議做某事，且提議者也是執行該提議的一員時，對方可能會說「Let's / Why don't we . . . ?」，而在轉述時我們可以採用以下句型：

| **suggest + 動詞 ing** | 或者 | **suggest + we should** + 原形動詞 |

- "Why don't we wait for them?"
- → I **suggested waiting** for them. / I **suggested we should wait** for them.

1 請完成間接問句。

1 John: "Where can I find the tickets for the show, please?"

John asked me where ....

....

2 My friend: "What time shall we meet?"

My friend asked me what time ....

....

3 Peter: "Why don't we play video games?"

Peter suggested ....

....

4 Rachel: "What about looking on Wikipedia?"

Rachel suggested that we ....

....

5 Sammy: "How much does this tablet cost?"

Sammy asked the assistant ....

....

6 "What does he have on his mind?"

I still wonder ....

....

7 "When are they coming?"

I'd like to know ....

....

8 Suzanne: "Why don't you take up a winter sport?"

Suzanne suggested ....

2 請改寫為間接問句。

0 "Did you enjoy the trip, John?" she asked.

She asked John if he had enjoyed the trip.

....

1 Amanda asked: "What time is Jane coming tomorrow?"

....

....

2 Angela asked: "Does Sammy like canoeing?"

....

....

3 Tom asked me: "Why didn't you go swimming last night?"

....

....

4 Sally asked Kate: "Is your brother working in Switzerland?"

....

....

5 I asked Sue: "Can you lend me your pen, please?"

....

....

6 The teacher asked: "Class, have you done your homework?"

....

....

3 請以間接問句改寫對話。

1 **Grandma:** "What's your school like?" **Me:** "It's great!"

Grandma asked me .... and I answered ....

2 "How long have you lived in Italy?" "For two years."

I was asked .... and I answered ....

3 **Dad:** "Did you know that more standing stones have been found near Stonehenge?"

Me: "No, I didn't."

Dad asked me if .... and I

answered that ....

4 **Pat:** "Have you ever been to Iceland?"

Me: "No, I've never been there. But I would like to go. I know it must be an amazing place."

Pat asked me if .... and I answered that I ....

.... and I added .... because ....

5 **Mom:** "Are you curious to know your exam results?" **Me:** "I can't wait!"

Mom asked me if .... and I answered that ....

4 請改寫為直述句。

1 Sarah told me she lived in a new house.

Sarah: ....

2 Ben asked David where he had studied Italian.

Ben: ....

3 Mom said she was very tired.

Mom: ....

4 Mr. Smith told Jason that he would arrive late the next day.

Mr. Smith: ....

5 Fiona asked me if Tom was working that afternoon.

Fiona: ....

5 請將下方段落改寫為對話。

Marco: "I met an old friend, Julie, the other day. She asked me when we had last seen each other. I told her that I thought it had been two years earlier. Then she asked me if I still lived in the same house near the main street. I said no, I'd moved to a new house. She wanted to know where it was and I told her it was in the suburbs. She asked if I liked it and I told her I loved it because it had a big garden and a conservatory."

Julie   Hi, Marco!

Marco   Hi, Julie! It's nice to see you again.

Julie   ....

Marco   ....

6 請以轉述句寫出 Yes/No 問句和答句。

0 "Do you go skating every day, Lisa?" asked Ellen. "Yes, I do," Lisa answered.

Ellen asked Lisa if/whether she went skating every day and Lisa answered that she did.

1 "Have you been to Athens before, Rick?" asked John. "No, I haven't," Rick answered.

....

2 "Are you having fun at the water park, children?" asked Emma. "Yes, we are!" the children said.

....

3 "Is your husband happy with his new motorbike, Sarah?" asked Matt.
"Yes, he's very happy," Sarah said.

....

4 "Did you come by train, Sylvia?" asked Mark. "No, I didn't. I came in the car," Sylvia answered.

....

5 "Do you have time to go for lunch, Julia?" asked Angela.
"Yes, I have," Julia said. "I suggest we go to the pub on the corner."

....

7 請將 1–6 與 A–F 配對成完整的句子。

..... **1** The doctor wanted to know   **A** if they had all understood the new lesson.

..... **2** The coach asked the team   **B** where they could find a nice place for their tent.

..... **3** The campers wondered   **C** if they had been exercising lately.

..... **4** The teacher asked the students   **D** when I was going to come home from college.

..... **5** The golf instructor wanted to know   **E** how long I had had those symptoms.

..... **6** My parents asked me   **F** if I had ever played before.

8 請以動詞 **suggest** 或 **recommend** 來寫出轉述句的提議。

0 "Why don't we go fishing next weekend?" said Luke.
Luke suggested going / that they went fishing the following weekend.

1 "How about eating at the new Thai restaurant tonight?" said Lewis.

....

2 "You should go to Rhodes next summer," said the tour operator.

....

3 "What about organizing a garage sale to raise some money?" asked Marion.

....

4 "You'd better not go out today, Peter," said his mother.

....

5 "Let's have a sleepover at my house on Saturday," said June.

....

6 "You should have a long brisk walk at least twice a week," said the therapist.

....

9 請將 **Wh** 問句改為間接問句。記得主要子句裡要使用括號裡動詞的簡單過去式。

0 Linda: "How are you going to travel to Portugal?" (ask)
Linda asked how we were going / would be going to travel to Portugal.

1 Ryan: "Where will they go on vacation next summer?" (wonder)

....

2 Olivia: "Who has booked the seats for the theater?" (want to know)

....

3 Carl: "What time are we meeting our guide for the city tour?" (ask)

....

4 Pamela: "When is Nancy leaving for Rome?" (want to know)

....

5 Simon: "Where would you like to go today?" (ask)

....

6 Mr. Wilson: "What is my son going to do when he leaves school?" (wonder)

....

1 請判斷下方各詞應搭配 **say** 還是 **tell**，並填入正確的類別中。

| the time | hello | no | something wrong | a lie | the truth |
| a word | the difference | a joke | me about it | thank you | goodbye |

SAY	**TELL**

2 請使用動詞 **say** 或 **tell** 的正確時態來完成句子。

1 You should always .... *please* and *thank you*.

2 Where's your mom? I want to .... goodbye to her.

3 They didn't .... me the truth about what had happened.

4 Vicky .... we were going to meet at 4:30.

5 Can you .... the difference between a bee and a wasp?

6 "Remember to take your keys," she .... him.

7 Could you please .... me what time it is?

8 "Don't forget your packed lunch," .... his mother.

9 My teacher always .... we must work hard for the exam.

10 Why didn't you .... me it was time to go?

3 請將 **1–8** 與 **A–H** 配對成完整的句子。

1 The science teacher told us   **A** not to drive on the icy road.

2 A police officer warned us   **B** visitors to the park to walk only along the path.

3 The doctor advised me   **C** not to come back late on Saturday night.

4 The zookeeper reminded the children   **D** to find information about global warming.

5 The ranger warned   **E** to do physical exercise and lose some weight.

6 Rachel's mother warned her   **F** not to swim far out to sea when it's rough.

7 The teacher asked the children   **G** not to feed the monkeys.

8 A life guard advised bathers   **H** to stop making all that noise.

1 .....   **2** .....   **3** .....   **4** .....   **5** .....   **6** .....   **7** .....   **8** .....

4 請以正確的代名詞、指示副詞和時間副詞，來完成意義相近的句子。

0 Weather forecaster: "There will be heavy rain tomorrow."

The weather forecaster said there would be heavy rain .....the following day..... .

1 Hilary: "I will go skiing this afternoon if it doesn't snow too hard."

Hilary said that .... would go skiing .... afternoon if it didn't snow too hard.

2 Andrew: "I can't come to see you next weekend. I'll be working."

Andrew said that .... couldn't come to see .... because .... would be working.

3 Danny: "Dad, we haven't watched this movie yet."

Danny told his dad that .... hadn't watched .... movie yet.

4 Ruth: "I really want to visit this art gallery. I like pop art."

Ruth said that .... really wanted to visit .... art gallery. She also said .... likes pop art.

5 PE teacher: "You aren't trying hard enough this term, Mike. Practice makes perfect."

The PE teacher told Mike that .... wasn't trying hard enough .... term. He added that practice makes perfect.

6 Shop assistant: "We don't have any blue jackets in stock. You should try again at the end of next week."

The shop assistant said .... didn't have any blue jackets in stock. She added that .... should try again at the end of ....

5 請進行所有必要更改，來寫出轉述句。

0 My best friend told me, "I'm happy to hear you are expecting a child!"

My best friend told me she was happy to hear I'm expecting a child.
....

1 Joan often says to her husband, "I don't like you lying on the sofa all day on Sundays."
....

2 The science teacher said, "Some dinosaurs were herbivores, others were carnivorous."
....

3 The sales manager remarked, "These data can't be correct! There must be a mistake!"
....

4 Alan keeps telling Nicole, "I want to find a better place to live and raise our children."
....

5 Mom always says, "Patience is a great virtue. Never forget it!"
....

6 My son sometimes tells me, "You are a great cook, Mom!"
....

7 Liza always says, "I'll become a great singer." And I think she will.
....

6 下方每個轉述句均有錯誤，請改寫出正確句子。

1 He said: "I will go to the mountains tomorrow." → He said that I would go to the mountains the day after.
....

2 She said: "I am happy for you." → She said she is happy for him.
....

3 I told him: "Don't play in your bedroom in those dirty shoes!" → I told him not play in his bedroom in those dirty shoes.
....

4 Sam said: "I met Jenny at the concert yesterday." → Sam said he had met Jenny at the concert yesterday.
....

5 Keira replied: "I don't want to pay extra money for this service." → Keira replied she doesn't want to pay extra money for that service.
....

6 He asked her: "Whose bike is it?" → He asked her whose bike was it.
....

7 He told me: "You and your family are very important to me." → He told me that I and my family are very important to me.
....

8 I said: "I'm going home because I feel sick." → I said I was going home because I feel sick.
....

7 請用下方動詞，進行必要更動，來改寫出轉述句。

| advised (x2)   explained   told (x4)   suggested   answered   asked |

1 Mom to the children: "Stop making all that noise. I'm working."

....

2 Ted to me: "Let's meet at the station at eight tomorrow morning."

....

3 The guide to the tourists: "The stones used to build Stonehenge were taken from very far away."

....

4 Sam to his friend Paul: "I'd like to stay a little longer. You can go home if you want to."

....

5 The teacher to her pupils: "This Norman castle was built in the 12th century."

....

6 My friend who lives in the USA to me: "I'm going to visit Yellowstone National Park next summer."

....

7 John to me: "Can you let me have a look at your history project?"
I to John: "Sorry, I can't. I've already handed it in."

....

....

8 The doctor to me: "Eat less and do physical exercise regularly."

....

8 請以下方動詞的簡單過去式，來完成短文。

| ask (x2)   say (x3)   remind   suggest   answer |

My sister ¹......................... me that tomorrow is Dad's birthday and ²......................... me if I was going to buy him a present. I ³......................... yes and ⁴......................... that we could buy a book or a classical CD. She ⁵......................... it was a good idea and that we might buy both a book and a CD. I then ⁶......................... who would go and buy them and guess what she ⁷.........................? She ⁸......................... "Here's my money. You go." Typical of my sister! So I'll go to the shopping mall later. I hope she won't criticize what I choose.

9 希拉蕊（Hilary）在旅行社工作。她傍晚下班回家後，都會告訴先生佛瑞德（Fred）當天上班的情況。請依照例句，將以下短文改為對話。

Hilary: Do you know who came into the agency today, Fred?
Fred: Of course not. How should I?
Hilary: ....

Hilary went back in the evening and told her husband Fred that a schoolmate of theirs had come into to the travel agency that day. Fred asked who it was and Hilary said it was Albert Swanson. Fred commented that they hadn't seen him since they had left school and asked her what he was like. Hilary said that he was very elegant and looked even younger than he was when they were at school. He seemed to be very rich, too, because he was interested in very expensive holiday resorts. Fred reminded Hilary of how scruffy Albert had looked when he was a student and asked Hilary if she was sure it was really Albert. Hilary said that Albert had recognized her, too. He had even suggested going out for a meal one day, the three of them and Albert's wife. Fred asked who Albert's wife was and Hilary answered that he would never guess. Albert's wife was Rose, the most beautiful girl in the school. Fred said he couldn't believe it because at that time Rose hadn't even wanted to sit next to Albert during lessons.

10 請使用提示用詞，且在不改變原句意的情況下，改寫為轉述句。

0 Arthur said to me: "I can't come to the countryside with you tomorrow."

TOLD Arthur told me he couldn't go to the countryside with me the next day.

1 Rachel asked me: "Do you want any more food for the picnic?"

KNOW ....

2 Tony said to his father: "I've had some trouble with my mountain bike recently."

TOLD ....

3 Damien asked her: "Are you happy with your new car?"

WANTED ....

4 A friend asked me: "Why did you give up fencing?"

WONDERED ....

5 The ranger said to Don: "Stay at home during the snowstorm."

WARNED ....

6 The instructor said to me: "You should go waterskiing in the summer."

ADVISED ....

7 Andrew said to the children: "Get out of that boat."

ORDERED ....

Reflecting on grammar

請研讀文法規則，再判斷以下說法是否正確。

		True	False
1	動詞 tell 必須搭配介系詞 to，放在人名或代名詞的前面；但 say 就不需要搭配任何介系詞。		
2	「tell thank you」是正確的說法。		
3	「She asked me to wait for her.」是正確的句子。		
4	「He said: "I'm leaving tomorrow."」這句話，如果我要在他還沒離開的同一天，表達轉述句，句子必須改為「He said he's leaving tomorrow.」；如果我在他已經離開後，才表達轉述句，則必須改為「He said he was leaving the next day.」。		
5	直述句如使用簡單現在式，改為轉述句後，就會變成過去完成式。		
6	如果要提議一起做某事，那麼動詞 suggest 後面可以接動詞 ing。		
7	「He said he was tired.」此句子裡雖然沒有寫出連接詞 that，但可以理解是被省略了。		
8	助動詞 do 需用於直接問句和間接問句。		
9	我們通常會使用連接詞 if 來轉述 Yes/No 問句，例如：「He asked me if I wanted a cup of tea.」。		
10	我們轉述 Wh 問句時，會先講動詞，再講主詞，例如：「I asked him whose coat was it.」。		

連接子句 Connecting Clauses

LESSON 1 反義子句和讓步子句 Adversative and concessive clauses

連接詞具有結合部分句子或部分短文的功能。我們已在 Unit 5 學過最常用於結合對等子句的連接詞 and、but 和 or，還有表達因果關係的 because 和 so（請參閱第 84 頁）。我們將於本單元了解其他類型的連接詞、介系詞和副詞及其用法。

反義子句

如果要引導一個子句讓它與另一個子句呈現**對比意義**，可以使用以下詞語：

but	• I like this song, **but** it's not my favorite. • I have no choice **but** to accept her offer.
however （放在句首或句尾）	• He finds math very hard. **However**, he's trying his best to understand it. • I didn't feel very well this morning. I went to school, **however**.
though （放於句尾，非正式）	It's a very nice dress. It's quite expensive, **though**.
yet	You have a good job, and **yet** you're always complaining.
on the one hand . . . (but) on the other (hand) . . .	**On the one hand**, I think it would be a good idea to study abroad, **but on the other** it would be hard to leave my family and friends.

1 請使用 but 連接兩個句子，且不能改變原句意義。

1 I studied hard. I didn't get a good mark, though.

....

2 He looks like a tough guy. He's very shy, however.

....

3 The movie was good. It was a bit slow, however.

....

4 The T-shirt they gave me for my birthday is nice. It's too short, though.

....

5 Emma liked Tom. She didn't really trust him, though.

....

6 I thought it would be sunny in Sicily in May. We had lots of rain, however.

....

7 They've had a lot of problems recently, and yet they've never complained.

....

8 It's a very nice house. It's away from the center, though.

....

2 請使用下方連接詞來完成短文。

because (x2)	and (x2)	but	or	so	however

Have you ever heard of a dodo or a quagga? Your answer could be no ¹............................ these animals are now extinct. The dodo was a bird ²............................ the quagga a kind of zebra. A lot of different animal species no longer exist. Many disappeared a long, long time ago, ³............................ others are in danger today ⁴............................ people hunt them ⁵............................ change their natural environment. The mountain gorillas of Zaire, for example, are in danger from the number of visitors coming to take photos of them. They disturb the primates and they don't reproduce, ⁶............................ their number is decreasing each year. ⁷............................, in some places things are changing for the better. Many animals are now protected ⁸............................ there are special reserves where they can live safely.

讓步子句

❶ 由 **although** 和 **even though** 所引導的**子句**，會讓主要子句的訊息變得**令人驚訝**或**出乎意料**。此時這個從屬子句可以放在主要子句的前面或後面，並以逗號相隔：

- **Although** he's only 22 years old, he's already a renowned chef.
- We won the match, **even though** we didn't play very well.

❷ 在口語英文裡也可用 **though** 達到相同意思：**Though** I studied hard, I didn't get a good mark.

FAQ

Q: even though 與 even if 的意思有差嗎？

A: 兩者意思很相近，是「即使」的意思，用來表示將義無反顧做某件事。但 **even though** 講的是**事實**，如說：「I want to read this novel, even though my friend says it is quite boring.」，而 **even if** 則是表達**可能**會發生，或可能不會發生的事，如：「We'll go to the stadium even if it rains.」。

下方幾個詞和 although 與 even though 意思相近，但後接的並非子句：

❶ 介系詞 **despite** 和 **in spite of**，使用時後面需要接上**名詞**或**動詞 ing**：

- **Despite** making a big effort, he didn't manage to lift the heavy case.
- **Despite** being so young, she's already a famous singer.
- He is still very active **despite** his age.
- **In spite of** the fact (that) she is so young, she's already a famous singer.

❷ 副詞 **however** 需放在形容詞或副詞的前面，等於「no matter how . . .」：

- **However** late it is, it's never too late.
- She always wears a T-shirt, **however** cold it is.
- **However** carefully the teacher explains physics, I still don't understand.

3 請使用 **even though**、**despite**、**although**、**in spite of** 或 **however** 來完成句子。
注意有些句子可同時使用兩個單字。

1 I'm going for a walk, ... it's raining.

2 .... studying so little, he usually manages to get good marks.

3 She bought the leather bag, ... it was expensive.

4 .... our room was quite small, it was neat and tidy.

5 .... hard he tries, he will never do it!

6 .... the fact it's a cheap restaurant, the food isn't bad.

7 I enjoyed my vacation .... the bad weather.

8 .... early they leave, they won't get there on time.

4 請將 **1–6** 與 **A–F** 配對成完整的句子。

..... **1** The restaurant has changed the menu,

..... **2** Although you might have to pay a bit more,

..... **3** Although it may seem incredible,

..... **4** Even if you didn't want to go,

..... **5** In spite of the fact he's nearly fifty,

..... **6** On the one hand I would like to forgive her,

A you would have to anyway.

B everything I told you is true.

C even though the old one was very popular.

D it will certainly be worth it to have a better room.

E but on the other I find it really hard to do.

F he's very fit and looks like someone in his thirties.

5 請使用提示用詞來改寫句子；注意不能改變原句意。

1 Jane got home late but she prepared dinner for everybody. (although)

....

2 The waiter was very kind. The food wasn't that good, though. (but)

....

3 I don't have an English-French dictionary, but I can look words up on the Internet. (though)

....

4 I don't know his wife, but I know his children. (however)

....

5 We had a great time although the weather wasn't very nice. (even though)

....

6 We got lost despite having a map of the city. (although)

....

7 No matter how good it may be, I will never be able to eat sushi. (however)

....

原因子句

我們可以使用下方詞語引導說明原因：

because（請參閱第 84 頁）	He arrived at work late **because** he had missed the bus.
since（較正式）	**Since** I lost my passport, I had to change my return flight.
as（較正式）	• **As** my computer wasn't working, I couldn't finish my report. • I can't call her **as** I don't have her number.
for（較正式）	I'm not going to pay him **for** he didn't do a good job.

1 請使用括號裡的單字，在筆記本上改寫出句意不變的句子。

1 Since the weather is so bad, the barbecue has been canceled. (as)

2 We didn't buy that computer because it was too expensive. (since)

3 As we didn't have any money for a taxi, we walked back home. (because)

4 As it was raining, we decided not to play tennis. (since)

5 Since our grandparents live there, we often go to Barcelona. (because)

6 We couldn't get there on time because there was a bus strike. (as)

連續子句

我們可以使用下方詞語引導說明結果：

so（請參閱第 84 頁）	I didn't feel very well, **so** I didn't go to school.
as a result / for this reason / **therefore / consequently**（較正式）	The theme park was very crowded. **As a result**, we had to line up for each ride.
so + 形容詞／副詞 + **(that)**	The line for the tickets was **so long that** we gave up and went home.
so as (not) to	They were quiet **so as not to** wake everybody up.
such a/an + 形容詞 + 名詞 + **(that)**	It was **such a great trip that** nobody wanted to go home.

2 請使用提示用詞完成意思相近的句子。

1 I couldn't wait any longer because it was too late.

   SO   It was too late, ...

2 I didn't have any money, so I couldn't buy anything.

   BECAUSE   I couldn't ....

3 We didn't have a good time at the party because we didn't know many people.

   SO   We didn't ....

4 My car broke down, so I went to work on my bike yesterday.

   BECAUSE   I went to ....

5 I'm going to eat less sugar because I want to lose weight.

   THEREFORE   I want to ....

6 His parents were furious with him because his school report was bad.

   THAT   His school report ....

3 請使用以下單字來完成句子。

so good   such a great   so often   so badly   so boring   so long   so lucky   so much

1 He eats .... that he's putting on weight.

2 She's .... singer! Everybody loves her voice.

3 He's .... at chess. He often wins a lot of money.

4 My friend is ....—he always wins things on the lottery.

5 The flight took .... that I had watched all the movies available by the time we landed.

6 My mother cooks fish .... that I'm getting fed up with eating it.

7 He played .... that he lost the match in less than half an hour.

8 The movie was .... that I fell asleep after a quarter of an hour.

目的子句

我們可以使用下方詞語引導說明某行為結果或目的：

to + 原形動詞	I'm going **to go** to London to improve my English. (NOT . . . for improve my English)
in order to（比單獨使用 to 還要正式）	**In order to** preserve the quality of the garment, dry-clean it only.
so that（常能引導含有情態助動詞的子句）	I'll use the big screen for my PowerPoint presentation **so that** everybody can see it.
so as (not) to	They finished all their work in the evening **so as to** be free the next day.

---

4 請將 1–6 與 A–F 配對成完整的句子。

..... **1** I'm going to enroll on a creative writing course

..... **2** She bought all the ingredients

..... **3** She left her country

..... **4** In order to qualify for the next Olympic Games,

..... **5** I will take a lot of photos during the trip

..... **6** She was ill and

A you'll have to improve your own personal record.

B therefore she had to cancel her vacation.

C so that I can improve my writing skills.

D to make an apple pie.

E to look for better opportunities and a new life.

F so that I will be able to show all the places I visited to my friends.

5 請圈出正確的用字。

1 The cafeteria was closed, **so / because** we couldn't get a drink.

2 Try to do your best **such / so as** to please your parents.

3 Ring the bell **for call / to call** room service.

4 They took the subway **because / so** they didn't want to walk.

5 **Therefore / Since** you have come late, you'll have to wait longer.

6 I always keep the TV volume low **so as not / in order** to disturb my neighbors.

7 I'm saving some money **so as to / so that** I can buy a motorbike.

8 John couldn't come with us **as a result / because** he was at home with flu.

9 They're working quite hard **therefore / in order to** pass the exam with a good mark.

10 Your company failed to send the offer by the fixed deadline, **consequently / because** we couldn't even examine it.

6 請以合適的連接詞來完成句子。

1 I've decided to become a vegetarian .... vegetables and cereal are a healthier diet.

2 I want to keep fit .... I work out in the gym every day.

3 .... I'm really interested in modern art, I'll visit the Tate Modern tomorrow.

4 I was very hungry last night .... I had skipped lunch.

5 I'll write him an email every day .... he'll remember me.

6 It's .... hot day today .... I won't go out till sunset.

7 The vacation in Kenya was .... adventurous .... everybody decided to go back there next year.

8 He did the dishes after dinner .... leave any mess for the morning.

LESSON 3 時間子句／順序副詞／建立論點的連接副詞
Time clauses; sequencing adverbs; linking words to build an argument

下方為**引導時間子句的主要連接詞**：

❶ when（……時），後面可以接簡單現在式、簡單過去式、現在完成式或過去完成式的動詞，但絕對不能使用 will 未來式。其他時間連接詞一樣適用此原則：
- **When** you see him, tell him I've gone to hospital. (**NOT** When you ~~will see~~ him)
- **When** I was young, I often went dancing.

❷ while（……時），通常會搭配現在進行式或過去進行式：
- **While** I'm writing this email, you can start making dinner.
- I broke my ankle **while** I was skiing.

> when 和 while 後面亦可接**動詞 ing**：
> - You have to be careful **when writing** in English　• I saw a fox **while cycling** in the country.

❸ as long as（只要）：I will love you **as long as** I live. (**NOT** as long as I ~~will live~~)

❹ until/till（直到）：I worked **until** it was dark.

❺ as soon as（一……就……）：I'll let you have the contract **as soon as** I get it signed.
(**NOT** as soon as I ~~will get it~~ . . .)

❻ before（……前），後面需接上動詞 ing 或子句如「主詞＋簡單現在式動詞」或「主詞＋簡單過去式動詞」：
- He delivers newspaper **before** he goes to school in the morning.
  Also before going to school
- He used to deliver newspaper **before** he went to school.

❼ after（……後），後面亦需接上動詞 ing 或子句：
He goes to school **after** he has delivered newspaper. **Also** after delivering

1 請圈出正確的用字。

1 Before / Until / After leaving for the weekend, I watered the plants.

2 Come on! You're always late! We must get to the movies **while / before / until** the movie starts.

3 Don't worry! You can stay here **while / as long as / when** you like.

4 Can you help me tidy up **before / as long as / as soon as** the party has finished?

5 Let's go for a walk in the park **until / while / after** the sun is still shining.

6 I can't go out **when / until / while** the cake is ready and out of the oven.

7 Until / As soon as / Before deciding what food to buy for the party, the girls had read a lot of recipes.

8 After / Until / While Rose was peeling the apples, her sister was whipping the cream.

2 請使用下方詞語來完成句子。

> until   while   when   as soon as   after   as long as

1 I like working in the garden .... I'm on vacation. I find it relaxing.

2 I'll wait .... half past ten. Mr. Brosnan should arrive then.

3 Please call me .... you get this message. It's urgent.

4 I cut my finger .... chopping parsley.

5 We can help you with the organization of the conference for .... you need us.

6 .... watching the movie, we went to bed.

順序副詞和片語

當要依照時間順序介紹事件、需要表達一連串指示的順序時，我們可使用以下副詞和時間用語：

- **first / at first**（首先）
- **then**（然後）
- **after that**（之後）（不能單用 after，因為 after 本身是介系詞，不是副詞！）
- **finally / in the end**（最後）

3 請使用副詞來完成下方的食譜。

To make a Caesar salad, [1].......................... roast a chicken breast, [2].......................... cut it into strips and put it into a bowl. [3].......................... , add some lettuce and some pieces of toasted bread, and [4].......................... season with salad cream to taste.

FAQ

Q: finally、at last 和 eventually 之間有何差別？

A: **finally** 帶有「清單裡的最後一個」或「最後要說的事」等意思；**eventually** 有「一段時間後的終點」或「一連串原因的結局」等意思；**at last** 則用於經過很長一段時間後，「終於發生某事」，尤其是因故延宕，或過程中有遭遇障礙等。

建立論點的連接副詞

當要列舉一連串論點，來表示支持或反對某事物時，就會使用以下副詞。這些副詞常用於書面：

- **firstly**（第一點）
- **secondly**（第二點）(用在前方有用過 firstly 時）
- **another point is**（還有一點是……）
- **in addition (to that)**（此外）
- **on top of that**（此外）(非正式用法）
- **finally / lastly / in conclusion**（最後）

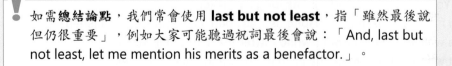

如需總結論點，我們常會使用 **last but not least**，指「雖然最後說但仍很重要」，例如大家可能聽過祝詞最後會說：「And, last but not least, let me mention his merits as a benefactor.」。

4 請使用下方連接副詞來完成短文。

| last but not least | before | Firstly | Another point | because | In addition | Secondly |

Our club would like to start a new course. Since a lot of people are now interested in healthy food, we are planning to organize a few evening classes on this topic. ¹.................................... , we need to find an expert who can talk about organic food. ².................................... , we have to find at least two chefs who can teach us how to cook healthy recipes. ³...................................., we need a place with a big kitchen ⁴... our premises don't have the necessary equipment.

⁵... is the fee. We should decide how much the course should cost ⁶.......................... advertising it. And ⁷.. , we have to discuss whether to advertise it in the local newspapers or on the radio as well.

要補充更多資訊或概念來強調論點，可用表示「**另外、此外、除此之外**」的**連接副詞**：

moreover（正式）	This is healthy food, and **moreover** it's organic.
what's more（非正式）	The hotel was very nice. **What's more**, it had a large pool.
also	If you want to lose some weight, you shouldn't just eat less, you should **also** do some exercise.
besides + 動詞 ing	**Besides being** very helpful, she's also a great friend.

5 請圈出正確的用字。

1 **Besides / Also / What's more** being good for you, bananas are also cheap.

2 I'm not very hungry. **Lastly / What's more / Finally**, this spaghetti is overcooked.

3 That restaurant is very expensive and **after that / besides / firstly** the service is very slow.

4 I don't feel like going out tonight. I'm quite tired. **Firstly / What's more / Lastly**, I have to get up early tomorrow morning.

5 You forgot to put the documents for the meeting in my folder. **Secondly / Moreover / Finally**, you gave me the wrong address.

6 **Moreover / Besides / Also** winning the match, my favorite team played incredibly well yesterday.

6 請以下方的連接副詞或順序詞來完成克漏字。

| as soon as (x2) | first of all | before | until | secondly | while |

1 .... deciding what slides to prepare for the presentation, we had looked for a lot of images.

2 I was drawing the graphs .... the secretary was keying in the figures referring to the sales.

3 We won't be able to go home .... we have finished analyzing these data.

4 We'll switch on the projector .... all the guests have taken their seats.

5 ...., we have to find a room big enough for all the participants; ...., we'll have to rent the conference equipment.

6 .... the presentation is over, the participants will move on to the garden to listen to a concert.

條件子句

如下所示，條件子句中看到類似 if（請參閱第 291 頁）的連接詞：

1 provided / providing (that) / as long as（只要）：
- I'll let you go out tonight **provided that** you are at home before midnight.

2 unless（除非）：引導具有肯定動詞的從屬子句，但後面或前面需接上否定的主要子句：
- I won't go **unless** you allow me to.
- I don't watch TV **unless** there's something really interesting on.

3 in case（以免）：Here's my phone number **in case** you need help.

4 if only（但願）
- ❶ 感嘆句裡的 if only 搭配**簡單過去式動詞**或情態助動詞 **would/could** 時，是表達渴望或後悔某事的意思：
  - **If only** I <u>had</u> a little more time! / **If only** she <u>would give</u> me another chance!
  （也可以說「I wish I had . . . / I wish she would give me . . .」；請參閱第 240 頁）
- ❷ 如果是搭配**過去完成式的動詞**，則是代表對某過往事件感到後悔：
  - **If only** I <u>had told</u> her!（也可以說「I wish I had told her.」；請參閱第 241 頁）

5 as if / as though（彷彿）：
- He started shouting **as if** he were mad.
- Her voice sounded **as though** she had been crying.

1 請將 1–6 與 A–F 配對成完整的句子。

..... **1** I can't help you   **A** provided you are back before midnight.
..... **2** Don't watch this movie   **B** in case we have to go for lunch.
..... **3** You can go out with your friends   **C** as if he had never tasted food before.
..... **4** Let's take some extra money   **D** if you don't like horror movies.
..... **5** He kept eating   **E** as if he was upset with us.
..... **6** Tom behaved strangely   **F** unless you show me exactly what you have to do.

2 請使用以下單字來完成句子。

if only   as long as   provided   as if (x2)   in case (x2)   unless

1 I'll drive, ... you tell me the way.

2 We can't come with you .... we get back before dinner.

3 You look .... you're going to give up.

4 .... we hadn't agreed to go! I'm so tired I just want to stay at home!

5 Pack some warm clothes .... the temperature drops.

6 She danced and danced .... there were no tomorrow.

7 Just .... you couldn't come, give me a ring.

8 The company can increase the sales .... they start selling products online.

比較子句

我們可採用以下方式來引導比較子句：

as + 形容詞／副詞 + as	It wasn't **as difficult as** I thought it would be.
as/like（非正式用法）	• Do **as** you like! • No one plays the violin **like** she does!
比較級形容詞或副詞 + than	The exam was **easier than** we expected.

3 請使用 than、as 或 as . . . as 來完成句子。

1 The exhibition was much more interesting .... we expected.

2 It must be a very rich area. There are .... many jewelry shops in this one street .... in my whole town.

3 Nobody understands her .... I do.

4 They behaved .... if nothing had happened.

5 When you go to another country, eat .... the locals do.

6 The local university is offering a much wider choice of courses .... before.

敘述子句和解釋子句

❶ **that** 是最廣為運用的連接詞,但因為我們能輕易了解 that 在子句裡的意義,因此實際上常**省略**:
- I thought **(that)** he was coming.　　• He promised **(that)** he would come.
- Did you know **that** she got married last month?

❷ **that is (to say)**(也就是說)等於正式書寫語文裡的縮寫 **i.e.**(源自拉丁文 id est),
目的在於更清楚說明某事物的意義:
- You can arrive any time before noon, **that's to say** from eight to twelve.

4 請使用 that、than 或 if 來完成短文。

Karen said [1]..................... she was going to do her Master's in Tokyo. Janet wanted to know [2]..................... she had to learn Japanese. Karen answered [3]..................... she spoke Japanese much better [4]..................... French. She promised [5]..................... she would invite Janet to stay with her. Janet thanked her and told her [6]..................... she had always wanted to visit Japan, but it was always more expensive [7]..................... she could afford.

使役動詞

以下幾個是表達「讓某人完成某事」的說法:

make sb do sth (表中立或強硬)	• Her story **made me cry**. • The teacher **makes us stay** at school after classes if we misbehave.(或被動語態 We are made to stay at school . . .)
let sb do sth / **allow sb to do sth**	• My parents don't **let me go** camping with my friends – that's not fair! • The teacher **allowed us to use** calculators during the test. (或被動語態 We were allowed to use . . . ;請參閱第 234 頁)
get sb to do sth (表說服)	My friend **got me to buy** an automatic transmission car and I'm happy with it.
compel/force sb **to do sth** (表義務或強制規定)	• A lot of people **were forced to leave** their jobs because of the crisis. • They **will be compelled to stay** at home. (常以被動語態表達,請參閱第 258 頁)
cause sth **(to happen)**(常表負面)	The heat and winds of the last few days **have caused the woods to catch** fire.

如需了解 get something done 或 have something done 的被動語態句型,請參閱第 318 頁。

請以動詞 **make** 的正確形式來完成句子。

1 I .... the kids tidy their room yesterday.

2 Jack often .... me miss the bus in the mornings. He's always late.

3 My wife .... me paint the kitchen last week. My back is still aching.

4 Having a big breakfast in the morning .... me feel energetic all day.

5 Will your manager .... you prepare next week's presentation?

6 Are you really going to .... me speak in public during the meeting?

7 My parents .... me go to piano lessons when I was little. I didn't enjoy them!

8 Don't .... me laugh!

9 Are you really .... him go to that party with people he can't stand?

10 The boss .... me attend a German course before sending me to the Bremen branch.

請以 **let、get 或 cause** 的正確形式來完成句子。

1 My husband .... me use his brand new car yesterday. It was great!

2 My sister .... the accident. She dropped a heavy pan on my foot!

3 The frost .... the lake to freeze.

4 The salesman .... us to buy a new dishwasher. He said ours couldn't be fixed.

5 The heavy rain .... the river to flood the village.

6 Will your brother .... you play with his new video game?

7 The principal .... me to attend this course on evaluation but I find it boring and useless.

8 Liza's parents .... her go on vacation on her own for the first time.

請使用下方動詞的正確時態來完成句子。

let	make	allow	get	cause	oblige

1 Her parents .... her to stay out until midnight last Saturday.

2 I .... to go. It was a work dinner with our German partners. I couldn't miss it.

3 My mom .... her hair done at the hairdresser's every week.

4 Our math teacher .... us do a test every week.

5 Why don't you .... them go? It's going to be a nice trip.

6 The freezing weather .... some of the plants in my garden to die.

請將根據句意，搭配合適的使役動詞來造句，記得使用括號內的時態。

1 My parents / not / me go out / in the evening. / That's not fair. *(simple present)*

....

2 This movie / very moving. / The ending / me cry. *(simple past)*

....

3 Mr. Basset / us go into his lab / next week. *(future)*

....

4 I / you to come / the swimming pool / with me / after work. / It's so relaxing! *(future)*

....

5 We / Tom sing a song / at the party / although he didn't want to. *(simple past)*

....

6 This is music / that / everybody dance! *(simple present)*

....

記得以下用法：

動詞 1 + 受詞 + 不定詞 to + 動詞 2
動詞 1 如：**ask、expect、want、would like、get、compel、oblige、allow、cause**
→ want / would like somebody to do something （請參閱第 240 頁）

感官動詞（表示全程目睹）或使役動詞 + 受詞 + 原形動詞
→ hear/see somebody do something （請參閱第 333 頁）

另外，使役動詞的被動語態必須使用不定詞用法「**to + 原形動詞**」：
- I **was made to do** something. / He **was seen to do** something.
  （如果行為的進行時間較長，亦可說「He was seen doing something.」）

9 請完成句子，使用下方動詞的原形動詞、動詞 **ing** 或 **to** + 原形動詞型態。

| clean | take | have | ring | make | phone | go | load | leave | run | learn |

1 The market is closing. I can see the produce seller .... his van.

2 I'd like my daughter .... her hair cut.

3 I'd like you .... part in the next meeting. We have .... some important decisions.

4 Sometimes we are made .... our classroom at the end of the lessons.

5 Mom expected us .... her as soon as we got to the airport.

6 Our friends wanted us .... to the theater with them, but we couldn't.

7 They were seen .... the restaurant at about ten last night.

8 The teacher made me .... the poem by heart.

9 I always let my dog .... freely on the hillside.

10 Sorry, I didn't hear the phone ....

10 請以合適的連接詞來完成句子。

1 Yes, you can buy those shoes, ... they don't cost more than £50.

2 I don't usually ask for help with my homework, ... it's a really difficult task.

3 Take your pullover jacket with you .... it gets colder.

4 He was behaving .... he was a little child.

5 .... I could play the piano like you!

6 This exercise is easier .... I thought.

7 He said .... he was going to help you .... you were in trouble.

8 No one makes a better apple pie .... you do.

9 .... hard I try, my English teacher is never satisfied with my work.

10 Switch on the oven .... you get home or the cake will never be ready for dinner.

ROUND UP 20

以下依功能分類，整理出連結句子的主要用詞，含**連接詞**和**副詞**。 延伸補充

對等連接詞

附加說明	排除在外	對比	原因	其中一個	結果	結果
and	nor	but	for	or	so	yet

> 句型 **主要子句 + 對等連接詞 + 主要子句**
>
> ❶ 結合同樣重要的**兩個子句**。
>
> ❷ 為了方便記憶，可記住縮寫字 FANBOY（**f**or–**a**nd–**n**or–**b**ut–**o**r–**y**et）。
>
> ❸ 連接詞 **yet** 和 **for** 的前面通常要加上**逗號**。

從屬連接詞

原因	目的	對比	時間	條件句、 間接問句	轉述句、 間接說辭、結果
as because for since	so so that	although though	after before until while when as as soon as	if / whether unless as long as provided whenever whatever	that

> 句型 **主要子句 + 從屬連接詞 + 次要子句**　　句型 **從屬連接詞 + 次要子句 + 主要子句**
> （兩句之間的逗號可有可無）　　　　　　　　（兩句之間一定要以**逗號**相隔）

相關連接詞

包括在內	其中一個	其中一個	包括在內	排除在外	比較、同等
both . . . and	either . . . or	whether . . . or	not only . . . but also	neither . . . nor	as . . . as

> 相關連接詞用來**結合兩個同等要素**，故前後一定各有一組用語。

連接副詞和轉折詞

結果	對比	附加說明	時間順序	再次強調
accordingly consequently therefore thus	still nevertheless however otherwise instead	also besides moreover furthermore	firstly secondly then next meanwhile finally	indeed

> 連接副詞和轉折詞是用來**連接句子或部分句子**，以增進語句的通順流暢度。由於這些詞會放在句子各處，因此稱「轉折詞」（transitional word，transitional 是過渡、變遷的意思）。

1 請使用以下對等連接詞來完成句子。

| so | yet | nor | and (x2) | for | or | but |

1　I love him .... I don't want to marry him.

2　I have some more free time this week, ... I'm going to play some sports.

3　It's a small car, ... it's very spacious.

4　I won't buy it, ... it's far too costly.

5　You can spend £500 .... have this TV set .... you can spend a little more .... have that one—it's much better!

6　She didn't want any fruit, ... would she eat the dessert.

2 請使用以下從屬連接詞來完成句子。

| as long as | that | if | though | so | until | so . . . that | because |

1　I'm going to London .... I've found a good job there.

2　This novel is quite good, ... some descriptions in it are rather boring.

3　I've set the alarm for six o'clock .... I won't oversleep.

4　They say .... the concert will be broadcast live tomorrow evening.

5　This cake is .... good .... everyone wants another slice.

6　I asked a passer-by .... he knew a good restaurant in that area.

7　They couldn't export any of their products .... they started selling them on the e-market.

8　You won't have any problems in high school .... you work hard enough.

3 請參考例句，將主要子句和從屬子句的位置互換。記得調整標點符號的用法。

0　As it's raining, I'm going to the movies this afternoon.
　　I'm going to the movies this afternoon as it's raining.
　　..

1　He didn't want anything else because he had eaten enough.
　　..

2　I went straight home after I finished school yesterday.
　　..

3　If you see anything strange, call me at once.
　　..

4　You can join us on our boat trip, provided you don't suffer from seasickness.
　　..

5　I won't try this dish whatever they say.
　　..

6　I went jogging for an hour before I went to the office this morning.
　　..

7　As long as it doesn't rain, I'll go for a bike ride later.
　　..

4 請用下方的連接詞、副詞或代名詞完成短文。

> If only   who   to   before   also   that   so   which (x2)

Two years ago, a friend of mine, [1]............................ pretended to be very well informed about financial matters, got me [2]............................ invest some of my money in certain funds [3]............................ apparently rewarded you with very high interest rates. [4]............................ I hadn't followed his advice! I've lost all the money I had invested that way. Luckily I hadn't put all of my money in those rotten funds, I had [5]............................ invested part of it in shares [6]............................ have performed very well on the stock market in the last few months, [7]............................ I have partly covered the losses. The lesson I've learned is [8]............................ you must be very well informed [9]............................ you do any kind of investment.

5 請閱讀下方卡士達醬的製作步驟，並將順序詞填入空格。

> first   finally   after that   then   until   next

Do you want to make proper custard?
Just follow these instructions.

Ingredients	
1 pint of milk	4 egg yolks
2 fl. oz. of cream	2 spoonfuls of corn flour
1 oz. of sugar	½ teaspoon of vanilla extract

[1]............................ bring the milk and the cream to simmering point. [2]............................ whisk the egg yolks with the sugar and the corn flour. [3]............................ , pour the hot milk and cream onto the eggs and sugar, whisking all the time. [4]............................ return to the pan and add the vanilla extract. Keep stirring with a wooden spatula [5]............................ thickened. [6]............................ , pour the custard into a jug and serve at once.

6 請閱讀文章，在空格填入正確的用詞。

> as a result   and   which   however   if   although   in spite of

The San Andreas Fault

The San Andreas Fault, [1]............................ extends for more than 600 miles (970 km) from Point Arenato to the Colorado Desert, is the most active fault in California. But what exactly is a fault? The Earth's surface consists of about 20 rigid plates of rock that move slowly past one another. This motion squeezes [2]............................ stretches the rocks at the edge of these plates. [3]............................ the force is too great, the rocks break and shift and an earthquake is caused [4]............................ .

The energy created travels away from the fault in seismic waves. In 1906, a horizontal movement of the earth's crust caused the terrible earthquake in the city of San Francisco. [5]............................ the number of studies on the matter, the reliable prediction of earthquakes is not possible yet. [6]............................ , scientists study history to try and guess how often a certain region can expect a catastrophe.

For example, California may expect a catastrophic earthquake once every 50 to 100 years. And, [7]............................ there was a quake in 1989, Californians are still on the alert, waiting for "the Big One."

7 請使用動詞 make、get 或 let 的合適形式，來完成短文。

When it's sunny, my parents [1]........................... my brother and me help them in the garden—I hate it! The front garden is small and has some flowers, so it's not that bad, but the back garden is very big and my parents [2]........................... us to grow vegetables there. We also have some apple and pear trees, mom [3]........................... us to pick the fruit for the family. Dad [4]........................... us mow the lawn once a month and mom [5]........................... us to weed the flower beds at the front. When she's too busy with her job, mom [6]........................... us water the plants—indoor and out—and dad [7]........................... my brother trim the hedge with him. Sometimes dad [8]........................... me drive his car—I much prefer this to doing gardening.

8 請使用以下動詞的正確時態，來完成短文。

| make | allow | hear | force | see | need | oblige | get |

1 Mom .... me to learn the piano even though I had no musical talent.

2 The math teacher .... us do a test every day. That's hard!

3 Mrs. Durrell .... her hair done in London every month.

4 Brian's parents .... him to stay out until midnight. He's so lucky!

5 I .... people buying the latest digital products at the fair yesterday.

6 David .... to get his suit dry-cleaned for tomorrow's meeting.

7 Ben felt .... to go. It was a work dinner and he couldn't miss it.

8 We .... the street sellers shouting on the market square early this morning.

Reflecting on grammar

請研讀文法規則，再判斷以下說法是否正確。

		True	False
1	and、nor 和 or 都是從屬連接詞。		
2	「on the one hand . . .」後面一定要接「on the other . . .」。		
3	although 負責引導讓步子句（有時稱為對比子句）。		
4	目的子句的句型通常是 for + 原形動詞。		
5	since、for、as 和 because 都是表達原因的連接詞。		
6	從屬子句不能放在主要子句前面，所以我們不能將從屬連接詞放在句首。		
7	「I'm going to tell him as soon as I'll see him.」是正確的句子。		
8	在 before 和 after 後面，可以接含有限定動詞的片語或動詞 ing。		
9	論述裡的最後一個重點，或一連串事件裡的最後一件事，通常以副詞 first 來引導。		
10	主動語態裡的使役動詞（make、get、let、cause），均具有相同句型：受詞 + 原形動詞。		

21 語序／片語動詞／構詞方法
Word Order, Phrasal Verbs and Word Formation

LESSON 1 肯定句和否定句的語序／主詞和動詞的倒裝用法
Word order in positive and negative sentences; inversion of subject and verb

肯定句的語序

❶ 肯定句的句型一般為**主詞 + 動詞 + 受詞**。

❷ **be** 動詞和 **become**、**feel** 和 **look** 等連綴動詞，後面可接**補語**，
就是補充主詞資訊的形容詞或名詞片語：
- They **are** very **nice**.（形容詞）
- He **became** a great chef.（名詞片語）

❸ **及物動詞**的後方先接**直接受詞**，再接其他間接受詞：
- I **met** John at the shopping mall yesterday.

FAQ

Q: 老師教我們以首字母縮寫字 SVOMPT 來記得句子裡的語序，但這是什麼意思呢？

A: SVOMPT 代表肯定句的語序用法，也就是：

Subject + **V**erb + **O**bject + **M**anner + **P**lace + **T**ime
（主詞 + 動詞 + 人事物受詞 + 方法 + 場所 + 時間）

當然，不是所有句子都會有間接受詞，但是只要句子裡有受詞，就要遵循上方的語序原則，例如：「I（主詞）have（動詞）a quick lunch（受詞）in the school cafeteria（場所）on Mondays.（時間）」。

go、**come**、**drive** 等表示移動的不及物動詞，則遵循 **SVPMT** 語序：

Subject + **V**erb + **P**lace + **M**anner + **T**ime （主詞 + 動詞 + 場所 + 方法 + 時間）

例如：「My parents（主詞）went（動詞）to London（場所）in their friends' car（方法）last Sunday.（時間）」。此外，**時間補語**也能放在**句首**，寫為「Last Sunday, my parents went to London in their friends' car.」。

1 請重新排序單字來造句。動詞的部分，如果是及物動詞（**transitive**），請於句尾框格寫 **T**；如果是不及物動詞（**intransitive**），請寫 **I**；如果是連綴動詞（**linking verb**），請寫 **L**。

☐ **1** leaving / He's / college / in / for / a / time / week's / .

....

☐ **2** I / today / great / feel / .

....

☐ **3** last / They / way / all / drove / the / Portugal / to / summer / .

....

☐ **4** bought / I / a / pretty / skirt / very / in / the / shop / little / .

....

☐ **5** famous / They / very / became / their / last / after / album / .

....

☐ **6** watch / We / on / videos / YouTube / often / .

....

☐ **7** the / We / to / shop / on / went / the / High / lunch / fish-and-chip / Street / for / .

....

☐ **8** vacation / They / are / on / the Netherlands / a / cycling / going / in / .

....

☐ **9** silly / at / night / party / last / He / very / pants / the / looked / in / those / .

....

☐ **10** went / a / bikes / on / We / for / our / ride / .

....

主詞和動詞倒裝

❶ 當句首出現 **never**、**seldom**、**rarely**、**hardly ever**、**nowhere**、**not only**、**no sooner . . . than . . .**、**only in this way**、**by no means** 等此類副詞或副詞片語，且句子為**否定句**或帶有**限制**意思時，即需採用與疑問句相同的句型，也就是「**助動詞／情態助動詞 + 主詞**」句型：

- **Rarely have I** listened to such great music.
- **Not only can you** come and see us any time, but you can also bring your brother.

如果沒有可用的助動詞或情態助動詞，我們就遵循問句的原則，補上**符合時態的助動詞 do**：

- **Hardly ever does she** arrive on time.
- **Never did they go** abroad for work.

> ❗ 如果句首先出現的從屬子句，開頭為 **not until** 或副詞 **only**（如 **only when**、**only if**、**only by doing so**），那麼就要**倒裝主要子句的主詞和動詞**：
> - **Only if** you work really hard, **will you** be able to achieve your goals.
> - **Not until** he spoke, **did I** realize who he really was.

❷ 其他主詞和動詞需要倒裝的情況如下：

  ❶ 當句首有**地方副詞**或**形容詞**；在此情況下，我們**不需要**補上助動詞：
  - **Here comes** the bride!　　• **Awful was** his anger.

  ❷ 當引導**條件句**，而**連接詞 if 已被省略**時：
  - **Should** I decide to go, I'll let you know.（也可寫作 If I decided to go；請參閱第 303 頁）

2 請將 **1–8** 與 **A–H** 配對成完整的句子。

●●

..... **1** Nowhere was a police officer　　　**A** than she was offered a job.

..... **2** Never have I seen　　　**B** have so many people migrated to Europe.

..... **3** No sooner had she got her degree　　　**C** to be seen.

..... **4** Only in this way will　　　**D** can social welfare be sustained.

..... **5** Rarely in modern times　　　**E** will you have the opportunity of meeting new people.

..... **6** Only if everybody pays their taxes　　　**F** the problem be solved.

..... **7** Only by joining the club　　　**G** have I seen such a beautiful landscape.

..... **8** Hardly ever　　　**H** such a beautiful sea.

❶ 否定句裡一定要出現**助動詞**或**情態助動詞**，我們才能加上 **not**：
- They **were** not / **weren**'t at home.（be 動詞）
- I **could** not / **couldn**'t hear what they said.（情態助動詞 could）

❷ 如果沒有可用的助動詞或情態助動詞，我們就補上**現在式助動詞 do/does**，或**過去式助動詞 did**：
- He **does** not / **doesn**'t like drawing.（like 的第三人稱單數簡單過去式）
- I **did** not / **didn**'t know.（know 的簡單過去式）

FAQ

Q: 我聽過有人說「I do like it.」，但肯定句裡也能使用 do 嗎？

A: 可以的，這樣寫是為了**強調動詞**。「I **do** like it」的意思和「I **really** like it.」相同。其他例子還有「She **does** look nice today!」、「You **did** buy that dress after all.」、「We **do** want to see it.」。

3 請將句子改寫為否定句，記得進行必要的文法變化。

0 There was someone in the room.   There wasn't anyone in the room.

1 The man was standing near the shop door. ....

2 There was something strange about him. ....

3 They discovered a Neolithic site in this area. ....

4 Tina looks happy today. ....

5 I'm thirsty. I need something to drink. ....

6 I have to work on weekends this month. ....

7 The visitors left the museum before five. ....

8 Karen will arrive at the end of December. ....

9 We could see the entrance of the building on the screen. ....

10 She went out with her boyfriend last night. ....

11 I have played tennis a lot recently. ....

12 They had already left the office. ....

LESSON 2 問句和簡答句 / 附加問句 / So do I 與 Neither do I 用法
Questions and short answers; question tags; *So do I / Neither do I*

疑問句：Yes/No 問句   → 圖解請見 P. 415

❶ Yes/No 問句的句首一定是**助動詞**或**情態助動詞**，後接主詞或其他用詞（如主要動詞、受詞等）。如果句子裡沒有情態助動詞或助動詞，我們在問句裡一樣補上現在式的 do/does，或過去式的 did。

❷ 此類問句通常是以簡答的方式回覆，如：

> **Yes 或 No + 主格代名詞 + 與問句相同的助動詞或情態助動詞**

- "**Have you** got any pets?" "No, **I haven't**."
- "**Can Janet** speak Spanish?" "Yes, **she can**."
- "**Did you** get there on time?" "Yes, **I did**."

切記！Yes/No 的後面一定要寫上**逗號**。

FAQ

Q: 簡答句為什麼會稱為簡答句呢？畢竟其實不算簡答啊，難道不能只回答 Yes 或 No 就好了嗎？

A: 之所以稱為簡答句，是因為比完整答句還短。在口語英文裡，我們有時候確實只會回應 Yes 或 No。但一般而言，我們還是會加上代名詞和助動詞，來確認肯定或否定的答句意思。

如果問句問的是**意見或臆測**，像是「Do you think she will come?」，即可回應「I think so. / I don't think so.」。其他可用的答句如下：

- I expect so.
- I guess so / I believe so.
- I hope so.
- I suppose so.
- I'm afraid so.

- I expect not.
- I guess not / I believe not.
- I hope not.
- I suppose not. / I don't suppose so.
- I'm afraid not.

其他問句與答句如下：

Would you like . . . ?（表邀約）	Yes, please. No, thank you.

Can I have . . . ?（表請求）	Yes, sure. No, sorry.

1 請先重新排序單字寫出問句，再根據括號裡的指示寫出答句；若為 (+) 則寫肯定答句，(−) 則寫否定答句。

1 like / do / painting / you / ? (+)

....

2 play / does / in / the / school / Rebecca / team / volleyball / ? (−)

....

3 the / are / going / home / boys / ? (−)

....

4 like / would / to / her / meet / you / ? (+)

....

5 did / boyfriend / present / your / you / give / a / ? (+)

....

6 laptop / got / has / with / Marion / her / her / ? (−)

....

2 請使用括號裡的動詞和指示，寫出肯定或否定的簡短答句。

1 Do you think she'll like our present? (hope / +) ....

2 Do you think the test will be difficult? (hope / −) ....

3 Will we really have to do all this work by tomorrow? (am afraid / +) ....

4 Are we going to have a longer vacation this year? (am afraid / −) ....

5 Is she coming tomorrow? (think / −) ....

6 Are they going to win the match? (guess / +) ....

7 Are we going to leave the office earlier tomorrow? (suppose / −) ....

8 Will Mr. Dreier join the meeting later today? (believe / +) ....

疑問句：Wh問句

1 Wh 問句的句型為：

> **Wh 疑問詞 + 助動詞或情態助動詞 + 主詞 + 主要動詞和其他補語**

2 Wh 疑問詞有 What、Where、When、Why 等。

3 如之前所說，如果句子裡沒有助動詞或情態助動詞，我們要在主詞前面補上 **do/does/did**。而答句的部分，可在不重複主詞和動詞的情況下，以完整答句或簡答句來回覆必要訊息：

- "**What** are you doing?" "I'm working."
- "**Where** should I go?" "To the bank."
- "**What** time does the movie on Screen 3 start?" "(It starts) at nine."

FAQ

Q: 我們為什麼要在問句裡加上 do？do 與此類問句有何關係呢？

A: do 作為主要動詞具有實質的意義，但當作助動詞時，就得捨棄那些字義，僅作「**提示**」用途。例如當問句句首是 **does**，這就代表即將提問和**第三人稱單數現在式**有關的人事物；若問句句首是 **did**，就表示即將提問與**過去**有關的人事物。

再看「What do you do?」這個問句，可以知道第一個 do 是提示用，第二個 do 則是主要動詞。

1 Wh 問句裡如果有介系詞，即需放在句尾：
- What are they talking **about**? (NOT About what are they talking?)
- Where do they come **from**? (NOT From where do they come?).

2 若 Who、What 或 Which 作為問句主詞，句型即與肯定句相同，也就是主詞 + 動詞：
- **Who** knows?　• **What** happened?　• **Which** is yours?

---

3 請重新排序單字來寫出問句，並將問句與 **A–H** 的答句配對。

1 station / do / to / we / how / get / the / ?

....

2 buy / when / you / your / did / car / ?

....

3 when / come / you / could / house / to / my / ?

....

4 laughing / why / you / were / ?

....

5 you / buy / which / of / T-shirts / those / did / ?

....

6 long / how / did / wait / them / you / for / ?

....

7 you / sell / to / apartment / your / going / are / ?

....

8 time / brother / home / what / did / your / night / last / get / ?

....

A I can come tomorrow, if that's okay with you.
B The striped one.
C Because I heard a good joke on the radio.
D I bought it last year.
E Just after midnight, I think.
F For over an hour.
G Go down this road and then turn right.
H Yes, I want to buy a bigger one.

1 ..... 　**2** ..... 　**3** ..... 　**4** ..... 　**5** ..... 　**6** ..... 　**7** ..... 　**8** .....

4 請使用下表用詞來寫出問句。

Wh 疑問詞	助動詞	主詞	動詞	補語	介系詞	
Where What Who When Why How	are is was were do does did	you they he Josh your friends Martina your family	get come go start running going to do looking waiting going	to the movies to school the guitar course in the holidays last night	to for at from with	?

附加問句　→ 圖解請見 **P. 417**

1 附加問句，也就是句尾補上**逗號**和**簡短的問句**，是用**提問來確認某事**。我們會在附加問句重複主要句子裡使用的助動詞或情態助動詞，再接上主格代名詞：It's raining, **isn't it?**

回應時則使用簡答句：

Yes, it is.（在下雨）/ No, it isn't.（沒有在下雨）

2 如果沒有可用的助動詞或情態助動詞，我們就補上現在式的 **do/does** 或過去式 **did**：

• You like Italian food, **don't you?**

3 附加問句具有下方規則：

肯定句，配否定附加問句：

• You **like** fantasy movies, **don't you?**

• Ben **can** swim, **can't he?**

否定句，配肯定附加問句：

• You **didn't** get a bad mark, **did you?**

• I **can't** be in two places at once, **can I?**

4 有時前半部分的句意顯而易見，故會**省略不寫**：

• Great match, isn't it?（省略了開頭的 It's a）

5 以非正式語言來說，我們會以「**Right?**」來確認句意：

• This is yours, **right?**

6 看看下方較為正式的祈使句附加問句如：

• Let's go, **shall we?**

• Pass the salt, **will you?**

簡短問句

如果要表現對某人剛說的話**感興趣**或**感到驚訝**，我們回答時可以使用**前面句子的助動詞或情態助動詞 + 主格代名詞**、再偶爾加上副詞「**Really?**」：

• "You know, Peter is in my class."

"**Is he?** That's great!"

（也可以說「Is he really?」或僅說「Really?」）

• "I've nearly finished the book!"

"Oh . . . **Have you really?** You're a quick reader."

5 請使用附加問句完成對話。

ON THE BUS

A Excuse me, this is the right stop for Piccadilly Circus, [1]...........................

B Yes, it is. Piccadilly Circus is just over there.

A Thank you very much.

B You aren't British, [2]...........................

A No, I'm Australian, from Melbourne!

383

AFTER A PARTY

David Fabulous party, [3].........................

Megan Yes, it was great.

David Er . . . can I take you home?

Megan Yes, that'd be nice.

David You live in New York City, [4].........................

Megan No, in Jersey City, actually. You've got a car, [5].........................

David Well, no. You don't mind going on my motorcycle, [6].........................

Megan Not at all. I love riding on motorcycles!

6 請使用附加問句完成句子。

1 Today is October 2nd, ...

2 Miss Johnson is the Sales Manager, ...

3 You've got a brother called Jack, ...

4 It wasn't such a long flight, ...

5 You don't mind walking, ...

6 Your guests arrived this morning, ...

7 You didn't call me earlier, ...

8 Max can play the guitar, ...

9 Let's order now, ...

10 He drives a taxi, ...

7 請根據各題文意寫出簡短問句。

0 "James is a very good mechanic." "......Is he?............"

1 "Daisy wants to become a web designer." ".........................."

2 "Do you know Tom is in India?"
   ".........................." "I didn't know."

3 "Dan would never behave like that." ".........................."

4 "I have never been here before." ".........................."

5 "He'll buy me some new clothes." ".........................."

6 "I can't go to the movies tonight." ".........................."

7 "I've already watched this movie." ".........................."

贊同與不贊同   → 圖解請見 **P. 415**

看看以下表達贊同與不贊同的句型

贊同肯定句	**So + 助動詞或情態助動詞 + 主詞** • "I'm taking this course." **"So am I."** • "I like rap." **"So do I."**
贊同否定句	**Neither/Nor + 助動詞或情態助動詞 + 主詞** • "I'm not taking this course." **"Neither am I."** • "I don't like jazz." **"Neither do I. / Nor do I."**
不贊同肯定句	**主詞 + 否定助動詞或情態助動詞** • "I'm happy with the exam results." **"I'm not."** • "I like this song." "Really? **I don't.**"
不贊同否定句	**主詞 + 肯定助動詞或情態助動詞** • "I'm not happy with the exam results." **"I am."** • "I don't like this song." "Really? **I do.**"

請參考一下更多例句：

• "We're going out for dinner tonight."
  "**So are we**. Let's go together, shall we?" / "**We aren't**. We're having dinner at home."

• "Jack wasn't on the school trip." "**Neither was his sister**. / Really? **His sister was.**"

8 請圈出表達贊同的答案。

1 I don't think it's a good idea.
- Ⓐ Neither do I.
- Ⓑ Neither don't I.
- Ⓒ Nor I do.

2 I can't wait any longer.
- Ⓐ Nor can I.
- Ⓑ Nor could I.
- Ⓒ So can I.

3 I'd like to work in a foreign country.
- Ⓐ So I would.
- Ⓑ So I'd like.   Ⓒ So would I.

4 I think you're right.
- Ⓐ So am I.
- Ⓑ So do I.
- Ⓒ So did I.

5 I loved the concert!
- Ⓐ So do we.
- Ⓑ So loved we.
- Ⓒ So did we.

6 Rick wants to learn French.
- Ⓐ So does Eliza.
- Ⓑ Nor does Eliza.
- Ⓒ Neither does Eliza.

9 請將 **1–7** 的說辭，和表達不贊同看法的 **A–G** 配對。

..... **1** I would like to have a part-time job.

..... **2** She likes to upload her photos on Facebook.

..... **3** I don't cook on the weekend. My husband does.

..... **4** I think he's the greatest rapper ever!

..... **5** We didn't enjoy the cruise on the Nile.

..... **6** We're ready to go. Are you?

..... **7** We thought the movie was really boring.

A I wouldn't. I'd rather work full time!

B I don't. He's not a good singer.

C Sorry, we aren't. We've just got up.

D My husband and I did! We loved it!

E We didn't. We thought it was good.

F Does she? Her boyfriend doesn't.

G Lucky you! Mine never does.

10 請根據括號裡的指示與主詞，按照題意寫出答句。
(=) 指答句要表示贊同；(≠) 指答句要表示不贊同。

0 I'm going to bed now.

(=) (we) .... So are we. ....

(≠) (we) .... We aren't. ....

1 They would like to leave early.

(≠) (their friends) ....

2 We often travel abroad for work.

(=) (we) ....

3 I'll give Kate a present for her birthday.

(=) (I) ....

4 My daughter loves ballet!

(≠) (my daughter) ....

5 I went to Brazil last year.

(=) (my son) ....

6 My teachers are quite nice.

(≠) (mine) ....

7 We've never been to Brazil.

(=) (we) ....

LESSON 3 構詞方法／字首和字尾 Word formation; prefixes and suffixes

複合名詞的構詞方法

許多複合名詞均以兩個單字構成，例如由 week 加 end 組成的 weekend，或以空格分開的 school year。複合名詞的第一個單字具有形容詞的**功能**，可用來說明第二個單字的**性狀**，例如 safety belt（安全帶）就是用 safety 來形容 belt，表示是能保護人身安全的皮帶。

Focus

請注意以下兩詞的差異：**a tea cup**（茶杯）指的是空容器，**a cup of tea**（一杯茶）則是裝有液體的容器。

a tea cup   a cup of tea

形成複數時，若複合名詞由**名詞 + 名詞**組成，就要在**第二個單字**後面加上 **s**，例如 tea bags 與 tennis rackets。不過如果複合名詞是由**名詞 + 副詞**或**名詞 + 介系詞**組成，**s** 就要加在**名詞後**，如 passers-by、brothers-in-law 等等。許多複合名詞用以表達以下情況：

歸屬關係	**the kitchen table**（kitchen + table 廚房裡的桌子 → 餐桌） **the school car park**（school + car park 學校裡的停車場） **the London Subway**（London + subway 倫敦的地下鐵） 請注意，此時兩個詞不具「持有」的關係，因此我們不使用所有格 's 來表達，也就是說不能寫作 London's Subway。
某物品的用途	**football boots**（football + boots 踢足球穿的鞋子 → 足球鞋） **wallpaper**（wall + paper 貼在牆上的紙 → 海報） **bathtub**（bath + tub 泡澡用的水缸 → 浴缸） **frying pan**（fry + pan 油炸用的平底鍋 → 煎鍋） **shopping bag**（shop + bag 購物用的袋子 → 購物袋） **fishing rod**（fish + rod 釣魚用的竹竿 → 釣魚竿） 如最後三個例子所示，這個情況下，第一個單字通常是動詞 ing。
某物體的材質	**a straw hat**（straw + hat 稻草做的帽子 → 草帽） **rubber boots**（rubber + boots 橡膠做的靴子 → 橡膠鞋） **a silk scarf**（silk + scarf 絲綢做的披巾 → 絲巾）
文學、音樂或電影類別	**crime stories**（crime + story 犯罪的故事） **rock music**（rock + music 搖滾音樂） **war movies**（war + movie 講述戰爭的電影）
時間用語或節慶	**the summer holidays**（summer + holiday 夏天的假期） **a weekend trip**（weekend + trip 週末的旅行） **an end-of-school party**（end-of-school + party 結業派對、期末派對）

我們常可看到複合名詞由三個以上的名詞組成：

a science-fiction movie / the World Football Championship / the UK Energy Resource Center

1 請將 **1–12** 的單字與 **A–L** 的單字配對，來形成複合名詞。注意某些單字可配對成不只一種複合名詞。

..... **1** washing   ..... **7** alarm

..... **2** swimming   ..... **8** front

..... **3** weather   ..... **9** contact

..... **4** post   ..... **10** shopping

..... **5** railway   ..... **11** table

..... **6** road   ..... **12** Christmas

A pool		**G** office	
B accident		**H** mall	
C machine		**I** door	
D clock		**J** station	
E cards		**K** lenses	
F forecast		**L** tennis	

2 請將下方各題改寫成複合名詞；注意，形容用的名詞必須是單數。

1 The team from the school

....

2 A holiday in the summer

....

3 A driver of taxi

....

4 A magazine about fashion

....

5 A garden where vegetables are grown

....

6 Vegetables from the garden

....

7 A glass for drinking wine

....

8 A room for conferences

....

9 A shop where shoes are sold

....

10 Boots to use when you ski

....

11 A resort where you go in the winter

....

12 A story that talks about love

....

13 A court where you play tennis

....

14 Music in the rock style

....

15 A screen you use with your computer

....

16 The door of your car

....

形容詞的構詞方法

許多性狀形容詞其實是字尾 ing 的**現在分詞**（像是 a marching band），或字尾 ed 的**過去分詞**（如 a broken arm）。切記！字尾是 **ing** 的形容詞具有**主動**語態的意思；字尾是 **ed** 的形容詞則有**被動**語態的意思。

動詞	字尾是 ing 的形容詞	字尾是 ed 的形容詞
interest	interesting	interested
relax	relaxing	relaxed
satisfy	satisfying	satisfied
tire	tiring	tired

注意，「Her story touched us all very deeply.」、「Her story was a touching story.」與「We were all touched by her story.」以上三個句子的意義均雷同。

Focus

有些形容詞的構成方式，是在**名詞**（如人體部位或衣物）後面加 **ed**，並在此名詞前加上**連字號**（-）及**另一個形容詞或名詞**，如「a dark-haired man」（深髮色男人）就是由 hair + ed 再用連字號把 haired 與 dark 連起來。

其他例子還有「a blue-eyed girl」（藍眼女孩）或「a long-legged dog」（長腿的狗）。

FAQ

Q: 我看過 a ten-year-old boy 的說法，但不是應該寫成複數的 a ten-years-old 嗎？

A: 不是的。**year** 在此作為**形容詞化的名詞**，不用改為複數。同樣的例子還有 a ten-pound note（10 英鎊的紙幣），而非寫作 a ten-pounds note。

有些形容詞可作為集合名詞，來表達整個單一類別的物品。此情況同理可證，不需加上 s 即具有複數意義，例如 the young、the rich、the poor。

3 請依照例句，用複合名詞來完成句子。

0 A shirt with short sleeves is a ....short-sleeved shirt........ .

1 A man with a big nose is a ....

2 A dog with short legs and a long tail is a ....

3 A girl with long hair is a ....

4 A hat with a wide brim is a ....

5 Shoes with high heels are ....

6 A baby who has just been born is a ....

7 A country that has been torn by war is a ....

8 A canal made by man is a ....

4 請將括號裡的單字改為 **ing** 或 **ed** 形式的形容詞，填入句子的空格中。

1 I was really .... when most of my students didn't have their books with them. (annoy)

2 Your disruptive behavior during the lesson was really .... (annoy)

3 The directions we were given were so .... that we couldn't find our way to the hotel. (confuse)

4 The action movie I saw last night was really .... (excite)

5 We had a .... day yesterday. We were so .... in the evening! (tire)

6 My friend is very .... in Irish folk music and dance. (interest)

7 He's really .... when he tells his jokes. He makes everybody laugh. (entertain)

8 Look at the .... sun. What a majestic sight! (rise)

9 We had a really .... evening, just chilling out with a takeout and a movie. (relax)

10 I was really .... by what you said. I couldn't understand your point at all. (confuse)

具有字首和字尾的單字

要變造單字，可**加上字首**或**字尾**，衍生出來的單字會與原字根的意義不同，例如：

字首 mis + 動詞 understand（理解）→ misunderstand（誤會）

有時加了字尾的單字，也會和原字具有不同的文法功能，例如從名詞變成形容詞：

名詞 beauty（美麗）+ 字尾 ful → 形容詞 beautiful（美麗的）

❶ 字首

以下列出主要字首，依功能劃分：

相反	dis–	dishonest / disappear	過多、瑕疵	over–	overestimate / overpopulated
	il– / ir–	illegal / irregular		under–	underestimate / underweight
	im– / in–	imperfect / inhospitable	預知、預測	fore–	foresee / foretell
	un–	unbelievable	數量、數字	mono–	monologue
重複	re–	rebuild / repay		bi–	bicycle
共同點、合作	co–	cooperation / coexist		tri–	triangle
減少、剝奪	de–	deforestation / defrost		poly	polysyllabic
成效不佳、執行不當	mis–	misbehavior / misfortune		multi–	multipurpose
	ill–	ill-equipped			

---

5 請在單字 **1–12** 的字首畫<u>底線</u>，並與 **A–L** 的字義配對。

..... **1** multitasking   ..... **5** dehydrate   ..... **9** trilogy

..... **2** forecast   ..... **6** disagree   ..... **10** ill-treated

..... **3** polytheistic religion   ..... **7** unfriendly   ..... **11** rearrange

..... **4** oversleep   ..... **8** undernourished   ..... **12** polyglot

A have a different idea	**G** in three parts
B treated badly	**H** not very sociable
C put things in a different way	**I** not well fed
D make dry by removing the water	**J** say what the future will be like
E doing more than one thing at a time	**K** someone who speaks many languages
F get up later than usual	**L** more than one god is worshipped

❷ 構成名詞的字尾

抽象概念		職業、人類從事的活動或物品功能	
–ness	happiness	–er / –or	employer / calculator
–ship	friendship	–ress	後接於某些職業的陰性名詞，如 waitress
–hood	childhood	–ee	employee
–ment	disappointment	–ist	novelist
–ance / –ence	performance / difference	–ian	politician
–y / –ity / –iety	jealousy / immunity / variety	–ant / –ent	assistant、superintendent
–tion / –ation	connection / combination		
–dom	boredom		

❸ 構成形容詞的字尾

特質或特性	–able / –ible	reliable / convertible	充盈	–ful	hopeful
	–ive	attractive	削減	–less	hopeless
	–ous	dangerous	技術性、科學或文化語言	–al	cultural / central
	–y	noisy		–ar	molecular
國籍（首字母一定要大寫）	–an / –ian	Mexican / Canadian		–ic / –ical	atomic / historical
	–ish	Polish	從方位基點衍生	–ern	northern / southwestern
	–ese	Portuguese			
減少、貶低		childish			
無法確切定義的顏色	–ish	reddish / yellowish			

❹ 構成動詞的字尾

有「促成」、「成為」意義

–ize / –ise【英式】（modernize / legalise【英式】）

–ify （purify）

–en （strengthen / widen / shorten）

❺ 構成副詞的字尾

–ly （mainly / generally）

許多副詞均為情狀副詞（softly / gently）

（請參閱第 174 頁）

6 請將括號裡的單字加上合適的字尾，來寫出職業或活動名稱。

1 A great .... is someone whose work never dies. (art)

2 Most .... think that human events go in cycles. (history)

3 The .... said that sales should increase. (direct)

4 Picasso is one of the greatest .... of all times. (paint)

5 The .... made all the children laugh with his tricks. (magic)

6 He's the .... in the band and she's the .... (drum / sing)

7 請在單字的字首和字尾畫底線，並在後方寫上詞性。如果是名詞，請寫 N；如果是動詞，請寫 V；如果是形容詞，請寫 ADJ；如果是副詞，請寫 ADV。

0 <u>un</u>favo<u>rable</u> ......(ADJ)..........

1 peaceful ....

2 rewind ....

3 impatiently ....

4 reorganization ....

5 unfortunately ....

6 disadvantage ....

7 insecurity ....

8 leadership ....

9 loneliness ....

8 請將括號裡的單字加上的 **ful** 或 **less** 字尾，來構成形容詞並完成句子。

1 Not answering her emails is .... (point)

2 The sunset is always a .... sight. (wonder)

3 There are lots of .... people sleeping on the park benches. (home)

4 Luckily, this pocket calculator has proved to be very .... (use)

5 Talking so loudly is really .... We can hear you very well when you talk normally. (use)

6 Be very .... when driving in the fog. (care)

7 He's a .... writer. He makes lots of spelling mistakes. (care)

8 Our company's CEO is a .... and confident woman. (power)

9 Patricia will never learn French. She's .... at foreign languages. (hope)

10 We hope this will be the start of a .... business relationship. (fruit)

9 請將畫底線的單字改為形容詞，來完成意義相近的句子。

1 These jeans are in <u>fashion</u>. → They're .... jeans.

2 He thinks only about him<u>self</u>. → He's a .... person.

3 There's a lot of <u>noise</u> in here. → It's a very .... place.

4 This drink has got <u>alcohol</u> in it. → It's an .... drink.

5 What you said doesn't <u>mean</u> anything. → What you said is ....

6 Such protests are without <u>precedent</u>. → Such protests are ....

7 It's a night <u>without clouds</u>. → It's a .... night.

8 Sara is a girl you can <u>rely</u> on. → Sara is a .... girl.

9 It's <u>not possible</u> to climb that mountain. → Climbing that mountain is ....

10 It's <u>difficult to predict</u> what he's going to do next. → He's very ....

LESSON 4 片語動詞 Phrasal verbs

❶ 片語動詞的結構是一個主要動詞，加上一或兩個介副詞，來賦予動詞特定的意義，例如 **Get on with** your work（= Continue . . . ）

❷ 此類動詞常用於口語英文。有時候觀察動詞和介副詞的意思，就能輕鬆猜到整個片語的意義，例如 give back（拿回來）或 go around（到處走）。

❸ 但若意思完全改變，非英文母語人士就會很難猜到的片語意義，例如 put up with 意指 tolerate（容忍），give in 意指 admit defeat（認輸），而容忍、認輸都和 put 或 give 本身的意思完全不相干。

FAQ

Q: 我真的沒辦法記住片語動詞。有沒有其他同義詞可以取代呢？

A: 其實片語動詞幾乎都可用同義動詞來替代，而且英文裡的此類單字多源自於拉丁文，如 **tolerate** 可取代 put up with；**arrive** 可取代 get to，**enter** 可取代 go in；**return** 可取代 go back。單字在英文裡比片語動詞正式，如果常使用此類單字，會讓人覺得你的英文造詣很高喔！

片語動詞根據及物與否分為：

1 不及物片語動詞（由「動詞＋介副詞構成」，且沒有直接受詞）：
- They all **stood up** when the principal **came in**.

2 及物片語動詞（後接直接受詞）：**Wake up** the kids.

片語動詞還有以下特性：

1 許多可**分隔使用**，也就是可以把直接受詞放在動詞和介副詞之間：
- **Tidy up** your room. / **Tidy** your room **up**.

2 如果受詞是**代名詞**，一定要放在動詞和介副詞之間：
- He read the book and then he **brought it back** to the library. (NOT ~~he brought back it~~)

3 如果介副詞是**介系詞**（for、at、to、into 等），就不能將片語動詞分隔為兩個部分：
- I **ran into** Kate this morning. (NOT ~~I ran Kate into~~)

4 某些片語動詞可後接**動詞 ing**：My father **gave up smoking** a couple of months ago.

UNIT 21 語序／片語動詞／構詞方法

FAQ

Q: 片語動詞可兼具多種意思嗎？

A: 可以的，這種情況很常見。以 **take off** 為例，如果當作不及物片語動詞使用，意指飛機起飛，如「My plane takes off in a few minutes.」；如果當作及物片語動詞使用，意指卸除、脫去，如「Take off your coat.」。

其他例子還有 **go off**，它可以是 go away（走開）、explode（爆炸）、stop working（失效）、fall asleep（睡著）甚至是 go bad（腐壞）的意思！因此要知道這種片語動詞的意思，只能透過上下文的內容來判斷。

常見不及物片語動詞

break out （令人不悅的事物）突然開始	**go back / come back / get back** 返回
call in 短暫拜訪	**go off** 離開、爆炸、腐壞
come in / go in 進入	**lie down** 平放、躺著休息
come out / go out / get out 離開（建物或居室空間）	**lie down** 平放、躺著休息
come up 上升；接近；開始成長	**look out / watch out** 小心
get off 離開（大眾運輸工具）	**stand up** 從坐下的姿勢站起來
get on (well) with 與……友善相處	**sit down** 從站立姿勢坐下
get on with / carry on with 繼續進行某事	**take off** （飛機）起飛
get up 起床	**wake up** 從睡眠狀態醒來
give in 認輸、投降	**wash up** 洗碗
go away / get away from 離開、逃離	**wash up** 洗碗

FAQ

Q: come out 和 go out 有什麼差別？

A: come out 和 go out 都有「**離開一個場所**」的意思。但已經**在場所外面**的人要使用 **come out**；仍在場所裡面的人則使用 **go out**。

come in 和 **go in** 一樣同理可證。在室內的人使用 come in，在室外的人則使用 go in。另外 **come up / go up** 和 **come down / go down** 也是一樣的道理。

1 Come .... , please. The door is open.

2 Let's .... in! It's cold outside.

3 Call .... tonight and we'll have a nice chat.

4 Never .... in without fighting!

5 I don't get .... very well with my new colleague.

6 You can't .... on like this. You should sleep more.

7 Wake .... ! It's late!

8 I sometimes wash .... after dinner.

9 We usually .... up at half past six a.m. on weekdays.

10 Please sit .... here, next to me.

11 If you have a headache, ... down on the sofa and get some rest.

12 Let's go .... now. We can take a walk to the beach.

13 Bye, Sam. Come .... soon!

14 The Second World War .... out in 1939.

15 Take .... your coat. It's quite warm in here.

16 Our plane .... off at eight. We have to be at the airport two hours before.

17 Go .... and leave me alone!

18 There's a lot of traffic. .... out before crossing the street!

19 Thank you for the nice presentation. You can go .... to your seat now.

20 The yoghurt will go .... if you don't put it in the fridge.

21 I don't always wake up when my alarm goes ....

22 .... out, everybody! There's a bull in that field!

23 You should .... up when the principal walks into the classroom.

24 Dave ran .... a dog by mistake while he was driving to work.

常見及物片語動詞

bring about 導致某事物發生	**put away** 將東西整齊歸位
bring back 帶回某人／某物； 將某物（禮物）送予某人	**put off** 延後
bring up 走在最後面； 教育；提起某事引起他人注意	**put on** 穿衣打扮
carry out 實行；完成某事務	**put out** 撲滅（火勢）
cut down 減少	**put up** 留宿某處
cut out 以裁切方式去除； 裁切為所需形體；省略；置之不理	**switch off** 關掉電源
fill in 完成（填妥表格）	**switch on** 打開電源
get across 使人了解	**take off** 脫去（衣物）
give out 分配	**take up** 開始追求（某職業、嗜好）
give up 停止；放棄	**try on** 試穿衣服是否合身
hand in 將某物拿給權威人士	**turn off** 轉動或切換開關來關水或關電
make up 捏造（藉口、故事）	**turn on** 轉動或切換開關；打開水龍頭或打開電源
pick up 接送某人；從地上撿起某物	**turn down** 減少或降低（音量、家電溫度） **turn up** 增加（音量、家電溫度）

搭配兩個介副詞的動詞

catch up with 迎頭趕上在前方的某人	**keep up with** 跟上、與……並駕齊驅
do away with 拆除；廢除	**look forward to** 以愉悅心情期待即將發生的事
get away with 做了不正當的事而沒被逮到	**put up with** 容忍、忍受
get by on/with 設法靠自己的經濟、知識或持有物來過活	**run out of** 用完某物品
get through with 結束某事物	**stand back from** 從某處退後、遠離某事物
go/come down with 感染某病症	**stand in for** 替代

2 請將介副詞移到受詞後面，來寫出意義相同的句子。

0 What has **brought about** this misunderstanding? What has brought this misunderstanding about?

1 **Bring back** the newspaper, will you? ....

2 **Fill in** this form, please. ....

3 **Hand in** your project by tomorrow. ....

4 It's cold. **Put on** your pullover. ....

5 Can I **try on** this coat, please? ....

6 **Switch on** the lights, it's dark. ....

7 **Put away** the glasses, please. ....

8 **Turn down** the TV. It's too loud. ....

3 請使用片語動詞，來寫出意義相同的句子。

1 Return as soon as you can!
Come .... !

2 Something's happened at work.
Something's come ....

3 I told them to enter.
I told them to come ....

4 However hard I try, I can't stop smoking.
I can't give ....

5 He invented a good story.
He made ....

6 Do you know what caused her depression?
Do you know what brought ....?

7 My grandparents raised eight children.
My grandparents brought ....

8 How can you tolerate his behavior?
How can you put .... ?

4 請選用下方的介副詞來完成句子。

away	with	down	forward	up (x2)	on	of

1 Keep up .... the good work!

2 We're looking .... to seeing him!

3 I'm running out .... gas, I'm afraid.

4 I have to catch .... with some work that I didn't get finished today.

5 How are you getting .... with your French?

6 They cheated during the test, but didn't get .... with it.

7 Last week she came .... with flu.

8 I can't keep .... with you. You're running too fast.

ROUND UP 21

1 下方句子中，有超過一個單字位置擺放錯誤，請以正確語序來改寫句子。

1 He doesn't like at all horror movies.

....

2 He didn't go last summer on vacation to the usual place.

....

....

3 Your sister speaks very well Spanish.

....

4 We thanked them for being to us so nice.

....

5 They spent in Africa two months last year.

....

6 What did you have yesterday for lunch?

....

7 They haven't been before to Turkey.

....

8 We spend usually our free time at the youth club or at the mall.

....

9 I today don't feel very well.

....

10 We're having in a week's time an exam.

....

11 What time does leave the next train?

....

12 From what platform does it leave?

....

2 下方句子均有錯誤，請以倒裝主詞和動詞的方式訂正。

0 You shouldn't smoke, nor you should drink alcohol.

You shouldn't smoke, nor should you drink alcohol.

1 Not only she was a great singer, she was also a fantastic dancer.

....

2 No sooner he had arrived than he started chatting and never stopped.

....

3 Only if you train hard, you will have a chance of winning the match.

....

4 Not until I got home in the evening I realized that my friend had left.

....

5 Never I have met such a silly boy as Tom.

....

6 Hardly ever they help with the housework. Their parents are really annoyed.

....

7 They came to the mountains, but not even once they tried to ski.

....

8 Only if you are nice to others, others will be nice to you.

....

3 請根據指示將句子改寫；**(+)** 代表肯定句，**(−)** 代表否定句，**(?)** 代表疑問句。

1 This isn't my first time in New York. (+)

....

....

2 They have a lot of friends here. (?)

....

....

3 We enjoyed the trip very much. (−)

....

....

4 The children have to be at school earlier tomorrow. (?)

....

....

5 The bus leaves on the half hour. (?)

....

....

6 They could find the answers to all of my questions. (−)

....

....

7 Tom and Lucy had dinner at home last night. (?)

....

....

8 There was a long line at the post office. (?)

....

....

9 My mom doesn't know my friend John. (+)

....

....

10 We didn't get up late this morning. (+)

....

....

4 請在各句後方補上附加問句。

1 You could have left before, ...

2 They've already had dinner, ...

3 You can't be sure of that, ...

4 You didn't study much yesterday, ...

5 Your parents don't speak German, ...

6 Your cousin Samantha lives near here, ...

7 That's her house, ...

8 They were all happy with their accommodation, ...

9 You've been to New York, ...

5 請根據指示，針對每個論述回覆；**(=)** 表示贊同，**(≠)** 表示不贊同。

0 We will be leaving soon. (=) ....So will I........... . It's time for me to go home too.

1 I like this song. (≠) .... I prefer the other one.

2 We went shopping yesterday. (=) .... We bought some nice shirts.

3 I didn't stay till the end. (≠) .... I thought it was a great conference.

4 We don't play hockey in my school. (=) .... We play volleyball.

5 I don't like hipster jeans. (=) .... I think they're horrible.

6 I couldn't help laughing! (=) .... I thought it was so funny!

7 My brother goes to primary school. (=) .... my brother. He's in Year 3.

8 My mother has retired from work. (≠) Mine .... She still works as a nurse.

9 Jack sings so well! (=) .... Steve. They both have great voices.

10 I didn't pay much for the flight. (≠) .... ! I paid nearly £200.

6 請參考下方字尾表，為表格中的單字加上字尾，來構成抽象名詞。並於必要時變化拼字方式。

-ness	-ship	-hood	-ment	-ation	-ance	-ity	-dom

	抽象名詞		抽象名詞		抽象名詞
sweet	sweetness	establish		liberate	
educate		possible		kind	
enjoy		credible		endure	
friend		hard		free	
leader		sister		excite	
perform		real		happy	

延伸補充

除了 Lesson 4 列過的，以下是其他常用的片語動詞：

be off 走開；下班	drop in at （偶爾）拜訪某處
be on 在電視上或電影院放映	drop in on （偶爾）拜訪某人
be over 完結	hang around 悠閒在某處附近等候或停留
be up to 做某事（有暗示偷偷摸摸的意思）、有能力做某事或適合做某任務	hang on 請某人短暫等候或放下手邊事務
break down 故障；情緒崩潰	hang on to 緊握某物；堅持與某事物為伴；保留某物
call off 取消	hang out 在某處停留很久的時間
come back 返回	set off 開始一趟旅程
come up with 找出答案；提議解決之道	shut up 關（門窗）；住嘴
cut off 中斷連接	work out 做運動

7 請將每個句子畫底線的動詞，改為上方 **延伸補充** 內意思相同的片語動詞。

1 The meeting has been <u>canceled</u>. ....

2 The car engine <u>stopped all of a sudden</u>. ....

3 They had been together for two years when they <u>parted</u>. ....

4 Will they <u>be able to do</u> this task? ....

5 What <u>are</u> you <u>doing</u>, children? Leave the cat alone! ....

6 Okay. I must <u>be going</u> now. ....

7 Mr. Romney is busy now. <u>Return</u> tomorrow, please. ....

8 We had a big problem, but our friends <u>found</u> a good remedy. ....

9 They <u>left</u> for Australia two days ago. ....

10 <u>Be quiet</u>, you two. Stop chatting. ....

11 I <u>do some exercise</u> in the gym once a week, doing weights and things like that. ....

12 <u>Hold</u> the rope tightly. ....

13 We like <u>spending our time</u> at the mall on Saturdays. ....

14 I saw a couple of boys <u>going up and down</u> the street. ....

15 It<u>'s</u> all <u>finished</u>! We won't have to think about it any more. ....

以下為 be + 過去分詞 + 介副詞的用法：

- **be done away with** 擺脫
- **be done in** 筋疲力盡
- **be done for** 處境非常不利；注定失敗
- **be done with** （+ 名詞或動詞 ing） 結束；完成
- **be fed up with** （+ 名詞或動詞 ing） 對某事物感到乏味或不開心
- **be worn out** 看起來或感覺很疲累；不能再用的

8 請將畫底線的單字，改為上方 延伸補充 內意思相同的用語。

1 I'll be happy when this job is over and <u>finished</u>. ....

2 I'm <u>too tired</u>. I can't work any longer today! ....

3 My shoes were <u>no longer useful</u> after I had walked all the way to Santiago de Compostela.

....

4 I <u>can't bear</u> my sons hanging around all day. ....

5 He's <u>exhausted</u> after a day's hard work! ....

6 Unless your school report is better this term, you'll be <u>in big trouble</u>. ....

7 All this paperwork should be <u>abolished</u>. ....

8 I <u>can't stand</u> this boring job. ....

Reflecting on grammar

請研讀文法規則，再判斷以下說法是否正確。

		True	False
1	SVOMPT 是幫助記憶肯定句語序的縮寫字。頭三個字母分別代表主詞、動詞和受詞。		
2	在肯定句裡，我們通常會將場所用語放在時間用語後面。		
3	否定附加問句通常接在肯定句後面，反之亦然。		
4	若某人說「I love ballet.」，表達贊同的說法會是「So am I.」。		
5	「When does the next bus leaves?」是正確的問句。		
6	在 waterproof jacket 此類「名詞 + 名詞」的複合名詞裡，第一個名詞具有形容詞的功能，用以說明或定義第二個名詞。		
7	underestimated 屬於含有字首和字尾的形容詞。		
8	字尾 hood 和 ness 用以構成表達職業或人類活動的名詞。		
9	句首如果是 never 等否定詞即需倒裝，也就是先寫出助動詞，再寫主詞。		
10	當受詞是代名詞，及物片語動詞一定要與質詞隔開。		

Revision and Exams 7 (UNITS 19 – 20 – 21)

1 請填空以下對話。

Neil So, [1].......................... was your vacation in Ireland?

Ellen Great! We really enjoyed ourselves!

Neil [2].......................... were you exactly?

Ellen We were in Galway for two weeks.

Neil Galway? It's on the west coast, [3].......................... it?

Ellen Yes, exactly. It's a beautiful place. There are a lot of things going [4]..........................
in the summer.

Neil What was the weather [5].......................... ? Windy and rainy, I guess.

Ellen Well, I was told the weather in that area was usually rainy, but in fact we had two weeks
of sun.

Neil That was lucky! Did you go to the Aran islands?

Ellen Yes, absolutely. We hired two bicycles and we went [6].......................... a trip around the
island of Inishmore. We also had a swim in the sea, even [7].......................... the water was
very cold!

Neil How I would have liked to have been with you! I love Ireland. Have you been there before?

Ellen No, this was our first time, but we want to go [8].......................... there next year.

2 到公司後，尼爾（**Neil**）將他和艾倫（**Ellen**）上述的閒聊告訴同事史提夫（**Steve**）。
請寫出他轉述的內容。

Neil Hi, Steve. Guess who I've just met. Ellen, do you remember her? She used to work in the
Accounts Department. I asked her what her vacation in Ireland was like and she said . . .

3 請使用下方片語動詞來完成對話。

get across	done in	come on	run out	give in	put up (x2)	make out

Paul Don't [1].......................... now, we're nearly there.

Dave But I'm [2].......................... . I can't walk any more.

Paul Can't you see the top? One more effort and we'll be there.
[3].......................... !

Dave I can't even [4].......................... the top in this mist.

Paul Stop complaining. You must learn to
[5].......................... with difficulties.

Dave But I can [6].......................... with difficulties. I realize now that I'm not trained. How
can I [7].......................... it .... to you?

Paul Okay, I see, but I know you can make it. Let's have some chocolate. It will help.

Dave Er . . . I didn't want to tell you, but we've [8].......................... of comfort food.

Paul Oh no! Do we have any water left?

Dave Yes, we've still got some water at least.

4 戴維（**Dave**）回家後，將上述爬山攻頂的對話告訴他的弟弟。請寫出戴維轉述的內容。

Dave You can't even imagine how difficult it was for me to get to the top. I thought I would
give in . . .

5 請使用下方單字，完成學校化學實驗室的規定。

but　if (x3)　after (x2)　or (x3)　before　and　when

Chemistry Lab Regulations

- The chemistry lab assistant will prepare the instruments you need for all experiments, [1].................. you must wash [2].................. clean them [3].................. use [4].................. return them to their shelves or cupboards.
- You must wear a protective smock [5].................. doing experiments in the lab. You don't have to wear one [6].................. you are attending a plenary lesson.
- You are allowed in the laboratory only [7].................. a teacher or the lab assistant is present.
- You must handle all instruments with care.
- You must tell the lab assistant [8].................. you find anything broken, missing [9].................. in the wrong place [10].................. you start working.
- You have to write a report [11].................. each experiment and hand it in to the chemistry teacher.
- You can't eat or drink [12].................. chew gum in the lab.

6 請閱讀下方短文，選出正確的答案。

I had never realized how odd English may sound to foreigners learning it [1]....... I had to learn a foreign language [2]....... . I studied some French [3]....... I was at school, but I didn't really learn it, [4]....... I never picked up the differences between English and a Latin language.

I've recently taken [5]....... an Italian course because I need it for my job, and one of the strangest things I'm learning is the order of words in a sentence. Adjectives often go [6]....... nouns in Italian but not always, and sometimes you can find a noun "surrounded" by adjectives, that is one adjective before it and a couple of adjectives after the same noun. Why is it so? I don't know. I'm going to buy a grammar book to see [7]....... I can find any explanations.

Another point is compounds. There aren't so many compounds in Italian [8]....... there are in English; for example, the word for *post office* sounds like "office postal," *mail box* is "the box of the mail," *racing car* is "a car to race" and so on. It drives me crazy! To translate from English into Italian, I have to sort of "undo" every compound and swap the position of the words, which slows me [9]....... quite a lot. I guess [10]....... an Italian person learning English will have to do the same, only vice versa.

1	Ⓐ as long as	Ⓑ until	Ⓒ when
2	Ⓐ myself	Ⓑ my own	Ⓒ me too
3	Ⓐ until	Ⓑ where	Ⓒ when
4	Ⓐ so	Ⓑ if	Ⓒ but
5	Ⓐ off	Ⓑ up	Ⓒ over
6	Ⓐ over	Ⓑ under	Ⓒ after
7	Ⓐ when	Ⓑ how	Ⓒ if
8	Ⓐ that	Ⓑ as	Ⓒ than
9	Ⓐ down	Ⓑ through	Ⓒ over
10	Ⓐ if	Ⓑ that	Ⓒ whether

7 你從網路型錄訂購一件防水外套，但到貨後卻有許多原因，讓你對產品感到不滿。以下列出你寫的部分型錄筆記。請以合適用語，寫出 **120–150** 字的客訴信。

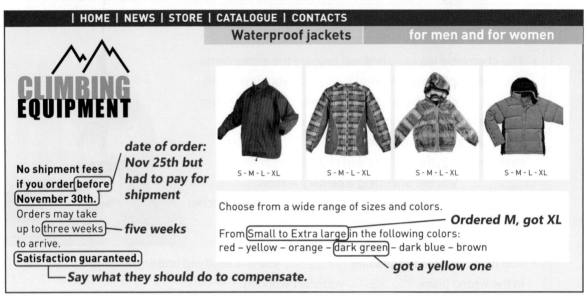

| HOME | NEWS | STORE | CATALOGUE | CONTACTS

Waterproof jackets　　　　　**for men and for women**

CLIMBING EQUIPMENT

S – M – L – XL　　S – M – L – XL　　S – M – L – XL　　S – M – L – XL

No shipment fees if you order [before] [November 30th.]
Orders may take up to [three weeks] to arrive.

date of order: Nov 25th but had to pay for shipment

five weeks

[Satisfaction guaranteed.]

Say what they should do to compensate.

Choose from a wide range of sizes and colors.

Ordered M, got XL

From [Small to Extra large] in the following colors:
red – yellow – orange – [dark green] – dark blue – brown

got a yellow one

8 請使用三個字以內的片語動詞完成意思相近的句子。

1 I can't stand people smoking while driving.

I can't .... people smoking while driving.

2 The annual conference has been postponed.

The annual conference has ....

3 Make sure that the children stay away from my flower beds.

Make sure that the children .... my flower beds.

4 We have no more paper for the photocopier. I must go and buy some immediately.

We have .... paper for the photocopier. I must go and buy some immediately.

5 Please complete this form if you want to apply for this job.

Please .... this form if you want to apply for this job.

6 I want to stop eating meat.

I want to .... meat.

7 Call in to see me next time you come to town!

.... see me next time you come to town!

8 We can execute your order by the end of the month.

We can .... your order by the end of the month.

9 請閱讀下方短文，選出正確的答案。

Last night I went to a Bob Dylan concert. I was there ⁰...B... 4 p.m., well ¹....... the concert started, ²....... I wanted to be near the stage, ³....... the stadium was already crowded. ⁴....... Bob started singing "Blowing in the Wind," his most famous hit, the audience started clapping ⁵....... everybody started singing along. ⁶....... he sang his "evergreen" songs, thousands of lights from cell phones appeared all over the stadium. ⁷....... Bob Dylan was famous in the 1970s ⁸....... I thought there wouldn't be a lot of young people at the concert, ⁹....... there were thousands of teenagers! ¹⁰....... being a great singer, Bob Dylan is also a cultural icon for all time.

0	Ⓐ on	Ⓑ at	Ⓒ until	Ⓓ till
1	Ⓐ after	Ⓑ before	Ⓒ until	Ⓓ soon
2	Ⓐ if	Ⓑ though	Ⓒ because	Ⓓ only if
3	Ⓐ but	Ⓑ case	Ⓒ unless	Ⓓ as soon as
4	Ⓐ Until	Ⓑ Unless	Ⓒ When	Ⓓ No sooner
5	Ⓐ however	Ⓑ though	Ⓒ but	Ⓓ and
6	Ⓐ When	Ⓑ However	Ⓒ But	Ⓓ Before
7	Ⓐ However	Ⓑ Even though	Ⓒ No sooner	Ⓓ Only if
8	Ⓐ and	Ⓑ but	Ⓒ as	Ⓓ like
9	Ⓐ secondly	Ⓑ firstly	Ⓒ until	Ⓓ in fact
10	Ⓐ Besides	Ⓑ When	Ⓒ As	Ⓓ Moreover

10 請閱讀短文，自行思考最貼切的單字填入空格。每一格僅能填入一個單字，可參考第 **0** 格。

A ⁰..........lot.......... of European students spend their summer picking fruit in farms all over the world. ¹.......................... being a healthy open-air activity, it is ².......................... an excuse to go ³.......................... for some time and have a vacation with other people. ⁴.......................... of the time, they live in a big group and learn to put ⁵.......................... with each other and become more tolerant. They have to adapt to things ⁶.......................... queuing up for the shower, sleeping in uncomfortable beds and working long hours. Some can't do ⁷.......................... their creature comforts and give ⁸.......................... after a few days. ⁹.......................... fruit picking is hard work, about half of the students decide to go ¹⁰.......................... to the same farm the following year.

11 請閱讀短文，依序將行末的大寫提示用詞，改為合適詞性的詞，再填入空格。

It is quite normal that there are ⁰.........disagreements..... in families and that there are

regular ¹.................................... between family members, as everyone has their own

ideas about what should happen when and how. In fact, it's almost ²................................

that most families actually manage to live together relatively happily. It is normal for

teenagers to fight for their ³.................................... and for parents to feel very

⁴.................................... towards them. Each family deals with the situation in a

⁵.................................... way.

AGREE

UNDERSTAND

BELIEVE

DEPEND

PROTECT

DIFFER

Towards Competences

有人請你寫一篇文章，內容要比較你所處地區生活概況的優缺點，此文章將發表於學校網站的「國際交流」單元。請使用合適的連接詞，寫出將近 200 字的通順短文。

Self Check 7

請選出答案，再至解答頁核對正確與否。

1 You .... me that the meeting was at three o'clock. Don't you remember?

   Ⓐ said   Ⓑ told   Ⓒ told to

2 If you .... me another lie, I won't talk to you any more.

   Ⓐ say   Ⓑ said   Ⓒ tell

3 .... thank you to your aunt. She's brought us a wonderful present.

   Ⓐ Say   Ⓑ Tell   Ⓒ Give

4 Don't forget .... goodbye to the manager when you leave the office.

   Ⓐ to say   Ⓑ to tell   Ⓒ to give

5 He told me .... for him in the hall.

   Ⓐ waiting   Ⓑ to wait   Ⓒ wait

6 They .... us to go to the lecture the following day.

   Ⓐ warned
   Ⓑ suggested
   Ⓒ reminded

7 She suggested .... together for the exam.

   Ⓐ to revise
   Ⓑ us to revise
   Ⓒ revising

8 The farmer .... us not to touch the electrified fence.

   Ⓐ warned   Ⓑ suggested   Ⓒ said

9 She said she .... her vacation in Greece the year before.

   Ⓐ is spending
   Ⓑ had spent
   Ⓒ would spend

10 Why didn't you tell them that you .... for Peru the next day?

   Ⓐ were going to leave
   Ⓑ have been going to
   Ⓒ would going to leave

11 Mark told us he would arrive late the .... day.

   Ⓐ after   Ⓑ previous   Ⓒ following

12 They asked me why .... to work night shifts.

   Ⓐ did I accept
   Ⓑ had I accepted
   Ⓒ I had accepted

13 I asked him if .... waterskiing.

   Ⓐ he did like   Ⓑ he liked   Ⓒ did he like

14 Mandy asked Jim why he .... her the night before.

   Ⓐ wouldn't phone
   Ⓑ hadn't phoned
   Ⓒ wouldn't have phoned

15 Terry asked Sara what she .... looking up in the dictionary.

   Ⓐ will be   Ⓑ would be   Ⓒ was

16 Margaret wanted to know why Bob had arrived late at work the day ....

   Ⓐ previous   Ⓑ before   Ⓒ following

17 .... he is quite young, he has already gained lots of experience in his field.

   Ⓐ But   Ⓑ In spite   Ⓒ Although

18 On the one hand, going jogging every day is healthy, but .... it could be risky if you suffer from heart disease.

   Ⓐ on the next
   Ⓑ on the other
   Ⓒ on another

19 .... I had forgotten my wallet, Sam had to pay for my train ticket.

Ⓐ As   Ⓑ So as   Ⓒ Though

20 We're going out .... some food for dinner.

Ⓐ to buying   Ⓑ for buy   Ⓒ to buy

21 Sara's going to attend evening classes .... she can improve her Chinese.

Ⓐ in order   Ⓑ so that   Ⓒ so as

22 When you ...., make sure you have all your documents with you.

Ⓐ will come
Ⓑ come
Ⓒ will be coming

23 Switch off the TV .... the movie is over.

Ⓐ until   Ⓑ as long as   Ⓒ as soon as

24 I'm really tired! ...., I have a terrible headache.

Ⓐ What's more
Ⓑ In addition to
Ⓒ Finally

25 Many animals are hunted for their skins. ...., they've become very rare.

Ⓐ Accordingly
Ⓑ Therefore
Ⓒ So why

26 You can have the afternoon off, ... you finish all your work by the end of the week.

Ⓐ unless   Ⓑ provided   Ⓒ as though

27 They .... us stay at school after classes when we need to use the media lab.

Ⓐ let   Ⓑ make   Ⓒ cause

28 Did they go .... ?

Ⓐ yesterday in the car to Glasgow
Ⓑ to Glasgow in the car yesterday
Ⓒ in the car yesterday to Glasgow

29 I like ....

Ⓐ very much reading detective stories
Ⓑ very much read detective stories
Ⓒ reading detective stories very much

30 "Do you think they'll increase our salaries?" "I hope ...."

Ⓐ yes   Ⓑ so   Ⓒ they are

31 Pass me the mint sauce, ... ?

Ⓐ shall I   Ⓑ shall you   Ⓒ will you

32 They don't belong to our sports club, ... ?

Ⓐ do they   Ⓑ don't they   Ⓒ they do

33 Let's go to the movies, ... ?

Ⓐ let we   Ⓑ shall we   Ⓒ do we

34 You haven't seen her, ... ?

Ⓐ haven't you   Ⓑ do you
Ⓒ have you

35 Look at that set of .... Aren't they beautiful?

Ⓐ cups for tea   Ⓑ cups of tea
Ⓒ tea cups

36 It's .... to drive through a red light.

Ⓐ unlegal   Ⓑ dislegal   Ⓒ illegal

37 I'm afraid you're .... about the matter.

Ⓐ disinformed   Ⓑ misinformed
Ⓒ uninformed

38 Please tell Ms. Tyrrell that the meeting has been ....

Ⓐ put on   Ⓑ put off   Ⓒ put away

39 Oh dear! I forgot to put the meat in the fridge and now it's ....

Ⓐ gone out   Ⓑ gone away   Ⓒ gone off

40 I don't know what happened to him. He just didn't turn ....

Ⓐ up   Ⓑ on   Ⓒ off

Assess yourself!

☐ 0 – 10   還要多加用功。

☐ 11 – 20   尚可。

☐ 21 – 30   不錯。

☐ 31 – 40   非常好!

1 Be 動詞｜簡單現在式

請使用下方單詞填空。

| the kitchen | they | Sheila and I | she | not |
| Tom and Susan | the dog | the children | it | am |

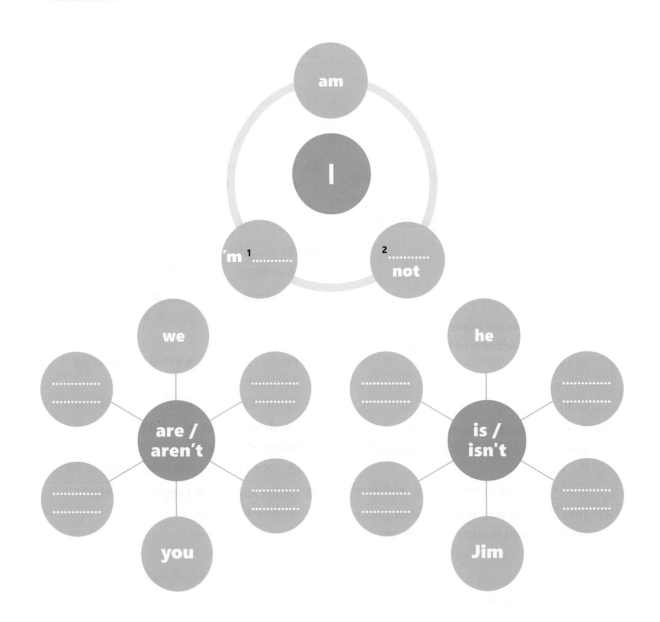

請寫出問句。　　　You are a doctor.　　It is late.

Are you a doctor?　　....... .... late?

2 動詞 Have Got | 簡單現在式

請使用下方單詞填空。

| they | we | it | you and Sally | the house | the children | she | the cat |

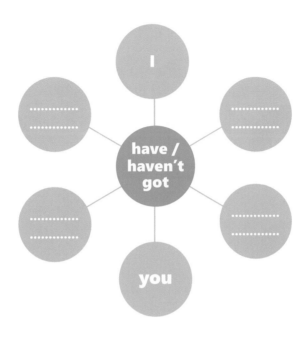

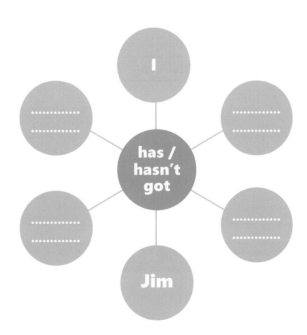

請寫出問句。

You have got a car.   He has got a dog.

Have you got a car?   .... got a dog?

3 簡單現在式｜肯定句

請使用下方單詞填空。

| they | we | it | Jim and I | the secretary | the clerks | she | the elevator |

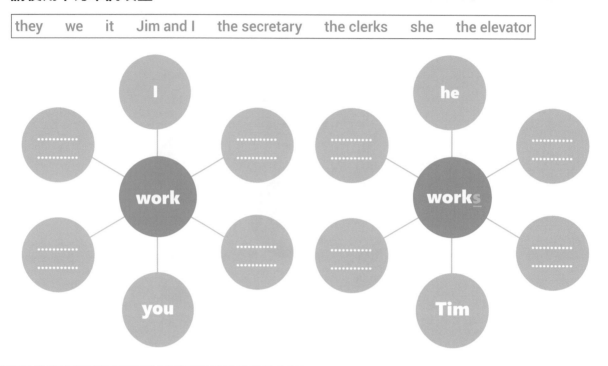

----

4 簡單現在式｜否定句

請使用下方單詞填空。

| she | Sabrina | you | Dave and Betty | it | Dad |

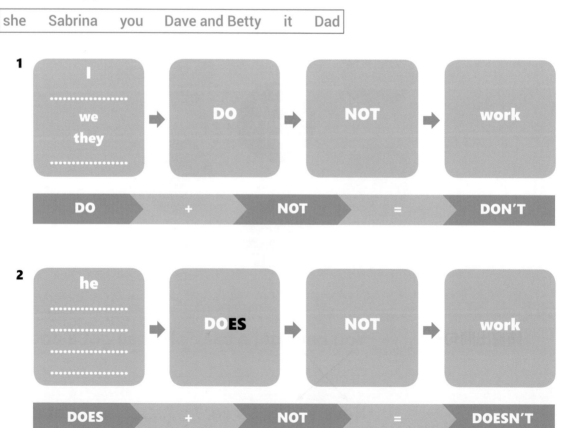

5 簡單現在式｜疑問句

請使用下方單詞填空。

| you | he | Claire and you | Jeff | it |

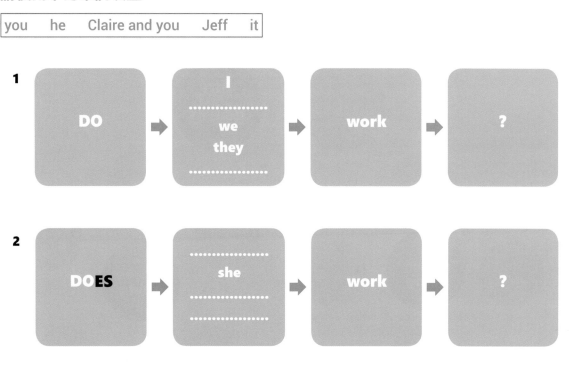

1

DO → I / we / they → work → ?

2

DO**ES** → she → work → ?

簡答句

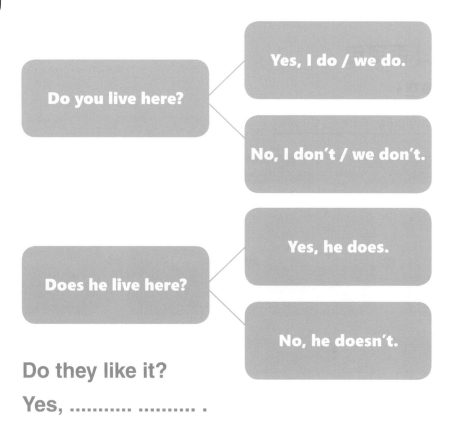

Do you live here?
- Yes, I do / we do.
- No, I don't / we don't.

Does he live here?
- Yes, he does.
- No, he doesn't.

Do they like it?
Yes, ...

6 現在進行式│肯定句

請使用下方單詞填空。

| are she we it the dog I is |

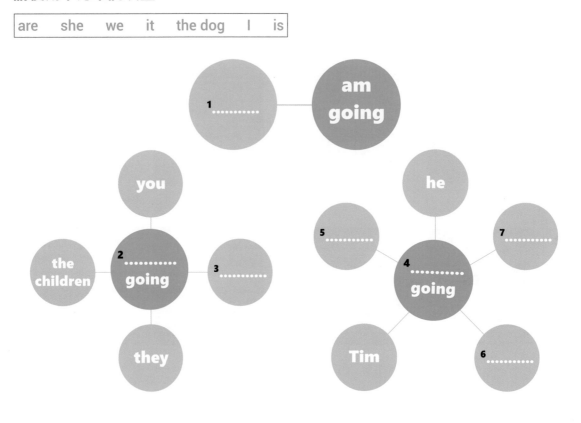

1. ....
   am going
2. .... going
3. ....
4. .... going
5. ....
6. ....
7. ....

you
the children
they
he
Tim

---

7 現在進行式│否定句

請使用下方單詞填空。

| you it the machines he Chuck |

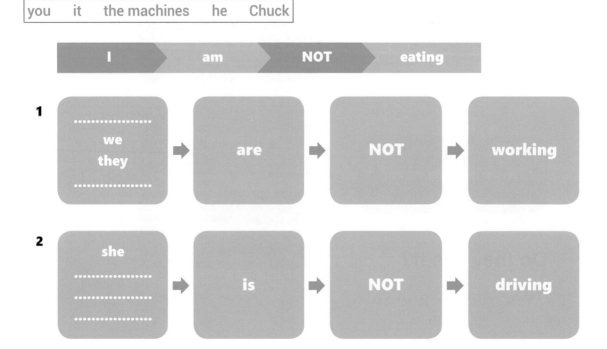

I → am → NOT → eating

1. .... we they .... → are → NOT → working

2. she .... → is → NOT → driving

8 現在進行式｜疑問句

請使用下方單詞填空。

| you | they | the students | Paul | it | the dog |

1

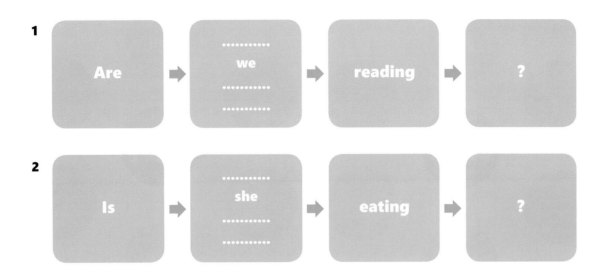

Are ➡ .... we .... ➡ reading ➡ ?

2

Is ➡ .... she .... ➡ eating ➡ ?

簡答句

Is he driving home?

Yes, he is.

No, he isn't.

Are you watching TV?

Yes, I am / we are.

No, I'm not / we aren't.

Are they going out?

No, ...

9 Be 動詞 | 簡單過去式

請使用下方單詞填空。

they	Dad and I	she	Tom and Susan	the web designer	the children	it	the town

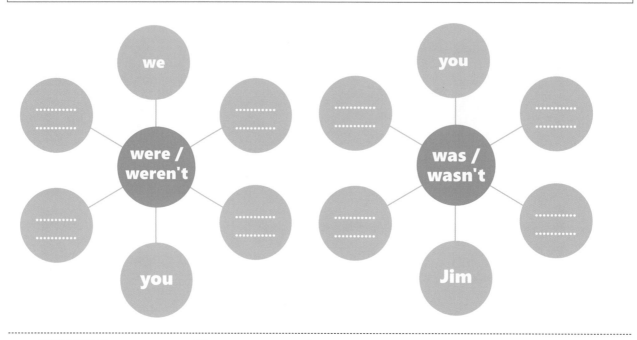

請寫出問句。

They were at home.　He was here.

Were they at home?　.......... .... here?

10 簡單過去式 | 肯定句

請使用下方單詞填空。

went	arrived	talked	drank	sat	watched
brought	did	lived	imagined	stayed	came

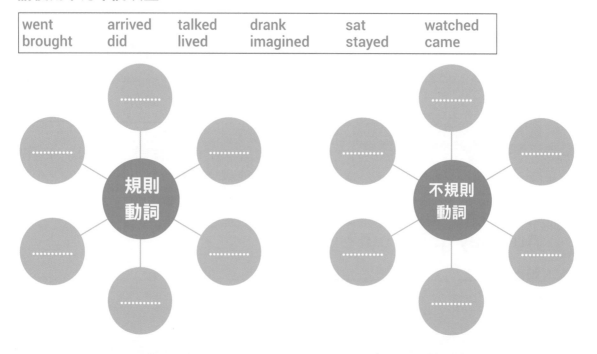

⑪ 簡單過去式｜否定句

請使用下方單詞填空。

she　he　you　it　they

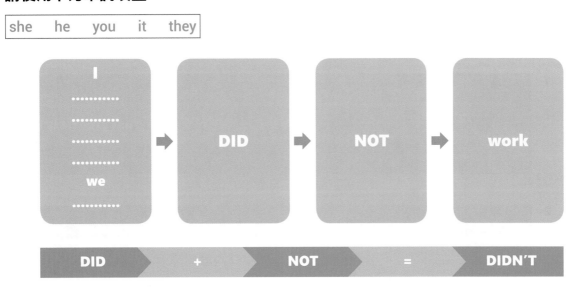

⑫ 簡單過去式｜疑問句

請使用下方單詞填空。

they　he　Claire　I　Jeff

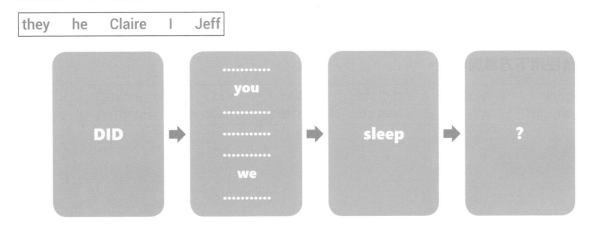

簡答句

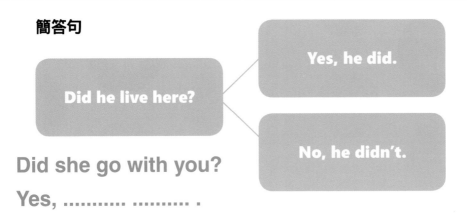

Did he live here?

Yes, he did.

No, he didn't.

Did she go with you?

Yes, ...

⓭ 現在完成式 | 肯定句和否定句

請使用下方單詞填空。

she	you	it	they

肯定句：I .... finished.   **否定句：**He .... gone!

⓮ 過去分詞

請使用下方單詞填空。

gone	washed	dictated	eaten	sat	looked
bought	done	stayed	cleared	listened	written

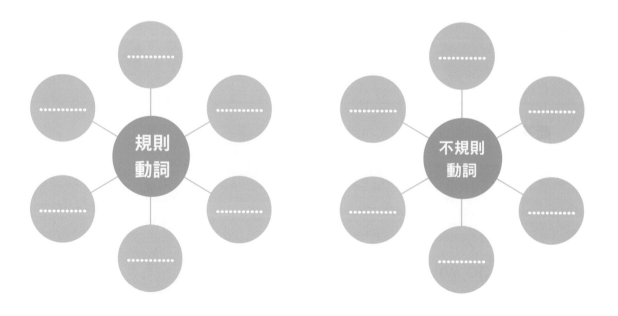

15 現在完成式｜疑問句

請使用下方單詞填空。

it	they	he	you

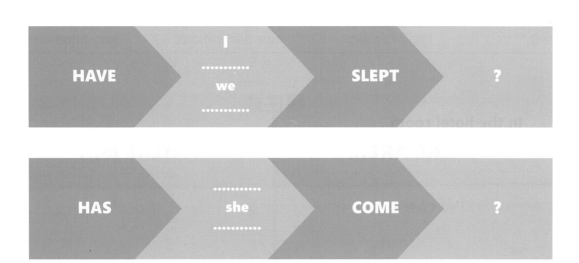

HAVE → I .... we .... → SLEPT → ?

HAS → .... she .... → COME → ?

簡答句

Has he been here for long?
— Yes, he has.
— No, he hasn't.

Have you ever been to Dublin?
— Yes, I/we have.
— No, I/we haven't.

Have they seen the movie?

No, ...

16 THERE IS / THERE ARE THERE WAS / THERE WERE

請使用下方詞彙來完成下表。

a double bed	two bedside tables	a big French window	nice pictures
a mirror	some shelves	a small wardrobe	some food
a DJ	lots of drinks	nice decorations	very good cocktails

現在式

In the hotel room

THERE ARE...

two chairs

....

....

....

THERE IS...

a desk

複數 ─────────────────── 單數

At last night's party

THERE WERE...

a lot of people

....

....

....

THERE WAS...

good music

....

....

....

過去式

# 17 贊同／不贊同

請看下表。
請以贊同或不贊同的簡答來完成下表。

贊同

否定說辭　　　　　　　　　　肯定說辭

I don't like thrillers.

Neither do I.

I like horror movies.

So do I.

I don't like historical novels.

1 ....

I like romantic novels.

2 ....

I don't like musicals.

Really? I do.

I like fantasy movies.

Really? I don't.

I don't like science-fiction stories.

3 ....

I like detective stories.

4 ....

不贊同

18 不定形容詞與代名詞 | some/any/no

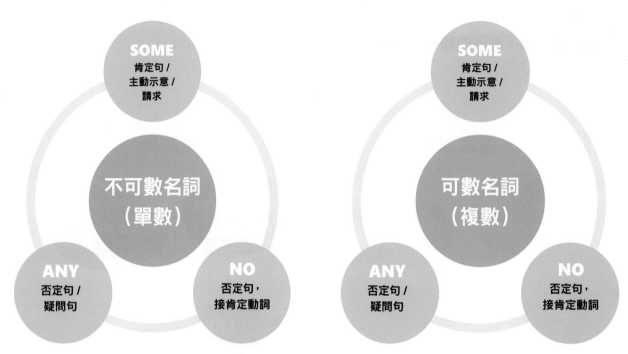

請使用不定形容詞完成句子。

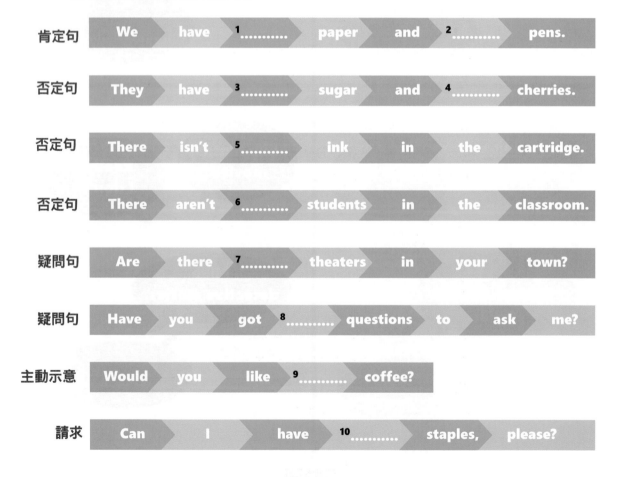

肯定句	We	have	1 .... paper	and	2 .... pens.		
否定句	They	have	3 .... sugar	and	4 .... cherries.		
否定句	There	isn't	5 .... ink	in	the	cartridge.	
否定句	There	aren't	6 .... students	in	the	classroom.	
疑問句	Are	there	7 .... theaters	in	your	town?	
疑問句	Have	you	got	8 .... questions	to	ask	me?
主動示意	Would	you	like	9 .... coffee?			
請求	Can	I	have	10 .... staples,	please?		

19 不定代名詞｜結合 some/any/no/every 的複合單詞

請完成下表。

		人物	事物	場所
		–body / –one	–thing	–where
肯定	some	somebody / someone	1	2
否定	no	3	4	5
否定 / 疑問	any	6	7	8
肯定 / 否定 / 疑問	every	9	10	11

-----

20 附加問句

請參考例句，完成下方附加問句。

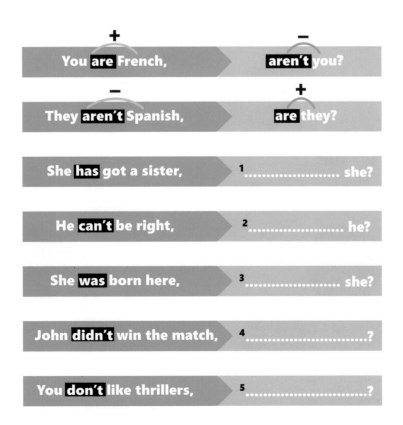

+	–
You **are** French,	**aren't** you?

–	+
They **aren't** Spanish,	**are** they?

She **has** got a sister,   1 .... she?

He **can't** be right,   2 .... he?

She **was** born here,   3 .... she?

John **didn't** win the match,   4 ....?

You **don't** like thrillers,   5 ....?

21 比較級

請使用下方形容詞的比較級來填空。

easy	fast	busy	comfortable	cheap	warm	expensive	pretty	early	fat
thin	nice	coarse	intelligent	young	hot	wide	gentle	flat	familiar

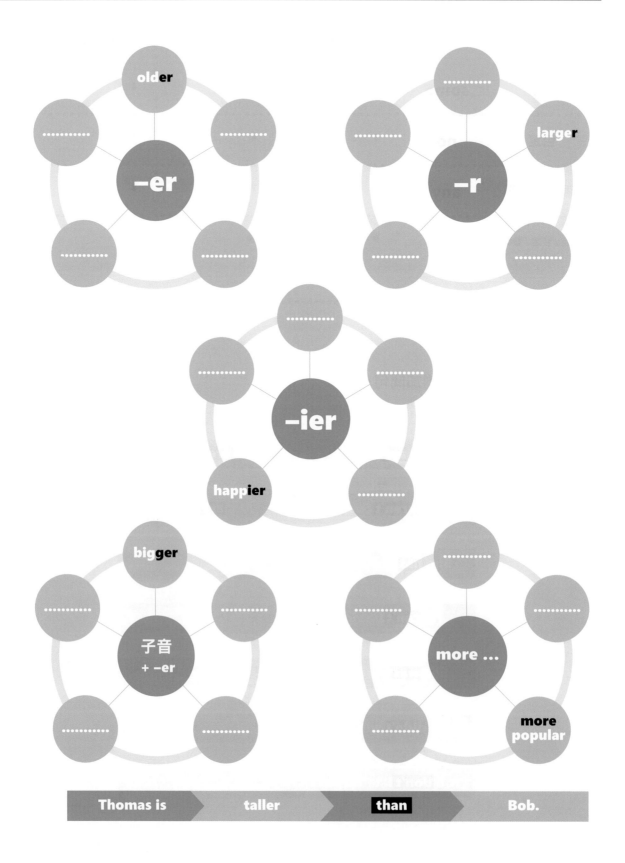

Thomas is taller **than** Bob.

418

22 最高級

請使用下方形容詞的最高級來填空

easy	fast	busy	comfortable	cheap	warm	expensive	pretty	early	fat
thin	nice	coarse	intelligent	young	hot	wide	gentle	flat	familiar

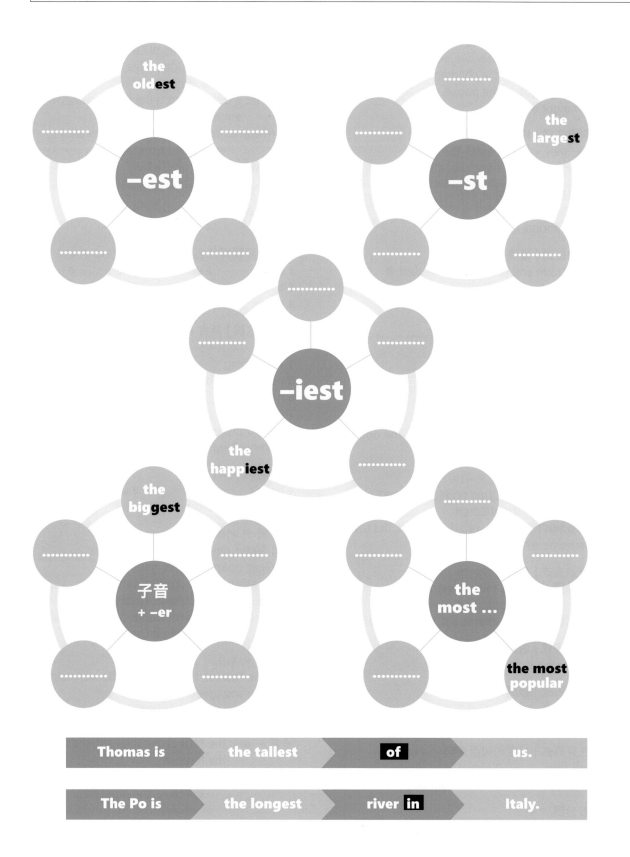

Thomas is → the tallest → **of** → us.

The Po is → the longest → river **in** → Italy.

圖解文法練習解答

1 **Be動詞 | 簡單現在式** P. 404
I: 1 not **2** am
are/aren't: they, Sheila and I, Tom and Susan,
the children
is/isn't: she, it, the dog, the kitchen
Is it late?

2 **動詞Have Got | 簡單現在式** P. 405
have/haven't got: they, we, you and Sally,
the children
has/hasn't got: it, the house, she, the cat
Has he got a dog?

3 **簡單現在式 | 肯定句** P. 406
work: they, we, Jim and I, the clerks
works: it, the secretary, she, the elevator

4 **簡單現在式 | 否定句** P. 406
1 you, Dave and Betty
2 she, Sabrina, it, Dad

5 **簡單現在式 | 疑問句** P. 407
1 you, Claire and you   **2** he, Jeff, it
Yes, **they do**.

6 **現在進行式 | 肯定句** P. 408
1 I   **2** are   **3** we   **4** is
5 she   **6** it   **7** the dog

7 **現在進行式 | 否定句** P. 408
1 you, the machines   **2** it, he, Chuck

8 **現在進行式 | 疑問句** P. 409
1 you, they, the students   **2** Paul, it, the dog
No, **they aren't**.

9 **Be動詞 | 簡單過去式** P. 410
were/weren't: they, Dad and I, Tom and Susan,
the children
was/wasn't: she, the web designer, it, the town
Was he here?

10 **簡單過去式 | 肯定句** P. 410
規則動詞：arrived, talked, watched,
lived, imagined, stayed
不規則動詞：went, drank, sat, brought, did, came

11 **簡單過去式 | 否定句** P. 411
you, she, he, it, they

12 **簡單過去式 | 疑問句** P. 411
I, he, Claire, Jeff, they
Yes, **she did**.

13 **現在完成式 | 肯定句和否定句** P. 412
1 you, they   **2** she, it
I **have** finished. / He **hasn't** gone!

14 **過去分詞** P. 412
規則動詞：washed, dictated, looked, stayed,
cleared, listened

不規則動詞：gone, eaten, sat, bought, done,
written

15 **現在完成式 | 疑問句** P. 413
1 you, they   **2** he, it
No, **they haven't**.

16 **THERE IS / THERE ARE**
THERE WAS / THERE WERE P. 414
there are: two bedside tables, nice pictures,
some shelves
there is: a double bed, a big French window,
a mirror, a small wardrobe
there were: lots of drinks, nice decorations,
very good cocktails
there was: some food, a DJ

17 **贊同／不贊同** P. 415
1 Neither/Nor do I.   **2** So do I.
3 I do.   **4** I don't.

18 **不定形容詞與代名詞 | some/any/no** P. 416
1 some   **2** some   **3** no   **4** no
5 any   **6** any   **7** any   **8** any
9 some   **10** some

19 **不定代名詞 | 結合 some/any/no/every 的複合單詞**
P. 417
1 something   **2** somewhere
3 nobody / no one   **4** nothing
5 nowhere   **6** anybody/anyone
7 anything   **8** anywhere
9 everybody/everyone   **10** everything
11 everywhere

20 **附加問句** P. 417
1 hasn't   **2** can   **3** wasn't
4 did he   **5** do you

21 **比較級** P. 418
-er: faster, cheaper, warmer, younger
-r: nicer, coarser, wider, gentler
-ier: easier, busier, prettier, earlier
子音 + -er: fatter, thinner, hotter, flatter
more . . . : more comfortable, more expensive,
more intelligent, more familiar

22 **最高級** P. 419
-est: the fastest, the cheapest, the warmest,
the youngest
-st: the nicest, the coarsest, the widest, the gentlest
-iest: the easiest, the busiest, the prettiest, the earliest
子音 + -est: the fattest, the thinnest, the hottest,
the flattest
the most . . . : the most comfortable, the most
expensive, the most familiar, the most
intelligent

英式英文與美式英文主要文法差異

英式英文和美式英文在字彙、發音、拼字與文法方面均有差異，這些區隔也可以在字典上查到。
以下列舉最明顯的差異。

① 當句子裡沒有特別指出時間，且搭配 **just**、**already**、**yet**、**ever**、**never** 等副詞時，美式英文較常使用**簡單過去式**，而英式英文較常使用**現在完成式**。

英式
- "**Have you seen** Jane?" "Yes, I**'ve seen** her."
- **Has** he **arrived** yet?
- I**'ve** never **tried** Thai food.

美式
- "**Did** you **see** Jane?" "Yes, I **saw** her."
- **Did** he **arrive** yet?
- I never **tried** Thai food.

② 美式英文不常使用 **have got / haven't got**。

英式
- **Have** you **got** a pen?
- I **haven't got** many friends here.

美式
- **Do** you **have** a pen?
- I **don't have** many friends here.

③ 英式英文比美式英文更常使用**附加問句**。

英式
- You're 16, **aren't you**?
- Don't be late, **will you**?

美式
- You're 16, **right**?
- Don't be late, **okay**?

④ 動詞 **need** 在英式英文較常身兼助動詞，美式英文則大多將 **need** 視為一般動詞。

英式 You **needn't** wait for me.

美式 You **don't need to** wait for me.

⑤ 美式英文較常使用情態助動詞 **should**，而非 **shall**。

英式
- What **shall** we do tonight?
- **Shall** I go now?

美式
- What **should** we do tonight?
- **Should** I go now?

⑥ **family**、**team** 與 **government** 等集合名詞，在英式英文裡可以是**單數**或**複數**，但在美式英文裡，只作為**單數**使用。

英式 John's family **is/are** leaving tomorrow.

美式 John's family **is** leaving tomorrow.

⑦ **get** 在英式英文裡的過去分詞是 **got**，在美式英文是 **gotten**。

英式 Your Spanish has **got** much better.

美式 Your Spanish has **gotten** much better.

⑧ 美式英文會以 **take** 取代 **have** 的用法，例如 **take a bath/shower/break** 等用語。

英式 I **have** a shower every morning.

美式 I **take** a shower every morning.

⑨ 美式英文會使用 **go get**、**go see** 的說法，英式英文則使用 **go and get**、**go and see** 的說法。

英式 **Go and get** the newspaper, please.

美式 **Go get** the newspaper, please.

⑩ 在美式口語英文裡，有些字尾 **ly** 的副詞，放在形容詞前面時，會去除字尾。

英式 She's **really** crazy.

美式 She's **real** crazy.

⑪ 美式英文裡的動詞 **help** 後面不接 **to**。

英式 Can you help me **to do** my homework?

美式 Can you help me **do** my homework?

標點符號

1 . 句點 full stop / period

放在句子結尾：He arrived yesterday.

2 , 逗號 comma

① 列舉一連串的不同要件：
He had ham, salad, apple pie, and a cup of tea.

② 區隔子句、評語：
My father, who works in Bristol, comes home on the weekend.

③ 放在引導性質的從屬子句後面：
When it stops raining, I'll go out to play.

④ 用於直述句：
"Come and see me," said Pete,
"I'll show you my new apartment."

3 : 冒號 colon

引導說明內容、清單或引述內容：
Martin Luther King started his famous speech with the words: "I have a dream . . ."

4 ; 分號 semicolon

① 放在兩個意思相關的主要子句之間：
I don't like eating in restaurants;
I prefer cooking my own meals.

② 用於排列一連串帶有逗號的語詞：
The characters in the play include Dennis, a London teenager; Debbie, his girlfriend; Mr. Johnson, Debbie's stepfather; and Ms. Ross, Dennis's mother.

5 ? 問號 question mark

放在直接問句的結尾：
How long will you be away?

6 ! 驚嘆號 exclamation mark

用於特別強調句意：What a lovely day!

7 . . . 省略號 dots/ellipsis

用以顯示不完整的句子、引述內容或清單：
I think I'll have roast beef, salad, some cake . . .

8 — 破折號 dash

用於分開一系列的同位語、插入語句或補充說明：
Spend a weekend in San Francisco—
the liveliest city of the Bay Area!

9 / 斜線／斜槓 slash/stroke

代表其他選擇：
Part-time / Full-time jobs as waiters/
waitresses. Apply inside.

10 - 連字號 hyphen

① 用於複合名詞和形容詞：
My mother-in-law is a bit absent-minded.

② 當字首的最後一個字母和單詞首字母是同一個母音，則需使用連字號隔開：
Co-operation is essential to get good results.

③ 當同一個單詞書面上要換行，也需以連字號分隔。

11 ( ) 括號 brackets/parentheses

提供額外資訊，尤其是交叉比對參考資料的時候：
Study the verb forms (see page 43).

12 ` ' 單引號 simple quotation marks／
" " 雙引號 double quotation marks

用以標出引言或直接敘述句：
"A witty portrait of literary life in New York"
Sunday Telegraph

13 , 撇號 apostrophe

用於縮讀形式和所有格：That isn't James's car.

14 A 大寫字母 capital / upper-case letter

以下英文用詞，開頭一定要用大寫字母：

① 專有名詞：
Paul Smith, my dog Rex, the Statue of Liberty, Mount Etna, Lake Erie

② 稱號頭銜和職業：
Mr. Bell, Ms. Derrick, Professor Dawson, Queen Elizabeth II

③ 星期幾的名稱、月分和節日：
Sunday, August, Easter

④ 說明國籍和語言的形容詞和名詞：
Brazilians speak Portuguese.

⑤ 在專有名詞前的家人稱謂：
Are you ready, Mom? Uncle Jim is waiting for us.

⑥ 書名、電影名稱、報章雜誌名稱等：
"The Good Life" by Jay McInerney is a moving novel.

語氣、時態和狀態

語氣	時態	狀態	例句
直述句	現在式	簡單式	I **call** him every day.
	過去式	簡單式	I **called** him yesterday.
	未來式	簡單式	I **will call** him tomorrow.
	現在式	進行式	I**'m calling** him right now.
	過去式	進行式	I **was calling** him when you arrived.
	未來式	進行式	I **will be calling** him tomorrow at this time.
	現在式	完成式	I **have** just **called** him.
	過去式	完成式	I **had called** him some time before you arrived.
	未來式	完成式	I **will have called** him by this time tomorrow.
	現在式	完成進行式	I **have been calling** him for an hour.
	過去式	完成進行式	I **had been calling** him for an hour when you arrived.
	未來式	完成進行式	By 5 p.m. I **will have been calling** him for an hour.
祈使句			**Come** here! **Don't talk**!
條件句	現在		I **would take** an umbrella if it rained.
	過去		I **would have taken** a taxi if I had been late.
假設句			If I **were** you, I would accept that job.
不定詞		簡單式	It is impossible **to save** money now.
		進行式	He seems **to be following** us.
分詞	現在		I heard a girl **singing** in the next room.
	過去		He came in, **followed** by his big dog.
動名詞		簡單式	I often spend my free time **reading**.
		完成式	He denied **having been** there.

can / could / be able to

簡單現在式	過去簡單式	未來式
• can/can't • am / am not able to • is/isn't able to • are/aren't able to	• could/couldn't • was/wasn't able to • were/weren't able to	• will/won't be able to

現在完成式	過去完成式	未來完成式
• have/haven't been able to • has/hasn't been able to	• had/hadn't been able to	• will/won't have been able to

條件句	條件句過去式
• could/couldn't • would/wouldn't be able to	• could/couldn't have • would/wouldn't have been able to

may / might / be allowed to

簡單現在式	過去簡單式	未來式
• may / may not • am / am not allowed to • is/isn't allowed to • are/aren't allowed to	• was/wasn't allowed to • were/weren't allowed to	• will/won't be allowed to

現在完成式	過去完成式	未來完成式
• have/haven't been allowed to • has/hasn't been allowed to	• had/hadn't been allowed to	• will/won't have been allowed to

條件句	條件句過去式
• might / might not • would/wouldn't be allowed to	• might have / might not have • would/wouldn't have been allowed to

must / have (got) to / need / be compelled/obliged to / should

簡單現在式	過去簡單式	未來式
• must/mustn't • need/needn't • don't/doesn't need to • have/haven't (got) to • has/hasn't got to • don't/doesn't have to	• had / didn't have to • need / didn't need to • was/wasn't compelled to • was/wasn't obliged to • were/weren't compelled to • were/weren't obliged to	• will/won't have to • will/won't be compelled to • will/won't be obliged to

現在完成式	過去完成式	未來完成式
• has/hasn't been compelled to • have/haven't been obliged to	• had/hadn't been compelled to • had/hadn't been obliged to	• will/won't have had to • will/won't have been compelled to • will/won't have been obliged to

條件句	條件句過去式
• should/shouldn't • would/wouldn't have to	• should/shouldn't have • would/wouldn't have had to

情態助動詞：條件句

第一類條件句

if 子句	主要子句
If I can . . .	I will . . .
If I want to . . .	I will . . .
If I must / have to . . .	I will . . .

- **If I can** stay one more day, **I will be** able to go on a sightseeing tour of the city.
- **If I want to** play in the final, **I will have** to train hard.
- **If I must / have to** wait so long, **I will** just **go** home and come back tomorrow.

第二類條件句

if 子句	主要子句
If I could . . . If I were able to . . .	I could . . . I would be able to . . . I might . . .
If I wanted to . . . If you would . . .	I would like to . . .
If I were to . . . （可能的情況） If I should . . . （可能的情況） If I had to . . . （義務）	I might . . . （可能）. . . I should . . . （個人義務） I ought to . . . （個人義務） I would have to . . . （因外在人事物衍生的義務）

- **If I could** find a better-paid job, **I would be** able to pay off my mortgage earlier.
- **If I should** win the race, **I should thank** the coach for his help.
- **If I had to** work on the weekend, **I would have to** ask someone to come and look after the kids.
- **If you wanted to** start a new business, **we might be** able to give you some financial backing.
- **If he were to** arrive earlier, **could you** please **meet** him at the airport?

第三類條件句

if 子句	主要子句
If I could have . . . If I had been able to . . .	I could have . . . I would have been able to . . . I might have . . .
If I had wanted to . . .	I would have liked to . . . （也可以說 I'd like to have + 過去分詞）
If I should have . . . If I had had to . . .	I should have . . . I ought to have . . . I would have had to . . .

- **If I had had to** pay a higher rent, **I would have had to** find a smaller apartment.
- **If I had been able to** ski, **I would have liked to** spend a holiday in the Swiss Alps.
- **If I had had to** wait for you any longer in the street, **I might have frozen** to death!
- **If I had** really **wanted to** reach the top, **I could** easily **have done** so.

不規則動詞：主動語態與被動語態

不定詞 to choose	**過去分詞** chosen	**現在分詞** choosing

主動語態

簡單過去式	現在過去式
I/You/We/They **choose** He/She/It **chooses**	I **am choosing** You/We/They **are choosing** He/She/It **is choosing**
簡單過去式	現在過去式
I/You/He/She/It/We/They **chose**	I/He/She/It **was choosing** You/We/They **were choosing**
簡單現在完成式	現在完成進行式
I/You/We/They **have chosen** He/She/It **has chosen**	I/You/We/They **have been choosing** He/She/It **has been choosing**
簡單過去完成式	過去完成進行式
I/You/He/She/It/We/They **had chosen**	I/You/He / She/It/We/They **had been choosing**
簡單未來式	未來進行式
I/You/He/She/It/We/They **will choose**	I/You/He/She/It/We/They **will be choosing**
簡單未來完成式	未來完成進行式
I/You/He/She/It/We/They **will have chosen**	I/You/He/She / It/We/They **will have been choosing**
be going to 未來式	以 be going to 表達過去的未來式
I'm **going to choose** You're/We're/They're **going to choose** He's/She's/It's **going to choose**	I/He/She/It **was going to choose** You/We/They **were going to choose**
條件句	條件句過去式
I/You/He/She/It/We/They **would choose**	I/You/He/She/It/We/They **would have chosen**

被動語態

簡單現在式	現在進行式
I **am chosen** You/We/They **are chosen** He/She/It **is chosen**	I **am being chosen** You/We/They **are being chosen** He/She/It **is being chosen**
簡單過去式	過去進行式
I/He/She/It **was chosen** You/We/They **were chosen**	I/He/She/It **was being chosen** You/We/They **were being chosen**
簡單現在完成式	簡單過去完成式
I/You/We/They **have been chosen** He/She/It **has been chosen**	I/You/He/She/It/We/They **had been chosen**
簡單未來式	未來完成進行式
I/You/He/She/It/We/They **will be chosen**	I/You/He/She/It/We/They **will have been chosen**
be going to 未來式	以 be going to 表達過去的未來式
I'm **going to be chosen** You're/We're/They're **going to be chosen** He's/She's/It's **going to be chosen**	I/He/She/It **was going to be chosen** You/We/They **were going to be chosen**
條件句	條件句過去式
I/You/He/She/It/We/They **would be chosen**	I/You/He/She/It/We/They **would have been chosen**

原形	簡單過去式	過去分詞
be	was, were	been
beat	beat	beaten
become	became	become
begin	began	begun
bend	bent	bent
bet	bet	bet
bind	bound	bound
bite	bit	bitten
blow	blew	blown
break	broke	broken
bring	brought	brought
broadcast	broadcast	broadcast/broadcasted
build	built	built
burn	burnt/burned	burnt/burned
burst	burst	burst
buy	bought	bought
catch	caught	caught
choose	chose	chosen
come	came	come
cost	cost	cost
cut	cut	cut
deal	dealt	dealt
dig	dug	dug
do	did	done
draw	drew	drawn
dream	dreamed	dreamed
drink	drank	drunk
drive	drove	driven
eat	ate	eaten
fall	fell	fallen
feed	fed	fed
feel	felt	felt
fight	fought	fought
find	found	found
fly	flew	flown
forecast	forecast	forecast
foresee	foresaw	foreseen
forget	forgot	forgotten
freeze	froze	frozen
get	got	got/gotten
give	gave	given
go	went	gone
grow	grew	grown
hang	hung/hanged	hung/hanged
have	had	had
hear	heard	heard
hide	hid	hidden
hit	hit	hit
hold	held	held
hurt	hurt	hurt
keep	kept	kept
kneel	knelt	knelt

原形	簡單過去式	過去分詞
know	knew	known
lay	laid	laid
lead	led	led
learn	learned	learned
leave	left	left
lend	lent	lent
let	let	let
lie	lay	lain
light	lit	lit
lose	lost	lost
make	made	made
mean	meant	meant
meet	met	met
pay	paid	paid
put	put	put
quit	quit	quit
read	read	read
ride	rode	ridden
ring	rang	rung
rise	rose	risen
run	ran	run
say	said	said
see	saw	seen
seek	sought	sought
sell	sold	sold
send	sent	sent
set	set	set
shake	shook	shaken
shine	shone	shone
shoot	shot	shot
show	showed	shown
shrink	shrank	shrunk
shut	shut	shut
sing	sang	sung
sit	sat	sat
sleep	slept	slept
smell	smelled	smelled
speak	spoke	spoken
spend	spent	spent
stand	stood	stood
steal	stole	stolen
swim	swam	swum
take	took	taken
teach	taught	taught
tell	told	told
think	thought	thought
throw	threw	thrown
understand	understood	understood
wear	wore	worn
win	won	won
write	wrote	written

圖解各類詞性

1 名詞、冠詞與動詞

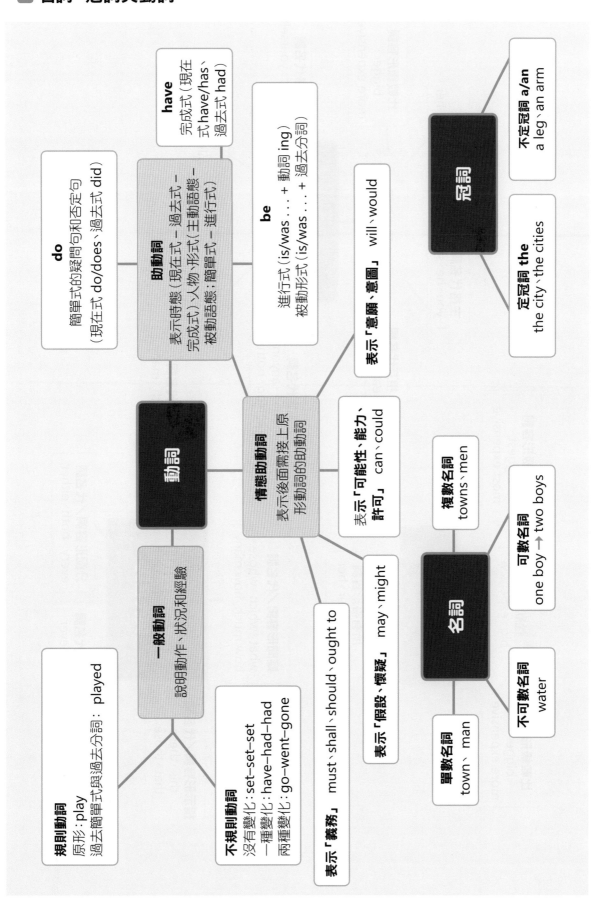

規則動詞
原形:play
過去簡單式與過去分詞:played

不規則動詞
沒有變化:set–set–set
一種變化:have–had–had
兩種變化:go–went–gone

一般動詞
說明動作、狀況和經驗

do
簡單式的疑問句和否定句
(現在式 do/does、過去式 did)

助動詞
表示時態(現在式 – 過去式 –
完成式)、形態(主動語態 –
被動語態;簡單式 – 進行式)

have
完成式(現在式 have/has、
過去式 had)

be
進行式(is/was ... + 動詞ing)
被動形式(is/was ... + 過去分詞)

動詞

情態助動詞
表示後面需接上原
形動詞的助動詞

表示「意願、意圖」 will、would

表示「可能性、能力、
許可」 can、could

表示「假設、懷疑」 may、might

表示「義務」 must、shall、should、ought to

名詞

單數名詞 town、man

不可數名詞 water

可數名詞 one boy → two boys

複數名詞 towns、men

冠詞

定冠詞 the the city、the cities

不定冠詞 a/an a leg、an arm

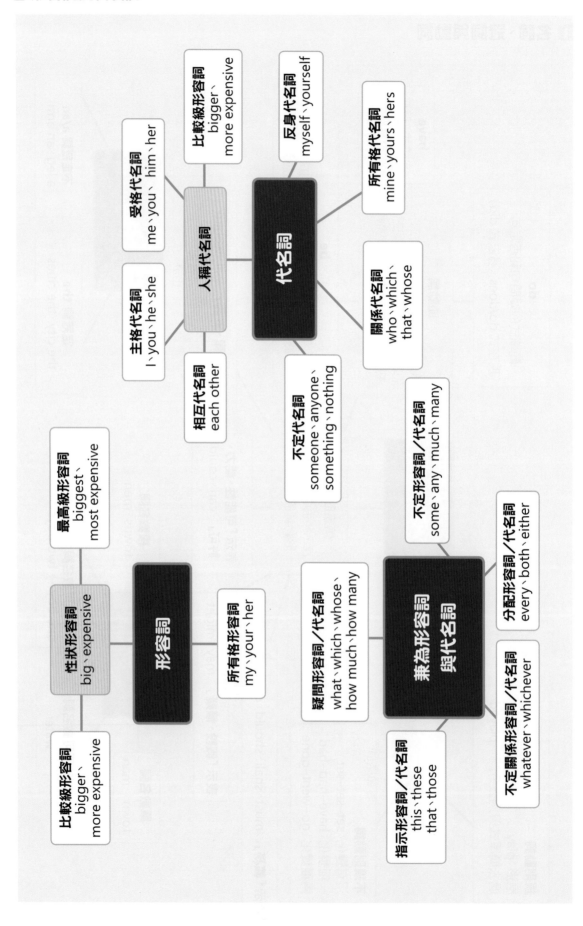

3 動詞、連接詞、連接副詞與介系詞

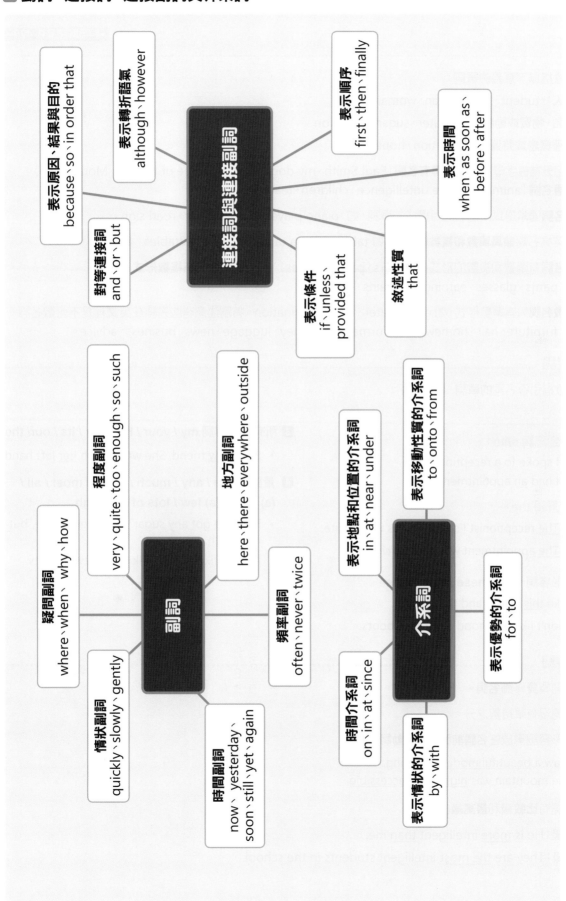

連接詞與連接副詞

表示原因、結果與目的
because、so、in order that

表示轉折語氣
although、however

表示順序
first、then、finally

表示時間
when、as soon as、before、after

對等連接詞
and、or、but

表示條件
if、unless、provided that

敘述性質
that

副詞

程度副詞
very、quite、too、enough、so、such

地方副詞
here、there、everywhere、outside

疑問副詞
where、when、why、how

頻率副詞
often、never、twice

情狀副詞
quickly、slowly、gently

時間副詞
now、yesterday、soon、still、yet、again

介系詞

表示移動性質的介系詞
to、onto、from

表示地點和位置的介系詞
in、at、near、under

表示優勢的介系詞
for、to

時間介系詞
on、in、at、since

表示情狀的介系詞
by、with

詞性重點整理

→ 圖解請見P. 429-431

1 名詞

1 名詞意指以下意義的單詞：

　① 某人：student、friend、man、woman

　② 物品、物質或動物：computer、sugar、dog、lion

　③ 某種概念或特質：imagination、hope、peace

2 名詞可分為首字母需大寫的**專有名詞**（Paul Smith、my dog Rex、the Statue of Liberty、Mount Etna），
　或**普通名詞**（animal、science、intelligence、children、teachers）。

3 **複合名詞**通常是以兩個名詞所構成的單詞，如：piano player、bank robber、road sign。

4 多數英文名詞**兼具單數和複數的形式**，如 table 可寫為a table（一張桌子）與tables（多張桌子）。

5 **可數名詞**有單數和複數的形式（car–cars、party–parties），但有些名詞**只有複數形式**，
　例如：pants、glasses、earnings、remains、contents。

6 **不可數名詞**只有單數形式，如 gold、water、fear、imagination。特別注意有些名詞在英文裡是不可數名詞，
　例如：furniture、hair、homework、information、money、luggage、news、business、advice。

2 限定詞

限定詞意指引導名詞的單詞，類型如下：

1 冠詞

　① 不定冠詞 **a/an**：
　　• I spoke to <u>a</u> receptionist.
　　• I had <u>an</u> appointment.

　② 定冠詞 **the**：
　　• <u>The</u> receptionist I spoke to was very polite.
　　• <u>The</u> appointment was at ten o'clock.

2 指示形容詞 **this / these / that / those**
　　• I like <u>this</u> T-shirt and these jeans.
　　• I don't like <u>that</u> hoodie or those boots.

3 所有格形容詞 **my / your / his / her / its / our/ their**
　　• She is <u>my</u> friend. She writes with <u>her</u> left hand.

4 量詞 **some / any / much / many / most / all / (a) little / (a) few / lots of / enough**
　　• Have we got any sugar? We've got <u>some</u>, but not <u>much</u>.
　　• I would like <u>a little</u> milk and a few biscuits.

3 形容詞

1 形容詞負責修飾**名詞**。

2 形容詞沒有單複數之分。

3 性狀形容詞需放在**名詞前面**或 **be 動詞後面**。
　　• I saw a <u>beautiful modern</u> building.
　　• The mountain was <u>high</u> and <u>inaccessible</u>.

4 形容詞有**比較級**和**最高級**的形式。

　比較級：He is <u>more</u> intelligent <u>than</u> me.

　最高級：They are <u>the most</u> intelligent students in the school.

4 人稱代名詞

1 人稱代名詞用以取代剛提及的名詞。此類單詞會因應句中功能而具有以下不同名稱：

① **主格代名詞**：I, you, he, she, it, we, you, they

② **受格代名詞**：me, you, him, her, it, us, you, them

③ **所有格代名詞**：mine, yours, hers, his, ours, yours, theirs

④ **反身代名詞**：myself, yourself, himself, herself, itself, ourselves, yourselves, themselves

2 其他常見代名詞如下：

① **關係代名詞** who, which, that, whose：I met the girl <u>who</u> lives next door.

② **疑問代名詞** who, what, whose, which：<u>What</u> did you get for your birthday?

③ **不定代名詞** someone/somebody, something, anyone/somebody, anything, no-one/nobody, nothing, everyone/everybody, everything：I didn't speak to <u>anybody</u> at the party.

④ **相互代名詞** each other, one another：How long have they known <u>each other</u>?

⑤ **分配代名詞** each, either, neither：Take one <u>each</u>.

5 動詞

1 動詞意指以下意義的單詞：

① **行為**：She <u>texts</u> me every evening.

② **狀況或情境**：It <u>is</u> a beautiful day.

③ **事件**：The war <u>broke out</u>.

④ **感官**：He <u>seems</u> a nice person.

2 動詞搭配主詞和一個或以上的補語，即可構成句子：
She（主詞）gave（動詞）presents（直接受詞）to all of us.（間接受詞）

3 及物動詞可後接受詞；不及物動詞無法後接受詞。
及物動詞：I <u>met</u> John in the market square.
不及物動詞：We <u>went</u> to London by train.

4 及物動詞有**主動語態**或**被動語態**：
主動語態：The earthquake <u>killed</u> more than two hundred people.
被動語態：More than two hundred people <u>were killed</u> by the earthquake.

5 看似動詞的用語如動名詞、不定詞、現在分詞與過去分詞等，由於並非句子裡闡述行為的單詞，因此不需搭配主詞。動名詞和不定詞通常可兼具名詞的功能，因此可作為句子的主詞或受詞。

6 **動名詞**的字尾有 **ing**：
- <u>Dancing</u> is a favorite pastime of mine.
- Do you enjoy <u>skiing</u>?

7 **不定詞**是 **to + 原形動詞**：
I started <u>to learn</u> some Chinese.

8 分詞字尾如果是 **ing**，即為**現在分詞**；如為 **ed**，即為**過去分詞**，如 following 與 followed。

9 動詞具有語氣、時態以及簡單式、進行式與完成式的狀態之別。

直述語氣
簡單現在式：I <u>call</u> him every day.
簡單過去式：I <u>called</u> him yesterday.
will 未來式：I <u>will call</u> him tomorrow.

進行式
現在進行式：I'm <u>calling</u> him right now.
過去進行式：I <u>was calling</u> him when you arrived.
未來進行式：I <u>will be calling</u> him tomorrow at this time.

完成式
現在完成式：I <u>have</u> just <u>called</u> him.
過去完成式：
I <u>had called</u> him some time before you arrived.
未來完成式：I <u>will have called</u> him by this time tomorrow.

完成進行式
現在完成進行式：
I <u>have been calling</u> him for an hour.
過去完成進行式：I <u>had been calling</u> him for an hour when you arrived.
未來完成進行式：
By 5 p.m. I will <u>have been calling</u> him for an hour.

祈使語氣 <u>Come</u> here! <u>Don't talk</u>!

條件語氣
I <u>would take</u> an umbrella if it rained.
I <u>would have taken</u> a taxi if I had been late.

假設語氣 If I <u>were</u> you, I would accept that job.

433

6 助動詞

助動詞是一種動詞，能構成其他動詞的時態、語氣和語態。英文裡的助動詞有 **be**、**have** 和 **do** 。

1 be 動詞的用途如下：

① 構成進行式：• He's watching the news.　　• I was cooking.　　• I'll be arriving by train.

② 構成被動語態：• This vase is made of glass.　　• He was named after his dad.

2 have 用於構成完成式：

• She has just arrived.　　• How long have you lived here?　　• We hadn't seen New York before.

3 do/does/did 的用途如下：

① 表達否定說辭：He doesn't work here.　　③ 表達否定問句：Don't you understand?

② 表達問句：Did you forget your keys?　　④ 強調語氣：• We do know him.

　　　　　　　　　　　　　　　　　　　　　　　　　　• She did tell me, but I forgot.

7 情態助動詞

情態助動詞可強調以下事項：

1 能力、可能性、許可和意願：can/could、may/might、will/would

• He can drive very well.　　　　　　• May I ask you a question?

• I can come tomorrow.　　　　　　　• She might not like this T-shirt.

• Could we have some sandwiches?　　• Will you dance with me?

2 義務和必要性：must、need、ought to、shall/should

• You must be punctual for your appointment.　　• We needn't go if it rains.

• She ought to apologize.　　　　　　　　　　　• What shall we do on the weekend?

• We should visit the newly opened museum.

8 片語動詞

片語動詞是由動詞後接一或兩個介副詞來構成，它的意思可能與動詞本身不同。

• They stood up when the teacher came in. (質詞與動詞不能分隔)

• Take off your coat. → Take your coat off. (質詞與動詞可以分隔)

• Keep up with the good work. (兩個質詞不能分隔)

9 使役動詞

1 使役動詞的**被動語態句**，用以表達**他人幫我們完成某事：have/get something done**

• She had her hair cut yesterday.　　• I have my car washed every Saturday.

2 使役動詞的**主動語態句**，用以表達**有人造成或允許某事發生：**

① make/have somebody do something (也可以說get/compel/force/cause somebody to do something)

• She made me cry.　　• I had the mechanic repair my car.　　• The frost caused the lake to freeze.

② let/allow/help somebody do something （也可以說help somebody to do something）

• Her parents let her stay out until midnight.　　• Can you help me do this math exercise?

10 介系詞

1 介系詞用以說明位置、某物的移動方向、事件的發生時間或執行某事件的方法。

介系詞後面可接名詞或代名詞，以下是介系詞的種類：

① 時間介系詞：at, in, on, during, since, for, till, until, before, after

② 場所介系詞：at, in, on, under, below, over, above, in front of, behind, between, near to

③ 表示移動性質的介系詞：to, from, into, out of, past, over, towards, along, through, up, down

④ 其他：with, without, by, for, of, about

2 介系詞雖然可作為片語動詞的一部分，但不能單獨存在來表達片語動詞的意思：
- I ran <u>into</u> Kate this morning.
- He tidied his room <u>up</u>.

11 副詞

1 副詞負責修飾動詞、形容詞或其他副詞。

2 情狀副詞的字尾通常是 **ly**。副詞可以有**比較級**和**最高級**的形式。

He plays the cello <u>beautifully</u>.（用以修飾動詞 plays）

They are <u>greatly</u> admired.（用以修飾形容詞 admired）

比較級：He is driving <u>more carefully</u> than usual.

最高級：Who can run <u>the fastest</u>?

3 副詞有以下種類：

①頻率副詞：Men and women haven't <u>always</u> had the same rights.

②程度副詞需搭配一個形容詞或其他副詞：
- The movie was <u>extremely long</u>.
- Today's test was <u>fairly easy</u>. We don't understand very well.

③時間副詞：What did you do <u>yesterday</u>?

④地方副詞：The children were playing <u>outside</u>.

⑤疑問副詞：<u>Where</u> did you go? <u>How</u> did you travel? <u>When</u> did you arrive? <u>Why</u> didn't you tell me?

⑥順序副詞：<u>First,</u> mix flour and butter. Then, add two tablespoons of water and mix to firm dough. <u>After that</u>, knead the dough briefly on a floured surface. <u>Finally,</u> wrap in plastic wrap and chill.

⑦連接副詞：
- The hotel had a large pool and it <u>also</u> had a golf course.
- This is healthy food, and <u>moreover</u> it's organic.

12 連接詞

連接詞負責連結片語、子句和句子，有分對等連接詞和從屬連接詞。

①對等連接詞：and, or, but, so, therefore
- We can visit the park <u>and</u> the zoo at the same time.
- Would you like tea <u>or</u> coffee?
- The journey was very long <u>but</u> interesting.

②從屬連接詞：

as、because、for、since（原因）、so、so that（目的）、although、though（對比）、after、before、until、while、when、as、as soon as（時間）、if、whether、unless、as long as、provided、whenever、whatever（條件句、間接問句）、that（轉述句、間接說詞、後果）

③相關連接詞：

both . . . and（包括在內）、either . . . or（其中一個）、whether . . . or（其中一個）、not only . . . but also（包括在內）、neither . . . nor（排除在外）、as . . . as（比較、同等）

13 感嘆詞

感嘆詞用以表達驚訝、喜樂、憤怒或其他情緒。
- Great!
- Well done!
- Ouch!
- Oh dear!
- What a beautiful day!
- What bad luck!
- How clever!
- How awful!

14 句子的基本要件

子句是由主詞 + 動詞（+ 補語）所構成，句子則是由主要子句加上一或多個對等子句或從屬子句所構成：
- <u>I'm late</u>（主要子句）<u>because I missed the bus</u>.（從屬子句）
- <u>When I was young,</u>（從屬子句）<u>I lived in Scotland</u>.（主要子句）
- <u>I did my homework,</u>（主要子句）<u>then I went out with my friends</u>.（從屬子句）

主詞：指執行動作／行為的人事物　　**She** bought a T-shirt. Did **you** buy anything?

受詞：指主詞執行動作後的結果　　She bought a **T-shirt**. Did you buy **anything**?

間接受詞：指動作接收者　　She bought a T-shirt for **Jim**. She bought **Jim** a T-shirt.

謂詞：指句子裡的動詞　　Jeremy **plays** rugby every Saturday.

ANSWER KEYS

UNIT 1

LESSON 1 P. 11 ....

1

-s	-es	-ies	-ves
boys	branches	strawberries	shelves
volcanos	volcanoes	countries	halves
oranges	matches	parties	calves
roofs	glasses	cavities	wives
novels	echoes	ladies	lives
drinks	foxes	libraries	thieves
earphones	wishes	babies	
rays			

2 1 Schools are closed today.　2 They're old churches.
3 Those cliffs are dangerous.　4 The shops are open
now.　5 Where are my keys?　6 They're great cities.
7 These stories are true.　8 Two cars are parked in the
street(s).

3 1 shelves　2 books　3 wall　4 bed　5 posters
6 singer(s)/actor(s)　7 actor(s)/singer(s)　8 sofa
9 armchairs　10 table　11 chairs　12 meals

4 1 cliffs　2 tomatoes/potatoes　3 potatoes / tomatoes
4 cherries　5 strawberries　6 cities　7 buses

5 1 children　2 pence　3 people　4 women　5 Geese
6 Mice　7 means　8 dice　9 fish　10 feet

6 1 are　2 is/are　3 are, is　4 is　5 are　6 is/are
7 is/are　8 is/are　9 are　10 is　11 is/are
12 is/are　13 are　14 are

LESSON 2 P. 14 ....

1

wool **U**	lemon **C**	egg **C**	ice **U**
window **C**	butter **U**	bottle **C**	beauty **U**
sandwich **C**	snow **U**	chair **C**	wine **U**
silver **U**	tea **U**	rain **U**	juice **U**
peace **U**	plastic **U**	biscuit **C**	gold **U**

2 **some** oil　　**some** bread　**some** sweets
some butter　**an** artichoke　**some** tomato sauce
an apple　　**a** banana　　**some** mayonnaise
some onions　**some** food　　**some** sugar

3 1 D　2 H　3 A　4 B　5 F　6 C　7 E　8 G

4
a jar of　　sweets, tomato sauce, mayonnaise
a bottle of　oil, tomato sauce
a kilo of　　bread, butter, artichokes, apples,
　　　　　　　onions, sugar, bananas
a bag of　　food, sweets, sugar
a packet of　sweets, sugar
a slice of　　bread, apple, onion

5 1 hair is　2 homework is　3 information, is
4 luggage, is　5 news is　6 furniture is
7 Business is　8 are, teas

LESSON 3 P. 16 ....

1 1 an　2 a　3 an　4 a　5 a　6 a　7 a　8 a　9 an
10 a　11 an　12 an　13 an　14 a　15 a　16 a
17 a　18 an　19 a　20 an　21 an

2 1 a　2 an　3 a　4 a　5 an　6 a　7 a, an　8 a, the
9 a　10 A/The　11 a　12 a　13 a　14 an　15 an　16 a

3 1 a　2 one　3 one, an　4 one/a　5 a, a　6 an
7 an/one　8 One　9 A　10 an

4 1 *Correct*　2 It's **a** beautiful day.
3 Serena is at home because she's got **a** cough.
4 Do you have ~~an~~ **a** high temperature?　5 *Correct*
6 *Correct*　7 What ~~an~~ **a** horrible day!
8 Mike, ~~a your friend's~~ **a friend of yours is /
one of your friends is** on the phone!
9 Sheila has got ~~a~~ brown hair and ~~a~~ brown eyes.
10 *Correct*

5 1 a　2 an　3 a　4 a　5 a　6 one

LESSON 4 P. 19 ....

1 1 the　2 a　3 a　4 the　5 the　6 an　7 a　8 the　9 a
10 the　11 the　12 the　13 the　14 the　15 an　16 the

2 1 The, a　2 a, a, The, a, the, an　3 a, the, the　4 the
5 The　6 the　7 the, the, a　8 the　9 the　10 A, a

3 1 //, //, //　2 The, the　3 the　4 //, //　5 the, the
6 The　7 //, the　8 //, the　9 //, //　10 //, //, the, the

4 1 A/The, an　2 An/The, an/the
3 A/The　4 A/The, a　5 A/The, a

5 1 the, //　2 The, the, the　3 The, the, the, the, the
4 //, //, the, //　5 The, the, the　6 the, //　7 //, the, //
8 The, //

6 1 ~~The~~ Mathematics is my favorite subject.
2 There's a good movie on at **the** movies this week.
3 The quiz starts **at** ~~the~~ 7:30.
4 Jason plays **the** drums.
5 Eleanor loves ~~the~~ nature.
6 I don't like ~~the~~ tennis.
7 These are ~~the~~ your sandwiches.
8 Sardinia is **a** beautiful island.

ROUND UP 1 P. 22 ....

1 1 wives　2 leaves　3 knives　4 lives　5 loaves
6 shelves　7 halves　8 thieves

2 1 is/are　2 are　3 are　4 are　5 are　6 is　7 is
8 are　9 is　10 is　11 are　12 is

3 1 P　2 P　3 S　4 S　5 S　6 P

436

4 1 fungi/funguses 2 hypotheses 3 analyzes
4 criteria 5 media

5 1 much 2 much 3 many 4 many 5 A 6 some

6 1 a cup of 2 a jar of 3 paper 4 bread
5 a slice of 6 a bottle of 7 beer 8 chocolate
9 a drop of 10 a box of

7 1 experience, experiences 2 business, businesses
3 damages, damage 4 fish, fishes 5 coffees, coffee
6 glass, glasses

8 1 the 2 a 3 a 4 the 5 the 6 an 7 the 8 the
9 a 10 the 11 a 12 the 13 an 14 an 15 an
16 the 17 the 18 the 19 a 20 a

9 1 the, the 2 The, a 3 a, a, The, the 4 the
5 the 6 The 7 a 8 the

Reflecting on grammar

1 F 2 T 3 F 4 T 5 F 6 F 7 F 8 T 9 F 10 T

UNIT 2

LESSON 1 P. 26 ....

1 1 She 2 He 3 We 4 They 5 you, It, it
6 you 7 They 8 It 9 They 10 You

2 1 She, she 2 They, They 3 I, I 4 They
5 You/We 6 they 7 He 8 We 9 You 10 He
11 She 12 you 13 we 14 you

3 1 D 2 H 3 G 4 F 5 A 6 C 7 B 8 E

4 1 My dad ~~he~~ always gets back home very late.

2 Ann likes cooking but (she) hates cleaning the kitchen.

3 On Saturdays they go shopping or (they) see their friends.

4 John and Kylie ~~they~~ have a lot of common interests.

5 Marion plays computer games or (she) reads a book in her spare time.

6 The movie ~~it~~ starts at 8:30 and (it) ends at eleven o'clock.

7 I love Japanese food but (I) don't like Indian food. It's too hot and spicy.

8 Mr. Ross leaves home at 7:30 every morning and (he) takes a bus to his office.

9 Jason ~~he~~ is late as usual.

10 Karen doesn't play the piano but (she) sings beautifully.

11 The children ~~they~~ go to the playground every afternoon.

5 1 It's 2 is 3 You're 4 It's 5 Who's, He's 6 I'm

LESSON 2 P. 28 ....

1 1 Camilla is/'s a nice old lady.
2 Brian is/'s thirsty.
3 Jack and Debbie are our next-door neighbors.
4 The dog is/'s outside in the garden.
5 Mark and I are cousins.
6 My parents are on vacation in Spain.
7 I am/'m very tired tonight.
8 You are/'re really funny.

2 1 're 2 's 3 are 4 's 5 's 6 's, 's 7 're 8 're
9 'm 10 are

3 1 thirsty 2 in a hurry 3 right 4 cold
5 scared 6 hungry 7 sleepy 8 hot

4 1 is/'s 2 am/'m 3 is/'s 4 are/'re 5 is/'s
6 am/'m 7 is/'s 8 is 9 are 10 are/'re

5 1 We aren't ready for the test. /
We're not ready for the test.

2 They aren't at home now. /
They're not at home now.

3 It isn't too late! / It's not too late.

4 Aman isn't at school today. /
Aman's not at school today.

5 I'm not afraid of the dark.

6 She isn't 17 years old. / She's not 17 years old.

7 My parents aren't at work.

8 I'm not very good at math.

6 1 aren't / 're not 2 aren't 3 'm 4 're
5 aren't 6 isn't / 's not 7 aren't 8 're

7 1 are 2 is/'s 3 is/'s 4 are not / aren't / 're not
5 is/'s 6 is/'s 7 am/'m 8 am no / 'm not
9 are/'re

8 1 Is 2 Are 3 Are 4 Am 5 Is 6 Are

9 1 Are, aren't / 're not 2 Is, is 3 Are, aren't / 're not
4 Am, are 5 Is, is 6 Is, isn't / 's not

10 1 Is Matthew Susan's cousin? Yes, he is.

2 Isn't he a good singer? Yes, he is.

3 Are your children at school today? No, they aren't / they're not. They're on vacation.

4 Is your sister's name Claire? Yes, it is.

5 Are Chris and Daniel twins? No, they aren't / they're not. Chris is older than Daniel.

6 Aren't Bob and Edward good friends? Yes, they are.

11 1 "Am I short?"
2 "Is it warm/hot in here?" /
"Are you warm/hot in here?"

3 Are you afraid of the dark?"

4 "Is your sister good at math?"

5 "Are you and Claire sisters?"

6 "Is Peter's office on the first floor?"

7 "Is Mark John's brother?"

8 "Are you hungry?"

LESSON 3 P. 32

1
1 There's 2 There isn't 3 There's 4 There are
5 There isn't 6 There aren't
7 There's, there isn't 8 There aren't

2
1 Are there, there are 2 Is there, there isn't
3 Are there, there are 4 Is there, there isn't
5 Is there, there is 6 Are there, there aren't

3
1 there 2 here 3 there 4 Here 5 here 6 here

4
1 ~~Here's~~ a great match tomorrow.
There's a great match tomorrow.

2 There ~~are~~ one table and four chairs in the kitchen.
There **is/'s** one table and four chairs in the kitchen.

3 "Is ~~there~~ your brother?" "No, he's at work."
"Is your brother there/here?" "No, he's at work."

4 "~~There is~~ a room for tonight? "Yes, there is."
"Is there a room for tonight? "Yes, there is."

5 Here ~~it is~~ your bill.
Here's your bill.

6 How many of you ~~there are~~?
How many of you **are there**?

7 ~~There are~~ any tickets left?
Are there any tickets left?

8 ~~There's~~ two bags on the table.
There are two bags on the table.

LESSON 4 P. 34

1
1 E 2 H 3 A 4 G 5 C 6 B 7 F 8 D

2
1 How old 2 How long 3 How many
4 How much 5 Why 6 How far
7 When 8 How 9 Where 10 How often

3
1 **D** What's your house like?
2 **H** Who are you talking to?
3 **A** What's the weather like?
4 **B** How is Peter now?
5 **C** What's your sister like?
6 **E** Where are you from?
7 **F** What are you talking about?
8 **G** Who is this present for?

4 *Suggested answers:*

1 What's your family like? 2 When is John at home?
3 Where's the party? 4 Who's Mr. Blackwell?
5 What's your favorite food?
6 What's your phone number?
7 Where's Silvia from? 8 How many people are there?
9 How much (money) have you got in your wallet?
10 Which car does Carol prefer?

5
1 How high is Mount Everest?
2 How long is the Mississippi River?
3 How deep is Loch Ness?
4 How big is the Isle of Wight?
5 How tall is your brother?
6 How wide is this table?

6
1 F 2 E 3 C 4 B 5 D 6 A

ROUND UP 2 P. 38

1
1 They are both from Korea.
2 She is 16 years old. 3 It is a big school.
4 He is Swedish. 5 We are friends.

2
1 It 2 she 3 she 4 She 5 they
6 It 7 you 8 I 9 I 10 It

3
1 There is a lamp and a book on my bedside table.
2 There are three cans of orangeade in the fridge.
3 There is a new boy in my class this year.
4 There are a lot of books in your rucksack!
5 There are only 12 students in the class today.
6 There are a lot of good songs on my MP3 player.

4
1 are 2 is/'s 3 is 4 are not / aren't / 're not
5 is 6 is/'s 7 am/'m 8 am/'m not 9 are/'re

5
1 is 2 it is/'s 3 be 4 is/'s 5 are 6 you are/'re
7 you are/'re 8 is/'s 9 is/'s 10 you are/'re 11 are

6
1 Susan and I ~~am~~ **are** students in this school.
2 Janet is 15 and her twin brothers ~~is~~ **are** 20.
3 – Who ~~are~~ **is** that man?
  – ~~She~~ **He**'s my uncle.
4 – ~~Is~~ **Are** you a member of the drama club?
  – Yes, ~~I'm~~ **I am**.
5 Thomas and his friend ~~is~~ **are** taking part in the
school tennis tournament.
6 The student's room ~~are~~ **is** on the first floor.
7 I know that policeman. ~~She's~~ **He's** a friend of my
brother's.
8 ~~Is~~ **Are** we going to the movies tonight?

7
1 There is / There's 2 you are 3 Are there 4 are
5 Here 6 It is / It's 7 here is / here's 8 It is / It's
9 you are 10 here is / here's

8
1 he 2 Is, isn't 3 far 4 isn't, she 5 She's / She is
6 Are, not 7 like 8 How

9
1 D 2 A 3 F 4 E 5 C 6 B

10
1 it is / it's not a good 2 it is / it's very upsetting to
3 because it is / it's Mom's 4 it is / it's okay by/with
5 it is / it's good for me 6 That's / That is the nicest
thing

11
1 It's 2 It's, That's 3 That's 4 it's 5 It's, That's
6 That's 7 It's, That's 8 It's

12
1 How much 2 How many 3 How old
4 Why 5 Where 6 When 7 How 8 Who
9 Which 10 How tall

Reflecting on grammar

1 T 2 F 3 T 4 F 5 F 6 F 7 T 8 F 9 F 10 F

UNIT 3

LESSON 1 P. 42 ....

1 1 those 2 these 3 those 4 that 5 that

2 1 That 2 this 3 that 4 that 5 This
6 this/that 7 This 8 that

3 1 He's a new student in this school.
2 This is good news!
3 These are our cell phones.
4 That's a great idea!
5 Give me those magazines, please.
6 That's all I need.
7 This is my best friend.
8 Who are those two guys over there?

4 1 Those 2 those/these 3 These/Those
4 these/those, these 5 that, This 6 these, that

LESSON 2 P. 44 ....

1 1 any, any 2 some 3 a 4 some 5 a 6 an
7 any 8 some

2 *Possible answers*
There's an important meeting this morning.
There's some good news in today's paper.
There's some fruit in the kitchen.
There's a post office just around the corner.
There are some children in the playground.
There are some fantastic beaches on this island.

3 1 some **R**   2 some **O**   3 some **R**
4 any **I**   5 any **I**   6 some **O**

4 1 any 2 no 3 any 4 none 5 no 6 any, none
7 no 8 any

5 **1** 1 some   2 any
2 1 any   2 some   3 some
4 some   5 some   6 any   7 Any
3 1 Any
4 1 any   2 some   3 any   4 some

LESSON 3 P. 46 ....

1 1 It's a <u>hot</u> day today.
2 There is a <u>small</u> church in my village. /
There is a church in my <u>small</u> village.
3 Are these chairs <u>comfortable</u>?
4 The <u>big</u> house in the square looks abandoned.
5 There are some <u>young</u> children in the park.
6 The view from the tower is <u>fantastic</u>.
7 Is this <u>famous</u> restaurant <u>expensive</u>? /
Is this <u>expensive</u> restaurant <u>famous</u>?
8 There is a <u>new</u> clothes shop on the <u>main</u> street.

2 1 There are two ~~bigs~~ **big** computer labs in our school.
2 Is ~~ready~~ your brother **ready** for his final exam?
3 *Correct*
4 *Correct*
5 Are ~~happy~~ your parents **happy** with your school results?

6 Mr. Ross always gives **interesting** speeches ~~interesting~~.
7 Some ~~youngs~~ **young** boys are playing in the park.
8 Correct

3 1 A blue and white, Chinese, porcelain fruit bowl
2 An abstract, large oil painting
3 A neoclassical, French, wooden chest of drawers
4 Five old, Italian, silver coffee spoons
5 A white and violet, Venetian, glass paperweight

4 1 The girls are wearing expensive, black, American,
leather jackets.
2 Here's a valuable, old, African, ebony elephant for
your collection.
3 Why don't you buy that simple, green, cotton dress?
4 Let's sit around this oval, dark green, plastic table.
5 The new teacher is a handsome, tall, young,
Canadian man. Everyone likes him!
6 His girlfriend has got long, straight, blonde hair.
7 There's a horrible, big, black spider in my bedroom.

LESSON 4 P. 48 ....

1 1 F 2 B 3 E 4 C 5 A 6 D

2 1 two hundred and twenty-five 2 hundreds
3 thousand 4 Thousands 5 million
6 two hundred and five pounds
7 hundred and thirty-three 8 two point five five
9 Thousands 10 Two thousand and seven

3 1 twentieth 2 fifth 3 thirteenth 4 sixteenth
5 twelfth 6 second 7 forty-ninth, fiftieth

4 1 1st January, 2000 (Br.E.)
2 23rd April, 2005 (Br.E.)
3 March 17th, 1969 (Am.E.)
4 July 4th, Independence Day (Am.E.)
5 9th November, 2011 (Br.E.)
6 30th January, 2014 (Br.E.)
7 January 1st, New Year's Day (Am.E.)

5 1 $^2/_9$ 2 $^4/_7$ 3 $^4/_{15}$ 4 $^7/_{18}$ 5 $^5/_8$ 6 $^3/_5$ 7 $^6/_{17}$ 8 $^2/_{11}$

6 1 zero 2 love 3 nil 4 oh 5 zero 6 zero
7 oh 8 zero 9 zero

ROUND UP 3 P. 52 ....

1 1 These are my friends.   2 Those are his dogs.
3 These are our sisters.   4 Those are your students.
5 Those are their cars.

2 1 any, some 2 some 3 any 4 Some 5 any
6 any 7 any, some 8 any 9 any, some 10 any

3 1 none 2 no 3 no 4 None 5 no 6 No
7 None 8 None

4 1 No shops <u>aren't</u> open today. It's a holiday.
No shops **are** open today. It's a holiday.
2 I <u>haven't</u> no homework to do for tomorrow.
I **have** no homework to do for tomorrow.

3 "No, there aren't <u>none</u>."
   "No, there aren't **any**."

4 <u>Not any</u> patients are allowed in this area.
   No patients are allowed in this area.

5 <u>None</u> journalists can get into the room.
   No journalists can get into the room.

6 It's no <u>any</u> use crying over spilt milk.
   It's **no use** crying over spilt milk.

7 The airport must be <u>any</u> 20 miles from here.
   The airport must be **some/about** 20 miles from here.

8 We're <u>some</u> good at painting.
   We're **no** good at painting.

5
1 Finnish, Latvian 2 Canadian 3 Thai
4 German 5 Belgium, Europe 6 the Netherlands

6
1 B 2 A 3 C 4 A 5 A 6 C 7 B 8 C 9 A
10 B 11 C 12 A 13 B 14 C

Reflecting on grammar

1 F 2 T 3 F 4 F 5 F 6 F 7 F 8 T 9 T 10 F

Revision and Exams 1   P. 56

1
1 the 2 // 3 // 4 the 5 // 6 // 7 an 8 the
9 a 10 // 11 // 12 a 13 a 14 // 15 the

2
1 are 2 am/'m 3 am not / 'm not 4 are
5 is/'s 6 are 7 are/'re 8 is/'s

3
1 oxen 2 sheep/cows 3 cows/sheep 4 are
5 ducks/geese 6 geese/ducks 7 deer
8 bushes 9 is 10 Are

4
1 B 2 C 3 C 4 C 5 A 6 B 7 C 8 B 9 A
10 A 11 A 12 A

5 *Suggested answers*
1 great, trendy 2 popular 3 colorful, eco-leather
4 cheap 5 Long-sleeved, black-white, cotton
6 incredible 7 short, tight, denim 8 long, low-
necked, blue 9 fantastic 10 long, glittery, evening

6
1 has 2 be 3 is 4 has 5 is 6 are 7 are

7
1 are 2 the 3 the 4 is 5 the 6 the 7 The 8 an
9 The 10 is 11 the 12 is

8
1 B 2 B 3 B 4 A 5 A 6 D 7 B 8 C 9 A 10 D

9
1 the 2 It 3 Some/Many 4 the 5 some
6 their 7 they 8 a 9 the 10 the

Self Check 1   P. 60

1 B	2 C	3 B	4 B	5 B	6 A	7 B	8 C
9 A	10 C	11 C	12 A	13 C	14 B	15 C	16 C
17 B	18 B	19 C	20 C	21 A	22 C	23 B	24 A
25 A	26 A	27 B	28 A	29 B	30 C	31 B	32 A
33 B	34 C	35 A	36 A	37 C	38 B	39 C	40 B

UNIT 4

LESSON 1   P. 62

1
1 My mother's got a part-time job.
2 They've got some relatives in Australia.
3 The contracted form can't be used in this sentence.
4 You've got great talent!
5 My brother's got a degree in physics.
6 She's got a very large house.
7 We've all got black hair in my family.
8 Julie's got a fantastic voice.

2
1 My sister has long, straight hair.
2 I've got a very bad headache.
3 I have a tattoo on my left arm.
4 We've got two tickets for the concert.
5 Our hotel has got an indoor pool.
6 Your dad has a good sense of humor.
7 We have got a big, black dog.
8 I've got your phone number.

3
1 Adam's **got** spiky hair.
2 *This sentence is correct.*
3 She's got **has** a shower every morning.
4 The children've **have (got)** blue eyes.
5 Dad's got **has** a rest in the afternoon.
6 Have got a good time at the party!
7 *This sentence is correct.*
8 *This sentence is correct.*

LESSON 2   P. 63

1
1 hasn't got 2 haven't got 3 has got
4 hasn't got 5 has got 6 have got
7 have got 8 has got, hasn't got

2
1 I haven't got any warm clothes with me.
2 She hasn't got a present for you.
3 The students don't have a break at 11 o'clock in the morning.
4 He hasn't got a lot of contacts on social media.
5 They don't have a vacation in July.
6 She doesn't usually have tea for breakfast.
7 My mother hasn't got blue eyes.
8 We haven't got tickets for the match.

3
1 My bedroom doesn't have a balcony, but it does have French windows. / My bedroom hasn't got a balcony, but it has got French windows.
2 The village has a post office, but it doesn't have a bank. / The village has got a post office, but it hasn't got a bank.
3 I don't have any trees in my garden, but I have lots of flowers. / I haven't got any trees in my garden, but I've got lots of flowers.
4 We don't have enough money for a pizza, but we have enough for a couple of sandwiches. / We haven't got enough money for a pizza, but we've got enough for a couple of sandwiches.

4 1 D 2 E 3 A 4 B 5 F 6 C

5
2 Does Ben have any good video games?
3 It's heavy! What do you have in your bag?
4 Do we have time to catch the next train?
5 Do you have any good music on your MP3 player?
6 Do you have any pink clothes?

6
1 My house has got solar panels on the roof.
2 I haven't got time to chat. I'm busy at the moment.
3 "Has Peter got a big family?"
  "Yes, he's got four children."
4 "What car have you got?"
  "I've got a hybrid car. It's very cheap to run."
5 London has got a population of over 8.3 million.
6 We haven't got much money. We must find an ATM.
7 "Have you got any preferences for your room?"
  "I'd like a non-smoking one, please."
8 "Has your school got a big playground?"
  "No, but it's got a very big gym."
9 "Have you got any hand luggage, madam?"
  "I've only got this handbag."
10 We haven't got any bread, but we've got some breadsticks.

LESSON 3 P. 66

1
1 **E** you, your   2 **A** Zimbabwe, Its
3 **G** Mr. Johnson, His   4 **F** Kate, Her
5 **D** We, Our   6 **B** My uncle and aunt, their

2
1 their 2 your 3 its 4 her
5 my 6 his 7 our 8 your

3
1 **His** house is on Darwin Road.
2 Emma's got a little brother. **His** name's Harry.
3 This farm belongs to my grandparents.
  It's **their** farm.
4 She's wearing **her** new red dress.
5 The hamster isn't in **its** cage!
6 My diary has got flowers on **its** cover.
7 I often have sleepovers at **my** friend's house.
8 John and Simon have **their** own fitness instructor.
9 Karen's got a sister. **Her** name is Davina.

4
1 yours 2 your, mine 3 His, his 4 theirs
5 hers 6 yours 7 ours 8 their

LESSON 4 P. 68

1
1 Whose are those scooters? /
  Whose scooters are those?
2 Whose is that coat? / Whose coat is that?
3 Whose is this telephone number? /
  Whose telephone number is this?
4 Whose are those suitcases? /
  Whose suitcases are those?
5 Whose is this magazine? / Whose magazine is this?
6 Whose is that idea? / Whose idea is that?

2 3, 1, 4, 2, 6, 5

3
1 a week's vacation
2 your brother's email address
3 my brothers' bedroom
4 one of Amy Winehouse's best songs
5 The clowns' tricks
6 Van Gogh's paintings
7 The principal's office

4
1 the kitchen walls   2 the laptop charger
3 the pen cap   4 the book cover
5 the door handle   6 the table legs
7 the computer screen
8 the TV remote control   9 the tree top

5
1 bicycle is white.   2 my father's computer.
3 eyes are beautiful.   4 the guides' backpacks.
5 smartphone is new.   6 computer is very good.

6
1 Rino's 2 chemist's 3 St. Peter's 4 doctor's
5 my friend's 6 baker's 7 dentist's
8 producer seller's

7
1 Two of the Smiths' neighbors 2 One of my brother's colleagues 3 Many of John's selfies 4 One of the Browns' friends 5 Four of my cousin's birthday presents 6 One of Peter's cousins 7 Some of the stamps of my father's collection

8
1 Albert and Maddie's 2 Albert and Daphne's
3 Joe and Alice's 4 Albert and Maddie's
5 Joe and Alice's 6 Joe and Alice's
7 Maddie and Jack's 8 Ann and Mark's
9 Maddie's 10 Jack's

9
1 *Correct*
2 I usually have two **weeks'** holiday in July.
3 *Correct*
4 Where are the **children's** backpacks?
5 Is James's brother a friend of **Thomas's**?
6 This isn't today's newspaper. It's **yesterday's**.
7 *Correct*
8 Two **of the** UK's top attractions are the Tower of London and Windsor Castle.
9 My office is five **minutes'** walk from the bus station.
10 *Correct*
11 *Correct*
12 *Knockin' on Heaven's* Door is **one of** Bob Dylan's most famous songs.

10
1 Mrs. 2 house 3 car 4 girlfriend 5 students'
6 bicycles 7 son 8 Mary and Lucy's
9 Peter's and John's 10 one of 11 Some of
12 your father's

ROUND UP 4 P. 72

1 *Possible answers*
I have six hundred names in my contact list.
I have big responsibilities in my new job.
We have some chips in our packed lunch.
We have a lot of homework for tomorrow.

They have three sons but no daughters.

Wimbledon Center Court has a movable roof.

Robert has a funny hat.

The black rhino has a gigantic horn.

That girl has a new email address.

That man has a beard and a mustache.

This mini-van has eight seats.

A dice has six faces.

The Statue of Liberty has a torch in her hand.

2 1 is 2 has (got) 3 is 4 is 5 is 6 is
7 have (got) 8 has (got) 9 have 10 have (got)

3 1 They don't have lunch at home on weekdays.

2 I haven't got / don't have a new car.
This is my old one.

3 Sheila hasn't got / doesn't have an umbrella with her.

4 The company hasn't got / doesn't have a new sales manager. Mr. Jones is still the Chief Buyer.

5 We don't have a sandwich for lunch on the weekend.

6 That man hasn't got / doesn't have a pass. Stop him!

7 My parents don't have a walk in the evening.
They're far too lazy.

8 I haven't got / don't have a cold. Why are you asking?

9 Mark doesn't have breakfast at home. He usually goes to a café next to his office.

10 Oh dear! I haven't got / don't have my wallet with me. Can you lend me some money?

4 1 O 2 P 3 G 4 P 5 A 6 P

5 1 Do you usually have a sandwich for lunch?

2 Have a nice stay

3 Has Gwen got measles?

4 What have you got in your packed lunch?

5 Have some more cookies / another cookies.

6 Are you having a break?

7 Let's have a walk.

8 Are you having a rest?

6 1 your 2 mine 3 mine 4 Whose 5 Hers 6 her
7 your 8 mine/his 9 his/mine 10 your
11 yours 12 ours 13 Our 14 our 15 your

7 1 <u>Has Pat usually</u> a snack during the break?
Does Pat usually have a snack during the break?

2 This is not <u>mine</u> tablet. This is not **my** tablet.

3 That's <u>her</u> bicycle in the garden.
That's **his** bicycle in the garden.

4 I'm going to the <u>dentists'</u> and I'll come back late.
I'm going to the **dentist's** and I'll come back late.

5 Let's print the <u>students's</u> reports before the end of the lessons.
Let's print the **students'** reports before the end of the lesson.

6 Why don't we read <u>a Dickens' novel</u> this year, Miss Pearson?
Why don't we read **one of Dickens' novels** this year, Miss Pearson?

7 "Whose <u>those cars are</u>?"
"Whose **are** those cars?" / "Whose cars **are** those?"

8 <u>Some my</u> friends are coming for dinner tonight.
Some of my friends are coming for dinner tonight.

8 1 tie of your father's
2 of my nephews is moving
3 walls bright yellow
4 of my sister's neighbors has a beautiful German shepherd
5 the children's toys are still in the
6 of the room was locked
7 (best) friend of his
8 of Thomas's are having a barbecue in the garden

9 1 ours 2 Their 3 his 4 His 5 Hers 6 their
7 their 8 their 9 Their 10 her

10 1 dentist's 2 produce seller's 3 baker's
4 butcher's 5 chemist's 6 hairdresser's

11 1 Sophocles' plays 2 St. James's Park
3 Dickens' biography 4 Prince Charles' residence
5 Mr. Fox's desk 6 Douglas's son

Reflecting on grammar

1 F 2 T 3 F 4 F 5 F 6 T 7 F 8 T 9 T 10 T

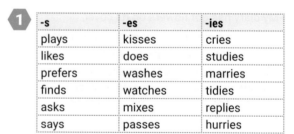

UNIT 5

LESSON 1 P. 76 ....

1 1 give 2 sit 3 Wait 4 have 5 Let's 6 Don't
7 Enjoy 8 Let's not go

2 1 Sit, don't jump 2 Don't lie 3 Walk, turn
4 Read, write 5 Don't tell 6 Don't be, remember

3 1 Let's make 2 Let's work
3 Let's not buy, Let's go 4 Let's not watch
5 Let's play 6 Let's have

LESSON 2 P. 77 ....

1

-s	-es	-ies
plays	kisses	cries
likes	does	studies
prefers	washes	marries
finds	watches	tidies
asks	mixes	replies
says	passes	hurries

2 1 Thomas studies Russian, too.

2 I go to university, too.

3 My cousin lives in Manchester, too.

4 I love antique furniture, too.

5 I get up at seven o'clock, too.

6 He misses his friends, too.

7 My boyfriend watches a lot of TV, too.

3 1 tidies 2 plays 3 washes 4 does
5 goes 6 misses 7 arrives 8 stays

4
1 check   2 doesn't wear   3 don't go
4 don't study   5 doesn't get

5
1 Frances doesn't dance very well.
2 She doesn't like romantic novels.
3 We don't have lunch at school.
4 They don't work in a hospital.
5 Catherine doesn't play the violin.
6 We don't go shopping on Mondays.
7 The movie doesn't start at 9:00.
8 He doesn't go to work by car.

6
1 doesn't have   2 doesn't go   3 doesn't play
4 don't, watch   5 don't work   6 don't go, don't work

7
1 Do, I/we do   2 Does, he doesn't   3 Do, they do
4 Does, he does   5 Do, we do   6 Does, she doesn't
7 Do, I/we don't   8 Do, they don't

8
1 When do you do your homework?
2 Where does your best friend come from?
3 What kind of music do they like?
4 How much does that smartphone cost?
5 Which song do you like best?
6 What do you have for breakfast?

9
A 6 B 3 C 1 D 5 E 2 F 4

10
1 time do you (usually) get up   2 do you go to
work   3 does, help   4 do you (usually) meet your
friends   5 do you go   6 does she live

11
1 ✗ Water ~~freeze~~ **freezes** at 0°C and ~~boil~~ **boils** at 100°C.
2 ✓   3 ✗ The match doesn't ~~starts~~ **start** at three o'clock.
4 ✗ This laptop ~~don't belongs~~ **doesn't belong** to the
teacher.   5 ✗ What **do** you think of this plan?   6 ✓
7 ✗ I ~~doesn't~~ **don't** agree with you.   8 ✓   9 ✓
10 ✗ He doesn't ~~believes~~ **believe** his team can win
today.   11 Does he ~~wants~~ **want** to go to the movies
with us?   12 ✓

LESSON 3 P. 81

1
1 We occasionally meet for a drink after work.
2 My brother is never at home in the evening.
3 Where do you usually have lunch?
4 He sometimes listens to classical music. /
Sometimes he listens to classical music. /
He listens to classical music sometimes.
5 I don't often go to the theater.
6 They are always at school in the morning.
7 My friend rarely eats meat.
8 We never see each other on weekends.

2 *Possible answers*
1 I always go to the market on Saturday morning.
2 I am / I'm never at home in the mornings.
3 I rarely play tennis on the weekend.
4 I usually sleep till late on Sunday morning.
5 I sometimes go to the theater with my friends.

3
1 They seldom have piano lessons in the morning.
2 Greg often surfs the Internet in the evening.
3 This train is usually on time.
4 Does Mom ever come back late from work?
5 Jill sometimes works on the weekend. /
Jill works on the weekend sometimes /
Sometimes Jill works on the weekend.

4
1 E   2 A   3 C   4 B   5 F   6 D

5 *Possible answers*
1 Where do your parents work?
2 How much does this book cost?
3 How does this machine stop?
4 What time do the shops open?
5 When does the yoga course start?
6 How often do you practice?

6
1 five days a week / on weekdays   2 twice a year
3 once a year   4 every day   5 twice a day
6 three times a year   7 four times a month

LESSON 4 P. 83

1
1 it   2 them   3 us   4 him   5 her   6 you
7 them   8 me

2
1 Are you talking to me?
2 Here's a present for you, Dad!
3 I don't know her very well.
4 I like it very much.
5 They are coming with us.
6 Can you wait for me, please?

3
1 She, him   2 us   3 it, her   4 He, it   5 him, He
6 her, She   7 they, them   8 them, They

4
1 because   2 so   3 and   4 or   5 so   6 or   7 and
8 because

5
1 and   2 but   3 so   4 or, and   5 or   6 and
7 because   8 so

6
1 Go to the science lab quickly because your
teacher is waiting for you.
2 Would you like/prefer an apple or an orange?
3 Come before five so we can have a nice chat.
4 Steve is a nice boy, but he's a bit lazy.
5 My son helps me at home, but he can't cook (though).

7
1 them   2 him   3 me   4 because   5 and   6 them
7 But   8 So   9 them   10 and   11 them   12 them
13 And   14 or

8
1 but   2 she   3 because   4 at   5 her   6 because
7 Their   8 in   9 and   10 and   11 them   12 Her
13 because   14 and   15 and   16 but   17 their
18 but   19 them   20 them

ROUND UP 5 P. 86

1
1 Always wear gloves and a mask. / It is important that
you always wear gloves and a mask. / It is important
for you to always wear gloves and a mask. /
It is essential that you always wear gloves and a
mask.

2 Don't park your car here. /
You mustn't park your car here.

3 Have some coffee. / Would you like some coffee? /
Do you want some coffee? / How about some coffee?

4 Let's go to the leisure center. / Why don't we go to
the leisure center? / What about going to the leisure
center? / Shall we go to the leisure center?

5 Let's have an ice cream. / How about having an ice
cream? / What about having an ice cream? /
Shall we have an ice cream?

6 Read this novel. It's really good.

7 Read the instructions before you start. /
You must read the instructions before you start. /
It is important for you to read the instructions
before you start. / It is essential that you read the
instructions before you start.

8 Let's talk about it. / How about talking about it? /
What about talking about it? / Shall we talk about it?

9 Never give up.

10 Come here, please.

2 1 E 2 A 3 F 4 G 5 H 6 B 7 C 8 D 9 J 10 I

3 1 P 2 A 3 S 4 OF 5 O 6 OF 7 S 8 P 9 A
10 OF 11 O 12 S

4 1 c 2 j 3 h 4 d 5 a 6 i 7 f 8 e 9 g 10 b

5 1 Do you have piano lessons (every Monday)?

2 Does she (ever) eat meat?

3 Do they like the mountains? / Do they spend any time
in the mountains? / Do they ever go to the Alps /
mountains?

4 What language(s) do you study (as a foreign language)?

5 How often do you have basketball practice?

6 Which dress do you prefer?

7 Where does your sister work? /
What does your sister do?

8 Where do your parents live?

9 What do you do on the weekend? /
When do you go jogging?

10 Do you (ever/often) go to the theater?

11 Do you ever go to the mountains in summer?

12 Where's the Sales Manager's office? /
Which floor is the Sales Manager's office on?

13 What does your grandfather do in the evening?

14 How often do you go to the movies? /
What do you do once a week?

6 1 Get me 2 Get me 3 go and see 4 can sign
5 you say 6 Turn down 7 give me 8 Why don't you

7 1 says 2 catches 3 sleep 4 catch 5 like 6 go
7 work 8 finish 9 gets up 10 goes 11 prefer

8 1 it/them 2 they 3 me 4 us 5 I 6 you 7 you

Reflecting on grammar

1 T 2 F 3 F 4 T 5 F 6 T 7 F 8 T 9 F 10 T

UNIT 6

LESSON 1 P. 90

1

putting	writing	reading
dancing	living	staying
transmitting	referring	dyeing
playing	rising	watching
entering	asking	hitting
trying	marveling (Am.E.)	committing
waiting	typing	painting
getting	leaving	answering
lying	thinking	behaving
working	suffering	stopping
changing	copying	shouting

2 1 **N** Playing tennis is one of his favorite activities.

2 **V** I'm having a geography lesson in a few minutes.

3 **N** She really loves working out in the gym.

4 **A** Oh dear! That's such a heartbreaking story!

5 **V** We're leaving for Paris next week.

6 **A** That is shocking news.

7 **V** Congratulations! You're doing a really great job.

8 **N** Most people are interested in learning English.

3 1 Dad is cooking an exotic meal tonight.

2 Knitting is Rachel's favorite hobby.

3 I enjoy drawing and painting / painting and drawing.

4 Her performance was so disappointing!

5 Learning Japanese is really challenging.

6 This is a deeply moving movie.

LESSON 2 P. 91

1 1 are doing 2 is wearing 3 is/'s having
4 are walking 5 is/'s watching 6 are playing
7 is/'s getting 8 am/'m writing
9 are/'re buying 10 is/'s texting

2 1 's filing 2 's studying 3 's talking 4 are running
5 's leaving 6 're lying 7 are staying 8 is having
9 's having 10 's working

3 1 The secretary isn't filing some/any documents.

2 My brother isn't studying at San Francisco
State University.

3 The President isn't talking to Congress right now.

4 The students aren't running to their class because
they're early / they aren't late.

5 The ship isn't leaving New York harbor.

6 We aren't lying in the sun.

7 My friends aren't staying at a four-star hotel
by the sea.

8 Ms. Sunis isn't having lunch at the moment.

9 Dad isn't busy right now.

10 Sam isn't working on the roof.

4 1 Julie isn't reading a magazine.

2 My parents aren't meeting their friends.

3 You aren't studying history.

4 They aren't drinking tea.

5 Ben isn't playing football.

6 I'm not going to the park this afternoon.

7 They aren't filing documents.

5
1 am not / 'm not studying, am/'m studying

2 is not / isn't playing   3 are cooking

4 am not / 'm not enjoying   5 are sleeping

6 am not / 'm not playing, am/'m, writing

7 are not / aren't going, are coming

6 1 E   2 D   3 A   4 F   5 B   6 C

7 1 Is your brother sleeping on the sofa? Yes, he is.

2 Are Jo and Tamsin acting in the school play?
Yes, they are.

3 Isn't she watching TV tonight? Yes, she is.

4 Are they having breakfast now? No, they aren't. /
No, they're not.

5 Isn't Tom ironing his shirts? No, he isn't. /
No, he's not.

6 Aren't you studying for your test tomorrow?
Yes, I am / we are.

7 Is the train leaving in ten minutes? No, it isn't. /
No, it's not.

8 Is Rob taking part in the tennis tournament?
Yes, he is.

8 1 Aren't/Are you staying at home (this afternoon)?

2 Are you going out?

3 Are you listening to your favorite rock band?

4 Aren't/Are you chatting with Tom?

5 Why aren't you doing any/your homework (today)?

6 Why are they running?

7 Who are you playing with? /
What are you doing with your little sister?

9 1 F   2 C   3 E   4 A   5 B   6 D

10 1 always   2 tonight   3 these   4 this/next
5 right   6 next/this   7 nowadays   8 tomorrow

11 1 is/'s, waiting   2 is/'s talking   3 is/'s sitting
4 (is) drinking   5 is/'s carrying   6 walking
7 isn't / is not, walking   8 is/'s running
9 is/'s hailing

LESSON 3 P. 96

1 1 I'm spending   2 Do you collect
3 You're always making   4 is not going   5 are visiting
6 usually eat   7 works   8 is watching

2 1 read, am/'m reading   2 does, is/'s cooking
3 cycles, is/'s raining, is/'s driving   4 shines
5 is/'s setting

3 1 Do, live   2 live   3 do you do   4 run   5 grow
6 'm staying   7 are opening   8 're having

4 1 can't hear   2 is enjoying   3 doesn't mind
4 are seeing   5 Do you like   6 Do you think
7 is having   8 knows   9 Do you want
10 Do you remember   11 enjoy

12 are you thinking

5 1 are you thinking   2 do you remember
3 don't know   4 lives   5 're/are cooperating
6 Don't you usually work   7 's/is enjoying

LESSON 4 P. 100

1 1 to eat   2 smoking   3 getting   4 talking
5 moving   6 eating   7 working   8 to have
9 driving   10 helping

2 1 eating   2 to have   3 to meet
4 to meet / meeting   5 watching   6 washing
7 skiing   8 to learn / learning   9 singing
10 drinking

3 1 Keep ~~to work~~ **working** and you'll get a promotion.

2 I'd love ~~touring~~ **to tour** the Australian outback.

3 He denied ~~to steal~~ **stealing** the gold necklace.

4 I'd like ~~talking~~ **to talk** to the manager, please.

5 My son always avoids ~~to help~~ **helping** with the
housework!

6 Don't forget ~~buying~~ **to buy** some bread for tonight.

7 Do you miss ~~to live~~ **living** in a big city?

8 I always stop ~~buying~~ **to buy** the newspaper on my
way to work.

9 I often fancy ~~to tour~~ **touring** Iceland in the summer.

10 Why don't we stop here ~~having~~ **to have** breakfast?

4 1 telling   2 to wake up   3 running   4 running
5 to be   6 to avoid   7 doing   8 to say

ROUND UP 6 P. 102

1 1 to find   2 to talk   3 to abandon   4 to go
5 to buy   6 to play   7 to do   8 to give   9 to leave
10 to become   11 to get up   12 to see

2 1 crying   2 smoking   3 acting, dancing / dancing,
acting   4 Cooking   5 rising   6 bullying   7 raising
8 talking

3 1 working   2 cooking   3 cleaning   4 to help
5 helping   6 to help   7 to stop   8 to employ
9 to help   10 paying

4 1 am staying   2 go   3 lie   4 don't swim
5 am going   6 am looking   7 are you doing
8 Are you studying

5 1 lives   2 works   3 gets   4 starts   5 finishes
6 gets   7 goes   8 meets   9 is/'s looking
10 is/'s staying   11 does not / doesn't have
12 is/'s having / has   13 is/'s getting up
14 is/'s going   15 is/'s dating
16 are/'re going back   17 wants

6 1 G   2 G   3 PP   4 PP   5 PP   6 PP

Reflecting on grammar

1 T   2 T   3 F   4 F   5 T   6 F   7 T   8 T   9 F   10 T

Revision and Exams 2 P. 106

1 1 Discover/Admire 2 Rent 3 admire/discover
4 Ride 5 observe 6 Finish 7 don't forget

2 1 Keep 2 Don't leave 3 Remember / Don't forget
4 Use 5 take 6 Put 7 Don't smoke
8 Don't forget / Remember

3 1 Are you having 2 keep 3 remember 4 learn
5 write 6 Write 7 helps 8 am/'m trying
9 am/'m writing 10 am/'m talking 11 do
12 are/'re using 13 are/'re 14 are/'re saying

4 1 lives 2 work 3 send 4 pass 5 organize 6 do
7 starts 8 sleeps 9 has 10 goes 11 meet 12 go

5 1 is/'s getting up, is/'s, sleeping
2 is/'s having, is/'s starting
3 are, working, is/'s passing, is/'s organizing
4 are/'re having
5 is/'s going, is/'s, working
6 are meeting, are/'re looking

6 1 span 2 offers 3 offers 4 are teaching
5 enroll 6 opens 7 closes
8 're / are carrying out 9 is 10 Visit

7 *Students' own answers*

8 1 but 2 take/share 3 because
4 don't 5 do 6 because/as 7 so 8 and

Self Check 2 P. 110

1 B	2 B	3 C	4 A	5 B	6 A	7 B	8 A
9 A	10 C	11 B	12 C	13 B	14 C	15 B	16 C
17 A	18 C	19 B	20 C	21 A	22 B	23 C	24 B
25 A	26 A	27 B	28 A	29 C	30 C	31 B	32 A
33 B	34 A	35 C	36 A	37 C	38 B	39 C	40 B

UNIT 7

LESSON 1 P. 112 ....

1 1 in 2 at 3 on 4 in 5 In, at 6 at 7 on 8 at

2 1 on 2 at 3 on 4 in 5 in 6 in 7 at 8 on
9 on 10 in 11 in 12 in, in

3 1 In, for 2 after 3 in, By 4 from
5 for, until 6 during, at 7 by 8 over
9 within 10 until

4 1 for 2 between 3 from, to 4 during 5 since
6 by 7 in 8 before

5 1 I often study **at** night.
2 Are you free on Monday **between** five **and** six /
from five **to** six?
3 What do you usually do **on** Christmas Day?
4 We have to hand in our essays **by** next Monday.
5 We like sleeping until late **on** Sundays.

LESSON 2 P. 114 ....

1 1 on 2 on, at 3 in 4 on, at 5 on
6 over/on, over 7 in, in

2 1 next 2 along 3 from 4 in front 5 around
6 off 7 between 8 opposite 9 behind
10 among

3 1 to 2 on, to 3 to 4 past 5 for 6 - - -
7 along 8 off

4 1 from 2 at 3 for 4 along 5 into, through
6 up to 7 away from 8 out of 9 to 10 as far as

5 1 down, as far as 2 into, on 3 at, across
4 off, at, along 5 past, on 6 to 7 up, from 8 to, on
9 along 10 towards

LESSON 3 P. 117 ....

1 1 by, on 2 of, of 3 on 4 about 5 like 6 of
7 with 8 by 9 without 10 for

2 1 ✔
2 Can you lend ~~to me~~ your credit card, Dad?
3 ✔
4 Samantha explained ~~me her plans~~ **her plans to me**.
5 ✔
6 ✔
7 ✔
8 They offered to us a very good meal.
9 ✔
10 We will deliver ~~our customers the goods~~ **the goods
to our customers** in two weeks.
11 We must report ~~the manager the theft~~ **the theft to
the manager**.
12 ✔

3 1 Can you give my friend a lift, please?
2 Can you lend me this book? I'd like to read it.
3 This sentence can't change.
4 Give your sister this paper, please.
5 If you like, I'll show you my photos.
6 They offered all the ladies a red rose.
7 This sentence can't change.
8 Have you sent Mr. Wayne an email yet?
9 My neighbor told everybody the news.
10 The coach asked the players their names.

LESSON 4 P. 119 ....

1 1 keen 2 Sorry 3 surprised 4 angry 5 popular
6 bored 7 afraid/scared, scared/afraid
8 interested 9 good 10 happy

2 1 about 2 with 3 to 4 on 5 with 6 from/to
7 with 8 with

3 1 Aren't you surprised **to** see me here?
2 My father is interested **in learning** how to surf
the Internet.

446

3 Mr. Higgins is really angry **with** his son because he has just broken the kitchen window.

4 I am very keen **on** English.

5 I am quite worried **about** the Spanish test. I haven't studied much.

6 I'm not very happy **with** my job. I would like a change.

7 Is she married **to** the new doctor?

8 Come on! You can't be scared **of** bugs. They're harmless.

9 She's always been very fond **of** her grandmother. She visits her every day.

10 We are really disappointed **by/at/with** the quality of this project.

11 Are you aware **of** all the risks involved in using chemicals?

12 He's responsible **for** the whole marketing department.

4 1 H 2 A 3 F 4 B 5 D 6 E 7 C 8 G 9 J 10 I

5 1 on 2 of 3 from 4 about 5 in 6 about
7 for 8 for 9 for 10 after

6 1 about 2 about 3 after 4 with, about/on
5 in 6 from 7 about 8 for 9 for 10 to, about

7 1 ask 2 apologize 3 agree 4 get used
5 complain 6 borrows 7 arguing 8 looking
9 shouting 10 thank

8 1 look around 2 look after 3 look up
4 looking into 5 looked at 6 looked for

9 1 having 2 get 3 waiting 4 going 5 seeing
6 be 7 meet 8 find 9 be 10 play 11 go
12 working 13 tell 14 being

ROUND UP 7 P. 124

1 1 at/on 2 in, in 3 at/on 4 at/on 5 on 6 on
7 on 8 in, in 9 in 10 on

2 1 without 2 on, to/from 3 about/on
4 for/from 5 by 6 to 7 to 8 at 9 in 10 on

3 1 I was born in **on** October 8th, 2005.

2 I don't like being home alone in the **at** night.

3 We usually go in **to** the mountains for a week on **in** August.

4 *No mistakes in this sentence.*

5 *No mistakes in this sentence.*

6 I will be at home between four to **and** five in the afternoon tomorrow.

7 *No mistakes in this sentence.*

8 Go until **up to / as far as** the traffic lights and then turn to left.

9 *No mistakes in this sentence.*

10 Do you often go jogging at **in the** morning?

4 1 He lent his son his cell phone.

2 Can you bring me that magazine, please?

3 Give my secretary your email address, will you?

4 They sent us a lot of photos when they were in Australia.

5 Will you please give your teacher this book?

6 We showed our friends our new car.

7 He sent his girlfriend a beautiful present for her birthday.

8 Take the beggar some money.

5 1 A 2 D 3 B 4 B 5 C 6 D 7 D 8 A 9 A 10 C

6 1 for 2 by 3 for 4 of 5 on 6 to, about 7 at
8 like 9 of 10 with

7 1 accusing 2 on 3 embarrassed 4 feel
5 on 6 of 7 for 8 of/about 9 for 10 protect

Reflecting on grammar

1 F 2 T 3 T 4 F 5 T 6 T 7 F 8 F 9 T 10 T

UNIT 8

LESSON P. 128

1 1 There wasn't a restaurant.
2 There were two playgrounds.
3 There was a beach.
4 There were lots of tourists.

2 1 was not / wasn't 2 was, was
3 was not / wasn't 4 were not / weren't
5 Was, was 6 was, was not / wasn't
7 was, were, were 8 Were, were

3 1 D 2 H 3 A 4 F 5 B 6 C 7 E 8 G

LESSON 2 P. 129

1

規則動詞		不規則動詞	
原形	過去式	原形	過去式
stop	stopped	have	had
help	helped	know	knew
play	played	leave	left
shout	shouted	meet	met
work	worked	go	went
try	tried	tell	told
refer	referred	take	took
quarrel (Br.E.)	quarrelled	read	read
submit	submitted	come	came
move	moved	speak	spoke

2 1 played 2 met 3 quarreled/shouted
4 worked, moved 5 read 6 tried, tried 7 took
8 had 9 helped 10 submitted

3 1 had 2 took 3 had 4 got 5 felt 6 spent
7 saw 8 drove 9 saw 10 flew
11 crossed over (*This is the only regular verb in the exercise.*) 12 came across 13 was

4 **a** 1 stayed, didn't meet 2 had, didn't go
3 watched, didn't go 4 went, didn't stay up

b 1 Mr. and Mrs. Steel didn't stay at home last night, they met their friends.

2 They didn't have dinner at home, they went to a restaurant.

3 They didn't watch a movie on TV, they went to the movies.

4 They didn't go to bed early, they stayed up late.

5 **1** Did, enjoy, I/we did   **2** Did, play, he didn't
3 Did, travel, they didn't   **4** Did, work, she did
5 Did, have, I/we didn't   **6** Did, come, he did

6 **1** We didn't like the movie at all.
2 Did you buy a return train ticket?
3 Didn't you check your emails this morning?
4 She didn't go out with Thomas last night.
5 Did she get up late on Sunday?
6 We didn't do our homework yesterday.
7 Did he repeat the same story over and over again?
8 They didn't want to leave the party so early.

7 **1** Where did you buy, How much did you pay
2 What did you do, Who did you go, How did you
3 When did you get here   **4** Where did you study, What did you study   **5** What did you do, How did you book

LESSON 3 P. 133

1 **1** last   **2** give   **3** opens, opened   **4** on
5 last   **6** last   **7** ago   **8** this   **9** before yesterday
10 last night

2 *Possible answers*
1 in March   **2** in 2015   **3** two days ago
4 last month   **5** yesterday   **6** at four o'clock
7 last week   **8** when I was 15   **9** in 2010
10 three months ago

3 **1** After   **2** First   **3** then   **4** After   **5** then
6 first   **7** After   **8** Finally

4 *Possible answer*
Last Saturday, we went on a trip to Canterbury. First, we visited the cathedral. Then we had lunch in a fast food restaurant. After that, we went around the shops and bought gifts. Finally, we had coffee and drove back home.

5 **1** First preheat the oven to 180°C.
2 To make the dough, mix the butter and sugar together.
3 When the butter and sugar mixture is light and fluffy, beat in the egg and slowly add the flour.
4 Then break up the chocolate into small pieces and put them into the mixture.
5 After greasing a baking sheet, put about 20 teaspoonfuls of the mixture onto it.
6 Then bake in the oven for 15 to 20 minutes until the cookies are golden brown.
7 Finally, put them on a wire rack to cool.

6 **1** Did your brother use to be a boy scout?
2 Jane used to dye her hair red when she was younger.
3 I used to study long hours when I was at college.

4 We didn't use to have cell phones or MP3 players.
5 My family used to run a youth hostel in the town center.
6 Where did you use to go dancing in the old days?

7 **1** used to have   **2** did not / didn't use to buy
3 used to make   **4** used to hang up
5 did not / didn't use to sleep
6 did not / didn't use to have   **7** used to act
8 used to sing

8 **1** There used to be a fountain in this park.
2 We used to wear a uniform when we were in/at primary school.
3 I went out after closing all the windows and switching off the lights.
4 Before going skateboarding in the park, I helped my grandma with the shopping.
5 My husband drove for five hours before stopping at a service area.
6 My father used to help me with my homework when I was little.
7 The last time I missed a day's work was two years ago.
8 I was last in bed with flu during the Christmas holidays three years ago.

LESSON 4 P. 136

1 **1** H   **2** E   **3** I   **4** F   **5** C   **6** G   **7** A   **8** D   **9** J   **10** B

2 **1** Were - wearing, was wearing   **2** Was - driving, was studying   **3** were - doing, was working
4 were - arguing, was making, was watching
5 wasn't driving, were going

3 **1** D   **2** A   **3** C   **4** F   **5** B   **6** G   **7** E

4 **1** While I was walking in the street, I saw a bad accident.
2 While we were all cheering, a group of hooligans invaded the football pitch.
3 While they were going home, they saw an old friend getting off the bus.
4 While the actors were getting ready for the shoot, the director suddenly left.
5 While I was doing my homework, my friend was waiting for me in the hall.
6 While I was talking to the English teacher, the principal came into the library.
7 While we were having a drink, a band started playing folk music.
8 While the exam students were still writing, the final bell rang.

5 **1** was cycling, saw
2 came / was coming, was baking
3 was trying, went off
4 opened, heard
5 was dreaming, jumped, woke - up
6 was playing, winning, started

ROUND UP 8 P. 140

1
1 was 2 were 3 was 4 was 5 were
6 weren't 7 was 8 were 9 weren't 10 was
11 wasn't 12 was 13 wasn't 14 wasn't

2
1 was born 2 studied 3 didn't go 4 was
5 married 6 had 7 left 8 became 9 started
10 wrote 11 founded 12 bought 13 retired
14 died

3
1 I would cycle to my grandma's every Sunday.
2 We used to learn nursery rhymes by heart when we were in primary school.
3 He would work six days a week for his former company.
4 My mother would cook fresh vegetables every day.
5 They used to go to an organic market to buy local cheeses when they lived in Lincoln.
6 I would walk a lot when I was younger.
7 She wouldn't take her sister with her.
8 My brother used to ride a big red motorcycle when he was young.

4
1 Five minutes ago 2 Three hours ago
3 Last night 4 Yesterday morning 5 Last week
6 Two months ago 7 Last year

5
1 were watching TV 2 was going back home
3 was waiting 4 went out 5 was 6 lasted
7 got back home 8 went to bed

6
1 spread 2 didn't reach 3 came 4 began
5 spread 6 grew 7 developed 8 started
9 became

7
1 Were - sleeping 2 was checking 3 did - get
4 got 5 Did - enjoy 6 had 7 met 8 did - meet
9 was walking 10 saw 11 was 12 knew
13 was 14 was 15 left 16 heard 17 was - doing

8
1 to 2 were 3 had 4 was 5 used 6 lot
7 While 8 After 9 As/Since/Because
10 danced

9
1 was sleeping 2 rang 3 answered
4 didn't hear 5 put 6 tried 7 rang 8 decided
9 was dialing 10 saw 11 was walking
12 (was) searching 13 answered 14 whispered
15 tried 16 was happening 17 was waiting
18 hid 19 was doing 20 was getting 21 heard

10 *Possible answer*
I was very scared, but I opened the door. My neighbor stood there with a torch in his hand and his cat under his arm. "I'm so sorry," he said. "I lost my cat and my cell phone. I just found them both in your garden shed . . . and I think my cat pressed the speed-dial number for your house by mistake. Did you get some strange phone calls?" I was very relieved, but it took quite a lot of explaining when the police arrived . . .

Reflecting on grammar

1 T 2 T 3 F 4 F 5 F 6 T 7 F 8 F 9 T 10 F

UNIT 9

LESSON 1 P. 144

1
1 've lost 2 haven't planted 3 've tried
4 's moved 5 haven't done 6 've had
7 haven't watered 8 've, liked 9 haven't washed
10 Have you ordered, haven't brought

2
1 **B** Have, checked   2 **C** have, bought
3 **D** Has, arrived   4 **F** Have, built
5 **A** Have, seen   6 **E** has, cooked

3
1 been 2 been 3 gone 4 been 5 gone
6 gone 7 gone 8 gone 9 been 10 been

4
1 ever 2 ever 3 ever 4 never 5 never 6 never

5
1 My son has never lived on his own before.
2 Have you ever thought of moving abroad?
3 I've never seen such a beautiful picture!
4 Have you done any research so far?
5 It's been hot and sunny all day today.
6 We have never been there.
7 Has your team won a match so far this year?
8 She has never worked in a restaurant before!

6
1 F 2 D 3 A 4 G 5 E 6 B 7 H 8 C

LESSON 2 P. 147

1
1 just 2 still 3 just 4 yet, yet 5 just
6 just/already, yet 7 yet, still 8 already
9 already

2 *Possible answers*
1 We have never tried bungee jumping.
2 They have already seen this movie.
3 I have just written my history project.
4 My sister has already read this novel.
5 He has just booked a flight to New York.
6 She has never played the xylophone.

3
1 She has already bought some bags of sweets for the kids.
2 She hasn't decorated the birthday cake yet.
3 She hasn't put the play tent up in the garden yet.
4 She has already organized some games.
5 She hasn't asked Martha for some more chairs yet.
6 She has already bought some balloons and party hats.

4
1 G 2 D 3 J 4 A 5 I 6 C 7 H 8 E 9 F 10 B

5
1 lived, came 2 have been 3 got up, didn't have
4 have lived 5 have read 6 hasn't been
7 have had, haven't found 8 stayed
9 didn't have, were 10 Have you ever been

6
1 **PP** I haven't tidied my bedroom yet.
2 **PS** She tidied her bedroom last Saturday.
3 **PP** Has Louise got back from France yet?
4 **PS** When did Louise get back from France?
5 **PP** Guess who I have just seen in town!

6 **PS**   I saw an old friend of mine at the theater last night.

7 **PP**   My brother has already graduated from high school.

8 **PS**   I graduated from high school last year.

7   1 had, was, Have you ever tried
   2 've already done, went, saw, haven't visited
   3 've just got back
   4 Have you booked, did
   5 've already bought, still haven't bought
   6 didn't go, 've already been
   7 've never been
   8 's just phoned, arrived

8   1 **Mark**   Have you ever visited the Tate Modern? / Have you visited the Tate Modern yet?
   Julie   Yes, I have.
   Mark   When did you go?
   Julie   I went there yesterday afternoon.

   2 **Adam**   Have you ever been camping?
   Rick   Yes, I have.
   Adam   Did you like it?
   Rick   Yes (, I did). It was a great experience.

   3 **Brad**   Have you ever been to Australia?
   Frances   Yes(, I have). I've been there twice.
   Brad   Did you stay long?
   Frances   I stayed for two weeks the first time and three weeks the second time.
   Brad   Which cities did you visit?
   Frances   I visited Sydney and Melbourne.

LESSON 3 P. 151 ....

1
FOR	SINCE
ten minutes	yesterday
two years	March, 2015
an hour	last month
centuries	last week
a long time	five o'clock
ages	1998

2   1 have lived, since   2 has been, since
   3 have known, for, since   4 have wanted, since
   5 have lived, since   6 has owned, for
   7 have/'ve been, since, have/'ve taught, for
   8 have worked, for, since

3   1 have you known   2 have/'ve known
   3 did you, see   4 saw   5 came   6 did he get married
   7 have they known   8 met   9 have been
   10 have you heard   11 haven't heard
   12 has/'s been

4   1 I haven't been to New York for ten years.
   2 We haven't had dinner in a restaurant since my birthday.

3 The last time I had a long holiday was the summer of 2020.

4 I bought this Harley Davidson three years ago.

5 I've been a Manchester City fan since I was five years old.

6 They became best friends a long, long time ago.

7 He was in a club for three hours last night, from 11 to 2 a.m.

8 We haven't had a heavy snowfall since the winter of 2014.

9 Carol and Richard met in 2019 and (they) got married in 2020.

10 They last played tennis together last year.

5   1 Mr. Reed has been teaching Class 3. They have designed a school web page.
   2 The students in Class 2 have been reading their study notes. They have revised things for their exams.
   3 The ICT teacher has been tutoring a small group. They have learned InDesign.
   4 Our English class has been looking at the present perfect. I/We have done this exercise.
   5 The headmaster has been writing end-of-term reports. He/She has nearly finished all the reports.
   6 Mrs. Seath has been revising French irregular verbs. She has read out a list of difficult verbs.

6   1 A   2 A   3 B   4 B   5 A   6 A   7 B   8 B

7   1 **D**   have/'ve been learning
   2 **F**   have/'ve been working
   3 **A**   have/'ve been waiting
   4 **H**   have/'ve been walking
   5 **B**   has been teaching
   6 **C**   have/'ve been trying
   7 **E**   has/'s been playing
   8 **G**   have/'ve been practicing

8   1 [Since when] have you been singing in the school choir?
   2 [Has] it been raining all afternoon [there]?
   3 [How long] have [the kids] been playing?
   4 Have [you] been studying [chemistry]?
   5 [How long] have you been eating [for]?
   6 [What kind of music] have [you] been listening [to]?
   7 [What] have you been doing [this afternoon]?
   8 [Since when] have you been working [on your computer]?

9   1 [I've] been working on this project [for] five days.
   2 [Peter] has/'s been working out in the gym [for] two hours.
   3 [I've been] telling you [over and over again] how to behave.
   4 [It's been] snowing [for] three hours, [since] 9 p.m.
   5 [The boys have] been swimming [for] an hour to train [for their next event].

10   1 Have, ordered; have, ordered
   2 have, been doing; have been sleeping; reading; watching; have you been watching; have been watching

3 's been cooking; has, been cooking; has made
4 haven't looked up; have, been reading; have, finished
5 Have, tried

LESSON 4 P. 159 ....

1 1 A 2 A 3 B 4 A 5 A 6 B

2 1 had, begun 2 got, had, gone
3 had eaten, walked 4 opened, had drunk
5 had, bought 6 came, had not / hadn't seen
7 had, got 8 had not / hadn't studied

3 1 **D** had been looking for 2 **A** had done
3 **H** had had 4 **B** had been
5 **G** had met 6 **C** had attended
7 **E** had been watching 8 **F** had been driving
9 **J** had been tidying 10 **I** had already finished

4 1 had been 2 had been 3 went 4 had
5 had been shouting 6 had been hoping
7 have 8 had been 9 got 10 had been

5 1 had not / hadn't been 2 had 3 'd/had been
looking forward 4 visited 5 'd/had never met
6 (had) organized 7 stayed 8 was 9 'd/had missed
10 was

ROUND UP 9 P. 164 ....

1 1 B 2 C 3 A 4 C 5 B 6 A 7 B 8 C

2 1 have/'ve been 2 has not / hasn't disappointed
3 have/'ve been 4 have already seen
5 have/'ve just come back 6 built 7 got 8 was
9 ate 10 bought 11 have not / haven't had
12 have/'ve always found / always find
13 have/'ve been teaching 14 have/'ve never felt
15 got 16 gave up 17 have/'ve ever done
18 has/'s already got 19 has/'s been telling me /
has/'s told me / tells 20 have/'ve booked

3 1 lived 2 was looking 3 came 4 'd/had found
5 (had) lived 6 couldn't / could not 7 asked
8 were imagining / imagined 9 broke 10 had thrown

4 1 started studying / to study three hours
2 While we were standing
3 I've/have/'d/had ever walked
4 's/has been working on her project since
5 When we got, were already open
6 we got to the theater, had already started.
7 's/has (only) been waiting for a short time
8 've/have (only) worked out little

5 1 got 2 realized 3 had happened 4 had broken
5 opened 6 had been moved 7 'd/had left 8 was
9 'd/had cleared up 10 left 11 phoned
12 'd/had been

6 1 decided 2 did not / didn't have 3 went
4 bought 5 had 6 decided 7 went 8 asked
9 could not / couldn't 10 searched 11 said
12 have/'ve lost 13 said 14 came 15 left
16 found 17 caught 18 went 19 asked

20 was / had been 21 told 22 'd/had lost
23 (had) missed 24 said 25 have/'ve found

7 1 'd/had had 2 ('d/had) interviewed
3 received 4 'd/had been looking 5 arrived
6 took 7 did not / didn't show 8 felt
9 have/'ve been working 10 have/'ve been

8 1 arrived 2 had already closed 3 had 4 was
5 were waiting 6 was 7 was going 8 had told
9 'd/had wanted 10 hadn't / had not left

9 1 danced / were dancing
2 'd/had been practicing 3 took part 4 were
5 were waiting 6 talked / were talking 7 was
8 'd/had never seen 9 had never danced
10 had performed 11 announced 12 had won
13 'd/had never been

Reflecting on grammar

1 F 2 F 3 F 4 T 5 T 6 T 7 T 8 F 9 F 10 T

Revision and Exams 3 P. 168

1 1 into 2 to 3 down 4 to 5 into 6 at 7 on
8 to 9 out of

2 Roy Brooks ~~gets~~ **got** up at 9:00 on Monday, May 11th,
2015 and ~~has~~ **had** breakfast on the terrace of his
penthouse overlooking the bay. He usually has a big
breakfast, but ~~this~~ **that** morning he only ~~has~~ **had** a cup
of green tea.

He ~~feeds~~ **fed** his dogs, two giant black Schnauzers,
and ~~plays~~ **played** with them for half an hour. After
~~washing and getting~~ dressed he **had washed** and (**he
had**) **got dressed**, he ~~leaves~~ **left** home at about 11:00
and ~~drives~~ **drove** to his office downtown. At 11:30, he
~~parks~~ **parked** his car in his office parking lot and ~~takes~~
took the elevator to the 27th floor, where his secretary
~~greets~~ **greeted** him with a cup of coffee.

He ~~doesn't~~ **didn't** have any lunch ~~today~~ **that day**. At
3:00, a South-American man ~~goes~~ **went** into Roy's
office and ~~they talk~~ **talked** for about an hour. Just
before the man ~~leaves~~ **left** the office, Roy ~~is shouting~~
had been shouting some words in Spanish. When the
man ~~leaves~~ **left**, Roy ~~is~~ **was** visibly upset and ~~makes~~
made a few telephone calls.

At 6:00, he ~~takes~~ **took** a taxi to The Fox and Hunter,
a fashionable bar on Columbus Avenue, where his
girlfriend Linda ~~is waiting~~ **had been waiting / was
waiting** for him. They ~~have~~ **had** a Martini, ~~leave~~
left the bar and ~~walk~~ **walked** to a nearby Chinese
restaurant, Chow Mei. They ~~have~~ **had** dinner there and
Roy ~~talks~~ **talked** to the Chinese restaurant manager
for quite a long time. At 10:30, a driver they ~~have~~ **had**
never seen before ~~picks~~ **picked** them up and ~~drives~~
drove them towards the harbor.

3 1 had been sitting 2 had 3 was 4 had been
5 has always been 6 reminded 7 were chatting

4 1 became 2 established 3 housed 4 withdrew
5 fell 6 became 7 were 8 gave 9 invaded

10 established   11 flourished   12 declined
13 entered   14 became   15 helped

5 1 B   2 A   3 B   4 A   5 B   6 B   7 A   8 A   9 A   10 A

6 1 A   2 C   3 B   4 A   5 D   6 A   7 B   8 A   9 B   10 C

7 1 have been our   2 used to be
3 've/have been sitting   4 had been cooking for
5 his favorite cartoons for hours
6 've/have known Susan for ten
7 have/'ve already tidied my
8 have/'ve just seen your sister

Self Check 3 P. 172

1 B	2 B	3 C	4 B	5 C	6 C	7 A	8 C
9 B	10 C	11 B	12 A	13 C	14 B	15 A	16 C
17 B	18 A	19 B	20 A	21 C	22 B	23 A	24 B
25 B	26 B	27 A	28 A	29 C	30 C	31 C	32 B
33 B	34 A	35 B	36 C	37 B	38 C	39 A	40 C

UNIT 10

LESSON 1 P. 174

1

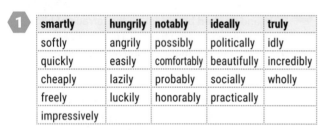

smartly	hungrily	notably	ideally	truly
softly	angrily	possibly	politically	idly
quickly	easily	comfortably	beautifully	incredibly
cheaply	lazily	probably	socially	wholly
freely	luckily	honorably	practically	
impressively				

2 1 well, quickly   2 correctly, perfect   3 good
4 simple   5 beautiful   6 delicious   7 hard, hardly
8 wonderfully

3 1 The computer system was **seriously** damaged
by a virus.
2 Harrison Ford is **totally** unrecognizable in this movie.
3 Your lasagna is good. You always cook it **incredibly**
well. / Your lasagna is **incredibly** good. You always
cook it well.
4 It's **highly** improbable that they will be here
tomorrow.
5 Dear me! It's **terribly** late. I must hurry up.
6 They have been **happily** married for over 20 years.

4 1 quietly   2 hard   3 carefully   4 early   5 easily
6 fast

5 1 Luckily   2 different, hardly   3 angrily
4 Lately, well   5 friendly   6 easily   7 carefully
8 correctly   9 delicious

LESSON 2 P. 177

1 1 I had quite a good result in yesterday's test.
2 Their performance was absolutely perfect.
3 We watched quite an enjoyable movie last night.

4 It's rather late, but the shop is still open.
5 They can dance pretty well.
6 Were there enough chairs for everybody?
7 The hotel was a fairly modern building.
8 This package holiday is way too expensive for
what it offers.

2 1 extremely   2 not very   3 not, at all   4 rather
5 too   6 fairly   7 too   8 enough

3 **basic:** ugly, happy, excited, scared, nice, sad
cold, nervous, angry, afraid
strong: marvelous, astonishing, furious
freezing, fantastic, frantic

4 1 so   2 really   3 quite   4 quite a hard
5 absolutely   6 really   7 such a   8 long enough

5 1 We had a really nice holiday last summer.
2 The palace was so big that we got lost.
3 He is quite a good actor.
4 It isn't warm enough to swim in the lake.
5 It's such a cute little dog.
6 It's rather a dull autumn day.

6 1 He's <u>enough old</u> to cook his own meals.
He's **old enough** to cook his own meals.
2 It's <u>a so exciting</u> thriller. It keeps you on edge
until the end.
It's **such an exciting** thriller. It keeps you on
edge until the end.
3 I could <u>hard</u> understand what she was saying.
I could **hardly** understand what she was saying.
4 The view from the hotel terrace is <u>very amazing</u>.
The view from the hotel terrace is **absolutely amazing**.
5 We bought <u>a quite cheap</u> dishwasher but it broke
after a couple of years.
We bought **quite a cheap** dishwasher but it broke
after a couple of years.
6 My son <u>likes a lot cooking</u>.
My son **likes cooking a lot**.

7 1 too   2 so, hardly   3 really   4 quite   5 much

LESSON 3 P. 180

1 1 a lot of / many   2 many, a lot of   3 much
4 many, many   5 a lot of   6 much

2 1 Too   2 too   3 many   4 much   5 too   6 many
7 too   8 much   9 much   10 much   11 too busy
12 too

3 1 many   2 many   3 much   4 many   5 plenty of
6 All   7 Most   8 enough   9 loads of   10 enough

4 1 There aren't enough sandwiches for all these people.
2 The room isn't big enough for the party.
3 We have seen enough of this movie.
4 He hasn't studied enough to pass this test.
5 Harry isn't old enough to have his own credit card.

5 1 many/enough   2 many/most   3 enough
4 much   5 many, enough   6 most, all

LESSON 4 P. 183 ....

1
1 little 2 a little 3 a few 4 a few 5 a few
6 few 7 a little 8 little

2
1 a few, none 2 much 3 hardly any 4 few
5 a little 6 a lot of 7 a few 8 Not many
9 hardly any 10 none

3
1 B 2 D 3 B 4 C 5 B 6 C 7 B 8 B

4
1 much information 2 warm enough
3 a few ethnic restaurants 4 much traffic
5 much traffic 6 take no risks
7 such an irresistible rhythm

5
1 a little 2 few 3 a little 4 very little 5 many
6 much 7 many 8 a few 9 no

ROUND UP 10 P. 186 ....

1
1 too/very/really 2 really/very 3 absolutely
4 quite 5 such, really/very 6 so 7 at all
8 slightly / a bit 9 slightly / a bit
10 really / rather / very / so / quite / slightly / a bit
11 just/absolutely/really, so

2
1 quietly 2 straight 3 fluently 4 beautifully
5 Luckily 6 well 7 hard 8 enthusiastically
9 unfortunately

3
1 all the 2 the whole 3 all 4 All of 5 all of / all
6 all 7 all / all of 8 The whole

4
1 It's too good to be true.
2 There's too much salt in the soup.
3 There isn't enough sugar in my coffee.
4 There's too much noise in this room.
5 The shops are too crowded on the first day of the sales.
6 There are too many people here today.
7 I haven't got enough money for the ticket.
8 This table isn't large enough.

5
1 some 2 some 3 How much 4 enough
5 any 6 How many 7 some 8 a little 9 finely
10 slowly 11 gently 12 delicious

6
1 very 2 (very) much 3 a few 4 fairly 5 any
6 (very) much 7 very / fairly 8 a few 9 actually
10 a little

7
1 a few 2 quite a 3 All of us 4 the most
5 all 6 quite 7 rather 8 so few 9 a bit
10 especially 11 whole 12 completely
13 slightly 14 definitely

8
1 Unfortunately 2 unpredictable 3 amazing
4 glowing 5 commonly 6 mainly

Reflecting on grammar

1 F 2 F 3 T 4 F 5 T 6 F 7 F 8 T 9 F 10 T

LESSON 1 P. 190 ....

1

形容詞 + er	形容詞 + ier	more + 形容詞
taller	healthier	more intelligent
slimmer	drier	more dangerous
smarter	heavier	more interesting
cheaper	happier	more successful
hotter	luckier	more important
brighter	prettier	more beautiful

2
1 This building is tall. The other one is taller.
2 This suitcase is heavy. The other one is heavier.
3 This T-shirt is cheap. The other one is cheaper.
4 Yesterday was hot. Today is hotter.
5 This boy is clever. The other one is cleverer / more clever.
6 This land is dry. The other (land) is drier.

3
1 cheaper than 2 cleverer / more clever than
3 more difficult than 4 more careful
5 more successful than 6 healthier, healthier
7 warmer, than 8 nicer, than 9 faster
10 kinder, kinder

4
1 far / a lot / much more exciting
2 far / much / a lot quieter 3 darker, darker
4 much / a lot / far more expensive, much / a lot / far more comfortable
5 much / a lot / far hotter 6 thinner, thinner

5 *Possible answers*
1 I think living in a big city is more exciting than living in the country, but living in the country is much cheaper.
2 I think adventure movies are far more exciting than comedies, but comedies are nicer.
3 I think cycling is a lot more tiring than walking, but cycling is much healthier.
4 I think traveling by train is more expensive than traveling by car, but traveling by car is far easier.
5 I think working in an office is more boring than working in the open air, but working in the open air is far more tiring.
6 I think doing yoga is a lot more relaxing than going jogging, but going jogging is much healthier.
7 I think golf is far more relaxing than football, but football is much better.

LESSON 2 P. 194 ....

1
1 Mr. Johnson's lessons are usually less boring than Mr. Riley's.
2 The blue coat is less expensive than the brown one.
3 My suitcase is less heavy than yours.
4 This building is a less modern style than the other one.

5 Today it's less warm than yesterday.

6 This TV series is less exciting than the one on Channel 4.

7 It's less likely to rain this afternoon.

2
1 She's just as beautiful as her sister.

2 Luckily I'm not so/as busy today as I was yesterday.

3 Bob Dylan is as famous as Bruce Springsteen.

4 This article is not so/as interesting as the one in *TIME* magazine.

5 The show was as exciting as a cold rice pudding!

6 Their latest concert was just as good as last year's.

7 The Rolling Stones were as popular as The Beatles in the 1960s.

3
1 Claire is as old as Karen.

2 Today is as hot as yesterday.

3 The blue jacket is not as expensive as the black jacket.

4 Their apartment is not as large as our apartment.

5 The history book is not as big as the grammar book.

6 The Ohio river is not as long as the Mississippi.

7 The Breithorn is not as high as Mont Blanc.

8 Phoenix is not as far from here as Los Angeles.

4
1 Cross-country skiing isn't as risky as alpine skiing or snowboarding.

2 A small tent isn't as comfortable as a campervan.

3 This song isn't as famous as the others on her latest album.

4 Baseball isn't as popular in Italy as football.

5 She hasn't been as successful in her career as her sister.

6 My scooter isn't as sporty as your motorcycle.

LESSON 3 P. 196 ....

1
1 the largest 2 the oldest 3 newest
4 the busiest 5 the most careful
6 the most exclusive 7 the most exciting
8 the smallest

2
1 in 2 of 3 in 4 of 5 of 6 in 7 in 8 of 9 in

3
1 This is one of the most exciting football matches we have ever seen.

2 Mrs. Ray is the most competent teacher I've ever met.

3 This is by far the best career opportunity Jack has ever had.

4 It's one of the most moving stories I've ever read.

4
1 **G** Last night's fireworks display was the most spectacular we had/'d ever seen.

2 **A** This is the biggest pumpkin they have/'ve ever grown.

3 **F** This is the most comfortable armchair I have/'ve ever tried.

4 **B** I have/'ve ever heard.

5 **C** That was the steepest path we had/'d ever walked up.

6 **E** I'm having fun in Ibiza. It's the most exciting holiday I have/'ve ever had.

7 **H** George thought that was the hardest exam he had/'d ever taken.

5
1 best 2 worst 3 oldest 4 farthest 5 best
6 latest 7 eldest 8 last 9 worst 10 farthest

6
1 the least useful thing 2 the least exciting match
3 the least amusing program
4 the least complicated person
5 the least interesting place 6 the least popular resort
7 the least expensive bag 8 the least relevant thing
9 the least flattering outfit 10 the least impressive attempt

LESSON 4 P. 200 ....

1
1 as 2 longest 3 more 4 later, longer 5 more
6 better 7 higher 8 less, than 9 more, more
10 farther, smaller

2
1 I'm sure I can run as fast as you.

2 This term I haven't studied as hard as last term.

3 Paula always works harder than everyone else.

4 The movie festival started later this year.

5 They climbed higher than ever before.

6 The last journey took us longer than usual.

7 He speaks the most quickly when he's nervous.

8 The earlier you leave, the less traffic you'll find.

3
1 Today we have as many guests in our restaurant as we had yesterday, 20. / Yesterday we had as many guests in our restaurant as we have today, 20.

2 We spent as much time to clean the house as (we did) to prepare dinner.

3 The conference room on the second floor has as many seats as the one on the first floor, 50. / There are as many seats in the conference room on the second floor as there are in the one on the first floor, 50.

4 There are as many fish in the aquarium as (there are) in the pond, 12.

5 Italy got as many gold medals as Belarus in the Baku 2015 European Games, ten.

6 Paul has as many elephants statuettes as Lawrence in his collection, 550.

4
1 less 2 more/better than, best 3 less, than, least
4 as much, as 5 as many, as 6 less, than
7 more than 8 less, less, than 9 as much as, more
10 more, than 11 more, than, the most 12 the least

5
1 more, than 2 more, more/less 3 less than
4 a lot more 5 harder/more, than 6 as much as

ROUND UP 11 P. 204 ....

1
1 many, the most 2 lots of, the most
3 a few, fewer 4 little 5 The less, the more
6 More and more 7 less 8 the most 9 few
10 less

2
1 most shaken   2 most harmless
3 most hidden   4 more bent   5 most renowned
6 best known   7 most hopeless   8 more helpful

3
1 A   2 B   3 C   4 A   5 B   6 C   7 A   8 C

4
1 Who jumped ~~the farther~~ **the farthest** in the last event?
2 Your girlfriend was the most elegant ~~in~~ **of** all the girls at last night's party.
3 ~~The most~~ **Most/More** people communicate through social networks these days.
4 Please drive more ~~carefuller~~ **carefully** than usual. There's a baby in the car.
5 Why didn't you study as hard ~~than~~ **as** usual?
6 Always try to do your ~~better~~ **best**.
7 I like this song ~~as~~ **more** than the other one.
8 Their ~~later~~ **latest** CD is much better than the previous one.
9 Which was the ~~worse~~ **worst** experience you've ever had, if I may ask?
10 Don't go any ~~farthest~~ **farther**. It could be dangerous.
11 The more people there are, the ~~loudest~~ **louder** you'll have to shout.
12 As ~~harder~~ **hard** as it seems, it will be worth it in the end.

5
1 the best   2 latest   3 eldest   4 youngest
5 later   6 longer

6
1 A   2 B   3 B   4 A   5 D   6 B   7 C   8 D   9 C
10 B   11 D   12 A

Reflecting on grammar

1 F   2 F   3 F   4 T   5 T   6 F   7 T   8 F   9 F   10 T

UNIT 12

LESSON 1   P. 208 ....

1
1 anything   2 anything/something, Anything
3 nothing   4 something, something   5 nothing
6 something   7 anything   8 something/anything
9 nothing   10 anything

2
1 someone   2 anyone   3 somebody   4 no one
5 anyone   6 anybody   7 anything   8 Nothing
9 Somebody, something   10 nothing
11 anything, nothing   12 something

3
1 John didn't tell me anything about what had happened last night.
2 There wasn't anybody who knew the right answer.
3 If we don't have a car, there's nowhere we can go.
4 We've bought nothing for Emily's birthday yet.
5 I don't have anything new to tell you.
6 I didn't see anybody in town yesterday.
7 We didn't go anywhere on the weekend, we stayed at home.
8 Sorry, there's nothing else I can do for you.

4
1 Nothing   2 anywhere   3 Nobody / No one
4 nowhere   5 Someone/Somebody
6 somewhere   7 anything   8 anyone/anybody
9 anywhere, somewhere   10 something
11 No one / Nobody   12 anyone/anybody

5
1 something of wrong → something wrong
2 aren't doing nothing → aren't doing anything
3 wasn't someone → wasn't anyone/anybody
4 anywhere interesting → anything interesting
5 anything → anyone/anybody
6 Anything other? → Anything else?
7 Let's go anywhere → Let's go somewhere
8 don't want nothing → don't want anything

LESSON 2   P. 211 ....

1
1 either   2 Most of, were   3 all   4 either/both
5 Neither   6 both   7 either   8 all   9 both
10 Either   11 all   12 all

2
1 each   2 both   3 Each   4 Neither, either
5 either, both   6 both   7 either   8 Neither
9 either   10 Neither

3
1 every   2 everyone/everybody
3 Everyone/Everybody   4 everywhere
5 everything, everything   6 everyone/everybody
7 Everything   8 everywhere   9 Every
10 Everyone/Everybody

4
1 ✗ Everyone I know likes reading.   2 ✓
3 ✗ All of them went to the same place for their holidays.   4 ✓   5 ✗ There's free WiFi in every room of the hostel.   6 ✗ If you want everything, you may end up with nothing.   7 ✓   8 ✓

5
1 everywhere   2 everyone/everybody
3 everything   4 both games   5 Most   6 All
7 Neither of us   8 anywhere   9 Both of them
10 Neither of them

LESSON 3   P. 214 ....

1
1 Simon and Rachel often help each other.
2 They didn't listen to each other. Both of them just went on talking.
3 Sally and I have been sending / have sent each other birthday cards for many years.
4 My neighbor and I often look after each other's cats when we're away.
5 Mark and Fiona are madly in love with each other.
6 When we met at the airport, we gave each other a big hug.

2
1 F   2 D   3 J   4 A   5 C   6 B   7 I   8 H   9 G   10 E

3
1 wherever   2 Whoever   3 whatever   4 whatever
5 Wherever   6 whenever   7 Whoever   8 Whatever

4
1 Anywhere you go on this island, you find people enjoying themselves.
2 You can go into any bars or restaurants wearing whatever you like.
3 Just call me any time you want.

4 Anything I cook, he finds something wrong with it.

5 Whoever touches my computer wouldn't dare do so again.

6 Whichever of you wants to work on this project should come to tomorrow's meeting.

7 Some cause happiness wherever they go, others whenever they go.

8 I take my tablet with me anywhere I go.

9 Tell whoever comes that I'm very busy these days.

10 Here's some money for your birthday. Buy whatever you like.

LESSON 4 P. 217 ....

1 1 C 2 H 3 F 4 A 5 G 6 B 7 D 8 E

2 1 yourself 2 myself 3 herself 4 themselves
5 ourselves 6 himself 7 itself 8 yourselves
9 ourselves 10 yourself

3 1 cut himself 2 enjoyed ourselves
3 washed itself 4 bought herself
5 ask yourself 6 found themselves
7 tied himself 8 hurt myself 9 scared themselves 10 cheered herself up

4 1 your 2 by 3 themselves 4 myself 5 himself
6 on 7 herself 8 yourself 9 own 10 herself

5 1 He was by himself all weekend.
2 They did it by themselves.
3 You can work by yourself today.
4 I traveled around France by myself.
5 I have never sung by myself before.
6 You can't leave a baby by itself in the house!
7 He was able to run the firm by himself.
8 I don't mind living by myself in my new apartment.
9 Don't worry. She's used to staying at home by herself.
10 Look at this beautiful cake! I decorated it by myself.

6 1 one 2 one 3 ones, ones 4 one 5 ones
6 one, one 7 one 8 one, ones

7 1 ✗ Lisa must learn to control **herself**. 2 ✓
3 ✗ "I like those boots." "Which **ones** do you mean?"
4 ✗ I always tell the children to wash **their hands** before eating. 5 ✓ 6 ✓ 7 ✗ We really enjoyed **ourselves** at the barbecue party.
8 ✗ Help **yourselves**, guys! There's food for everyone.
9 ✗ The twins hurt **themselves** when their treehouse fell down. 10 ✓

8 1 jacket 2 one 3 one 4 size 5 pants
6 ones 7 pants/ones 8 cake 9 one 10 one 11 one

9 1 the best one 2 a new one 3 A French one
4 Which one 5 another one 6 a similar one

ROUND UP 12 P. 222 ....

1 1 some 2 all 3 someone 4 anyone 5 No one
6 any 7 someone 8 everybody 9 anyone
10 anyone 11 some 12 all

2 1 Both - and 2 Most 3 every 4 Each
5 neither - nor, something 6 each other
7 Nothing 8 Each

3 1 either 2 neither 3 either 4 Neither
5 Neither 6 Either

4 1 **Each** of these sentences contains a mistake. Find it and correct the sentences.
2 Most of the tourists who visit Juliet's house in Verona **leave** a love message.
3 He's new here. He doesn't know **anybody** yet.
4 Everybody **likes** this cake. It's very popular with my family.
5 **Everybody/Everyone**, clap your hands and give our host a warm welcome.
6 Either John **or** Jack must have left his coat behind.
7 You can have **whatever** you like; it's all free.
8 Whoever **wants** to join me on my adventure is welcome.

5 1 wherever 2 Whoever 3 whenever
4 whatever 5 Wherever 6 however

6 1 F 2 D 3 A 4 B 5 C 6 E

7 1 D 2 A 3 C 4 A 5 B 6 D 7 B 8 C 9 B 10 C

8 1 Every 2 whatever 3 something
4 whoever 5 each 6 own 7 any more

9 1 everywhere, somewhere 2 Most 3 own
4 someone, where 5 Wherever 6 another
7 both 8 somewhere 9 anything
10 anything, nothing

10 1 C 2 A 3 C 4 A 5 D 6 C

Reflecting on grammar

1 F 2 T 3 F 4 T 5 T 6 T 7 F 8 F 9 T 10 F

Revision and Exams 4 P. 226

1 1 none 2 Both 3 and 4 quite 5 many
6 Neither 7 nor 8 such a 9 both

2 1 the most exclusive 2 hotter than
3 so/as cold 4 milder 5 farther
6 darker/longer 7 longer/darker 8 tastier
9 fewer 10 the best

3 1 everyone 2 whenever 3 myself 4 somewhere
5 nothing 6 something 7 both 8 anything

4 1 anyone 2 either 3 faster 4 very 5 best
6 more 7 herself 8 anything 9 both 10 all
11 anything 12 ones 13 ones 14 How many
15 Anything 16 much 17 many 18 How much

5 1 each other 2 Everybody 3 lots of 4 both
5 Neither 6 each other 7 Neither 8 each other
9 everybody 10 himself

6 1 A 2 C 3 C 4 D 5 B 6 C 7 A 8 C 7 D 8 A

7 1 Both 2 all 3 quite/very/extremely/rather/really
4 most 5 someone 6 All 7 Everyone/Everybody
8 best

8
1 last day of the crew / movie crew's last day
2 the best in the class
3 the fastest driver   4 is nothing John
5 don't have anything   6 mind either English cheddar
7 a lot of free/empty   8 Each/Every student
9 isn't enough space/room   10 such a funny movie
11 Nobody runs as fast as   12 There isn't anybody

Self Check 4 P. 230

1 B	2 C	3 B	4 A	5 B	6 B	7 C	8 A
9 C	10 B	11 C	12 A	13 C	14 B	15 C	16 B
17 B	18 A	19 B	20 A	21 C	22 A	23 A	24 C
25 B	26 C	27 B	28 A	29 C	30 C	31 C	32 A
33 B	34 A	35 B	36 C	37 B	38 A	39 B	40 C

UNIT 13

LESSON 1 P. 232 ....

1
1 Sam ~~cans~~ **can** ski well because his father is a ski instructor.
2 They might ~~to~~ arrive a bit late tonight.
3 ~~Does he will~~ **Will he** go to university after secondary school?
4 You ~~don't should~~ **shouldn't** go to bed so late every night!
5 ~~Do we may~~ **May we** hand in our assignment next week, Miss?
6 Joe can ~~drives~~ **drive** us to the restaurant. His car's bigger than ours.

2
1 can't   2 Could, could   3 couldn't
4 Can/Could, can't   5 can/could
6 can't, couldn't/can't   7 Could, Could   8 Couldn't
9 can't   10 Can/Could   11 Could

3
1 Can/Could you look after my dog today?
2 Could he walk when he was (13) months old?
3 Can/Could you help me paint the kitchen?
4 Can/Could I have a coffee and some milk, please?
5 Can I drive your car?
6 Can you close/shut the door, please?
7 Can/Could you tell me the way to Euston Station?
8 Could they go on holiday last summer?

4
1 I   2 P   3 R   4 A   5 R   6 A   7 P   8 I

5
1 I'm sorry I won't be able to come to the conference next week. I'll be away on business.
2 I didn't manage to get to the top of the mountain. It was too hard for me.
3 We aren't / We're not allowed to park on this side of the road.
4 Students aren't / are not permitted to smoke in the school grounds.
5 Have you been able to talk to the manager?
6 Will it be possible for us to see the house later this afternoon?

7 We won't be allowed to enter the club. We aren't dressed properly.

LESSON 2 P. 235 ....

1
1 My favorite basketball team may win the championship this year.
2 They may arrive any minute now.
3 We might not go on vacation with our parents next summer.
4 I may not be able to come to your graduation next week.
5 The local council might not organize a summer festival this year.
6 We may not join the drama club this year.

2
1 Maybe your brother knows our new colleague.
2 Perhaps they will / they'll spend next weekend in Paris.
3 It's likely that Tom will leave early tomorrow morning. /
Tom is / Tom's likely to leave early tomorrow morning.
4 Maybe Mary will want to go to the zoo next Sunday.
5 It's unlikely that Melanie will go to John's party if you're not going. /
Melanie is / Melanie's unlikely to go to John's party if you're not going.
6 Perhaps Jim and I will visit the new museum on Saturday morning.
7 It's likely that we will / we'll join the carnival tomorrow if it's sunny. /
We're / We are likely to join the carnival tomorrow if it's sunny.
8 Ben will probably decide to retire next year.
9 Maybe we will not / won't have time to go.
10 My sister is likely to join the yoga club. /
It's likely that my sister may join the yoga club.

3
1 I   2 Pr   3 Pr   4 I   5 W   6 Pr   7 Pe   8 W   9 Pr   10 W

4
1 My friends might organize a barbecue in their garden next Sunday.
2 Peter may not marry Jane. They're so different.
3 Ted and Sue may enjoy their vacation in Florida.
4 Greg may/might buy a new suit for the wedding.
5 We may join our friends in the pub tonight.
6 Lily might not leave Marshall. She still loves him.
7 My father may/might give me some money to buy a present for Jenny.
8 The tourist guide may organize an excursion to the island.
9 Mr. Ross may put off his lesson to next week.
10 The twins might not wear the same clothes at the wedding tomorrow.

LESSON 3 P. 238

1
1 Will you have lunch with me today?
2 Would you like a sandwich, Jack?
3 Would you bring me the menu, please?
4 Will/Would you pass the salt, please, Susan?
5 Will you help me make dinner, please, Harry?
6 Would you like a drink?

2 1 C 2 D 3 B 4 A 5 E

3
1 Mr. Hanley wants Ms. Dell to make an appointment with Ms. Bradley on Tuesday morning.
2 Tom and Claire's parents don't want them to get back late tonight. /
Our parents don't want Tom and Claire to get back late tonight.
3 John's mother doesn't want him to play video games all afternoon.
4 Tess wants Nella to invite David to her party.
5 My brother wants me to lend him ten dollars.

4
1 I wish it would stop raining.
2 I wish it wasn't/weren't so hot.
3 I wish I was/were lying on a beach.
4 I wish I/we could have some snow.
5 I wish I could paint better.
6 I wish I could sing like her.

5
1 We wish our favorite team would win the championship.
2 I wish I were/was 10 cm taller.
3 We wish our neighbors were not / weren't so noisy.
4 Dan wishes he had a brand new car.
5 I wish my husband had more free time.
6 Our teacher wishes he/she could retire at the end of this school year.

6
1 I/We wish we had been luckier!
2 Ben and Karen wish they hadn't gone out trekking in the bad weather.
3 Dinah wishes she hadn't worn her gold necklace last night. /
Dinah wishes she hadn't lost her gold necklace last night.
4 Mike wishes he had gone to university after high school.
5 I wish I hadn't forgotten the appointment with an important customer.
6 I wish they had gone to the club with me. /
I wish I had gone to the club with them. /
I wish they hadn't gone to the club without me.

7 1 D 2 A 3 F 4 B 5 C 6 E

8 *Suggested answers*
1 I wish my girlfriend was/were here.
2 I wish I could go out with my friends tonight.
3 I wish I hadn't eaten raw fish last night.
4 I wish I'd learned to ski when I was young.
5 I wish I could be a pop singer.

LESSON 4 P. 243

1 1 G 2 F 3 E 4 D 5 B 6 A 7 C

2 1 like 2 would like 3 Would, like 4 would like
5 like 6 Do, like

3 1 would prefer 2 would rather 3 would rather
4 would rather 5 would prefer 6 would prefer
7 would rather 8 would prefer

4 1 D 2 F 3 G 4 A 5 B 6 H 7 C 8 E

5
1 I'd like ~~that James washes~~ **to wash** my car. It's so dirty!
2 They would rather ~~spending~~ **spend** the weekend in London than at home doing gardening.
3 He would prefer **to** go to a rock concert. He doesn't like house music very much.
4 Would you like ~~coming~~ **to come** to my birthday party next week?
5 "What would you like to drink?" "I **'d/would** like a soft drink."
6 Do we really have to go out with Ben and Louise? I ~~had~~ **would** rather eat out with you alone.
7 Our instructor would like ~~we trained~~ **us to train** three times a week.
8 It's so cold that I ~~had~~ **'d/would** prefer **to** stay at home tonight.
9 "Would you like ~~sitting~~ **to sit** on the terrace?" "Oh yes, that would be nice."
10 "Do you want to drink some water?" "Well, er . . . I'd rather ~~to~~ have some juice."

ROUND UP 13 P. 246

1 1 can 2 couldn't 3 can't 4 can't 5 can't
6 could 7 can't 8 can 9 can/could 10 can

2 1 can't have been 2 may have gone
3 can't have been 4 can't have been
5 may have arrived 6 can't have been
7 may have finished 8 may have had
9 can't have run 10 may have handed in

3
1 I couldn't help but cry
2 couldn't help telling
3 might be able to help
4 may visit
5 can't have recognized
6 would rather buy
7 wish I could have
8 wishes (that) she'd learned to play
9 may be
10 would prefer to call

4
1 Will you be able to do it?
2 You won't be allowed to come back after midnight.
3 They haven't been allowed to go.
4 You may not be allowed to use your calculator.
5 She has managed to get here on time.
6 It's likely that it will snow tonight.

458

7 I don't know if I will be able to come.

8 She will probably be late.

9 Could you talk to him about his horrible behavior?

10 They might be able to help organize the catering for your garden party.

5 1 He will be able to leave early tomorrow because there's a train at 6:30 a.m.

2 Visitors were only allowed to see / could only see the rooms on the first floor.

3 I was able to fix my bike on my own eventually.

4 I won't be allowed to stay out late in the evening.

5 I won't be able to come, I'm sorry.

6 I see you have managed to make this elaborated chocolate cake.

7 "Have you been able to talk to Mr. Bailey yet?" "No, I haven't."

8 I won't be able to park my car in front of the restaurant.

9 We won't be able to go to Sally's wedding next month.

10 We were likely to go to the Halloween party. / It was likely that we went to the Halloween party

6 1 Ben, Will you dig the garden, please?

2 Would you mind telling/tell me where Castle Street is?

3 Would you wait / mind waiting in the line, please?

4 Would you fasten your seat belts, please?

5 Would you follow me to the elevator, please?

6 Will you go to the football match with me?

7 Will/Would you go to the art exhibition with me, please?

8 Would you sign at the bottom of the form, please?

7 1 She 'd like her mom to make her a big chocolate cake for her birthday.

2 I'd like my parents to book me a cruise.

3 Bill wants his friends to organize a fancy-dress party.

4 My son would like the university to give him a grant to study in Berlin.

5 My brother wants me to lend him my new laptop.

6 The citizens want the city council to build a new indoor swimming pool.

Reflecting on grammar

1 F 2 T 3 T 4 T 5 T 6 F 7 T 8 F 9 F 10 T

UNIT 14

LESSON 1 P. 250 ....

1 1 B 2 D 3 E 4 A 5 F 6 C

2 1 to get up early 2 mustn't talk in the library
3 don't have / need to bring 4 don't have to tell
5 don't have to bring 6 have to hand in your essays

3 1 We had to carry a lot of books to classes.

2 They didn't have to hurry to catch their train.

3 She will/'ll have to work very hard to prepare for the exam.

4 I will/'ll have to buy a new car; mine is very old now.

5 It must have been love!

6 He has had to study all the irregular verbs for the test.

7 I have to mow the lawn every week.

4 1 F 2 E 3 A 4 G 5 C 6 D 7 B

5 *Suggested answers*

1 Do you have to work on the weekends?

2 Must I cut/mow the grass/lawn?

3 Do you have to wear a uniform at work?

4 When do I/we have to hand in my/our project(s)?

5 Can/May I/we sit on these sofas?

6 Do you have to buy/get a new computer?

LESSON 2 P. 253 ....

1 1 needs 2 don't need 3 Do, need 4 need
5 needs 6 needn't 7 didn't need 8 needed
9 Do, need 10 needn't 11 will need / need
12 need

2 1 You may need to reserve a table.

2 They don't need to / needn't go.

3 This coat needs to be dry-cleaned.

4 You don't need to / needn't be there before nine o'clock.

5 All passengers need to be informed about the safety rules.

6 We didn't need to call / needn't have called the doctor for our mother.

3 1 are to show 2 is to talk 3 is to be signed
4 are to vote 5 is to meet 6 Am - to get out

4 1 have to, has to 2 don't need 3 is to 4 need
5 must / have to 6 needs

LESSON 3 P. 255 ....

1 1 D 2 E 3 A 4 C 5 B

2 1 Take the number 15. It's quicker.

2 Let's get some drinks and snacks.

3 No, I've got some. Get some chips.

4 Let's go to the Multiplex.

5 Would three o'clock be okay?

6 You needn't cook tonight. I'll get pizza.

3 1 Shouldn't you be working at the moment?

2 Should I bring a large bag?

3 Shall we watch this DVD?

4 Should I/we bring her some flowers?

5 Shall we ask Mark to our party?

6 Should they walk or (should they) take the bus?

4 1 ought 2 should 3 'd better 4 shouldn't
5 should 6 Shall I

5 1 had better 2 had better 3 ought
4 had better not 5 had better not
6 had better 7 ought not 8 had better

LESSON 4 P. 258 ....

1 1 was due 2 is obliged 3 was forced 4 is due
5 is/was due 6 'm/am forced/obliged

2 1 owe 2 owed/owes 3 was bound
4 owe 5 are bound 6 are/were bound

3 1 due 2 alerted 3 compelled to
4 been forced 5 take off 6 will be obliged

4 1 F 2 E 3 H 4 D 5 B 6 C 7 A 8 G

ROUND UP 14 P. 260 ....

1 1 obligation or necessity
2 deduction
3 permission
4 requests for instructions
5 advice
6 requests for others to do something
7 obligation or necessity
8 prohibition
9 requests to have something

2 1 mustn't tell 2 must fasten 3 must win
4 mustn't forget 5 must drive 6 must book
7 must be 8 mustn't leave 9 must tidy
10 must hurry

3 1 has to 2 had to 3 didn't / did not have to
4 Do/Did, have to 5 had to 6 didn't / did not
have to 7 have to 8 have to

4 1 **D** must   2 **C** don't have
3 **F** must   4 **A** must/should
5 **E** should   6 **B** don't have

5 1 can, mustn't 2 mustn't, can
3 must, don't have to

6 1 doesn't have to drive 2 mustn't walk
3 doesn't have to wear
4 mustn't leave 5 don't have to wash

7 1 must have won 2 must have been
3 must have had 4 must have been
5 must have got up 6 must have cost

8 1 You can't have gone on vacation with no money.
2 There must be a report on yesterday's athletics
competition in the local newspaper.
3 He can't be over 65. He's still working!
4 He must be fit, as he is a PE teacher.
5 There must be some coffee left. I bought it yesterday.
6 You can't have recharged the cell phone battery
last night; it's gone flat already.
7 She can't be her mother; she's far too young.
8 That must have been the manager who just left.

9 1 ought 2 owe, owe 3 should / ought to / must
4 better, should / ought to / must
5 forced/obliged/compelled 6 ought
7 don't have 8 due 9 supposed/allowed
10 shall 11 Should, should 12 obliged/forced

10 1 C 2 C 3 A 4 B 5 A 6 A 7 B 8 C 9 C 10 B

11 1 must 2 have to 3 have to / must
4 have to / must 5 don't have to
6 should/must 7 must 8 due

12 1 Our bus is due to arrive in the next few minutes.
Hurry up!
2 They were forced to leave their home because
of the flood.
3 "How much do I owe you?" "Eight pounds."
4 You'd better to come to work on time if you want to
keep your job.
5 Tess suggested having lunch together tomorrow. /
Tess suggested that we/they (should) have lunch
together tomorrow.
6 You look tired. Shall I to cook for you tonight?

Reflecting on grammar

1 F 2 T 3 T 4 T 5 F 6 F 7 T 8 F 9 T 10 T

UNIT 15

LESSON 1 P. 264 ....

1 1 B/C 2 C 3 B/C 4 C 5 A 6 A

2 1 We are/'re visiting the Tate Gallery at three o'clock.
2 Are you going shopping this afternoon?
3 I am/'m having dinner at a Greek restaurant tonight.
4 What time are you going to work tomorrow?
5 When are you having your exam?
6 We are/'re getting married next Saturday.
7 I am/'m seeing the optician at half past ten tomorrow.
8 They are/'re leaving for New York next week.
9 Who are you meeting at ten o'clock?
10 Where are you having lunch today?

3 1 F 2 P 3 F 4 F 5 P 6 P 7 F 8 P

4 1 get 2 have 3 meet 4 walk 5 visit 6 have
7 have 8 meet

5 1 starts / is starting 2 am/'m going
3 arrive / are / 're arriving 4 are, doing
5 am/'m leaving, leaves 6 is singing
7 am/'m having 8 are/'re spending

LESSON 2 P. 267 ....

1 1 are not / aren't going to work 2 am/'m going to get
3 is/'s going to take 4 Are, going to buy 5 are/'re
going to move 6 are, going to watch 7 is not / isn't
going to apply 8 are, going to live

2 1 **A** going to get married   **B** getting married
2 **A** not working   **B** not going to work
3 **A** going to bring   **B** bringing

3
1 is going to be   2 am going to tell
3 isn't going to do   4 aren't going to change
5 are, going to take

4
1 He is/'s going to be an engineer when he grows up.
2 Get an umbrella. It is/'s going to rain.
3 I am/'m going to plant some fruit trees in my garden this coming spring.
4 We are/'re going to clean out the garage on the weekend.
5 Stop chatting! The lesson is/'s going to start.
6 Look at those grey clouds. It is/'s going to rain soon.
7 Today you are / 're going to work in pairs.

LESSON 3 P. 269

1
1 She will get there by noon.
2 It will not happen again.
3 The sun will set at 7:30 tonight
4 I will always be with you.
5 It will be cold and cloudy / cloudy and cold tomorrow.
6 We will not survive on this money for a whole week.
7 Go ahead, I will follow you.
8 Everything will be ready by three o'clock.

2
1 Will, find, you will   2 Will, work, they won't
3 Will, be, it won't   4 Will, stay, I will
5 Will, have, I won't   6 Will, like, she will
7 Will, win, they will   8 Will, make, they will

3
1 will probably   2 sure   3 will   4 be   5 will be
6 start   7 hope   8 get   9 the game last   10 have

4

樂觀預測	悲觀預測
Unemployment will be higher than now.	Unemployment will be lower.
There will still be wars.	Everybody will have enough to eat.
Air pollution will be worse.	There will be no more wars.
There will still be hunger and poverty.	There will be less air pollution.
There will be new diseases.	There will be a cure for most illnesses.

5 1 E 2 A 3 F 4 H 5 B 6 C 7 G 8 I 9 J 10 D

6
1 I'll always ~~am~~ **be** on your side. You can be sure of this.
2 I don't think it will ~~to~~ rain today.
3 ~~Between~~ **In** five days we'll be at the seaside. I can't wait!
4 We'll be best friends for ~~always~~ **ever**.
5 I'm busy now. I'll talk to you ~~next~~ **later**.
6 The climate will ~~get probably~~ **probably get** warmer in the future.
7 I ~~willn't~~ **won't** fight with my brother again, I promise!
8 Where ~~I will~~ **will I** meet Mr. Johnson?
9 Don't worry. They'll arrive ~~soon~~ **sooner** or later.
10 Do you think you'll be free the day ~~next~~ **after** tomorrow?

7
1 C 2 F 3 E 4 A 5 H 6 B 7 D 8 G
Red: 2, 8, A, B, C, G
Blue: 1, 3, 5, 7, D

LESSON 4 P. 273

1
1 will/'ll be lying   2 will/'ll be relaxing
3 enjoying   4 will/'ll be working
5 will/'ll be cleaning   6 cooking

2
1 **C** Will you be doing
2 **G** Will you be going out
3 **E** will they be going
4 **A** will you be leaving
5 **B** will Robert be having
6 **F** Will you be traveling
7 **D** Will you be using

3
1 will have left   2 will/'ll have taken
3 will/'ll have become   4 will/'ll have learned
5 will/'ll have finished   6 will have disappeared

4
1 will/'ll have finished   2 will/'ll be feeling
3 Will, be reading   4 will/'ll have recovered
5 will be using   6 will/'ll, have eaten

ROUND UP 15 P. 276

1
1 will win   2 I'll carry   3 will set   4 are you meeting, are meeting   5 Will you open   6 will
7 I'll   8 are leaving   9 will come   10 be lying

2
1 am/'m doing   2 Are you going to be
3 will rain
4 will/'ll never come   5 are you going to do
6 am/'m going to buy   7 will win   8 is/'s flying
9 will/'ll meet   10 am/'m having

3
1 will be flying   2 will be   3 will leave
4 will be flying   5 will be flying   6 will arrive

4
1 be feeling   2 have been using
3 be interviewing   4 have finished
5 be eating   6 be doing

5 1 B 2 C 3 B 4 C 5 C 6 A 7 C 8 A 9 B 10 C

6
You   What are you going to do next summer?
Susan I'm going (to go) to Cannes to take a French course.
You   How long will you / are you going to stay there in Cannes?
Susan Three weeks. Would you like to go/come with me?
You   I'd like to, but I have to work this summer.
Susan What are you going to work as, and where are you going to work?
You   I'm going to work as a receptionist in a hotel in Geneva.
Susan I'll bring you a present from Cannes.

7
1 Sarah was going to be an actress when she was younger.
2 I wasn't going to study abroad.

3 They were going to share their apartment with a friend.

4 We were going to have an appointment for the next day, but he didn't turn up.

5 We were going to have the party at the local Youth Club, but it was not available.

6 It looked as if it was going to rain last night, but it didn't .

8 1 be doing 2 be working 3 be 4 Will
5 have moved 6 Will they be 7 will they have
8 have finished 9 be thinking 10 will decide
11 want 12 will 13 be 14 be working 15 will

9 1 By this time tomorrow, I'll **be** hiking in the Alps.
2 *Correct*
3 I hope my children ~~will have been leaving~~ **will be leaving** in a peaceful world.
4 The sea level ~~will be steadily risen~~ **will be steadily rising / will steadily rise** in the next fifty years.
5 *Correct*
6 *Correct*
7 "What ~~will you have done~~ **will you be doing** in ten years' time?"
8 *Correct*

Reflecting on grammar

1 T 2 T 3 F 4 F 5 T 6 F 7 F 8 T 9 T 10 F

Revision and Exams 5 P. 282

1 1 would like 2 studying 3 she's going to apply
4 wouldn't like 5 wants to 6 she'd rather go
7 she's going to learn 8 would prefer 9 has
10 be allowed 11 would like her 12 needs

2 1 am/'m going to have 2 will/'ll ask
3 am/'m going to answer
4 will/'ll probably ask 5 am/'m going to tell
6 will/'ll be 7 will/'ll get

3 1 will/'ll be dealing 2 will/'ll have to
3 Will I have to 4 will/'ll have to
5 Will I have to 6 Will I have to 7 will/'ll have to
8 Did you work 9 worked

4 1 Do, have/need 2 want 3 wants/needs 4 must
5 Do, want/need 6 don't / do not have
7 have/need 8 mustn't / must not 9 had
10 need/have 11 do, have/need
12 don't / do not have/need

5 *Student's own answer*

6 1 B 2 B 3 C 4 B 5 C

7 1 B 2 B 3 D 4 B 5 A 6 C 7 B 8 D 9 C 10 B

8 1 will/'ll have gone 2 am/'m seeing
3 will not / won't have 4 ought to
5 Do you want me to 6 is not / isn't due
7 had/'d better not sunbathe
8 are bound to happen 9 would organize trips out

10 I'd / I would rather stay
11 We don't / do not have 12 I might visit
13 can't be Tom's 14 must be Ben's father
15 you're having an appointment with
16 There's no need

Self Check 5 P. 286

1 B	2 C	3 A	4 B	5 C	6 B	7 C	8 A
9 A	10 B	11 C	12 B	13 B	14 A	15 A	16 C
17 A	18 A	19 B	20 C	21 B	22 B	23 C	24 A
25 B	26 C	27 A	28 A	29 C	30 B	31 B	32 A
33 C	34 A	35 C	36 B	37 C	38 A	39 B	40 C

UNIT 16

LESSON 1 P. 288

1 1 Would you go to the swimming pool with me?
2 It would be better to stay at home today.
3 Jim would not try white-water rafting.
4 I wouldn't go kayaking in this weather.
5 Would you help me lay the table?
6 Would you climb a really / really climb a steep mountain face?

2 1 Wouldn't, help 2 wouldn't, do 3 would, say
4 Would, do 5 would, be 6 wouldn't, accept

3 1 I **hoped** they **would** arrive for the beginning of the movie.
2 They **promised** they **would** call around this week.
3 Ann **thought** she **would/'d** take up rowing.
4 They **knew** they **would/'d** need a lot of training before going trekking in Nepal.
5 Tom **said** he **would** look for a new job soon.
6 We **knew** they **would** fight for their rights.
7 Luke **said** he **would/'d** invite us to try kayaking.
8 Jim **promised** he **would/'d** have a haircut before the wedding.

4 1 We would have liked to go shopping. /
We would have liked to have gone shopping.
2 I might have attended a German course.
3 Would you have spent all that money on a pair of shoes?
4 You should have been more careful.
5 They could have run faster.
6 I wouldn't have driven so fast.
7 We might have bought a new car after the summer.
8 They could have called after the match.

5 1 like 2 taken 3 put off 4 told 5 go 6 rest
7 arrived 8 be

6 1 be working 2 be studying 3 be joking
4 be waiting 5 be traveling
6 be winning 7 be serving 8 be having

LESSON 2 P. 291

1 1 D 2 A 3 G 4 H 5 C 6 B 7 E 8 F

2 1 improves 2 shows 3 like 4 buy 5 opens
6 get 7 feel 8 tell

3 1 rains, will not / won't go
2 will/'ll have, doesn't rain
3 will not / won't have, do not / don't want
4 will/'ll do, ask
5 will/'ll go, find
6 spend, will not / won't have
7 leave, will/'ll get
8 don't study, will not / won't be able
9 come, will go
10 will fall, keeps

4 1 continue, will/'ll be obliged 2 need, will/'ll be
3 competes, will/'ll go 4 snows, will not / won't go
5 mix, get 6 will be, get 7 stops, will/'ll go
8 die, don't / do not give 9 look, get
10 will/'ll get, don't / do not do

LESSON 3 P. 293

1 1 would 2 wouldn't 3 broke 4 could
5 wouldn't 6 would be

2 1 tried, enjoy 2 lived, would 3 would have, didn't
4 wouldn't, knew 5 go, wouldn't be
6 didn't study, wouldn't 7 wouldn't, could
8 weren't, would go

3 1 had 2 worked 3 would tell 4 was/were
5 didn't turn up 6 would/'d travel 7 could 8 felt
9 would you do 10 arrived

4 1 would be, got 2 would dye, allowed
3 improved, would be 4 didn't have, would I do
5 Would you buy, didn't cost
6 wouldn't go, didn't look after
7 knew, would/'d ring 8 won, would/'d - give
9 were, wouldn't trust 10 found, would/'d take
11 would/'d be, didn't / did not invite
12 would/'d have, was/were

5 1 **D** Type 1 2 **G** Type 3 3 **A** Type 2 4 **F** Type 3
5 **B** Type 1 6 **C** Type 3 7 **H** Type 2 8 **E** Type 3

6 1 hadn't made, would/'d have got
2 would/'d have worn, had/'d told
3 had/'d known, would not / wouldn't have ordered
4 would/'d have washed, 'd/had read
5 would not / wouldn't have broken, had/'d stayed
6 had invested, would/'d have made

7 1 If I went out tonight, my parents would be angry.
2 If I had/'d had my car yesterday, I could have gone to the mall.
3 If my mom (would) let me, I would/'d love to have a tattoo.
4 If I got on with my brother, I would/'d see him.

5 If I was/were rich, I could buy a big house.
6 If she hadn't / had not gone to the party, she would not / wouldn't have met her future husband.

LESSON 4 P. 297

1 1 **E** can 2 **A** may 3 **F** may
4 **B** can 5 **C** may 6 **D** may

2 1 could 2 would/'d have to 3 might
4 would/'d have to 5 would/'d like to
6 could 7 could 8 might

3 1 would/'d have liked, hadn't / had not spent
2 hadn't / had not left, would/'d have had
3 'd/had waited, 'd/would have been
4 might/would have visited, had been
5 could/might/would have won the race, 'd/had trained
6 should have told, knew
7 'd/would have reported, 'd/had known
8 might have been, hadn't / had not left

4 1 E 2 D 3 F 4 C 5 A 6 B

5 1 "Would he have passed his driving test?"
"Yes, if he'd practiced more often."
2 "Would they have enjoyed white-water rafting?"
"Yes, if they hadn't been so scared."
3 "Would the team have won the competition?"
"Yes, if one of them hadn't hurt his/her/their leg."
4 "Would you have sailed to the island yesterday?"
"Yes, if we'd known it would be windy. / was going to be windy."
5 "Would she have gone to Sally's party?"
"Yes, if she'd known (that) Peter was there."

6 1 had been able to, would have told, would be
2 had had to, wouldn't have accepted
3 was/were obliged, would choose, would play
4 had been / were able to, would have tried
5 had worked, could have got
6 could have found, would/might have been able to

7 1 E 2 D 3 B 4 C 5 A *Student's own answer*

8 1 book 2 will get 3 booked 4 would get
5 had booked 6 would have got

9 1 shouldn't, should 2 would, could 3 would
4 wouldn't 5 should, would/could
6 could, wouldn't 7 would, could

10 1 If he went to the opera, he would certainly enjoy it.
If he had gone to the opera, he would certainly have enjoyed it.
2 You wouldn't spend too much if you bought things in the sales.
You wouldn't have spent too much if you had bought things in the sales.
3 They would talk to him if they saw him.
They would have talked to him if they had seen him.

4 If you had a day off, we would go on a trip to the lake. If you had had a day off, we would have gone on a trip to the lake.

5 If she didn't turn up on time, we would leave without her. If she hadn't turned up on time, we would have left without her.

6 If you tried hard, you would certainly succeed. If you had tried hard, you would certainly have succeeded / have certainly succeeded.

11 1 You should have <u>told</u> me that you were not coming.

2 If I <u>had</u> brought my packed lunch with me, I would have shared it with you.

3 If you <u>liked</u> Japanese food, you would try the sushi in this restaurant. / If you like Japanese food, you <u>should</u> try the sushi in this restaurant. It's excellent!

4 What do you suggest I <u>could</u> do to improve my English?

5 If I had <u>had</u> more time, I would have prepared something special for dinner.

6 I was afraid she <u>might not</u> love me any more.

7 What would I <u>have done</u> if I had been you? / What would I do if I <u>was/were</u> you? I just don't know! You should ask someone else.

8 I would <u>have</u> thanked them for their great hospitality if I had seen them.

ROUND UP 16 P. 302 ....

1 1 I wouldn't have told him a lie.

2 You should have been more careful!

3 He could have helped you.

4 They can't/couldn't have been so silly!

5 She may/might have known the truth.

6 I'd have liked to see them / I'd like to have seen them.

7 Which one would you have chosen?

8 They might have been lucky.

9 It can't/couldn't have been Doug!

2 1 is going to melt

2 am not going to read / won't be reading

3 are going to stop

4 am going to read

5 will be leaving / am going to leave

6 are going to watch / will be watching

7 will be having / are going to have

8 am going to book / will be booking

9 are going to build

10 am going to make / will be making

3 1 rise 2 will become 3 will melt 4 melts
5 will rise 6 will be 7 don't find 8 don't limit
9 will increase 10 continues 11 will become
12 won't be able

4 1 Should I arrive late, please save a seat for me.

2 Should I decide to go, I'll let you know.

3 Had we enough money, we would buy this car.

4 Had they any children, they wouldn't be able to go out every evening.

5 Should it rain hard, we wouldn't go out.

6 Had they traveled more, they would be more open-minded.

5 1 don't 2 want 3 are 4 might 5 would
6 open 7 be 8 could

6 1 would have left 2 would choose 3 would take
4 would play 5 didn't pass 6 would be
7 would have slept
8 would have known / would know

7 1 would have happened 2 had won
3 Would the American colonies have been
4 had ruled 5 had been 6 had won
7 would have been speaking
8 would have backed
9 would have gained
10 Would the French Revolution have broken out
11 wouldn't have studied 12 will be

8 1 can, have 2 try, 'll, know
3 give, will be, teach, will be
4 have, have, will, have, have, have, will have
5 wasn't/weren't, would, be 6 judged, would live

Reflecting on grammar

1 T 2 T 3 T 4 F 5 F 6 T 7 T 8 T 9 T 10 F

UNIT 17

LESSON 1 P. 306 ....

1 1 Sports equipment is sold in this store.

2 Designer clothes are made in this factory.

3 Cars aren't produced here any more.

4 The national anthems are played before each game.

5 French, German and Italian are spoken in Switzerland.

6 Prizes are given to all winners.

7 Computers are used in the marketing lessons.

8 The orchestra is directed by a very young woman.

9 He is considered a real math genius!

10 The United Kingdom is made up of Scotland, England, Wales and Northern Ireland.

2 1 Is the movie directed by Steven Spielberg?

2 Are school uniforms paid for by the families?

3 The notice is not / isn't written in my language.

4 Dice are not / aren't used for this game.

5 Is Spanish taught in their school?

6 These sunglasses are not / aren't made in Italy.

7 Is the UNO Tower made of glass and steel?

3 1 Coffee is ground and then (it is) packed into tins.

2 These bags are made in Florence.

3 Carnival is celebrated in February.

4 The rooms are cleaned by Mrs. Jones every morning.

5 Where are these tomatoes imported from?

4 1 is played 2 is being played 3 are specified
4 are being built 5 is included
6 is being refurbished 7 are being raised
8 is being served

5 1 is transformed 2 is chewed 3 is swallowed
4 is mixed 5 is completed 6 is called
7 are not / aren't needed 8 are expelled

6 1 are invited 2 are asked 3 are filed
4 is forbidden 5 be borrowed 6 are fined

LESSON 2 P. 309

1 1 were written 2 was named 3 were explored
4 was conquered 5 was defeated
6 was designed 7 was invented 8 was created
9 was built

2 1 Who was *The Last Supper* painted by?
2 When was the first Liverpool to Manchester railway opened?
3 Who was replaced by Miss Ross in the English class yesterday?
4 What was your first dog called?
5 How many languages was his novel translated into?
6 How were the glasses packed? Where were they shipped to?
7 Who was *Brick Lane* written by?

3 1 The Walt Disney Company created both Mickey Mouse and Donald Duck.
2 Thomas Edison invented the light bulb.
3 They were repairing the main road, so we came by a different route.
4 They built higher walls in New Orleans after Hurricane Katrina destroyed part of the city.
5 The storm damaged lots of cars last night.
6 The rock star's fans cheered him all the way to his hotel.
7 They arrested Rosa Parks in Montgomery, Alabama, in 1955 because she had sat in a bus seat reserved for white people.
8 They called an ambulance immediately after the accident.
9 They made a mistake.

4 1 has been inaugurated 2 was opened
3 Has she ever been invited 4 was chosen
5 has been repaired 6 has just been cleaned
7 has not / hasn't been announced
8 was released 9 was stolen

5 1 Have, been
2 had been canceled
3 has not / hasn't been repaired
4 has not / hasn't been reached
5 has been announced

6 had, been done, had been cooked, had been set, had been decorated

7 have been reserved

8 had been made

LESSON 3 P. 312

1 1 is not / isn't going to be appointed
2 will be taken 3 will have been chosen
4 are/'re going to be asked
5 will not / won't be published 6 will be released
7 are going to be sold 8 will be held

2 1 You will certainly be declared innocent.
2 His next movie is going to be filmed in New Zealand.
3 The rooms of the old mansion will be redecorated next year.
4 An interesting exhibition is going to be opened later this month.
5 A concert will be organized in his memory.
6 This old building is going to be demolished.
7 Who's going to be chosen for the main role in the musical?
8 The names of the winners will be announced tomorrow.
9 A traditional meal with local wines will be served to everyone.
10 I think your proposal will be taken seriously.

3 1 must not 2 can/could 3 must 4 may/can
5 can/could/may 6 couldn't 7 would

4 1 The apples should be cut into halves.
2 The car needs to be washed today.
3 The ball can't be touched with the hands in soccer.
4 I should have been informed!
5 Your application form might have been lost.
6 An agreement ought to be reached.
7 Dinner might be served in the garden this evening.
8 It can't have been made in three minutes.

5 1 Can a boat be hired for the lake?
2 Must all expenses be paid in advance?
3 Can a little butter be added to the sauce?
4 Should everyone be punished?
5 Can it be cooked in the microwave?

6 1 Your essay should have been written more carefully.
2 We might have been invited to his party.
3 The onions should have been chopped more finely.
4 They might have been chosen for the part.
5 We should have been informed about any problems.

7 1 D 2 B 3 G 4 H 5 F 6 C 7 A 8 E

LESSON 4 P. 315

1 1 give → given 2 were → was 3 ✓
4 offer → offered 5 ✓ 6 ✓ 7 credit → credited

2 1 She was sent red roses.
2 Susan was told a nice story.

3 We were sent an invitation to the opening of a new shop.

4 We were granted a 30% discount on last year's clothes.

5 Paul was shown the cathedral by the bishop.

6 Caroline was asked to pick him up at the airport.

7 The children were given some nice illustrated books.

8 I was taught how to model clay.

3 1 They told us 2 They were known to be
3 You are supposed to be 4 He was found to be
5 painting is considered to be
6 villa is said to belong

4 1 PR 2 PA 3 PR 4 PA 5 PR 6 PR 7 PR 8 PA

5 1 has been credited 2 was 3 had been taught
4 ran 5 was devastated 6 was given

6 1 Martha Miller is thought to be an interesting artist.

2 John Landis was thought to be / have been a rich art dealer.

3 The stolen painting is supposed (by the police) to have already been sold.

4 Their works are known to be the most expensive in the gallery.

5 The painter is known to be / have been given a new canvas and some watercolors.

6 The fakers are supposed to have moved to South America by now.

7 The owner of the art gallery is believed to be very wealthy.

7 1 D 2 F 3 A 4 B 5 C 6 E

8 1 I want to get these photos printed.

2 She must get her jacket dry-cleaned.

3 I need to get this shirt ironed.

4 We need to get our computer repaired.

5 My mom wants to have the kitchen extended.

6 My parents want to have a new satellite dish installed.

7 Laura must have her nails manicured before the wedding.

8 She must have a hole in her tooth filled.

9 I need to get the car washed.

10 We must get the grass cut this weekend.

ROUND UP 17 P. 320 ....

1 1 主動語態、過去進行式
2 被動語態、過去完成式
3 被動語態、未來完成進行式
4 主動語態、條件句過去式
5 主動語態、現在完成進行式
6 主動語態、簡單過去式
7 被動語態、過去be going to未來式
8 被動語態、簡單未來式

2 1 washes, washing, washed
2 cuts, cutting, cut
3 lives, living, lived
4 writes, writing, wrote, written

5 enjoys, enjoying, enjoyed

6 cries, crying, cried

7 comes, coming, came, come

8 spends, spending, spent

9 sees, seeing, saw, seen

10 says, saying, said

3 1 is being sent 2 was - rewarded
3 had been lost 4 will be spent
5 were being served 6 have been demolished

4 1 All your emails will be replied to.

2 The children will be looked after by a new babysitter tonight.

3 This song has been played a hundred times on the radio today.

4 The schedule might have been changed.

5 Their car is going to be sold.

6 Big dams are being built in Venice.

7 The equipment in the science lab must not be used by students without permission.

8 A charity concert has been organized by the club members.

5 1 Hot meals were served at all times in the restaurant.

2 The cake had to be stored in a cool place.

3 Very good bargains could be found on Prime Day.

4 This dish was prepared in the traditional way.

5 All of the carpets were hand-woven in Morocco.

6 The sauce needed to be prepared in advance.

7 The scarves in the shop window were all hand-painted.

8 The bags and belts were made of real leather.

6 1 He was offered a movie contract. / A movie contract was offered to him.

2 You will be sent two copies of the contract. / Two copies of the contract will be sent to you.

3 New students are shown the syllabus. / The syllabus is shown to new students.

4 The children are going to be taught a nursery rhyme. / A nursery rhyme is going to be taught to the children.

5 She has been awarded with an Oscar. / An Oscar has been awarded to her.

6 Each council member was passed a folder of documents. / A folder of documents was passed to each council member.

7 Sara has been told the story of this strange room. / The story of this strange room has been told to Sara.

8 The children are being given some snacks for the break. / Some snacks are being given to the children for the break.

7 1 the oven be switched off?

2 was *Julius Caesar* written by?

3 was this song composed by?

4 was she given the prize?

5 can be done now?

6 languages are spoken here?

7 his paintings be sold (at the next auction)?

8 this apartment going to be rented?

8 1 devastated 2 repaired 3 cleaned up
4 cut, dyed, restyled 5 done 6 washed, ironed

9 1 The students were ~~gave~~ **given** some new books.
2 ~~Have~~ **Were** the stadium gates opened at 6 p.m. for the concert?
3 The Sagrada Familia ~~were~~ **was** designed by Antoni Gaudi.
4 The movie will be ~~was shooted~~ **shot** in Central Italy.
5 The dog was supposed to **be** missing.
6 A radio station ~~has~~ **was** established by Marconi on the Isle of Wight.

Reflecting on grammar

1 F 2 F 3 F 4 T 5 T 6 F 7 T 8 T 9 F 10 T

UNIT 18

LESSON 1 P. 324

1 1 who 2 which 3 who 4 who 5 which 6 who
7 which 8 who

2 1 That is the lady who ~~she~~ owns the flower shop in the High Street.
2 Aren't these the earrings ~~for that~~ **(that)** you've been looking **for** for ages? / Aren't these the earrings for ~~that~~ **which** you've been looking for ages?
3 The doctor ~~for who~~ **whom** you're waiting has just arrived. / The doctor ~~for who~~ **(whom)** you're waiting **for** has just arrived.
4 I'm sure this is the boy ~~which~~ **whose** father works in the bank next to my office.
5 Can't you see that car? The one ~~who~~ **which/that** is parked in front of that gate?
6 Isn't he the artist ~~which~~ **(that/whom/who*)** we met at yesterday's opening in Leo's art gallery?

Although whom is correct here, who would be used in most colloquial situations.

3 1 (who) 2 – 3 (that) 4 – 5 – 6 –, –
7 (which) 8 (that)

4 1 (who) 2 (which) 3 who 4 whose 5 (which)
6 whose 7 which 8 which

5 1 The friend I usually play tennis with has broken his arm falling off his bike.
2 The colleagues my mother works with gave her a beautiful necklace on her birthday.
3 The e-book we were talking about yesterday got an important award.
4 The café we are going to tonight was opened two hundred years ago!
5 Jack and Beatrix are going to buy the house they have been dreaming of for a long time.
6 The document I had been looking for for two days was in a drawer in my office.
7 The colleague I travel to work with every day is ill this week.

8 The large order we have been looking forward to has finally arrived.

6 1 That is the boy whose father is a renowned web designer.
2 The phone call I was waiting for came too late.
3 He's the man you saw at the pub last night.
4 This is the new scanner I'm going to buy.
5 That's the history teacher who gives us a lot of homework.
6 This is the lady who gave me her old digital camera.
7 The car which/that was found near the park is Mr. Beckett's.
8 The house Carol lives in is really smart.

7 1 Comfort food is a kind of food that/which makes you feel better, like chocolate and cookies.
2 Skydiving is a sport in which you jump from a plane and fall a long way down before opening your parachute.
3 A skydiver is a person who does skydiving.
4 A hoverboard is an electric scooter that/which is used in pedestrian areas.
5 A drone is an aircraft without a pilot that/which is controlled from the ground.
6 Paintball is a game in which people shoot balls of paint at each other.
7 A QR Code is a type of matrix barcode that/which consists of black modules arranged in a square grid that / which can be read by a camera or a scanner.
8 A crocoburger is a hamburger that/which is made with crocodile meat.

LESSON 2 P. 328

1 ***Non-defining clauses:***
1 The Sullivans, who live opposite us, have just bought a new car.
2 My washing machine, which is quite old, keeps breaking down.
4 My son's friends, who are often at our house, are very pleasant young people.

Sentences 3, 5, 6 and 7 are defining clauses and do not need commas.

2 1 whose 2 who 3 who 4 whom/who
5 which 6 whom/who 7 who 8 which

3 1 Our French teacher, who/whom we all liked very much, retired last month
2 Mr. and Ms. Martin, who/whom I met in Spain last summer, are a married couple.
3 That is a self-portrait which/that my father painted 20 years ago.
4 Do you know the name of that model whose photo was on the front cover of Vanity Fair last week?
5 Mr. Owen, who I work for / for whom I work, is the financial manager of our company. /
I work for Mr. Owen, who is the financial manager of our company.
6 I've got two younger sisters who I get on well with / with whom I get on well.

7 *Cats*, which has been on in theaters all over the world for years, is a very famous musical. /
Cats, which is a very famous musical, has been on in theaters all over the world for years.

8 I hate novels which/that tell silly love stories.

9 The friends I study with every day are very good at math and help me a lot. / The friends with whom I study every day are very good at math and help me a lot. / The friends whom I study with every day are very good at math and help me a lot.

10 The desk I work at is stacked with books and papers. / The desk at which I work is stacked with books and papers. / The desk which I work at is stacked with books and papers.

LESSON 3 P. 330 ....

1
1 All 2 what 3 all that 4 what 5 why 6 how
7 what 8 where 9 when 10 where 11 why
12 in which

2
1 how 2 why 3 (that/where) 4 (that)
5 (when/that) 6 (that) 7 when 8 where
9 where 10 why

3
1 Everybody liked the food I had cooked, which was quite surprising.
2 Connie passed her driving test, which she didn't quite expect.
3 They didn't come to the concert, which was a shame.
4 Sam will have to work next Sunday, which is quite unusual.
5 A lot of students in our school do voluntary work, which is really admirable.
6 Quite a number of start-up companies have opened in our town, which is good news.

4
1 Why don't you tell me all ~~which~~ **that** you know?
2 Give me one reason ~~because~~ **why** I should help them.
3 This is the place ~~on~~ **in which / where** I saw the accident.
4 An Indie Market is a place ~~in~~ where all the traders are independent.
5 Why don't you tell me ~~way~~ **how** you solved the problem?
6 This is the time ~~at~~ **when / at which** the ghost is said to appear in the Big Hall.
7 I couldn't see ~~that which~~ **what** she was wearing under her coat.

LESSON 4 P. 332 ....

1
1 standing 2 two people cycling 3 sitting
4 his mom buying something
5 playing football

2
1 Feel 2 hear 3 tastes 4 watched 5 smell
6 heard

3
1 I heard the kids laughing.
2 I smelled something sweet baking / being baked.
3 I saw two men open the door of the bank.
4 He felt a cold wind blowing in the street.

5 I noticed two people leave the room before the end of the lecture.
6 We saw the waiter drop a pile of plates.
7 I didn't hear anyone/anybody knock at the door.
8 I heard the girl playing the violin.

4
1 crash 2 standing 3 gossiping 4 burning
5 call/calling 6 waiting

5
1 He was seen throwing stones.
2 She was heard singing a beautiful song.
3 They were heard opening the garage door late at night.
4 Someone was noticed walking up and down the street.
5 He was heard to whistle.
6 You have been seen copying during the exam.
7 Some young people were noticed hanging around late last night.
8 Jack was seen to get on a train at the station.
9 The baby was heard crying at night.
10 They were heard laughing like mad.

6
1 Draw a picture of one of the animals mentioned in the story.
2 The news was in an article published in a local magazine.
3 We're going to rent an apartment overlooking the sea.
4 The path leading to the waterfall is very steep.
5 My friend's notes, taken at the conference, were very clear.
6 Try to explain the words highlighted in the text.
7 Do you know the lady sitting in the last row?
8 Do you know that girl eating an ice cream?

7
1 This is the e-book that/which was illustrated by my father.
2 There were lots of kids who were playing games on the web.
There are more and more people who are using open-source software.
4 I met Linda when/while she was looking for a new digital camera in the store.
5 There was a dark spot that/which was covering the PC screen.
6 He was looking at the images that/which were printed in color.
7 They usually double-check the information that/which is found on Wikipedia.
8 This is the new software that/which was created by a group of students aged 16.

ROUND UP 18 P. 336 ....

1
1 C 2 F 3 A 4 B 5 D 6 E

2
1 who 2 whom/who 3 who 4 who 5 which
6 whose 7 who/whom 8 which 9 which 10 whose

3
1 The text I was working with suddenly vanished from the screen.

2 Who are the people you are waiting for?

3 The house they live in is super technological.

4 The people she went to the meeting with went home early.

5 The e-book we were talking about got an important award.

6 The music you are listening to is played by the London Symphony Orchestra.

7 The kind of life they had got used to was going to change.

8 The baby I looked after last summer is now nearly one year old.

4 1 There are moments in which I would like to live on a desert island.

2 This is the university at which both my husband and I studied years ago.

3 I don't know the reason for which she left her job.

4 Last Friday was the day on which we moved to the new office.

5 Three o'clock is the time at which you can meet the sales manager.

6 Unfortunately there isn't a place in/at which you can camp near here.

7 The country in which they speak Urdu is Pakistan.

8 Can you give me a good reason for which I should have a healthier life?

5 1 This is a hut we stayed in for the night / where we stayed for the night.

2 This is a hot chocolate (which/that) we drank to make ourselves warm.

3 This is the view (which/that) we had from the top of the mountain.

4 This is a little lake where we stopped for a picnic.

5 These are my trekking boots, which were muddy at the end of the day.

6 This is the mountain peak (that/which) we could reach.

7 These are our friends who climbed the mountain with us.

8 This is our guide, who led us to the top.

9 This is a marmot (which/that) we saw in a meadow.

6 1 which is broadcast
2 who are always directed
3 which are mostly composed
4 which usually come
5 which is accompanied
6 which are set

7 1 Things are not always done the way I like.

2 I'm the one who spoke to you on the phone yesterday.

3 "Goodbye Mr. Holland" is a good movie which came out in 1995.

4 A hero is someone who does his duty every day.

5 She is the girl whose mother is a famous painter.

6 Is this the present which Dad bought for you?

8 1 – 2 (which) 3 (whom) 4 – 5 (which) 6 –
7 (which) 8 –

9 1 That was all (that) we could do.

2 I'm so curious. Tell me <u>what</u> you know.

3 He's the one (<u>that/who/whom</u>) I was waiting for.

4 We're leaving tomorrow, <u>which</u> makes me very sad.

5 My house is the place <u>in which/where</u> I most like to be.

6 Come and see those girls <u>who/that</u> are dancing so well.

7 Cupertino is the town Apple has its headquarters / <u>in which</u> Apple has its headquarters. / <u>where</u> Apple has its headquarters.

8 Tigers are animals <u>which/that</u> are in danger of extinction.

10 1 who 2 which 3 whose 4 who/whom
5 which/that

11 1 Our rep, whom/who you met last week, will offer you favorable contracts.

2 The technician who has repaired my computer is really good.

3 Tom, who I am studying with today, is a whiz at IT!

4 The homepage which was created by one of our programmers is updated every week.

5 The printer (that) we have in our office is also a scanner and a photocopier.

Reflecting on grammar

1 T 2 T 3 F 4 T 5 F 6 F 7 F 8 T 9 T 10 T

Revision and Exams 6 P. 340

1 1 want 2 would/'d buy 3 pay 4 have 5 get
6 'd/had known 7 had/'d managed

2 **Three languages are taught** in my school: French, German and Spanish. I'm learning one, German. **We are made to work very hard by Ms. Hofer, the German teacher:** of course, **only German must be spoken** during her lessons. **We are given lots of grammar exercises** to do every day. **We are also asked** to read a new book and write a review of it every month, then **each of our reviews is discussed** in the class. **Good results can be obtained** with Ms. Hofer only if you study really hard. If you want to learn a language very well, the best thing to do is go to a country where **it is spoken**. But **a language can be learned** quite well in school too, if you have a teacher like mine!

3 1 living 2 come 3 getting 4 getting
5 say/saying 6 looking 7 leading 8 sitting
9 waiting

4 1 B 2 C 3 A 4 B 5 B 6 C 7 A
8 B 9 D 10 B

5 1 what 2 where 3 who/whom
4 –/that/which 5 where 6 where 7 which
8 where 9 who 10 –/that/which
11 –/that 12 which/that

6 1 which was begun by France and Britain in 1987
2 only seven years to finish the Eurotunnel.

3 officially opened by Queen Elizabeth II and French President François Mitterand

4 in commercial service was started first

5 which came later that year, was started on December 22nd,

6 was named "Top Construction Achievement of the 20th Century" in March 1999.

7 1 who 2 had 3 wouldn't 4 be 5 which
6 which 7 if 8 hadn't 9 were 10 were

Self Check 6 P. 344

1 A	2 B	3 C	4 B	5 B	6 A	7 C	8 A
9 A	10 C	11 A	12 B	13 A	14 C	15 B	16 A
17 B	18 C	19 B	20 C	21 B	22 C	23 C	24 B
25 C	26 B	27 A	28 A	29 C	30 C	31 C	32 A
33 B	34 A	35 C	36 C	37 B	38 A	39 C	40 B

UNIT 19

LESSON 1 P. 346

1 1 Tell 2 say 3 Say 4 telling 5 tell 6 say
7 Say 8 tell

2 1 her 2 to him 3 she said 4 not to be late
5 says 6 me 7 said 8 told us

3 1 I was told to wait until they came back.
2 She is said to be a great artist.
3 We were told to reach the conference room before nine.
4 The lecturer is said to be one of the best in his field.
5 The Board of Directors was/were told to meet in the afternoon.
6 Serena Williams is said to be one of the best tennis players ever.

LESSON 2 P. 348

1 1 She told them to wait for the coach in the car park. / (that) they should wait for the coach in the car park.
2 She told them to walk in a line while they were in town. / (that) they should walk in a line while they were in town.
3 She told them to hold their friend's hand when they crossed the street. / (that) they should hold their friend's hand when they crossed the street.
4 She told them not to walk around on their own. / (that) they shouldn't walk around on their own.
5 She told them to bring their packed lunch. / (that) they should bring their packed lunch.
6 She told them not to forget to bring an anorak and a hat. / (that) they shouldn't forget to bring an anorak and a hat.
7 She told them to wear comfortable shoes. / (that) they should wear comfortable shoes.

8 She told them to remind their parents to pick them up at 6 p.m. in front of the school. / (that) they should remind their parents to pick them up at 6 p.m. in front of the school.

2 1 asked 2 reminded 3 advised 4 ordered
5 warned

3 1 Mike advised me/us to use sunscreen in this heat.
2 The ranger reminded the visitors not to feed the animals.
3 The teacher told the children to stop making so much noise.
4 The police warned the drivers not to drive up the mountain in that snow.
5 The receptionist advised the hotel guests to leave their valuables in the hotel safe.

4 1 says, look 2 thinks, has passed 3 would like
4 says, will be 5 going 6 dates back

5 1 's/has just found 2 she wants, she finishes
3 I need, I want my dreams 4 he's / he is going
5 the next test is on Monday, October 11th

6 1 she quite likes 2 she's / she has made
3 she went to see 4 she's / she has 5 been out
6 She's / She has bought
7 it's / it is quite windy there
8 she isn't / is not coming back
9 she's / she has got to study
10 she'll come back 11 will be away
12 you'll be 13 will call her 14 hello to you

LESSON 3 P. 351

1 1 she wouldn't / would not be back, the next/ following day
2 their, would be, (that) they'd/would be going
3 she had spent her, earlier/before
4 he would phone me the following/next day, he arrived
5 he had booked his, the previous week / the week before

2 1 they had been to a new Thai restaurant the previous Saturday / the Saturday before, had been really good.
2 Jane said to me she always travels by herself and added that way she's more open to meeting new people.
3 I told my secretary I was going to leave earlier the following/next day.
4 They said they had been to the museum that morning.
5 The receptionist told us she/he was afraid she/he wouldn't be able to get seats for that night's show.
6 Mom said she couldn't go to bed early that night and added she still had a lot of work to do.

3 1 was 2 wrote 3 sounded 4 said 5 were
6 were 7 could 8 move 9 got 10 has lived

4 1 The law in 1865 stated that slavery was abolished all over the United States.

2 The suspect claimed that he was at home all day on June 1st and added that he hadn't seen anyone except for his wife.

3 The physics teacher explained yesterday that the speed of a body is the distance it covers over a period of time.

4 Critics remarked that the famous composer's new symphony was not very original.

5 *Possible answer*

This is the report of the March 15th meeting. The Sales Manager stated that some of the customers would like a new, more technological product. They were asking for an even lighter waterproof jacket. The Purchasing Manager remarked that, in that case, they had to buy a different kind of fabric to meet their requirements. The Production Manager suggested that the machines should be updated too if they wanted to manufacture a new product. The Finance Manager said that he/she thought they had to draw up a business plan. He/She added that the costs couldn't exceed the benefits. The Sales Manager remarked that they also needed to carry out a survey so that they had real data to analyze. The Finance Manager explained that the survey had to be included in the costs. He/She added they could send questionnaires because interviews would be more expensive.

LESSON 4 P. 354 ....

1
1 he could find the tickets for the show.
2 we should meet.
3 that we (should/could) play video games. / playing video games.
4 (could) look on Wikipedia.
5 how much the/that tablet cost.
6 what he has/had on his mind.
7 when they are / they're coming.
8 taking up a winter sport / that I/we (should)take up a winter sport

2
1 Amanda asked what time Jane was coming the following/next day.
2 Angela asked if/whether Sammy liked/likes canoeing.
3 Tom asked me why I hadn't gone swimming the night before.
4 Sally asked Kate if/whether her brother was working in Switzerland.
5 I asked Sue if/whether she could lend me her pen.
6 The teacher asked the class if/whether they had done their homework.

3
1 what my school was like, that it was great
2 how long I had lived in Italy, for two years
3 I knew that more standing stones had been found near Stonehenge, I didn't
4 I'd ever been to Iceland, I'd never been there, that I'd like to go, I knew it must be an amazing place
5 I was curious to know my exam results, I couldn't wait

4
1 **Sarah**   "I live in a new house."
2 **Ben**   "Where did you study Italian, David?"
3 **Mom**   "I'm/am very tired."
4 **Mr. Smith** "Jason, I will/'ll arrive late tomorrow."
5 **Fiona**   "Is Tom working this afternoon?"

5
Julie   Hi, Marco!
Marco   Hi, Julie! It's nice to see you again.
Julie   When did we last see each other?
Marco   I think it was two years ago.
Julian Do you still live in the same house near the main street?
Marco   No, I've moved to a new house.
Julie   Where is it?
Marco   It's in the suburbs.
Julie   Do you like it?
Marco   I love it because it has a big garden and a conservatory.

6
1 John asked Rick if/whether he had been to Athens before and Rick answered that he hadn't.
2 Emma asked the children if/whether they were having fun at the water park and they answered that they were.
3 Matt asked Sarah if/whether her husband was happy with his new motorbike and she answered that he was.
4 Mark asked Sylvia if/whether she had come by train and she answered that she hadn't and that she'd come in the car.
5 Angela asked Julia if/whether she had time to go for lunch and she answered she had. She suggested going / that they go to the pub on the corner.

7 1 E 2 C 3 B 4 A 5 F 6 D

8
1 Lewis suggested eating / that they ate at the new Thai restaurant that night.
2 The tour operator recommended going / that they/we go to Rhodes the following summer.
3 Marion suggested organizing / that they/we organized a garage sale to raise some money.
4 Peter's mother suggested (to him) that he shouldn't / had better not go out that day.
5 June suggested having / that we had a sleepover at her house the following Saturday.
6 The therapist recommended having / that he/she/we/I should had a long brisk walk at least twice a week.

9
1 Ryan wondered where they would go / be going on vacation the following summer.
2 Olivia wanted to know who had booked the seats for the theater.
3 Carl asked what time we were meeting our guide for the city tour.
4 Pamela wanted to know when Nancy was leaving for Rome.
5 Simon asked where I/we would like to go that day.
6 Mr. Wilson wondered what his son was going to do when he left school.

1 **SAY:** hello, no, something wrong, a word, thank you, goodbye

TELL: the time, a lie, the truth, the difference, a joke, me about it

2 1 say 2 say 3 tell 4 said 5 tell 6 told 7 tell 8 said
9 says 10 tell

3 1 D 2 A 3 E 4 G 5 B 6 C 7 H 8 F

4 1 she, that 2 he, me/us the following weekend, he
3 they, that 4 she, that, she 5 he, that
6 they, I/we, the following week

5 1 Joan often says to her husband that she doesn't like him lying on the sofa all day on Sundays.
2 The science teacher said that some dinosaurs had been herbivores, others had been carnivorous.
3 The sales manager remarked that those data couldn't be correct. There must have been a mistake.
4 Alan keeps telling Nicole that he wants to find a better place to live and raise their children.
5 Mom always says that patience is a great virtue. We should never forget it.
6 My son sometimes tells me that I am a great cook.
7 Liza always says that she will/'ll become a great singer. And I think she will.

6 1 He said that ~~I~~ **he** would go to the mountains the day after.
2 She said she ~~is~~ **was** happy for him.
3 I told him not **to** play in his bedroom in those dirty shoes.
4 Sam said he had met Jenny at the concert ~~yesterday~~ **the previous day / the day before**.
5 Keira replied she ~~doesn't~~ **didn't** want to pay extra money for that service.
6 He asked her whose bike ~~was it~~ **it was**.
7 He told me that I and my family are very important to ~~me~~ **him**.
8 I said I was going home because I ~~feel~~ **felt** sick.

7 1 Mom told the children to stop making all that noise. She was working.
2 Ted suggested meeting / that we (should) meet at the station the next/following morning at eight.
3 The guide told the tourists that the stones used to build Stonehenge had been taken from very far away.
4 Sam told his friend Paul that he'd like to stay a little longer, and added that he could go home if he wanted to.
5 The teacher explained to her pupils that that Norman castle had been built in the 12th century.
6 My friend who lives in the USA told me he/she was/is going to visit Yellowstone National Park next / the following summer.

7 John asked me if he could have a look at my history project. I answered that he couldn't because I'd already handed it in.
8 The doctor advised me to eat less and do physical exercise regularly.

8 1 reminded 2 asked 3 said 4 suggested
5 said 6 asked 7 answered 8 said

9 **Hilary** Do you know who came into the agency today, Fred?
Fred Of course not. How should I?
Hilary It was a schoolmate of ours.
Fred Who was it?
Hilary It was Albert Swanson.
Fred We haven't seen him since we left school. What's he like?
Hilary He's very elegant and looks even younger than he was when we were at school. He seems to be very rich, too, because he's interested in very expensive holiday resorts.
Fred Do you remember how scruffy Albert looked when he was a student? Are you sure it was really Albert?
Hilary Albert recognized me, too. He suggested going out for a meal one day, the three of us and his wife.
Fred Who's Albert's wife?
Hilary You'll never guess. His wife is Rose, the most beautiful girl in the school.
Fred I can't believe it! Rose didn't even want to sit next to Albert during lessons then.

10 1 Rachel wanted to know if/whether I wanted any more food for the picnic.
2 Tony told his father that he'd had some trouble with his mountain bike a short time before.
3 Damien wanted to know if/whether she was happy with her new car.
4 A friend wondered why I had given up fencing.
5 The ranger warned Don to stay at home during the snowstorm.
6 The instructor advised me to go waterskiing in the summer.
7 Andrew ordered the children to get out of the boat.

Reflecting on grammar

1 F 2 F 3 T 4 T 5 F 6 T 7 T 8 F 9 T 10 F

UNIT 20

LESSON 1 P. 362 ....

1 1 I studied hard, but I didn't get a good mark.
2 He looks like a tough guy, but he's very shy.
3 The movie was good, but it was a bit slow.
4 The T-shirt they gave me for my birthday is nice, but it's too short.

5 Emma liked Tom, but she didn't really trust him.

6 I thought it would be sunny in Sicily in May, but we had lots of rain.

7 They've had a lot of problems recently, but they've never complained.

8 It's a very nice house, but it's away from the center.

2 1 because 2 and 3 but 4 because 5 or
6 so 7 However 8 and

3 1 even though / although 2 Despite / In spite of
3 even though / although 4 Although / Even though
5 However 6 Despite / In spite of 7 despite /
in spite of 8 However

4 1 C 2 D 3 B 4 A 5 F 6 E

5 1 Although Jane got home late, she prepared dinner for everybody.

2 The waiter was very kind, but the food wasn't that good.

3 I don't have an English-French dictionary. I can look words up on the Internet, though.

4 I don't know his wife; however, I know his children.

5 We had a great time, even though the weather wasn't very nice.

6 We got lost, although we had a map of the city.

7 However good it may be, I will never be able to eat sushi.

LESSON 2 P. 365

1 1 As the weather is so bad, the barbecue has been canceled.

2 We didn't buy that computer since it was too expensive.

3 We walked back home because we didn't have any money for a taxi.

4 Since it was raining, we decided not to play tennis.

5 We often go to Barcelona because our grandparents live there.

6 We couldn't get there on time as there was a bus strike.

2 1 so I couldn't wait any longer
2 buy anything because I didn't have any money
3 know many people, so we didn't have a good time at the party
4 work on my bike yesterday because my car broke down
5 lose weight; therefore, I'm going to eat less sugar
6 was so bad that his parents were furious with him

3 1 so much 2 such a great 3 so good
4 so lucky 5 so long 6 so often 7 so badly
8 so boring

4 1 C 2 D 3 E 4 A 5 F 6 B

5 1 so 2 so as 3 to call 4 because 5 Since
6 so as not 7 so that 8 because 9 in order to
10 consequently

6 1 because 2 so 3 As/Since/Because
4 because 5 so (that) 6 such a, that
7 so, that 8 so as not to / in order not to

LESSON 3 P. 367

1 1 Before 2 before 3 as long as 4 as soon as
5 while 6 until 7 Before 8 While

2 1 when 2 until 3 as soon as 4 while
5 as long as 6 After

3 1 first 2 then 3 After that 4 finally

4 1 Firstly 2 Secondly 3 In addition 4 because
5 Another point 6 before 7 last but not least

5 1 Besides 2 What's more 3 besides
4 What's more 5 Moreover 6 Besides

6 1 Before 2 while 3 until 4 as soon as
5 First of all, secondly 6 As soon as

LESSON 4 P. 370

1 1 F 2 D 3 A 4 B 5 C 6 E

2 1 provided 2 unless 3 as if 4 If only 5 in case
6 as if 7 in case 8 as long as

3 1 than 2 as, as 3 as 4 as 5 as 6 than

4 1 that 2 if 3 that 4 than 5 that 6 that 7 than

5 1 made 2 makes 3 made 4 makes 5 make
6 make 7 made 8 make 9 making 10 made

6 1 let 2 caused 3 caused 4 got 5 caused 6 let
7 got 8 let / will let

7 1 allowed 2 was obliged 3 gets 4 makes
5 let 6 caused

8 1 My parents do not / don't let me go out in the evening. That's not fair!

2 This movie was very moving; the ending made me cry.

3 Mr. Basset is going to / will let us go into his lab next week.

4 I will/'ll get you to come to the swimming pool with me after work. It's so relaxing!

5 We made Tom sing a song at the party, although he didn't want to.

6 This is music that makes everybody dance!

9 1 loading 2 to have 3 to take, to make
4 to clean 5 to phone 6 to go 7 leaving
8 learn 9 run 10 ring

10 1 as long as 2 unless 3 in case 4 as if 5 If only
6 than 7 that, as / because / since
8 than 9 However 10 as soon as

ROUND UP 20 P. 374

1 1 but/yet 2 so 3 but/yet 4 for 5 and, or, and 6 nor

2 1 because 2 though 3 so 4 that 5 so, that
6 if 7 until 8 as long as

3
1 Because he had eaten enough, he didn't want anything else.
2 After I finished school yesterday, I went straight home.
3 Call me at once if you see anything strange.
4 Provided you don't suffer from seasickness, you can join us on our boat trip.
5 Whatever they say, I won't try this dish.
6 Before I went to the office this morning, I went jogging for an hour.
7 I'm going for a bike ride later, so long as it doesn't rain.

4
1 who 2 to 3 which 4 If only 5 also 6 which
7 so 8 that 9 before

5
1 First 2 Then 3 After that / Next
4 Next / After that 5 until 6 Finally

6
1 which 2 and 3 If 4 as a result 5 In spite of
6 However 7 although

7
1 make 2 get 3 gets 4 makes 5 gets
6 makes 7 makes 8 lets

8
1 forced 2 makes 3 gets 4 allowed/allow
5 saw 6 needs 7 obliged 8 heard

Reflecting on grammar

1 F 2 T 3 T 4 F 5 T 6 F 7 F 8 T 9 F 10 F

UNIT 21

LESSON 1 P. 378 ....

1
1 I He's leaving for college in a week's time.
2 L I feel great today.
3 T They drove all the way to Portugal last summer.
4 T I bought a very pretty skirt in the little shop .
5 L They became very famous after their last album.
6 T We often watch videos on YouTube.
7 I We went to the fish-and-chip shop on the High Street for lunch.
8 I They are going on a cycling vacation in the Netherlands.
9 L He looked very silly in those pants at the party last night.
10 I We went for ride on our bikes.

2
1 C 2 H 3 A 4 F 5 B 6 D 7 E 8 G

3
1 The man wasn't / was not standing near the shop door.
2 There wasn't / was not anything strange about him.
3 They didn't / did not discover a Neolithic site in this area.
4 Tina doesn't / does not look happy today.
5 I'm / I am not thirsty. I don't / do not need anything to drink.
6 I don't / do not have to work on weekends this month.
7 The visitors didn't / did not leave the museum before five.

8 Karen won't / will not arrive at the end of December.
9 We couldn't / could not see the entrance of the building on the screen.
10 She didn't / did not go out with her boyfriend last night.
11 I haven't / have not played tennis a lot recently.
12 They hadn't / had not left the office yet.

LESSON 2 P. 380 ....

1
1 "Do you like painting?" "Yes, I/we do."
2 "Does Rebecca play in the school volleyball team?" "No, she doesn't."
3 "Are the boys going home?" "No, they aren't. / No, they're not."
4 "Would you like to meet her?" "Yes, I/we would."
5 "Did your boyfriend give you a present?" "Yes, he did."
"Did you give your boyfriend a present?" "Yes, I did."
6 "Has Marion got her laptop with her?" "No, she hasn't."

2
1 I hope so. 2 I hope not. 3 I'm afraid so.
4 I'm afraid not. 5 I don't think so. 6 I guess so.
7 I suppose not.   8 I believe so.

3
1 G How do we get to the station?
2 D When did you buy your car?
3 A When could you come to my house?
4 C Why were you laughing?
5 B Which of those T-shirts did you buy?
6 F How long did you wait for them?
7 H Are you gong to sell your apartment?
8 E What time did your brother get home last night?

4 *Possible answers*
Where did you go in the holidays?
What were your friends going to do last night?
Who is Martina looking for?
When does he start the guitar course?
Why are they running?
How did you get to the movies?

5
1 isn't it? 2 are you? 3 wasn't it? 4 don't you?
5 haven't you? 6 do you?

6
1 isn't it? 2 isn't she? 3 haven't you? 4 was it?
5 do you? 6 didn't they? 7 did you? 8 can't he?
9 shall we? 10 doesn't he?

7
1 Does she? 2 Is he really? 3 Wouldn't he?
4 Haven't you? 5 Will he? 6 Can't you?
7 Have you?

8
1 A 2 A 3 C 4 B 5 C 6 A

9
1 A 2 F 3 G 4 B 5 D 6 C 7 E

10
1 Their friends wouldn't. 2 So do we. 3 So will I.
4 My daughter doesn't. 5 So did my son.
6 Mine aren't. 7 Neither/Nor have we.

LESSON 3 P. 385

1 1 C 2 A 3 F, J 4 G 5 B, J 6 B 7 D 8 I
9 K 10 H 11 L 12 E

2 1 The school team 2 A summer holiday
3 A taxi driver 4 A fashion magazine
5 A vegetable garden 6 Garden vegetables
7 A wine glass 8 A conference room
9 A shoe shop 10 Ski boots 11 A winter resort
12 A love story 13 A tennis court
14 Rock music 15 A computer screen
16 Your car door

3 1 big-nosed man 2 short-legged, long-tailed dog
3 long-haired girl 4 wide-brimmed hat
5 high-heeled shoes 6 new-born baby
7 war-torn country 8 man-made canal

4 1 annoyed 2 annoying 3 confusing 4 exciting
5 tiring, tired 6 interested 7 entertaining
8 rising 9 relaxing 10 confused

5 1 multitasking **E**   2 forecast **J**
3 polytheistic religion **L** 4 oversleep **F**
5 dehydrate **D**   6 disagree **A**
7 unfriendly **H**   8 undernourished **I**
9 trilogy **G**   10 ill-treated **B**
11 rearrange **C**   12 polyglot **K**

6 1 artist 2 historians 3 director(s) 4 painters
5 magician 6 drummer, singer

7 1 peaceful   **ADJ**
2 rewind   **V**
3 impatiently   **ADV**
4 reorganization   **N**
5 unfortunately   **ADV**
6 disadvantage   **N**
7 insecurity   **N**
8 leadership   **N**
9 loneliness   **N**

8 1 pointless 2 wonderful 3 homeless 4 useful
5 useless 6 careful 7 careless 8 powerful
9 hopeless 10 fruitful

9 1 fashionable 2 selfish 3 noisy 4 alcoholic
5 meaningless 6 unprecedented 7 cloudless
8 reliable 9 impossible 10 unpredictable

LESSON 4 P. 390

1 1 in 2 go 3 in 4 give 5 on 6 carry/go 7 up
8 up 9 wake/get 10 down 11 sit/lie 12 out
13 back 14 broke 15 off 16 takes 17 away
18 Watch 19 back 20 off 21 off 22 Look
23 stand 24 over

2 1 Bring the newspaper back, will you?
2 Fill this form in, please.
3 Hand your project in by tomorrow.
4 It's cold. Put your pullover on.

5 Can I try this coat on, please?
6 Switch the lights on, it's dark.
7 Put the glasses away, please.
8 Turn the TV down. It's too loud.

3 1 back as soon as you can 2 up at work
3 in 4 up smoking 5 up a good story
6 about/on her depression
7 up eight children 8 up with his behavior

4 1 with 2 forward 3 of 4 up 5 on 6 away
7 down 8 up

ROUND UP 21 P. 394

1 1 He doesn't like horror movies at all.
2 Last summer, he didn't go on holiday to the usual place. / He didn't go on holiday to the usual place last summer.
3 Your sister speaks Spanish very well.
4 We thanked them for being so nice to us.
5 Last year, they spent two months in Africa. / They spent two months in Africa last year.
6 What did you have for lunch yesterday?
7 They haven't been to Turkey before.
8 We usually spend our free time at the youth club or at the mall.
9 I don't feel very well today.
10 We're having an exam in a week's time.
11 What time does the next train leave?
12 What platform does it leave from?

2 1 Not only was she a great singer, she was also a fantastic dancer.
2 No sooner had he arrived than he started chatting and never stopped.
3 Only if you train hard will you have a chance of winning the match.
4 Not until I got home in the evening did I realize that my friend had left.
5 Never have I met such a silly boy as Tom.
6 Hardly ever do they help with the housework. Their parents are really annoyed.
7 They came to the mountains, but not even once did they try to ski.
8 Only if you are nice to others will others be nice you.

3 1 This is my first time in New York.
2 Do they have a lot of friends here?
3 We didn't enjoy the trip very much.
4 Do the children have to be at school earlier tomorrow?
5 Does the bus leave on the half hour?
6 They couldn't find the answers to all of my questions.
7 Did Tom and Lucy have dinner at home last night?
8 Was there a long line at the post office?
9 My mom knows my friend John.
10 We got up late this morning.

4 1 couldn't you? 2 haven't they? 3 can you?
4 did you? 5 do they? 6 doesn't she? 7 isn't it?
8 weren't they? 9 haven't you?

5 1 I don't 2 So did we 3 I did 4 Neither/Nor do we
5 Neither/Nor do I 6 Neither/Nor could I
7 So does 8 hasn't 9 So does 10 I did

6

	抽象名詞
educate	education
enjoy	enjoyment
friend	friendship
leader	leadership
perform	performance
establish	establishment
possible	possibility
credible	credibility
hard	hardship, hardness
sister	sisterhood
real	reality
liberate	liberation
kind	kindness
endure	endurance
free	freedom
excite	excitement
happy	happiness

7 1 called off 2 broke down 3 broke up 4 be up to
5 are, up to 6 be off 7 Come back
8 came up with 9 set off 10 Shut up
11 work out 12 Hang on to 13 hanging out
14 hanging around 15 is/'s, over

8 1 done with 2 worn out / done in 3 worn out
4 am / 'm fed up with 5 worn out / done in
6 done for 7 done away with 8 am/'m fed up with

Reflecting on grammar

1 T 2 F 3 T 4 F 5 F 6 T 7 F 8 F 9 T 10 T

Revision and Exams 7 P. 398

1 1 how 2 Where 3 isn't
4 on 5 like 6 on
7 though 8 back

2 **Neil** Hi, Steve. Guess who I've just met. Ellen, do you
remember her? She used to work in the Accounts
Department. I asked her what her holiday in Ireland
was like and she said that they really enjoyed
themselves. She explained that they were in Galway
for two weeks, on the west coast, and said that it's a
beautiful place and that there are a lot of things going
on in the summer. I asked her what the weather had
been like and she replied that she had been told the
weather in that area was usually rainy, but in fact they
had had two weeks of sun. I asked her if they had been
to the Aran Islands, and she said that they had. She

added that they had hired two bicycles and had been
on a trip around the island of Inishmore. She said that
they had even swum in the sea, even though the water
had been very cold. I told her I would have liked to have
been with them because I love Ireland. I asked her if
they had been there before, and she answered that it
had been their first time, but they wanted to go back
there next year / the following year.

3 1 give in 2 done in 3 Come on 4 make out
5 put up 6 put up 7 get, across 8 run out

4 You can't even imagine how difficult it was for me to
get to the top. I thought I would give in, but Paul told
me not to give in then, as we were nearly there. I told
him that I was done in and I couldn't walk any more,
but he asked me if I couldn't see the top. He said that
with one more effort, we would be there, and told me
to come on. I complained that I couldn't even make out
the top in that mist, but he told me to stop complaining
and said that I should learn to put up with difficulties.
I said that I could put up with difficulties, but I realized
then that I wasn't trained. I asked him how I could get
that across to him. He said that he saw, but added that
he knew I could make it. He suggested we had some
chocolate and said it would help, but I said that I hadn't
wanted to tell him, but we'd run out of comfort food.
He asked if we had any water left, and I replied that we
did still have some water at least.

5 1 but 2 or 3 after 4 and 5 when 6 if 7 if
8 if 9 or 10 before 11 after 12 or

6 1 B 2 A 3 C 4 A 5 B 6 C 7 C 8 B 9 A 10 B

7 ***Student's own answer***

8 1 put up with 2 been put off 3 keep off
4 run out of 5 fill in 6 give up eating
7 Pop / Drop in to 8 carry out

9 1 B 2 C 3 A 4 C 5 D 6 A 7 B 8 A 9 D 10 A

10 1 Besides 2 also 3 away/abroad 4 Most
5 up 6 like 7 without 8 up 9 Although
10 back

11 1 misunderstandings 2 unbelievable
3 independence 4 protective 5 different

Self Check 7 P. 402

1 B	2 C	3 A	4 A	5 B	6 C	7 C	8 A
9 B	10 A	11 C	12 C	13 B	14 B	15 C	16 B
17 C	18 A	19 A	20 C	21 B	22 B	23 C	24 A
25 B	26 B	27 A	28 B	29 C	30 B	31 C	32 A
33 B	34 C	35 C	36 C	37 B	38 B	39 C	40 A

作　　者	Lucy Becker / Carol Frain / Karen Thomas
譯　　者	劉嘉珮
校　　對	陳慧莉／許嘉華／黃詩韻
編　　輯	王采翎
主　　編	丁宥暄
內文排版	林書玉
封面設計	林書玉
製程管理	洪巧玲
發 行 人	周均亮
出 版 者	寂天文化事業股份有限公司
電　　話	02-2365-9739
傳　　真	02-2365-9835
網　　址	www.icosmos.com.tw
讀者服務	onlineservice@icosmos.com.tw

2020年12月　初版一刷
郵撥帳號 1998620-0　寂天文化事業股份有限公司
劃撥金額600（含）元以上者，郵資免費。
訂購金額600 元以下者，請外加郵資65元。
〔若有破損，請寄回更換，謝謝。〕

國家圖書館出版品預行編目(CIP)資料

焦點英文文法完全練習/Lucy Becker, Carol Frain,
Karen Thomas作；劉嘉珮譯. -- 初版. -- [臺北市]：寂
天文化, 2020.12
　　面；　公分
譯自：Grammar Matrix
ISBN 978-986-318-950-3
1.英語 2.語法
805.16　　　　　　　　　　　　　　109016795